The Television Detectives' Omnibus

◆

GREAT TALES OF CRIME AND DETECTION

The
TELEVISION DETECTIVES'
Omnibus

GREAT TALES OF CRIME AND DETECTION

Edited by
PETER HAINING

ARTUS BOOKS
LONDON

First published in Great Britain in 1992 by Orion,
an imprint of Orion Books Ltd.
This edition published by Artus Books,
Orion Publishing Group, Orion House,
5 Upper St Martin's Lane,
London WC2H 9EA

ISBN 1 898799 02 4

Printed in England by Clays Ltd, St Ives plc

CONTENTS

◆

CONTENTS

ACKNOWLEDGEMENTS

For
JEREMY BRETT
'The' Television Detective

INTRODUCTION

———◆———

The Television Detective has been one of the favourites of viewers almost since the advent of the small screen in the living room over fifty years ago, just prior to the outbreak of the Second World War. It was on the evening of October 1, 1936 that the BBC inaugurated what was the world's first permanent television service, transmitting pictures from their rudimentary studios at the Victorian hill-top pile known as Alexandra Palace to those fortunate enough to possess television sets and living within the limited range of the North London transmitter.

This was not only the dawn of the 'Television Age' but also the middle of the 'Golden Age' of the Detective Story, and the appearance of policemen and private detectives on the new medium was not so much a matter of if but when. Indeed, ever since August when the BBC had given their first public demonstration of 'talking pictures on television', transmitting tiny, flickering, grey and white images from Alexandra Palace to Olympia where over seven thousand people had queued to gaze wide-eyed at this amazing new development in broadcasting, programme planners had been well aware of the general public's taste for the crime story.

Since 1930, in fact, a host of new writers had taken the detective tale in new and exciting directions: John Dickson Carr with his 'locked room mysteries'; John Creasey with his police procedural novels; while in America Raymond Chandler had made the 'Hardboiled Dick' a household name, Erle Stanley Gardner had introduced the famous attorney Perry Mason, and Rex Stout's fat, misogynistic sleuth Nero Wolfe had taken crime readers by storm. Add to these the contributions of Brett Halliday (with Mike Shayne), George Simenon (introducing the redoubtable Maigret) and Dashiell Hammett and the entire *Black Mask* school of rough-house writers and it was, indeed, a 'Golden Age'.

That year of television's debut was also a time when murder and violence were very much in the headlines. Hitler and his Nazi Party were sweeping all opposition before them and had entered the Rhineland; Mussolini had proclaimed his Fascist Empire in Italy; and Civil War had broken out in Spain. In Russia, Stalin had executed a number of his former allies in show trials, and in London an assassin had even tried to shoot the soon-to-abdicate King Edward VIII.

The television receivers with which the fortunate few watched the BBC's first programmes – a mixture of news broadcasts, documentaries, plays, variety shows and extracts from the latest films – would appear odd indeed to modern viewers. What audiences looked at were small square boxes housing either a flask-shaped cathode ray tube which faced the viewer or else a vertical tube projecting a picture onto a mirror. The largest of these screens were twenty-two inches by eighteen, but the majority were almost half this size at ten by eight inches. For those who could afford them, this new novelty was priced at 100 guineas (when the average wage was £3 per week) and they were almost impossible to view except in a room with the curtains drawn.

Programmes were transmitted intermittently from the middle of the afternoon to a news programme at nine o'clock which was usually in sound only. Breaks between transmission either left the screen blank, showing a 'Test Card', or during the evening, a restful shot of a potter's wheel or slowing-turning windmill which were, to all intents and purposes, the forerunners of today's commercial breaks!

BBC Radio – which had been on the air since 1922 – had already utilised the popularity of detective stories in the form of plays and adaptations of the books of writers like Agatha Christie, Dorothy L. Sayers, Edgar Wallace and Leslie Charteris, thereby making their works familiar to an even larger audience. It was not until the Spring of 1937, however, that the first 'serial' detective made his bow on radio in May 1937 in the weekly programme, *Monday At Seven*. The series was called 'Inspector Hornleigh Investigates' in which the hero interrogated various witnesses to a crime, one of whom would make a fatal slip during the conversation. These dramatic sketches would end with the announcer asking listeners, 'Are you as astute as Inspector Hornleigh? The mistake of the guilty man will be disclosed later in the programme.'

This pioneer programme was the brainchild of BBC scriptwriter Hans W. Priwin, and starred S. J. Warmington as Inspector Hornleigh and Ewart Scott as his assistant, Sergeant Bingham. They were the first 'Holmes and Watson' of radio and in August 1937 became the first duo on television. The radio programme, in fact, became so popular that, the following year, it was turned into a stage play with John Longdon, and in 1939 the first of three Hornleigh films was made with Gordon Harker in the lead role.

By all accounts, the TV version of Inspector Hornleigh on August 7 with Warmington and Scott duplicating their radio roles was a static performance in which detectives and suspects were shown, head only, against a nondescript background which may have been intended to represent a police station interview room. The fifteen minute 'live' programme suffered from several of the complaints familiar in the early days of TV – the end of a sound boom was visible in a number of shots, one of the suspects moved off camera before a second camera had taken over the story, and the perspiration which dripped from the unhappy Inspector's face from the battery of lights above him was visible for all to see. For whatever reason, he did not return to repeat his cross examination.

Short-lived 'Inspector Hornleigh Investigates' on TV may have been, but it nevertheless marked the debut of the series detective on television – a tradition that has now endured and prospered for 55 years.

It was perhaps only right that the first of the detectives from crime fiction to make his debut on television should have been the great Sherlock Holmes. The only surprising feature of this was that it occurred not in Britain, but America, where television was still even more in its infancy in the late Thirties. The production was an adaptation of the case of *The Adventure of the Three Garridebs* which the newly formed National Broadcasting Company (NBC) put out 'live' as a trial broadcast in New York on the evening of November 27, 1937. Unlike 'Inspector Hornleigh Investigates', this was a broadcast which included film inserts of London – including the Great Detective and Dr Watson riding in a hansom cab through the streets – and two sets representing Holmes' flat in Baker Street and the home of the ornithologist, Nathan Garrideb. The actors, too, were in full period costume and thoroughly rehearsed.

Although it is undeniably true that the American production also left something to be desired in terms of quality, it was a considerable improvement on the BBC's programme, and the newspaper reports the following day perceptively hinted at a great future lying ahead for the sleuth on the small screen. It is, therefore, with this tale that I have chosen to start my fifty-year Omnibus collection of short stories featuring the great television detectives.

The first crime fighters on television were, with rare exceptions, to be found in special productions like the BBC's *Play of the Week* and the American anthology series such as *Suspense, The Web* and *Alfred Hitchcock Presents* which came into their own once the Second World War was over for both nations. It was not until the Fifties that the famous investigators from the printed page really began to make an impact on TV, and such was the success of these productions that they often made the heroes familiar to new audiences outside the realms of crime fiction aficionados. In recent years, some literary detectives owe their international fame very much to their adaptation for the small screen.

In the pages which follow, then, are to be found the most popular detectives from crime fiction who have starred in their own TV series, each represented by what I believe to be the most significant short story in which they appeared. Each is introduced with details of the character, his or her creator and the series they inspired, as well as, where appropriate, details of other radio, film and even stage adaptations.

Television has also, of course, created many of its own now-famous crime fighters – the list is far too long to include here – and although a considerable number have subsequently been featured in books and short stories, they fall outside the scope of this, already very substantial, collection. The success of this Omnibus might well, though, call for an anthology of these other policemen, amateur detectives and private eyes. The spy, who also has a long tradition on TV, likewise falls outside our boundaries and perhaps similarly deserves a separate collection.

It was Sherlock Holmes who stated in *The Sign of Four* that detection is – or ought to be – an exact science which should be treated in the same cold and unemotional manner. Indeed, he reprimanded his chronicler Dr Watson, 'You have attempted to tinge it with romanticism, which produces much the same effect as if you worked a love-story or an elopement into the fifth proposition of Euclid.'

Although I am second to none in my admiration for the Great Detective, I have to confess that I am glad that Watson, and all the other recounters of the cases which will be found in these pages, did not take this message to heart. For it is the very spirit of romance, the mystery of crime, and the excitement of detection, which makes the detective in print or on television irresistible . . .

PETER HAINING,
May, 1992.

The Adventure of the Three Garridebs

◆

SIR ARTHUR CONAN DOYLE

Sherlock Holmes was not only the first detective from crime fiction to appear on television in America in 1937, but, courtesy of the current Granada TV series starring the definitive Holmes, Jeremy Brett, is now by far the longest running serial in the history of the medium. The tall, aesthetic detective with his hawk-like features, remarkable intellect and extraordinary powers of observation and deduction, is today listed among the half-dozen most famous characters in literature. His deerstalker hat and curled pipe are images familiar all over the world: while the fact that he prides himself on his athleticism and is an excellent boxer and fencer seems curiously at odds with his taste for cocaine. It was apparently in the year 1881 that he set himself up as the world's first consulting detective at 221B Baker Street and became friendly with Dr John H. Watson who was thereafter to be his trusty accomplice and faithful scribe. Holmes has survived several attempts on his life – including a famous one at the Reichenbach Falls instigated by his creator, Sir Arthur Conan Doyle (1859–1930) but not successfully carried out by his arch-enemy, Professor Moriarty – and after a lifetime of exemplary crime detection has now apparently settled into comfortable retirement in Sussex where he lives to this day tending his bees.

The Baker Street sleuth has, of course, been featured in films almost since the birth of that medium, making his bow in 1903 in Sherlock Holmes Baffled *and since then portrayed by many famous stars including William Gillette, John Barrymore, Eille Norwood, Clive Brook, Arthur Wontner, Basil Rathbone, Peter Cushing and Robert Stephens. His TV debut was in the NBC hour-long 'live' adaptation of* The Adventure of the Three Garridebs *on November 27, 1937, with two well-known radio broadcasters, Louis Hector and William Podmore as Holmes and Watson. In the years since then he has appeared on television in virtually every country in the world and been played by a similar galaxy of excellent actors including Alan Wheatley, Douglas Wilmer, Peter Cushing, Tom Baker and Ian Richardson in the UK; Ronald Howard, Basil Rathbone, Stewart Granger, Leonard Nimoy and Larry Hagman in the USA; plus Christopher Lee in a German series, Radovan Lukavsky on Czech TV and Vassily Livanov in the first Russian Sherlock Holmes serial. The choice of* The Adventure of Three Garridebs *by NBC for their viewers was a natural enough one with its plot of fraud and attempted murder revolving around an American family. And whatever shortcomings the production may have had, the* New York Times *was still able to report enthusiastically the next morning, 'Sherlock Holmes sleuthed around the television cameras at Radio City in the most ambitious experiment in teleshowmanship so far attempted in the air over New York . . . and the ingenious welding of film and studio production offered an interesting glimpse into the future of a new form of dramatic art.' The paper might also have added that there could now be no doubt that a new era of the detective story on television was about to begin . . .*

IT may have been a comedy, or it may have been a tragedy. It cost one man his reason, it cost me a blood-letting, and it cost yet another man the penalties of the law. Yet there was certainly an element of comedy. Well, you shall judge for yourselves.

I remember the date very well, for it was in the same month that Holmes refused a knighthood for services which may perhaps some day be described. I only refer to the matter in passing, for in my position of partner and confidant I am obliged to be particularly careful to avoid any indiscretion. I repeat, however, that this enables me to fix the date, which was the latter end of June, 1902, shortly after the conclusion of the South African War. Holmes had spent several days in bed, as was his habit from time to time, but he emerged that morning with a long foolscap document in his hand and a twinkle of amusement in his austere grey eyes.

'There is a chance for you to make some money, friend Watson,' said he. 'Have you ever heard the name of Garrideb?'

I admitted that I had not.

'Well, if you can lay your hand upon a Garrideb, there's money in it.'

'Why?'

'Ah, that's a long story – rather a whimsical one, too. I don't think in all our explorations of human complexities we have ever come upon anything more singular. The fellow will be here presently for cross-examination, so I won't open the matter up till he comes. But meanwhile, that's the name we want.'

The telephone directory lay on the table beside me, and I turned over the pages in a rather hopeless quest. But to my amazement there was this strange name in its due place. I gave a cry of triumph.

'Here you are, Holmes! Here it is!'

Holmes took the book from my hand.

' "Garrideb, N.," ' he read, ' "136 Little Ryder Street, W." Sorry to disappoint you, my dear Watson, but this is the man himself. That is the address upon his letter. We want another to match him.'

Mrs Hudson had come in with a card upon a tray. I took it up and glanced at it.

'Why, here it is!' I cried in amazement. 'This is a different initial. John Garrideb, Counsellor at Law, Moorville, Kansas, USA.'

Holmes smiled as he looked at the card. 'I am afraid you must make yet another effort, Watson,' said he. 'This gentleman is also in the plot already, though I certainly did not expect to see him this morning. However, he is in a position to tell us a good deal which I want to know.'

A moment later he was in the room. Mr John Garrideb, Counsellor at Law, was a short, powerful man with the round, fresh, clean-shaven face characteristic of so many American men of affairs. The general effect was chubby and rather childlike, so that one received the impression of quite a young man with a broad set smile upon his face. His eyes, however, were arresting. Seldom in any human head have I seen a pair which bespoke a more intense inward life, so bright were they, so alert, so responsive to every change of thought. His accent was American, but was not accompanied by any eccentricity of speech.

'Mr Holmes?' he asked, glancing from one to the other. 'Ah, yes! Your pictures are not unlike you, sir, if I may say so. I believe you have had a letter from my namesake, Mr Nathan Garrideb, have you not?'

'Pray sit down,' said Sherlock Holmes. 'We shall, I fancy, have a good deal to discuss.' He took up his sheets of foolscap. 'You are, of course, the Mr John Garrideb mentioned in this document. But surely you have been in England some time?'

'Why do you say that, Mr Holmes?' I seemed to read sudden suspicion in those expressive eyes.

'Your whole outfit is English.'

Mr Garrideb forced a laugh. 'I've read of your tricks, Mr Holmes, but I never thought I would be the subject of them. Where do you read that?'

'The shoulder cut of your coat, the toes of your boots – could anyone doubt it?'

'Well, well, I had no idea I was so obvious a Britisher. But business brought me over here some time ago, and so, as you say, my outfit is nearly all London. However, I guess your time is of value, and we did not meet to talk about the cut of my socks. What about getting down to that paper you hold in your hand?'

Holmes had in some way ruffled our visitor, whose chubby face had assumed a far less amiable expression.

'Patience! Patience, Mr Garrideb!' said my friend in a soothing voice. 'Dr Watson would tell you that these little digressions of mine sometimes prove in the end to have some bearing on the matter. But why did Mr Nathan Garrideb not come with you?'

'Why did he ever drag you into it at all?' asked our visitor, with a sudden outflame of anger. 'What in thunder had you to do with it? Here was a bit of professional business between two gentlemen, and one of them must needs call in a detective! I saw him this morning, and he told me this fool-trick he had played me, and that's why I am here. But I feel bad about it, all the same.'

'There was no reflection upon you, Mr Garrideb. It was simply zeal upon his part to gain your end – an end which is, I understand, equally vital for both of you. He knew that I had means of getting information, and, therefore, it was very natural that he should apply to me.'

Our visitor's angry face gradually cleared.

'Well, that puts it different,' said he. 'When I went to see him this morning and he told me he had sent to a detective, I just asked for your address and came right away. I don't want police butting into a private matter. But if you are content just to help us find the man, there can be no harm in that.'

'Well, that is just how it stands,' said Holmes. 'And now, sir, since you are here, we had best have a clear account from your own lips. My friend here knows nothing of the details.'

Mr Garrideb surveyed me with not too friendly a gaze.

'Need he know?' he asked.

'We usually work together.'

'Well, there's no reason it should be kept a secret. I'll give you the facts as short as I can make them. If you came from Kansas I would not need to explain to you who Alexander Hamilton Garrideb was. He made his money in real estate, and afterwards in the wheat pit at Chicago, but he spent it in buying up as much land as would make one of your counties, lying along the Arkansas River, west of Fort Dodge. It's grazing-land and lumber-land and arable-land and mineralized-land, and just every sort of land that brings dollars to the man that owns it.

'He had no kith nor kin – or, if he had, I never heard of it. But he took a kind of pride in the queerness of his name. That was what brought us together. I was in the law at Topeka, and one day I had a visit from the old man, and he was tickled to death to meet another man with his own name. It was his pet fad, and he was dead set to find out if there were any more Garridebs in the world. "Find me another!" said he. I told him I was a busy man and could not spend my life hiking around the world in search of Garridebs. "None the less," said he, "that is just what you will do if things pan out as I planned them." I thought he was joking, but there was a powerful lot of meaning in the words, as I was soon to discover.

'For he died within a year of saying them, and he left a will behind him. It was the queerest will that has ever been filed in the State of Kansas. His property was divided into three parts, and I was to have one on condition that I found two Garridebs who would share the remainder. It's five million dollars for each if it is a cent, but we can't lay a finger on it until we all three stand in a row.

'It was so big a chance that I just let my legal practice slide and I set forth looking for Garridebs. There is not one in the United States. I went through it, sir, with a fine-toothed comb and never a Garrideb could I catch. Then I tried the old country. Sure enough there was the name in the London Telephone Directory. I went after him two days ago and explained the whole matter to him. But he is a lone man, like myself, with some women relations, but no men. It says three adult men in the will. So you see we still have a vacancy, and if you can help to fill it we will be very ready to pay your charges.'

'Well, Watson,' said Holmes, with a smile, 'I said it was rather whimsical, did I not? I should have thought, sir, that your obvious way was to advertise in the agony columns of the papers.'

'I have done that, Mr Holmes. No replies.'

'Dear me! Well, it is certainly a most curious little problem. I may take a glance at it in my leisure. By the way, it is curious that you should have come from Topeka. I used to have a correspondent – he is dead now – old Dr Lysander Starr, who was Mayor in 1890.'

'Good old Dr Starr!' said our visitor. 'His name is still honoured.
Well, Mr Holmes, I suppose all we can do is to report to you and let
you know how we progress. I reckon you will hear within a day or
two.' With this assurance our American bowed and departed.

Holmes had lit his pipe, and he sat for some time with a curious
smile upon his face.

'Well?' I asked at last.

'I am wondering, Watson – just wondering!'

'At what?'

Holmes took his pipe from his lips.

'I was wondering, Watson, what on earth could be the object of this
man in telling us such a rigmarole of lies. I nearly asked him so – for
there are times when a brutal frontal attack is the best policy – but I
judged it better to let him think he had fooled us. Here is a man with an
English coat frayed at the elbow and trousers bagged at the knee with a
year's wear, and yet by this document and by his own account he is a
provincial American lately landed in London. There have been no
advertisements in the agony columns. You know that I miss nothing
there. They are my favourite covert for putting up a bird, and I would
never have overlooked such a cock pheasant as that. I never knew a Dr
Lysander Starr of Topeka. Touch him where you would he was false. I
think the fellow is really an American, but he has worn his accent
smooth with years of London. What is his game, then, and what
motive lies behind this preposterous search for Garridebs? It's worth
our attention, for, granting that the man is a rascal, he is certainly a
complex and ingenious one. We must now find out if our other
correspondent is a fraud also. Just ring him up, Watson.'

I did so, and heard a thin, quavering voice at the other end of the
line.

'Yes, yes, I am Mr Nathan Garrideb. Is Mr Holmes there? I should
very much like to have a word with Mr Holmes.'

My friend took the instrument and I heard the usual syncopated
dialogue.

'Yes, he has been here. I understand that you don't know him . . .
How long? . . . Only two days! . . . Yes, yes, of course, it is a most
captivating prospect. Will you be at home this evening? I suppose your
namesake will not be there? . . . Very good, we will come then, for I
would rather have a chat without him . . . Dr Watson will come with
me . . . I understood from your note that you did not go out often . . .
Well, we shall be round about six. You need not mention it to the
American lawyer . . . Very good. Goodbye!'

It was twilight of a lovely spring evening, and even little Ryder

Street, one of the smaller offshoots from the Edgware Road, within a stone-cast of old Tyburn Tree of evil memory, looked golden and wonderful in the slanting rays of the setting sun. The particular house to which we were directed was a large, old-fashioned, Early Georgian edifice with a flat brick face broken only by two deep bay windows on the ground floor. It was on this ground floor that our client lived, and, indeed, the low windows proved to be the front of the huge room in which he spent his waking hours. Holmes pointed as we passed to the small brass plate which bore the curious name.

'Up some years, Watson,' he remarked, indicating its discoloured surface. 'It's *his* real name, anyhow, and that is something to note.'

The house had a common stair, and there were a number of names painted in the hall, some indicating offices and some private chambers. It was not a collection of residential flats, but rather the abode of Bohemian bachelors. Our client opened the door for us himself and apologized by saying that the woman in charge left at four o'clock. Mr Nathan Garrideb proved to be a very tall, loose-jointed, round-backed person, gaunt and bald, some sixty-odd years of age. He had a cadaverous face, with the dull dead skin of a man to whom exercise was unknown. Large round spectacles and a small projecting goat's beard combined with his stooping attitude to give him an expression of peering curiosity. The general effect, however, was amiable, though eccentric.

The room was as curious as its occupant. It looked like a small museum. It was both broad and deep, with cupboards and cabinets all round, crowded with specimens, geological and anatomical. Cases of butterflies and moths flanked each side of the entrance. A large table in the centre was littered with all sorts of debris, while the tall brass tube of a powerful microscope bristled up amongst them. As I glanced round I was surprised at the universality of the man's interests. Here was a case of ancient coins. There was a cabinet of flint instruments. Behind his central table was a large cupboard of fossil bones. Above was a line of plaster skulls with such names as 'Neanderthal,' 'Heidelberg,' 'Cromagnon' printed beneath them. It was clear that he was a student of many subjects. As he stood in front of us now, he held a piece of chamois leather in his right hand with which he was polishing a coin.

'Syracusan – of the best period,' he explained, holding it up. 'They degenerated greatly towards the end. At their best I hold them supreme, though some prefer the Alexandrian school. You will find a chair here, Mr Holmes. Pray allow me to clear these bones. And you, sir – ah, yes, Dr Watson – if you would have the goodness to put the

Japanese vase to one side. You see round me my little interests in life. My doctor lectures me about never going out, but why should I go out when I have so much to hold me here? I can assure you that the adequate cataloguing of one of those cabinets would take me three good months.'

Holmes looked round him with curiosity.

'But do you tell me that you *never* go out?' he said.

'Now and again I drive down to Sotheby's or Christie's. Otherwise I very seldom leave my room. I am not too strong, and my researches are very absorbing. But you can imagine, Mr Holmes, what a terrific shock – pleasant but terrific – it was for me when I heard of this unparalleled good fortune. It only needs one more Garrideb to complete the matter, and surely we can find one. I had a brother, but he is dead, and female relatives are disqualified. But there must surely be others in the world. I had heard that you handled strange cases, and that was why I sent to you. Of course, this American gentleman is quite right, and I should have taken his advice first, but I acted for the best.'

'I think you acted very wisely indeed,' said Holmes. 'But are you really anxious to acquire an estate in America?'

'Certainly not, sir. Nothing would induce me to leave my collection. But this gentleman has assured me that he will buy me out as soon as we have established our claim. Five million dollars was the sum named. There are a dozen specimens in the market at the present moment which fill gaps in my collection, and which I am unable to purchase for want of a few hundred pounds. Just think what I could do with five million dollars. Why, I have the nucleus of a national collection. I shall be the Hans Sloane of my age.'

His eyes gleamed behind his great spectacles. It was very clear that no pains would be spared by Mr Nathan Garrideb in finding a namesake.

'I merely called to make your acquaintance, and there is no reason why I should interrupt your studies,' said Holmes. 'I prefer to establish personal touch with those with whom I do business. There are few questions I need ask, for I have your very clear narrative in my pocket, and I filled up the blanks when this American gentleman called. I understand that up to this week you were unaware of his existence.'

'That is so. He called last Tuesday.'

'Did he tell you of our interview to-day?'

'Yes, he came straight back to me. He had been very angry.'

'Why should he be angry?'

'He seemed to think it was some reflection on his honour. But he was quite cheerful again when he returned.'

'Did he suggest any course of action?'

'No, sir, he did not.'

'Has he had, or asked for, any money from you?'

'No, sir, never!'

'You see no possible object he has in view?'

'None, except what he states.'

'Did you tell him of our telephone appointment?'

'Yes, sir, I did.'

Holmes was lost in thought. I could see that he was puzzled.

'Have you any articles of great value in your collection?'

'No, sir. I am not a rich man. It is a good collection, but not a very valuable one.'

'You have no fear of burglars?'

'Not the least.'

'How long have you been in these rooms?'

'Nearly five years.'

Holmes's cross-examination was interrupted by an imperative knocking at the door. No sooner had our client unlatched it than the American lawyer burst excitedly into the room.

'Here you are!' he cried, waving a paper over his head. 'I thought I should be in time to get you. Mr Nathan Garrideb, my congratulations! You are a rich man, sir. Our business is happily finished and all is well. As to you, Mr Holmes, we can only say we are sorry if we have given you any useless trouble.'

He handed over the paper to our client, who stood staring at a marked advertisement. Holmes and I leaned forward and read it over his shoulder. This is how it ran:

HOWARD GARRIDEB.

Constructor of Agricultural Machinery.

Binders, reapers, steam and hand plows, drills, harrows, farmers' carts, buckboards, and all other appliances.

Estimates for Artesian Wells.

Apply Grosvenor Buildings, Aston.

'Glorious!' gasped our host. 'That makes our third man.'

'I had opened up inquiries in Birmingham,' said the American, 'and my agent there has sent me this advertisement from a local paper. We must hustle and put the thing through. I have written to this man and told him that you will see him in his office to-morrow afternoon at four o'clock.'

'You want *me* to see him?'

'What do you say, Mr Holmes? Don't you think it would be wiser? Here am I, a wandering American with a wonderful tale. Why should he believe what I tell him? But you are a Britisher with solid references, and he is bound to take notice of what you say. I would go with you if you wished, but I have a very busy day to-morrow, and I could always follow you if you are in any trouble.'

'Well, I have not made such a journey for years.'

'It is nothing, Mr Garrideb. I have figured out your connections. You leave at twelve and should be there soon after two. Then you can be back the same night. All you have to do is to see this man, explain the matter, and get an affidavit of his existence. By the Lord!' he added hotly, 'considering I've come all the way from the centre of America, it is surely little enough if you go a hundred miles in order to put this matter through.'

'Quite so,' said Holmes. 'I think what this gentleman says is very true.'

Mr Nathan Garrideb shrugged his shoulders with a disconsolate air. 'Well, if you insist I shall go,' said he. 'It is certainly hard for me to refuse you anything, considering the glory of hope that you have brought into my life.'

'Then that is agreed,' said Holmes, 'and no doubt you will let me have a report as soon as you can.'

'I'll see to that,' said the American. 'Well,' he added, looking at his watch, 'I'll have to get on. I'll call to-morrow, Mr Nathan, and see you off to Birmingham. Coming my way, Mr Holmes? Well, then, good-bye, and we may have good news for you to-morrow night.'

I noticed that my friend's face cleared when the American left the room, and the look of thoughtful perplexity had vanished.

'I wish I could look over your collection, Mr Garrideb,' said he. 'In my profession all sorts of odd knowledge comes useful, and this room of yours is a storehouse of it.'

Our client shone with pleasure and his eyes gleamed from behind his big glasses.

'I had always heard, sir, that you were a very intelligent man,' said he. 'I could take you round now, if you have the time.'

'Unfortunately, I have not. But these specimens are so well labelled and classified that they hardly need your personal explanation. If I should be able to look in to-morrow, I presume that there would be no objection to my glancing over them?'

'None at all. You are most welcome. The place will, of course, be shut up, but Mrs Saunders is in the basement up to four o'clock and would let you in with her key.'

'Well, I happen to be clear to-morrow afternoon. If you would say a word to Mrs Saunders it would be quite in order. By the way, who is your house-agent?'

Our client was amazed at the sudden question.

'Holloway and Steele, in the Edgware Road. But why?'

'I am a bit of an archæologist myself when it comes to houses,' said Holmes, laughing. 'I was wondering if this was Queen Anne or Georgian.'

'Georgian, beyond doubt.'

'Really. I should have thought a little earlier. However, it is easily ascertained. Well, good-bye, Mr Garrideb, and may you have every success in your Birmingham journey.'

The house-agent's was close by, but we found that it was closed for the day, so we made our way back to Baker Street. It was not till after dinner that Holmes reverted to the subject.

'Our little problem draws to a close,' said he. 'No doubt you have outlined the solution in your own mind.'

'I can make neither head nor tail of it.'

'The head is surely clear enough and the tail we should see to-morrow. Did you notice nothing curious about that advertisement?'

'I saw that the word "plough" was misspelt.'

'Oh, you did notice that, did you? Come, Watson, you improve all the time. Yes, it was bad English but good American. The printer had set it up as received. Then the buckboards. That is American also. And artesian wells are commoner with them than with us. It was a typical American advertisement, but purporting to be from an English firm. What do you make of that?'

'I can only suppose that this American lawyer put it in himself. What his object was I fail to understand.'

'Well, there are alternative explanations. Anyhow, he wanted to get this good old fossil up to Birmingham. That is very clear. I might have told him that he was clearly going on a wild-goose chase, but, on second thoughts, it seemed better to clear the stage by letting him go. To-morrow, Watson – well, to-morrow will speak for itself.'

Holmes was up and out early. When he returned at lunch-time I noticed that his face was very grave.

'This is a more serious matter than I had expected, Watson,' said he. 'It is fair to tell you so, though I know it will only be an additional reason to you for running your head into danger. I should know my Watson by now. But there *is* danger, and you should know it.'

'Well, it is not the first we have shared, Holmes. I hope it may not be the last. What is the particular danger this time?'

'We are up against a very hard case. I have identified Mr John Garrideb, Counsellor at Law. He is none other than "Killer" Evans, of sinister and murderous reputation.'

'I fear I am none the wiser.'

'Ah, it is not part of your profession to carry about a portable Newgate Calendar in your memory. I have been down to see friend Lestrade at the Yard. There may be an occasional want of imaginative intuition down there, but they lead the world for thoroughness and method. I had an idea that we might get on the track of our American friend in their records. Sure enough, I found his chubby face smiling up at me from the Rogues' Portrait Gallery. James Winter, *alias* Morecroft, *alias* Killer Evans, was the inscription below.' Holmes drew an envelope from his pocket. 'I scribbled down a few points from his dossier. Aged forty-four. Native of Chicago. Known to have shot three men in the States. Escaped from penitentiary through political influence. Came to London in 1893. Shot a man over cards in a night club in the Waterloo Road in January, 1895. Man died, but he was shown to have been the aggressor in the row. Dead man was identified as Rodger Prescott, famous as forger and coiner in Chicago. Killer Evans released in 1901. Has been under police supervision since, but so far as known has led an honest life. Very dangerous man, usually carries arms and is prepared to use them. That is our bird, Watson – a sporting bird, as you must admit.'

'But what is his game?'

'Well, it begins to define itself. I have been to the house-agents. Our client, as he told us, has been there five years. It was unlet for a year before then. The previous tenant was a gentleman at large named Waldron. Waldron's appearance was well remembered at the office. He had suddenly vanished and nothing more been heard of him. He was a tall, bearded man with very dark features. Now, Prescott, the man whom Killer Evans had shot, was, according to Scotland Yard, a tall, dark man with a beard. As a working hypothesis, I think we may take it that Prescott, the American criminal, used to live in the very room which our innocent friend now devotes to his museum. So at last we get a link, you see.'

'And the next link?'

'Well, we must go now and look for that.'

He took a revolver from the drawer and handed it to me.

'I have my old favourite with me. If our Wild West friend tries to live up to his nickname, we must be ready for him. I'll give you an hour for a siesta, Watson, and then I think it will be time for our Ryder Street adventure.'

It was just four o'clock when we reached the curious apartment of Nathan Garrideb. Mrs Saunders, the caretaker, was about to leave, but she had no hesitation in admitting us, for the door shut with a spring lock and Holmes promised to see that all was safe before we left. Shortly afterwards the outer door closed, her bonnet passed the bow window, and we knew that we were alone in the lower floor of the house. Holmes made a rapid examination of the premises. There was one cupboard in a dark corner which stood out a little from the wall. It was behind this that we eventually crouched, while Holmes in a whisper outlined his intentions.

'He wanted to get our amiable friend out of his room – that is very clear, and, as the collector never went out, it took some planning to do it. The whole of this Garrideb invention was apparently for no other end. I must say, Watson, that there is a certain devilish ingenuity about it, even if the queer name of the tenant did give him an opening which he could hardly have expected. He wove his plot with remarkable cunning.'

'But what did he want?'

'Well, that is what we are here to find out. It has nothing whatever to do with our client, so far as I can read the situation. It is something connected with the man he murdered – the man who may have been his confederate in crime. There is some guilty secret in the room. That is how I read it. At first I thought our friend might have something in his collection more valuable than he knew – something worth the attention of a big criminal. But the fact that Rodger Prescott of evil memory inhabited these rooms points to some deeper reason. Well, Watson, we can but possess our souls in patience and see what the hour may bring.'

That hour was not long in striking. We crouched closer in the shadow as we heard the outer door open and shut. Then came the sharp, metallic snap of a key, and the American was in the room. He closed the door softly behind him, took a sharp glance around him to see that all was safe, threw off his overcoat, and walked up to the central table with the brisk manner of one who knows exactly what he has to do and how to do it. He pushed the table to one side, tore up the square of carpet on which it rested, rolled it completely back, and then, drawing a jemmy from his inside pocket, he knelt down and worked vigorously upon the floor. Presently we heard the sound of sliding boards, and an instant later a square had opened in the planks. Killer Evans struck a match, lit a stump of candle, and vanished from our view.

Clearly our moment had come. Holmes touched my wrist as a signal, and together we stole across to the open trapdoor. Gently as we moved, however, the old floor must have creaked under our feet, for the head of our American, peering anxiously round, emerged suddenly from the open space. His face turned upon us with a glare of baffled rage, which gradually softened into a rather shamefaced grin as he realized that two pistols were pointed at his head.

'Well, well!' said he, coolly, as he scrambled to the surface. 'I guess you have been one too many for me, Mr Holmes. Saw through my game, I suppose, and played me for a sucker from the first. Well, sir, I hand it to you; you have me beat and – '

In an instant he had whisked out a revolver from his breast and had fired two shots. I felt a sudden hot sear as if a red-hot iron had been pressed to my thigh. There was a crash as Holmes's pistol came down on the man's head. I had a vision of him sprawling upon the floor with blood running down his face while Holmes rummaged him for weapons. Then my friend's wiry arms were round me and he was leading me to a chair.

'You're not hurt, Watson? For God's sake, say that you are not hurt!'

It was worth a wound – it was worth many wounds – to know the depth of loyalty and love which lay behind that cold mask. The clear, hard eyes were dimmed for a moment, and the firm lips were shaking. For the one and only time I caught a glimpse of a great heart as well as of a great brain. All my years of humble but single-minded service culminated in that moment of revelation.

'It's nothing, Holmes. It's a mere scratch.'

He had ripped up my trousers with his pocket-knife.

'You are right,' he cried, with an immense sigh of relief. 'It is quite superficial.' His face set like flint as he glared at our prisoner, who was sitting up with a dazed face. 'By the Lord, it is as well for you. If you had killed Watson, you would not have got out of this room alive. Now, sir, what have you to say for yourself?'

He had nothing to say for himself. He only lay and scowled. I leaned on Holmes's arm, and together we looked down into the small cellar which had been disclosed by the secret flap. It was still illuminated by the candle which Evans had taken down with him. Our eyes fell upon a mass of rusted machinery, great rolls of paper, a litter of bottles, and, neatly arranged upon a small table, a number of neat little bundles.

'A printing press – a counterfeiter's outfit,' said Holmes.

'Yes, sir,' said our prisoner, staggering slowly to his feet and then sinking into the chair. 'The greatest counterfeiter London ever saw. That's Prescott's machine, and those bundles on the table are two thousand of Prescott's notes worth a hundred each and fit to pass anywhere. Help yourselves, gentleman. Call it a deal and let me beat it.'

Holmes laughed.

'We don't do things like that, Mr Evans. There is no bolt-hole for you in this country. You shot this man Prescott, did you not?'

'Yes, sir, and got five years for it, though it was he who pulled on me. Five years – when I should have had a medal the size of a soup plate. No living man could tell a Prescott from a Bank of England, and if I hadn't put him out he would have flooded London with them. I was the only one in the world who knew where he made them. Can you wonder that I wanted to get to the place? And can you wonder that when I found this crazy boob of a bug-hunter with the queer name squatting right on the top of it, and never quitting his room, I had to do the best I could to shift him? Maybe I would have been wiser if I had put him away. It would have been easy enough, but I'm a soft-hearted guy that can't begin shooting unless the other man has a gun also. But say, Mr Holmes, what have I done wrong, anyhow? I've not used this plant. I've not hurt this old stiff. Where do you get me?'

'Only attempted murder, so far as I can see,' said Holmes. 'But that's not our job. They take that at the next stage. What we wanted at present was just your sweet self. Please give the Yard a call, Watson. It won't be entirely unexpected.'

So those were the facts about Killer Evans and his remarkable invention of the three Garridebs. We heard later that our poor old friend never got over the shock of his dissipated dreams. When his castle in the air fell down, it buried him beneath the ruins. He was last heard of at a nursing-home in Brixton. It was a glad day at the Yard when the Prescott outfit was discovered, for, though they knew that it existed, they had never been able, after the death of the man, to find out where it was. Evans had indeed done great service and caused several worthy CID men to sleep the sounder, for the counterfeiter stands in a class by himself as a public danger. They would willingly have subscribed to that soup-plate medal of which the criminal had spoken, but an unappreciative Bench took a less favourable view, and the Killer returned to those shades from which he had just emerged.

The Death Cry

◆

ARTHUR B. REEVE

The first television detective series to be launched in America also came from NBC and featured Craig Kennedy, a consulting detective who employs psychoanalytical techniques and a knowledge of chemistry to solve his cases – factors which earned him the soubriquet of 'the American Sherlock Holmes'. For a number of years between the two World Wars, Kennedy was undoubtedly the most popular sleuth in America, and the stories about him are still highly regarded as the first to link Freudian psychology to detection almost two decades before psychoanalysis gained widespread public acceptance.

Kennedy was created by Arthur B. Reeve (1880–1936), a trained lawyer who abandoned his profession to write when he sensed a growing interest in the use of science in crime detection, and created the first story about his hero, The Silent Bullet, in 1912. Thereafter, Craig Kennedy rapidly became famous as the first Scientific Detective, thanks to a string of best-selling novels and various silent film serials made between 1915 and 1936, starring Arnold Daly. When, however, the detective was transferred to television by producer Adrian Weiss in 1952 as Craig Kennedy, Criminologist, Donald Woods, a Canadian-born star of B-movie crime dramas was cast in the lead for the twenty-six half-hour programmes. This series was later shown in Britain where Reeve's mysteries had already become the first by an American to gain a wide readership. Kennedy is a man of action as well as thought, as he demonstrates in solving the following murder mystery which was adapted for the TV series and, as the reader will find, has more than a little in common with that famous Holmesian adventure, 'The Hound of the Baskervilles' . . .

I.

T HE Three Pines Hotel stood high on the mountainside in the heart of the Catskills, a gaunt and rambling structure that loomed ghost-like and white in the night. Moonlight filtered weakly through the great pines that towered over it; and this moonlight – bluish haze in the night – gave the hotel a weird and forbidding aspect.

It was the third week of the summer season; yet from the hotel came no music or laughter, no animation or gaiety such as in years past in summer seasons. The low structure with its several wings stood silent and grim in the night. Lights shone from a few of its windows, but the lights seemed lifeless; and over the great white rambling building a shroud of impenetrable silence seemed to hang. Encompassing this shroud of silence was the sense of some indefinable dread, stark and ominous and eerie.

Craig Kennedy brought his roadster to an abrupt stop in front of the hotel.

The big wide veranda was lighted, but no one sat in any of the numerous chairs scattered over it. Lights came from the first-floor windows. On the second floor a window here and there was lighted, but most of them were dark.

Kennedy stepped out of his roadster and stood in the shadows of the trees along the road. For some time he remained immovable, his body tense and his eyes on the second-floor windows.

Suddenly he caught his breath. A window in the upper part of the building opened. It was the window of an unlighted room. The dull scraping of the frame going up broke the stillness of the night. In the moonlight Kennedy could see the white outline of the window as it went up slowly.

The long, dark form of a man – or was it a woman? – protruded far out the window. The hands went down to the ledge that ran along the front of the hotel beneath the second-floor windows. Someone walked out on the porch. The dark form darted back into the darkened room. The window thudded down.

Kennedy shrugged and walked across the road and up on the porch. The person who had come out on the porch was gone. Kennedy went directly into the lobby and up to the desk.

A tall, pale-faced man with the air and the voice and the clothes of a successful hotel clerk stood behind the desk.

'The manager of the hotel, Mr Condon,' said Kennedy. 'I have an appointment with him.'

The eyes of the clerk appraised Kennedy coldly. 'You – you are Mr Kennedy?'

Kennedy nodded.

'Ah – then, Mr Kennedy, you may go right up into Mr Condon's private office. He is waiting for you. First door, right.'

Kennedy turned and started for the door to the right. He looked around the lobby. Everything about it bespoke luxury and comfort. A few people were sitting in chairs, staring silently at him. Their faces were set and drawn; they had little of the demeanour or ease of guests of an exclusive summer hotel.

Kennedy opened the door to the manager's office. A young man, not far past thirty, sat behind a desk. His face was frank and pleasant-looking, though there were lines on it from worry and lack of sleep.

'Kennedy!' he exclaimed as he got up quickly and rushed to meet him. 'I'm glad you've come!'

Craig took his hand, smiled, then sat down on the desk.

'Yes, Condon, thanks! The head office of the hotel in the city asked me to get up here as quickly as I could. What's happened? Your place looks like a funeral parlour!'

'It will be a cemetery in another week if things don't change!' exclaimed Condon. 'Did they tell you anything yet?'

'Only to get up here as quickly as I could and find out what was the trouble, cost what it might. No; they gave me no particular information. Said it would come better from you.'

Condon sat down wearily.

'I guess maybe,' he said, 'it mightn't have got under my skin so much if it wasn't that this is my first year as manager. And it looks as if it will be my last.'

'Oh, come now,' broke in Kennedy. 'There may be someone who wants this to be your last year.'

Condon merely shook his head.

'I'll give you an idea of what has happened. The season opened with every prospect of a big summer. The hotel filled rapidly. Then on Thursday of the first week came the first intimation of what was to come. It was a trivial thing and I thought nothing of it at the time.

'Miss Worthington, an old maid, was awakened about three in the morning by the sound of someone in her room. Miss Worthington is very hysterical and she ran out in the hallway screaming, woke up all the other guests. We investigated but could find no evidence of anyone having been in her room. I put it down to a bad dream. But the following night George Branford, an old guest, complained that someone was in his room.

'Branford didn't make much of a scene, but he did tell the other people. Of course Miss Worthington talked about nothing but the man in her room. At first the guests took it as a joke. But when Branford told his story, people began to get puzzled. You know, Kennedy, how such things grow with the telling. In a few days Miss Worthington had been attacked – and Branford's life had been threatened, so it seemed.

'Well, five days passed and nothing happened. Then came that ungodly scream. I heard it. Everyone in the hotel heard it. I can't describe it. It was inhuman, terrifying. It lasted for a full minute. Coming as it did in the dead of night and waking everybody from sleep, it was nerve-racking in view of the nervous state of the guests already.

'This week, Kennedy, it came again! Philip Coulter, an old guest of the hotel, was awakened by someone moving in the dark. But when he turned on the lights he was the only person in the room. Yet on the bed-clothes there was blood! He felt his neck. There was blood there!

'Now, the strange part of all this. Coulter's door was locked and bolted from the inside. No key could have moved that night bolt. His window was up only a few inches. There is a ledge along the front of the building. But this ledge is only a few inches wide, and round on the top. Only a bird could have walked this ledge. How that person entered Coulter's room is the greatest mystery of the whole thing.'

Kennedy merely shrugged. It was obvious why they had said nothing at the city office. 'I see. The scream and the attack on this man Coulter have driven away all your guests.'

'All but eight,' nodded Condon wearily. 'Just eight left – and we are right in the middle of the season.'

'You have checked up on all the guests?' suggested Kennedy. 'You are sure none of them was behind these queer things?'

'We've checked every one and we've searched every inch of this hotel,' Condon replied positively. 'We have no idea where the scream comes from or who is behind it. Neither can we explain the blood on Coulter's bed-clothes. Frankly, we are completely stumped.'

'Any queer guests?' queried Kennedy.

Condon smiled.

'You always have odd characters in a summer hotel. We have Madam Certi with us now.'

'Madam Certi? Who is she?'

'A very fine old lady who talks with the dead. She claims to be a great spiritualist, but really is a very sweet and very fine old lady.'

'I see,' noted Kennedy dryly. 'She is still here?'

'Yes; all the screams and other things have worried her very little.'

'Any other peculiar guests?'

'Professor Mundo is a queer old character. Claims to be a great scientist.'

'You have checked up on these two people?'

'In every detail, I'd say. They could have had nothing to do with the presence of someone in the different rooms or the screams.'

'This scream,' Kennedy remarked thoughtfully, 'what do you make of it yourself? You're worldly-wise, Condon.'

Condon actually shuddered. 'It's the most ungodly thing, Kennedy, you ever heard! So damnably ungodly that if you once hear it, you'll never be able to forget it – or describe it.'

Kennedy smiled and Condon flushed with resentment.

'You may laugh at me. Kennedy, but – ' he checked himself. 'I don't know what is behind all of it. But I am convinced an attempt was made to murder Coulter. How or by what means I don't know – unless someone was trying to choke him and he woke up.'

Kennedy passed it by. 'Let's get down to business, Condon. Where does this scream come from, in your opinion?'

'Why, it usually – '

Condon never finished the sentence. From somewhere in the depths of that great hotel came a wailing cry. It started low and dismal; a chanting wail, weird and unearthly. Then it increased in volume until it was a screeching, hideous scream, like neither human being nor animal.

All colour fled from Condon's face. He raised himself in his chair, trembling. 'My God!' he cried hoarsely. 'Talk of the devil – there it is now!'

Kennedy with a leap was out of his own chair and out in the deserted lobby. The unearthly scream was dying away slowly. It was coming from somewhere on the second floor, apparently. Kennedy was up the stairs, two steps at a time.

A man was running down the hallway. Kennedy recognized him as the pale-faced clerk down at the desk. His eyes were wild and his lower lip was twitching.

'God, man!' he cried. 'It came from Mr Coulter's room!'

An old man, small and wizened, dressed in the uniform of a hotel porter, joined them. He looked at the clerk and at Kennedy a bit stupidly, then started for Coulter's room on a dog-trot.

Kennedy and the clerk followed. At room 256 the old man tried the door. It was locked. He shouted. No answer. The clerk fumbled nervously for his pass-key but couldn't find it. Kennedy shoved him aside and tried the door with his shoulder. It didn't give. He backed away and threw his body against it. It crashed – and he catapulted into the room with it.

When Kennedy got to his feet he looked around. His body stiffened and a whispered oath escaped his lips.

Lying face down on the floor, his neck covered with blood, was a grey-haired man. The bed-clothes were still wrapped around his pyjama-clad body.

Kennedy turned the body over.

The face of the man was blue and distorted as if he had died in either great pain or great fear.

That moment Condon came rushing into the room.

'Anything happen?' he was crying breathlessly.

'This old man,' returned Kennedy, taking his hand off the heart, 'has been murdered!'

'Murdered?' repeated Condon, aghast. 'Mr Coulter!'

2.

Kennedy lost no time getting into action. He sent Condon and the clerk to check up on every person in the hotel. Then he sent the old servant, whose name was Peter, to get the keys to the two suites adjoining that of the murdered man.

Next Kennedy made a rapid but thorough examination of the murder suite. The bedroom where the body of Coulter lay on the floor, with the bed-clothes still wrapped about his legs just as he had either crawled or been pulled out of the bed, was the second room of the suite. The other was smaller, apparently a study. There was a desk in it, a large number of books, and a couple of easy-chairs.

Quick investigation showed nothing that interested Kennedy much except that the windows of the study were locked. He turned back into the bedroom and noted that the door he had crashed had a night bolt on it, and that the bolt had been slipped closed evidently when he crashed the door in.

The windows to the bedroom were up, but one look out of the windows convinced Kennedy that it would have been a physical impossibility for anyone to walk along the ledge below them. The ledge was less than two inches wide, and the top of it was round. The transom to the hall was closed. Apparently, a careful examination of the window, the door and the floor gave no clue as to how the murderer had entered the room.

Then Kennedy turned his attention to the dead man. He brushed some of the blood away from the jugular vein. Under the blood near the base of the throat he saw something that made the lines of his face tighten. There were two little holes – no larger than a pin-point and about half an inch apart. They were black, and apparently the blood on the dead man's throat had come from them.

For some moments Kennedy studied these little holes. Then he stood up, his eyes still staring at the face of the murdered man. His own face was hard and tense; two little lines formed around his mouth.

He looked at the broken door, at the night bolt that had been slipped on, and the closed transom; he turned his face slowly and studied the open windows. His lower lip was sucked in between his teeth. Suddenly it came out with a subdued flop.

He turned and walked deliberately back into the study.

Seizing the telephone, Kennedy put in a call for the sheriff of the county. It was some minutes before he got him.

'Sheriff,' Kennedy shot out in sharp staccato, 'this is Craig Kennedy, of New York City. There's been a murder up at the Three Pines Hotel. Bring a couple of men with you. We'll need them. And the coroner. If you can't get the coroner right away, bring a good doctor along. And I can use a good fingerprint man if you have one available.'

He hung up and walked back into the bedroom.

Condon was standing in the door; old Peter was with him.

'Have – have you found anything, Kennedy?' asked Condon hoarsely. 'I have all the guests rounded up in the lobby downstairs.'

'I've just called the sheriff, Condon,' replied Kennedy. 'He'll be over at once.'

Condon's youthful face wore a positively frightened look which suddenly turned to consternation.

'The sheriff?' he repeated. 'Man, isn't it enough to have this happen without broadcasting – '

'Condon,' retorted Kennedy sternly, 'this is murder – hotel business or no hotel business. Have you the keys to the adjoining rooms?'

'I suppose you're right,' muttered Condon. 'Here they are.'

Kennedy turned to old Peter, whose mouth was gaping with terror, his eyes riveted on the body on the floor.

'Stay at this door, Peter,' ordered Kennedy. 'Condon, you and I are going to have a look at these rooms.'

Old Peter muttered a protest which Kennedy ignored as he turned to the adjoining suite to the right.

It was a small room and had been vacant a week. There was no connecting door to the Coulter suite.

Examination netted nothing. The window was down and locked. There were no indications that anyone had been in the room since it had been vacated.

'That other suite to the left,' explained Condon as Kennedy turned to it, 'is occupied by a young married couple, Mr and Mrs Frederick Pilcher. They took it the first week of the season and remained. They're downstairs. You can go in – on your own responsibility.'

'I'll take it,' decided Kennedy.

The Pilcher suite was laid out in similar manner to the Coulter suite, a bedroom and a second room, in their case a lounging-room, feminine in every detail.

Kennedy examined the furniture carefully, then went over to the window. It was wide open. This window was next to the bedroom where Coulter had been murdered. He looked back. The transom of the hall door was open.

'What do you know about this couple?' asked Kennedy.

'Nothing more than that they have been guests since we opened, and appear to be very pleasant young people. They seem to have plenty of money and to be well connected in the city.'

Kennedy nodded but said nothing. He walked into the lounging-room. Two glasses half-filled with liquor were on a table by a chaise-longue; a cigarette was still smouldering in an ash-tray.

'The Pilchers were up here when the murder was committed,' Kennedy remarked. 'Did they hear anything?'

'I talked to both of them,' Condon replied. 'The first thing they heard was the scream.'

Kennedy walked back into the bedroom. Over by the door he picked up a small piece of black leather. He looked at it, then smiled.

'That's interesting,' he muttered. 'Come back to Coulter's room.'

Condon looked at the piece of leather, his face a blank. Then he followed Kennedy out of the room.

Old Peter was still guarding the death room, his body atremble and his face colourless. Kennedy walked deliberately over to the head of the bed and pointed down at the floor.

'I left that piece of leather on the floor for a reason,' he said. 'I'm glad I did, now. If you will look closely, you will see that this piece in my hand corresponds to the piece on the floor.'

Condon looked down. Lying near the bed was a piece of black leather about an inch wide and perhaps an inch and a half long. A piece had been torn from one end of it, and the leather in Kennedy's hand corresponded to the part torn off.

Condon shook his head wearily. 'I don't understand it. The door was locked and bolted from the inside. No chance to get through the windows. How did the murderer get in?'

'That,' said Kennedy, 'is what I'm figuring out.'

'Simply couldn't be done,' Condon asserted, 'unless the murderer flew through the window.'

'Oh,' Kennedy retorted, 'just exercise your imagination.'

Condon was about to reply, but he no more than framed his lips. The scream of a woman out in the hallway sent both Kennedy and himself in a rush to the door.

Her hair down and streaming behind her, her face distorted with fear, a tall woman, very tall and very slim, arms outstretched, was running wildly.

'Miss Worthington!' Condon cried. 'What's happened?'

'Oh – oh – oh!' she wailed. 'I saw it! I saw it!'

'Saw what?' demanded Kennedy.

'I saw it! A great big black *thing*! It came after me. Oh!'

'Miss Worthington,' Condon soothed, 'if you have seen anything or know anything, calm yourself. You must tell Mr Kennedy. He's a detective.'

'A detective!' The words came from the old maid's mouth in an awed whisper. 'All right – I will tell, if I must. I was coming down from my room as you ordered and I passed Madam Certi's door – and it was there! I saw it! A great big black creature moving down the hall! I screamed – and it disappeared. I just ran and kept on screaming – and here I am!'

'You are here, all right, Miss Worthington,' said Kennedy. 'But what was the great black creature? Man or woman?'

'Oh – oh – oh!' She started to wail again. 'I didn't stop to look. It was big and it was moving fast. That's all I saw. I wasn't stopping to see anything else!'

Voices were coming from downstairs as of people entering the hotel, the sounds of heavy feet on the porch.

'The sheriff,' Condon muttered, frowning. 'If only we could have kept the authorities out of this!'

'Take Miss Worthington down with you,' Kennedy ordered. 'And

Peter also. Tell the sheriff to send a man up at once to take charge of this room. I'll stay until he comes.'

Condon, Miss Worthington and old Peter went downstairs and Kennedy went back to the room. He knelt down on the floor near the piece of leather. For some time he studied it; then he picked it up with his handkerchief, wrapped the linen around it carefully and put it in his pocket.

Again he knelt and studied the floor around the bed. He brushed back the nap of the rug in different spots. Finally he smiled grimly and got up.

A moment later two men entered. One was a short, heavy-set man, a deputy-sheriff. The other was tall, thin-faced and grey-haired; he had shell-blue eyes that gave him a soft, kindly look. He was carrying a small black leather bag.

'I am Doctor Greeley,' the tall man announced to Kennedy. 'Sheriff Blount asked me to help out on this case. The coroner is down at the other end of the county and can't be reached.'

Nervously the other man added, 'The sheriff sent me up to keep watch over the dead.'

Kennedy's instructions were brief. He told the doctor to make as quick an examination of the dead man as possible in the hotel to determine the cause of death. He told the deputy to remain in the room and allow no one to enter.

Then Kennedy went downstairs.

3.

Sheriff Blount was not the usually accepted type of country sheriff. He was young, an ex-service man, keen, alert and business-like. He wore a well-tailored suit and a soft grey hat.

Condon had given the sheriff the details of the murder by the time Kennedy got down.

'Doctor Greeley has told you why he is here, I suppose,' Sheriff Blount greeted Kennedy cordially. 'I have no finger-print expert but I brought along powder and impression paper. I believe you must be an expert yourself, and I know the technique pretty well.'

Kennedy smiled. Everything about this young sheriff pleased him. 'That's all right. We can go over things and see what we find. There likely won't be any prints, but we might run into something.'

'How was Coulter murdered really? Poison?'

'It looks very much that it was, Sheriff. Two little holes over the jugular vein indicate poison, and the face is blue. Doctor Greeley should be able to give a report soon.'

Kennedy was looking at the lobby as he spoke. Huddled like sheep, with silent, drawn faces, the seven guests sat in chairs.

'I want you to see that no one leaves this hotel, Sheriff,' he went on. 'Naturally you are in charge of the case. I'll help you all I can in clearing up this mystery.'

'You mean *I'll* help *you*.' The sheriff was quick to appreciate Kennedy's tact.

Kennedy and the sheriff walked over to the guests in a half-circle in big easy-chairs. In the centre sat Madam Certi, stout, grey-haired, almost queenly. Her round, fat little face with her small blue eyes looked kindly. Her eyes wandered from one guest to another in patronizing, motherly fashion.

Next to her, on her right, sat Professor Mundo, a little dried-up old man with a heavy head of iron-grey hair and a thin, twitching face. His grey eyes shifted rapidly from one to another. To her left sat George Branford, a typical New York broker, sleek, self-satisfied, with an outwardly frank, open face.

To the left of Branford were the Frederick Pilchers, the occupants of the suite next to the murdered man. Mrs Pilcher was a girl somewhere in her late twenties, slim, graceful, with a cold, sharp face of the classical type rather than the frank open beauty of the outdoor girl. There was something in her, the movements of hands and head, that bespoke the stage.

Pilcher himself was small of body, and his face was weak. It was obvious he was largely under the influence of his wife.

At the left of Professor Mundo sat Burroughs Matthews, young and handsome and slightly bored by the whole proceedings. Next to him was Godfrey Nelson, a man somewhere in his fifties, with a full red face and heavy body. Money and success in business had left their mark on him.

Then at the right end of the half-circle, her hair still down and her face white, her lips still twitching, sat Miss Worthington. Her teeth were clicking and she kept her silence only by great effort.

Condon stood at the other end of the half-circle and at his side was George McGuire, the pale-faced clerk. Old Peter paced back and forth behind them like a nervous animal in a cage.

'A murder has been committed in this hotel,' began the sheriff quietly. 'We shall have to ask each one of you to remain in the hotel until the investigation has been completed.'

'I – I knew it was murder!' Miss Worthington let out a wail that might have been heard all over the hotel.

Burroughs Matthews smiled in his bored manner. Madam Certi gave a little gasp of fear. The others just stared in a helpless, grim manner.

'I knew some of us would be murdered!'

'The trains are still running,' Matthews observed. 'If you were so frightened, why didn't you leave?'

Miss Worthington promptly started to sob. Madam Certi gave Burroughs Matthews a reproving look.

'Mr Kennedy will desire to question you,' Blount went on.

'There will be no questions from me now,' Kennedy cut in. 'I want you all to go to your rooms and remain there. When I want any of you, I'll send for you.'

'How long do we have to stay here?' Branford, the broker, rose. 'I have to get back to New York tomorrow.'

'Perhaps you may,' returned the sheriff. 'We'll see.'

'I – I am willing to co-operate.' Godfrey Nelson got up slowly, stammering. 'But one man has been killed. Can we be safe if we go back to our rooms?'

'Well, you may remain in the lobby if you wish,' Kennedy conceded. 'One or the other.'

'I won't go to my room alone!' wailed Miss Worthington. 'Someone tried to kill me two weeks ago. I won't go alone!'

Matthews laughed. 'Then take some brave man with you.'

'A man – in my room!' Miss Worthington blushed very red and walked to the other end of the lobby and sat down.

Branford and Nelson started up the stairs slowly. Madam Certi rose, her fat little body wobbling.

'Ah, Mr Kennedy,' she gushed. 'I have heard a great deal of you as a detective. I am so glad to be here in this crisis and to be able to help. You know I do many things not understood by the human mind. I know I can work with you.'

'I have heard of you, Madam Certi,' Kennedy replied quietly. 'I am sure we will be able to work together.'

The coldness of his tone was not lost on Madam Certi. For a fleeting second the sweet, kindly look on her face became a dark, animal-like scowl that passed as quickly as it came. She smiled sweetly and wobbled away.

Professor Mundo followed, walking with short, nervous strides. His eyes were on the floor, his thin face twisted.

Burroughs Matthews remained seated. 'If there is any excitement to break the tedium, I hope you'll let us in on it, Kennedy.'

'I shall. You may be sure of that.'

Kennedy turned to Condon. 'What became of old Peter as our backs were turned?'

'Why – he has disappeared.' Condon looked helplessly about. 'A queer old duck. Comes and goes like a ghost.'

'Never mind, now,' Kennedy bustled. 'The sheriff and I are going to the cellar. Show us the cellar stairs.'

'The cellar!' Condon gasped. 'There – there isn't anything down there – I am sure.'

'And I,' Kennedy insisted coldly, 'am sure there is!'

4.

Slowly and carefully Kennedy and Sheriff Blount went down the stairs that led to the cellar. A worn electric bulb did not exactly flood the cellar with light. At the foot of the steps was a furnace on a clean cement floor. But beyond this under the different wings of the building the shadowy, yawning mouths of passageways loomed dark and sinister.

They had proceeded scarcely as far as the heater when Kennedy's body suddenly stiffened. Somewhere in the jet blackness of one of those shadowy passageways something was moving. There was the almost inaudible sound of feet.

Kennedy's automatic was out in an instant as he strode towards the shadowy part of the cellar.

'Go to the other side of the furnace and the coal bins, Blount!' he muttered. 'And keep your eye peeled.'

There was a swish of air. Something cracked the weak light bulb and plunged the whole cellar into deep darkness. A body was moving in that shadow. Another swish – and a guttural groan from Blount as he went down.

The same instant Kennedy's automatic blazed orange-red. He lunged forward, fairly diving into the dangerous darkness as with his other hand he whipped out his flashlight and sent a long streak of white light along the floor and walls.

The wavering streak of the flash revealed nothing, and he turned it back on Blount staggering to his feet, a thickening red trickle spreading down his forehead.

Whoever it was, whatever it was, had disappeared in the second before Craig could flash his light.

'What – hit – me?' gasped Blount.

'The person who missed me in the dark – just as I must have missed him in the dark, also,' returned Kennedy.

'Person?' Blount tried weakly to laugh it off. 'That was no person. It was a monster of some kind as near as I could make it out. Then something hit me.'

Kennedy shook his head. 'It was a very human person,' he insisted, 'a person who knows this cellar well and can move with the speed of a greyhound.'

Craig was helping Blount to rise. 'How are you?'

'All right – just groggy.'

'Got to get you upstairs to Doctor Greeley right away.' Kennedy advanced nevertheless, flashing his light on the walls.

The rock walls looked just as they had been left after the cellar was blasted. No cement had been put on them and no attempt had been made to smooth them over. Jagged rocks stuck out of the wall. Cracks appeared here and there.

'Come,' Kennedy decided, 'I've got to get you up to the doctor, pronto. Hulloa!'

His flashlight was playing on the floor where there was a thin covering of dust and dirt. Over at that end outlines of Kennedy's and Blount's footprints were visible. What Kennedy was looking at was another strange outline in the dust.

It was a round outline, more or less irregular. These outlines of strange-looking footprints came from a passage under the north wing. There were none on the smooth cement floor. But they went in on the other side, up the service stairs in the back – and were lost.

'Whoever made those prints disappeared quickly up those stairs,' concluded Kennedy, 'didn't stop or turn back. He just came, smashed the light, cracked your head and went! Come on, Sheriff, I must get you up to the doctor. This cellar will bear exploring, later.'

By the time they got up to the Coulter suite through the now deserted lobby, Doctor Greeley had completed his examination of the body, now on the bed and covered by a sheet. The doctor was just closing his medicine bag.

Doctor Greeley squinted his eyes and looked at the sheriff.

'What's happened to you, Blount?'

'A ghost cracked me on the head in the cellar – a great big ghost that can run like hell!'

'Well, you come right over here under this light and let me have a look at you. H'm. A nasty blow. But I'll give you something to relieve the pain and then I'll dress it for you.'

'By the way, Doctor,' Kennedy nodded toward the bed, 'what's the verdict?'

'The man died by poison that was injected into his veins,' replied the doctor, working rapidly over the sheriff. 'By what means it was injected, I do not know. It entered the jugular vein through two little holes that might have been made by some form of hypo-needle – and might not. He died almost instantly when the poison coursed through the blood stream.'

'There was a struggle,' Kennedy reconstructed, 'and in the struggle Coulter was pulled off the bed. What caused the blood on his neck?'

'A series of very fine scratches, Kennedy. Very mysterious, those scratches. You have to look very closely to see them now. I didn't get them myself at first.'

'I see,' Craig nodded. 'Just how can you connect those scratches with the two holes on the neck?'

'That, Kennedy,' Greeley avoided, 'is a matter for you to puzzle out. I am a doctor, not a detective.'

Kennedy held up his hand and listened. An instant later he was out in the hall, past the door, where he scowled because the deputy sheriff was not there. An instant later he was in the Pilcher suite, where he had heard someone entering.

Standing in the lounge-room by a little escritoire was Mrs Pilcher, her face pale and her lips quivering. She stared at Kennedy helplessly. All the cold cockiness she had displayed down in the lobby was gone.

'You are looking for something, Mrs Pilcher?' inquired Kennedy courteously. 'It was hardly necessary for you to wait until the deputy sheriff had been enticed away, then sneak through the halls to get it.'

'I came to get some night-clothes! I don't intend to sleep in this room tonight!' She was quick with the excuse.

'Night-clothes – in the escritoire?'

Her cold thin face flushed angrily. But in her eyes there was a helpless stare, and she was stammering.

'I am afraid, Mrs Pilcher,' said Kennedy, 'that I have already on my first visit to your room found what you are searching for to conceal.'

Her face paled. 'What – what do you mean?' she gasped.

Kennedy merely smiled. 'I think you know.'

Staring, with mouth gaping open, she gave a little cry of fear, then rushed out the door and down the hall.

'There you are, Blount,' pronounced the doctor. 'By the way, an old man who looks like a servant came with a message for your deputy. He asked me to watch. I almost forgot about it.'

'Get hold of your deputy, Sheriff. Tell him not to leave his post even if he's blasted from it!' muttered Craig.

Condon, breathing heavily as if he had been running, came up the hall. 'Madam Certi wants to see you in her rooms at once, Kennedy. It's important, she says, very important.'

5.

Madam Certi's suite was in the south wing, overlooking the great mountain that rose in the rear of the hotel. It consisted of two rooms: a bedroom and a front room larger than in most suites.

This front room was filled with strange-looking furniture which Madam at her own expense moved up at the beginning of the summer in a small van. Odd-shaped chairs that rose only a few inches from the floor, teak tables weirdly shaped, black curtains that hung from the ceiling putting the room at all times in dark and shadow. At one end was a dais, somewhat like a throne of an ancient queen. Black curtains from the ceiling almost hid the throne chair.

Madam Certi, clothed in a long, flowing white robe, her head covered by a veil-like hood, met Kennedy and the sheriff at the door.

'Ah, Mr Kennedy,' she crooned in a soft whisper. 'You have come to Madam Certi and it is well. For I will make the dead speak and when they speak you will learn much.'

'So, you got me here to show me a little spiritualism,' he smiled. 'I thought it was something important.'

An angry scowl flitted over the round, fat face of Certi. 'I will show you,' she reproved, 'how Mr Coulter was killed, because I have talked with him and he will appear to you.'

'Talking with spirits won't get us anywhere,' growled Blount. 'Even a scientist like Professor Mundo might – '

'Ah, Professor Mundo,' Madam Certi interrupted softly. 'You wish to see him? He is here right now.'

One of the curtains moved. The small wizened form of Professor Mundo appeared. His face was pale and he was trembling.

The lights went out. From the dais came the voice of Certi. 'You will now see Madam Certi call the dead to speak! You will now see how Madam Certi can help you, Craig Kennedy!'

Silence, eerie and oppressive. The voice of Madam Certi came in a low droning. Her words were incoherent.

Blount started toward the door. Kennedy's arm shot out, stopping him.

'Wait a minute!' Craig whispered. 'It may all have some meaning.'

Madam Certi's voice grew higher and plainer.

'Speak, departed one, speak, for there are those here who would know of thy death.'

An effusion of amber rays fell upon the white-cloaked figure of Madam Certi. Then the rays dimmed. It was some light effect no doubt rigged up by Professor Mundo.

'Speak, spirit of John Coulter, speak!'

'She's crazy as hell,' Blount muttered in disgust. 'She – '

He didn't finish the sentence. As the light faded from Madam's face and figure, another light appeared to her right, at first just a soft glow; then as it grew stronger the outlines of a white face appeared in the light.

Blount gave a gasp of surprise. It certainly did strongly resemble the face of John Coulter, the murdered man.

'You are with friends, Mr Coulter,' she droned. 'You may speak and tell them what you told me.'

Coulter's face was vivid and ghastly. The lips actually began to move, as the light shimmered over the face.

'I was murdered.' The voice was hollow, metallic, like a voice from a radio-drama telephone. 'I was murdered by a fiend who kills through means more hideous than those of the Dark Ages.' The voice died away in a groan.

'Speak on!' urged Madam Certi. 'There are those who would avenge thy murder.'

The lips of the ghastly vision moved again.

'Study well the marks on my neck and you will see – '

Even the voice of the dead was interrupted. Somewhere through the hallway the low wail of the death scream, the scream that had followed Coulter's death, broke the air. It rose to a high pitch, a weird, unearthly scream of death. It rang through the hotel, increasing in volume until it was an inhuman, terrifying screech.

The face of John Coulter disappeared. The light went out.

Kennedy made a leap for the door of the suite.

'Stay here, Blount! Don't let them escape!' he cried.

The door was locked. Kennedy fumbled, found the light-switch and flooded the apartment with light. The Madam was gone from the throne. Blount poked the curtain. Mundo was not there, either.

Outside, somewhere on the second floor, the weird, death-like scream was dying into a pitiful moan. A woman was yelling hysterically. Footsteps of men in the hall could be heard.

Kennedy crashed the lock with a succession of slugs from his automatic. As he leaped into the hall he looked back.

'The head's a wax figure, made up – lips move on wires!' shouted Blount, who had torn aside another curtain.

Kennedy could hear people talking excitedly somewhere in the south wing. He strode down, swerved at the first turn. McGuire, the pale-faced clerk, and Condon were before a door. Old Peter came around a corner and joined them.

'It's Branford's room!' Condon muttered huskily as Kennedy strode up quickly.

McGuire was turning the lock with his pass-key. The door opened. No night bolt had been shot this time.

Kennedy pushed the clerk unceremoniously aside and took a step into the room. The lights were out. His hand fumbled for the light-switch, found it, snapped it on.

Lying on the floor, near the window, clad in pyjamas, and with some bed-covers wound around his legs, was the body of George Branford. He lay partly on his side, his face toward them.

The face was blue and distorted, twisted out of shape, as if, like Coulter, Branford had died in some great pain or fear.

Kennedy walked over to the body and looked down at the neck. Blood was over it. He knelt down and brushed the blood away from the jugular vein. There, as in the case of Coulter, were two little black holes, no larger than a pinhead!

Kennedy got up. His face was set and hard. Lines played about his mouth. His eyes narrowed to slits.

Condon in the doorway was staring, terror-stricken, at Branford's body. McGuire, at his side, the colour completely gone from his face, was fidgeting nervously. Old Peter had disappeared again.

'Whose is the next suite?' Kennedy waved his hand in the direction of the corner in the hall.

Condon wet his lips. 'The Pilchers,' he replied.

'You gave them a room next to Branford?'

'Yes. They requested it.'

'And on the other side?'

'Empty.'

Kennedy went to the window and looked out. It was the front of the hotel, still, although around a turn in the hall. He was about to say something as Sheriff Blount burst into the room.

'They're gone! They've disappeared!' Blount cried. 'Not in their rooms – not anywhere in the hotel!'

'I'm not surprised,' returned Kennedy quietly.

A woman suddenly flung open the door of her room far down the hall. Her hair was streaming and her teeth chattered, as her eyes were staring wild with fear.

It was Miss Worthington.

'Look! Look!' she cried in a crescendo. 'It went through the lobby! Look – out the window!'

Kennedy turned to the window. The road that ran in front of the Three Pines was flooded with a soft moonlight that penetrated a bit through the trees that lined the road. A form, dark and moving with the swiftness of an animal, was disappearing into the trees.

Kennedy took one good look; then with a spring he was through the door of the room.

Miss Worthington, with the sight of the dead body of Branford lying on the floor, groaned and slumped into a swoon in the arms of Condon, who caught her.

'Check them all as far as you can, Sheriff,' Kennedy called back over his shoulder as he ran. 'Have them all in the lobby.'

A matter of seconds and he was out and across the road in front of the hotel.

6.

The moonlight filtered through the great pines that covered the mountainside in fleeting, darting shafts of light. In places it cut through the trees with the brightness of day; in other places it failed to penetrate and the darkness was jet-black and heavy.

Kennedy dashed through the trees. No sign of the form appeared. He came to a narrow path that wound in and out among the trees like a wriggling snake. He followed it.

It was taking him far down the mountain and out across a little plateau. Here and there the moon lighted his way; at other times he was plunging through a darkness so intense he could scarcely see the trees before him.

Blindly he followed the path. He had no idea whether the person he had seen disappear in the trees was in front of him or far to his right or left. He plunged on, his mind mystified at what he had seen from the window.

The person who had disappeared among the trees was no dark form or monster. Kennedy's one good look told him that. But what he had seen was even more puzzling than if it had been the dark form of some monster. The man who plunged into the pines was Burroughs Matthews!

Slowly in Kennedy's mind there had been forming a solution to the strange murders. But this solution was so weird, so terrifying that at first he had refused to give it credence. The séance of Madame Certi had given him an inkling that it was true. And yet in this solution Burroughs Matthews had had no place. But now he was following the young man, who was rich and cultured and very much bored with life. Kennedy wondered vaguely where this chase was taking him.

Suddenly Kennedy stopped. He was in the darkness of the trees; but out in front of him was an open space, flooded brightly by the moonlight. An old stone fence was around the open space and the grass grew wild and high over the fence.

Inside the enclosure was a small mound. An old tombstone leaned grotesquely in the tall, wild grass.

Kneeling down by this tombstone was the slender, youthful form of Burroughs Matthews.

Kennedy remained in the darkness of the trees and watched. The young man was tugging at the tombstone. Then suddenly he stopped, took a piece of paper from his pocket and began writing on it. He made only a few notes. Then he jumped up suddenly, ran through the grass away from Kennedy, disappearing over the stone fence.

Had he heard something?

Kennedy did not follow him. For several minutes he remained standing in the shadow of the trees. Then he struck out into the open, leaped the stone fence and thrashed through the grass to the lone grave.

It was an old-fashioned round-topped tombstone with the grass swaying weirdly about it. The inscription read:

> GYPSY JONES
> Born August 12, 1871
> Died July 22, 1924
> So have I lived unknown
> So shall I die unknown

Kennedy studied the strange inscription. He took a pencil from his pocket and copied it in a notebook. He slipped the book back into his pocket and turned to retrace his steps.

Something was moving in the grass to his right. Instantly he went down flat on his stomach. He lay still, his body tense and ready for a spring. But only the silence of the night greeted him. The tall grass waved lazily in the soft breeze. A little to his right the old tombstone seemed to lean weirdly, loosened.

Somewhere in front of him he had seen the grass move. But now there was no sign of life there. Slowly he crawled forward on his stomach; it was difficult work in the grass. His automatic was ready but he wasn't firing blindly and giving the advantage of knowing where he was. He moved forward several yards flat on the ground.

Somewhere in front of him there came a harsh, inhuman laugh. Two cold hands with powerful fingers went round his throat. He felt fingernails tearing at his skin. He drew his legs under his body for one supreme lunge forward to throw off his strange attacker.

But he never got his legs under his body. From behind, what seemed in the darkness a form, huge and grotesque, loomed over him, poised in the air a second, then crashed down on his head, and he saw no more.

Kennedy came to, later, with someone shaking his body violently. He opened his eyes, but the pain in his head was too great.

Someone was leaning over him. At first he could not recognize who it was. Then the outlines of a young and handsome face came to him. He blinked his eyes again. It was Burroughs Matthews!

'I came out for a quiet walk,' said Matthews, 'and I run right into excitement! Someone must have been trying hard to kill you, Kennedy. You have me to thank that they didn't.'

'I don't know,' Kennedy muttered as he struggled to his feet, 'whether I should thank you – or arrest you as a material witness.'

'Neither is very important right now,' returned Matthews.

'Why were you trying to remove that tombstone – and why did you stop?'

'Just curiosity,' Matthews answered in a bored manner. 'I heard someone coming. So I started away. When I heard a struggle I came running back. The tombstone was gone. You were lying on the ground and some baffling-looking person in the dark was going over the fence. That's all. Come, I'll get you back to the hotel.'

7.

As Kennedy and Matthews walked into the lobby of the hotel the four remaining guests were seated in a circle at the far end. Sheriff Blount and Condon were with them.

Mr and Mrs Pilcher sat close together on a small couch, their eyes on the floor. Mrs Pilcher had lost much of her brazen attitude. She did not look up as Kennedy placed Matthews next to her.

Godfrey Nelson, his full, red face drawn and haggard, sat directly across from them. Miss Worthington, hysterical and crying softly to herself, sat near Condon. She insisted on his holding her hand, which the young manager did with a scowl.

'Burroughs Matthews is not to leave this hotel, Sheriff,' indicated Kennedy. 'Have one of your men with him all the time. I have something important to discuss with you and Condon now.'

The Pilchers looked up at Matthews, surprised and puzzled. Godfrey Nelson stared at the young man. Even Miss Worthington stopped crying to look at him.

Matthews smiled and nonchalantly lighted a cigarette.

'Sweet man, you are,' Matthews laughed dryly. 'I save your life – and then you virtually place me under arrest!'

Kennedy said nothing. He turned and walked into Condon's private office with the young manager. Blount motioned to one of his men, whispered his orders, and followed them closely.

In the office Kennedy shut the door himself, then turned to the other two. 'I want all the information you have about one Gypsy Jones buried down there on the plateau.'

Condon looked blank at him. Sheriff Blount was puzzled.

'Gypsy Jones?' the sheriff repeated. 'You mean that fellow who lived like a hermit on this mountain when the hotel was being built?'

'I imagine so,' Kennedy encouraged. 'There was a tombstone down there with his name on it, his dates and a queer inscription underneath. I followed Burroughs Matthews down there after the murder of Branford. Someone knocked me unconscious. When I came to, Matthews was there – the tombstone was missing.'

'Missing!' Blount repeated, then wrinkled his forehead. 'I don't remember a great deal about Gypsy Jones. I was pretty young when he died. But as a boy I can remember the strange old man who lived on this mountain like a hermit.'

'Oh, I've heard of him,' Condon put in. 'Yes; he died the year the hotel was opened. I have heard of this Gypsy Jones. Why, Godfrey Nelson was a guest of the hotel the year that Gypsy Jones died. He was supposed to have known him.'

'Did Coulter know this Gypsy Jones?'

Condon wet his lips and nodded. 'Yes,' he said at length. 'Coulter knew him, I believe. So did Branford. Coulter, Branford and Nelson are our oldest guests. They've spent every summer here since the place opened.'

'Get Godfrey Nelson in here,' Kennedy ordered.

A few minutes later Nelson entered the room, his round, red face a bit pale and his eyes roving anxiously.

'Tell us all you know about Gypsy Jones, Nelson,' Kennedy demanded briskly. 'All.'

'Gypsy Jones?' Nelson repeated. He was sparring for time. His eyes met Kennedy's. 'Why – why,' he decided to surrender, 'it was ten years ago he died. Yes, I knew him. A strange character. In fact, I was present at his death. People around here considered him insane. He lived in an old shack that has since been torn down. He was buried near the shack.'

'Coulter and Branford knew him,' prompted Kennedy.

'Why – yes; they knew him as I did.'

'You were guests,' prompted Kennedy again, 'the first year.'

'Yes, we three often tramped over the mountains. I think it was Branford who first ran across Gypsy Jones. Jones was an old man with a fine, intellectual face. We were convinced Gypsy Jones was not his real name, that he was a man of breeding and culture – perhaps a man with a past he was trying to forget.'

'Did you learn his real name?' demanded Kennedy.

Nelson hesitated, then decided it was best to tell. 'Yes – his real name was Sir Charles Wainwright. He was an Englishman.'

'An Englishman? Why was he buried as Gypsy Jones – and on that lonely spot?'

Godfrey Nelson shook his head. 'It was his last wish,' he replied earnestly. 'Coulter and I were with him just before he died. He was delirious and it was then that we heard his real name. But before he died he was himself again. He asked us if he had talked. We told him he had. Then he made us solemnly promise that he would be buried as Gypsy Jones and that his name would for ever remain a secret with us.'

The breaking of a confidence to a dying man seemed to worry Nelson.

'When a man is dying,' he went on, on the defensive, 'a person respects his wishes. So he was buried there as he wished. Why, he dictated the inscription for his tombstone. The three of us respected the oath. I am talking now only because the law is forcing me to talk. What mystery was behind this poor man's life, I don't know. What that may have to do with these terrible murders, I can't conceive.'

'It has very much to do,' asserted Kennedy. 'Coulter, Branford and you are, or should be, the only persons who knew the real identity of this man. And now someone is very anxious, for some reason, to see each of you die before you can tell.'

Nelson paled and bit his lip. 'You mean,' he said weakly, 'I am to die, also?'

'You,' asserted Kennedy grimly, 'are scheduled to die next. But if you do as I instruct, you have nothing to fear.'

Nelson's lips twitched. His face was imploring.

'You,' Kennedy instructed, 'are to remain in this hotel. But you are not to go to your room alone, or any other room, under any circumstances. You are to remain down here in the lobby and Sheriff Blount will assign one of his best men to remain with you. If you fall asleep, there will be someone awake near you. You may go back into the lobby now.'

Godfrey Nelson got up slowly and walked out of the room.

'But, Kennedy,' the sheriff remonstrated, 'how could a man like Gypsy Jones be connected in any way with these murders? He died ten years ago. He was half crazy and – '

'Three men knew who he was; two of these men are dead.' Kennedy was positive. 'If we're not careful the third will die.'

'Yes, but that death scream – '

'I have a theory about that; it may seem fantastic and weird just now. Those two pieces of leather gave me my first hunch. I think it is going to take us back down-cellar.'

'Let's go, then, and get it over.' The sheriff rubbed his sore head ruefully.

Kennedy shook his head. 'I am not ready yet. First I must check up on some facts that have aroused my suspicions. To do that I must go to New York immediately.'

8.

Kennedy's roadster cut through the night with the speedometer registering better than seventy much of the time. He slumped in the seat wearily, his face set. For the first time since the attack near the lone grave he realized the strain.

Intermittently far behind him came the subdued roar of a powerful car.

He crossed the Hudson by the Peekskill Bridge. On this wide road he was shooting the gas to his motor. The illuminated dial of his wrist-watch gave two-thirty as the time when he hit the Bronx River Parkway.

Stil, now and then, that subdued roar of a powerful car.

It was ten minutes to four when he pulled up before the granite, pillared and domed building on Centre Street which was Police Headquarters.

He was there probably not more than twenty minutes, making requests for information in the morning, telephoning and checking up on an address he had taken from the register at the Three Pines.

He examined the automatic in his left coat pocket, checked the ammunition in the clip, then did the same with the automatic in his shoulder holster.

His plan of campaign set, Kennedy nodded to the officer at the main entrance, ran down the steps, and shot his roadster slithering uptown on the East Side, with little to hinder him but a few cruising night-hawk taxis.

Eyes on the mirror, he finally satisfied himself that he was not being followed. Only then did he turn, shoot across town to Second Avenue, finally pulling up at a corner in the upper forties.

No sign of life moving on the street. Across, an apartment house loomed. It was not a new building. There was, however, an air of exclusiveness about it, a look that set it apart from the cheaper tenements surrounding it.

For some time Kennedy studied the building. There was just one light from a window on the fifth floor. Perhaps someone had forgotten to switch off the light. Otherwise it was dark.

Finally, Kennedy crossed the street. A coloured boy was dozing in a chair by the elevator.

Kennedy twirled a five-dollar bill in his hands. 'Apartment 513,' he said peremptorily, stepping into the car.

The coloured boy was wide awake now. He looked greedily at the five-dollar note, then uncertainly at Kennedy. Casually Kennedy slipped his hand from his left coat pocket and turned up the left lapel of his coat. A shield which he wore by courtesy of the police commissioner, gleamed.

The coloured boy swallowed hard, took the bill, shot the car upward to the fifth floor.

'Don't bang the door, Rastus,' Kennedy admonished as the boy hesitated. 'Shoot down – but keep awake, if I should ring.'

'Yas, suh!' The boy was still pop-eyed over the shield.

The moment the elevator was gone, Kennedy, noting that 506 was before him, turned and walked quietly until he stopped before a door numbered 513.

He pressed the buzzer. There was no answer. He pressed again and listened again. Only the deep impressive silence of night.

He tried the door. It was locked, of course. With a quick look up and down the hall, he took a piece of steel from his pocket. It was only a matter of minutes before he sprung the lock, and the door opened.

A wall of darkness greeted him. With his hand on the automatic in his holster, Kennedy felt his way down a long narrow corridor. This was the Pullman type of apartment.

At the end he came out on a large room facing the street. Enough light feebly filtered in from the street to give a shadowy outline of the furniture.

Kennedy stood, his body rigid, right hand still gripping his automatic. His ears strained, but only an eerie silence greeted him.

Then he walked over to the wall, felt along it until he came to the light-switch, turned it, and the room was flooded with light. A moment he stood, his body tense and ready for action, eyes and ears alert for any sound or movement.

It was the living-room of the apartment. From all indications it had not been used for some time. A coat of city dust covered tables, chairs and bookcases.

He went over to a bookcase, and glanced cursorily at the books. Suddenly his attention was drawn to a book out of the top of which stuck several pieces of paper. He removed it from the bookcase. The slips of paper showed that someone had the habit of marking places in the book in this manner. He opened to the marked places rapidly. Then he found another and still another book similarly marked.

All the markers were at descriptions of poisons!

Kennedy piled the books up on a chair and turned to the apartment for further investigation.

He turned into a room off the living-room, a small study, with a desk at the window also opening on the street. A letter file on the desk was open, drawers were pulled out, papers, letters, documents were scattered about.

Someone had been there before him! He thought of the roar of the high-powered motor behind him on the road. He reached up to feel the electric light bulb. It was still hot. Someone had been there only minutes ago!

His left hand still on the bulb overhead and his right on the gun in his shoulder holster, a body came hurtling at him through the semi-darkness of the room.

He had turned and drawn with the speed of lightning. But the suddenness of the attack sent his shot wild as he felt thin arms encircling him with the insane power of a maniac. The impetus of the attack knocked the automatic from his hand. He might have reached for the other in his coat pocket, but he needed both arms to fight off the maniacal clutch of those wiry arms.

Together they went to the floor. Silently, grimly they struggled, each trying for a strangle hold. The body under Kennedy was slippery and quick as a cat. Kennedy's hands went to the person's neck. Once he had it he might either reach the gun on the floor with his right hand or the gun in his pocket with the left.

He had it! The gun on the floor was only six inches away.

The body slipped out from under him with an incredible eeliness. His right hand had the gun – but his left was only gripping the floor.

He threw his body backward and made a dive in the darkness for the legs that must be there. The lunge through the dark for his unknown assailant was futile. There came a bang – and out in the hallway a dry, inhuman laugh. No other sound.

Kennedy was on his feet, his body against the door. It was the door that had banged shut. It did not give. His flashlight had been smashed in the scuffle. He felt along the wall for the switch, turned it, and flooded the little room with light. A closet door was open.

He smiled a cold, bitter smile as he saw the desk and floor covered with papers, scattered in every direction. That must have been the fifth-floor light he had seen. The intruder had been working as he entered, must have retreated into the closet, and catapulted himself out the instant Kennedy's back was turned.

As Kennedy wrenched at the closed door he realized there was a snap-lock on the other side. The outside apartment door banged. Should he shoot the lock and pursue?

His eye lighted on a burned piece of paper, a letterhead torn across the top. Gun in hand, he picked it up.

Engraved in old English across the top were the words:

Sir Charles Wainwright
42 Haversham Road
Whitehall
London, England

The typed part had been burned in the little fireplace, along with other charred paper.

He turned to the lock, shot it open, and dashed down the hall, both guns in his hands. In the hall he thought for a moment. The assailant had just enough start to enable him to make a getaway down the fire-stairs.

He turned back and dashed to the front windows. The first rays of dawn were breaking. Down on the street he could make out a tall, thin form scurrying from the street door.

A cold, satisfied smile played over Kennedy's face. The form he had seen scurrying out and around the corner was none other than McGuire, the tall, pale-faced clerk at Three Pines!

He felt for the paper in his pocket, picked up the books on the chair, switched out the lights, and went out leisurely.

9.

It was forenoon when Kennedy got out of bed at his apartment on Riverside Drive.

His man, Parker, had three telegrams and notations of two telephone calls that had come in that morning.

Kennedy scanned the telegrams casually and stuffed them into his pocket. Then he called back twice on the telephone. Already, breakfast, still steaming, had arrived from the restaurant downstairs.

He was eating leisurely and Parker was busying himself about the diggings, when suddenly Parker stopped short.

'Oh, by the way, sir, begging your pardon, sir,' Parker interjected apologetically, 'Police Headquarters telephoned while you were in the bath and asked that you be informed they have arrested Madam Certi and a Professor Mundo and are having them held, sir. I made no notation and I forgot to tell you, sir.'

Kennedy frowned.

'Stupid!' he exclaimed. 'Headquarters is the last place I want Madam Certi and Professor Mundo held.'

'And, sir, they said, I believe, that they arrested them at Madam Certi's apartment. I understood them to say they made the arrest at five this morning when Madam Certi and the professor entered the apartment.'

'Hand me the telephone, Parker – I must have them released at once – no, it can wait. I shall be at headquarters several hours before I am able to drive back to Three Pines. You'll probably see me in the early morning hours, Parker. Tell people I am out of town, that's all. Use your discretion.'

'Thank you, sir. Good-bye, sir,' Parker bowed as Kennedy strode out to his roadster which had already been sent around from the garage, washed, greased, oiled and generally tuned up.

It was about four when Kennedy swung into his roadster down at Centre Street and started back to the Three Pines Hotel in the Catskill Mountains. When finally he left the city behind he kept his car at an easy speed and appeared in no great hurry to get back to the hotel.

His face no longer wore a puzzled look. In the rumble of the car were piled the books with their telltale slips of paper as markers. He had various strips of leather. And in his breast pocket was a voluminous sheaf of telegrams and radiograms.

Shortly past seven he parked his roadster in front of the Three Pines. Sheriff Blount was waiting on the veranda.

Ignoring the locked rumble seat and its precious evidence, Kennedy locked the car as the sheriff came down the steps.

'Madam Certi and Professor Mundo came back an hour ago,' the sheriff announced, modulating his voice. 'Someone drove them back from New York and they have gone directly to Madam Certi's room and have locked themselves in. Something queer is going on in there. Strange noises are coming from the room.'

'Anything happen since I left?' Kennedy inquired.

'Happen? Plenty! Mrs Pilcher tried to commit suicide. That's just one of the many things that have happened.'

'Tried to commit suicide?' Kennedy repeated quickly.

'I don't understand it,' Blount returned. 'But, then, there isn't anything I do understand about this whole damned case. Yes; Mr Pilcher came running wildly down the stairs about noon, shouting that his wife had taken poison. I got Doc Greeley up here and sure as hell she had taken some poison. The Doc was able to bring her around after pumping out her stomach. She's upstairs now and won't speak to anyone. Her husband's been acting queer ever since.'

'What else happened?' Kennedy asked keenly.

'About everything you could think of,' Blount answered wearily. 'Old Peter came back and then disappeared again. And then that damned scream! It came again – right after Madam Certi and Professor Mundo came back and locked themselves in the room.'

'The scream!' Kennedy exclaimed. 'Who's been killed?'

'Nobody was killed. But the scream sent the old maid, Miss Worthington, into hysterics. Doc Greeley took her home with him. I hope Mrs Greeley gets her quiet. She used to be a nurse, you know. I know what I'd do with her if I had my way – solitary and straitjacket!'

'Quite scientific, quite scientific,' Kennedy ignored. 'What about Godfrey Nelson? You gave my heart a jump when you mentioned that scream.'

'Oh, Nelson has hardly stirred from his chair in the lobby. Just sits there like a man who is about to be electrocuted.'

Kennedy by this time was walking into the lobby, Blount following, shoulders sagging a bit and face tired.

Godfrey Nelson was the only person except his guard in the lobby at the moment. He was sitting in a large easy-chair, his hands gripping the arms of the chair and his eyes staring first one way, then another.

'And my friend, McGuire, the clerk?' Kennedy asked, seeing no one behind the desk. 'Has he come back yet?'

'Come back?' Blount exclaimed. 'Where did he go?'

'On a rather long trip,' Kennedy avoided dryly. 'Is he in the hotel now?'

'I saw him a few minutes ago. Up in his room, I guess. He's not on duty at this hour.'

'I see.'

Burroughs Matthews was walking down the stairs at the moment with his usual bored nonchalance.

'Ah, there you are, Kennedy!' he greeted. 'I say, Mrs Pilcher has been asking for you. She wants very much to talk to you, refuses to talk to Sheriff Blount. It seems her conscience is troubling her. So, you see, Kennedy, I haven't run away yet – and we haven't found the tombstone either.'

'When the time comes, Matthews,' Kennedy retorted, 'that block of brownstone may upset somebody as if it were thrown at them. Come on, Sheriff; we'll both go up and see what Mrs Pilcher has to say.'

Matthews shrugged and walked over to Nelson and sat down beside him. Kennedy and Blount ascended the wide stair.

Mrs Pilcher was in bed. Her face wore a death-like pallor and her eyes were wild and glassy. Her husband sat near the bed. His thin face was turned to her and his eyes seemed to bore like gimlets. He looked up at Kennedy and Blount as they entered. But there was nothing friendly about his look.

Kennedy went over by the bed and stood by her.

'There is something – something I must tell you, Mr Kennedy,' she murmured. Her voice was weak and had a far-away note in it as she opened her eyes, then closed them again. 'I wanted to die – so I wouldn't have to tell it – but they wouldn't let me – and now I have to tell – '

Her voice died away in a feeble moan. She looked at her husband. His eyes were flashing fire and hatred.

She shook her head as if to gather her thoughts. 'Fred,' she said to her husband, 'we – I must tell!'

He rose stiffly, his thin lips pressed tightly.

'Ethel!' His voice cut the air like a sharp knife.

She raised her head and body a little, gave a frightened scream, then fell back on the bed in a swoon.

Her husband turned to Kennedy and Blount. 'I am sorry, gentlemen,' he said in a smooth, oily voice, 'but Mrs Pilcher is still delirious. She doesn't know what she is doing.'

Kennedy shot a withering look at Pilcher.

'Mrs Pilcher doesn't need a doctor,' he said curtly. 'Mrs Pilcher needs a friend right now!' He massaged her temples.

Kennedy turned as her eyelids fluttered, and walked out of the room. Blount hesitated, looked at the pale face of the woman, her breathing so low it could just be distinguished, then followed quickly.

'What do you make of it?' He jerked his head backward.

'She'll never talk as long as that husband is around, and we can't very well see her now without his being in the room.'

From far up the hall came a low moan, a moan as of pain.

'Madam Certi!' Blount muttered with a scowl. 'That's been going on ever since she came back.'

The moaning suddenly ceased. Someone was talking in a low, chanting voice. The voice stopped and the moan resumed.

'Talking with the dead!' Kennedy exclaimed. 'It won't get us anywhere to disturb her now.'

He looked at his wrist-watch. 'First we're going out to the car. You're going to help me carry some stuff into Condon's office where I can lock it up. Then I'll take you down-cellar and solve the weird part of these murders!'

10.

Condon's private office was empty when Kennedy and Blount entered, their arms full, from the car.

'Condon is up in his room,' Blount explained. 'He went up just before you came back. He is fagged out.'

'Just as well.' Kennedy closed the door and locked it on the inside. 'We have the office to ourselves. I can explain certain things that I want to tell you.'

Kennedy laid the books on the desk and took the sheaf of telegrams and radiograms from his pocket.

'I found out, Blount,' he began, 'that Gypsy Jones who lies buried out there is going to figure as the key to this case.'

Kennedy selected one radiogram in particular.

'I found out, for one thing,' he went on, 'that the Wainwright estate in England is a very large one. The last heir died in London. The money is now looking for someone to go to.'

'The Wainwright estate?' Blount inquired, puzzled.

'Yes. It seems that Sir Charles Wainwright, the chap buried out there as Gypsy Jones, left his ancestral home when he was a young man. He had some trouble with his family over his escapades and changed his name. His estrangement and all preyed on his mind – finally drove him to lead the life of a hermit up in these mountains.'

Kennedy paused. Blount was all ears.

'But,' Kennedy added impressively, 'before he started to lead that life, he had married under the name of Jones in New York. To this marriage was born a son. That son is now living in New York. Under the law this son would inherit the entire Wainwright estate if he could establish the fact that his father, this Gypsy Jones, was Sir Charles Wainwright. That son has no suspicion, even, who his father really was!'

The sheriff framed his lips for a low whistle.

'There is, however, a certain other collateral heir to this vast estate who, if the identity of Gypsy Jones is never known, will inherit the fortune. Thus you have the reason why someone is frantically busy to murder the three men who could swear that Gypsy Jones was really Sir Charles Wainwright. This person happens to be right in this hotel!'

Kennedy spread out the telegrams before Blount.

'The whole story can be found in these telegrams and radiograms. I had Police Headquarters wireless Scotland Yard for the complete information. They got a prompt answer. Those books I took out of an apartment of the person who has murdered two people and hopes to murder the third.'

Blount fumbled the messages nervously.

'Yes,' Kennedy repeated, 'the moment Godfrey Nelson leaves that chair and goes upstairs, he will be a dead man!'

'Phew!' Blount was reading the messages, trying to digest them. 'Then you know what that scream is?'

'We'll find out about that weird part of it all in the cellar,' Kennedy nodded. 'I've had a hunch all along what it was. But it wasn't until I read a couple of volumes in the Police Academy up the street from headquarters that I was convinced.'

Impatiently Kennedy slipped the books and other stuff into the safe, shoved the telegrams in his pocket, unlocked the door and then locked it again.

'Better have your automatic ready, Sheriff,' he said ominously as they approached the cellar stairs; 'you might have to use it down here any moment. Be prepared for some fast work!'

'OK, Kennedy!' said the sheriff, grimly following as Kennedy opened the door.

The cellar under the north wing of the hotel was brightly lighted now with a hundred-power lamp. Sheriff Blount had put it down there during the day.

The stone walls of the cellar, left exactly as they had been blasted out of the side of the mountains, loomed ruggedly in the brilliant light, a wall of jagged rocks. Here and there large cracks appeared in the rock, and at several different places dampness seeped through.

The dusty floor of the cellar was covered with footprints this time, none now distinguishable from the others in the mass. Old pieces of broken furniture strewed the floor, and boxes with an accumulation of dust were piled against the wall.

Kennedy moved swiftly along the east wall of the cellar, his face tense, his automatic in his right hand.

Blount followed, a look of bewilderment on his face as Kennedy gave up trying to study the footprints and started tapping the wall with an old stick. The taps echoed sharp and clear through the cellar.

Suddenly he stopped. He stepped back and surveyed the wall. On his face was a puzzled look.

'It's there,' he said, 'somewhere in that wall!'

Blount looked at him. 'What's there?' he demanded.

Kennedy said nothing. He just surveyed the cellar wall. To the right in the direction of the main cellar old boxes were piled against the wall. To the left the jagged rocks extended to another cross-corridor of the cellar about twenty feet.

'Hidden very well,' he muttered to himself. 'Better than I had expected.'

Blount now merely looked. Kennedy picked up a rock to tap the wall. Then he got down on his knees and started tapping the wall from the bottom.

He stopped. The clear sharp taps on the rock had a hollow sound. He got up and tapped the wall clear to the top.

'It's here all right!' he cried. 'Give me a hand, Blount.'

Blount started toward the wall to do so, then stopped suddenly. His body froze in his tracks, his face lost all colour. Even Kennedy paled a bit and took an involuntary step backward.

From somewhere beyond that jagged wall of rock there came the wailing unearthly scream, the scream that had followed the murders of both Coulter and Branford.

At first it was low and indistinct and far away; then it increased in volume, a screeching, blood-freezing scream, inhuman, piercing, weird enough to set on edge with terror the nerves of the most intrepid human being. Then it died away into a mournful, sad moan; died away, it seemed, into the very bowels of the earth.

For seconds after it ceased, a deep, oppressive silence hung over the cellar. Blount stared at the wall, his eyes wild and his face a death-like grey. Kennedy wet his lips and in spite of himself gave a quick, nervous laugh.

'We've found it, all right,' he said slowly. 'Now we'll have to find out how to get on the other side of this wall.'

'Good God, man,' groaned Blount, 'you're not going there?'

'As soon as I can find a way,' returned Kennedy.

He was tearing at the jagged rocks. He loosed a rock and then some dirt. He paused. That did not seem very practical. A moment and he began moving some large but comparatively light wooden crates piled up alongside the wall. Back of them was a huge piece of slate-rock. He pried at it with a stick, and the slate swung outward on hinges. A dark, yawning opening was revealed that led to a cave-like room back of the rock wall.

'Be ready for anything, Blount!' Kennedy cautioned. 'This thing was evidently built for a cold room in the summer and a root cellar in the winter – without a doubt overlooked when the new hotel syndicate took over the hotel. Now – watch out!'

A gust of dank musty air came from the yawning hole. There was something fetid, mephitic, bestial in it. Black as jet, the yawning cavern opened in front of Kennedy and Blount.

Kennedy turned slightly to see that the sheriff was following close behind. Then he deliberately stepped forward into the darkened hole and disappeared in the blackness.

II.

Kennedy walked straight ahead some ten feet before he stopped. The darkness was so intense that he could see absolutely nothing. Inside the dungeon-like room, the air was warm and there was an odour of either animal or human presence, the odour mixed with the dank, heavy air of the underground cavern.

He threw the white beam of his flashlight around in the darkness. It fell on a jagged rock wall and then on an old table. He flashed it on the other side of the cave. Another wall, and near the wall an old couch.

He threw the light back on the table. There was a candle-stub on the table. He took a step over to it and lighted it. At first the flame of the candle flickered weakly; then it gained strength and cast a wavering light around the dungeon.

Sheriff Blount was standing near the entrance, where the light from the now brightly lighted cellar died away into the darkness of the cave. Blount walked closer to Kennedy.

'What is this?' he asked. 'There is a bed!'

Kennedy was examining a bottle that stood on the table. He pulled the cork, poured out a bit on the table-top, and smelled it carefully.

'I thought so!' he exclaimed to himself. 'It's all working out. That's the poison marked in the books.'

He examined the cave closely. The rock floor was damp and there was considerable straw scattered over it. Suddenly he reached down and pulled something heavy out of the darkness under the couch. It was a large, flat rock.

'Our tombstone!' he cried. 'The murderer hid it here!'

He studied it under the light, especially the wording of the inscription.

'Sir Charles was romantic,' he smiled grimly. 'He wanted to die unknown and unsung. But he wanted the world to know that he died unknown and unsung.'

'Yes. What do you make of this room?' Blount was not romantic. 'It still leaves a great deal to be solved about those strange murders.'

'It won't; not when we've found the thing we came here for,' Kennedy replied. 'That bottle of poison tells a great deal. I think the floor will tell more.'

Kennedy swung the beam of light on the floor. 'Pieces of leather – a strap clawed and chewed until it's cut!' he cried.

'Look!' Blount exclaimed. 'There's meat down here, too! You mean to tell me that this is a den for an animal?'

Kennedy had no chance to answer. A dark form suddenly moved swiftly out of a black hole in the wall. It was a large form, and it shot across the shadowy cave like a streak. It was out of the door before either Kennedy or Blount could blaze away at it.

'Good God! What is it?' Blount cried.

Kennedy was out of the cave dashing through the cellar at top speed, Blount some twenty feet behind him.

Kennedy did not stop to seek where it had gone. He had but one thought in his mind. He took the cellar steps two at a time.

Godfrey Nelson was there, safe with his guard.

'Get another man with him, too, Sheriff, quick!'

Blount called another of his deputies. 'But, Kennedy,' he whispered aside, 'what was that dark form?'

'An animal,' Kennedy avoided.

'It looked like a bear to me,' exclaimed the sheriff.

'We're too late!' Kennedy grabbed at Blount's arm.

Upstairs the piercing, heart-rending scream of some human being in great mental or physical pain broke the silence.

'The thing has struck!' Kennedy muttered.

The piercing human scream suddenly ceased. Kennedy was at the foot of the stair and up two steps at a time again.

The hallway on the second floor was empty. No sounds came from any room. Blount came up, out of breath, and stopped.

Then came the second scream, this time the weird, inhuman scream that started in a low wail and increased until it echoed and re-echoed in the night. It was the scream of death – inhuman, terrifying, unearthly.

It came from a room down the hall. With a spring Kennedy was at the door of that room. The scream was dying away.

'Too late!' he whispered to Blount. 'Too late – but perhaps it is best that we are!'

Blount now had the pass-key out of his pocket. He unlocked the door and pushed it open. Kennedy rushed into the room. It was dark and he could see nothing, but from the darkness came the low dying sound of that inhuman scream. Two yellow-green luminous spots in the darkness!

Kennedy found the light-switch and snapped it on. Blount was standing beside him.

'God save us!' the young sheriff whispered hoarsely, 'a cat – a giant cat!'

Lying on the floor, the body wrapped in the bed-clothes, was a human form. It was impossible to tell whether it was a man or a woman. But sitting on the shoulder of the person, its teeth firmly implanted in the neck, was a huge grey cat.

'Look out!' Kennedy yelled to Blount.

The huge cat had raised its head and looked at Kennedy and Blount. Its mouth was open and bloody. Its teeth were long and fang-like.

The creature's body doubled for a spring.

Kennedy's automatic roared. The bullet caught the great cat in the head just as it started to spring. Its body stiffened. An unearthly scream came from it. The body fell back, quivered a little and lay still.

'I don't under – it's infernal – it's all so damned unreal!' stammered Blount. 'Who is that in the bed-clothes?'

'The murderer of Coulter and Branford,' said Kennedy quietly.

'But the cat?' Blount was still stunned. 'What about the cat?'

'The means used to commit a perfect murder,' Kennedy explained casually. 'Rather a long story – too long for now.'

Blount continued to stare at the dead person in the bed-clothes. Then he shuddered, bit his lip, walked over and pulled the clothes from the face.

'Miss Worthington!' he exclaimed in a low whisper. 'It can't be possible!'

'But it is possible,' said Kennedy, 'only it doesn't happen to be Miss Worthington. That was simply a name used for convenience up here to murder Coulter and Branford. Her real name was Lucille Wainwright, a distant relative in the Wainwright family.'

'She just slipped in from the doctor's,' muttered Condon in the doorway.

Pale-faced McGuire back of him turned and fled up to his room.

Blount started to pull the bed-clothes back over the face of the dead woman. As he did so clumsily the sheet brushed the blood on the neck. Two little black holes were there, caused by the cat's teeth. He shuddered and walked to the door.

As he passed the table he saw a duplicate pass-key on it.

'The instant that cat came into the room,' said Kennedy, 'she knew the game was up – and deliberately let the cat complete the death list!'

'I'll call a deputy, Kennedy, to guard the body,' said Blount. 'I'm going down – to get a breath of fresh air!'

12.

Five minutes later Kennedy sat in the little private office downstairs with Condon and Sheriff Blount. Blount was still pale. Condon wore a perplexed look.

Kennedy had the messages on the desk and had taken the books and other stuff out from where he had locked them up.

'German criminology, Condon,' Kennedy was explaining, 'records in large number the cases of murder by the Sino-Cat. I brought along a book from the library at the Police Academy. Briefly and clearly stated, the Sino-Cat is a huge ferocious blood-sucking cat, although literally the term means a cat from China, or the Malay Peninsula. Out in our own country districts we find similar cats killing chickens and sucking eggs. The Sino-Cat, given a chance, will suck the blood of a human being.'

Kennedy fingered the pages of the book.

'They approach so softly,' he went on, 'that the victim is seldom conscious of what is going on until the cat has a firm hold on the neck and it is too late. The cat will crawl on a sleeping person, then suddenly strike for the jugular vein, and suck the blood like a vampire.'

Blount was slowly shaking his head, shivering.

'The blood-sucking cat,' Kennedy continued, 'is far more prevalent than is generally believed. It is particularly so in Asia. In our cats it is just a perverted twist. In Asia it's a terrible reversion to type. And the use of such cats to kill people has been known for ages. In western Europe it has undoubtedly given rise to many vampire legends and beliefs. The application of the poison on the fangs and claws is possible because of the ease in giving a cat an antidote, and also because this particular poison is deadly only in the blood stream, not in the digestive tract. In the first attack on Coulter Miss Worthington tried to make her beast kill without the poison. It failed, and she resorted to the more dangerous and deadly expedient, about which she had read.'

He turned to the books.

'When I was in New York I visited Miss Worthington's apartment. I found there many books with marked passages on poisons; several on the subject of vampires and cats. I suppose it was from these books she devised her diabolical plan of killing the three men who stood in her way to a fortune.'

'And at last the cat turned on her?' Condon queried.

Kennedy nodded. 'Yes. Having been to her room many times before, and always associating her presence with food, it sprang through the open transom. Deprived of blood so long, it turned on its owner; that's all.'

He paused.

'As I explained to Blount, Miss Worthington's name really was Lucille Wainwright. She knew the secret of Coulter, Branford and Nelson. I can believe that her discovery of that cavern down in the cellar gave her the first idea about hiding a blood-sucking cat there. The other parts of her plan were easily worked out, like allowing the cat to crawl along the narrow ledge to an open window, then drawing it back with a long leash before it could be discovered. In each case there was an empty room next to that of the murder victim. And the murderess, by means of her pass-key, was able to gain admission to all the rooms.'

Blount nodded.

'The screaming of the cat,' Kennedy continued, 'was caused by the fact that its victims died almost instantly when the poison was injected into the blood stream. The cat, with a good hold on the jugular vein, was angered when the blood flow stopped, as it naturally would after death.'

Sheriff Blount wet his lips and continued to regard Kennedy as someone uncanny. 'But,' he asked, 'how in the world did you happen to suspect her?'

'I suspected her from the first,' Kennedy replied, 'when, as you'll remember if you think back, she came running down the hall, screaming she had seen something black go from Madam Certi's room. Well, it so happened that she came from a different direction than Madam Certi's room. I figured if one part of her story was a lie, it was all lies. The finding of the pieces of leather strap gave me a hunch about an animal. The murderess evidently wanted to convey that impression – a tactical blunder on her part. For somehow I immediately associated a cat with Miss Worthington. Another thing. Those roundish footprints in the cellar. I knew at once they were faked. Some person was wearing something to make weird footprints. Their size gave away the fact it was a woman. Madam Certi was too fat to move as that person did. Mrs Pilcher didn't have the strength.'

'So,' Blount said, admiringly, 'you put a lot of things together and suspected Miss Worthington. I am dumb.'

'Oh, not so dumb, Sheriff. It really wasn't until I gained entrance to the apartment of Lucille Wainwright in New York, saw pictures and handwriting that corresponded to Miss Worthington's face and her handwriting on the register here that it was certain. After that, it was merely a matter of figuring out how the murders had actually been committed.'

'She faked the hysterics,' Condon considered, 'went to Doctor Greeley's, then sneaked back here, to get Godfrey Nelson.'

Kennedy nodded, and Condon went on. 'But Madam Certi and the Pilchers?'

'Take the Pilchers first,' Kennedy replied. 'Very simple. The murder of Coulter put them in a bad spot. The truth is, Mr and Mrs Pilcher are not the respectable young married couple you believed them to be. They are blackmailers. I found letters to prove it, and Mrs Pilcher knows I have them. They came here to blackmail Coulter and Branford. Their transom was open the night of the Coulter murder. Miss Worthington just tossed in a piece of the leather strap such as I found in Coulter's room and down in the cellar, a piece torn and chewed by the cat. She was wise to their blackmail scheme and took advantage of it. It was the fact she knew I knew so much and it might incriminate her that drove Mrs Pilcher to attempt suicide. The disgrace would ruin both of them.'

'And Madam Certi?' Blount inquired.

'Just a publicity-seeking old fool,' laughed Kennedy. 'The same applies to Professor Mundo. If Madam could stage something and get by with it, she knew when I solved the case, she could claim part of the credit and her reputation would be made. Only unfortunately the second murder frightened them out of their wits.'

Blount was dumbfounded.

'When people kill with Sino-Cats, they got me beat!' he admitted. 'I had it figured out either old Peter did it or that slicker, Burroughs Matthews.'

Kennedy smiled. 'Old Peter was just suspicious of everyone. That accounts for his strange disappearances. Matthews had stumbled over the old lone grave. His curiosity gave him a hunch but he didn't know what it was. He was there at the lone grave when Miss Worthington, dressed as a man, tried to kill me.'

'I say, Kennedy, but, disguise or no disguise, she wasn't strong enough to carry away that brown stone!' Matthews had stuck his head in the door and was listening. 'There was another there. How about it?'

Far up under the eaves of the hotel came the echo of a shot. Before they could start to locate it, Old Peter was running breathless down from the quarters assigned to the help.

'It – it's Mr McGuire – shot hisself!' he gasped.

'The answer to your question, Matthews, is there,' Kennedy remarked quietly. 'McGuire was really the secret husband of Miss Worthington, a crooked, smart London solicitor.'

'Hope I don't dream of blood-sucking cats,' shivered the sheriff uncomfortably.

'I've a long drive ahead of me tonight to New York,' Kennedy smiled back. 'Do you know what I think would do you a lot of good? Let's go out in the bar and have a night-cap!'

The Footprint in the Sky

◆

JOHN DICKSON CARR

The first British detective series, Colonel March of Scotland Yard, reached the TV screens in the autumn of 1953 and brought back to the country one of its best-known expatriate stars, Boris Karloff, to play the amiable, pipe-smoking solver of bizarre crimes. Karloff, famous for his monster roles in Hollywood horror movies, was actually beneath the grease-paint a genuine English gentleman who loved cricket and appreciated fine wines, and was therefore ideally cast as Colonel March, the head of the Yard's Department of Queer Complaints (known in the Force as D-3), whose task is to solve what are said to be impossible crimes. Behind his unassuming eyes and bushy moustache, the Colonel (who had actually served in the Army prior to his appointment) possesses a razor sharp mind and a memory packed with the most obscure information which invariably comes in handy when tackling the extraordinary cases put before him.

The BBC TV series, which ran for twenty-six half-hour episodes, was based on the series of stories about The Department of Queer Complaints, written from 1940 onwards by the American-born crime writer, John Dickson Carr (1900–1977). Carr, who is widely regarded as one of the pre-eminent writers of the 'impossible crime' story, discovered detective fiction in the library of his lawyer father and became a life-long fan of Sherlock Holmes and G. K. Chesterton's Father Brown. Carr later married an English girl and settled in England, where he began his long and productive career. During the Second World War he was responsible for scripting one of the best-remembered shows on British radio, Appointment With Fear, in which the sepulchral voice of actor Valentine Dyall did full justice to Carr's macabre narratives. In 1951, Carr returned to live in America where he continued writing about his three most popular crime solvers, Dr Gideon Fell, Sir Henry Merrivale and Colonel March who, he once revealed, was based on a friend of his named Major C.J.C. Street, formerly of the British Army and also a mystery story writer under the pen-name, John Rhode. Of all the Colonel's cases, The Footprint in the Sky, *which was screened as an episode of the series in January 1954, is probably the best and certainly the 'queerest' . . .*

SHE awoke out of confused dreams; awoke with a start, and lay staring at the white ceiling of her bedroom for a minute or two before she could convince herself it was anything but a dream.

But it was a dream.

The cold, brittle sunlight poured in at the open window. The cold, brittle air, blowing the curtains, stirred a light coating of snow on the window sill. It stirred briskly in that little, bare room; it should have set the blood racing, and Dorothy Brant breathed it deeply.

Everything was all right. She was at the country cottage, where she and Dad and Harry had come down for the skating on the frozen lake; possibly even a little mild skiing, if the snow came on according to the weather forecast. And the snow had fallen. She should have been glad of that, though for some reason the sight of it on the window sill struck her with a kind of terror.

Shivering in the warm bed, the clothes pulled up about her chin, she looked at the little clock on her bedside. Twenty minutes past nine. She had overslept; Dad and Harry would be wanting their breakfast. Again she told herself that everything was all right: though now, fully awake, she knew it was not. The unpleasantness of yesterday returned. Mrs Topham next door – that old shrew and thief as well . . .

It was the only thing which could have marred this weekend. They had looked forward to the skating: the crisp blades thudding and ringing on the ice, the flight, the long scratching drag as you turned, the elm trees black against a clear cold sky. But there was Mrs Topham with her stolen watch and her malicious good manners, huddled up in the cottage next door and spoiling everything.

Put it out of your mind! No good brooding over it: put it out of your mind!

Dorothy Brant braced herself and got out of bed, reaching for her dressing gown and slippers. But it was not her dressing gown she found draped across the chair; it was her heavy fur coat. And there were a pair of soft-leather slippers. They were a pair of soft-leather moccasins, ornamented with bead-work, which Harry had brought back from the States; but now the undersides were cold, damp, and stiff, almost frozen. That was when a subconscious fear struck at her, took possession, and would not leave.

Closing the window, she padded out to the bathroom. The small cottage, with its crisp white curtains and smell of old wood, was so quiet that she could hear voices talking downstairs. It was a mumble in which no words were distinguishable: Harry's quick tenor, her father's slower and heavier voice, and another she could not identify, but which was slowest and heaviest of all.

What was wrong? She hurried through her bath and through her dressing. Not only were they up but they must be getting their own breakfast, for she could smell coffee boiling. And she was very slow; in spite of nine hours' sleep she felt as edgy and washed-out as though she had been up all night.

Giving a last jerk of the comb through her brown bobbed hair, putting on no powder or lipstick, she ran downstairs. At the door of the living room she stopped abruptly. Inside were her father, her cousin Harry, and the local Superintendent of Police.

'Good morning, miss,' said the Superintendent.

She never forgot the look of that little room or the look on the faces of those in it. Sunlight poured into it, touching the bright-coloured rough-woven rugs, the rough stone fireplace. Through side windows she could see out across the snow-covered lawn to where – twenty yards away and separated from them only by a tall laurel hedge, with a gateway – was Mrs Topham's white weather-boarded cottage.

But what struck her with a shock of alarm as she came into the room was the sense of a conversation suddenly cut off; the look she surprised on their faces when they glanced round, quick and sallow, as a camera might have surprised it.

'Good morning, miss,' repeated Superintendent Mason saluting.

Harry Ventnor intervened, in a kind of agony. His naturally high colour was higher still; even his large feet and bulky shoulders, his small sinewy hands, looked agitated.

'Don't say anything, Dolly!' he urged. 'Don't say anything. They can't make you say anything. Wait until – '

'I certainly think – ' began her father slowly. He looked down his nose, and then along the side of his pipe, everywhere except at Dorothy. 'I certainly think,' he went on, clearing his throat, 'that it would be as well not to speak hastily until – '

'*If* you please, sir,' said Superintendent Mason, clearing his own throat. 'Now, miss, I'm afraid I must ask you some questions. But it is my duty to tell you that you need not answer my questions until you have seen your solicitor.'

'Solicitor? but I don't want a solicitor. What on earth should I want with a solicitor?'

Superintendent Mason looked meaningly at her father and Harry Ventnor, as though bidding them to mark that.

'It's about Mrs Topham, miss.'

'Oh!'

'Why do you say "Oh"?'

'Go on, please. What is it?'

'I understand, miss, that you and Mrs Topham had "words" yesterday? A bit of a dust-up, like?'

'Yes, you could certainly call it that.'

'May I ask what about?'

'I'm sorry,' said Dorothy; 'I can't tell you that. It would only give the old cat an opportunity to say I had been slandering her. So that's it! What has she been telling you?'

'Why, miss,' said Superintendent Mason, taking out a pencil and scratching the side of his jaw with it, 'I'm afraid she's not exactly in a condition to tell us anything. She's in a nursing-home at Guildford, rather badly smashed up round the head. Just between ourselves, it's touch and go whether she'll recover.'

First Dorothy could not feel her heart beating at all, and then it seemed to pound with enormous rhythm. The Superintendent was looking at her steadily. She forced herself to say:

'You mean she's had an accident?'

'Not exactly, miss. The doctor says she was hit three or four times with that big glass paperweight you may have seen on the table at her cottage. Eh?'

'You don't mean – you don't mean somebody *did* it? Deliberately? But who did it?'

'Well, miss,' said Superintendent Mason, looking at her still harder until he became a huge Puritan face with a small mole beside his nose. 'I'm bound to tell you that by everything we can see so far, it looks as though you did it.'

This wasn't happening. It couldn't be. Afterward she remembered, in a detached kind of way, studying all of them: the little lines round Harry's eyes in the sunlight, the hastily brushed light hair, the loose leather wind-jacket whose zip fastener was half undone. She remembered thinking that despite his athletic prowess he looked ineffectual and a little foolish. But then her own father was not of much use now.

She heard her own voice. 'But that's absurd!'

'I hope so, miss. I honestly hope so. Now tell me: were you out of this house last night?'

'When?'

'At any time.'

'Yes. No. I don't know. Yes, I think I was.'

'For God's sake, Dolly,' said her father, 'don't say anything more until we've got a lawyer here. I've telephoned to town; I didn't want to alarm you; I didn't even wake you – there's some explanation for this. There must be!'

It was not her own emotion; it was the wretchedness of his face which held her. Bulky, semi-bald, worried about business, worried about everything else in this world – that was John Brant. His crippled left arm and black glove were pressed against his side. He stood in the bright pool of sunlight, a face of misery.

'I've – seen her,' he explained. 'It wasn't pretty. Not that I haven't seen worse. In the war.' He touched his arm. 'But you're a little girl, Dolly; you're only a little girl. You couldn't have done that.'

His plaintive tone asked for confirmation.

'Just one moment, sir,' interposed Superintendent Mason. 'Now, miss! You tell me you *were* outside the house last night?'

'Yes.'

'In the snow?'

'Yes, yes!'

'Do you remember the time?'

'No, I don't think so.'

'Tell me, miss: what size shoes do you wear?'

'Four.'

'That's a rather small size, isn't it?' When she nodded dumbly, Superintendent Mason shut up his notebook. 'Now, if you'll just come with me?'

The cottage had a side door. Without putting his fingers on the knob, Mason twisted the spindle round and opened it. The overhang of the eaves had kept clear the two steps leading down; but beyond a thin coating of snow lay like a plaster over the world between here and the shuttered cottage across the way.

There were two strings of footprints in that snow. Dorothy knew whose they were. Hardened and sharp-printed, one set of prints moved out snakily from the steps, passed under the arch of the powdered laurel-hedge, and stopped at the steps to the side door of

Mrs Topham's house. Another set of the same tracks – a little blurred, spaced at longer intervals where the person had evidently been running desperately – came back from the cottage to these steps.

That mute sign of panic stirred Dorothy's memory. It wasn't a dream. She had done it. Subconsciously she had known it all the time. She could remember other things: the fur coat clasped round her pyjamas, the sting of the snow to wet slippers, the blind rush in the dark.

'Yours, miss?' inquired Superintendent Mason.

'Yes. Oh, yes, they're mine.'

'Easy, miss,' muttered the Superintendent. 'You're looking a bit white round the gills. Come in here and sit down; I won't hurt you.' Then his own tone grew petulant. Or perhaps something in the heavy simplicity of the girl's manner penetrated his official bearing. 'But why did you do it, miss? Lord, why did you do it? That's to say, breaking open that desk of hers to get a handful of trinkets not worth ten quid for the lot? And then not even taking the trouble to mess up your footprints afterward!' He coughed, checking himself abruptly.

John Brant's voice was acid. 'Good, my friend. Very good. The first sign of intelligence so far. I presume you don't suggest my daughter is insane?'

'No, sir. But they were her mother's trinkets, I hear.'

'Where did you hear that? You, I suppose, Harry?'

Harry Ventnor pulled up the zip fastener of his wind-jacket as though girding himself. He seemed to suggest that he was the good fellow whom everybody was persecuting; that he wanted to be friends with the world, if they would only let him. Yet such sincerity blazed in his small features that it was difficult to doubt his good intentions.

'Now look here, old boy. I *had* to tell them didn't I? It's no good trying to hide things like that. I know that, just from reading those stories – '

'Stories!'

'All right: say what you like. They always find out, and then they make it worse than it really was.' He let this sink in. 'I tell you, you're going about it in the wrong way. Suppose Dolly did have a row with the Topham about that jewellery? Suppose she *did* go over there last night? Suppose those are her footprints? Does that prove she bashed the Topham? Not that a public service wasn't done; but why couldn't it have been a burglar just as well?'

Superintendent Mason shook his head. 'Because it couldn't, sir.'

'But why? I'm asking you, why?'

'There's no harm in telling you that, sir, if you'll just listen. You probably remember that it began to snow last night at a little past eleven o'clock.'

'No, I don't. We were all in bed by then.'

'Well, you can take my word for it,' Mason told him patiently. 'I was up half the night at the police station; and it did. It stopped snowing about midnight. You'll have to take my word for that too, but we can easily prove it. You see, sir, Mrs Topham was alive and in very good health at well after midnight. I know that too because she rang up the police station and said she was awake and nervous and thought there were burglars in the neighbourhood. Since the old lady does that same thing,' he explained with a certain grimness, 'on the average of about three times a month, I don't stress *that*. What I am telling you is that her call came in at twelve-ten, at least ten minutes after the snow had stopped.'

Harry hesitated, and the Superintendent went on with the same patient air: 'Don't you see it, sir? Mrs Topham wasn't attacked until after the snow stopped. Round her cottage now there's twenty yards of clean, clear, unmarked snow in every direction. The only marks in that snow, the only marks of any kind at all, are the footprints Miss Brant admits she made herself.'

Then he rose at them in exasperation.

' 'Tisn't as though anybody else could have made the tracks. Even if Miss Brant didn't admit it herself, I'm absolutely certain nobody else did. You, Mr Ventnor, wear size ten shoes. Mr Brant wears size nine. Walk in size four tracks? Ayagh! And yet somebody did get into that cottage with a key, bashed the old lady pretty murderously, robbed her desk, and got away again. If there are no other tracks or marks of any kind in the snow, who did it? Who must have done it?'

Dorothy could consider it, now, in almost a detached way. She remembered the paperweight with which Mrs Topham had been struck. It lay on the table in Mrs Topham's stuffy parlour, a heavy glass globe with a tiny landscape inside. When you shook the glass globe, a miniature snowstorm rose within – which seemed to make the attack all the more horrible.

She wondered if she had left any fingerprints on it. But over everything rose Renée Topham's face, Renée Topham, her mother's bosom friend.

'I hated her,' said Dorothy; and, unexpectedly, she began to cry.

Dennison Jameson of the law firm of Morris, Farnsworth & Jameson, Lincoln's Inn Fields, shut up his brief case with a snap. He was putting on his hat and coat when Billy Farnsworth looked into the office.

'Hullo!' said Farnsworth. 'You off to Surrey over that Brant business?'

'Yes.'

'H'm. Believe in miracles, do you?'

'No.'

'That girl's guilty, my lad. You ought to know that.'

'It's our business,' said Jameson, 'to do what we can for our clients.'

Farnsworth looked at him shrewdly. 'I see in your ruddy cheek. Quixotry is alive again. Young idealist storms to relief of good-looker in distress, swearing to – '

'I've met her twice,' said Jameson. 'I like her, yes. But, merely using a small amount of intelligence on this, I can't see that they've got such a thundering good case against her.'

'Oh, my lad!'

'Well, look at it. What do they say the girl did? This Mrs Topham was struck several times with a glass paperweight. There are no fingerprints on the paperweight, which shows signs of having been wiped. But, after having the forethought to wipe her fingerprints carefully off the paperweight, Dorothy Brant then walks back to her cottage and leaves behind two sets of footprints which could be seen by aerial observation a mile up. Is that reasonable?'

Farnsworth looked thoughtful. 'Maybe they would say she isn't reasonable,' he pointed out. 'Never mind the psychology. What you've got to get round are the physical facts. Here is the mysterious widow Topham entirely alone in the house; the only servant comes in by day. Here are one person's footprints. Only that girl could have made the tracks; and, in fact, admits she did. It's a physical impossibility for anybody else to have entered or left the house. How do you propose to get around that?'

'I don't know,' said Jameson rather hopelessly. 'But I want to hear her side of it first. The only thing nobody seems to have heard, or even to be curious about, is what she thinks herself.'

Yet, when he met her at the cottage late that afternoon, she cut the ground from under his feet.

Twilight was coming down when he turned in at the gate, a bluish twilight in which the snow looked grey. Jameson stopped a moment at the gate, and stared across at the thin laurel-hedge dividing this property from Mrs Topham's. There was nothing remarkable about this hedge, which was some six feet high and cut through by a gateway like a Gothic arch. But in front of the arch, peering up at the snow-coated side of the hedge just above it, stood a large figure in cap and waterproof. Somehow he looked familiar. At his elbow another man evidently the local Superintendent of Police, was holding up a camera; and a flashbulb glared against the sky. Though he was too far away to hear anything, Jameson had a queer impression that the large man was laughing uproariously.

Harry Ventnor, whom he knew slightly, met Jameson at the door.

'She's in there,' Harry explained, nodding toward the front room. 'Er – don't upset her, will you? Here, what the devil are they doing with that hedge?'

He stared across the lawn.

'Upset her?' said Jameson with some asperity. 'I'm here, if possible, to help her. Won't you or Mr Brant give some assistance? Do you honestly think that Miss Brant in her rational senses could have done what they say she did?'

'In her rational senses?' repeated Harry. After looking at Jameson in a curious way, he said no more; he turned abruptly and hurried off across the lawn.

Yet Dorothy, when Jameson met her, gave no impression of being out of her rational senses. It was her straightforwardness he had always liked, the straightforwardness which warmed him now. They sat in the homely, firelit room, by the fireplace over which were the silver cups to denote Harry's athletic and gymnastic prowess, and the trophies of John Brant's earlier days at St Moritz. Dorothy herself was an outdoor girl.

'To advise me?' she said. 'You mean, to advise me what to say when they arrest me?'

'Well, they haven't arrested you yet, Miss Brant.'

She smiled at him. 'And yet I'll bet that surprises you, doesn't it? Oh, I know how deeply I'm in! I suppose they're only poking about to get more evidence. And then there's a new man here, a man named March, from Scotland Yard. I feel almost flattered.'

Jameson sat up. He knew now why that immense figure by the hedge had seemed familiar. 'Not Colonel March?'

'Yes. Rather a nice person, really,' answered Dorothy, shading her eyes with her hand. Under her light tone he felt that her nerves were raw. 'Then again, they've been all through my room. And they can't find the watch and the brooch and the rings I'm supposed to have stolen from Aunt Renée Topham. Aunt Renée!'

'So I've heard. But that's the point – what are they getting at? A watch and a brooch and a couple of rings! Why should you steal that from anybody, let alone from her?'

'Because they weren't hers,' said Dorothy, suddenly looking up with a white face, and speaking very fast. 'They belonged to my mother.'

'Steady.'

'My mother is dead,' said Dorothy. 'I suppose it wasn't just the watch and the rings, really. That was the excuse, the breaking point, the thing that brought it on. My mother was a great friend of Mrs Topham. It was "Aunt Renée" this and "Aunt Renée" that, while my mother was alive to pamper her. But my mother wanted me to have those trinkets, such as they were. Dear Aunt Renée Topham coolly appropriated them, as she appropriates everything else she can. I never knew what had happened to them until yesterday.

'Do you know that kind of woman? Mrs Topham is really charming, aristocratic and charming, with the cool charm that takes all it can get and expects to go on getting it. I know for a fact that she's really got a lot of money, though what she does with it I can't imagine: and the real reason why she buries herself in the country is that she's too mean to risk spending it in town. I never could endure her. Then, when my mother died and I didn't go on pampering Aunt Renée as she thought I should, it was a very different thing. How that woman loves to talk about us! Harry's debts and my father's shaky business. And *me*.'

She checked herself again, smiling at him. 'I'm sorry to inflict all this on you.'

'You're not inflicting on me.'

'But it's rather ridiculous, isn't it?'

' "Ridiculous," ' said Jameson grimly, 'is not the word I should apply to it. So you had a row with her?'

'Oh, a glorious row. A beautiful row. The grandmother of all rows.'

'When?'

'Yesterday. When I saw her wearing my mother's watch.'

She looked at the fire, over which the silver cups glimmered.

'Maybe I said more than I should have,' she went on. 'But I got no support from my father or Harry. I don't blame Dad: he's so worried about business, and that bad arm of his troubles him so much sometimes that all he wants is peace and quiet. As for Harry, *he* doesn't really like her; but she took rather a fancy to him, and that flatters him. He's a kind of male counterpart of Aunt Renée. Out of a job? – well, depend on somebody else. And I'm in the middle of all this. It's "Dolly, do this," and "Dolly, do that," and "Good old Dolly; she won't mind." But I do mind. When I saw that woman standing there wearing my mother's watch, and saying commiserating things about the fact that we couldn't afford a servant, I felt that something ought to be done about it. So I suppose I must have done something about it.'

Jameson reached out and took her hands. 'All right,' he said. 'What did you do?'

'I don't know! That's just the trouble.'

'But surely — '

'No. That was one of the things Mrs Topham always had such sport with. You don't know much when you walk in your sleep.

'Ridiculous, isn't it?' she went on, after another pause. 'Utterly ludicrous. But not to me! Not a bit. Ever since I was a child, when I've been overtired or nervously exhausted, it's happened. Once I came downstairs and built and lit a fire in the dining room, and set the table for a meal. I admit it doesn't happen often, and never before with results like this.' She tried to laugh. 'But why do you think my father and Harry looked at me like that? That's the worst of it. I really don't know whether I'm a near-murderer or not.'

This was bad.

Jameson admitted that to himself, even as his reason argued against it. He got up to prowl round the room, and her brown eyes never left him. He could not look away; he saw the tensity of her face in every corner.

'Look here,' he said quietly, 'this is nonsense.'

'Oh, please. Don't you say that. It's not very original.'

'But do you seriously think you went for that woman and still don't know anything about it now?'

'Would it be more difficult than building a fire?'

'I didn't ask you that. *Do* you think you did it?'

'No,' said Dorothy.

That question did it. She trusted him now. There was understanding and sympathy between them, a mental force and communication that could be felt as palpably as the body gives out heat.

'Deep down inside me, no, I don't believe it. I think I should have waked up. And there was no — well, no blood on me, you know. But how are you going to get round the evidence?'

The evidence. Always the evidence.

'I did go across there. I can't deny that. I remember half waking up as I was coming back. I was standing in the middle of the lawn in the snow. I had on my fur coat over my pyjamas; I remember feeling snow on my face and my wet slippers under me. I was shivering. And I remember running back. That's all. If I didn't do it, how could anybody else have done it?'

'I beg your pardon,' interposed a new voice. 'Do you mind if, both figuratively and literally, I turn on the light?'

Denis Jameson knew the owner of that voice. There was the noise of someone fumbling after an electric switch; then, in homely light, Colonel March beamed and basked. Colonel March's seventeen stone was swathed round in a waterproof as big as a tent. He wore a large tweed cap. Under this his speckled face glowed in the cold; and he was smoking, with gurgling relish, the large-bowled pipe which threatened to singe his sandy moustache.

'Ah, Jameson!' he said. He took the pipe out of his mouth and made a gesture with it. 'So it *was* you. I thought I saw you come in. I don't want to intrude; but I think there are at least two things that Miss Brant ought to know.'

Dorothy turned round quickly.

'First,' pursued Colonel March, 'that Mrs Topham is out of danger. She is at least able, like an after-dinner speaker, to say a few words; though with about as much coherence. Second, that out on your lawn there is one of the queerest objects I ever saw in my life.'

Jameson whistled. 'You've met this fellow?' he said to Dorothy. 'He is the head of the Department of Queer Complaints. When they come across something outlandish, which may be a hoax or a joke but on the other hand, may be a serious crime, they shout for him. His mind is so obvious that he hits it every time. To my certain knowledge he has investigated a disappearing room, chased a walking corpse, and found an invisible piece of furniture. If he goes so far as to admit that a thing is a bit unusual, you can look out for squalls.'

Colonel March nodded quite seriously. 'Yes,' he said. 'That is why I am here, you see. They thought we might be interested in that footprint.'

'That footprint?' cried Dorothy. 'You mean –?'

'No, no; not your footprint, Miss Brant. Another one. Let me explain. I want you, both of you, to look out of the window; I want you to take a look at the laurel-hedge between this cottage and the other. The light is almost gone, but study it.'

Jameson went to the window and peered out.

'Well?' he demanded. 'What about it? It's a hedge.'

'As you so shrewdly note, it is a hedge. Now let me ask you a question. Do you think a person could walk along the top of that hedge?'

'Good lord, no!'

'No? Why not?'

'I don't see the joke,' said Jameson, 'but I'll make the proper replies. Because the hedge is only an inch or two thick. It wouldn't support a cat. If you tried to stand on it, you'd come through like a ton of bricks.'

'Quite true. Then what would you say if I told you that someone weighing at least twelve stone must have climbed up the side of it?'

Nobody answered him; the thing was so obviously unreasonable that nobody could answer.

Dorothy Brant and Dennis Jameson looked at each other.

'For,' said Colonel March, 'it would seem that somebody at least climbed up there. Look at the hedge again. You see the arch cut in for a gate? Just above that, in the snow along the side of the hedge, there are traces of a footprint. It is a large footprint. I think it can be identified by the heel, though most of it is blurred and sketchy.'

Walking quickly and heavily, Dorothy's father came into the room. He started to speak, but seemed to change his mind at the sight of Colonel March. He went over to Dorothy, who took his arm.

'Then,' insisted Jameson, 'somebody did climb up on the hedge?'

'I doubt it,' said Colonel March. 'How could he?'

Jameson pulled himself together. 'Look here, sir,' he said quietly. '"How could he?" is correct. I never knew you to go on like this without good reason. I know it must have some bearing on the case. But I don't care if somebody climbed up on the hedge. I don't care if he danced the tango on it. The hedge leads nowhere. It doesn't lead to Mrs Topham's; it only divides the two properties. The point is, how did somebody manage to get from here to that other cottage – across sixty feet of unbroken snow – without leaving a trace on it? I ask you that because I'm certain you don't think Miss Brant is guilty.'

Colonel March looked apologetic. 'I know she isn't,' he answered.

In Dorothy Brant's mind was again that vision of the heavy paperweight inside which, as you shook it, a miniature snowstorm arose. She felt that her own wits were being shaken and clouded in the same way.

'I knew Dolly didn't do it,' said John Brant, suddenly putting his arm round his daughter's shoulder. 'I knew that. I told them so. But –'

Colonel March silenced him. 'The real thief, Miss Brant, did not want your mother's watch and brooch and chain and rings. It may interest you to know what he did want. He wanted about fifteen hundred pounds in notes and gold sovereigns, tucked away in that same shabby desk. You seem to have wondered what Mrs Topham did with her money. That is what she did with it. Mrs Topham, by the first words she could get out in semi-consciousness, was merely a common or garden variety of miser. That dull-looking desk in her parlour was the last place any burglar would look for a hoard. Any burglar, that is, except one.'

'Except one?' repeated John Brant, and his eyes seemed to turn inward.

A sudden ugly suspicion came to Jameson.

'Except one who knew, yes. You, Miss Brant, had the blame deliberately put on you. There was no malice in it. It was simply the easiest way to avoid pain and trouble to the gentleman who did it.

'Now hear what you really did, Miss Brant,' said Colonel March, his face darkening. 'You did go out into the snow last night. But you did not go over to Mrs Topham's; and you did not make those two artistic sets of footprints in the snow. When you tell us in your own story that you felt snow sting on your face as well as underfoot, it requires no vast concentration, surely, to realize that the snow was still falling. You went out into it, like many sleepwalkers; you were shocked into semi-consciousness by the snow and the cold air; and you returned long before the end of the snowfall, which covered any real prints you may have made.

'The real thief – who was very much awake – heard you come back and tumble into bed. He saw a heaven-sent opportunity to blame you for a crime you might even think you had committed. He slipped in and took the slippers out of your room. And, when the snow had stopped, he went across to Mrs Topham's. He did not mean to attack her. But she was awake and surprised him; and so, of course, Harry Ventnor struck her down.'

'Harry – ' The word, which Dorothy had said almost at a scream, was checked. She looked round quickly at her father; then she stared straight ahead; then she began to laugh.

'Of course,' said Colonel March. 'As usual, he was letting his – what is it? – his "good old Dolly" take the blame.'

A great cloud seemed to have left John Brant; but the fussed and worried look had not left him. He blinked at Colonel March.

'Sir,' he said, 'I would give my good arm to prove what you say. That boy has caused me half the trouble I ever had. But are you raving mad?'

'No.'

'I tell you he couldn't have done it! He's Emily's son, my sister's son. He may be a bad lot; but he's not a magician.'

'You are forgetting,' said Colonel March, 'a certain size-ten footprint. You are forgetting that interesting sight, a smeared and blurred size-ten footprint on the side of a hedge which would not have held up a cat. A remarkable footprint. A disembodied footprint.'

'But that's the whole trouble,' roared the other. 'The two lines of tracks in the snow were made by a size four shoe! Harry couldn't have made them, any more than I could. It's a physical impossibility. Harry wears size ten. You don't say he could get his feet into flat leather moccasins which would fit my daughter?'

'No,' said Colonel March. 'But he could get his hands into them.'

There was a silence. The Colonel wore a dreamy look, almost a pleased look.

'And in this unusual but highly practical pair of gloves,' the Colonel went on, 'Harry Ventnor simply walked across to the other cottage on his hands. No more than that. For a trained gymnast – as those silver cups will indicate – it was nothing. For a rattle-brained gentleman who needed money it was ideal. He crossed in a thin coating of snow, which would show no difference in weight. Doorsteps, cleared of snow by the overhanging roof, protected him at either end when he stood upright. He had endless opportunities to get a key to the side door. Unfortunately, there was that rather low archway in the hedge. Carrying himself on his hands, his feet were curved up and back over the arch of his body to balance him; he blundered, and smeared that disembodied footprint on the side of the hedge. To be quite frank, I am delighted with the device. It is crime upside down; it is leaving a footprint in the sky; it is – '

'A fair cop, sir,' concluded Superintendent Mason, sticking his head in at the door. 'They got him on the other side of Guildford. He must have smelled something wrong when he saw us taking photographs. But he had the stuff on him.'

Dorothy Brant stood looking for a long time at the large, untidy blimp of a man who was still chuckling with pleasure.

Then she joined in.

'I trust,' observed Dennis Jameson politely, 'that everybody is having a good time. For myself, I've had a couple of unpleasant shocks today; and just for a moment I was afraid I should have another one. For a moment I honestly thought you were going to pitch on Mr Brant.'

'So did I,' agreed Dorothy, and beamed at her father. 'That's why it's so funny now.'

John Brant looked startled – but not half so startled as Colonel March.

'Now there,' the Colonel said, 'I honestly do not understand you. I am the Department of Queer Complaints. If you have a ghost in your attic or a footprint on top of your hedge, ring me up. But a certain success has blessed us because, as Mr Jameson says, I look for the obvious. And Lord love us! – if you have decided that a crime was committed by a gentleman who could walk on his hands, I will hold under torture that you are not likely to succeed by suspecting the one person in the house who has a crippled arm.'

The Adventure of the Emperor's Dice

◆

ELLERY QUEEN

The cases of private detective Ellery Queen, which had run on CBS radio since 1939, also successfully made the transition from the air waves to the TV screen in 1954 in what was to prove the first of three television adaptations to date. The somewhat self-opinionated young sleuth with his mental agility and eye for detail, was described as 'the logical successor to Sherlock Holmes' when he made his debut in print in 1929 in The Roman Hat Mystery, *and proved a popular TV star – especially with female viewers – when played by the debonair actor, Hugh Marlowe. Queen is ostensibly a writer, with a personal secretary, Nikki Porter, but is never happier than when helping out his father, Inspector Richard Queen, solving a crime.*

The byline on all the Ellery Queen stories concealed the identities of Frederic Dannay (1905–) and Manfred B. Lee (1905–1971), two New York-born cousins who began their working lives as advertising copywriters until their collaboration on The Roman Hat Mystery *won first prize in a 1928 literary competition and set them on the course which was to make 'Ellery Queen' (they chose the same name for both character and author in the hope that it would be more memorable to readers) hugely popular in novels and short stories, as well as in his own magazine and on radio, films and TV. The first TV series,* The Adventures of Ellery Queen *(also known as* Mystery Is My Business*) ran for thirty-two-half-hour episodes, and was followed in 1971 by* Ellery Queen: Don't Look Behind You *a ninety-six-minute colour special by NBC with Peter Lawford which was to have been the pilot for a new series, although this did not materialize. Three years later, NBC tried again with twenty-two-hour-long mysteries starring Jim Hutton which were considerably more successful. A unique element of*

the series was a break in which viewers had the chance to work out
their own solutions before the young detective revealed all in a final
confrontation with the suspects in a locked room. A feature of many of
Ellery Queen's cases has also been the detective's ability to unravel a
'dying message' in which the murder victim, just before their death,
leaves a critical clue either in writing or through an object held in the
hand. Such a clue will be found in The Adventure of the Emperor's
Dice *which was one of the featured episodes in the* 1954 *Hugh*
Marlowe TV series.

WHEN Caligula became emperor of the world he nominated
Incitatus his consul, Incitatus being his horse. On evidence such
as this, the grandson of Tiberius is considered by historians to have
been crazy. The conclusion is questionable. Consuls in Caligula's day
exercised high criminal jurisdiction; obviously, a man could turn his
back on his horse. There have been appointments, and not only in
Roman history, far less astute.

We are told, too, that Caligula had his adopted son, Lucius,
murdered; that he commanded citizens who displeased him to enter
the arena; that at the imperial gaming tables this legate of Tiberius's
mighty treasury played with crooked dice; and so on. That these are
the historical facts seems indubitable, but do the facts warrant the
historian's conclusions? We have already disposed of the episode of
the praetorian horse. As for Lucius, by Tiberius's will he was
Caligula's co-heir; and an emperor who murders his co-heir before his
co-heir can murder him may be considered of nervous temperament,
or overcautious, but he is certainly not irrational. Turning one's
enemies into gladiators combines private interest with the public
pleasure and is the sign of a political, not a psychotic, mind. And while
loading one's dice is indefensible on moral grounds, there is no
denying the fact that the practice reduces the odds against the dicer.

In short, far from being a lunatic, Caligula was a man of uncommon
sense; demonstrating what was to be proved – namely, *Caveat lector*.

We now leap nineteen centuries.

It was the time of the vernal equinox, or thereabout; in fine, the last
day of the third month of the Queenian calendar, and a night of
portents it was, speaking in wind, thunder, and rain. Even so, Mark
Haggard's voice could be heard above the uproar. Haggard was

driving a leaky station-wagon along the Connecticut road with the hands of a charioteer, sawing away at the wheel and roaring oaths against the turbulent heavens as if he were Martius himself. The Queens and Nikki Porter could only embrace one another damply and pray for midnight and the rise of a saner moon.

Ellery did not pine for Connecticut week-ends at unmapped homes occupied by unexplored persons. He had too cartographic a memory of hosts floating about in seas of alcohol or, as happened with equal frequency, forty-eight becalmed hours of Canasta. But the Inspector appeared sentimental about this one.

'Haven't seen Mark, Tracy, or Malvina Haggard since their dad kicked off ten years ago,' the Inspector had said, 'and I hadn't much contact with Jim's children before that except when they were little. But if they've turned out anything like Jim or Cora . . .'

'They rarely do,' Ellery had said nastily. 'Anyway, did Mark Haggard have to include me in?'

'Jim and I went through the police academy together, son. I was Jim Haggard's best man when he married Cora Maloney in – yep, 1911, just forty years ago. I can see the big lug now,' said the Inspector mistily, 'standing in front of the preacher in his monkey suit . . . Cora buried Jim in that suit, Ellery.'

'Hadn't he gained any weight? But I still don't see why – '

'Ellery's too lofty to mix with ordinary folks, Inspector,' Nikki had put in gently. 'Too much of a brain, you know. It gets *so* bored. Besides, he knows I can't go unless he does – '

'All right!' howled Ellery; and so here they were, and he hoped they were both thoroughly satisfied.

It had begun with a train that was late, a whistle-stop station that was wrong, no taxi service, and an hour's wait in splashy darkness. Then their host found them, and even the Inspector began to look as if he regretted the whole thing. Haggard was a staring man with a week's black stubble, given to sudden convulsions of laughter, and he drove like a madman.

'Can't tell you how happy I was to hear from you, Mark,' said the old gentleman, bouncing and hanging on to his denture. 'I feel like a heel having neglected your mother so long. It'll be good seeing Cora again.'

'In hell,' screamed Mark Haggard, rocketing over a patch of ice left over from the last snowfall.

'What did you say, Mark?'

'Ma's in hell!'

'Oh, I'm sorry to hear it,' the Inspector said confusedly. 'I mean, when did she – ?'

'Two years ago.'

'But not in the hot place,' muttered the Inspector. 'Not Cora.'

Mark Haggard laughed. 'You didn't know her. You don't know any of us.'

'Yes, people change,' sighed the Inspector. Then he tried to sound chatty again. 'I remember when your father resigned from the Force, Mark. Your mother was against it. But he'd inherited all that money, and I guess it went to his head.'

'What makes you think his head was any different before, Inspector? He was crazy. We're all crazy!'

Ellery thought that was an extremely bright remark.

'Is it much further, Mark?' asked the old gentleman desperately.

'Yes, I'm so very wet,' said Nikki in a gay voice.

'Threw money around like a maniac,' said Mark Haggard angrily. 'The great collector! Who did he think he was – Rosenbach?'

'Books?' asked Ellery, rousing himself.

'My father? He could hardly read, Gambling collection! Crummy old roulette wheels, medieval playing cards, ancient dice – junk filled the whole Gun Room. Get over on your side of the road, you — —!'

'Sounds like a – harmless enough – hobby,' said Nikki jouncily. The other car was lost in the weeping night. Lightning showed them Haggard's face. Nikki closed her eyes.

'Harmless?' chortled their host. 'Nothing about our family is harmless. Including the ancestral dump that Pop inherited from Uncle Jonas.'

'I suppose,' said Nikki, keeping her eyes shut, 'you live in a haunted house, Mr Haggard?'

'Yes!' said Mark Haggard gleefully.

Nikki screeched. But it was only another icy drop pelting the side of her neck.

'Any ghost I know?' asked the Inspector wittily.

'It's the ghost of an unsolved murder mystery.'

'Murder mystery!'

'Unsolved?' said Ellery.

'The house was then occupied by a family of five,' chuckled their chauffeur, 'a father, a mother, and three grown children. The two sons were bugs on hunting and they had a regular arsenal. One night the father's body was found in the gun-room. He'd been shot to death. It couldn't have been suicide, the servants were away, and from the physical evidence an outside murderer was out of the question. It had to be someone in the house that night, and the only ones in the house that night were the mother and the three grown children. Revolting, hey?'

Ellery stirred.

'Humour him!' whispered Nikki.

'Mark's just making this up,' said Inspector Queen heartily. 'Mark, I'm soaked to the hide. Have you lost your way?'

Haggard laughed again. But then he hurled the station-wagon around another car, cursing, and Ellery shuddered. 'And the best part of it was that nobody ever suspected the father'd been murdered. Not even the police.'

'You see?' said the Inspector in a beamy voice. 'Fairy tales. Mark, get there!'

'But keep talking,' said Ellery. 'Just how was the murder concealed?'

'Simplest thing in the world. One of the sons was a medical doctor and the other was an undertaker. The son who was a doctor made out a false death certificate and the son who was an undertaker prepared the body for burial.' Haggard's laugh mingled with the rain and the thunder. 'So murder didn't out after all. And it won't unless somebody can read those three clues.'

'Oh, there were clues,' said Ellery.

'This has gone far enough,' said the Inspector sharply. 'Are you sure, Mark, you're not driving around in circles?' He peered through a window, but they might have been crossing the Styx.

'What were they, Mark?'

'Ellery,' moaned Nikki.

'The bullet which killed the father came from a .38 revolver. There were two .38 revolvers in the Gun Room. So the two .38s were clues –'

'Ballistics check-up,' mumbled the Inspector.

'Oh, no,' chuckled Mark Haggard. 'The bullet passed right through the body and smashed against the bricks of the fireplace. And both guns had been cleaned after the murder.'

'And the third clue?'

'You'll love it, Ellery. It was found by the sons in their father's hand.'

'Oh? What was it?'

'A pair of dice. Very famous bones they are, too, bloody as hell.' And Haggard laughed and laughed.

After a moment Ellery said, 'All this happened . . . when did you say, Mark?'

'I didn't. Ten years ago.'

'Ten – !' The Inspector checked himself.

'Would you care to see the two revolvers and the dice?'

'Do you have them?'

'Oh, yes,' said Mark. 'In a wooden box at home.'

'Now that's going too far!' exploded the Inspector. 'Mark, either stop this foolishness or turn around and drive us back to the railroad station!'

Mark Haggard laughed again. The lightning flashed, and for a photographic instant they saw his lumpish eyes, the blueness about the black stubble, the dance of his hands on the wheel.

Ellery heard Nikki's teeth. 'M-Mister Haggard,' she chattered, 'what do you and your brother do-do for a living?'

'Tracy is a physician,' Haggard cried, 'and I'm an undertaker.' The station-wagon slid to a cascading stop, throwing them violently forward. Mark Haggard sprang into the darkness, and from the darkness they heard him shout, 'Get out, get out. We're here!' like some demon commanding them to his pleasure.

This was the beginning of an historic night . . . darkest history. They could make out nothing of the house, but a porch creaked underfoot and things banged somewhere gleefully. Ellery could feel the revolt in Nikki as she held on to him. Mark Haggard's right fist crashed repeatedly against an invisible door.

'Damn you, Malvina, open the door! Why'd you lock it?'

A creature in a white negligee of the flowing drapery variety stood there, holding aloft in her left hand – Nikki giggled something about a left-handed Statue of Liberty – a candle in a black candlestick. The face behind the candle was blanker than her robe. Only the eyes had life, a peering kind of life.

'I'm glad you've come back, Mark,' she said in a perfectly lifeless voice. 'The lights went out and then a hot flash followed me all over the house. Wherever I went, it was hot, and it burned, Mark, it burned me. Why did the lights go out?'

'Hot *what*?' muttered the Inspector.

Haggard tried a wall switch. 'Power failure – !'

'It burns, Mark,' his sister intoned.

'Malvina, these are some people visiting us. Give me that candle! I'll get a couple of flashlights.' Mark Haggard's right hand seized the candlesick and the flame darted off, leaving them in darkness, with the white-robed woman.

'Malvina, you remember me, don't you?' The Inspector might have been wheedling a child. 'Your father's friend? Richard Queen?'

'No.' That was all she said, in the toneless tones; after that inhuman sound, no one said anything. They shivered in the dark among their weekend bags, waiting dully for Mark Haggard's return. The house was deathly cold, with a dampness that attacked like acid.

Mark returned in another rage. 'No lights, no heat, no dinner prepared, Tracy gone out on a sick call, servants off somewhere – Malvina! Where the devil are Bessie and Connors?'

'They left. They were going to kill me. I chased them with a kitchen knife and they ran away. And Tracy went away, too. My own brother a doctor, and he doesn't care that the hot flashes burn me . . .' They heard a horrible snuffling and they realized the creature was crying.

Mark thrust a flashlight into Ellery's hand, wielding his own in crazy swoops that touched bare floors, shrouded furniture, his weeping sister. 'Stop it or you'll have another fit – ' She had it, on the floor, writhing like a frying soul, and screaming, screaming. 'No – ! If Tracy hadn't – *No!* I'll handle her alone. Go to your rooms – head of the stairs. You'll find some bread to eat and a can of sardines in the kitchen – '

'Couldn't eat a thing,' mumbled Inspector Queen. 'Wet clothes . . . go to bed . . .'

But Haggard was gone, running with his sister in his arms, her draperies trailing, the beam of light painting wild parabolas on the darkness. The Inspector said simply, 'We'd better get dry, rest awhile, and then clear out.'

'How about now?' said Nikki. 'I sometimes enjoy being wet, and I'm not in the least bit tired. I'm sure we could call a cab – '

'While a ten-year-old unsolved murder drifts around the premises crying for its mate?' Ellery glanced up into the black hole of the staircase, his jaw out. 'I'm sticking the week-end.'

Inspector Queen was stretched on one of the icy twin beds, and Nikki whimpered in the bedroom beyond – she had promised hysterics at the suggestion that in the interests of propriety the communicating door be shut – when the men's door burst open and light invaded the room. From the other room Nikki squealed, and the Inspector heaved twelve inches towards the ceiling. Ellery dropped a shoe, definitely.

But it was only Mark Haggard, grinning. He was carrying an electric lantern in one hand and a battered old wooden box the size of a cigar humidor in the other. 'The clues to the murder,' he chuckled. 'Old Mark Elephant!' He slammed the box down on the highboy nearest the door.

Haggard kept looking at Ellery, teeth glittering from the underbrush of stubble. The Inspector scrambled out of bed in his nightshirt as Ellery slowly opened the box.

Two rusty revolvers, Colt .38s, nested in the box. On them lay a small squarish case that looked like gold.

'The dice,' said Mark Haggard, smiling. 'Open it.'

'Hold the light higher,' Ellery said. His father craned over his shoulder.

Two crystalline red dice incised in gold sparkled up at them from a bed of purple velvet.

'They look like jewels,' exclaimed the Inspector.

'That's what they are,' said Mark. 'Square-cut rubies with pure gold dots inset. These dice are almost as old as the Christian era. Supposed to have been the personal property of the Roman Emperor Caligula. We gave them to Pop for his gambling collection.'

'This inscription in the case?' Ellery squinted. 'Hold the lantern up a bit, Mark . . . *To Dad, from Mark, Malvina, and Tracy, on His Ruby Wedding Anniversary.* In what way, Mark, were these dice a clue to – ?'

But Haggard was gone in the arctic night of the hall.

The Inspector heard the sounds first. He reached across the abyss between their beds and touched Ellery on the shoulder. It was a little past three. Ellery awoke instantly.

'Ellery. Listen.'

It was still raining, jungle music by a thousand drums. The wind slammed a shutter somewhere. In the next room Nikki's bed springs complained as she turned desperately over.

Then Ellery heard a floorboard give way and in the same moment ghastly lightning made the bedroom spring alive. A man was standing at the highboy, his right hand reaching for the box Mark Haggard had brought to the room a few hours before. With the first crack of thunder Ellery jumped out of bed and hurled himself across the room. His shoulder hit the intruder below the knees and the man toppled with a cry, striking his head against the highboy.

Ellery sat on him.

'Tracy Haggard!' Inspector Queen leaned over them, trying to hold the beam of his flash steady. From the other room Nikki was wailing, 'What was that? What happened?' Dr Haggard was a small, neat, greying man with a clever face; when his eyes opened they were pale and rather glassy. 'This is a fine way to meet again after all these years, Tracy,' growled the Inspector. 'What's the idea of playing sneak thief in your own house?'

'Mark's box of clues, Dad,' murmured Ellery. 'Apparently when Tracy Haggard got home, he learned that his brother had blabbed to us about the ten-year-old murder and left the clues in here. He's tried to get them back and dispose of them before we can dig too deeply into the crime.'

'I don't know why I didn't destroy those guns and dice years ago,' said Dr Tracy Haggard, calmly enough. 'Ellery – you are Ellery, aren't you – would you mind removing the *derrière* from my alimentary canal? You're not exactly a featherweight.'

'Then it's true.' Ellery did not stir.

'And I attended Jim's funeral and never suspected,' said Inspector Queen bitterly. 'Tracy, which one of you shot your father? And for God's sake, why?'

'I don't know the answer to either question, Inspector. It's been unholy hell . . . the four of us living together all these years, knowing one of us did it . . . It sent Mother to her grave.' Tracy Haggard tried to rise, failed, and hardened his stomach muscles. 'I'm glad she's dead and out of it. And I suppose you saw what it's done to Malvina and Mark. Mark was always a little batty, but Malvina had a promising career in the theatre when this happened, and she cracked.'

'What's going *on* in there?' shrieked Nikki.

'Dr Haggard, your brother made no bones about the murder of your father,' said Ellery. 'Does Mark want the truth to come out?'

'When Mother died,' said Tracy Haggard coolly, 'the three of us split the income of a very large trust fund. By will, if there were only two of us, the income would be that much greater per individual. Mark is always broke – gambling mostly. Does that answer your question?'

'Won't anybody talk?' howled Nikki. 'I *can't* come in there!'

'That's why he asked us up here, is it?' snarled the Inspector. 'To pin Jim's death on you or Malvina. Mark must feel pretty safe . . .'

'We're going to try to oblige your brother, Doctor.' Ellery got off his host and reached for the box of clues.

Dr Haggard rose, tight-lipped. 'In the middle of the night?'

'Dad, get a robe on and throw me mine . . . Why, yes, Doctor. Would you take us to the room where your father was shot to death?'

They trooped downstairs to the nervous accompaniment of the electric lantern, Ellery hugging the box, Nikki in a woolly robe and scuffs insisting that death would be instantaneous if she were to stay upstairs alone. Towards the rear of the main hall Tracy Haggard paused before a heavy door.

'Understandably, none of us ever goes in here. Nothing's been touched since the night of the crime.' Dr Haggard unlocked the door, threw it open, and stepped aside. 'I might add,' he said dryly, 'that neither Mark nor I has done any hunting since . . . at least with any of these weapons.'

The walls of the gun-room flanking the one door were hung with racks of shotguns, rifles, and small arms. On the other walls were cases containing James Haggard's gambling collection, and a great many larger gambling objects were grouped about the room. A thick coat of dust covered everything.

'Just where was your father's body found?' Ellery murmured.

'Seated behind that desk.'

The desk was an elaborate production of inlaid woods, with gunstock-shaped legs and a sheathing of hammered gunmetal. A matching chair with a braided leather seat stood behind it.

'Was he facing this door, Dr Haggard?'

'Squarely.'

'The only door, notice,' snapped Inspector Queen, 'so the odds are the killer stood in the doorway when he fired the shot. Just one shot, Tracy?'

'Just one shot.'

Ellery opened Mark's box and removed the two rusty revolvers. 'I see the gunracks are numbered. In which rack, Doctor, were these .38s normally kept?'

'This one came from the rack immediately to the right of the door.'

'To the right of the door, Doctor? You're positive?'

'Yes, this rack is numbered one. The other .38 was kept in the rack immediately to the left of the door. This one here, the rack numbered six.'

'Gun Exhibit A, right of door, rack number one. Gun Exhibit B, left of door, rack number six.' Ellery frowned. 'And it must have been done by one of those two guns, Mark said . . . These ruby dice, Doctor – what did they have to do with the murder?'

'Caligula's dice? We found them in Dad's hand.'

'In his *hand*?' exclaimed Nikki. 'I didn't really believe your brother when he said that – '

'My examination of his body indicated that he lingered a few minutes before dying. You'll notice that one of the wall cases behind the chair is open and empty. That's where the Emperor's Dice, as Dad used to call them, were displayed. When the shooter left, Dad must have managed to reach up, open the case, and take out the ruby dice. Then he died.'

'But why would he do a thing like that?' asked Nikki.

'Dad had police training. He was leaving a clue to his killer's identity. But we never could figure out whom the dice indicated. They'd been a gift from all three of us.'

'Seems like an awfully peculiar anniversary gift to one's parents,' Nikki said coldly.

'The dice were for Dad. We gave Mother a ruby pendant.'

'Well, I don't get it,' the Inspector said irritably. 'Clues, ruby dice, emperors! Ellery, can you make anything out of this hash?'

'Let's hope he won't,' said Dr Haggard. 'I could kill Mark for this stunt . . .'

'The way you killed your father, Dr Haggard?' asked Nikki.

Tracy Haggard smiled. 'Shows how insidious Mark's little propaganda scheme is.' He shrugged and disappeared in the black hall.

The Inspector and Nikki were staring into the darkness when Ellery said abruptly, 'You and Nikki go to bed.'

'What are you going to do?' asked his father.

'Stay down here,' said Ellery, rolling the historic dice between his palms, 'until I throw a natural.'

Malvina Haggard screamed on and off for the remainder of the night, and the angry voices of the brothers raised in bitter argument penetrated to the gun-room, but from that room there was no sound but the sound of rattling bones, as if the bimillennial ghost of the gambling Emperor himself had returned to dice with Ellery. And finally, at the first smudge of the cold and streaming dawn, the sound stopped, and Ellery came upstairs and methodically roused the household, inviting them all – even the demented woman – to join him on the scene of the old crime. Something in his manner quietened Malvina and she drifted downstairs with the others docilely.

They took places about the desk in the dusty gun-room, Mark viciously alive, Malvina somnolent, the doctor suspended watchfully, and Nikki and Inspector Queen trying to contain their excitement.

'The case,' announced Ellery, 'is solved.'

Mark laughed.

'Damn you, Mark!' That was his brother.

Malvina began to croon a wailing tune, smiling.

'I've been throwing these ruby dice for hours,' continued Ellery, 'with the most surprising result.' He shook the dice briskly in his cupped right hand and rolled them out on the desk.

'Nine,' said Tracy Haggard. 'What's surprising about that?'

'Not merely nine, Dr Haggard. A three and a six.'

'Well that's nine!'

'Temper, Tracy,' laughed Mark. Ellery rolled again.

'Eleven. Remarkable!'

'Not merely eleven, Dr Haggard – a five and a six.' And Ellery rolled a third time. 'And there's seven – a one and a six. Never fails.'

'What never fails?' asked Nikki.

'The six, my pet. I've made several hundred rolls while you were tossing around upstairs, and while one of these dice behaves with self-respecting variability, the other comes up 6 every time.'

'Crooked! Loaded!' said Inspector Queen. 'Who'd you say these dice used to belong to?'

'According to Mark, to Gaius Cæsar, better known as Caligula, Emperor of Rome from AD 37 to 41. And it may well be true, because Caligula was one of history's most distinguished dicing cheats.'

'And what does all this mean to you, Ellery?' asked Mark Haggard softly.

'Your father left these dice as a clue to the one of you who shot him. There are two dice, there were two .38 revolvers. Theory: The dice were meant by your father to refer to those two revolvers. But we now find that one of these dice is "loaded" – your word, Dad – while the other is not. Conclusion: Jim Haggard meant to convey the message that *the murderer loaded one of these revolvers.*'

'Wonderful,' said Mark Haggard.

'Ridiculous,' said Tracy Haggard. 'Of course he loaded one of them! But which one?'

Malvina Haggard kept smiling and crooning her little tune, keeping time with her sharp white fingers.

'The loaded dice,' explained Ellery, 'always turns up at the number six, and one of the revolvers comes from a gunrack numbered six. It seems obvious that the revolver associated with the number six was the one the murderer "loaded" . . . in other words, the one he chose to fire the fatal bullet into Jim Haggard.'

'And a fat lot of good that does you,' sneered Tracy Haggard. 'How can knowing which of the two .38s killed Dad possibly tell you which one of us murdered him?'

'In which direction in relation to the door,' inquired Ellery, 'is rack number six located?

'The rack to the left of the doorway,' the Inspector said slowly. 'To the *left* . . .'

'Killer opens door, to his right is a rack with a .38, to his left a rack with a .38. We now know he chose the .38 from the left-hand rack. What kind of person, when he has a choice of either side, automatically chooses an object to his left side? Why, a left-handed person, of course. And that pins the murder on . . .' Ellery stopped.

'Just marvellous,' gloated the Inspector. 'How this boy of mine comes through! Eh, Nikki?'

'Every time!' said Nikki worshipfully.

'And that pins the job on which one, son?' The old gentleman rubbed his palms together.

'It was *supposed* to pin the crime on Malvina,' said Ellery, 'who held the candle prominently aloft in her left hand when she greeted us – as commented upon by Miss Nikki Porter, aloud – whereas the brothers conscientiously demonstrated by various actions during the night that they're both right-handed. Unfortunately, gentlemen and ladies, I'm going to prove a disappointment to you. Aside from a number of tremendous, not to say laughable, improbabilities in the plot, there was one enormous flaw.'

'Plot? Flaw?' spluttered Inspector Queen.

The brothers glared. Even Malvina's clouded intelligence seemed shocked to clarity by Ellery's tone.

'I was told,' murmured Ellery, 'that the ruby dice were a gift to Jim Haggard on the occasion of Mr and Mrs Haggard's ruby wedding anniversary – '

'Sure they were, Ellery,' said the Inspector. 'You saw the inscription in the case yourself!'

'And you told me, Dad, that you'd been the best man at your old friend Jim Haggard's wedding forty years ago. You even mentioned the date – 1911.'

'Yes, but I don't see,' began his father doubtfully.

'You don't? How long ago was Jim Haggard murdered?'

'Ten years ago, Ellery,' said Nikki. 'That's what they said.'

'Married forty years ago, died ten years ago – so Jim Haggard could have been married no longer than thirty years at the time of his death. But ruby weddings commemorate which anniversary? Don't strain yourselves – ruby wedding is the *fortieth*. I must therefore inquire,' said Ellery politely, 'how Mr and Mrs Haggard could have been presented with gifts commemorating forty years of marriage if when Mr Haggard died he'd only been married thirty years. No answer being forthcoming, I must conclude the error in mathematics lies in the figures surrounding Mr Haggard's "death"; and this is confirmed by the dice, which these two innocent eyes saw in their gold case, dear children, proving that your parents celebrated an anniversary this very year. So I'm delighted to announce – as if you didn't know it – that your parents are very much alive, my friends, and that the whole thing has been a hoax! You lied, Mark. You lied, Tracy. And Malvina, your performance as Ophelia completely vindicates Mark's judgement that you had a promising career on the stage.

'And *you*, my worthy father.' Inspector Queen started. 'You ought to apply for an Equity card yourself! Didn't you tell me emotionally that you attended Jim Haggard's funeral ten years ago? So you're one of this gang, too . . . and so are you, Nikki, with your screams and your squeals and the dramatic way in which you pointed out for my benefit the crucial fact that Malvina is left-handed.'

There was a vast silence in Jim Haggard's gun-room.

'All cooked up,' said Ellery cheerfully. 'The wild night ride, the prevailing lunacy, the lights that atmospherically failed, the carefully deposited dust in the gun-room, and all the rest of it – cooked up by my own father, in collusion with his precious pals, the Haggard family! Object: Apparently to lead me to deduce from the herrings strewn across the trail, that Malvina killed her father. Then Jim Haggard could pop out of whatever closet he's skulking in with dear Cora and show me up for the gullible fathead I presumably am. My own father! Not to mention my faithful amanuensis. Reason totters and whimpers: Why? I restored her to her throne when I remembered the date.'

Ellery grinned. 'Yesterday was the last day of March. Which makes to-day,' and Ellery applied his outspread hand to the end of his nose and, using his thumb as a pivot, gently waved his celebrated fingers in their petrified direction, '*April Fool!*'

Too Many Have Lived

◆———————◆

DASHIELL HAMMETT

Sam Spade, the 'hardboiled dick' who first appeared rather inauspiciously in the pages of the pulp detective magazine, Black Mask, in 1929, is today one of the most famous detectives in American fiction. The story in which he appeared, The Maltese Falcon, later became a best-seller in hardcovers, but Spade's enduring fame was perhaps most firmly ensured when Humphrey Bogart portrayed him in John Huston's 1941 movie which has been called 'the finest private eye film ever made.' Bogart's is certainly the image of him that remains forever imprinted in the mind. Spade is, though, so well known that crime lovers tend to think of him as the protagonist of scores of books and films . . . while in fact there is only one other short novel and two stories about this tough character with his bony jaw and v-shaped face which are said to make him look like 'a blond Satan'. Certainly, too, his reputation has been enhanced by a radio series, Sam Spade, which was broadcast by CBS in 1946, starring Howard Duff; and then in a number of specially scripted cases for the weekly, half-hour CBS TV series, Suspense, the first crime and detection anthology programme on American TV, which ran from 1949 to 1953. Howard Duff repeated his role on the small screen, and although he was decidedly less aggressive towards woman than Bogart had been, he still displayed a nicely cynical disregard for loaded guns and vicious gangsters. (Suspense later returned in the Sixties as an hour-long film series hosted by Sebastian Cabot, though it only featured one Sam Spade episode, starring Richard Conte.)

Spade, described by one of his adversaries as, 'wild, astonishing, unpredictable, amazing', was created by Dashiell Hammett (1894–1961) who worked for seven years with the Pinkerton Detective

*Agency – keeping tabs on gangster Nick Arnstein during one case, and
investigating the rape charges against the famous actor, Fatty
Arbuckle, during another – which provided him with the material for
his hardboiled stories, though not, surprisingly, the model for Sam
Spade. 'He was an idealised figure,' Hammett explained when asked,
'in the sense that he is what most of the private detectives I've worked
with would like to have been.' The story which follows about this
unique private detective is one that was featured in* Suspense *in* 1953.

T HE man's tie was as orange as a sunset. He was a large man, tall
and meaty, without softness. The dark hair parted in the middle,
flattened to his scalp, his firm, full cheeks, the clothes that fit him with
noticeable snugness, even the small, pink ears flat against the sides of
his head – each of these seemed but a differently coloured part of one
same, smooth surface. His age could have been thirty-five or forty-five.

He sat beside Samuel Spade's desk, leaning forward a little over his
Malacca stick, and said, 'No. I want you to find out what happened to
him. I hope you never find him.' His protuberant green eyes stared
solemnly at Spade.

Spade rocked back in his chair. His face – given a not unpleasantly
satanic cast by the v's of his bony chin, mouth, nostrils, and thickish
brows – was as politely interested as his voice. 'Why?'

The green-eyed man spoke quietly, with assurance: 'I can talk to
you, Spade. You've the sort of reputation I want in a private detective.
That's why I'm here.'

Spade's nod committed him to nothing.

The green-eyed man said, 'And any fair price is all right with me.'

Spade nodded as before. 'And with me,' he said, 'but I've got to
know what you want to buy. You want to find out what's happened to
this – uh – Eli Haven, but you don't care what it is?'

The green-eyed man lowered his voice, but there was no other
change in his mien: 'In a way I do. For instance, if you found him and
fixed it so he stayed away for good, it might be worth more money to
me.'

'You mean even if he didn't want to stay away?'

The green-eyed man said, 'Especially.'

Spade smiled and shook his head. 'Probably not enough more

money – the way you mean it.' He took his long, thick-fingered hands from the arms of his chair and turned their palms up. 'Well, what's it all about, Colyer?'

Colyer's face reddened a little, but his eyes maintained their unblinking cold stare. 'This man's got a wife. I like her. They had a row last week and he blew. If I can convince her he's gone for good, there's a chance she'll divorce him.'

'I'd want to talk to her,' Spade said. 'Who is this Eli Haven? What does he do?'

'He's a bad egg. He doesn't do anything. Writes poetry or something.'

'What can you tell me about him that'll help?'

'Nothing Julia, his wife, can't tell you. You're going to talk to her.' Colyer stood up. 'I've got connections. Maybe I can get something for you through them later . . .'

A small-boned woman of twenty-five or six opened the apartment door. Her powder-blue dress was trimmed with silver buttons. She was full-bosomed but slim, with straight shoulders and narrow hips, and she carried herself with a pride that would have been cockiness in one less graceful.

Spade said, 'Mrs Haven?'

She hesitated before saying 'Yes.'

'Gene Colyer sent me to see you. My name's Spade. I'm a private detective. He wants me to find your husband.'

'And have you found him?'

'I told him I'd have to talk to you first.'

Her smile went away. She studied his face gravely, feature by feature, then she said, 'Certainly,' and stepped back, drawing the door back with her.

When they were seated in facing chairs in a cheaply furnished room overlooking a playground where children were noisy, she asked, 'Did Gene tell you why he wanted Eli found?'

'He said if you knew he was gone for good maybe you'd listen to reason.'

She said nothing.

'Has he ever gone off like this before?'

'Often.'

'What's he like?'

'He's a swell man,' she said dispassionately, 'when he's sober; and when he's drinking he's all right except with women and money.'

'That leaves him a lot of room to be all right in. What does he do for a living?'

'He's a poet,' she replied, 'but nobody makes a living at that.'

'Well?'

'Oh, he pops in with a little money now and then. Poker, races, he says. I don't know.'

'How long've you been married?'

'Four years, almost' – she smiled mockingly.

'San Francisco all the time?'

'No, we lived in Seattle the first year and then came here.'

'He from Seattle?'

She shook her head. 'Some place in Delaware.'

'What place?'

'I don't know.'

Spade drew his thickish brows together a little. 'Where are you from?'

She said sweetly, 'You're not hunting for me.'

'You act like it,' he grumbled. 'Well, who are his friends?'

'Don't ask me!'

He made an impatient grimace. 'You know some of them,' he insisted.

'Sure. There's a fellow named Minera and a Louis James and somebody he calls Conny.'

'Who are they?'

'Men,' she replied blandly. 'I don't know anything about them. They phone or drop by to pick him up, or I see him around town with them. That's all I know.'

'What do they do for a living? They can't all write poetry.'

She laughed. 'They could try. One of them, Louis James, is a – a member of Gene's staff, I think. I honestly don't know any more about them than I've told you.'

'Think they'd know where your husband is?'

She shrugged. 'They're kidding me if they do. They still call up once in a while to see if he's turned up.'

'And these women you mentioned?'

'They're not people I know.'

Spade scowled thoughtfully at the floor, asked, 'What'd he do before he started not making a living writing poetry?'

'Anything – sold vacuum cleaners, hoboed, went to sea, dealt blackjack, railroaded, canning houses, lumber camps, carnivals, worked on a newspaper – anything.'

'Have any money when he left?'

'Three dollars he borrowed from me.'

'What'd he say?'

She laughed. 'Said if I used whatever influence I had with God while he was gone he'd be back at dinnertime with a surprise for me.'

Spade raised his eyebrows. 'You were on good terms?'

'Oh, yes. Our last fight had been patched up a couple of days before.'

'When did he leave?'

'Thursday afternoon; three o'clock, I guess.'

'Got any photographs of him?'

'Yes.' She went to a table by one of the windows, pulled a drawer out, and turned towards Spade again with a photograph in her hand.

Spade looked at the picture of a thin face with deep-set eyes, a sensual mouth, and a heavily lined forehead topped by a disorderly mop of coarse blond hair.

He put Haven's photograph in his pocket and picked up his hat. He turned towards the door, halted. 'What kind of poet is he? Pretty good?'

She shrugged. 'That depends on who you ask.'

'Any of it around here?'

'No.' She smiled. 'Think he's hiding between pages?'

'You never can tell what'll lead to what. I'll be back some time. Think things over and see if you can't find some way of loosening up a little more. Bye.'

He walked down Post Street to Mulford's book store and asked for a volume of Haven's poetry.

'I'm sorry,' the girl said. 'I sold my last copy last week' – she smiled – 'to Mr Haven himself. I can order it for you.'

'You know him?'

'Only through selling his books.'

Spade pursed his lips, asked, 'What day was it?' He gave her one of his business cards. 'Please. It's important.'

She went to a desk, turned the pages of a red-bound sales-book, and came back to him with the book open in her hand. 'It was last Wednesday,' she said, 'and we delivered it to a Mr Roger Ferris, 1981 Pacific Avenue.'

'Thanks a lot,' he said.

Outside, he hailed a taxicab and gave the driver Mr Roger Ferris's address . . .

The Pacific Avenue house was a four-storey, greystone one set behind a narrow strip of lawn. The room into which a plump-faced maid ushered Spade was large and high-ceilinged.

Spade sat down, but when the maid had gone away he rose and began to walk around the room. He halted at a table where there were three books. One of them had a salmon-coloured jacket on which was printed in red an outline drawing of a bolt of lightning striking the ground between a man and a woman, and in black the words *Coloured Light, by Eli Haven.*

Spade picked up the book and went back to his chair.

There was an inscription on the flyleaf – heavy, irregular characters written with blue ink:

> *To good old Buck, who knew his coloured lights,*
> *in memory of them there days.*
> *Eli*

Spade turned pages at random and idly read a verse:

> STATEMENT
>
> *Too many have lived*
> *As we live*
> *For our lives to be*
> *Proof of our living.*
> *Too many have died*
> *As we die*
> *For their deaths to be*
> *Proof of our dying.*

He looked up from the book as a man in dinner clothes came into the room. He was not a tall man, but his erectness made him seem tall even when Spade's six feet and a fraction of an inch were standing before him. He had bright blue eyes undimmed by his fifty-some years, a sunburned face in which no muscle sagged, a smooth, broad forehead, and thick, short, nearly white hair. There was dignity in his countenance, and amiability.

He nodded at the book Spade still held. 'How do you like it?'

Spade grinned, said, 'I guess I'm just a mug,' and put the book down. 'That's what I came to see you about, though, Mr Ferris. You know Haven?'

'Yes, certainly. Sit down, Mr Spade.' He sat in a chair not far from Spade's. 'I knew him as a kid. He's not in trouble, is he?'

Spade said, 'I don't know. I'm trying to find him.'

Ferris spoke hesitantly: 'Can I ask why?'

'You know Gene Colyer?'

'Yes.' Ferris hesitated again, then said, 'This is in confidence. I've a chain of picture houses through northern California, you know, and a couple of years ago when I had some labour trouble I was told that Colyer was the man to get in touch with to have it straightened out. That's how I happened to meet him.'

'Yes,' Spade said dryly. 'A lot of people happen to meet Gene that way.'

'But what's he got to do with Eli?'

'Wants him found. How long since you've seen him?'

'Last Thursday he was here.'

'What time did he leave?'

'Midnight – a little after. He came over in the afternoon around half past three. We hadn't seen each other for years. I persuaded him to stay for dinner – he looked pretty seedy – and lent him some money.'

'How much?'

'A hundred and fifty – all I had in the house.'

'Say where he was going when he left?'

Ferris shook his head. 'He said he'd phone me the next day.'

'Did he phone you the next day?'

'No.'

'And you've known him all his life?'

'Not exactly, but he worked for me fifteen or sixteen years ago when I had a carnival company – Great Eastern and Western Combined Shows – with a partner for a while and then by myself, and I always liked the kid.'

'How long before Thursday since you'd seen him?'

'Lord knows,' Ferris replied. 'I'd lost track of him for years. Then, Wednesday, out of a clear sky, that book came, with no address or anything, just that stuff written in the front, and the next morning he called me up. I was tickled to death to know he was still alive and doing something with himself. So he came over that afternoon and we put in about nine hours straight talking about old times.'

'Tell you much about what he'd been doing since then?'

'Just that he'd been knocking around, doing one thing and another, taking the breaks as they came. He didn't complain much; I had to make him take the hundred and fifty.'

Spade stood up. 'Thanks ever so much, Mr Ferris. I – '

Ferris interrupted him: 'Not at all, and if there's anything I can do, call on me.'

Spade looked at his watch. 'Can I phone my office to see if anything's turned up?'

'Certainly; there's a phone in the next room, to the right.'

Spade said. 'Thanks' and went out. When he returned he was rolling a cigarette. His face was wooden.

'Any news?' Ferris asked.

'Yes. Colyer's called the job off. He says Haven's body's been found in some bushes on the other side of San Jose, with three bullets in it.'

He smiled, adding mildly, 'He *told* me he might be able to find out
something through his connections . . .'

Morning sunshine, coming through the curtains that screened Spade's
office windows, put two fat, yellow rectangles on the floor and gave
everything in the room a yellow tint.

He sat at his desk, staring meditatively at a newspaper. He did not
look up when Effie Perine came in from the outer office.

She said, 'Mrs Haven is here.'

He raised his head then and said, 'That's better. Push her in.'

Mrs Haven came in quickly. Her face was white, and she was
shivering in spite of her fur coat and the warmth of the day. She came
straight to Spade and asked, 'Did Gene kill him?'

Spade said, 'I don't know.'

'I've got to know,' she cried.

Spade took her hands. 'Here, sit down.' He led her to a chair. He
asked, 'Colyer tell you he'd called the job off?'

She stared at him in amazement. 'He what?'

'He left word here last night that your husband had been found and
he wouldn't need me any more.'

She hung her head and her words were barely audible. 'Then he did.'

Spade shrugged. 'Maybe only an innocent man could've afforded to
call it off then, or maybe he was guilty, but had brains enough and
nerve enough to – '

She was not listening to him. She was leaning towards him, speaking
earnestly: 'But, Mr Spade, you're not going to drop it like that? You're
not going to let him stop you?'

While she was speaking his telephone bell rang. He said, 'Excuse
me,' and picked up the receiver. 'Yes? . . . Uh-huh . . . So?' He pursed
his lips. 'I'll let you know.' He pushed the telephone aside slowly and
faced Mrs Haven again. 'Colyer's outside.'

'Does he know I'm here?' she asked quickly.

'Couldn't say.' He stood up, pretending he was not watching her
closely. 'Do you care?'

She pinched her lower lip between teeth, said 'No' hesitantly.

'Fine. I'll have him in.'

She raised a hand as if in protest, then let it drop, and her white face
was composed. 'Whatever you want,' she said.

Spade opened the door, said, 'Hello, Colyer. Come on in. We were
just talking about you.'

Colyer nodded and came into the office holding his stick in one hand, his hat in the other. 'How are you this morning, Julia? You ought to've phoned me. I'd've driven you back to town.'

'I – I didn't know what I was doing.'

Colyer looked at her for a moment longer, then shifted the focus of his expressionless green eyes to Spade's face. 'Well, have you been able to convince her I didn't do it?'

'We hadn't got around to that,' Spade said. 'I was just trying to find out how much reason there was for suspecting you. Sit down.'

Colyer sat down somewhat carefully, asked, 'And?'

'And then you arrived.'

Colyer nodded gravely. 'All right, Spade,' he said; 'you're hired again to prove to Mrs Haven that I didn't have anything to do with it.'

'Gene!' she exclaimed in a choked voice and held her hands out toward him appealingly. 'I don't think you did – I don't want to think you did – but I'm so afraid.' She put her hands to her face and began to cry.

Colyer went over to the woman. 'Take it easy,' he said. 'We'll kick it out together.'

Spade went into the outer office, shutting the door behind him.

Effie Perine stopped typing a letter.

He grinned at her, said, 'Somebody ought to write a book about people sometime – they're peculiar,' and went over to the water bottle. 'You've got Wally Kellogg's number. Call him up and ask him where I can find Tom Minera.'

He returned to the inner office.

Mrs Haven had stopped crying. She said, 'I'm sorry.'

Spade said, 'It's all right.' He looked sidewise at Colyer. 'I still got my job?'

'Yes.' Colyer cleared his throat. 'But if there's nothing special right now, I'd better take Mrs Haven home.'

'OK, but there's one thing: According to the *Chronicle*, you identified him. How come you were down there?'

'I went down when I heard they'd found a body,' Colyer replied deliberately. 'I told you I had connections. I heard about the body through them.'

Spade said, 'All right; be seeing you,' and opened the door for them.

When the corridor door closed behind them, Effie Perine said, 'Minera's at the Buxton on Army Street.'

Spade said, 'Thanks.' He went into the inner office to get his hat. On his way out he said, 'If I'm not back in a couple of months tell them to look for my body there . . .'

Spade walked down a shabby corridor to a battered green door marked '411'. The murmur of voices came through the door, but no words could be distinguished. He stopped listening and knocked.

An obviously disguised male voice asked, 'What is it?'

'I want to see Tom. This is Sam Spade.'

A pause, then: 'Tom ain't here.'

Spade put a hand on the knob and shook the frail door. 'Come on, open up,' he growled.

Presently the door was opened by a thin, dark man of twenty-five or six who tried to make his beady dark eyes guileless while saying, 'I didn't think it was your voice at first.' The slackness of his mouth made his chin seem even smaller than it was. His green-striped shirt, open at the neck, was not clean. His grey pants were carefully pressed.

'You've got to be careful these days,' Spade said solemnly, and went through the doorway into a room where two men were trying to seem uninterested in his arrival.

One of them leaned against the window sill filing his fingernails. The other was tilted back in a chair with his feet on the edge of a table and a newspaper spread between his hands. They glanced at Spade in unison and went on with their occupations.

Spade said cheerfully, 'Always glad to meet any friends of Tom Minera's.'

Minera finished shutting the door and said awkwardly, 'Uh – yes – Mr Spade, meet Mr Conrad and Mr James.'

Conrad, the man at the window, made a vaguely polite gesture with the nail file in his hand. He was a few years older than Minera, of average height, sturdily built, with a thick-featured, dull-eyed face.

James lowered his paper for an instant to look coolly, appraisingly at Spade and say, 'How'r'ye, brother?' Then he returned to his reading. He was as sturdily built as Conrad, but taller, and his face had a shrewdness the other's lacked.

'Ah,' Spade said, 'and friends of the late Eli Haven.'

The man at the window jabbed a finger with his nail file, and cursed it bitterly. Minera moistened his lips, and then spoke rapidly, with a whining note in his voice: 'But on the level, Spade, we hadn't none of us seen him for a week.'

Spade seemed mildly amused by the dark man's manner.

'What do you think he was killed for?'

'All I know is what the paper says: His pockets was all turned inside out and there wasn't as much as a match on him.' He drew down the ends of his mouth. 'But far as I know he didn't have no dough. He didn't have none Tuesday night.'

Spade, speaking softly, said, 'I hear he got some Thursday night.'

Minera, behind Spade, caught his breath audibly.

James said, 'I guess you ought to know. I don't.'

'He ever work with you boys?'

James slowly put aside his newspaper and took his feet off the table. His interest in Spade's question seemed great enough, but almost impersonal. 'Now what do you mean by that?'

Spade pretended surprise. 'But you boys must work at something?'

Minera came around to Spade's side. 'Aw, listen, Spade,' he said. 'This guy Haven was just a guy we knew. We didn't have nothing to do with rubbing him out; we don't know nothing at all about it. You know, we – '

Three deliberate knocks sounded at the door.

Minerva and Conrad looked at James, who nodded, but by then Spade, moving swiftly, had reached the door and was opening it.

Roger Ferris was there.

Spade blinked at Ferris, Ferris at Spade. Then Ferris put out his hand and said, 'I *am* glad to see you.'

'Come on in,' Spade said.

'Look at this, Mr Spade.' Ferris's hand trembled as he took a slightly soiled envelope from his pocket.

Ferris's name and address were typewritten on the envelope. There was no postage stamp on it. Spade took out the enclosure, a narrow slip of cheap white paper, and unfolded it. On it was typewritten:

You had better come to Room No. 411 Buxton Hotel on Army St at 5 PM this afternoon on account of Thursday night.

There was no signature.

Spade said, 'It's a long time before five o'clock.'

'It is,' Ferris agreed with emphasis. 'I came as soon as I got that. It was Thursday night Eli was at my house.'

Minera was jostling Spade, asking, 'What is all this?'

Spade held the note up for the dark man to read. He read it and yelled, 'Honest, Spade, I don't know nothing about that letter.'

'Does anybody?' Spade asked.

Conrad said 'No' hastily.

James said, 'What letter?'

Spade looked dreamily at Ferris for a moment, then said, as if speaking to himself, 'Of course, Haven was trying to shake you down.'

Ferris's face reddened. 'What?'

'Shake-down,' Spade repeated patiently; 'money, blackmail.'

'Look here, Spade,' Ferris said earnestly; 'you don't really believe what you said? What would he have to blackmail me on?'

' "To good old Buck" ' – Spade quoted the dead poet's inscription –

' "who knew his coloured lights, in memory of them there days." ' He looked sombrely at Ferris from beneath slightly raised brows. 'What coloured lights? What's the circus and carnival slang term for kicking a guy off a train while it's going? Red-lighting. Sure, that's it – red lights. Who'd you red-light, Ferris, that Haven knew about?'

Minera went over to a chair, sat down, put his elbows on his knees, his head between his hands, and stared blankly at the floor. Conrad was breathing as if he had been running.

Spade addressed Ferris: 'Well?'

Ferris wiped his face with a handkerchief, put the handkerchief in his pocket, and said simply, 'It was a shake-down.'

'And you killed him.'

Ferris's blue eyes, looking into Spade's yellow-grey ones, were clear and steady, as was his voice. 'I did not,' he said. 'I swear I did not. Let me tell you what happened. He sent me the book, as I told you, and I knew right away what that joke he wrote in the front meant. So the next day, when he phoned me and said he was coming over to talk over old times and to try to borrow some money for old times' sake, I knew what he meant again, and I went down to the bank and drew out ten thousand dollars. You can check that up. It's the Seamen's National.'

'I will,' Spade said.

'As it turned out, I didn't need that much. He wasn't very big-time, and I talked him into taking five thousand. I put the other five back in the bank next day. You can check that up.'

'I will,' Spade said.

'I told him I wasn't going to stand for any more taps, this five thousand was the first and last. I made him sign a paper saying he'd helped in the – in what I'd done – and he signed it. He left sometime around midnight, and that's the last I ever saw of him.'

Spade tapped the envelope Ferris had given him. 'And how about this note?'

'A messenger boy brought it at noon, and I came right over. Eli had assured me he hadn't said anything to anybody, but I didn't know. I had to face it, whatever it was.'

Spade turned to the others, his face wooden. 'Well?'

Minera and Conrad looked at James, who made an impatient grimace and said, 'Oh, sure, we sent him the letter. Why not? We was friends of Eli's, and we hadn't been able to find him since he went to put the squeeze to this baby, and then he turns up dead, so we kind of like to have the gent come over and explain things.'

'You knew about the squeeze?'

'Sure. We was all together when he got the idea.'

'How'd he happen to get the idea?' Spade asked.

James spread the fingers of his left hand. 'We'd been drinking and talking – you know the way a bunch of guys will, about all they'd seen and done – and he told a yarn about once seeing a guy boot another off a train into a canyon, and he happens to mention the name of the guy that done the booting – Buck Ferris. And somebody says, "What's this Ferris look like?" Eli tells him what he looked like then, saying he ain't seen him for fifteen years; and whoever it is whistles and says, "I bet that's the Ferris that owns about half the movie joints in the state. I bet you he'd give something to keep that back trail covered!"

'Well, the idea kind of hit Eli. You could see that. He thought a little while and then he got cagey. He asked what this movie Ferris's first name is, and when the other guy tells him, "Roger," he makes out he's disappointed and says, "No, it ain't him. His first name was Martin." We all give him the ha-ha and he finally admits he's thinking of seeing the gent, and when he called me up Thursday around noon and says he's throwing a party at Pogey Hecker's that night, it ain't no trouble to figure out what's what.'

'What was the name of the gentleman who was red-lighted?'

'He wouldn't say. He shut up tight. You couldn't blame him.'

'Uh-huh,' Spade agreed.

'Then nothing. He never showed up at Pogey's. We tried to get him on the phone around two o'clock in the morning, but his wife said he hadn't been home, so we stuck around till four or five and then decided he had given us a run-around, and made Pogey charge the bill to him, and beat it. I ain't seen him since – dead or alive.'

Spade said mildly. 'Maybe. Sure you didn't find Eli later that morning, take him riding, swap him bullets for Ferris's five thou, dump him in the – ?'

A sharp double knock sounded on the door.

Spade's face brightened. He went to the door and opened it.

A young man came in. He was very dapper, and very well proportioned. He wore a light topcoat and his hands were in its pockets. Just inside the door he stepped to the right, and stood with his back to the wall. By that time another young man was coming in. He stepped to the left. Though they did not actually look alike, their common dapperness, the similar trimness of their bodies, and their almost identical positions – backs to wall, hands in pockets, cold, bright eyes studying the occupants of the room – gave them, for an instant, the appearance of twins.

Then Gene Colyer came in. He nodded at Spade, but paid no attention to the others in the room, though James said, 'Hello, Gene.'

'Anything new?' Colyer asked Spade.

Spade nodded. 'It seems this gentleman' – he jerked a thumb at Ferris – 'was – '

'Any place we can talk?'

'There's a kitchen back here.'

Colyer snapped a 'Smear anybody that pops' over his shoulder at the two dapper young men and followed Spade into the kitchen. He sat on the one kitchen chair and stared with unblinking green eyes at Spade while Spade told him what he had learned.

When the private detective had finished, the green-eyed man asked, 'Well, what do you make of it?'

Spade looked thoughtfully at the other. 'You've picked up something, I'd like to know what it is.'

Colyer said, 'They found the gun in a stream a quarter of a mile from where they found him. It's James's – got the mark on it where it was shot out of his hand once in Vallejo.'

'That's nice,' Spade said.

'Listen. A kid named Thurber says James comes to him last Wednesday and gets him to tail Haven. Thurber picks him up Thursday afternoon, puts him in at Ferris's, and phones James. James tells him to take a plant on the place and let him know where Haven goes when he leaves, but some nervous woman in the neighbourhood puts in a rumble about the kid hanging around, and the cops chase him along about ten o'clock.'

Spade pursed his lips and stared thoughtfully at the ceiling.

Colyer's eyes were expressionless, but sweat made his round face shiny, and his voice was hoarse. 'Spade,' he said, 'I'm going to turn him in.'

Spade switched his gaze from the ceiling to the protuberant green eyes.

'I've never turned in one of my people before,' Colyer said, 'but this one goes. Julia's *got* to believe I hadn't anything to do with it if it's one of my people and I turn him in, hasn't she?'

Spade nodded slowly. 'I think so.'

Colyer suddenly averted his eyes and cleared his throat. When he spoke again it was curtly: 'Well, he goes.'

Minera, James, and Conrad were seated when Spade and Colyer came out of the kitchen. Ferris was walking the floor. The two dapper young men had not moved.

Colyer went over to James. 'Where's your gun, Louis?' he asked.

James moved his right hand a few inches towards his left breast, stopped it, and said, 'Oh, I didn't bring it.'

With his gloved hand – open – Colyer struck James on the side of the face, knocking him out of his chair.

James straightened up, mumbling, 'I didn't mean nothing.' He put a hand to the side of his face. 'I know I oughtn't've done it, Chief, but when he called up and said he didn't like to go up against Ferris without something and didn't have any of his own, I said, "All right," and sent it over to him.'

Colyer said, 'And you sent Thurber over to him, too.'

'We were just kind of interested in seeing if he did go through with it,' James mumbled.

'And you couldn't've gone there yourself, or sent somebody else?'

'After Thurber had stirred up the whole neighbourhood?'

Colyer turned to Spade. 'Want us to help you take them in, or want to call the wagon?'

'We'll do it regular,' Spade said, and went to the wall telephone. When he turned away from it his face was wooden, his eyes dreamy. He made a cigarette, lit it, and said to Colyer, 'I'm silly enough to think your Louis has got a lot of right answers in that story of his.'

James took his hand down from his bruised cheek and stared at Spade with astonished eyes.

Colyer growled, 'What's the matter with you?'

'Nothing,' Spade said softly, 'except I think you're a little too anxious to slam it on him.' He blew smoke out. 'Why, for instance, should he drop his gun there when it had marks on it that people knew?'

Colyer said, 'You think he's got brains.'

'If these boys killed him, knew he was dead, why do they wait till the body's found and things are stirred up before they go after Ferris again? What'd they turn his pockets inside out for if they hijacked him? That's a lot of trouble and only done by folks that kill for some other reason and want to make it look like robbery.' He shook his head. 'You're too anxious to slam it on them. Why should they – ?'

'That's not the point right now,' Colyer said. 'The point is, why do you keep saying I'm too anxious to slam it on him?'

Spade shrugged. 'Maybe to clear yourself with Julia as soon as possible and as clear as possible, maybe even to clear yourself with the police, and then you've got clients.'

Colyer said, 'What?'

Spade made a careless gesture with his cigarette. 'Ferris,' he said blandly. 'He killed him, of course.'

Colyer's eyelids quivered, though he did not actually blink.

Spade said, 'First, he's the last person we know of who saw Eli alive, and that's always a good bet. Second, he's the only person I talked to before Eli's body turned up who cared whether I thought they were holding out on me or not. The rest of you just thought I was hunting for a guy who'd gone away. He knew I was hunting for a man he'd killed, so he had to put himself in the clear. He was even afraid to throw that book away, because it had been sent up by the book store and could be traced, and there might be clerks who'd seen the inscription. Third, he was the only one who thought Eli was just a sweet, clean, lovable boy – for the same reasons. Fourth, that story about a blackmailer showing up at three o'clock in the afternoon, making an easy touch for five grand, and then sticking around till midnight is just silly, no matter how good the booze was. Fifth, the story about the paper Eli signed is still worse, though a forged one could be fixed up easy enough. Sixth, he's got the best reason for anybody we know for wanting Eli dead.'

Colyer nodded slowly. 'Still – '

'Still nothing,' Spade said. 'Maybe he did the ten-thousand-out-five-thousand-back trick with his bank, but that was easy. Then he got this feeble-minded blackmailer in his house, stalled him along until the servants had gone to bed, took the borrowed gun away from him, shoved him downstairs into his car, took him for a ride – maybe took him already dead, maybe shot him down there by the bushes – frisked him clean to make identification harder and to make it look like robbery, tossed the gun in the water, and came home – '

He broke off to listen to the sound of a siren in the street. He looked then, for the first time since he had begun to talk, at Ferris.

Ferris's face was ghastly white, but he held his eyes steady.

Spade said, 'I've got a hunch, Ferris, that we're going to find out about that red-lighting job, too. You told me you had your carnival company with a partner for a while when Eli was working for you, and then by yourself. We oughtn't to have a lot of trouble finding out about your partner – whether he disappeared, or died a natural death, or is still alive.'

Ferris had lost some of his erectness. He wet his lips and said, 'I want to see my lawyer. I don't want to talk till I've seen my lawyer.'

Spade said, 'It's all right with me. You're up against it, but I don't like blackmailers myself. I think Eli wrote a good epitaph for them in that book back there – "Too many have lived." '

The Case of the Irate Witness

◆————————◆

ERLE STANLEY GARDNER

Perry Mason, the most famous attorney in crime fiction, has appeared in over eighty novels and rarely been off the screen for fifty years since his movie debut in The Case of the Howling Dog *made by Warner Brothers in 1934, starring Warren William. The handsome, bulky and very single-minded Los Angeles lawyer who will only take on the cases of those he is convinced are innocent, also appeared in the Forties on radio in a Monday-to-Friday night serial on CBS with John Larkin; but then became an international celebrity in 1957 thanks to television and his portrayal by Raymond Burr. The CBS series lasted for a decade – 245 black and white, hour-long episodes – earning Burr an Emmy Award and also making stars of Barbara Hale as Perry's secretary, Della Street, and William Hopper playing private detective Paul Drake, who does much of Mason's investigative work. A re-make in 1973,* The New Adventures of Perry Mason, *which ran for thirteen, one-hour episodes, was less successful, although a new dimension was added with scenes outside the office and courtroom – the failure probably attributable to the less charismatic cast of Monte Markham, Sharon Acker and Albert Stratton. In 1990, NBC reunited Raymond Burr and Barbara Hale once again in a one hundred and twenty-minute special,* Perry Mason: The Case of the Defiant Daughter, *which recreated the best elements of the original and proved, according to a* Variety *review, 'there is little doubt about Mason's drawing power among whodunit fans.'*

Erle Stanley Gardner (1889–1970), the creator of the persuasive attorney, had himself been a practising lawyer often taking on seemingly hopeless cases, before he decided to write fiction and became one of the best-selling writers of all time. He was initially a

prolific contributor to the pulp magazines, but it was the appearance of
Perry Mason in The Case of the Velvet Claws *in 1933 – in which he*
was actually more of a private detective than a lawyer – that signalled
the start of his world-wide fame. Curiously, Gardner only wrote one
short story about his distinguished lawyer, The Case of the Irate
Witness *(1953), but, just like most of the eighty novels, it, too, was*
used in the long-running original TV series.

THE early-morning shadows cast by the mountains still lay heavily
on the town's main street as the big siren on the roof of the Jebson
Commercial Company began to scream shrilly.

The danger of fire was always present, and at the sound, men at
breakfast rose and pushed their chairs back from the table. Men who
were shaving barely paused to wipe lather from their faces; men who
had been sleeping grabbed the first available garments. All of them ran
to places where they could look for the first telltale wisps of smoke.

There was no smoke.

The big siren was still screaming urgently as the men formed into
streaming lines, like ants whose hill has been attacked. The lines all
moved toward the Jebson Commercial Company.

There the men were told that the doors of the big vault had been
found wide open. A jagged hole had been cut into one door with an
acetylene torch.

The men looked at one another silently. This was the fifteenth of
the month. The big, twice-a-month pay-roll, which had been brought
up from the Ivanhoe National Bank the day before, had been the
prize.

Frank Bernal, manager of the company's mine, the man who ruled
Jebson City with an iron hand, arrived and took charge. The
responsibility was his, and what he found was alarming.

Tom Munson, the night watchman, was lying on the floor in a back
room, snoring in drunken slumber. The burglar alarm, which had
been installed within the last six months, had been bypassed by means
of an electrical device. This device was so ingenious that it was
apparent that, if the work were that of a gang, at least one of the
burglars was an expert electrician.

Ralph Nesbitt, the company accountant, was significantly silent.

When Frank Bernal had been appointed manager a year earlier, Nesbitt had pointed out that the big vault was obsolete.

Bernal, determined to prove himself in his new job, had avoided the expense of tearing out the old vault and installing a new one by investing in an up-to-date burglar alarm and putting a special night watchman on duty.

Now the safe had been looted of a hundred thousand dollars and Frank Bernal had to make a report to the main office in Chicago, with the disquieting knowledge that Ralph Nesbitt's memo stating that the antiquated vault was a pushover was at this moment reposing in the company files.

Some distance out of Jebson City, Perry Mason, the famous trial lawyer, was driving fast along a mountain road. He had planned a weekend fishing trip for a long time, but a jury which had waited until midnight before reaching its verdict had delayed Mason's departure and it was now eight-thirty in the morning.

His fishing clothes, rod, wading boots, and creel were all in the trunk. He was wearing the suit in which he had stepped from the courtroom, and having driven all night he was eager for the cool, piny mountains.

A blazing red light, shining directly at him as he rounded a turn in the canyon road, dazzled his road-weary eyes. A sign, *STOP – POLICE*, had been placed in the middle of the road. Two men, a grim-faced man with a .30-30 rifle in his hands and a silver badge on his shirt and a uniformed motorcycle officer, stood beside the sign.

Mason stopped his car.

The man with the badge, deputy sheriff, said, 'We'd better take a look at your driving licence. There's been a big robbery at Jebson City.'

'That so?' Mason said. 'I went through Jebson City an hour ago and everything seemed quiet.'

'Where you been since then?'

'I stopped at a little service station and restaurant for breakfast.'

'Let's take a look at your driving licence.'

Mason handed it to him.

The man started to return it, then looked at it again. 'Say,' he said, 'you're Perry Mason, the big criminal lawyer!'

'Not a criminal lawyer,' Mason said patiently, 'a trial lawyer. I sometimes defend men who are accused of crime.'

'What are you doing up in this country?'

'Going fishing.'

The deputy looked at him suspiciously. 'Why aren't you wearing your fishing clothes?'

'Because,' Mason said, and smiled, 'I'm not fishing.'

'You said you were going fishing.'

'I also intend,' Mason said, 'to go to bed tonight. According to you, I should be wearing my pyjamas.'

The deputy frowned. The traffic officer laughed and waved Mason on.

The deputy nodded at the departing car. 'Looks like a live clue to me,' he said, 'but I can't find it in that conversation.'

'There isn't any,' the traffic officer said.

The deputy remained dubious, and later on, when a news-hungry reporter from the local paper asked the deputy if he knew of anything that would make a good story, the deputy said that he did.

And that was why Della Street, Perry Mason's confidential secretary, was surprised to read stories in the metropolitan papers stating that Perry Mason, the noted trial lawyer, was rumoured to have been retained to represent the person or persons who had looted the vault of the Jebson Commercial Company. All this had been arranged, it would seem, before Mason's 'client' had even been apprehended.

When Perry Mason called his office by long-distance the next afternoon, Della said, 'I thought you were going to the mountains for a vacation.'

'That's right. Why?'

'The papers claim you're representing whoever robbed the Jebson Commercial Company.'

'First I've heard of it,' Mason said. 'I went through Jebson City before they discovered the robbery, stopped for breakfast a little farther on, and then got caught in a road-block. In the eyes of some officious deputy, that seems to have made me an accessory after the fact.'

'Well,' Della Street said, 'they've caught a man by the name of Harvey L. Corbin, and apparently have quite a case against him. They're hinting at mysterious evidence which won't be disclosed until the time of trial.'

'Was he the one who committed the crime?' Mason asked.

'The police think so. He has a criminal record. When his employers at Jebson City found out about it, they told him to leave town. That was the evening before the robbery.'

'Just like that, eh?' Mason asked.

'Well, you see, Jebson City is a one-industry town, and the company owns all the houses. They're leased to the employees. I understand Corbin's wife and daughter were told they could stay on until Corbin got located in a new place, but Corbin was told to leave town at once. You aren't interested, are you?'

'Not in the least,' Mason said, 'except that when I drive back I'll be going through Jebson City, and I'll probably stop to pick up the local gossip.'

'Don't do it,' she warned. 'This man Corbin has all the earmarks of being an underdog, and you know how you feel about underdogs.'

A quality in her voice made Perry suspicious. 'You haven't been approached, have you, Della?'

'Well,' she said, 'in a way. Mrs Corbin read in the papers that you were going to represent her husband, and she was overjoyed. It seems that she thinks her husband's implication in this is a raw deal. She hadn't known anything about his criminal record, but she loves him and is going to stand by him.'

'You've talked with her?' Mason asked.

'Several times. I tried to break it to her gently. I told her it was probably nothing but a newspaper story. You see, Chief, they have Corbin dead to rights. They took some money from his wife as evidence. It was part of the loot.'

'And she has nothing?'

'Nothing. Corbin left her forty dollars, and they took it all as evidence.'

'I'll drive all night,' he said. 'Tell her I'll be back tomorrow.'

'I was afraid of that,' Della Street said. 'Why did you have to call up? Why couldn't you have stayed up there fishing? Why did you have to get your name in the papers?'

Mason laughed and hung up.

Paul Drake, of the Drake Detective Agency, came in and sat in the big chair in Mason's office and said, 'You have a bear by the tail, Perry.'

'What's the matter, Paul? Didn't your detective work in Jebson City pan out?'

'It panned out all right, but the stuff in the pan isn't what you want, Perry,' Drake explained.

'How come?'

'Your client's guilty.'

'Go on,' Mason said.

'The money he gave his wife was some of what was stolen from the vault.'

'How do they know it was the stolen money?' Mason asked.

Drake pulled a notebook from his pocket. 'Here's the whole picture. The plant manager runs Jebson City. There isn't any private property. The Jebson company controls everything.'

'Not a single small business?'

Drake shook his head. 'Not unless you want to consider garbage collecting as small business. An old coot by the name of George Addey lives five miles down the canyon; he has a hog ranch and collects the garbage. He's supposed to have the first nickel he ever earned. Buries his money in cans. There's no bank nearer than Ivanhoe City.'

'What about the burglary? The men who did it must have moved in acetylene tanks and – '

'They took them right out of the company store,' Drake said. And then he went on: 'Munson, the watchman, likes to take a pull out of a flask of whiskey along about midnight. He says it keeps him awake. Of course, he's not supposed to do it, and no one was supposed to know about the whiskey, but someone did know about it. They doped the whiskey with a barbiturate. The watchman took his usual swig, went to sleep, and stayed alseep.'

'What's the evidence against Corbin?' Mason asked.

'Corbin had a previous burglary record. It's a policy of the company not to hire anyone with a criminal record. Corbin lied about his past and got a job. Frank Bernal, the manager , found out about it, sent for Corbin about eight o'clock the night the burglary took place, and ordered him out of town. Bernal agreed to let Corbin's wife and child stay on in the house until Corbin could get located in another city. Corbin pulled out in the morning, and gave his wife this money. It was part of the money from the burglary.'

'How do they know?' Mason asked.

'Now there's something I don't know,' Drake said. 'This fellow Bernal is pretty smart, and the story is that he can prove Corbin's money was from the vault.'

Drake paused, then continued: 'The nearest bank is at Ivanhoe City, and the mine pays off in cash twice a month. Ralph Nesbitt, the cashier, wanted to install a new vault. Bernal refused to okay the expense. So the company has ordered both Bernal and Nesbitt back to its main office at Chicago to report. The rumour is that they may fire Bernal as manager and give Nesbitt the job. A couple of the directors don't like Bernal, and this thing has given them their chance. They dug out a report Nesbitt had made showing the vault was a pushover. Bernal didn't act on that report.' He sighed and then asked, 'When's the trial, Perry?'

'The preliminary hearing is set for Friday morning. I'll see then what they've got against Corbin.'

'They're laying for you up there,' Paul Drake warned. 'Better watch out, Perry. That district attorney has something up his sleeve, some sort of surprise that's going to knock you for a loop.'

In spite of his long experience as a prosecutor, Vernon Flasher, the district attorney of Ivanhoe County, showed a certain nervousness at being called upon to oppose Perry Mason. There was, however, a secretive assurance underneath that nervousness.

Judge Haswell, realizing that the eyes of the community were upon him, adhered to legal technicalities to the point of being pompous both in rulings and mannerisms.

But what irritated Perry Mason was in the attitude of the spectators. He sensed that they did not regard him as an attorney trying to safeguard the interests of a client, but as a legal magician with a cloven hoof. The looting of the vault had shocked the community, and there was a tight-lipped determination that no legal tricks were going to do Mason any good *this* time.

Vernon Flasher didn't try to save his surprise evidence for a whirlwind finish. He used it right at the start of the case.

Frank Bernal, called as a witness, described the location of the vault, identified photographs, and then leaned back as the district attorney said abruptly, 'You had reason to believe this vault was obsolete?'

'Yes, sir.'

'It had been pointed out to you by one of your fellow employees, Mr Ralph Nesbitt?'

'Yes, sir.'

'And what did you do about it?'

'Are you,' Mason asked in some surprise, 'trying to cross-examine your own witness?'

'Just let him answer the question, and you'll see,' Flasher replied grimly.

'Go right ahead and answer,' Mason said to the witness.

Bernal assumed a more comfortable position. 'I did three things,' he said, 'to safeguard the payrolls and to avoid the expense of tearing out the old vault and installing a new vault in its place.'

'What were those three things?'

'I employed a special night watchman; I installed the best burglar alarm money could buy; and I made arrangements with the Ivanhoe National Bank, where we have our payrolls made up, to list the number of each twenty-dollar bill which was a part of each payroll.'

Mason suddenly sat up straight.

Flasher gave him a glance of gloating triumph. 'Do you wish the court to understand, Mr Bernal,' he said smugly, 'that you have the numbers of the bills in the payroll which was made up for delivery on the fifteenth?'

'Yes, sir. Not *all* the bills, you understand. That would have taken too much time, but I have the number of all the twenty-dollar bills.'

'And who recorded those numbers?' the prosecutor asked.

'The bank.'

'And do you have that list of numbers with you?'

'I do. Yes, sir.' Bernal produced a list. 'I felt,' he said, glancing coldly at Nesbitt, 'that these precautions would be cheaper than a new vault.'

'I move the list be introduced in evidence,' Flasher said.

'Just a moment,' Mason objected. 'I have a couple of questions. You say this list is not in your handwriting, Mr Bernal?'

'Yes, sir.'

'Whose handwriting is it, do you know?' Mason asked.

'The assistant cashier of the Ivanhoe National Bank.'

'Oh, all right,' Flasher said. 'We'll do it the hard way, if we have to. Stand down, Mr Bernal, and I'll call the assistant cashier.'

Harry Reedy, assistant cashier of the Ivanhoe Bank, had the mechanical assurance of an adding machine. He identified the list of numbers as being in his handwriting. He stated that he had listed the numbers of the twenty-dollar bills and put that list in an envelope which had been sealed and sent up with the money for the payroll.

'Cross-examine,' Flasher said.

Mason studied the list. 'These numbers are all in your handwriting?' he asked Reedy.

'Yes, sir.'

'Did you yourself compare the numbers you wrote down with the numbers on the twenty-dollar bills?'

'No, sir. I didn't personally do that. Two assistants did that. One checked the numbers as they were read off, one as I wrote them down.'

'The payrolls are for approximately a hundred thousand dollars, twice each month?'

'That's right. And ever since Mr Bernal took charge, we have taken this means to identify payrolls. No attempt is made to list the bills in numerical order. The serial numbers are simply read off and written down. Unless a robbery occurs, there is no need to do anything further. In the event of a robbery, we can reclassify the numbers and list the bills in numerical order.'

'These numbers are in your handwriting – every number?'

'Yes, sir. More than that, you will notice that at the bottom of each page I have signed my initials.'

'That's all,' Mason said.

'I now offer once more to introduce this list in evidence,' Flasher said.

'So ordered,' Judge Haswell ruled.

'My next witness is Charles J. Oswald, the sheriff,' the district attorney announced.

The sheriff, a long, lanky man with a quiet manner, took the stand. 'You're acquainted with Harvey L. Corbin, the defendant in this case?' the district attorney asked.

'I am.'

'Are you acquainted with his wife?'

'Yes, sir.'

'Now, on the morning of the fifteenth of this month, the morning of the robbery at the Jebson Commercial Company, did you have any conversation with Mrs Corbin?'

'I did. Yes, sir.'

'Did you ask her about her husband's activities the night before?'

'Just a moment,' Mason said. 'I object to this on the ground that any conversation the sheriff had with Mrs Corbin is not admissible against the defendant, Corbin; furthermore, that in this state a wife cannot testify against her husband. Therefore, any statement she might make would be an indirect violation of that rule. Furthermore, I object on the ground that the question calls for hearsay.'

Judge Haswell looked ponderously thoughtful, then said, 'It seems to me Mr Mason is correct.'

'I'll put it this way, Mr Sheriff,' the district attorney said. 'Did you, on the morning of the fifteenth, take any money from Mrs Corbin?'

'Objected to as incompetent, irrelevant, and immaterial,' Mason said.

'Your Honour,' Flasher said irritably, 'that's the very gist of our case. We propose to show that two of the stolen twenty-dollar bills were in the possession of Mrs Corbin.'

Mason said, 'Unless the prosecution can prove the bills were given Mrs Corbin by her husband, the evidence is inadmissible.'

'That's just the point,' Flasher said. 'Those bills *were* given to her by the defendant.'

'How do you know?' Mason asked.

'She told the sheriff so.'

'That's hearsay,' Mason snapped.

Judge Haswell fidgeted on the bench. 'It seems to me we're getting into a peculiar situation here. You can't call the wife as a witness, and I don't think her statement to the sheriff is admissible.'

'Well,' Flasher said desperately, 'in this state, Your Honour, we have a community-property law. Mrs Corbin had this money. Since she is the wife of the defendant, it was community property. Therefore, it's partially his property.'

'Well now, there,' Judge Haswell said, 'I think I can agree with you. You introduce the twenty-dollar bills. I'll overrule the objection made by the defence.'

'Produce the twenty-dollar bills, Sheriff,' Flasher said triumphantly.

The bills were produced and received in evidence.

'Cross-examine,' Flasher said curtly.

'No questions of this witness,' Mason said, 'but I have a few questions to ask Mr Bernal on cross-examination. You took him off the stand to lay the foundation for introducing the bank list, and I didn't have an opportunity to cross-examine him.'

'I beg your pardon,' Flasher said. 'Resume the stand, Mr Bernal.'

His tone, now that he had the twenty-dollar bills safely introduced in evidence, had a gloating note to it.

Mason said, 'This list which has been introduced in evidence is on the stationery of the Ivanhoe National Bank?'

'That's right. Yes, sir.'

'It consists of several pages, and at the end there is the signature of the assistant cashier?'

'Yes sir.'

'And each page is initialled by the assistant cashier?'

'Yes, sir.'

'This was the scheme which you thought of in order to safeguard the company against a payroll robbery?'

'Not to safeguard the company against a payroll robbery, Mr Mason, but to assist us in recovering the money in the event there was a holdup.'

'This was your plan to answer Mr Nesbitt's objections that the vault was an outmoded model?'

'A part of my plan, yes. I may say that Mr Nesbitt's objections had never been voiced until I took office. I felt he was trying to embarrass me by making my administration show less net returns than expected.' Bernal tightened his lips and added 'Mr Nesbitt had, I believe, been expecting to be appointed manager. He was disappointed. I believe he still expects to be manager.'

In the spectators' section of the courtroom, Ralph Nesbitt glared at Bernal.

'You had a conversation with the defendant on the night of the fourteenth?' Mason asked Bernal.

'I did. Yes, sir.'

'You told him that for reasons which you deemed sufficient you were discharging him immediately and wanted him to leave the premises at once?'

'Yes, sir. I did.'

'And you paid him his wages in cash?'

'Mr Nesbitt paid him in my presence, with money he took from the petty-cash drawer of the vault.'

'Now, as part of the wages due him, wasn't Corbin given these two twenty-dollar bills which have been introduced in evidence?'

Bernal shook his head 'I had thought of that,' he said, 'but it would have been impossible. Those bills weren't available to us at that time. The payroll is received from the bank in a sealed package. Those two twenty-dollar bills were in that package.'

'And the list of the numbers of the twenty-dollar bills?'

'That's in a sealed envelope. The money is placed in the vault. I lock the list of numbers in my desk.'

'Are you prepared to swear that neither you nor Mr Nesbitt had access to these two twenty-dollar bills on the night of the fourteenth?'

'That is correct.'

'That's all,' Mason said. 'No further cross-examination.'

'I now call Ralph Nesbitt to the stand,' District Attorney Flasher said. 'I want to fix the time of these events definitely, Your Honour.'

'Very well,' Judge Haswell said. 'Mr Nesbitt, come forward.'

Ralph Nesbitt, after answering the usual preliminary questions, sat down in the witness chair.

'Were you present at a conversation which took place between the defendant, Harvey L. Corbin, and Frank Bernal on the fourteenth of this month?' the district attorney asked.

'I was. Yes, sir.'

'What time did that conversation take place?'

'About eight o'clock in the evening.'

'And, without going into the details of that conversation, I will ask you if the general effect of it was that the defendant was discharged and ordered to leave the company's property?'

'Yes, sir.'

'And he was paid the money that was due him?'

'In cash. Yes, sir. I took the cash from the safe myself.'

'Where was the payroll then?'

'In the sealed package in a compartment in the safe. As cashier, I had the only key to that compartment. Earlier in the afternoon I had gone to Ivanhoe City and received the sealed package of money and the envelope containing the list of numbers. I personally locked the package of money in the vault.'

'And the list of numbers?'

'Mr Bernal locked that in his desk.'

'Cross-examine,' Flasher said.

'No questions,' Mason said.

'That's our case, Your Honour,' Flasher observed.

'May we have a few minutes indulgence?' Mason asked Judge Haswell.

'Very well. Make it brief,' the judge agreed.

Mason turned to Paul Drake and Della Street. 'Well, there you are,' Drake said. 'You're confronted with the proof, Perry.'

'Are you going to put the defendant on the stand?' Della Street asked.

Mason shook his head. 'It would be suicidal. He has a record of a prior criminal conviction. Also, it's a rule of law that if one asks about any part of a conversation on direct examination, the other side can bring out all the conversation. That conversation, when Corbin was discharged, was to the effect that he had lied about his past record. And I guess there's no question that he did.'

'And he's lying now,' Drake said. 'This is one case where you're licked. I think you'd better cop a plea, and see what kind of a deal you can make with Flasher.'

'Probably not any,' Mason said. 'Flasher wants to have the reputation of having given me a licking – wait a minute, Paul. I have an idea.'

Mason turned abruptly, walked away to where he could stand by himself, his back to the crowded courtroom.

'Are you ready?' the judge asked.

Mason turned. 'I am quite ready, Your Honour. I have one witness whom I wish to put on the stand. I wish a subpoena *duces tecum* issued for that witness. I want him to bring certain documents which are in his possession.'

'Who is the witness, and what are the documents?' the judge asked.

Mason walked quickly over to Paul Drake. 'What's the name of that character who has the garbage-collecting business,' he said softly, 'the one who has the first nickel he'd ever made?'

'George Addey.'

The lawyer turned to the judge. 'The witness that I want is George Addey, and the documents that I want him to bring to court with him are all the twenty-dollar bills that he has received during the past sixty days.'

'Your Honour,' Flasher protested, 'this is an outrage. This is making a travesty out of justice. It is exposing the court to ridicule.'

Mason said, 'I give Your Honour my assurance that I think this witness is material, and that the documents are material. I will make an affidavit to that effect if necessary. As attorney for the defendant, may I point out that if the court refuses to grant this subpoena, it will be denying the defendant due process of law.'

'I'm going to issue the subpoena,' Judge Haswell said, testily, 'and for your own good, Mr Mason, the testimony had better be relevant.'

George Addey, unshaven and bristling with indignation, held up his right hand to be sworn. He glared at Perry Mason.

'Mr Addey,' Mason said, 'you have the contract to collect garbage from Jebson City?'

'I do.'

'How long have you been collecting garbage there?'

'For over five years, and I want to tell you – '

Judge Haswell banged his gavel. 'The witness will answer questions and not interpolate any comments.'

'I'll interpolate anything I dang please,' Addey said.

'That'll do,' the judge said. 'Do you wish to be jailed for contempt of court, Mr Addey?'

'I don't want to go to jail, but I – '

'Then you'll remember the respect that is due the court,' the judge said. 'Now you sit there and answer questions. This is a court of law. You're in this court as a citizen, and I'm here as a judge, and I propose to see that the respect due to the court is enforced.' There was a moment's silence while the judge glared angrily at the witness. 'All right, go ahead, Mr Mason.' Judge Haswell said.

Mason said, 'During the thirty days prior to the fifteenth of this month, did you deposit any money in any banking institution?'

'I did not.'

'Do you have with you all the twenty-dollar bills that you received during the last sixty days?'

'I have, and I think making me bring them here is just like inviting some crook to come and rob me and – '

Judge Haswell banged with his gavel. 'Any more comments of that sort from the witness and there will be a sentence imposed for contempt of court. Now you get out those twenty-dollar bills, Mr Addey, and put them right up here on the clerk's desk.'

Addey, mumbling under his breath, slammed a roll of twenty-dollar bills down on the desk in front of the clerk.

'Now,' Mason said, 'I'm going to need a little clerical assistance. I would like to have my secretary, Miss Street, and the clerk help me check through the numbers on these bills. I will select a few at random.'

Mason picked up three of the twenty-dollar bills and said, 'I am going to ask my assistants to check the list of numbers introduced in evidence. In my hand is a twenty-dollar bill that has the number L 07083274 A. Is that bill on the list? The next bill that I pick up is number L 07579190 A. Are any of those bills on the list?'

The courtroom was silent. Suddenly, Della Street said, 'Yes, here's one that's on the list – bill number L 07579190 A. It's on the list, on page eight.'

'What?' the prosecutor shouted.

'Exactly,' Mason said, smiling. 'So, if a case is to be made against a person merely because he has possession of the money that was stolen on the fifteenth of this month, then your office should prefer charges against this witness, George Addey, Mr District Attorney.'

Addey jumped from the witness stand and shook his fist in Mason's face. 'You're a cockeyed liar!' he screamed. 'There ain't a one of those bills but what I didn't have it before the fifteenth. The company cashier changes my money into twenties, because I like big bills. I bury 'em in cans, and I put the date on the side of the can.'

'Here's that list,' Mason said. 'Check it for yourself.'

A tense silence gripped the courtroom as the judge and the spectators waited.

'I'm afraid I don't understand this, Mr Mason,' Judge Haswell said, after a moment.

'I think it's quite simple,' Mason said. 'And I now suggest the court take a recess for an hour and check these other bills against this list. I think the district attorney may be surprised.'

And Mason sat down and proceeded to put papers in his brief case.

Della Street, Paul Drake, and Perry Mason were sitting in the lobby of the Ivanhoe Hotel.

'When are you going to tell us?' Della Street asked fiercely. 'Or do we tear you limb from limb? How could the garbage man have – ?'

'Wait a minute,' Mason said. 'I think we're about to get results. Here comes the esteemed district attorney, Vernon Flasher, and he's accompanied by Judge Haswell.'

The two strode over to Mason's group and bowed with cold formality.

Mason got up.

Judge Haswell began in his best courtroom voice. 'A most deplorable situation has occurred. It seems that Mr Frank Bernal has – well – '

'Been detained somewhere,' Vernon Flasher said.

'Disappeared,' Judge Haswell said. 'He's gone.'

'I expected as much,' Mason said.

'Now will you kindly tell me just what sort of pressure you brought to bear on Mr Bernal to – ?'

'Just a moment, Judge,' Mason said. 'The only pressure I brought to bear on him was to cross-examine him.'

'Did you know that there had been a mistake in the dates on those lists?'

'There was no mistake. When you find Bernal, I'm sure you will discover there was a deliberate falsification. He was short in his accounts, and he knew he was about to be demoted. He had a desperate need for a hundred thousand dollars in ready cash. He had evidently been planning this burglary, or, rather, this embezzlement, for some time. He learned that Corbin had a criminal record. He arranged to have these lists furnished by the bank. He installed a burglar alarm, and, naturally, knew how to circumvent it. He employed a watchman he knew was addicted to drink. He only needed to stage his coup at the right time. He fired Corbin and paid him off with bills that had been recorded by the bank on page eight of the list of bills *in the payroll on the first of the month.*

'Then he removed page eight from the list of bills contained in the payroll *of the fifteenth*, before he showed it to the police, and substituted page eight of the list for the *first of the month* payroll. It was that simple.

'Then he drugged the watchman's whiskey, took an acetylene torch, burned through the vault door, and took all the money.'

'May I ask how you knew all this?' Judge Haswell demanded.

'Certainly,' Mason said. 'My client told me he received those bills from Nesbitt, who took them from the petty-cash drawer in the safe. He also told the sheriff that. I happened to be the only one who believed him. It sometimes pays, Your Honour, to have faith in a man, even if he has made a previous mistake. Assuming my client was innocent, I knew either Bernal or Nesbitt must be guilty. I then realized that only Bernal had custody of the *previous* lists of numbers.

'As an employee, Bernal had been paid on the first of the month. He looked at the numbers on the twenty-dollar bills in his pay envelope and found that they had been listed on page eight of the payroll for the first.

'Bernal only needed to abstract all twenty-dollar bills from the petty-cash drawer, substitute twenty-dollar bills from his own pay envelope, call in Corbin, and fire him. His trap was set.

'I let him know I knew what had been done by bringing Addey into court and proving my point. Then I asked for a recess. That was so Bernal would have a chance to skip out. You see, flight may be received as evidence of guilt. It was a professional courtesy to the district attorney. It will help him when Bernal is arrested.'

Walk Softly, Strangler

◆

ROBERT HART DAVIS

Charlie Chan, the gentle Chinese-Hawaiian-American Inspector of the Honolulu Detective Bureau, appeared in almost fifty Hollywood feature films before making his television debut in – of all things – a British-made series of thirty-nine half-hour episodes screened in 1957 and starring J. Carrol Naish. The extraordinary profusion and popularity of the Charlie Chan movies is all the more remarkable when it is recalled that the original creator of the character, Earl Derr Biggers (1844–1933), only wrote six novels about the aimiable, chubby sleuth. Notwithstanding this, his adventures provided the basis for several radio series, a long-running comic strip, and all the film and TV adaptations. When he first appeared in print in 1925 in The House Without A Key, *Charlie provided a striking contrast to the sinister Orientals who were appearing in much contemporary fiction, and his courteous manners and broken English, not to mention his awesome intelligence, made him immensely popular. Strangely, not a single actor of Chinese extraction has so far played the character – Warner Oland, Sidney Toler, Roland Winters and Peter Ustinov appearing in the screen roles; with Walter Connolly, Ed Begley and Santos Ortega in the Charlie Chan radio series which ran from 1932 into the mid-Fifties. J. Carrol Naish, the American-born actor who came to England to make* The New Adventures of Charlie Chan *for ITC in 1957, was actually the descendant of a long line of Irish peers, and he had travelled extensively in Europe before moving to Hollywood and breaking into films first as a stuntman, then in a variety of B-movies. He later established himself as a versatile character actor, specializing in playing foreigners. His characterization of the Honolulu detective was certainly more accomplished and better*

*received than the subsequent 1971 TV production, Charlie Chan:
Happiness Is A Warm Gun, a ninety-six-minute colour production
starring Ross Martin which because of poor writing and unsuitable
casting doomed the series it was supposed to herald.*

*Despite the enormous popularity of Charlie Chan, Erle Derr
Biggers resisted all the offers to write more than the six novels about
his character, much preferring – like Sir Arthur Conan Doyle before
him – to work on his mainstream novels and plays for the theatre. It is,
though, for the little Oriental sleuth that he will always be remembered, and the story about Chan which follows is based on an episode
from the 1957 series and is written in the style of the original books by
the scriptwriter, Robert Hart Davis.*

M EI T'ang Wu's face was as impassive as a mask of pale gold.
Only the slight narrowing of her eyelids and a tautness at the
corners of her lotus blossom lips revealed the fury that lurked behind
it. Even her low pitched, faintly husky voice was under rigid control.

'Ah-Nah,' she said to the younger, slighter, less beautiful woman
confronting her, 'how did this find its way to the carpet?'

'This' was a tiny insect of intricately wrought gold with diamond
eyes and wings of transparent amber set in thread-like gold frames. It
lay in the palm of her outstretched left hand, barely covering the span
between the heart and life lines upon that velvetlike surface.

There was tension in the younger woman's voice as she replied, 'It
was not there when I vacuumed the room this morning.'

'Obviously. If it had been, the vacuum would have picked it up. I
should not have found it . . . or found *this*.'

She opened the palm of her right hand and unfolded the fine linen
handkerchief upon it. Within its folds lay what looked like a ginseng
root, marvellously ugly and intricate to the final whisker, its surface
dotted twice, once with what looked to be a replica of the golden fly in
her left hand, the other a gauzy dragonfly of like expensive elements.

Ah-Nah's dismay became confusion. She said, 'I don't understand.'

The ageing screen star thrust both hands toward Ah-Nah, said, 'Take
a closer look.'

Ah-Nah did so, a scowl on her pretty Sino-American face revealing
shortsightedness as well as concentration. After a long, silent moment,

she straightened up, here eyes wide, and said, 'This is a copy. Very good, too.'

'But not good enough,' said the former film star. 'What was jade is alabaster – soapstone. What was gold, what were diamonds, are – who knows?'

'But who – ' Ah-Nah began, then stopped in utter dismay.

'Never mind for now, Ah-Nah. Let us examine the contents of the other jars.'

The room in which the two women stood was as fantastic as the dragon patterns of solid gold thread woven into the richly embroidered antique mandarin robe that sheathed Mei T'ang's slim, still elegant body from throat to heels. She was more than seventy years old – how much more was a carefully kept secret – and looked not a day older than thirty-eight. She moved with the sinuous ease and grace of a well conditioned young woman of twenty-eight.

Surrounding them, atop richly lacquered ebony cabinets, stood a long row of old-fashioned apothecaries' jars each two feet high and half as much in diameter, looking oddly out of place against the costly Chinese cloud tapestries that covered most of the walls, leaving room only for two large casement windows to the north plus the two doors.

At the bottom of each jar lay a different form of plant or animal life, enduring endlessly without preservative since each was, or had been, a masterpiece of the jeweller's art, each exotic vegetable or root adorned with some form of insect life reproduced in mineral and metal on the base of perfectly selected and carved jade. Here were small carp with ruby eyes, scales lustrous with the rich red hue of Shansi gold, dried frogs of clouded green jade, glittering coiled snakes of jet and silver with more golden flies on their outstretched tongues.

The collection, as both women knew, was insured for more than a million dollars and this was a mere token estimate of its actual cash value in the present day collectors' market – it was, at any rate, beyond value if only because it was unique and therefore irreplaceable, unmatchable. Or it had been before it was debased by substitution.

Now all of the originals were gone . . . enough to represent a theft far surpassing the value of any of the celebrated Brinks' armoured truck robberies of years gone by. Ah-Nah made notes as her mistress took inventory of each of the hundred or more objects that reposed in the bottoms of the large jars.

Only once, toward the end of the chore, did Ah-Nah speak. Then it was to say, 'Your company – the guests will be arriving soon.'

With a quick, impatient angry gesture – the first visible evidence of the rage that burned within her – Mei T'ang said, 'Keep them in the conservatory. Give me the list – we have done enough. Now I must talk to the thief.'

When the woman had silently departed, her mistress stood briefly in thought. Then, with a deep breath that lifted the small, still firm breasts beneath the brocaded mandarin jacket, she glided to the ebony table that stood in room centre, lifted the telephone handset from its top and began to dial a number.

Behind her, the second dark door opened silently and her dialling was interrupted by a gently mocking voice that said, 'There is no need to call, loved one. I am here. I must confess to welcoming this confrontation, now that it has come. I never dreamed it would take you so long to find me out.'

Before Mei T'ang could reply, the silken steel-hard fingers were around her throat and her breathing was abruptly cut off. Nor did she breathe again in this world.

II

Dr Eric Svorenssen, DDS, lifted his foot from the pedal, thus halting the deadly drone of the dental drill, and stood back, beaming proudly at the patient in the chair. Beneath the pale straw thatch of his thinning hair, his face resembled an inverted russet pear set atop the larger inverted pear of his body, an erstwhile athlete quite happily gone to seed via enjoyment of the good things of middle life.

He said, 'That should do it for now, Charlie. We'll have the abutment inlay ready when you come back Thursday. It wasn't so bad, was it?'

Chan said, 'Mouth feel like boxing glove but unable to hit back at tormentor.'

Dr Svorenssen flicked the tip of his bulbous nose with a thumbnail, said, 'Come on Charlie. You speak better English than I do. Save the Confucius Say bit for your admiring public.'

He turned away.

Chan said, rubbing his jaw with thumb and forefinger and feeling as if there were nothing there, 'Not speak good English with face full of Novocaine. Tongue fill mouth to point of detonation.'

Removing his white jacket, for this was his final appointment of the afternoon, Dr Svorenssen said, 'If I hadn't used Novocaine, you'd feel a lot worse.'

'Perhaps – but cure sometimes worse than sickness.'

The need for new bridgework was part of the reason for the

presence in Los Angeles of the veteran Inspector of the Honolulu Detective Bureau. The other part being the first American showing of some spectacular samples of pre-Confucian Chinese art unearthed by the busy archaeologists of Mao Tse-tung's People's Government.

Chan had found, over a period of more than two decades, that Eric Svorenssen, while not possessed of the most delicate of dental touches, did work that lasted. If his technique was 'shoot 'em full of Novocaine and then blast,' it worked. Once a Svorenssen bridge was in, it stayed in. He was knowledgeable, thorough, and remarkably more skilful than his battering ram methods suggested.

Donning a resplendent sports jacket in a vivid Saxony gun club check while his pretty little Swedish assistant helped Chan into his light pongee coat, Dr Svorenssen said, 'Let me give you a lift to the hotel, Charlie.'

'Too much trouble,' said Chan. 'Out of your way.'

Eric Svorenssen lived in one of the pale pink towers of Park La Brea, less than four blocks from his office in the Desmond Tower, overlooking that stretch of Wilshire Boulevard called the 'Miracle Mile' for reasons unknown save to the developers who hung the title upon it. Chan had taken a small suite at the Hollywood Roosevelt, a good two miles to the north-northeast.

'I'm going your way,' said Svorenssen, opening the door that led to the foyer of his office and bidding a cheerful farewell to his receptionist. Neither believing nor disbelieving, Chan saw no reason for further protest. He told himself he would do more than the same for his friend whenever he chose to visit the Islands.

They drove north in the dentist's black Mercedes through the used-car-lot wastelands of La Brea Avenue. Not until they were halted for a red light at Willoughby did either of them speak again.

Then Doctor Svorenssen said, 'You remember Mei T'ang Wu, Charlie?'

'*Hearts of Palm* favourite film for many years. Much in love with her,' said Chan. 'Is she dead?'

'She's very much alive,' said Svorenssen. 'I've been taking care of her teeth for almost thirty years. She's still the most beautiful Oriental woman I have ever seen.'

'Chinese flower slow to fade,' said Chan, a reminiscent glow lending warmth to his usually inscrutable dark eyes. 'Very good news, my friend. With the years, my list of personal idols reads like the casualty list of the Fort Pillow Massacre.'

'And *that's* the truth,' said Svorenssen sadly, negotiating a lane change to avoid a stalled moving van. Certain his friend had not brought up the former film star's name idly, Chan waited for the explanation. It came as they passed Santa Monica Boulevard.

'Mei T'ang is entertaining this afternoon,' Svorenssen said. 'I'm taking you there now – if you don't mind, Charlie.'

'Have I a choice?' Chan countered cryptically.

'None,' said his friend. 'She called earlier to ask me to bring you. Mei T'ang have problem – damn you, you've got me talking your pidgin!'

Chan masked a smile of amusement, said, 'Wise man watch self near poison oak or catch same.' A pause, then, 'Eric, you know I'm not in Hollywood for business, apart from the damnable business of my bridgework.'

'I hope you'll see her,' said Svorenssen. 'Otherwise, I'll take you to the hotel. But she sounded distressed when she called – and angry.'

'Every intention of accepting. Chance to meet idol of youth not to be neglected.'

'Who said that?' Svorenssen asked, 'Confucius or Lao T'se?'

'Charlie Chan,' said the detective with a trace of smugness. Then, 'Does she still live in fabulous House of Wu?'

'You'll see for yourself in about two minutes,' said Svorenssen as he drove past Hollywood Boulevard to take the right turn at Franklin.

Like any normal American-bred youth of his era, Charlie Chan had been a devotee of the late silent and early talking films and had devoured his fill of the ecstatic fan magazines that flourished between the two World Wars. He had feasted his eyes on picture layouts of Rudolph Valentino's *Falcon's Lair*, on Harold Lloyd's terraced palace, on Nazimova's Garden of Allah – and on exotic Mei T'ang Wu's *House of Wu*, in many ways the most remarkable of all Hollywood eyries of the great days of the so-called film capital.

Built in 1932 a mere two blocks northwest of Grauman's Chinese Theatre, it was neither solely a private residence, a hotel nor an apartment house but, in the purported words of its sleekly glamorous creator, 'combines the best features of all, functionally and artistic-ally.'

Since Mei T'ang was of Chinese ancestry like himself, albeit California rather than Hawaiian born, the young Charlie Chan had been one of her most loyal and devoted fans.

He had seen her in at least a score of her filmed epics, from the early, and silent, *Kowloon Nights* to her final appearance as *Mother Goddan* in a technicolor revival of John Colton's *Shanghai Gesture*. Yet, despite his avid interest and his reading of hundreds of publicity stories that purported to tell 'the truth' about her private life, Mei T'ang remained a cipher, an enigma – which, with the passage of time and the growth of sophistication, Charlie Chan had come to accept as an integral part of her carefully contrived public image.

Inscrutable and Oriental . . . of the real Mei T'ang, Chan had long ago reluctantly accepted the sad fact that he knew nothing at all. And now, after so many years, so much bemused speculation, he was to meet her in the flesh.

Chan suppressed a surge of immature curiosity about the mystery. In view of the fact that he was so soon to meet his long-time idol and that she had asked to see *him*, he decided against questioning Dr Svorenssen about her, preferring not to cloud his own first impressions with those of anyone else.

Fortunately, as they turned south from Franklin, a car pulled out from a parking place near the corner – for otherwise the block was jammed all the way to Hollywood Boulevard at the foot of the gentle slope. Behind them as they emerged, rose the steeper slope of the Hollywood Hills. Facing them, directly across Sycamore Drive, was the fabled House of Wu.

Its lower surfaces masked by twin palisades of small cypresses, its upper three stories rose square and plain and somewhat weathered and disappointing to the detective. It was faced with brick of a burnt orange hue, with black shutters and portico. Only the pagoda-like upcurve of the entrance top suggested the Orient in any way.

Nor did its appearance improve upon closer approach. The bricks were stained with years of usage and the black surface of the portico revealed chips and scars that showed the natural light coloured wood beneath the lacquer.

III

While they waited, after Dr Svorenssen pushed the bell for admittance, another couple joined them at the double front door. They were man and woman, both past middle age and waging a losing battle against the encroachments of time. Despite a deep suntan and an obviously dyed black moustache, the man's face, like his protruding belly, had run to flab, as had the lady's countenance beneath over-heavy makeup and a bright henna frame of thinning curls, although her stomach was rigidly corseted to give her body the overall appearance of a short, thick salami.

'Going to Mei T'ang's?' the lady asked. At Dr Svorenssen's assent, she began to spout an involved reminiscence of having first met the actress at Malibu Breach in a mixup of cabanas, a discourse mercifully cut short by the buzz of the admittance signal.

In a city whose interior surfaces are devoted to the promulgation of a merciless maximum of light, the inside of the House of Wu was, to Charlie Chan, pleasantly sombre and shabby. It looked lived in and enjoyed. Nor was any plaster visible save on the ceiling. The walls were covered with deep orange floral paper, the interior woodwork, like that of the exterior, was black.

Halfway down the passage that ran the east-west length of the building, staircase and elevator faced one another. The plump, hennaed lady pushed the lift button in a flurry of jewelled bracelets and wrapped her lynx stole around her with a regality that failed to come off.

When the elevator failed to respond instantly, she muttered something about 'these old buildings.' Her escort smiled apologetically beneath his bravely dyed moustache.

After a few moments, the lady said, 'I'm going to walk it. Come on, Harold, it's good for your figure.'

With an eloquent glance at Charlie Chan and Eric Svorenssen, Harold followed her up the carpeted staircase in silence. The dentist watched their progress until they were well out of sight and murmured, 'It doesn't require a detective to spot a henpecked husband.'

'Not husband,' said Chan.

The dentist blinked his surprise, said. 'How can you be sure?'

'No ring in nose,' said Chan.

'Oh, *brother!*' moaned Dr Svorenssen. 'Charlie, sometimes you're harder to take than the Chinese water torture.'

Following a series of creaks and sighs, the elevator door slowly opened in front of them and they got in. Svorenssen punched the top button and, with another series of dolorous protests, the lift began an unsteady ascent that reminded Chan of the hideous time when, despite eloquent protest, he had been coerced into riding the back of a mule to the bottom of the Grand Canyon and then back up to its top.

There was, to a passenger in this elevator, a somewhat similar sense of being trapped on the brink of imminent disaster.

At the second floor, amid another series of sounds of deep emotional disturbance, it halted jarringly and settled at a slight tilt. The door opened and a man and woman got in – not the two who had defected to the staircase.

The woman who entered wore the rags of a once-handsome face like a gallant scarecrow, made no attempt to hide the scars of time beyond such diversion of viewer interest as was afforded by an elegant rep-silk pants suit of dark blue decorated vividly with poker hands.

She lighted up at sight of Dr Svorenssen, seized both his hands and cried, 'Doc, you old Torquemada – and how are *your* eyeteeth?'

'Happily long gone and unmourned,' replied the dentist, kissing the colourful apparition on one tan leathery cheek.

'Let a fellow in, will you?' said another voice, a voice rich, deep and slightly querulous. It belonged to a tall, languid, superbly elegant man whose features bore the familiar landmarks of long film stardom. It was, Chan recognized, Gilman Roberts, whose success as a player of scores of suave villainous roles on both the small and large screens was matched only by his emergence as a leading American cultural champion; as antique buyer for a major department store chain and a cookbook author.

The creaking elevator protested even more loudly at this addition to its load, but joviality rode the rest of the way to the roof with Chan and Dr Svorenssen. Yet there was something in the caged atmosphere that caused the detective inspector's psychological neck hairs to tingle a minor alarm.

It had entered the ancient lift with the newcomers – an overnote of heartiness in Gilman Roberts' drawling accents, a withdrawal by the ravaged lady in poker hand silk. Before the lift passed the third floor on its way to the top of the House of Wu, Chan was quite certain that these two detested one another.

He thought, *Love turned to hate is deepest of all hatreds . . .*

Briefly, out of long habit, he speculated as to which of them, man or woman, had originally done what to the other and which had paid the heaviest penalty, might still be paying it. Then he dismissed the thoughts as none of his business and therefore unworthy of his time.

As the decades moved past him with increasing rapidity, Chan found himself getting more and more wary of wasting what his mind, if not his body, told him was an ever-decreasing margin of life.

He dismissed that thought as being miserly and even less worthy than the one that had prompted it. As in many other observations on the mystery of living, Chan's three principal mentors – Confucius, Lao T'se and Li Tai Po, were agreed that the hoarding of anything is the most useless of human instincts, since by its very nature it prevents the miser from enjoying what he saves.

Still, there was a current between tall man and ravaged lady, he thought, as they at last left the Toonerville lift . . .

. . . to emerge in a glassed roof garden of an infinite variety of Chinese blooms, shrubs and dwarf trees, set in hydroponic beds of purest quartz pebbles whose liquid nutrients made the atmosphere as richly humid as the flowers made it rich in scent. On the gravelled walks of the conservatory and in a rectangular centre area, groups of men and women conversed, smoked and sipped drinks of various hues.

Opposite the elevator door, which had creaked shut behind them, was a bar of ebony with gleaming silver fittings, being served by a young Asian in a close fitting, bright red, high collared jacket.

What used to be called a Sun Yat Sen jacket, Chan thought ruefully, before it became revived as a Mao – inevitably he was reminded of the old French aphorism to the effect that, the more things change, the more they remain the same. Somewhere in the middle distance, he could hear the shrillness of the fat henna-head's voice reminding her husband that their doctor had warned him never to take more than two cocktails.

Hell hath no fury like a wife unchecked, he thought, deciding the paraphrase had some merit.

A young Chinese-American woman, her face bland and pleasant within its border of closely bound black hair, her slender body graceful within its sheath of black watered silk, approached them and greeted Dr Svorenssen warmly before turning to Chan.

She bowed, said, 'Inspector Chan, I am Ah-Nah, Madame Wu's companion. She wishes to see you before she receives her other guests. I'm so glad you could come.'

She spoke softly, swiftly, both as if she did not wish to be overheard and as if she wished to waste a minimum of time on the rituals of formality. Chan looked down at her, liked what he saw, then turned to his friend.

'Go ahead, Charlie,' said Svorenssen. 'If Mei T'ang wants to see you first, she will. Meanwhile, I'll try to keep the bar from falling over.'

As the former film star's companion preceded him along a path that led to a Chinese blue wall pierced by an ornate closed door of red lacquer and gold, Chan saw that, for all her grace, she moved with the tautness of tension. Thus far, he concluded, Mei T'ang's little party had not proved to be exactly a relaxed and relaxing occasion.

Having opened the ornate door and ushered Chan inside, Ah-Nah left him there. The room he found himself in was long, low-ceilinged and twilight dim. Off-white walls were hung with priceless tapestries and lined, here and there, with almost equally rare low cabinets, brightly carved and painted on an ivory lacquer base.

His hostess sat on a sort of throne chair on a small dais at the far end of the room, her hands planted firmly around the ends of the knobs.

She wore a richly brocaded mandarin robe whose wealth of gold threading seemed to flicker with light even in the half-dark room. As Chan drew slowly close to her, she made no sign of greeting. Shadowed by some angle of the dim indirect lighting, her face was inscrutable.

As he came closer, it seemed to Chan that Mei T'ang was still a very beautiful woman – until he got close enough to see that she was a very dead one.

IV

Chan stood perfectly still, staring at the body of his hostess. His first thought, there in the dim light, was that she must have been dead long enough for rigor mortis to have set in. In the soft warmth of the room's temperature, however, this would require a matter of hours since her demise. But it seemed unlikely that, with a party to prepare for, the former screen star would have placed herself on her lacquered throne so early, or that her absence would not have been noticed and her body discovered long before the guests began arriving.

He took two steps forward and peered more closely at the corpse. From the discoloration of her face, he had no doubt that she had been strangled. Also, this close but quick examination revealed that she had not been dead as long as Chan first thought. Extending a tentative forefinger, he touched the exquisite fabric of the mandarin coat that covered her once famous body from throat to heels.

Although the surface of the silk was sleek and soft, he could feel the stiff sizing beneath. And the embroidery, intricately laced with real gold thread, was firm and heavy. It was the robe, rather than rigor mortis, that was holding her body upright and in place.

First message from the corpse, he thought. Mei T'ang Wu had been quite freshly killed. It occurred to him that she would not be able to enjoy the inevitable notoriety that must follow so sensational a demise – not at least on any earthly plane.

Stepping backward, he regarded the body as a whole, for the first time noted the pair of black gloves that lay in its lap. Whose – the murderer's gloves or those of the victim? Discovery would have to await the arrival of the police.

Chan glanced around the room, saw the small ivory plastic telephone resting on one of the priceless cabinets that lined the lower walls. He crossed to it, paused for a moment to clear his thoughts before picking up the handset. Then he punched Central Police

Headquarters and asked to speak to Captain Pat Jarvis. It took less than two minutes to get Jarvis on the line, two minutes during which the room's silence grew increasingly oppressive.

'Who is it?' barked the captain's voice.

'Charlie Chan at your service.'

'For Christ's *sake!*' said Jarvis. 'I thought you were tending your ladybugs in Hawaii. Are you in town on holiday or working?'

Chan explained precisely where he was and what he was doing. Jarvis said, '*Jesus!*' Then, 'Stand by, I'd better take this one myself. Mei T'ang Wu? My God, I must have seen a dozen of her pictures. Can you play watchdog till I get there?'

'Can watch body but not guests,' said Chan.

'Do just that, Charlie. Stand by.'

Chan hung up. His feelings at this moment were curiously mixed. In his long and illustrious career as a police detective, he had been forced to deal repeatedly with every variety of those human failings that are labelled crimes by the law he served. Save on the rare occasions when it could be justified, he considered murder one of the three most evil types of felony.

The snuffing out of another human life to him was unforgivable unless the slayer was forced to kill in self defence. The other two categories he found most loathsome were kidnapping and blackmail because of the continuing unhappiness they inevitably caused not only their victims but those most closely associated with slayer and slain.

All in all, however, murder was the worst . . .

To Chan, there was nothing romantic about murder. It was dirty and all too often meant interminable toil before a murderer was brought to justice. Not infrequently, Chan had wondered, after dealing with a most atrocious killing, if the very filth whose cleansing was his job had not rubbed off on his own psyche. He who digs in dirt seldom keeps clean fingernails.

Though Chan tried to force himself to feel disgust a faint thrill of excitement tugged at his nerve ends, made taut the muscles of his stomach. Here was a body, dead, strangled, and a killer at large. It was with difficulty that Chan reminded himself he was not a Los Angeles detective but a mere vacationer from Honolulu, that his proper role in this affair must be that of discoverer of the crime and thus only a witness for the prosecution.

The tautness in his nerve ends persisted, causing him to shrug and sigh and, from long habit, to look carefully about the exotic room in which he stood face to face with the corpse of Mei T'ang Wu. From long experience, he knew that, if corpses had messages to give the experienced investigator, so, more often than not, did the immediate environment in which they were found.

Moving softly, silently and with deceptive swiftness, Chan took a look around. He left the gloves on the dead woman's lap alone. It was not his job in any way to touch the body. The reading of whatever further messages it might convey was up to the trained scientists of the coroner's office and the police scientific crime analysts.

He examined the soft, priceless carpet that filled the room almost from wall to wall and on which the late film star's throne rested. As he moved, something bright was reflected in the dim light, something that winked up at him out of the deep pile of the carpet slightly to the left of the throne. He moved toward it, bent down, drawn by another sparkling highlight, picked it up.

It was a golden house fly with diamond eyes and tiny wings of transparent white jade framed in golden wire that retraced each tiny segment of the insect's flight appendages. A magnificent work of the jeweller's art, one that, even there in the carefully arranged artificial twilight, bore the unmistakable stamp of having been manufactured in the land of his ancestors.

He was still peering at it, entranced, when his concentration was shattered by a knock at the door.

Chan moved to answer it but, as he did so, the knock sounded again – from behind him. It had come from the far side of a less conspicuous portal, set in the wall opposite the elaborate entrance through which he had come – a door Chan had taken for that of a closet.

He took it for granted that it was the police that were knocking – and again was wrong. Even his brief vacation, he decided, had made him careless as he was all but engulfed by an invasion of a half-dozen men and women in starched and spotless white uniforms, pushing before them a pair of portable steel tables on wheels, tables laden wth an assortment of covered steel food containers, cutlery, plates and paper napkins.

An immense black man rendered over seven feet tall by an enormous chef's hat said, 'Jason Hollywood Catering – do we set up in here?'

For once, the veteran detective inspector was nonplussed. Taking his silence for assent, the chef said, 'Lay it out, team,' and the room became as busy as the celebrated Walt Disney version of Santa's workshop under the unseeing eyes of the corpse, while the redolence of fine cooking filled the death chamber.

To Chan's relief, at that moment the burly shoulders of Captain Patrick Jerome Jarvis blocked the doorway through which the caterers had just erupted, backed by a pair of uniformed policemen. He, too, looked in speechless dismay at the unwanted activity, then spotted Charlie Chan and came over to him.

'For Chrissakes,' he said, 'who ordered the food?'

'Not unworthy self,' said Chan. 'Comestibles precede coppers by gnat's eyelash.'

Captain Jarvis's sunbronzed countenance contracted in a wince. He said, 'If *that* came from Confucius, I'll eat my Borsalino, feather and all.'

'Difficult to prove origin of wise saying,' said Chan. Then, lapsing into excellent English, he gave Jarvis a rundown on what he knew in two concise paragraphs, concluding with, 'Suggest you move caterers out of room.'

'I'd better send them back where they came from,' Jarvis said, and did so. Not until this was done was any sort of procedural order attained.

Watching, Chan was interested to discover that the door through which they had made their surprise entrance led to a windowless central foyer on which fronted a large freight elevator with quilt-hung walls to prevent furniture damage. He noted that another door, across from the throne room entrance, stood ajar and entered it to discover himself in the late film star's study-laboratory with its curious jars of various Chinese medicinal roots and the dried bodies of what had been lizards, frogs and fish.

His nostrils dilated as he smelled the fading after-aroma of some personal scent. Perfume it was not, the odour was too light for a perfume's heavy base. It could have been that of a lady's cologne or of a man's after-shave lotion – he could not be sure. Nor could he identify the brand, which he might have done had he entered the room a few minutes earlier.

All he was sure of was that he would recognize it if he encountered it again. It had a lilac base, whether real or manufactured he could not be certain, though the odds were heavily in favour of the synthetic article. He only hoped a number of the guests in the conservatory were not wearing it.

Peering into the nearest of the old-fashioned apothecaries' jars, Chan discovered that the twisted orchid root it contained had a pair of spots upon its otherwise intact surface. Closer examination revealed them to be lifesized insects, apparently crafted of jewels and precious minerals and metals.

He opened his left hand, which still contained the handsome, elegant and beautifully crafted artificial housefly he had picked up beside the throne chair of Mei T'ang Wu. He studied it, looked again at the insects on the exotic root in the jar, then carried it to a casement window through which the late afternoon sunlight streamed at a flat angle from over the shoulder of Laurel Canyon.

Until then, Chan's senses had been in a state of general alert. Now they moved into narrower focus and intensified.

One by one, he examined the elements of Chinese pharmaceutics in the jars, moving from one to another, studying each in turn, until the eleventh he examined held his interest. He had already determined that no two of the jewelled insects were alike – just as no two of the objects on which they rested were similar.

What held Chan's attention was a curiously carved ginseng root, gnarled and twisted like a deformed parsnip. On its curved surfaces reposed a pair of flies, one of which, from his relatively distant point of vision, seemed the twin of the jewelled insect he had picked up from the carpet in the other room. He looked from the gem in his hand to that in the jar, frowning.

Strange, Chan thought, *no other two alike . . .*

V

It was a puzzle whose solution would have to wait opportunity for closer examination. At the moment, with no standing, official or otherwise, in the investigation, Chan had no desire to disturb anything in the rooftop apartment where murder had so recently been committed.

He should have turned the insect over to Pat Jarvis. But the two lapses in his thinking – that of taking for granted first that the door in the death room led to a closet rather than to the freight elevator foyer, second that the caterers were the police, had led to this third lapse.

Chan itched to get a closer look at the strange contents of the jars since he had never seen anything like them, had never heard of such strange examples of what appeared to be the ancient craft of Chinese jewel-making lifted to its highest plane – beautiful baubles for a Han emperor or a Mongol prince grown sufficiently effete by residence in China to have developed a taste for *objets d'art* of such refinement and such delicacy.

This strange room, like the reception room where Mei T'ang's body presumably still sat on its throne chair in death, had another door. This one, Chan determined to open before another invasion caught him offguard.

Chan moved cautiously – but not cautiously enough. As he peered through the partly opened portal, a large dark cloth was flung over his head, effectively blanketing both his vision and his breath. A pair of invisible arms pinioned him briefly, then he was flung back into the laboratory-study onto his rump in a most undignified fashion.

When Chan got the cloth, a large lavender bath towel, from his head, he was sitting on the carpet, facing the door through which he had just peered. It was again closed, enigmatic, mocking. The crumpled towel which he had been holding in his hand he dropped beside him.

It did not surprise him to discover that the priceless insect jewel had vanished.

*　　*　　*

Chan took a number of deep breaths before rising to his feet with unexpected grace for a man of stocky figure. He was reminding himself with every ounce of wisdom he and his ancestors had amalgamated that he must not allow anger to cause him to lose further control of self.

For Chan was bone-angry. This last humiliation, coming on top of his previous lapses, had heaped injury on top of insult. Nor did the fact that the injury was limited to his pride make it any the less painful.

And this, too, rankled the usual serenity of his soul.

As his deductive faculties became operative once again, he realized all too clearly that he must have been observed, at least while he was in this strange room. Otherwise, how could he have been ambushed so neatly – and how would his observer have known he held the jewelled insect in his hand?

The questions answered themselves – but they failed to indicate who had observed him, or how.

He opened the door again, this time without untoward incident, and discovered himself to be in a bathroom equipped with lavender face and hand towels, washcloths and toilet tissue. In contrast to the other rooms he had visited in the House of Wu, there was nothing Oriental about either the plumbing or the bathroom decor. Neatly folding the towel that had blinded him, Chan replaced it on the rack alongside the shower-tub.

Then he examined the door to the laboratory he had just left. It opened and closed without sound. This, at any rate, accounted for the fact of his being observed, if not the identity of whoever had spied on him. Only the memory of the faint scent remained . . . unidentifiable in the melange of perfume trails that assailed his nostrils in what was evidently the powder room for the reception.

The other door to the bathroom was abruptly opened, bringing with it a ground swell of conversation from the conservatory. The raddled but still attractive lady in the blue pants suit with the bright poker hands looked at him with sardonically uplifted left eyebrow.

'Really, Mr Chan!' she said. 'It never occurred to me, in all the years I have followed your career, that you did your sleuthing in a ladies' lounge.'

Chan mustered the shattered remnants of his poise to reply, 'Strange house offer strange trails. Excuse, please.'

He slid past her near-famine-thin figure to return to the conservatory, where the guests were milling about in apparent confusion. He noted the two uniformed policemen guarding the main elevator entrance, wondering what steps his friend Captain Jarvis had taken to hold possible witnesses for questioning. It occurred to him that a long evening lay ahead for most of them – long and hungry since the caterers had been so summarily sent back where they came from.

Appetizers were reduced to a few greasy crumbs on the serving platters, but the drinks continued to flow without interruption. Chan suppressed a smile, realizing that Captain Jarvis was evidently proceeding on the old *in vino veritas* assumption. 'In wine is truth.'

He hoped it worked. In his own considerable experience of crime allied with alcohol, Chan had long since reached the conclusion that the combination all too often resulted in *in vino vast confusion*.

Dr Svorenssen spotted him and came over, to thrust a drink in his hand and say, 'Charlie, will you please tell me what in hell is going on?'

Chan sipped his drink carefully, said, 'Charlie Chan like three monkeys – see no evil, hear no evil – above all speak no evil. Besides, Charlie Chan not know.'

'Come *off* it, Charlie,' said Svorenssen. 'Ah-Nah took you to see Mei T'ang. You've been gone almost an hour. And the police have been holding us here for the past forty minutes.'

The elderly couple who had taken the stairs up instead of the elevator approached and the hennaed wife said, 'Why can't we leave? This is a violation of our civil rights. I won't stand for it. Harold, *speak* to somebody!'

Her voice was shrill and cut through the sound in the glass-roofed conservatory like a laser beam. As if in answer to it, a young plainclothes officer moved front and centre before the portable bar and announced that all who wished to depart could do so as soon as they had left their names, addresses and telephone numbers with the officers at the door.

The hennaed henpecker gave a triumphant toss of her head and trumpeted. 'You see, Harold – all it takes is a little gumption!'

'Watch your language, Rosina darling,' drawled the elegant Gilman Roberts, who had just joined the group. 'You're dating yourself. *Gumption!* Really . . .' He looked after the departing couple in wonderment before turning to Chan.

'We really *would* like to know what has happened,' the actor said. 'I suppose somebody stole one of Mei T'ang's precious pretties – although this – ' with a sweeping gesture that indicated the policemen at the portals ' – does seem a classic case of over-reaction, even for a lady as volatile as Mei T'ang.'

Chan regarded the tall, elegant actor impassively. It was evident from his question, however indirectly delivered, that word of the murder of their hostess had not yet been announced to the assembled guests. The Honolulu chief of detectives therefore held his own silence. He felt he had no right to interfere with the procedure established by Pat Jarvis, even though, personally, he would have liked to watch and weigh reactions to its announcement.

At that moment, the shrill voice of the hennaed henpecker again cut through the moist, perfumed air of the conservatory, as she cried, 'If you don't let us out *right now*, I'll see to it that Harold has your badge.'

'Ah, gumption!' sighed Gilman Roberts. 'What violence is committed in thy name.'

Dr Svorenssen, whose attention had been temporarily diverted by the overloud exit of the elderly couple, returned his attention to Chan and repeated his demand to know what was going on. Chan blandly ignored him and said to the tall actor, 'Would like identity of loud lady just leaving.'

'Believe it or not,' replied Roberts, 'the little man she bosses around is a veteran Hollywood producer. The name is Heinemann – Harold Heinemann. That of his louder, though not necessarily better, half is Rosina. Would you believe she was once a star in *Our Gang* comedies?'

Chan said, 'Husband boss people around all day. Wife boss husband around all night – right?'

'That's about it,' said the actor. 'As a matter of fact, Harold has been signed to produce the picture this party is all about.'

Chan looked accusingly at Dr Svorenssen, said, 'You not tell Charlie movie involved.'

'So solly, Cholly,' said Svorenssen. 'Not lemember evelything.'

'Oh, shut up, Eric,' said Roberts. 'Not funny.' Then, to Chan, 'It's one of those hit-or-miss deals everything in pictures seems to be nowadays. We make a feature film. If it goes, we use it to pilot a TV series. If they don't spot the series opposite a show with a high Nielson rating, it runs a few seasons and we all get rich and go to Switzerland and lie around on our numbered bank accounts. If it doesn't go, we pick ourselves up and look for another vehicle.'

'And Mei T'ang will star?' Chan asked.

'She will *co-star* – ' Roberts stressed the word hard ' – with me. You see, in this sort of movie, in a . . .'

Whatever else the actor was about to say was interrupted by the abrupt opening of the lacquered doors to the throne room followed by the emergence of the ravaged lady in the poker-hand pants suit. Closing them abruptly behind her, she paused in silence until she had the attention of all in the conservatory save for a few drunks otherwise occupied in potted palm alcoves.

'Kids,' she said in her husky, penetrating, somewhat gravelled voice, 'you can all go home now. Our hostess has been murdered!'

The room hushed.

VI

Eric Svorenssen pointed the forefinger of his highball holding hand at Chan and said, 'You *knew!* Why didn't you tell us?'

Gil Roberts said, 'Probably, Doc, because he had orders not to.'

Despite the languidness of his stance and the drawl of his voice, the actor spoke with authority. Svorenssen deflated and said, 'Is that so, Charlie?'

Chan sipped his drink and said nothing. Gil Roberts, muttering an excuse, took off after the lady in the pokerhands pant suit, who was heading for the passenger elevator.

Chan said, 'Who's the lady in the pants suit?'

Svorenssen said, 'That's Claudia Haynes. She has an overbite due to an uncorrected faulty occlusion when she was a child.'

Shaking his head, Chan said, 'Doc, I asked who she was, not for her dental chart.'

'Sorry, Charlie, but I'm all shook up. Is Mei T'ang really dead?'

Chan nodded, repeated his question about the woman who had made the announcement, who was slipping into the elevator with Gil Roberts securely latched to her elbow.

Eric Svorenssen, his face drained of colour, said, 'Now she'll never get the eyetooth root-canal work done. Charlie, you wouldn't believe – '

'Who is she, Doc?' Chan committed the rare rudeness of an interruption.

'Oh . . .' Svorenssen snapped out of it, said, 'Claudia? She's an agent, what they call a package dealer. She's the one who put the deal together.' He put down his near-empty glass on a small table, said, 'Charlie, excuse me. I think I'm going to be sick.'

Looking after the dentist until he disappeared in the lavender bathroom at a trot, the Hawaiian detective inspector turned his attention to the reactions of the others in the conservatory. For the moment, it was still a tableau, with most of those present still frozen into immobility by shock at Claudia Haynes's abrupt announcement. A sort of non-conversation piece, he thought, wishing he knew who they all were.

Even as he watched, the tableau broke up. Voices rose on every side, voices expressing disbelief for the most part as the message took its time to sink in. Then the noise level rose higher and the guests, like Caesar's Gaul, divided themselves into three parts.

One group headed for the elevator to give names and addresses to the police guard stationed there. Another headed back to the bar, while a third milled aimlessly about.

Strange scene, strange happening, Chan thought, wondering who, if any among them, might have information that could lead to the identity of the person unknown by whom the crime had been committed. He heard one woman, denied the use of a telephone by the police, say, 'But if I don't get this to Sheila first, I'm off her payroll.'

Sheila, Chan surmised correctly, was almost certainly a screen gossip columnist. He was reminded again of the inevitable notoriety that must follow the dramatic murder of such a famed, exotic public personality as Mei T'ang Wu had been.

It was a crime that demanded a quick solution for many reasons, not the least of them police prestige. He began to map out proper procedure and again was forced to remind himself of his entire lack of any status, official or private, since his possible client was the victim.

A voice at his elbow said, 'Inspector Chan?'

It brought him out of his brief reverie. A tall, reedy young man in a grey suit and blue sports shirt stood beside him, added, 'Sir, Captain Jarvis wants to see you.'

As the detective ushered him through the bright lacquered door, Mei T'ang's companion, Ah-Nah, was ushered out. She said nothing to Chan as they passed, but her luminous dark eyes looked up eloquently into his with what he took to be a silent appeal for help.

The twilight of Mei T'ang's reception room had been banished and the lights were on bright and full. The body had already been removed and, despite the fact there were a half dozen persons present, the long chamber felt strangely empty. Even Pat Jarvis seemed to feel the eerie personality vacuum created by the departure of the former star's corpse. In death, her presence still dominated her surroundings as it had in life.

Jarvis said, 'This one looks like a ring-tailed doozy.' Then, to a pair of technicians busy by the now empty throne chair, 'Don't forget to dust the gloves for latents.' And, back to Chan, 'Anything you've got, Charlie.'

Chan gave it to him from the beginning in Dr Svorenssen's office. When he got to the episode of the lavender bath towel and the theft of the jewelled fly, Jarvis slapped the flat of a hand hard against the priceless antique chest on which he was resting his rump.

'Son of a *bitch!*' he said. 'Right under our *noses!* How do you like *that* for nerve?'

'Not much,' said Chan. He lapsed into his pidgin to add, 'Humble self much embarrassed.'

'*You're* embarrassed!' said the captain of detectives. 'How the hell do you think *I* feel? I don't suppose you have any idea who did it?'

Chan shook his head, told him about the perfume, concluded, 'Not much of a clue, I fear. Sorry.'

'Not your fault, Charlie,' said Jarvis, shaking his head like a mastiff emerging from the Santa Monica surf. Then, 'And those God damned caterers . . . You know, Charlie, if I can find who called them for delivery at that precise moment, I believe we'd have this case wrapped up.'

'Problem with call?'

'You can say *that* again! We don't even know it came from this building. Just a voice, apparently female, demanding immediate service. For a job like this, the Jason service has a stand-by system so they won't clutter up a party they're hired for until they're needed.'

Chan said, 'Would give much to know what Mei T'ang wished to see humble self about.'

'You and me both!' Captain Jarvis paused, scowled at the tapestry on the opposite wall. Then he said, 'Charlie, I don't know how to ask this of you!'

Chan said, 'Best way – ask. Then Charlie tell yes or no.'

'I wish you'd stop the doubletalk,' said the police captain. 'How the hell can *I* ask a favour of *you*? You may be out of your jurisdiction, but you still outrank me, and I want your help.'

'What do you want me to do?'

'Just stay with it. You have an inside track to begin with because

Mei T'ang asked to see you. *You* found the body, *found the jewelled fly*, you called me. Do what comes naturally, learn what you can. Frankly, we're stumped.'

'Case early,' said Chan. 'Time needed for key.' Then, 'I'd like to know more about those jade and gold objects the fly came from.'

'I haven't had time to examine them thoroughly,' said Jarvis, standing upright. 'Let's take a look at them right now.'

They left the scene of the murder, crossed the service elevator foyer to the laboratory. On the way, Chan remarked, 'The black gloves – did they yield anything?'

'Don't expect much from them, Charlie, even after the lab boys have tested them. They're on sale in every department store in Los Angeles – and in at least half the small clothing shops.'

'Men's or women's?' Chan asked.

'Women's – but that doesn't necessarily mean a thing – as you very well know.' They reached the laboratory and Captain Jarvis looked at the weird jewels in the big glass jars. He said, 'Jesus, what in the hell are they?'

Chan gave him his theory. When they reached the ginseng root, he pointed out the two flies, revealed the one whose duplicate he had found by the throne.

Jarvis squinted at it, said, 'It could have fallen from one of the other weirdoes.'

'I think not – no other two are alike.' He pointed at the bizarre object in the jar before them, said, 'I'd like to examine this one more closely, please.'

'Go ahead, Charlie, though I'm damned if I see how it ties in with the murder.'

Chan unscrewed the light metal lid of the jar without difficulty, plunged a hand in and withdrew the jewelled ginseng root. The moment his fingers caressed the sleek surface, he knew that it was not jade he was holding. It felt colder, greasier, totally different in texture. With each second of manual contact, the resemblance to jade grew increasingly superficial.

He turned his attention to the two jewelled flies and here no tactile test was needed. Viewed closely, they were obviously inferior imitations of the brilliantly crafted insect he had picked up from the carpet by the dead film star's throne. Neither the gold nor the diamonds were genuine and the wired-in wing surfaces were mica rather than thin slices of white jade.

Chan explained what he had discovered, concluded, 'Perhaps suggest something to agile police brain.'

'Hell, yes,' said Jarvis. 'Suggest substitution to agile police brain. I wonder how many of them are phoneys.'

'Leave to expert hands,' said Chan, 'but suggest many if not all. Meanwhile, wonder if dead lady have keen eyesight.'

'Okay, Charlie – and thanks. So far, this case has more questions than answers.'

'Ask right questions – get right answers,' said Chan.

'Confucius?'

'No, Socrates,' was the reply.

VII

In the conservatory, Charlie Chan found Svorenssen waiting for him almost alone in the recently filled room. The dentist, looking unhappily sober, was staring with gloom at the pale dregs of the highball in his right hand.

Chan said, 'No need to wait, Doc. We're right near my hotel.'

'I have a message for you,' said Svorenssen. 'Ah-Nah – Mei T'ang's companion – wants to talk to you.'

'So. . . ?' said Chan, remembering clearly the look of appeal she had sent his way when they passed in the doorway.

'She had to go out – something about the funeral arrangements. I took the liberty of telling her where you are staying.'

'That's okay, Doc. I want to talk to her.'

'Also, we're invited to a sort of wake at Claudia's apartment downstairs. I told you I'd ask you, so now I've done it and you can refuse.'

'On the contrary – I accept,' Chan told him.

Recalling his precarious ride up in the elevator, Chan elected to walk the stairs down to the second floor. There were perhaps a baker's dozen of guests in the shank lean agent's apartment, which covered one third of one side of the passage that divided lengthwise the lower floors of the building. While this made Claudia Haynes's residence considerably smaller than that of Mei T'ang, with the conservatory aside, it was still a large old-fashioned apartment.

Claudia had furnished it comfortably with a hodge-podge of antiques and newer pieces that somehow managed to achieve a precarious harmony – light cane-back French Provincial chairs cheek by jowl with dark, heavy carved Spanish tables. A pair of curved elephant tusks, their tips almost reaching the ceiling, rose like parentheses on either side of the wide doorway between living and dining rooms.

Chan spotted a genuine Fernand Leger among the paintings and photographic blowups of film personalities and movie stills that were spotted casually along the walls.

Claudia greeted them at the door, glass in hand, gave Eric Svorenssen an embrace and then said to the detective, 'Well, Charlie Chan, who dun it?'

Chan replied, 'Identity of murderer await police announcement. Till then, no can say.'

He had long since run out of replies to a question so often asked that it bored him – but that he was too polite to ignore. He was ushered into a study to the right of the living room and ensconced on a worn brown leather sofa, where Gil Roberts placed a drink in his fist.

The actor said, 'Claudia's cellar runs entirely to vodka and Fresca, so I took the liberty of bringing yours for you.'

'Many thanks,' said Chan. He sipped the drink, found it palatable, then said to the towering deputy host, 'Tell me, what is a package dealer, Hollywood style, please.'

Roberts dropped gracefully to a hassock close to the sofa, hugged a well tailored knee, said, 'That could be a long order, Mr Chan, but I'll try to be brief. A package dealer, Hollywood style, is usually an agent who puts his – in Claudia's case, her – clients together on a project which is then peddled to a studio or an independent distributor as a whole.'

'In case of the vehicle for Mei T'ang and yourself?'

'Claudia had Mei T'ang and myself as clients – also a half dozen other actors. She owned the screen play, which is the only thing she paid for, had Larry Kettering to direct and tied in Harold Heinemann as producer. She had the Ace-Keystone people ready to supply studio facilities and two major distributors begging for options on the finished product. It was a ripe vehicle.'

'Name of vehicle?' Chan asked.

The actor shrugged. 'Who knows what it would have been called by the time it came out? The working title was *Lady of Jade*.'

'Most fitting,' said the detective. 'Who put up the money to bring back such an old star?'

Claudia Haynes swung into the foreground, taking over from Gil Roberts. She said, 'Mei T'ang was putting up the big nut. Ever since Bette Davis made her comeback in *Baby Jane* and Crawford in *Sweet Charlotte*, she's been bugging me to put her back together again in a suitable vehicle.'

The antagonism between actor and agent etched in acid Gil Roberts' tone as he said, 'That's not entirely true, Clau-Clau, darling – you did at least half the bugging yourself. How long *is* it since you swung a big package deal?'

Venom crackled silently in the air like static electricity. Claudia snapped, 'Look who's talking! How long has it been since you've been even a semi-regular in a TV series?'

Roberts beamed at her happily, jiggled the ice in his glass as he looked down at Claudia from his great height and murmured sweetly, 'It has long been my fond belief that it's up to a competent agent to get client parts.'

For a moment, Chan thought Claudia was going to fling her glass in Gil Roberts' handsome face. She took a deep breath, then said, 'It's up to the client to make good . . .'

It was weak and she knew it, for she turned to Chan and said, 'Sorry, Charlie. We must sound like a flock of jackals squabbling over a dead tiger.' Then, to Roberts, 'By the way, where were *you* when Mei T'ang was strangled?'

Roberts' smile widened. He lifted his glass and said, 'As far as I know, I was with you, sweetie. I told Captain Jarvis as much upstairs. What did *you* tell him?'

'None of your damned business, you overstuffed Westphalian smoked butt,' said Claudia, on which tone the scene ended as its two chief players drifted apart.

Chan cogitated over what he had just seen and heard, sipping his highball sparingly. Had Claudia's final retort been a trifle too vehement? He wondered, thought *mebbeso, mebbeso* and was grateful neither Dr Svorenssen not Pat Jarvis was present to hear him utter the pidgin aloud.

He wondered if Claudia's final lashout had not covered a very real relief at Roberts' admission that he had covered her for the time of the murder by providing her with an alibi. Until then, Chan had only mildly considered the movements of possible suspects at the time of the murder, leaving such research to Captain Jarvis and his interrogators.

Now, he could not help wondering. After all, he had been closer to the crime, both in space and in time, than had any other officer of the law, official or otherwise. Point by point, he went over what had happened that afternoon, from the moment he and Dr Svorenssen approached the orange-brick apartment house the murdered film star had built.

His dentist friend returned with a freshly filled glass and said, 'Charlie, there's a call for you.' He indicated a telephone on a low refectory table across the room, a phone hitherto masked from the detective by a clump of people busily arguing whether a celebrated current male screen star were a non-actor or the genuine article.

Chan said, 'Excuse me, please.' He picked up the handset, said, 'Hello – Chan here.'

'This is Ah-Nah, Madame Wu's companion. Doctor Svorenssen says you are at the Hollywood Roosevelt.'

'That's right,' said Chan. He was about to give the number of his suite when a feminine voice remembered from upstairs cut in on another extension.

'Will you get the hell off this God damn line?' it said angrily. 'I've got to get through to Sheila.'

'One moment, please,' said Chan. Then, to Ah-Nah, 'Are you still there, Miss?'

'Yes.'

'Nine-sixteen,' said Chan.

'Are you going to get off this copulating line or do I call operator and *cut* you off?' said the intruding voice angrily.

'It's already past eleven,' said Ah-Nah, sounding confused. 'I'll meet you in the hotel at midnight.'

'I'll tear out the line if you don't get off,' said the lady who wanted to talk to Sheila.

'What's your room number?' Ah-Nah asked.

'*Nine-sixteen!*' Chan could not be sure whether he got through or not because the intruder chose that moment to kill the call.

He returned to Doctor Svorenssen, said, 'If Ah-Nah calls back after I leave, tell her I'm at the hotel.'

'Right on!' said the dentist, who had recovered his interrupted cocktail-hour glow.

Chan wandered through the apartment, taking in the scene. He spotted three other telephones, one of them in use by a horse-faced female in a splashy flowered print that reminded him of that long-ago era when chintz furniture covers were well in style. Standing behind her, he was debating a suitable reprisal against this one-track lady whose determination had probably ruined his call from Ah-Nah.

But as soon as the thoughts of reprisal rose, Chan dismissed them with some sense of shame as not merely unworthy of his ancestors but unworthy of himself.

Chan lingered another half hour, awaiting a call-back from Ah-Nah, then decided it would be wise to stroll the two blocks to his hotel.

Entering the lobby from the Hollywood Boulevard side, he looked around for the young woman, failed to see her. It occurred to him that he had better go upstairs, in case she had heard him correctly despite their garbled conversation, to see if she were waiting in the corridor outside his room. By his wristwatch, it was exactly six minutes past twelve when he entered the elevator.

Entering his room, Chan called the desk and left a message to have Ah-Nah call him when she arrived and asked for him. Then, feeling suddenly fatigued and let down after the events of the past seven hours, he took off his shoes and socks and jacket and loosened his shirt. Stretching out on the sofa, he turned on a tolerable late-show movie and settled down to wait.

When he awakened, it was past five in the morning and his head felt stuffed with cotton. Fearing lest he might have slumbered through Ah-Nah's call, Chan called the desk and was informed nobody had asked for him. Weighing the unpredictability of young women in general and Ah-Nah in particular, he got out of his clothes, donned unbleached raw silk pyjamas and went to bed.

VIII

Chan was sitting on the edge of the bed, pondering the events of the evening before, when Pat Jarvis called him from the Hollywood Police Station on Wilcox Avenue, just below Sunset.

Following a brief exchange of greetings, the captain said, 'Charlie, I had the department Oriental expert up at Mei T'ang's place early this morning. He rates those weird stone vegetables at less than a grand.'

Chan scratched his chest beneath his pyjamas, glanced at his wristwatch on the bedside table, said, 'Still early, Pat. So it's just junk then.'

'Worth the metal and alabaster, plus some curiosity value as murder relics,' said Jarvis.

Chan said, 'The fly I found by the body was not junk. Again I suggest a substitution. Otherwise, why the attack on me and theft of the jewelled fly?'

'Charlie, I know, I know – but I've got to go along with the estimate.'

'Then how do you account for the real one?'

'I don't,' said Jarvis. 'But we've got a murderer to find – and fast – before this case is blown up out of all proportion.'

'Ah,' said Chan. 'I remember the botch of the early-Twenties murder of William Desmond Taylor. You don't want to repeat that one, right?'

'Damned right,' said Jarvis.

'What can I do to help?'

'Right now, just keep digging. We need all the A-one help we can get. And you're just the man who can help me now!'

Chan said, quickly before Jarvis could hang up. 'The girl called me at Claudia Haynes's last night – the companion. She made an appointment to see me here at the hotel, but didn't keep it. I've been worried.'

'Forget that one, too,' said Captain Jarvis. 'We had her back here till past two o'clock, then drove her home.'

'Much relieved,' said Chan. He hung up.

However, he was far from relieved by Jarvis's call. As he showered, then shaved with the electric razor his oldest grandchild had given him for Christmas, he compared the case in its present condition to a plate full of soft noodles – loose ends in every direction.

There was one such end that he could investigate – the matter of the jewelled animals, insects and vegetables in the apothecaries' jars that the police expert had summarily pronounced to be junk. However, *he* had seen, held and briefly possessed the exquisitely crafted jewelled fly whose near-worthless replica adorned the carved ginseng root.

Chan knew it was not junk.

He ordered a Continental breakfast sent up. The hour was barely past nine – too early to call the party he had in mind. Following the light meal, he arranged with the hotel desk for the rental of a Chevrolet. Only then did he call Hei Wei Chinn, one of the authorities on antique Chinese artifacts he had flown to Los Angeles to see in connection with a viewing of the archaeological exhibition from the People's Republic.

'I await your visit with impatience,' said Hei Wei Chinn. He and Chan had been friends since the bygone time when the Oriental art dealer operated a small shop in Honolulu. 'When can I expect you?'

'Directly – if my visit at this time will not cause you inconvenience.'

'Oh, come on over, Charlie,' said the dealer.'Hell, I'm dying to see you after so many years.'

Hei Wei Chinn, like his modest shop on South Robertson Boulevard, just below Pico, looked well used. His lean frame was flattered by a finely tailored suit of Hongkong silk, his shoes were obviously bench made, his tie an *objet d'art* of vivid and wondrous resplendence.

Taking Chan back to his office, he produced, via a brisk Chinese girl assistant, a rare gunpowder tea in cups so thin as to be almost transparent, and there they chatted of former times and present problems.

When the conversation had been steered to the latter subject, Chan told his old friend about the murder.

'I heard about it on the TV news this morning,' said Hei Wei Chinn. 'A tragedy. I had no idea you were involved, however, Charlie.'

'Yes and no,' said Chan. 'But there is one point, perhaps a trivial one, on which perhaps you can enlighten me out of your great wisdom.'

He went on to describe the murdered star's strange collection and the jewelled insect he had found – and lost. He also gave the report of the police expert, concluding with, 'Chinn, did you ever hear of such a collection of curios in your study of Chinese works of art? For the fly I picked up was definitely a work of art.'

'How did it feel?' Hei Wei Chinn asked.

Chan understood the question perfectly. Without hesitation, he replied, 'It felt old – perhaps centuries old – which the ginseng root I handled did not.'

Both men knew well the value of the sense of touch in estimating the age of such objects, both were sensitive to the invisible patina of antiquity in the texture of all objects. While hardly as unerring in such estimates as his expert friend, more than once the veteran detective inspector had been able to assign an object to its proper century deep in the past.

Chinn looked thoughtful and fell silent for a pause of at least thirty seconds. Then he said, 'It is just possible – maybe . . .'

He picked up the phone and asked the girl to get him a number in Beverly Hills. After long preliminaries, the conversation was conducted in a North China dialect of which the Honolulu-born detective grasped only a few words. When Chinn hung up, he regarded his visitor with the trace of a complacent smile upon his lips.

He said, 'That was the deputy mission chief of the cultural mission from the People's Republic now in Los Angeles.'

'Yes?' said Chan following a three-beat pause.

'I asked him if he had ever heard of such a collection of jewels. He denied it. Then I told him you still had the jewelled fly and that I had examined it and pronounced it a genuine antique masterpiece.'

'Go on,' said Chan after another pause. 'What was his reply?' He looked at the dealer.

'He made me hold while he consulted somebody else. I detected a faint tone of excitement in his voice. When he came back, I asked him if he wished to examine it. He said, "No need. It is imitation." How do you like that?'

'I think Honourable Hei Wei Chinn should be detective instead of humble self,' said Chan.

'In the importing of cultural antiques, the dealer grows used to criminals,' said Chinn. 'Forgers, smugglers, thieves, fences, even murderers – all in a day's work. What do you make of it?'

'Just what you do, my friend,' said Chan.

The deputy mission chief had first denied knowing of a collection like that in Mei T'ang's apothecary jars. Then he had insisted that Chan's phantom fly was a fake. The implications were obvious – someone, almost certainly whoever had stolen the originals and replaced them with cheap facsimiles – had already made or was making a deal with the Communist mission. Their experts must at least have examined the goods and found every insect in place.

Chan said, 'If you learn anything further about the collection, I hope you will let me know. I suspect a close connection between the thief and the murderer of Mei T'ang.'

'Don't worry – I'll dig till it hurts,' promised the dealer. 'Who knows? Perhaps this fabulous collection of priceless articles may pass through my hands.'

'Keep eye on dollar – old age tranquil,' said Chan.

'Oh, cut it out, Charlie,' said his friend. '*I'm* not that old yet. And there's more than a possible buck involved here. My curiosity is aroused.'

'Don't let it sleep until it has led you to the truth,' said Chan.

Shortly afterwards, the visit was concluded and Chan drove the small rental Chevrolet slowly back toward the House of Wu. He remained curious about Ah-Nah, the dead lady's companion, wishing enlightenment as to why she had sought the midnight appointment and why she had not sought him out later in the hotel, when the police were through questioning her.

There was also the matter of discovering the craftsmen who had made the bogus jewels. It was quite possible that the girl, if she were in any way implicated in the robbery, might have some information on the subject. Nor did he rule out the possibility of Ah-Nah being the actual thief herself, though he doubted that the girl, alone, would have the resources to arrange a secret sale to the Chinese People's Republic.

There were a pair of LAPD cars parked outside the apartment house, each with a single uniformed officer idling at the wheel, presumably to watch those who entered and left the building as well as to monitor possible calls from Headquarters. Chan found a space halfway down Sycamore Drive and walked back.

Alone in the downstairs hallway, he paused, recalling in detail what had occurred on his first entry less than twenty-four hours earlier. He had entered with Doc Svorenssen, found the Heinemanns waiting for the rickety elevator to make its precarious way from the top floor. The oddly matched producer and his strident hennaed wife had tired of waiting and taken the stairs – at any rate, Mrs Heinemann had and her husband had tagged dutifully along.

The car arrived, Chan and Svorenssen had ridden upward – to be halted at the second floor by Claudia Haynes and Gil Roberts, who had accompanied them the rest of the precarious way to the murdered woman's rooftop conservatory. Chan remembered vividly the un-mistakable aura of bristling hostility between actor and agent, hostility barely held under wraps due to the presence of the other two in the car.

This time, Chan's solitary ride to the penthouse apartment was uninterrupted by anything save the protests of the senile machinery of the elevator – protests that again made him wish he had taken the stairs. He was met at the top by a uniformed policeman and policewoman, the latter looking trim and remarkably smart in her blues.

Ah-Nah, he learned, had departed at six-fifteen that morning. Yes, she had been alone. Yes, there had been a telephone call. It had come from a public phone booth near Hollywood and Vine. Yes, she had been driven away in a waiting car. No, she had not been followed. There had been only one police car on duty downstairs and there were no orders for either detainment or pursuit of the young woman. So they had let her go.

Chan knew better than to register vocally the frustration that he felt. It was, all too often, the story of his own life – his professional life at any rate. No matter how efficient the bureaucratic organization, there were inevitably unplanned-for contingencies, usually at some key point in the course of an investigation. It was too bad one arose so early.

He desired to examine again the collection of bogus jewelled objects in the dead woman's 'laboratory', was informed that, after dusting for fingerprints, they had already been conveyed to the far better equipped facilities of the department's top Oriental expert.

Had there been any subsequent word on the young woman's whereabouts? There had been none. *Strike out on two fronts*, Chan thought unhappily.

He decided to take the stairs down and not the elevator.

IX

At the second floor, Charlie Chan paused. The door to Claudia Haynes' apartment was ajar and, through it, he could hear voices in angry argument – one masculine, one feminine – the voices of Gil Roberts and the agent. He waited where he was, seeking to make out words, but both parties were talking simultaneously and all he could pick up, apart from obscenities, was the anger underlying the words.

As Chan moved along the worn carpet along the hallway between the staircases, the tall actor stormed out, his habitual languor destroyed by his very evident rage. He swung back towards the door and said, 'Without me, there'll be no package, you doublecrossing whore, and you know it. I'm in whether you like it or not.'

He swung back, saw Chan standing there, said without a trace of embarrassment, 'Maybe you can talk some sense into the washed-up old bag!'

Roberts' long legs devoured the down staircase three steps at a time. Chan had no trouble imagining that he could see steam arising from the actor's invisible footprints on the well worn carpet. He turned back. Claudia Haynes, looking ravaged-chic in cream-collared Cossack blouse and light blue pants, stood in the doorway, squinting at him through the smoke from a cigarette in a long ivory holder.

She said, 'You wish to see me, Inspector? Come right on in. This appears to be visiting day.'

There was no residue of anger in her manner as she led him crisply inside, sat him down in a leather chair opposite her script- and phone-laden desk and offered Chan a drink, which he refused. One of the three phones rang and she picked up the right one unerringly, delivered what sounded like a knowledgeable assessment of some young actress for a specific part.

While she chatted, Chan wondered if Gil Roberts shed his fury as easily as she appeared to. When she hung up, apologized, put her phones on the answer service, he asked her.

'Oh,' she said, 'Gil will sulk for a couple of hours – until something else turns up to occupy the monorail that passes for his mind. As for me, I blow my top at least a dozen times a day – it's expected of me in this business. If I *really* let myself get worked up, I'd have been buried years ago.' A pause, then, '*Now!* What was it you wanted to see me about?'

By this time, the veteran detective inspector had his questions ready. He said, 'I was wondering what effect the murder of your star will have on the package deal that was mentioned last night?'

She turned over her bony free hand atop the desk in another incisive gesture, said, 'Catastrophic – unless I can turn it to our advantage.'

'How do you propose to do that?'

'I'm not proposing to – I'm *doing* it,' she said and he noted a rigid, near-bulldog set to her jawline. 'I had no wish to see Mei T'ang killed – she was my best client and one of my best friends in bygone years, and she was helping finance her proposed comeback. But what's done is done and life must go on. So do income taxes.'

'Alas, true!' Chan punctuated her pause.

'Let's call a spade a spade, shall we, Inspector? There is going to be a tremendous burst of scandal over the killing. Every old lover in Mei T'ang's life – and there were a number of them, I can assure you – will be hauled out of the media morgues, dusted off and dragged into the spotlight. Her old pictures will be pulled out of film storage warehouses and reshown at specialty theatres and on television late shows. Until her murderer is caught, Mei T'ang will once again be big news . . . and when her murderer is brought to trial, she'll be even bigger news.

'Now my job, as I see it, is to put this film together and get it booked and shot before the second wave comes. If we do that, we ride the crest right up onto the Moneysville shoreline. I've been at it, hot and heavy, since six this morning, calling New York, then calling Chicago and so on, working right across the country with the time zones. And it's going to work. If you had come in half an hour earlier, I couldn't have taken time to see you.'

'I understand,' said Chan, wondering at this woman's chilled-steel opportunism, 'and I congratulate you.' Then, 'I see you work alone. You have no secretary?'

'Not in years, except for special rush jobs – and then I hire a Kelly Girl. With all the automatic aides industry has supplied in recent years, I'm saved the bother of breaking in a new girl and losing her to a studio or to some stud with king-sized equipment every six months. If the correspondence is too much for me, I tape it and ship it out to a professional typists' bureau less than six blocks away on Sunset.

'Believe me, it's easier – and cheaper in the long run. And there are no personality rubs.' Claudia discarded her cigarette and placed her folded hands on the desk, added, '*Now!* Anything else?'

'One further question occurs – how are you going to make the film with the star dead?'

'That,' she said with a lip-curl of triumph, 'is my secret. Sorry, but it has nothing to do with the crime or who committed it, Inspector.'

'One more thing – was Mr Gil Roberts one of Mei T'ang's many lovers?'

Claudia opened her hands with a what-else gesture, said, 'Oh, Gil had his turn in the royal sack.' There was a *who-didn't?* tone in her voice.

Chan said, 'I'd like to talk to him. Could you give me his address?'

'Of course.' She scribbled with a bright green ballpoint on a sheet of initialled notepaper, added as she thrust it across the desk at him, 'If you're thinking of seeing him now, I wouldn't. He lives way up in Laurel Canyon and he won't be home till after five. He has a whole slew of appointments.'

'Thank you, Miss Haynes.' He was dismissed, so he rose and left. Returning to the hotel, he found a half dozen messages from Eric Svorenssen, asking him to call the dentist's office the instant he came in.

Chan called the number Claudia had given him, was informed by the answering service Gil Roberts used that he would not be taking calls until late that afternoon. He then called Svorenssen, and was invited to enjoy luncheon at a Chinese restaurant the dentist had found on Pico Boulevard, close to Doheny Drive.

Regretfully, Chan declined, for he knew his friend's unerring instinct for ferreting out superfine restaurants in unlikely neighbourhoods. But he knew, also, that the afternoon would be consumed with the doubtless irresistible food, and there was something he wished to do before five o'clock – namely, to pay a visit to Gil Roberts' hilltop eyrie whether the actor was at home or not.

So he contented himself with eating lunch alone in the hotel grill, where the cooking, while of good quality, was lacking in the subtle and exotic flavours that represented his ancestral homeland to the Honolulu born Sino-American. While he ate, he considered the possibilities of the tall actor being the murderer of his former mistress – always granting the truth of Claudia's statement that he had been one of Mei T'ang's lovers.

Chan knew something of Roberts' career, first as a performer of suave villains in the A-movies of two decades ago, later as a star in the superior classic horror films that had emerged from the declining Hollywood studios during the Sixties. Recently, as the fad waned, Roberts' public appearances had been confined to television guest shots and panel shows, on which he had served as at best a semi-regular.

Just how the murder of Mei T'ang would affect Roberts' career, Chan had no idea. He had not brought up the subject with Claudia, having no desire to indicate to that astute female intellect the direction his thoughts were taking. Nor had she given any indication of considering Roberts as a suspect.

Chan doubted that she would have revealed such suspicions, if they existed – not, at least, if she felt revelation might in any way impair the precious package deal she was so energetically attempting to paste back together. He had long since learned that the female, under certain conditions, is far more ruthless than the male.

Roberts could have killed Mei T'ang. Certainly, he had the strength. Had he had the opportunity? Familiar with the House of Wu as he was, he undoubtedly knew and almost certainly had used, the service elevator. The question of motive remained. If he were the treasure thief, if he had been caught and accused by his former mistress, it would do. Even if he were not the thief, if Mei T'ang had decided to dismiss him from her comeback film, the motive for murder might be sufficient.

In any event, Chan felt a desire to talk to the actor on his home ground, at least to look over the ground for himself. His lunch completed and signed for, the detective recovered his Chevvy from the parking garage in the hotel basement and set out for the address Claudia had given him.

To Chan, unaccustomed to the lane-narrow vagaries of driving through the corkscrew maze of the Hollywood Hills, the trip was reminiscent of both the elevator in the House of Wu and his too-well-remembered ride down and up the Grand Canyon gorge on muleback. He lost his way twice as the rented car slowly scaled the heights, and when he finally found the proper street, he was little better off.

It was barely wide enough for a single car, rose at an alarmingly steep angle to curve out of view from below around a gorse-grown shoulder cut out to resemble the abutment of a miniature gorge. Had it not been for the mailbox at the foot of the driveway, bearing the name *Roberts*, Chan might not have found it at all.

Nor, when he reached the turnaround at driveway's end was he much better off. The canted roof of a house was barely visible over the brow of the hilltop, beyond which the San Gabriel Mountains, on the far side of the San Fernando Valley, were wreathed in smog of a mustard-gas yellow. To his left, with doors yawning emptily, was a frame two-car garage, filled with the sort of automotive debris that inevitably accumulates in such accommodations.

Chan got out, discovered a steep path that led over the apparent edge of the world between garage and house roof. Negotiating it gingerly, he found himself standing on a small entry in front of a chalet-type residence. The front door was locked and his ringing of the doorbell went unanswered.

Thanks to the building's cantilevered construction, sticking right out of the hillside's north face, there was not even opportunity to walk around it and see what he could see. Nor was there any apparent means of entry, barring the crashing of the door, which was iron-braced and seemed of solid construction.

So it was back up the steep path to reclaim his car and drive back down the twisting hillside road. He paused to look at the open garage, which held nothing more interesting than an old life saver bearing the legend *Lucille II* and a pair of surfboards marked *His* and *Hers*.

Feeling somewhat foolish at having thus wasted his time and missed an excellent lunch with his dentist friend, Chan rolled the rented car down the hill. So sharp was the turn that he did not see the other car blocking his path just around the bend until he was barely able to brake in time to avoid a collision. Thus preoccupied, he was unable to avoid, or even to see in time, the assailant who moved swiftly upon him from the side, grabbed him by the throat with a cruelly knowledgeable stranglehold and pulled him out of the car.

Chan's head struck the top of the front window with a blazing bump, causing him to black out.

X

When Chan recovered his senses, he was lying comfortably on a daybed covered with a bright Navajo blanket next to a picture window that offered, beyond a narrow porch, a breath-taking panorama of the smog-wreathed San Fernando Valley. His head throbbed from the bump on his forehead and his throat felt as it had not felt since the memorable occasion in his youth when he had worn a stiff old-fashioned evening collar three sizes too small to a formal police banquet in Honolulu.

Turning his head painfully away from the window, he saw the elegant form of Gil Roberts regarding him from a near-by lounge chair. The actor was wearing slacks and a pale blue turtleneck pullover and a sardonic expression. A cigarette smouldered in his long fingered left hand.

Seeing that Chan's eyes were open, the actor said, 'We were expecting visitors, but we had no idea it would be you, Inspector. Are you all right?'

'Apart from an abominable headache and a sore neck, I believe I'll survive.'

'Annie!' called Roberts. 'Will you bring our visitor two aspirins and the good brandy.'

The girl appeared, looking clean scrubbed and very much like a Los Angeles high school undergraduate of Chinese ancestry – pretty, healthy, young. As Roberts poured a generous portion of fine, virtually unobtainable old London Dock brandy into a broad beamed old fashioned glass, he said, 'Best cure for a sore throat in the world.'

Chan accepted the medication gratefully, chasing the aspirins with the liquid velvet of the strong liquor. Only then did he ask one of the questions that had been troubling him since regaining consciousness.

He said, 'Thankful for rescue. You see attacker?'

'There were two of them,' said the actor. 'I was on the garage roof. Unfortunately Annie had orders not to answer the door or it wouldn't have happened. When I yelled at them and jumped from the roof, the man holding you dropped you and ran to his car. The other was driving and backed away fast.'

Chan said, 'Did you recognize either of them?'

'The only one I saw was your attacker. I didn't see his face. The other stayed in the car.'

'The driver could have been a woman?'

Roberts shrugged, sipped the brandy he had poured for himself, said, 'It could have been. Even from my observation post, the view around the driveway curve was blocked beyond a certain point. You can check it out for yourself.'

'No need,' said Chan, who had mentally photographed the immediate exterior of the Roberts eyrie. 'You were expecting visitors?'

'A number of people were looking for Annie,' said the actor. 'I wanted her here where I knew she'd be relatively safe.'

'Safe from whom, and what?' said Chan, regarding the girl thoughtfully.

'From whoever killed her mother yesterday,' said Roberts quietly.

Chan nodded. His head still hurt but his mind and his senses were functioning. Although there were great surface differences between this scrubbed looking Sino-American schoolgirl type and the exotic companion of the slain film star, he had almost instantly recognized that the same girl was playing both roles.

He said, 'I wondered about the Ah-Nah, since it means virtually no name at all in Chinese.' Then, to the girl directly, 'You wished to see me last night. I have worried about you.'

She said, 'The police asked so many questions. It got so late I feared I would wake you, Inspector.'

'Why did you wish to see me?'

'I was confused. I felt I needed wise advice.'

'I feel complimented,' said Chan with a nod that briefly brought back his headache. *Must not nod*, he thought, *till head is better*. Then, 'You are confused no longer?' he asked her.

'I feel much more sure about things,' the girl said simply, looking at the actor with a glow of soft adoration.

Chan said, 'Sometimes a young woman needs a father even more than she needs a mother.'

Roberts opened his hands, said, 'So you guessed. Oh, well, I was going to tell you anyway since you're here.'

Chan said, 'Certain unmistakable bone structure similarities. Also, an ambiance of affection, not of lust.' Then, again to the girl, 'How long have you known?'

'Only since I called her early this morning and told her some long concealed truths,' said the actor. 'Annie's position was – well, peculiar. At the time her mother and I were lovers, we were both big stars – and in those days the Breen office rode hard herd on Hollywood where scandal was concerned. Remember what happened to Ingrid Bergman?'

Chan nodded. Then he said, 'You are Mei T'ang's heir – heiress?'

'Her only one,' said Roberts, 'apart from a few small bequests.'

'How long were you with her as companion?' Chan inquired.

'Only the last four years. Mother kept me in boarding schools and camp until I was eighteen.'

Chan said, 'Why are you in danger – rather, what reason do you have to believe you are in danger?'

The girl said, 'The same reason mother was in danger, and *she* was killed.'

Chan said. 'The stolen treasure in the apothecary jars?'

The girl nodded. 'It was very, very valuable. My mother was offered the chance to collect them only because she had a friend very high in the Nationalist government who was forced to flee to America in 1949. They were part of a very old, entirely unique Imperial palace treasure. Her friend needed money, mother needed a tangible investment.'

Roberts said, 'Poor Annie thought I was the thief. She also suspected me of murdering her mother.'

The girl said, 'The last thing she did was show me a jewelled fly she had found in the lab. Then we checked on the collection and found the originals were all stolen. Then she told me it was time she confronted the thief. She sent me to take care of the guests and to send you in to see her when you arrived.'

Chan nodded, said, 'Why did you suspect your father?'

The girl said, 'I didn't know he was my father then. I knew he and mother were not friendly and that he had access to the treasure and knew what it was. I knew his career was not going well.'

'How did you convince her you were not the thief?' said Chan to the actor.

'The thefts must have been going on for some time,' said Roberts, refilling his tumbler with brandy. 'My bank account had been dwindling steadily save for occasional deposits when I was paid for a TV job or picked up a residual check for reruns of old movies. There would have been some indication of unexplained periods of prosperity had I been the thief. I'm simply not a man who can hide the fact he has money. I enjoy spending it too much.'

'That is true,' said Annie. 'Remember, I have known him a long time now. And I heard mother talk about him.'

Chan hid a smile at the girl's proud naiveté. Yet he believed Gil Roberts. This man was not one to conduct a prolonged felony. To the girl, he said, 'Why did it take your mother so long to discover the thefts?'

The girl said, 'She seldom examined them. Her eyesight was very bad. She refused to get glasses until very recently.'

'Ah . . .' said the detective. 'And how did your father convince you he was not the murderer?'

'He reminded me that he saw me on the ground floor when the murder must have been committed. Just after mother dismissed me, I had to help one of the guests get parked outside.'

'I was on my way in to pick up Claudia,' said the actor. 'We said hello in passing. It will hold.'

'Perhaps,' said Chan. 'I hope so.' His head was clearing under the double impact of the brandy and the aspirins. It would hurt for a day or so – but he had endured worse. As for his throat, the discomfort was entirely external, thanks to his fortuitous rescue. Chan did not feel proud of himself at that moment. Twice he had been surprised by an unexpected assailant. Twice he had been easily taken.

The first time, he had lost the jewelled fly. The second time, he had lost consciousness, might well have lost his life. He pondered the purpose of his unseen assailant. He questioned Roberts further about the man he had seen, but the actor could not or would not give further details.

He said, 'In the first place, Inspector, I was too busy trying to save your life to pay attention to details. In the second place, the view to the south is all screwed up.'

Chan let it go. He said, to both of them, 'Did anyone else see you greet one another at the time of the murder, when you met downstairs?'

They looked at one another thoughtfully. After a moment, the girl said, 'There were Mr and Mrs Hillburn, I think. Remember?'

'Lloyd and Jeannie!' said the actor, looking relieved. 'Of course – they said hello as they went in.'

'There were others around,' the girl added. 'But I don't remember them for sure. Do you, Gil?' she asked, looking at her father.

Roberts shrugged wearily, said, 'It was a large party.'

Chan filed the names in his memory. Pat Jarvis could check it out more easily than he could. Personally, Chan felt quite certain the alibi would stand up. The question remained – whether it was a true one or had been arranged after the event. That, Jarvis could check out, too. There was another question he considered asking his benefactors, but he decided to hold it until the father-daughter story was found to hold water – or not.

Instead, he asked the girl about the jewelled fly. How, he said, had it happened to fall off?

Annie said promptly, 'I have considered that. I believe the diameter of the neck of the jar and the shape of the jade ginseng root, plus perhaps the thief's hurry, caused it to be knocked loose.'

Smart girl, Chan thought. He said, 'How firmly was it fastened to the root?'

'Like all the insects on the genuine jewels, it was not glued or nailed. There were tiny prongs on the tips of the legs that fitted into matching holes and slots in the jade.' She paused, looking at Roberts.

Chan nodded. This was entirely in keeping with the period and craftsmanship of the creation of the unique treasure. The superb artisans who did the actual carving would have scorned rivets or staples as unlike nature.

To Roberts, he said, 'Miss Haynes – you are old friends?'

The actor nodded, made a wry grimace, said, 'Old – *si*. Friends – not exactly. Claudia was my agent when I got started in Hollywood, as she is now. She was Mei T'ang's agent, too. That's how we met.'

Roberts paused, sighed, added, 'Claudia and I were an item until I fell in love with your mother, Annie. I probably would have married Claudia if she'd let me. But Claudia was all business and felt it might hurt my career – and her comission cut of same.'

'And after you fell in love with Mei T'ang?' Chan asked.

'The relationship was not so good. In fact, it might be said to have curdled. Claudia is a very possessive woman.'

'Yet she remained your agent?'

'Not by choice, said the actor. 'She had me lashed to an iron-bound contract. As I just said, she's a very possessive woman.'

'Perhaps you can clarify one thing that puzzles me,' said Chan.

'If I can,' the actor replied.

'Just how is Miss Haynes proposing to put her package deal together now that her Bette Davis-Joan Crawford is gone?'

From the look the girl and the actor exchanged, Chan sensed that he had touched a vital spot. There was a long, uncomfortable silence before Roberts replied.

Then he said, 'Claudia wants to exploit the publicity over the murder to put Annie in her mother's role.'

Chan blinked. Again he was surprised, not this time by a criminal action but by the utter cold-bloodedness of the agent's proposal. He said, 'Isn't Annie a little young?'

The actor said, 'That's the core of the idea – to have Annie playing her own mother playing a part old enough to be her grandmother. Claudia considers it a masterstroke. Remember, she thinks almost entirely in terms of exploitation.'

'You think it might work?'

'It *could*,' said Roberts. 'But it would hardly be a sound basis for launching Annie on a screen career. Such stunts seldom are.'

Chan turned to the girl. 'How do you feel about it?'

She hesitated, said, 'I don't really know. Everything is happening so fast.'

'Can she act?' Chan asked the actor.

Roberts said, 'Well enough. She's had training and has enough inherited talent. Given good direction . . .'

He let it hang. Nor did he, the detective noticed, cite which parent she might have inherited her talent from. Chan suppressed a smile at such tacit if typical actor-egotism, said, 'How about the director, and the others involved? How do they feel?'

Roberts said, 'It's too soon to tell. Kettering, the director, will probably go along, if I know him – and I do.'

'And the producer – Mr Heinemann?'

'So far, an unknown quantity,' Roberts told him. 'But he's an unemployed producer, so he'll probably fall in line by the time Claudia puts pressure on him.'

'How about *you*?' Chan asked Roberts.

'How do I feel about acting with my daughter?' Roberts replied.

'How would any actor feel? I'm delighted.'

'Then the relationship would be acknowledged?'

'Certainly. One thing about Claudia – she keeps abreast of the times. The poor thing has to, otherwise she's practically breastless. Oops – sorry! That was in bad taste. But she feels that things sexual in Hollywood have come a long way since poor Ingrid's time of troubles. Therefore . . .'

Roberts might have run on forever, had not Chan politely asked permission to use the phone. He called Jarvis, told him where he was and of the attack on his person. Jarvis swore mightily and promised to arrange a police guard of the driveway. Otherwise, he had little to reveal of the progress of the case save that the routine investigation was progressing.

Chan had heard this too often not to know its hidden meaning – that nothing was progressing satisfactorily. He hung up, called the hotel, was informed Hei Wei Chinn had left three messages requesting the detective inspector to call him back.

XI

Charlie Chan decided to make that one from the hotel and took his leave with appropriate expressions of thanks. As he worked his way down the twisting hill roads, this time without interference, it occurred to him that his most recent experience had been most curious on several counts, including the lack of description of his attacker and the spate of apparently honest information that threatened to leave him in greater confusion than ever. Damn it, he thought, he liked both father and daughter. If, indeed, they *were* father and daughter. But he felt quite certain important elements of the truth had been skilfully evaded or disguised.

In short, he didn't wholly believe either of them – nor had he the means of sifting truth from falsehood until he could move from a firmer foundation of fact.

Hei Wei Chinn picked him up at the hotel at seven in his cream coloured Continental. Through a smog free twilight, he headed west toward Santa Monica. The evening was pleasantly warm, as Southern California evenings are supposed to be and so seldom are, and the parking lot of the restaurant was washed by a cool breeze from the ocean.

The restaurant was ornate, a concrete and tile pagoda, and the food was more ornate still. The meal the antique dealer had ordered in advance consisted of a mere nine courses and came close to Chan's flavour-memories of true Mandarin cuisine.

The two chief dishes among a welter of delicate lesser platters were a whole haddock baked to flaky firmness and drenched in a sauce of soy base enriched with diced fruits, both fresh and candied, in zestful combination. And a pair of small Pekin ducks, one cooked in rich sauces with a stuffing of fresh green pine needles, the other roasted slowly with only a small cup of rare brandy inside so that the fumes of the liquor would permeate the bird from its core outward.

Not until the last of the preserved fruits that concluded the magnificent repast was consumed did Chan's host refer to the purpose of their trip – beyond that of the dinner they had just concluded. Leaning back against his side of the booth, he looked at his Bulova wristwatch and said, 'We have an appointment with Hiu Sai at ten.'

'Business – or pleasure?' said the detective inspector.

'My pleasure – your business,' said Hei Wei Chinn. 'Hiu Sai is a very special custom craftsman. I believe he can be of help to us in the matter of the imitations. When I reminded him of certain highly suspect *objets d'art* that have been sold as originals in the last few years, he consented to see us.'

Chan said, 'My friend, if you are taking me to the man who made the substitute treasures of Mei T'ang, it is eighteen minutes to ten right now.'

'Hiu Sai lives close at hand,' said Hei Wei, signalling for the check.

As they got back into the car, he said, 'You shouldn't have hurried us. Good food lies more easily on a restful stomach. Besides, I hate to be early.'

'Sometimes wise man ape early bird to good advantage – get worm,' said Chan, his face perfectly straight.

'Shut *up*, Charlie,' said Hei Wei, putting the cream coloured car into drive.

Hiu Sai's modest abode on a shadowy street close to the borderline between Santa Monica and Venice was dark, lit only by an isolated street lamp of low wattage halfway down the block, which shed only enough light to identify the name and number on the battered aluminium mailbox in front.

'That's funny,' said Hei Wei as he pulled smoothly to a stop. 'He promised to be here.'

Chan got out of the car in silence. His eyes followed the twin tracks of concrete that led to the garage door at the left of the two storey frame house. The door had been raised and the garage yawned an empty rectangle of darkness.

'I don't like this, Charlie,' said Hei Wei, standing at his elbow.

Chan studied the front of the house. It certainly seemed empty. He lifted his eyes towards the second storey, seeking an open window. All were closed and though the night was warm, there was smoke issuing from a stout brick chimney at the right end of the roof.

He sighed, said, 'I have the feeling I'm about to risk a judicial investigation for the violation of Hiu Sai's rights of property.'

Motioning Hei Wei to remain where he was, Charlie Chan climbed the three steps to the small front porch carefully, stepping atop the riser to avoid creaks. Gently, he tried the door, found it locked. He peered in the two front windows but, though the blinds were not drawn, could see nothing since the interior lights were out.

Leaving the porch, Chan walked around the house to the back door, which opened readily when he turned the knob. He stepped inside, closed his eyes and counted slowly to twenty, to permit them to adjust to the greater darkness. When he opened them, he could discern dimly that he stood in a kitchen. The smell of something burning was noticeable, but the heat was not in the stove, which was unlit.

The lights went on suddenly. Hei Wei had entered behind him, found the switch, turned it on. Ignoring his friend, Chan continued to sniff silently. There was an acid odour to the unseen fire that suggested to him only one thing – film recently incinerated.

He said, 'Where is the other stove?'

Hei Wei looked at his friend in perplexity, then said, '*Oh!* There's an annealling oven in the workshop in the basement.'

It proved, for Chan, an interesting room. He was intrigued not merely by the fact that it was an entirely modern electronic workshop in the anachronistic old frame house – but by the several natures of the articles its owner was in the process of reproducing.

Here were a leather seated wooden chair of mediaeval times, a wide variety of urns in various stages and hues of lustre, old armour (or new armour made old), terra cotta likenesses of Etruscan warrior heads with their wild looking headgear and eyes even longer and wider and more staring than those of the early Egyptian Dynasties.

More immediately interesting to Chan was an apparent object on which the vanished simulator appeared to be currently at work. Held in a vice on a workbench was a block of what looked like amber in which a pair of mating dragon-flies were eternally caught in the act. Atop the bench was a metallic lamp containing a milk white tube that filled its rectangular face.

Hei Wei said from beside him, 'So *that's* how he does it! Sometimes

Hiu Sai's workmanship is crude but his measurements are always correct.'

'What is it, Chinn?' the detective asked.

Hei Wei did not answer in words. Instead, he pushed a metal button below the white tube, which instantly came to life as a three-dimensional colour reproduction of what purported to be the original of the amorous insects. He stepped back, continuing to look at it admiringly.

'Son of a bitch!' he said. 'Look at that! He can make facsimiles without having the object itself for study.'

In a corner, they found a filing cabinet partially filled with labelled containers that held other tri-di film capsules. One conspicuous gap in the file was, to Chan, like a cavity in an otherwise perfect set of teeth. He hardly needed information as to what was or had been burned in the annealling oven at the far end of the room to make an educated guess. It was obviously film.

Chan said, 'Did you frighten Hiu Sai, Chinn?'

The dealer shrugged, said, 'I got the impression over the phone that I annoyed rather than frightened him. He's very secretive about his work, you see.'

'I see,' said Chan, 'and I can see why.' He indicated the oven, added, 'Is there any chance of saving anything burning in there?'

Chinn snorted. 'At two thousand degrees, Fahrenheit? You must be joking.'

A small sound from the doorway brought both men up short.

XII

'What the hell do you think you're doing here?' said a soft Southern voice. 'You're under arrest.'

A pair of uniformed policemen stood there, Smith & Wesson Magnums very much at the ready. Chan raised his hands with a sigh, saw Hei Wei do likewise.

To the arresting officers, Chan said, 'If you will have somebody call Captain Jarvis of the Hollywood Station and tell him you have arrested Charlie Chan . . .'

He got no further. The patrolman who had checked their search snorted his disbelief, said, 'And I'm Dick Tracy. You'd better come with us.'

It took time. Jarvis had retired for the night and not until close to twelve did anyone identify Chan to the satisfaction of the Santa Monica precinct. A neighbour of the missing Hiu Sai had seen the break-in and phoned an alarm.

'Next time,' said the lieutenant on night duty, 'let us know in advance. We'll be glad to cooperate, Inspector.'

'In Kingdom of Heaven,' said Chan, 'cooperation not competition, law of land.'

Back in the antique dealer's big car, Hei Wei said, 'Why the fortune cookie motto, Charlie?'

'People expect it of me,' said Chan. 'Cannot leave laughing , leave smiling.' He gave Hei Wei a broad smile.

'Pardon me while I retch,' said Hei Wei, turning east on Broadway. 'Where to now, Charlie?'

'Home – to hotel. And thanks for a fine dinner and a most instructive evening.'

'You call that instructive?' said Hei Wei. 'All but getting arrested? What good did it do?'

'It showed us the efficiency of the Santa Monica Police,' said Chan. 'It also showed us that someone called Hiu Sai to warn him of our impending arrival.'

'Now who would do a thing like that?' said Hei Wei. 'You give me the creeps.'

'Possibly a man named Hei Wei Chinn,' said Chan.

'*Me* – who was tapping my phone?'

'Remember, you called and made the appointment,' said Chan. 'It is just possible Hiu Sai decided to call his employer on the Mei T'ang treasure substitution and ask for advice.'

'*Son of a bitch*!' said Hei Wei, pounding the wheel with the base of a hand. Then, contrite moments later, 'Who did Hiu Sai call?'

'That,' said Chan, 'is the sixty-five thousand dollar question.'

'Don't you mean sixty-four thousand dollar question?' Hei Wei asked.

'Because of its importance, I decided to up the ante,' said Charlie Chan.

'I buy you the best Chinese dinner in Los Angeles,' lamented Hei Wei, 'and you turn me into a straight man!'

'Cholly so solly,' said Chan.

Both men began to laugh . . .

But Chan was not laughing when he reached the Hollywood Roosevelt. His face was as serious as his thoughts when he stepped to a lobby phone and gave the operator Claudia Haynes' number. During the seemingly wasted time of their arrest, his mind had been in overdrive. He had been reweighing the crucial minutes during the Mei T'ang party when the murder must have been committed.

He was quite certain that he and Svorenssen had arrived after the crime – but not by much. He once again used his disciplined near-total recall to run over everything he had seen, heard and smelled before and during that critical period.

Claudia's contralto growl came through, said, 'Who is it?'

'Inspector Chan,' he replied. 'Sorry to wake you.'

'You didn't,' said the agent. 'Who in hell can sleep with Mei T'ang's murderer still loose?'

Wearing a pink quilted house coat, she received Chan. A loaded highball was in one hand, a loaded cigarette holder in the other. She offered him a drink, which he refused, led him to the living room and turned down the sound on the colour television, which was running a James Bond type spy spoof.

Flinging her undernourished limbs on the leather sofa, she said, 'At your service.'

Claudia Haynes, Chan judged, was not drunk but had reached an uninhibited plateau of semi-intoxication. He said, 'You remember yesterday afternoon when you and Gil Roberts got in our elevator?'

'I'm not bloody likely to forget!' she replied. A visible shudder shook her thin shoulders.

'How long were you with Roberts before you got into the elevator, Miss Haynes?'

'Not long,' she said. 'In recent years, I see as little of Gil as possible, apart from professional considerations.' Then, with a shrug, 'A buck's a buck as you well know, and while Gil's value as a property is not what it was, ten per cent of his earnings is more than I can afford to give up.'

Ignoring the extraneous matter, Chan said, 'Do you remember which direction he came from?'

'Not bloody likely! He rang my doorbell just as I was about to leave and go upstairs to Mei T'ang's party.'

'And you had been at home until then?'

The agent revealed her exasperation, said, 'While I am fully aware of the importance of repeated questioning in an investigation of this nature, I was not aware that there was no legal proviso against boring the interrogatee to death.

'I've been through it with you, I've been through it with the police. Yes, I was at home. No, I have no witnesses to prove it, unless a check of my phone calls will serve that purpose. All I can tell you is what I already have.'

'Thank you, Miss Haynes.'

'Make that *Ms*, Inspector. I'm tired of sounding like the Virgin Queen.'

'As you wish,' replied Chan, thinking that here, indeed, was a fine specimen of a Woman's Lib leader born, perhaps, a decade or two too early. At the moment, Claudia was showing her age via the bags under her eyes and the heavy lines etched around her mouth.

'One thing more,' he said, 'if you can.'

'*If* I can,' she replied.

'I would like the address and phone number of the Heinemanns. I have yet to bore them with my questions.'

'Touché,' said the agent, rising from the couch with just a hint of a list to starboard.

While she went to her office to write down the information, Chan took the liberty of calling Gil Roberts, and was rewarded with the irritating buzz of a busy signal.

He hung up as Claudia returned bearing a piece of notepaper as well as a newly refilled highball. He said, 'May I continue to use the phone, Ms Haynes? Local calls only.'

'You may call Timbuctu if you wish,' she replied, handing him the paper with the Heinemann information. 'My phone bills, as an agent, are astronomical anyway.'

Chan dialled the Hollywood Detective Bureau, identified himself, inquired if there was still a patrolman on watch at the hilltop residence of Gil Roberts. Frowning, he hung up, dialled operator and asked for a cut-in on the busy Roberts line – to be informed that it was off the hook.

For a long moment, Chan stood lost in thought while Claudia regarded him curiously. Then he dialled the number of the producer and his wife that Claudia had just given him. Rosina Heinemann's ear-piercing shrill uttered a loud *Hello* in his left ear.

'Inspector Chan,' he told her. 'I apologize for such a late call but it is most important.'

'It's okay,' she said. 'Harold and I haven't been able to sleep since Mei T'ang was killed. What's on your mind, Inspector?'

He glanced at Claudia, saw that she was watching him and listening, narrow eyed. He said, 'I'd like to pay you a visit, please.'

'When?'

'Right now, if I may. Believe me, Mrs Heinemann, but it is most important.'

'Well, I don't know,' said the producer's wife. 'It's awfully late.'

'Please forgive my insistence,' said Chan. 'It's urgent.'

She gave in, saying, 'Well since Harold and I are still awake, I guess it's okay. But you'd better hurry. We just took a pill.'

'I'll be there directly, and thanks,' he said. 'Just stay awake till I get there.'

He hung up, turned to Claudia, said, 'How do I get there?'

She said, 'From here, the best route is to take Cahuenga to Berry Drive. There's a short cut through the Outpost, but you'll never find it unless you've been there before.' She rose again, said, 'I'll get you a map.'

She brought a road map back with her, spreading it out on the coffee table. Using a ballpoint, she traced the intricate convolutions of the hill-roads that would take him to the desired address. Chan studied it, memorized its curves, then paused to look at a spot on the chart just south and west of the indicated address.

He said, 'I believe I'm confused. Is this where I must go?'

Claudia crowded close to him to look. Her scent a heavy jasmine, was unfamiliar to his nostrils. She redirected the pen to its previous spot, said, 'That's not where the Heinemanns live. That's Gil Roberts' house. It may look close but it's about a quarter mile straight up from Harold and Rosy's'

'Sorry,' Chan said, masking the excitement that rose within him. 'I'd better get going.'

'You'll never find it if you can't read the map better than that, Inspector,' said Claudia, moving toward the door. 'I'll drive you there. I'll be ready in about ten minutes.'

She was back in less than five, wearing slacks and a grey sweater with an incongruous pastel mink stole slung over her shoulders. Chan, who had moved away from the telephone, regarded her with respect. He needed only one more piece in the puzzle to lock it up, and that piece could wait until morning.

Claudia said, pulling keys from the gold-mounted clutch-bag she was carrying, 'Let's put the show on the road, Inspector.'

XIII

Claudia Haynes took off from the underground garage beneath the House of Wu like a skyrocket, spinning her tiny yellow Porsche around curves and up grades with a speed that would have had Chan's insides up in his throat had he not quickly sensed that the agent was one of those rare drivers of either sex whose reflexes match her impulse for speed.

As they shot up the Outpost's corkscrews toward Mulholland Drive, Chan wondered if she was testing his nerve as a strong willed woman seeking any means of asserting her superiority – or was she pushed by some less obvious, less inner-directed motivation?

It was in part to discover this and other facets of Claudia Haynes that had prompted Chan so readily to accept her offer to be his chauffeur – plus the good and sufficient reason that she would probably get him to his destination much more rapidly than he could hope to do himself.

Chan also wondered if he would have arrived at the solution to the mystery of the strangling of Mei T'ang any more quickly if he had got around to talking to the Heinemanns earlier. Probably not, he decided . . . and there was still going to be a great deal to seek out and sort out once the strangler was safely under lock and key.

Merely thinking of those vicelike fingers made his own throat ache where they had gripped it that afernoon. His brush with death had been closer than he liked to think about. Had the killer not been interrupted . . .

'Hold onto your hat, Charlie,' said Claudia as she half-skidded the sports car over what looked like the rim of eternity. 'Here we go again.'

They followed a staggering series of s-curves at what seemed to Chan like a ninety degree drop, so steep that with each swerve of the front wheels he feared the rear of the Porsche would leave the rough pavement to somersault them arse over teakettle down the hill. Then, taking an abrupt left turn, Claudia powered the Porsche up to a briefer series of curves, swung right and skidded to a sudden halt on a well graded turnaround in front of a pair of bolted garage doors.

They were in a hillside recess, the night sky above them virtually shut out by the foliage of overhanging trees. Save for the faint glow of a distant street light – *again*, Chan thought, recalling the similar dim situation of Hiu Sai's deserted Santa Monica establishment – they were in a virtual enclosure of darkness.

The hillside rose to their left. To their right, barely visible stone steps led to a balustraded terrace that ran the length of a house that seemed embedded in the hill itself. No light shone in any of the windows.

Claudia's finger closed, clawlike, on Chan's right bicep. In a stage whisper, she said, 'I don't like it. You just talked to them, didn't you?'

'I talked to Mrs Heinemann,' said the detective inspector, his own voice low.

'Something must have happened,' said the agent.

'Maybe nothing has happened,' said Chan.

She stared at him in the darkness for a long moment then whispered. 'I can do without riddles, thank you. I'm going to take a look.'

'You'd be wiser to wait here,' he said, but it was too late. Claudia had already slipped out of the car and was making her way toward the balustrade that led to the front door of the house. From the fact that her footfalls were silent, he judged that she was wearing soft-soled slippers. Was it luck – or forethought? At the moment, Chan was not sure.

Three times already in this case, Chan had been caught with his guard down – once by the unseen assailant who had robbed him of the jewelled fly in Mei T'ang's bathroom, once by the strangler outside of Gil Roberts' hilltop house who had all but killed him, once by the Santa Monica police in Hiu Sai's workroom.

Three times was more than enough. He had no intention of being caught off-guard again . . .

The crux of the entire case, he was convinced, was the strange treasure of ancient Chinese jewels and jadecraft that had been stolen from the murdered actress' 'laboratory' and replaced with shoddy substitutes. Taken from the falling Republic of Nationalist China at the time of the Communist takeover, Mei T'ang had purchased the jewels honestly enough for an as yet unlisted sum of money.

The cultural representatives of the People's Republic currently in Los Angeles were willing to pay a large sum for their recovery and return to the land of their creation, according to his friend Hei Wei Chinn. They had virtually concluded a deal with whoever had managed the slow theft and replacement of the *objets d'art*.

Mei T'ang's poor eyesight, plus the screen-star vanity that forbade her wearing glasses for so long, had rendered both the theft and the substitution relatively simple for the thief. The murdered star had allowed no one in the treasure room – her 'laboratory' so called – save certain trusted individuals, and these only in her own presence. Otherwise, the bizarre chamber was kept under lock and key.

It occurred to Chan, as he quickly reviewed the basis of the case, that the old adage anent the Crusaders' wives' chastity girdles that has come down as, 'Love laughs at locksmiths,' would be more applicable as '*Lust* laughs at locksmiths.' Lust for loot as well as for romantic fulfilment.

Certainly, someone close to Mei T'ang had arranged access to the treasure chamber during the late star's absence, had had the unique and priceless gems tri-di photographed, returned them and done the substitutions one by one. The slow theft had been scheduled to coincide with the visit of the cultural mission from the People's Republic – or had it been the other way round?

At the moment, Chan considered this immaterial.

It had been Mei T'ang's misfortune to visit the oculist and have herself fitted for glasses just before the deal was complete. Whether the jewelled fly had been knocked or jarred free of its tiny slots on the surface of the jade ginseng root, while being brought back from the photographer, or when its substitution with the imitation ginseng root occurred, was also immaterial at this point.

Newly keen of vision, the erstwhile actress had discovered it on the eve of her reception – and this had led directly to her discovery of how she had been victimized. It had also led directly to her murder, in a form so dramatic that it hinted more at extemporal desperation than at the careful planning that had been a feature of the treasure thefts.

The importance of the jewelled fly to the thief was self-evident. It remained the only concrete evidence that Mei T'ang's treasure, purchased under the counter, had ever actually existed – or that it had remained in her possession right up to the time of her death.

Small wonder the thief, who was also almost certainly the killer, had run the appalling risks attendant upon assailing Chan with the lavender towel in his victim's bathroom. It had been vital that the tiny gem be recovered lest the whole crime be unveiled before the loot was paid for.

The problem assailing Chan was – who could have known he had it? The answer, of course, was – whoever had spied on him via the silent bathroom door. This, all of it, was the *corpus delicti*, the body of the crime.

Now it was time to bring the party or parties responsible into camp and into court where justice due would be meted out. Apparently it was up to him to see that this was done.

His eyesight now fully attuned to the tree-shaded darkness, Chan followed Claudia's progress as she slithered, a darker exclamation point against the deep shadow of the house itself, along the facade toward the front door. There, she apparently found the door unlocked, for she vanished within the house, seeming to flow through it.

'Interesting,' murmured Chan. He remained where he was, waiting for some visible or at least audible reaction to the agent's entry. But there was none.

Chan decided it was time for him to get into the action now that Claudia had committed herself. Moving with the greatest of care to avoid making any noise since, unlike the agent, he was not wearing soft-soled shoes, he avoided the balustrade steps that led to the front door. Instead, he worked his way along the side wall, hoping to find some sort of opening between the garage and the house, with the steep hillside immediately at its back. Chan was quite certain there had to be a rear entry, if only for delivery of groceries to such a sizeable house on a hill.

He found it, a wooden lattice gate that led to a path barely a yard wide between the rear wall of the house and the concrete revetment against the hillside to prevent landslides following spring rains. More important, at the end of this apparently blind alley, just short of the other end of the house, he found a concrete stairway leading steeply upward toward the scarp of the hill.

The light was better here than in the tree shaded front of the house. Chan could even see a narrow oblong section of night sky, complete with stars and scudding cotton clouds. He paused, checking his bearings, making sure of a return route should he need one in a hurry. To his right, a ground floor rear window was open. He waited, just short of it, for some sound or other sign of life inside the house. But there was none.

Chan wondered what Claudia Haynes was doing in there and if she was alone. If she was not, she had to be engaged in some sort of stalking game he very definitely wanted no part of.

Not unless he was sure *he* was the stalker. Chan had been stalked enough in the last thirty-six hours!

With continuing, practised care against involuntary noisemaking, Chan bent low to slip past the open window and went on to the concrete staircase at the end of the alleyway. When he reached their top, he discovered that less than two feet separated him from the roof of the producer's hillside mansion.

It was almost a flat roof, slanted enough to let rainwater flow off it into drains in the passageway at the rear of the house he had just traversed. About a dozen feet in from either end rose a massive chimney of light brick to a height of eight feet or more.

Chan hesitated. Since there was such easy external access to the roof, he doubted that there would be an internal opening. Hence, if he opted to use it and the cover of its chimneys while awaiting the imminent detonation he expected, he would be cut off from immediate and perhaps vital participation in whatever occurred inside the house.

At that moment, he heard the snap of a branch or large twig somewhere in the impenetrable brush tangle of the hillside above. At least one question was answered for the detective inspector – he had arrived ahead of the expected invaders. He would also be in plain view when the invaders drew nearer.

His decision taken from him, Chan leapt nimbly and silently for the roof and moved quickly to the far side of the nearer of the big brick chimneys.

It took Chan less than a second to discover that he was not alone in his cover, when he felt the muzzle of a revolver shoved into the small of his back and a voice whispered, 'Hands at the nape of your neck, you bastard – and shut *up!*'

This time, although apparently caught offguard, Chan was physically and psychologically prepared for any sort of unexpected attack. He had little time even for the highly specialized disciplines of defence and counterattack without any weapon save his mind, spirit and body, that were a part of his lifelong conditioning.

But so unskilled was the attack that he scarcely needed such disciplines. Instead, falling to his hands and knees, he kicked upward with unerring savage accuracy at the elbow of the arm that held the gun. Its owner let out a hiss of anguish and the hand-weapon, a small automatic, described a slow parabola against the sky. Rising to his knees, Chan caught the weapon before it could clatter to the roof and pushed both his attacker and himself back behind the cover of the chimney and its shadows.

He whispered, 'Mr Heinemann, I hope I didn't hurt you.'

'Charlie *Chan!*' the producer gasped. 'What the hell? I sure wasn't expecting you to be here at – '

The rest of his speech was abruptly cut off when Chan clapped a hand over his mouth and whispered, nodding toward the steep hillside, 'Company coming.'

XIV

Had Annie worn blackface or a dark mask, it is doubtful that either of the men on the roof would have seen her at all. Clad in a dark jumpsuit, she was virtually invisible as she emerged from the nightswept hillside behind her at the top of the revetment and moved silently down the steps to the rear of the house.

There was a low whistle from below them, followed by a soft call, 'Hey! It's me – *Annie!*'

Then came the sound of a door being unlocked and a sudden indirect glow as the lights went on, followed by a trio of voices in words of greeting – all of them feminine, all of them as easily recognizable to Chan as they were to his companion.

Claudia's husky contralto said, 'How did you manage to leave Gil?'

'Unconscious,' said Annie.

'You're sure he's out of the picture?' Claudia asked. 'I've known him to make a fast recovery when I thought he was passed out cold.'

'A little laudanum can be a girl's best friend,' Annie replied. Then, 'What about the son of heaven? I thought you told me over the phone you were driving him here.'

For the first time, Rosina Heinemann's shrill rasp made itself heard. 'Harold's taking care of him.'

'But Harold's a *pussycat!*' cried the girl. 'After all, Charlie Chan has a reputation for knowing how to handle himself.'

'Harold has his little surprises,' said his wife. 'He won a raft of combat medals in World War Two.'

'Just the same, let's check it out,' said Annie. 'I don't want Chan running for the police at this stage of the game.'

'The child's right,' said Claudia. 'Let's check it out. Where do we look?'

'Harold's on the roof,' said Mrs Heinemann. 'We'd have heard some noise if anything had gone wrong. Claudia, why didn't you bring him inside with you?'

'I thought he'd follow,' the agent replied. 'He started to, but I lost him. *Merde!*' said Claudia. 'Come on. We can't settle anything until we're sure.'

The voices faded and there were sounds of movement two stories below. Heinemann looked at the detective inspector, said, 'We've got less than fifteen seconds. Do you think you can trust me to make it look good?'

Chan said, 'No, but it looks as if I'll have to.'

He pulled the clip from the automatic, emptied it, put the bullets in a jacket pocket. Then he unloaded the cylinder, tossed that bullet up onto the hillside and replaced the empty clip before returning it to the producer. By the time the women appeared at the top of the concrete steps, he made a convincing captive with his hands clasped at the back of his neck and Heinemann standing behind him, covering his back with the automatic.

'Nice work, Harold,' said Claudia. 'Sorry, Chan, but you were making things uncomfortable and we have a lot to do.'

'What shall I do with him?' Harold asked.

There was a brief, whispering huddle – then Rosina said. 'Put him in the garage and tie him up in one of the cars. Then start the motor running.'

They stood aside as Harold pushed him down the concrete steps and watched by the glow of the lights in the house as the producer marched him along the narrow back passage to the trellis gate that led to the garage area of the estate.

Heinemann said, 'Open Sesame,' in front of the garage door, which rose in response to the sound of his voice to reveal a dark cavern with the rear elevations of a large Cadillac and a Country Squire station wagon.

Chan glanced quickly over his shoulder to see if they were being watched, saw that Annie was standing on the balustraded terrace with the other two women behind her.

'They don't seem to trust one another too well,' Chan said as the door closed silently behind them after Heinemann had switched on the garage lights.

'That's putting it mildly,' said the producer. He lowered the gun, added, 'Sorry to have to play such a performance with you, Charlie Chan. I know all about you, of course.'

'That is more than humble self know,' intoned the detective inspector.

'At least I've read almost everything that's been printed about you over the years. And your performance in disarming me up there on the roof more than lives up to advance notices.'

'Then you're not going to tie me up and leave me to the tender mercies of the soothing carbon monoxide?' Chan asked.

'And let those three furies have your murder hanging over me?' the producer countered, slipping the unloaded automatic into the waistband of his well cut slacks. 'Rosy's got enough on me already – never mind what – or I'd never have gone along with this cockamamie scheme in the first place.'

'Perhaps trouble with the Internal Revenue?' said Chan.

'Perhaps,' said Heinemann. 'At any rate, it's bad enough to justify cutting a few corners.'

'But not enough to risk a murder rap,' said Chan.

'No way,' the producer replied.

Heinemann went to the big Cadillac and got the motor going with the windows rolled halfway down. Then he did the same with the Country Squire.

'Between the two of them,' he said, 'they should do the job on a bound man in a garage this size. Let me go out first and see if anyone's still watching.'

Chan didn't like it. He had a hunch that, once the garage door was closed, it would open only to its master's (or mistress's) voice pattern. But he could shut the motors off so there was no danger of asphyxiation. He simply had no desire to be trapped.

It was a chance he had to take. So Chan took it. If his relief when the garage door went up again in a few moments failed to show on his inscrutable face, it was none the less real. He got out the instant the producer switched off the garage lights and the two of them made their way silently along the passage behind the house to the open rear window.

Claudia was striding the carpet, smoking a cigarette in her long holder as usual, sounding off to the others. She said, '. . . interest from now on lies in reviving the picture and exploiting it for every cent we can make. Otherise, this whole effort is up the spout. I don't think any of us want that, or can afford it. So what I propose is – '

Annie interrupted her to ask Rosina Heinemann, 'What about the fellow who made the fakes?'

'He's on his way to Brazil by now. He called to tell me Chan was coming to see him, so I told him to burn the photos and take off. He's been well paid and he has no desire to be pulled in as accessory to a murder. He's got a record for fraud as long as your arm.'

'One thing about a life of crime,' said Annie over the rim of a highball. 'You do meet such a nice level of people.'

'*Merde!*' said Claudia impatiently. 'What *I* want to see is some money. Without it, we're nowhere. We already spent a small fortune as it is – with no return.'

Rosina shrilled, 'Harold's meeting the Red China culture guy tomorrow – today, I mean, for the payoff.'

'By rights,' said Annie, 'it's *my* money. After all, I'm mother's chief legatee.'

'Honey,' said Claudia hoarsely, 'until the murder of your mother is solved, you've got about as much chance of inheriting a piece of toilet paper as you have of cashing in. That's one little trap the law lays for matricides – or any kind of murderer.'

'Don't look at me that way,' said Annie angrily. 'You seem to think I killed mother.'

'*Didn't* you, darling?' The agent's voice cut like a surgeon's scalpel.

There was a moment of thick silence in the room. Somewhere, on the hillside above them a cicada began strumming its jew's harp incessantly, to be joined by a swelling chorus of like-minded members of the species. But their tedious sound was insufficient to drown out the retort of the suddenly furious girl.

'You know perfectly well I didn't strangle Mei T'ang,' she cried, 'since you did it yourself. I *saw* you slipping into the elevator in the conservatory as I was greeting the guests.'

'I wasn't even inside the apartment proper. I left my cigarette holder

in my own pad and went back to get it. That's when Gil Roberts rang
my bell and I came back up with him.'

'*Gil!*' cried Rosina Heinemann. 'I never thought he had the guts to
kill a fly unless the script demanded it.'

'He didn't do it,' said the girl. 'I had to take the next elevator down
to take care of somebody's parking problem and met him coming in.'

XV

Charlie Chan had increasingly suspected that the alibi Annie and her
new-found father had given one another that afternoon, while he was
in the girl's house, was a phoney. He was quite sure it was the tall actor
who had half-strangled him and pulled him from his car unconscious.

After all, the empty garage indicated that Roberts, or the girl, or
both of them had been out somewhere while he poked around their
hillside place and found it empty. Now he wondered why he had been
attacked at all and why, in the circumstances, the attack had not been
carried through to a finish.

If, in fact, Gil Roberts was not the murderer, then only one real
possibility remained. And here, again, was a hitch. Vividly, Chan
remembered the Heinemanns standing in the ground floor hallway of
the House of Wu, awaiting the return of the interminable elevator to
take them aloft. They had been waiting where they were for some little
time, for he had not seen them enter the building as he and Doc
Svorenssen came up the walk.

He had not seen them – and he would have remembered Rosina
Heinemann's flaming hennaed hairdo had he seen it – because the
producer and his wife had not been outside the building. They had
come downstairs, probably by the service elevator, and were making
their official re-entry as guests at the party.

Only then did it occur to Chan that he was in far greater danger than
he had supposed. Evidently Heinemann had not carried out his wife's
instructions to put him out of the way for keeps because he hoped one
of the women could be neatly framed for the murder he had already
committed himself – that of Mei T'ang. But now such a possibility was
vanishing in front of his eyes.

On a sound level between the zum-zumming of the cicadas and the
voices of the women in the room, Chan heard the low growl of a barely
touched police car siren. When he dialled them on the alternate line in
Claudia's apartment, while she called Rosina to set up the meeting as
she dressed, he had asked them to be on hand at two-thirty. That hour

was gone, but not by much according to the phosphorescent dial on his Bulova.

There was something else nagging the periphery of his conscious-ness – a faint, all too familiar, scent of some sort of cologne or toilet water, an odour with a lilac base. At first, as they watched and listened at the window, Chan had been reasonably sure that it came from within the room, wafted through the open window by a current of air.

But, some moments before, Harold Heinemann had moved warily around the detective inspector and was standing wide of the window at his left side. Unquestionably, since what breeze there was came from the direction of the producer, he had to be the user of the scent – hence Chan's towel attacker in Mei T'ang's guest bathroom.

As far as Chan was concerned, this put the seal on the case. This and the conversation of the women in the late night talk he had so carefully arranged while making its participants believe they had arranged it themselves.

It was time to make his move – and he made it none too early. Apparently forgetting the gun was unloaded, the producer was in the act of pulling it from his waistband as Chan swung toward him in an explosion of frenetic activity that belied the placidity of his normal movements.

He stamped a heel down hard on Heinemann's left foot, hooked one of his own arms through his opponent's right elbow, jamming his gun hand, and drove his free elbow with rare precision, full into Heinemann's solar plexus, doubling him up without an ounce of air left in his lungs.

He was holding the producer thus, doubled over, when a patrolman came through the latticeworked gate and along the passage and shone a flashlight on the little tableau.

Chan said, 'You can take his gun, officer. It is not loaded.'

It was then that Charlie Chan was caught with his guard down for the fourth time since his involvement in the Mei T'ang murder began. As he removed the automatic from Heinemann's fingers, the officer's forefinger became caught in the guard and accidentally pressed the trigger.

The pistol detonated with a blast all the more startling because it was totally unexpected, causing both Chan and the officer to duck low as the bullet ricocheted angrily from wall to wall between house and revetment, finally to whine away to silence.

*   *   *

'Okay, Charlie,' said Doc Svorenssen, removing the spit inhalator and the cotton wadding from his mouth, 'that will do it.'

'Mouth dry as camel's tail,' said Chan, working his lips and tongue furiously to regain lost feeling. Outside, the view of the Miracle Mile from the dentist's window consisted mostly of smog. His new bridge felt tight, but he knew that would pass.

'Tell me, Charlie,' said Svorenssen, untying his white apron behind him, 'If you had known Harold Heinemann had reloaded his popgun with a spare clip, would you have been quite so nonchalant about the whole thing?'

Chan took his time answering. Once again, he reviewed the entire case. Heinemann was the murderer, of course, abetted by sweet Rosina of the hideously shrill voice – though which of the two had actually suggested the conspiracy that ended in Mei T'ang's murder would probably never have been known by anyone save the two principals.

The producer's career had been slipping but his life style had not. Hence, his tangle with the Internal Revenue Service and the State of California Franchise Tax Board. If Heinemann did not come up with a six-figure sum by June 15th, he was inevitably due to take crippling penalties, perhaps a prison term, for fraudulent returns.

At first, the picture Claudia and Mei T'ang wanted him to produce seemed like manna from heaven. He had had no other offers in two years and needed work – and the pay it would bring – desperately. However, most of his fee was to come out of subsequent profits, and it quickly developed that Mei T'ang's promise to finance the film, at least in part, was not to be fulfilled – and without the star's backing, in this case, no one else could be obtained.

It was out of his background that the conspiracy to steal her priceless collection of one-of-a-kind Chinese antique imperial baubles, replace them with imitations and peddle the originals to the Red Chinese cultural mission was born.

As Chan had suspected, the deal was all but completed when the erstwhile star determined to sacrifice her vanity at long length and be fitted for spectacles. Mei T'ang was motivated by her need to read the proposed script herself, an act that had further steeled her determination to have nothing to do with the film's financing.

Then she had discovered the jewelled fly and summoned Heinemann for a showdown, knowing him to have been the only person who could have had opportunity actually to commit the thefts over so long a period. Result – her own murder.

Mrs Heinemann, morally at least as guilty as her husband, had summoned the caterers in a well designed move to impede immediate police investigation with confusion. She had used Jason Catering herself many times while entertaining at her hillside house and was well aware of the stand-by system and near-instantaneous response by which the outfit operated so successfully in Hollywood.

This strident lady with hennaed hair was sufficiently involved as an accomplice in the actual crimes to find a prison term awaiting her – not as long as that of her husband but one which would probably use up what remained of her natural life.

Actual ownership of the fabulous treasure whose substitution was the immediate cause of the murder would remain with its purchasers –the Bureau of Culture of the Chinese People's Republic. After all, they had paid for it and, if the deal was tainted, there was heavy pressure from certain high American government circles to prevent any effort intended to halt its return to the land where it was created.

The others involved in the conspiracy, drawn into it by less directly felonious motives, would probably get off more lightly. Gil Roberts, it appeared, was not involved at all – for the fortunate reason none of the other members of the conspiracy had felt able to trust him.

As for his attack on Chan, Roberts had ruefully explained, 'Hell, I was afraid it was the murderer after Annie. She told me her life was in danger. When I heard a car start where no car was supposed to be as I was coming back, I blocked the driveway with my heap and yanked you out of yours by the throat. When I saw it was you, I damn near passed out.'

A pause, then, 'What do you suppose will happen to Annie? I guess in a way it's my fault.'

'As I understand it, her mother never gave you the chance,' said Chan, thereby lifting the fallen star's spirits immeasurably.

According to the Hollywood trade papers which Chan had examined that very afternoon in his dentist's reception room, Roberts alone of the lethal little group had emerged professionally unscathed. According to a page-five news squib, the tall actor had been cast in two television series segments and had the inside track for a second lead in an upcoming feature film.

Chan's thoughts returned to the here and now. Doc Svorenssen, wearing one of his patented ultra-loud sports jackets – this one in a plaid the like of which the Highlands never saw – grinned at Chan amiably, his blue eyes alight.

Putting an arm around his friend's shoulders, the dentist said, 'Hey, Charlie, since this is your last night on the mainland, how'd you like to come to a party with me?'

'I'd love to,' said Chan, 'but I'm taking a six p.m. plane to Honolulu right now. If you'd care to come along, I'll take you to nice party in Honolulu. Chop, chop.'

'Okay – but at least let me drive you to the airport,' said Svorenssen, an offer that Chan was glad to accept.

En route, Svorenssen said, 'Hey you didn't answer my question.'

'Which question?'

'Whether you'd have been quite so nonchalant about taking Heinemann if you'd known he'd reloaded his gun?'

'Cholly,' said Chan, 'assert better part of valour, – take the Fifth . . .'

Marlowe Takes on the Syndicate

◆

RAYMOND CHANDLER

'Hamlet in a dirty mac' is just one of the descriptions that has been given to Philip Marlowe, the archetypal private eye, a lonely, slightly seedy man, but intelligent and intensely loyal to those who seek his help. Trouble is, of course, very much the business of this tall, fortyish man with grey eyes and a jaw of stone who first appeared in 1939 in The Big Sleep *and has been immortalized in the cinema by such leading actors as Dick Powell, Humphrey Bogart, James Garner, Elliott Gould and Robert Mitchum. In 1949, a long running weekly radio series,* The Adventures of Philip Marlowe *with Van Hefflin was aired by CBS, to be followed ten years later by the private eye's TV debut in* Philip Marlowe, *a twenty-six episode series of half hour stories made by NBC and starring Philip Carey, a former US Marine and B-picture actor whose starring roles had included* I Was a Communist for the FBI *(1951) and* Man Behind The Gun *(1952). In 1984, LWT in England took the gamble of making* Marlowe – Private Eye *with Los Angeles exteriors but London sets and scored a notable success. The dozen, hour-long stories were well served by the acting of Powers Boothe whose tough looks mixed with a staunch integrity captivated audiences on both sides of the Atlantic. Marlowe has also been played on the London stage by Robert Powell in* Private Dick, *a spoof about the detective investigating the theft of a Chandler manuscript.*

Raymond Chandler (1888–1959), the Chicago-born writer who was educated in England, began his writing career in Los Angeles after being made insolvent in the oil industry and contributed several stories to the American pulp crime magazines in which the embryonic Marlowe began to emerge. Chandler's fame came with the publication of The Big Sleep *and this was followed by six more Marlowe novels and a number of short stories, of which* Marlowe Takes On The Syndicate *(aka* The Pencil*) is arguably the best and has been adapted for both TV series.*

THE fat man sidled past me into my thinking parlour, sat down carefully, prowled in his pocket and came out with a bill. Clean and new. One thousand dollars.

'Ever save a guy's life, Marlowe?'

He had a rusty voice. I'd have placed him as a mobster second-grade if I'd been asked. For once I was right. If he carried a gun it was inside his pants. His coat was too tight to hide the bulge of an underarm holster.

'What goes?' I asked.

'I heard you played level with customers, Marlowe.'

'That's why I stay poor.'

'I still got two friends. You make it three and you'll be out of the red. You got five grand coming if you pry me loose.'

'From what?'

'You're talkative as hell. Don't you pipe who I am?'

'Nope.'

'Never been East, huh?'

I was getting tired of it. 'Stop being so goddam cagey or pick up your grand and be missing.'

'I'm Ikky Rosenstein. I'll be missing but good unless you can figure some out. Guess.'

'I've already guessed. You tell me and quick. I don't have all day to watch you feeding me with an eye-dropper.'

'I ran out on the Syndicate. The high boys don't go for that. To them it means you got information you figure to peddle, or you lost your nerve. Me, I lost my nerve. I had it up to here.' He touched his Adam's apple.

'I scared and hurt guys,' he went on. 'I never killed nobody. That's nothing to the Syndicate. I'm out of line. So they pick up the pencil and they draw a line. I got the word. The operators are on their way. I tried to hole up in Vegas. Figured they'd never expect me to lie in their own joint. They outfigured me. When I took the plane to LA there must have been somebody on it. They know where I live.'

'Move.'

'No good now.' I knew he was right.

'Why haven't they taken care of you already?'

'They don't do it that way. Always specialists. Don't you know how it works?'

'More or less. A guy with a hardware store in Buffalo. A guy with a small dairy in Kansas City. Always a good front. They report back to New York or somewhere. When they fly West again they have guns in their briefcases. They don't sit together. Could be lawyers or tax sharpies . . . anything that's well mannered and inconspicuous . . .'

'Correct as hell. And when they land they'll be steered to me. They got ways. If I go to the cops somebody will know about me. They could have a couple of Mafia boys right on the City Council for all I know. It's been done. The cops will give me twenty-four hours to leave town. And my nice friends will have a car waiting to take me home . . . only not home.'

I had my pipe lit and going well. I frowned at the grand. I could use it, my account could kiss the sidewalk without stooping.

'Suppose I could figure an out for you. What's your next move?'

'I know a place . . . if I could get there without being tailed. A good-sized place, but still pretty clean.'

'Uh-huh.' I said. 'Wichita last I heard.'

He scowled at me. 'Get smart, Marlowe but not too damn smart.'

'I'll get as smart as I want to. Don't try to make rules for me. If I take this on there aren't any rules. And don't cross me. I might leak information. When's their plane in?'

'It's nine hours from New York. Probably in about five-thirty.'

'Might come by San Diego or Frisco. More planes. I need a helper . . . I know a girl. Daughter of a police chief who got broken for honesty . . .'

'Goddam Marlowe, you got no right risking her.' Ikky said angrily. 'Women ain't built for rough stuff.'

I was so astonished my jaw hung halfway to my waist.

'The man's got a heart,' I said, snapping the thousand-dollar note. 'Sorry. No receipt. I can't have my name in your pocket. And there won't be any rough stuff if I'm lucky. Now give me your address and all the dope you can think of.'

He did. He was a pretty good observer. Trouble was the Syndicate would know what he had seen. The operators would be strangers to him.

He got up silently, and put his hand out. I had to shake it but what he had said about women made it easier. His hand was moist. Mine would have been in his spot. He nodded, and went out silently.

*   *   *

The little house in Bay City was as neat as a fresh pinafore. It was in a quiet street . . . if there are any quiet streets in this beatnik generation when you can't get through a meal without some stomach singer belching out love or a Hammond organ jazzing it up.

I'd have mortgaged my left leg to live in a house like that. I didn't think I ever would.

The bell chimed inside and after a while she opened the door. She had grey-blue eyes, dark red hair and fine bones in her face. There was usually bitterness in her eyes.

She couldn't forget that her father's life had been destroyed by a gambling ship mobster, that her mother had died too.

She was able to suppress the bitterness when she wrote nonsense about young love for the shiny magazines, but this wasn't her life. She didn't really have any life.

She had an existence without much pain and enough oil money to make it safe.

But in a tight spot she was as cool and resourceful as a good cop. Her name was Anne Riordan.

She stood to one side and I passed her pretty close. But I have rules too. She shut the door, parked herself on the davenport, went through the cigarette routine – and here was one doll who had the strength to light her own cigarette.

'I need your help.' I said.

'That's the only time I ever see you.'

'I've got a client, an ex-hood, who used to be a trouble-shooter for the Syndicate . . .'

She moved her legs around, not provocatively – she wasn't the type – but it made it difficult for me to think straight just the same. I swallowed hard and went on . . .

'His name's Ikky Rosenstein, and he's not anything I like except one. He got mad when I said I needed a girl helper. That's why I took the job. To a real mobster a woman means no more than a sack of flour.'

'So far you've told me a whole lot of nothing. Perhaps you need a drink.'

'I don't in the morning – except sometimes, and this isn't one of them. Ikky has been pencilled.'

'So what can I do?'

'Help me spot their plane and see where they go – the operators assigned to the job. You know what they look like?'

'Oh sure. I meet killers every day.' She grinned. While she was grinning I took four long steps across the tan rug, lifted her and put a kiss on her mouth. She didn't fight me, but she didn't go all trembly either. I went back and sat down.

'They'll look like anybody in a quiet well-run business or profession and they'll be polite when they want to be. They'll have briefcases with guns in them that can't possibly be traced.

'When and if they do the job they'll drop the guns. They'll probably use revolvers, maybe even automatics. No silencers because they can jam a gun and the weight makes it hard to shoot accurately. They won't sit together on the plane, but once off it they may pretend to know each other and simply not have noticed before.

'They may shake hands and walk away and get into the same taxi. I think they'll go to a hotel first. Then move somewhere from which they can watch Ikky's movements. They won't be in any hurry unless Ikky moves. That would tip them off that Ikky's been tipped off. He has a couple of friends left . . . he says.'

'Will they shoot him from this room across the street . . . assuming there is one?'

'No. From three feet away. They'll walk up behind him, and say "Hallo, Ikky" and fill him with lead. Then they'll drop the guns and hop into the car they have waiting.'

'But,' said Anne, 'if you pull it off they'll send operators to you.'

'They don't kill a legit. Remember the top mobsters are businessmen. They only get really tough when they have to.

'If you spot the operators, or think you have, follow them if you can do it safely. Not otherwise. If it's a hotel check in and keep calling me until you get me.'

'You're the damndest guy,' she said, 'women do anything for you. How come I'm still single at twenty-eight?'

'I'm too bad to deserve a woman like you,' I said. 'We have to save a man's life. I'm going.'

She watched me leave with a grave face.

*   *   *

At Los Angeles International Airport you can't get close to the planes unless you're leaving on one. You see them land, but you have to wait at a barrier to see the passengers. And you can get callouses walking from TWA to American.

I copied an arrival schedule and prowled around like a dog who's forgotten where he's put his bone. Planes came. Planes went. I passed Anne a number of times. She ignored me.

At five-forty-five they must have come. Anne disappeared. I gave it half an hour just in case, then drove the crowded miles to Hollywood and my office. I had a drink and sat. At six-forty-five the phone rang.

'I think so,' she said. 'Beverley Western Hotel. Room 410. Couldn't get any names. I didn't like to ask questions.

'But I rode up in the elevator with them and spotted their room. I walked right on past them when the bellman put a key in their door and then downstairs with a bunch of women from the tea room. I didn't bother to take a room.'

'What did they look like?'

'Quiet suits, white shirts, nothing flashy. You wouldn't look at them twice. Will you take over and follow them?'

'If they're the right men they'll follow me. I already took an apartment across Poynter Street from Ikky. Well, so long. Anne. See you.'

'When you need help.' She hung up.

I called Ikky. He was out. I had a drink from the office bottle and called again. This time I got him. I told him the score up to then, said I hoped Anne had picked the right men, and told him about the apartment I'd taken. 'Do I get expenses?' I asked.

'Five grand ought to cover the lot.'

'If I earn it and get it. I heard you had two hundred and fifty thousand,' I said at a wild venture.

'Could be, pal. But it'll have to cool for a long time.'

I said I had cooled a long time. Of course, I didn't expect to get four thousand dollars, even if I pulled off the job. Men like Ikky would steal their mother's gold teeth.

I spent the next half hour trying to think of a plan. I couldn't. It was almost eight and I needed food. I didn't think the boys would move that night.

I was ready to leave when the buzzer sounded.

I opened the communicating door to the waiting-room. A small tight-looking man, hands behind his back, smiled at me but he wasn't good at it.

'You Marlowe?'

'Who else?'

He brought his right hand round fast with a gun in it. He stuck the gun in my stomach.

'Lay off Ikky Rosenstein,' he said in a voice to match his face, 'or you can get your belly full of lead.'

He pushed the gun into my stomach. But he was an amateur. If he'd stayed four feet away he might have had something. I took the cigarette out of my mouth and held it carelessly.

'What makes you think I know any Rosenstein?'

'Wouldn't you like to know.' He laughed. The empty triumph of the feeling of power that comes from a fat gun in a small hand.

'It would be fair to tell me.'

As his mouth opened for another crack I dropped the cigarette and swept a hand. I got my thumb behind the trigger and my hand over his. I kneed him in the groin, twisted his arm to the right, and I had his gun. I hooked a heel behind his heel, and he was on the floor blinking in surprise and pain. He rolled from side to side groaning.

I yanked him to his feet. I had six inches and forty pounds on him. They ought to have sent a bigger, better messenger. 'Let's go into my thinking parlour,' I said. 'Next time don't go near enough to a prospect to let him get your gun hand. I'll just see if you've got any more iron.'

He hadn't. I pushed him through the door and into a chair. His breath wasn't quite so rasping. 'Next time,' he said between his teeth. 'Next time.'

'Don't be an optimist. You don't look the part.'

I poured him a Scotch in a paper cup, broke his .38 and dumped the cartridges into the desk drawer. I clicked the chamber back and laid the gun down.

'Now, how did you get here?'

'Go chase yourself.'

'Don't be a crumb. I can get you for armed assault. Know what would happen then? You'd be out on a writ or bail and that's the last anyone would hear of you. The biggies don't go for failures. Now, who sent you and how did you know where to come?'

'Ikky was covered,' he said sullenly. 'I trailed him here easy. Why is he seeing a private eye? People want to know.'

'More.'

'Go to hell.'

I got up. 'I don't have to get you for armed assault. I can smash it out of you now.'

'If I get knocked about a couple of real tough monkeys will drop around. If I don't report back, same thing. You ain't holdin' no real high cards,' he said.

'You haven't anything to tell. If this guy Ikky came to see me you don't know why.'

'He come to get you to try to save his hide.'

'Who from?'

'That'd be talking.'

'Go right ahead. Your mouth seems to work fine. And tell the boys any time I front for a hood that'll be the day.' You have to lie a little once in a while in my business.

'You think you're a lot of man,' he sneered.

I laughed in his face, grabbed his right wrist and twisted it back. He began to squawk. I hauled a wallet out of his breast with my left hand.

I let him go. He grabbed for his gun on the desk and I bisected his upper arm with a hard chop. 'You can have your gun when I give it to you,' I told him. 'Now be good or I'll bounce you just to amuse myself.'

In the wallet was a driver's licence made out to Charles Hickson. Useless. Punks like him usually have a slangy pseudonym. They probably called him Tiny or Marbles. Or even just 'you.'

'Hell,' I said, 'there must be an economy campaign on if they sent you to do more than pick up cigarette ends.'

'Go chase yourself.'

'All right, mug. Beat it. Here's your gun.'

He gave me the dirtiest look he had in stock and strolled to the door nonchalant as a high-class girl with a new mink stole. Then he gave me the beady eye. 'Stay clean, tinhorn, tin bends easy.' With which blinding piece of repartee he drifted out.

After a while I locked up and left. I saw no one who looked like a life-taker. I drove home, packed a suitcase, then stored my car at a garage where they're almost fond of me and picked up a Hertz Chevrolet. I drove this to the sleazy apartment I'd rented opposite Ikky, dumped my suitcase and went to dinner at Victor's. I ordered a double with fresh limes and drank it. I was as hungry as a schoolboy.

*   *   *

On the way back to Poynter Street I did a lot of weaving with a gun on the seat beside me. As far as I could tell no one was trying to tail me. I stopped at a Sunset service station and made a couple of calls. I caught Bernie Ohls just as he was going home.

'Marlowe, Bernie. We haven't had a fight in years. I'm getting lonely!'

'Well, get married. I'm chief investigator for the sheriff's office now. I don't hardly speak to private eyes.'

'Speak to this one. I could get killed.'

'You expect me to interfere with the course of nature?'

'Come off it, Bernie. If I call you come running. I'm trying to save an ex-mobster from a couple of executioners.'

'The more they mow each other down, the better I like it.' We exchanged a couple of mild insults and hung up.

I dialled Ikky's number. 'OK, talk,' he said in his unpleasant voice.

'Marlowe. Be ready to move at midnight. Your boy friends are holed up at the Beverley Western. They won't try tonight. They don't know you've been tipped.'

'Sounds chancy.'

'It wasn't meant to be a Sunday-school picnic. And you've been careless, Ikky. You were followed to me. That cuts our time.'

He was silent, I heard him breathing. 'You're in for trouble, friend,' he said.

'When not? I'll come about midnight. Get your car into a side street and make a business of locking it up. Leave your suitcases out back in the alley. Douse your lights about ten and rumple the bed. And leave some luggage behind. Won't look so planned.' He grunted another OK. I hung up.

I took a long gander before I drove to my sleazy second-floor apartment on Poynter. I sat in the dark watching from my window. Like on Sunset, I saw nothing to worry me. A couple of medium-class girls were strolling outside Ikky's and a man about Ikky's build went into the apartment house. I couldn't spot anybody watching anything.

At midnight I walked a couple of blocks watching for a tail, and then went to Ikky's dive. He opened the door with a gun in his hand. There were two suitcases near the door, a third by the far wall.

I lifted one of the two by the door. 'Let's stash these in the alley. We go out by the front door. In case we're covered we're just two guys going out together. Keep your hands in your pockets and your gun in your right. If anybody calls out your name behind . . . turn fast and shoot. I'll do the same.'

'I'm scared,' he said rustily.

'Me, too, if it helps any.'

It went like a dream. We parked the suitcases and walked along Poynter as casual as a wife out buying a birthday tie. We picked up Ikky's hire car and got the suitcases. Nobody made a move. A traffic light not working, a boulevard stop or two, and we were on the Freeway, with Ikky doing a quiet seventy. We took Route 66 to Pomona. So far nothing.

'This is enough for me. I'll grab a bus back,' I said.

Ikky stopped the car midway of a block in the business section and handed me four thousand-dollar bills. 'I don't feel I've earned all that,' I said. 'It was too easy.'

He laughed with a kind of wry amusement on his pudgy face. 'Don't be a sap. I have it made. You didn't know what you was walking into. What's more, your troubles are just beginning. The Syndicate has eyes and ears everywhere. Perhaps I'm safe if I'm damn careful. Perhaps I ain't as safe as I think I am. Either way, you did what I asked. Take the dough. I got plenty.'

I took it and put it away. He drove to an all-night service station and we were told where to find the bus stop. 'There's a cross-country Greyhound at two-twenty-five a.m.,' the attendant said, looking at a schedule. 'They'll take you, if they got room.'

Ikky drove to the bus stop. We shook hands, and he went gunning down the road towards the Freeway. I looked at my watch and found a liquor store still open and bought a pint of Scotch. Then I found a bar and ordered a double with water.

My troubles were just beginning, Ikky had said. He was so right.

*   *   *

I got off at the Hollywood bus station, grabbed a taxi and drove to my office. I asked the driver to wait a few moments. At that time of night he was glad to.

Up in my office I pawed the floor for mail and found nothing but a narrow box. Special Delivery, with a Glendale postmark. It contained nothing but a freshly sharpened pencil, the mobster's mark of death.

I looked at the pencil. Maybe it meant I was marked for execution. But I didn't take it too hard. When they mean it they don't send it to you. I took it as a sharp warning to lay off. There might be a beating arranged. From the Syndicate's point of view that would be good discipline. That could be the message.

But I didn't aim to take any working over from a couple of graduate toughies. I thought of going to my house on Yucca Avenue. Too lonely. Anne's place in Bay City? Worse. If they got wise to her spotting the operators who came after Ikky, real Syndicate men would think nothing of smashing her around. Or worse.

It was the Poynter Street place for me, across from the apartment house I'd got Ikky out of. Easily the safest place now.

I went down to the taxi I had waiting and had him drive me within three blocks of the dump. Went upstairs, undressed, and slept raw. Nothing bothered me but a broken spring. That bothered my back.

I went to sleep with a gun under my pillow, which is a bad place when the pillow is as thick and soft as a typewriter pad.

The gun bothered me. So I transferred it to my right hand. Practice had taught me to keep it there even sleeping.

I woke up with the sun shining. I felt like a piece of spoiled meat. I struggled into the bathroom and doused myself with cold water, then wiped off with a towel you couldn't have seen if you held it sideways. This was a really gorgeous apartment.

There was nothing to eat and if I went out Miss-Nothing-Marlowe might miss something. I had a pint of Scotch. I looked at it, smelled it. But I couldn't take it for breakfast on an empty stomach, even if I could reach my stomach, which was floating up somewhere near the ceiling.

I looked in the pantry in case a previous tenant had left a crust of bread in a hasty departure. Nope. I wouldn't have liked it anyway. Not even with Scotch on.

I dressed and drove the car I'd hired to an eatery. The waitress was sore, too. She flashed a cloth over the counter and let me have the last customer's crumbs in my lap.

'Look, sweetness,' I said, 'save the crumbs for a rainy day. All I want is two eggs – three minutes – no more – a tall tomato juice, a slice of your famous concrete toast, a big happy smile, and don't give anybody else any coffee. I might want it all.'

'I got a cold,' she said, 'don't push me around. I might crack you one.'

'Let's be pals. I had a rough night, too.'

She gave me a half smile and went through the swing doors sideways. It showed more of her curves, which were ample, even excessive. But I got the eggs the way I liked them. I swallowed them, drank two cups of coffee, and was about to leave the toast for a tip, but changed my mind and left a quarter instead. That brightened her. It was a joint where you left a dime or nothing. Mostly nothing.

* * *

Back at my window on Poynter nothing had changed. At about eight-thirty a.m. the man who I thought resembled Ikky came out of the apartment-house across the way. Two men got out of a blue saloon. They were quietly dressed and had soft hats pulled low over their foreheads. Each jerked out a revolver.

'Hey, Ikky,' one of them called out.

'So long, Ikky,' said the other.

Gunfire racketed between the houses. The two men rushed for their car and were off, going west. In no time at all they were completely gone. It was a nice, swift, clean job.

There was only one thing wrong.

They had shot the wrong man.

I got out fast. Almost as fast as the killers. There was a smallish crowd gathered. I didn't need to join it. I knew the man was dead . . .

the boys were pros. Anyway, I'd already heard sirens in the distance. So somebody else had been working fast . . . with a telephone. It was too early for the cops to be going to lunch.

I jammed my suitcase into the car. The neighbourhood was not my piece of shortcake any more. I could imagine the questions.

'What took you there, Marlowe? Got a flop of your own, ain't you. . . ?'

And on and on. Policeman's dialogue. It comes out of an old shoe-box. They just keep boring in until you miss on a detail. Then they rub their hands, say 'Careless, weren't you.' And start all over again.

The less I had of that the better. . . . I went to my office. It was full of nothing but stale air. I sat in my chair and disadmired myself. Then I remembered the pencil. I made certain arrangements under my desk with a .45 before I dialled Bernie Ohls at the sheriff's office.

'Marlowe. I'm in real trouble,' I said.

'You must be used to it by now.' He was sour.

'This kind you don't get used to. I'd like to come over and tell you.'

'You in the same office?' asked Bernie.

'The same.'

'I'll drop in.'

He hung up. When he arrived he didn't bother with my elegant waiting-room. He came through my personal door and scowled his way to the visitor's chair.

'OK. Give.'

'Ever hear of Ikky Rosenstein? An ex-mobster who got disliked by the mob. They put a pencil through his name and sent the usual two toughs. He hired me to get him away.'

'Nice, clean work.'

'Look,' I went on, 'he's entitled to his life as long as he hasn't killed anyone. He told me he hadn't.'

'And you believed it? When do you start teaching Sunday School?'

'I didn't believe or disbelieve. There was no reason for not taking on the job.'

'Uh-huh. Let's have the facts. Make a little time, too.'

'At midnight I got Ikky out and left him in Pomona. Then I moved into the dump on Poynter I'd taken to watch his place.'

'Why . . . if he'd gone?'

'Because someone sent me this' – I took the pencil out of my drawer – 'and some little squirt came here and stuck a gun in my stomach. I thought Poynter Street was safer after that.'

Bernie stood up and stared at me for a long moment. 'I don't think they'll bother with you now. They've gunned the wrong guy. The

Syndicate will be very quiet for a while. You haven't told me anything I can act on, Phil. I'll talk to Homicide. I don't think you're in trouble. But you saw the killing. They'll want that.'

He went out and I sat wondering if I'd been a dope to talk to him. But I might easily have been on a murder charge. Anyway, five thousand greenbacks said it was worth while taking Ikky's troubles on. But they can be wrong, too.

* * *

Somebody banged on my door. It was a uniform holding a telegram. I signed for it and tore it open.

It said: 'On way to Flagstaff. Mirador Motor Court. Been spotted. Come fast.'

I tore the wire into small pieces and burned it in my big ashtray. Then I called Anne Riordan, who had helped me spot the operators assigned to kill Ikky. 'Funny thing happened,' I told her, and told her about the funny thing.

'I don't like the pencil,' she said. 'And I don't like the wrong man being killed. You should never have touched it, Phil. You'd better come down here for a while.'

'You don't get the point,' I said. 'I'm not through with the job. The homicide boys have to know where I am, and if they do, all the crime beat reporters will know too. The cops might still even decide to make me a suspect. Nobody who saw the shooting is going to put out a description that means anything. The American people know better than to be witnesses to gang killings.'

The buzzer sounded in the outside room. I told Anne I had to hang up. I opened the communicating door and an elegantly dressed middle-aged man stood six feet inside the outer door.

He wore a pleasantly dishonest smile, a white Stetson, and a beautifully tailored cream-coloured flannel suit.

'Mr Marlowe?'

I nodded.

'I'm Foster Grimes. I run the Rancho Esperanza in Las Vegas. Hear you got a little involved with Ikky Rosenstein.'

'Won't you come in?'

He strolled past me into my office. His appearance told me nothing. A prosperous man who liked or felt it good business to look a bit Western.

I flicked a wrist at the customer's chair and sat down in my antique squeaker.

'Where is Ikky now, if you know?'

'I don't know, Mr Grimes.'

'How come you messed with him?'

'Money, Mr Grimes.'

'A damned good reason,' he smiled. 'How far did it go?'

'I helped him leave town. I'm telling you this, although I don't know who the hell you are, because I've already told an old friend-enemy of mine, a top man in the Sheriff's Office.'

'What's a friend-enemy?'

'Law men don't go around kissing me, but I've known him for years, and we are as much friends as a private star can be with a law man.'

'I told you who I was. We have a unique set-up in Vegas. We own the place except for one lousy newspaper editor. We let him live because killings aren't good business any more.'

'Like Ikky Rosenstein.'

'That's not a killing. It's an execution. Ikky got out of line.'

'So your gun boys had to rub the wrong guy. They could have hung around a little to make sure.'

'They would have, if you'd kept your nose where it belonged. They hurried. We don't appreciate that. We want cool efficiency.'

'Who's this great, big, fat "we" you keep talking about?'

'Don't go juvenile on me, Marlowe.'

'Okay. Let's say I know.'

'Here's what we want.' He reached into his pocket and drew out a loose bill. He put it on the desk on his side. 'Find Ikky and tell him to get back in line and everything is okay. With an innocent by-stander gunned, we don't want any trouble or any extra publicity. It's that simple.

'You get this now,' he nodded at the bill. It was a grand. Probably a thousand dollars was the smallest bill they had. 'And another when you find Ikky and give him the message. If he holds out – curtains.'

'Suppose I say take your goddam grand and blow your nose with it?'

'That would be unwise.' He flipped out a Colt Woodsman with a short silencer on it. A Colt Woodsman will take one without jamming.

'I never left Vegas,' he said calmly. 'I can prove it. You're dead in your office chair and nobody knows anything. Just another private eye that tried the wrong pitch. Put your hands on the desk and think a little.'

'Just to sink a little lower in the social scale, Mr Grimes, I ain't putting no hands on no desk. But tell me about this.'

I flipped the nicely sharpened pencil across to him. He grabbed it after a swift change of the gun to his left hand – very swift.

I said: 'It came to me by special delivery mail. Think I've never heard about the pencil?'

He frowned and tossed the pencil down. Before he could shift his gun back to his right hand I dropped mine under the desk and grabbed the butt of the .45 I'd fixed there.

'Look under the desk, Mr Grimes. You'll see a .45 in an open-end holster. Even if you could shoot me through the heart the .45 would still go off from a convulsive movement of my hand.'

'Looks like a Mexican standoff,' he said, quietly holstering his gun. 'Nice smooth work Marlowe. Find Ikky and don't be a drip.'

'Tell me something, Mr Grimes. Why pick on me? Apart from Ikky, what did I ever do to make you dislike me?'

He thought a moment, or pretended to. 'The Larsen case. You helped send one of our boys to the gas chamber. That we don't forget. We had you in mind as a fall guy for Ikky. You'll always be a fall guy, unless you play it our way.'

'I might decide to do it your way, Mr Grimes, but I have to think. As for the Larsen case, the cops did all the work. I just happened to know where he was. I don't guess you miss him terribly.'

'We don't like interference.' He stood up. He put the grand note casually back in his pocket.

'I'll be in Vegas, Marlowe. In fact, I never left Vegas. No we don't give a damn about Larsen personally. We *do* give a damn that some punk private eye put the cops on to him.'

He nodded and went out.

I did some pondering. Then I called Anne Riordan again.

'I'm going to look for Ikky. I have to. If I don't call you in three days, get hold of Bernie Ohls. I'm going to Flagstaff, Arizona. Ikky says he will be there.'

'You're a fool,' she yelled. 'It's some sort of trap.'

'A Mr Grimes, of Vegas, visited me with a silenced gun. I beat him to the punch, but I won't always be that lucky. If I find Ikky and report to Grimes the mob will let me alone.'

'You'd condemn a man to death?' She was incredulous.

'No. He won't be there when I report. He'll have to buy forged papers and fly to Europe. He'll have a damned dull life staying alive. But for him it's either hide or get the pencil.'

'What about your own pencil?'

'Just a bit of scare technique.'

'And you don't scare, you wonderful, handsome brute.'

'I scare. But it doesn't paralyse me. So long. Stay single until I get back.'

'Damn you, Marlowe!'

She hung up on me. I hung up on myself. Saying the wrong thing is one of my specialities.

*   *   *

I made Phœnix by evening, and parked myself in a motorcourt on the outskirts, shut myself in a phone booth, and started to call the Mirador in Flagstaff.

How silly could I get? Ikky might be registered under any name from Cohen to Woichehovski.

I called, anyway, and got nothing but as much of a smile as you can get on the phone. So I asked for a room the following night. Not a chance unless someone checked out.

Flagstaff is too near the Grand Canyon. Ikky must have arranged in advance. That was certainly something to ponder, too.

At six-thirty next morning I shaved and showered and had breakfast and took off for Flagstaff. I got there by lunchtime and there was Ikky in the restaurant eating mountain trout. I sat down across from him.

He looked more than somewhat surprised to see me.

It was then I rumbled it. He wasn't Ikky Rosenstein at all.

I didn't say anything. I still needed time to sort it all out. So I sat down opposite the mobster who said he was Ikky Rosenstein.

I ordered mountain trout and ate it from the outside in, which is the proper way. Boning spoils it a little.

'What gives?' he asked me, with his mouth full. A delicate eater.

'You read the papers?'

'Just the sporting section.'

'Let's go to your room and talk about it. There's more than that.'

We paid for our lunches and went along to a nice double. The motor courts are getting so good that they make a lot of hotels look cheap. We sat down and lit cigarettes.

'The two hoods got up too early and went over to Poynter Street. They hadn't been briefed carefully enough. They shot a guy who looked a little like you.'

'That's a hot one,' he grinned. 'But the cops and the Syndicate will find out. So the tag for me stays on.'

'You must think I'm dumb,' I said. 'I am.'

'You did a first-class job, Marlowe. It's nice to have a helper.'

'You mean sucker.'

His face tightened. 'I don't catch. And give me back some of that five grand, will you? I'm shorter than I thought.'

'I'll give it back to you when you find a hummingbird in a salt shaker.'

'Don't be like that,' he almost sighed, and flicked a gun into his hand. I was already holding one in my side pocket.

'I oughtn't to have boobed off,' I said. 'Put the heater away. It doesn't pay any more than a Vegas slot machine.'

'Wrong. Them machines pay the jackpot every so often. Otherwise – no customers.'

'Every so seldom you mean. Listen, and listen good.'

He grinned. His dentist was tired waiting for him.

'The set-up intrigued me,' I went on, debonair as The Saint in a Charteris story. 'But, gradually I saw the little touches that flaw the picture. Why would you come to me at all? The Syndicate isn't that naive. Why would an old hand like you let anybody trail you?

'Why was someone so slick with a telephone after the gunning on Poynter? And how come you're surprised to see me today when you wired me to come fast? Then why was the pencil sent to me? Big dangerous threat. It reinforced the rest. But like I told your choir boy from Vegas, they don't send them when they mean them.

'By the way, he had a gun too. I had to make him put it away. He was nice about that. He started waving grands at me to find out where you were and tell him.'

'I don't know what the hell you're talking about. I just know it's too long.'

'Well, allow me to put it in English. Some poor jerk from the East Side called Ikky Rosenstein grows up in the lower grade of the Syndicate. But he's not rotten enough. So he tries to break loose. He comes out to LA and gets himself a cheap job, changes his name and lives quietly in a cheap apartment house.

'But somebody spots him. So the Syndicate say: "He can't do this to us. It's a small operation because he's small. But it annoys us. Bad for discipline. Call a couple of boys."

'But what boys do they call? A couple who've been around too long.

'So, although they don't know it, the boys they call are on their way out. But it would be kind of cute to frame a guy they already don't like, for sending a mobster named Larsen into Death Row.'

'The Torri brothers are real hard boys. They proved it – even if they did make a mistake,' my rusty-voiced friend blurted.

'Mistake nothing. They got the real Ikky Rosenstein. You're just a singing decoy in this deal. And as of now you're under arrest for murder. You're worse off than that. The Outfit will habeas corpus you out of the clink and blow you down.'

His finger tightened on the trigger. I shot the gun out of his hand. My gun in my coat pocket was small, but accurate at that distance. And it was one of my days to be accurate myself.

He made a faint moaning sound and sucked at his hand. I went over and kicked him hard in the chest. Being nice to killers is not part of my repertoire.

I took a pair of cuffs out of my pocket and snapped them on him. Then I went to the telephone.

Flagstaff was big enough to have a police force. The DA might even have his office there. This was Arizona, a poor State, relatively. The cops might even be honest.

I had to stick around for a few days, but I didn't mind that as long as I could have trout caught eight thousand or nine thousand feet up. I called Anne Riordan and Bernie Ohls.

The Arizona DA was a young keen-eyed man, and the Chief of Police was one of the biggest men I ever saw.

*   *   *

When I got back to LA I took Anne to Romanoff's for dinner and champagne.

'What I can't see,' she said over a third glass of bubbly, 'is why they dragged you into it; why they set up the fake Ikky Rosenstein. Why didn't they just let the two life-takers do their job?'

I said: 'I couldn't prove it. But I'd say this Larsen guy that I helped send to the gas chamber was bigger than he seemed to be. If Larsen was bigger than anyone thought the Syndicate would have had my name on a waiting list.'

'But why wait?' she asked. 'They'd go after you quickly.'

'They can afford to wait. So when they were good and ready they sent the phony Ikky. He had sufficient money to interest me. And he was supposed to have me on the spot when the real Ikky was eliminated. I was, too, but not the way the Syndicate figured.

'Their stooge made a fast telephone call, sure. I just happened not to hang around. I got out fast and rang Bernie Ohls at the sheriff's office.

'After that they had to make me lam out of town and get the cops hot-footing after me. That was why they wired from Flagstaff and why the visit from the Vegas smartie. Only they were too fast for themselves.

'I was out of town before the Homicide boys knew I was involved. Bernie and the sheriff's office never exactly hold back information from the city men . . . but then, they never exactly run in with it.'

I never knew what name 'Ikky' was born with, but anyway he broke under pressure and named the two gunmen – after I had already named them, the Torri brothers. But nobody could find them. They never went home. And you can't prove conspiracy on one man.

So the law had no real charge against 'Ikky.' They could have got him for some trifle, but they had a better idea. They left him to his friends. They turned him loose.

Where is he now? My hunch says nowhere.

Anne Riordan was glad it was all over and I was safe. Safe – that isn't a word you use in my trade.

Not – Tonight – Danger

◆

BRETT HALLIDAY

*There is a curious link between Raymond Chandler's Philip Marlowe
and Brett Halliday's rugged, red-headed Miami private eye, Mike
Shayne – for in 1942 the seventh Shayne movie,* Time To Kill, *was
actually based on an adaptation of the Marlowe mystery,* The High
Window, *which had just been published, the explanation being that
the stock of available Halliday novels had already been exhausted!
The Florida detective also made his debut in print the same year as
Marlowe in* Dividend on Death *and caught the interest of vast
numbers of readers with his mixture of clever thinking and dextrous
use of his fists. Less than two years after the publication of this novel,
Lloyd Nolan became the first of the two screen Mike Shaynes (Hugh
Beaumont was the second from 1946) in* Michael Shayne, Private
Detective, *a title that was also adopted for a weekly radio series with
Jeff Chandler in the lead role. In 1960, ABC Television introduced
Michael Shayne to viewers in a series of thirty-two hour-long stories
with Richard Denning, a blond, handsome and athletic former
leading man in Hollywood movies like* Assignment Redhead *(1956)
playing Shayne. For the TV series, though – which was shot in exotic
Miami locations – Denning had to put on weight and also dye his
hair.*

*Brett Halliday (1904–   ) spent a checquered career in the Army,
construction camps and oil fields before starting to supplement his
income by contributing to the pulp magazines in the late Twenties.
He enjoyed only limited success until his creation of Mike Shayne
who, he later confessed, was based on a larger-than-life character he
had met in Mexico while they were both working on an oil tanker.
Halliday has written almost seventy novels about his red-headed*

sleuth but surprisingly few short stories. Not – Tonight – Danger provided the basis for one of the episodes in the 1960 TV series.

THE telephone in Michael Shayne's Miami apartment began ringing as the redhead entered shortly after eleven o'clock.

A man's voice answered Shayne. A precise, cultivated voice, with an unmistakable New England accent; it sounded thin and agitated.

'Is that Michael Shayne, the detective? Thank heavens I've reached you. This is Mr Schoolman speaking. Harold Schoolman.' The voice was reproving, as though Shayne were expected to apologize for having been out.

Shayne grinned slightly and said, 'I don't know you, do I?'

'No. I'm staying at the Splendide Hotel on Miami Beach. Something terrible has happened, Mr Shayne. I must consult you.'

Shayne glanced at his watch and tugged at the lobe of his left ear. 'If you want to come here?' he said tentatively. 'If it can't wait until morning?'

'It definitely cannot.' The precise voice became agitated again. 'You see I . . . I hardly know how to say this, Mr Shayne. I . . .' There was a sound of a desperate gulp at the other end of the wire. 'I've done a horrible thing. I'm . . . a thief.'

'Wait!' Shayne came alert fast. 'Splendide Hotel? Are you telling me you snatched the Montalba diamond this afternoon?'

'Good heavens, no! Nothing like that, Mr Shayne. I wasn't even present at the concert when it happened, though my wife was. This is another matter entirely, but extremely embarrassing to me. I'm only a few blocks from your place at the moment, Mr Shayne. If I could come up and explain. . . ?'

Shayne said, 'Come along.'

For a moment he'd thought luck might be pushing something important his way. The fabulous Montalba medallion, boldly stolen from the Duchess at the Hotel Splendide that afternoon, was insured for two hundred grand. There would be a nice reward.

He was sure it must be Boston when Mr Harold Schoolman arrived a short time later. He was a slight, middle-aged man with a bulging forehead and rimless glasses. From the dull gleam of his discreetly polished shoes to the neat bow tie, he was the embodiment of bleak, down-East decorum and probity.

He gave Shayne a limp hand. 'This is the most upsetting experience of my life. I find myself a criminal, Mr Shayne. Inadvertently, but a criminal nonetheless. I implore you to find the owner of the stolen property and return it at once.'

'Sit down and tell me all about it.' Shayne moved back to his chair. 'A spot of brandy to settle your nerves?'

'No, thank you. I seldom indulge after dinner.' Mr Schoolman sat on the edge of a chair, reached in a side pocket and brought into view a small, exquisitely beautiful *petit point* evening bag with enamelled gold clasp and a loop of thin gold chain.

'I bought this for my present wife last Christmas. Note the distinctive, pastoral design, after Watteau. It cost three hundred dollars, Mr Shayne, and you see there's a chain to go over the wrist for safety while it is being carried.'

Shayne nodded and watched the Bostonian's strained face with some amusement.

'But my wife is exceedingly careless. She refused to use the chain, though I repeatedly warned her how easily a sneak thief might snatch it from under her arm. She was ... ah ... a member of the WAC before we were married, and the experience gave her quite an unfeminine feeling of self-sufficiency, I fear.

'I decided she should be taught a lesson. We were leaving the hotel at nine o'clock for a party here in Miami. It was raining hard and there was a crowd under the marquee waiting for cabs, pressed close together to avoid the rain.

'I left Alice to slip the doorman a dollar bill, and when I pushed back to her side I saw the expensive bag just begging to be stolen. So I took it, Mr Shayne. It was just as I had warned her. She had tucked the bag carelessly in the crook of her white fur sleeve, and she was not even aware it had been taken.

'At that moment, some hearty football types shouldered their way between us and I momentarily lost sight of Alice. The doorman waved that he had a cab and we both pushed forward through the jam and drove away with the bag securely in my pocket.

'I then put my little plan into effect. Peering in my wallet, I said, "Nothing smaller than a ten for the driver. Do you have a dollar bill in your bag, my dear?"'

Harold Schoolman paused in his recital and swallowed hard. 'Mr Shayne, you will never guess what happened.'

Shayne grinned at him, 'Your wife answered, "Yes, dear," and took a bill from her Watteau bag. You thrust your hand into your pocket and realized you were no longer a respectable member of society, but had become a sneak thief. In the crowd, you mistook another woman for your wife, one wearing a similar white fur jacket and with a similar evening bag. So you snatched the wrong one. Isn't there some identification inside?'

'There was nothing inside the bag.'

'Nothing?' Shayne took the bag in his big hands. It was empty except for a small torn piece of coarse, greyish paper, with a margin on the right and portions of printed lines on the left.

'Only that,' said Schoolman despondently. 'A piece torn from a galley proof, with proofreader's corrections on the margin. Why any woman would carry it in her evening bag is beyond my comprehension.'

'Galley proof?' said Shayne sharply. 'How do you know?'

'It's obvious,' said Schoolman impatiently. 'I'm a publisher in Boston, you see. It can hardly be anything else with those proof corrections in the margin.'

He pointed to the top pencilled marks. 'Quotation marks, you see. The next is the printer's symbol for more space. Then a single quote that has evidently been omitted, and the final mark indicates that a dollar sign should be inserted.'

Shayne nodded. 'Three of the printed words are underlined. *Not*. *Tonight*. And *danger*. Looks like a message. You have any galley proofs in the hotel, Mr Schoolman?'

'Certainly not. We're here on vacation. And when I'm home, I seldom bring work from the office. A message? Yes. My wife deduced that, also. But what can it mean?'

Shayne shrugged. 'That's what we'll have to find out. Were there many women wearing white fur coats like your wife's?'

'Possibly. I didn't notice. I didn't see my wife's face when I took the bag, of course. I was standing behind her. I saw the white fur and the familiar bag and naturally assumed . . .'

'I'd like to talk to your wife,' said Shayne briskly, 'and see if she noticed anything you didn't.'

'Yes. Of course.' Mr Schoolman looked at his watch and stiffened. 'I must be getting back to the hotel. I expect a long distance call at twelve fifteen from my daughter in Boston – from my first marriage. I left Alice at the party while I came here, and she promised to meet me in our suite at twelve thirty. Would you like to see her?'

'Very much,' said Shayne. His grey eyes were bleak as he studied the scrap of paper with three words underlined. He replaced it in the bag, tossed off the rest of his drink, and rose. 'I'll drive you to the Beach,' he said.

It had stopped raining. A golden moon was riding high overhead as they reached the ocean-side hotel. Shayne parked his car in the driveway and looked at his watch – a little after midnight. As they entered the luxurious lobby, he said, 'Suppose you go up to wait for your call. I'll nose around downstairs a while and join you in half an hour.'

'Very well. Our suite is 610. Do you think . . . *can* you determine ownership of the bag and return it without publicity?'

'I'll try. There can't be too many Watteau bags in one hotel.'

As Schoolman hurried toward the elevator, Shayne strolled across a lobby that suggested the Arabian Nights in a gaudier moment, to a nail-studded, leather door. He knocked and entered.

A pudgy man, seated at a desk, looked up at the redhead with a soft, wise smile. 'Hi, Mike. What brings you here?'

'Hello, Branson.' Shayne slid one hip onto a corner of the security officer's desk. 'Had any robberies lately?'

The man flushed. 'Maybe you'd like to take over the job of riding herd on a crazy Spanish Duchess and her quarter-million-dollar diamond she insists on displaying like a glass bauble.'

'How did it happen? All I got was a flash over the radio.'

Branson shrugged. 'A benefit concert in the main ballroom. A hundred or more guests milling around and I've got two men helping me cover it. I'm on the Duchess myself, but you can't breathe down her neck every moment. So it happened at the punch bowl. A dame stumbled into her just as she was drinking a cup of punch. It spilled on her and there was a lot of confusion. A minute later she screams her damned medallion is missing. She's been begging for this for years, Mike. Wears it dangling from her neck on a thin chain.

'There were four persons close enough to clip the chain. A Mrs Davis from Atlanta, who stumbled against her . . . insisted she was pushed. A Myrtle Hodson, unemployed secretary, who crashed the party. Lucille Lasalle, the movie actress, and . . . John Tarleton, who registered here yesterday.'

'Gentleman John? Good Lord, Branson!'

'Gentleman John Tarleton,' Branson agreed wearily. 'With a record of arrests in every major world capital for suspected jewel thefts, and nary a conviction. Sure he got it. Right under my nose. I recognized him at once and grabbed him. We also grabbed the three women fast and they agreed to be searched, after we explained that John is suspected of always working with a woman confederate to whom he passes the loot. No soap. Tarleton pulled off another perfect one.'

'So he passed the diamond and the chain clipper to some other woman before you got to him?'

'To any one of two or three dozen who pushed forward when the punch spilled. He had sixty seconds. That's all Tarleton needs.'

'Arrest him?'

'How the devil could we? We had to let him go with an apology. All we can do is tail him and wait for him to contact his confederate. Monitor his telephone line. He can't as much as speak to a dame without us grabbing her.'

'You didn't search all the other guests?'

'Lord, no. We'd be up to our necks in lawsuits if we did.'

'And you didn't search the Duchess either?'

Branson's mouth dropped open. 'It was *her* diamond.'

Shayne shrugged. 'You're positive it was genuine? I suppose she keeps it in your safe and you had a chance to inspect it carefully?'

'As a matter of fact, no. Each of our master suites is equipped with a small wall safe with a combination known only to the guest. She kept it there. What are you getting at, Mike? You suspect any funny business?'

'No. I dropped in on something else entirely. Any idea how many of your guests wear white fur coats?'

Branson scowled. 'There were exactly three at this afternoon's shindig. I know because the Duchess wore one and I checked the others to make it easier to keep an eye on the diamond.'

'Who wore the other two coats?'

'Miss Lasalle, and a woman from Boston. Mrs Schoolman. Why?'

'I don't know.' Shayne drew the Watteau bag from his pocket. 'Did your eagle eye notice any of these floating around this afternoon . . . preferably in conjunction with a white fur coat?'

Branson picked it up with a frown. 'You can't expect a man . . .'

'Frankly, no. What I really hoped was that this one had been reported stolen this evening. About nine o'clock. While a lot of your guests were jammed up outside waiting for cabs.'

'Sorry.' Branson looked completely bewildered. 'Nothing like that was reported stolen.'

Shayne said, 'See what you make of the paper inside.' He lit a cigarette and studied Branson's face while he took out the scrap.

'Three words underlined,' Branson mused. 'Could be some sort of message. A warning?'

'Could be,' agreed Shayne, cheerfully. 'You say you've got men on Tarleton. What were his movements this evening?'

Branson shuffled papers on his desk, picked one up, and read: 'Directly to his room when we released him at five thirty. Stayed until eight. Ordered two drinks and a sandwich from Room Service. Down to lobby at eight twelve. Bought newspaper and cigar. Sat alone in chair and read until nine six. Spoke to no one. Went out at nine six where there was a crowd waiting for taxis as you seem to know. Stayed on fringe of crowd, closely observed, for ten minutes, then evidently changed mind about going out in rain. Returned to room. I've got men on both front and rear exits and he hasn't showed again.' Branson sighed. 'He's undoubtedly laughing at us.'

'Probably. One thing more. Do you have any way of knowing whether either the Duchess of Montalba or your movie queen wore their white fur coats out of the hotel about nine o'clock?'

'No. They're not being tailed. We could ask them, I guess . . .'

The telephone interrupted him. He barked, 'Security Office,' listened a moment while his pudgy face went doughy. 'I'll be up at once. Stay right there.' He put down the phone and told Shayne heavily: 'Harold Schoolman has just been murdered upstairs.'

The woman who confronted them in the ivory and gold sitting room of Suite 610 was obviously fighting hard to hold back tears that seeped from under her eyelids. Like her husband, Alice Schoolman seemed to carry a wintry climate with her. The crisp, freshly waved hair was the sad brown of autumn leaves. The blue eyes were pale as ice, with a network of fine wrinkles at the corners.

She looked an oldish thirty-five, with tensely anguished features and blue-veined slender hands that twisted together as she stepped mutely aside to show them the figure of her husband, slumped on the floor beside a small table where a portable typewriter stood.

The upper rear of Schoolman's head was crushed, and blood still flowed from the gaping wound onto the carpet. A heavy, bloodstained whiskey decanter lay beside the body. From his position, it appeared that Schoolman had been seated in a chair before the typewriter, with his back to the door, when the fatal blow was struck. A single sheet of white notepaper was in the typewriter with the figures 2 and 3 typed on it.

The Bostonian had died instantly, and certainly not more than ten minutes before the detectives arrived. Mrs Schoolman's white fur coat lay on the floor just inside the door, with a pair of long white gloves and a Watteau bag beside it.

'I returned from a party just a few minutes ago,' she explained swiftly. 'I expected Harold to be in because he was expecting a telephone call. I rang the bell but he didn't answer. I thought he was on the phone, and used my key. He . . . was like that. I knew he was . . . gone, so I called the operator.' She slumped into a chair, covering her face with both hands.

Shayne said, 'I'll cover the door, Branson. Go through the suite and see if he's hiding. It's been only minutes . . .'

Branson nodded and strode away. Shayne stood quietly by the open door, looking at neither the corpse nor the weeping widow, his ragged red brows low over hooded eyes and a look of intense concentration on his rugged features.

Branson returned, shaking his head. 'All clean. And now you come clean, Mike. You've been asking a lot of questions about white fur coats and fancy bags. What's it all about?'

Shayne shook his red head impatiently. 'I still don't know. Check Tarleton's room. Is it on this floor?'

'One above.' Branson turned to the phone. Shayne looked down bleakly at the dead man and the typewriter. 'Did you or your husband use this machine, Mrs Schoolman.'

'I . . . mostly. H-Harold could only hunt and peck.'

'What do the figures two and three mean to you? Can you think why your husband might have typed those out before he was killed?'

'I don't know,' she said brokenly. 'A message? But *what*?'

Branson came from the phone. 'Gentleman John is in the clear again. He's been on the phone in his room chatting with a friend in New York for the past twenty minutes.'

Shayne nodded. A trace of the tightness left his face. He took out the *petit point* evening bag that Schoolman had given him and asked Alice Schoolman, 'Ever see this before?'

She looked at it with dilated eyes. 'It's like mine on the floor. Isn't it the one Harold grabbed by mistake, thinking it was mine? Didn't he explain that to you?'

'He told me.' Grimly, Shayne opened the bag and withdrew the scrap of paper and read, '*Not – tonight – danger*. He also showed you this. Do you agree these are proofreader's marks in the margin?'

'I suppose so. He said they were. He was a publisher, you know.'

Shayne told Branson: 'Ask the Duchess and Miss Lasalle to come here at once bringing their *petit point* bags with them. Have one of your men bring Tarleton also.'

'Mike, I've got to know . . .'

'You want to get back that diamond medallion,' Shayne reminded him harshly. 'And clean up the murder. Get them here.' He turned and stalked into the bedroom where he pulled a brocaded cover from one of the beds and brought it back to cover the body.

Branson turned from the phone. 'Miss Lasalle is out. Her maid insists she has only jewelled evening bags. The Duchess refuses to come and denies owning a bag like these.'

Shayne was looking down at the torn scrap of paper and the two digits on the sheet in the typewriter. 'I think I know why Schoolman typed those two figures before he died. Where is the private safe in this room?'

Alice Schoolman gestured to an inconspicuous silver dial in the wall above the divan. Shayne went to it slowly, asking her, 'What is the combination?'

'The combination?' she faltered. 'I don't . . . know. Harold set it this morning and didn't tell me.'

Shayne scowled unbelievingly. 'He didn't tell you? Why?'

'I don't know, really.'

Shayne swung to Branson. 'Can you get the combination?'

'Not a chance. Each guest sets his own when he checks into a suite. It's a simple one. Just two figures on the dial. You make two full turns to the right and stop. Then back to the second figure you've chosen. If Mrs Schoolman doesn't know, we'll have to get an expert to open it.'

Shayne turned the dial two full circles to the right, stopped on two. Branson intervened when Shayne started to turn back to three.

'Not that way. The first digit has to be larger. You can't turn back past zero.'

Shayne frowned, made two more complete turns, stopped at three. He turned back to two. Nothing happened. He turned from the safe to see Alice Schoolman waching, pallid and frightened.

Shayne strode to the typewriter and studied the scrap of paper again. He looked down musingly at the typewriter and pushed one of the keys with his forefinger. An eight appeared next to the two and three already on the sheet. He pressed another key and had four figures in a row: two, three, eight, four.

He told Branson grimly: 'That's the real message that was hidden in the bag Schoolman stole. Not the three underlined words. They were camouflage to draw attention away from the four pencilled symbols in the margin. Quotation marks, a space symbol, single quote, a dollar sign . . .'

He pointed to the symbols on the top row of the top line of keys. 'Right in front of us. A beautifully simple code. The same key that has quotes is also the figure two. The space symbol is a three. A single quote and a dollar sign – eight and four.'

'Two, three, eight, four,' repeated Branson. 'So what?'

'Try eight and four on the wall safe,' said Shayne grimly. 'When it opens, reach inside and take out the diamond medallion that Gentleman John snatched this afternoon and passed on to his confederate for safe keeping while he was being searched.'

Branson was on his way to the safe when Alice Schoolman was out of her chair and on him like an avenging fury, clawing his face and screaming hysterically, every iota of Boston calm forsaking her.

'She had to kill her husband,' Shayne told Branson later. 'As soon as she walked into the suite and saw him at the typewriter picking out the two and the three. He'd evidently remembered the proof marks and just noticed the juxtaposition of those symbols and numbers on the top row of keys. She knew the jig was up right then. Twenty-three and the combination to the safe in the suite.'

'What was the twenty-three for?' asked Branson.

'Twenty-three hours. Eleven o'clock. Don't forget she was in the WAC and learned the military way of reckoning time. Those were the two items of information she had to pass on to Tarleton after bringing the diamond up and putting it in her own safe this afternoon. The two things they couldn't set beforehand when they planned this coup so carefully in Boston where Tarleton picked her as his accomplice and made love to her. They couldn't afford to see each other or speak together after reaching the hotel, yet Tarleton had to know when the suite would be vacant and the combination Schoolman selected this morning.

'Tarleton knew he'd be watched every moment after the robbery, and bought her another Watteau bag as a means of passing the information. She had them *both* with her when she went down tonight, the decoy bag under her arm.

'Imagine how Tarleton must have felt when he followed her from the lobby to pick up his information . . . and had to stand helplessly by while her uncomprehending husband snatched the bag from her in front of his eyes. To teach his wife a needed lesson on the perils of carelessness,' Shayne ended sardonically.

It's in the Bag

ORSON WELLES

The enigmatic Harry Lime, a sinister figure on the edge of the law in postwar Vienna, so captured the public imagination when he appeared, played by Orson Welles, in the 1949 movie version of Graham Greene's murder mystery, The Third Man, *that he subsequently became the hero of both a radio and TV series, albeit somewhat sanitized. The enduring fame of the movie is probably due as much to the haunting zither music of the theme tune as Welles' comparatively brief appearance as the sinister Lime, but the versatile actor-director-writer became so fascinated by the character that in 1951 he part-scripted and starred in* The Lives of Harry Lime, *a series of fifteen half-hour radio plays for the BBC. In the new reincarnation, Lime became more of a private investigator devoting his energies to solving mysteries in Europe – although he always ensured getting well paid for his services and was not averse to breaking the law when the occasion demanded. In 1959, BBC Television in association with an American company, National Telefilm Associates, began production of* The Third Man, *a series of what would ultimately become seventy-seven half-hour episodes, which introduced Lime to the small screen. The suave English actor Michael Rennie who had begun his film career as an extra in the British picture* Secret Agent *(1936) became an international star as a result of playing Lime as a smooth, international operator with a special talent for helping pretty young women in distress. As Rennie explained it, 'Justice is Harry Lime's major concern, his primary motive.'*

Several of the stories which were created for the BBC radio series were later adapted for the Michael Rennie TV productions including It's In The Bag *by Orson Welles himself. The actor introduced the original performance with this intriguing prologue: 'It all happened on a train going through the Balkans from Istanbul to Belgrade. There's a mysterious veiled woman in it – naturally – and the whole thing ends up with me losing a suitcase full of money and getting a medal for doing it!' Now read on . . .*

THE Orient Express – the Central Line that is – runs between Istanbul and Paris. I had left Istanbul because all I got there was a kick in the pants and a polite invitation to leave town. I wanted as much mileage between me and Turkey as possible so I had my ticket booked all the way.

It's one of those famous trains, you know, like the Flying Scotsman, the Chief, the 20th Century, the Blue Train and the Trans-Siberian. In the bad old days before the war the Orient Express – particularly as far as Athens – could be relied on to provide a better cross-section of weird animals than a travelling circus. But now, in the bad new days, the travelling companions you're likely to find yourself with are rarely more than faces to break the monotony of the landscape.

Take my own neighbour – a little Greek in a suit that looked as if it had been clipped out of a comic strip. His face, if you could call it a face, was just something that grew a few inches north of his neck. The only feature to indicate which side was front was a pair of eyes that looked like black-currants swimming in lemon-juice. Altogether not the prettiest companion I could have chosen and a personality about as charming as a wad of yesterday's chewing-gum.

His name was Stathacopoulos and he travelled with as many provisions as a fair-sized delicatessen. This was lucky as it transpired that I'd missed the last sitting for dinner, and he insisted on my sharing his. But he had plenty of what he was pleased to call the 'wine of my country', which, although tasting a little like concentrated essence of candy store with a bit of cough medicine thrown in, had the kick of the proverbial army mule. I took very little and he took quite a lot, and pretty soon Greece's most relentless conversationalist was beginning to nod.

'Well, if you don't mind, old man,' I said, 'I think I'll just turn off the light and try to catch up on a little shut-eye.'

For some reason this alarmed him.

'No, no, the light must remain on; in the dark I might go off to sleep.'

'Do you a world of good, old man.'

'Tell me the truth, Monsieur. If you had ten thousand dollars in your pocket, would you go to sleep?'

'I've got more than that,' I said, 'a whole lot more. And it doesn't keep me from sleeping. And call me Harry.'

'How much more?' he asked.

'A hundred thousand.'

'A hundred thousand dollars, Harry?'

'That's right. Well, thanks for the picnic, old man, and be sure to wake me up when we get to Belgrade.'

I pretended to go to sleep and my grubby little friend, after picking his nails nervously with the broken blade of a penknife, settled down to watch me closely. I observed all this out of the corner of one slightly open eye and went on with a lot of fake snores for his benefit, praying all the time that the wine would finally be too much for him and he'd nod off. But there was no chance of that. No. He was going to stay awake if it killed him. *I* could have killed him out of sheer desperation.

Finally, he leaned over and shook me. What was I going to do with my money when we got to the border, he wanted to know. His money was the result of some black market wangling, and he didn't want the authorities to know about it. I spun him a yarn about my own activities – counterfeiting. My printer, I told him, was a Pole, my watermark specialist came from Roumania, and my engravings were done by a former chief technician of the German mint. Then I pulled out a wad of bills and let him examine them in detail.

Ten minutes later, with the assistance of another bottle of the local hooch, I allowed myself to be drawn into a business deal. Fifty thousand bucks' worth of nice, crisp Yugoslav banknotes to be sold to Mr Stathacopoulos at twenty-five per cent of face value if my partner in Belgrade would agree to it. I arranged to get out at the next stop and phone Belgrade.

When the train pulled into the next whistle stop, I made like a bird for the station-master's office. From where I sat by the window I could see my little Greek watching me from the train compartment. As the station-master got my call through, I gave Stathacopoulos the old OK sign, and he produced a grin that looked as if his teeth hurt him.

'Border Police?' I said in a forced voice into the receiver. 'This is a tip. Don't ask who I am. There's a counterfeiter in compartment twenty-five of the Orient Express. I can't tell you his name. He's carrying a hundred thousand dollars' worth of forged banknotes.'

Back in the compartment, I told the Greek that the deal was on, but that we would have to hurry as I had to get off at the next stop to meet another client. We both brought out our money and were beginning to count it, when the compartment door was thrown open. In no time the compartment was full of cops, all shouting instructions at once. One finally ordered me in English: 'Hands up, and do not touch that counterfeit money.'

By this time the Greek was hysterical. 'It's not mine, I tell you, it's not mine. It's his, it's all his.'

'Is that true,' asked the English-speaking policeman.

I admitted it.

'That's right, it's not mine,' cried the Greek. 'I am an honest business man. I don't deal in false currency. I am a Greek subject. I insist on my constitutional rights . . .' He was still talking like that when they took both me and the money off the train.

When the jail door shut behind me I gave one minute's silence to the memory of a certain little Greek who must have discovered by then that he'd talked himself out of ten thousand bucks. And so to bed.

Came the dawn; came the sweet scent of cabbage soup and black bread; came the chief of police. He was full of apologies.

'My dear Mr Lime, a thousand pardons! Belgrade have just informed us that your banknotes are in perfect order. How those silly train guards could ever have mistaken them for counterfeit is beyond me.'

'Me too.'

'I offer you, on behalf of the People's Democracy of Yugoslavia, my apologies.'

And so, after a ball with the chief of police and one or two of the local celebrities – female celebrities that is – I found myself back on the Orient Express with Mr Stathacopoulos's ten thousand bucks to finance the trip.

Only this time there was a difference. In place of Mr Stathacopoulos's family reminiscences and fried fish, we are now sharing a compartment with a fine-looking chick, pickled in *Bandit* by Piquet and stacked like a proud frigate. Like the classic lady of mystery, she was even wearing a veil – but not so much of it that you couldn't appreciate what lay behind. I was just figuring a way to get through the camouflage when she got the first word in ahead of me.

'I wonder if you could perhaps have the goodness to help me down with my bag? It is rather heavy.'

Of course, I was delighted. But she had been exaggerating, the way girls will: it wasn't heavy at all. In fact, it hardly weighed more than my own little bag that didn't contain anything except fifty thousand bucks and a toothbrush. And don't think that I took my eyes off my own little bag for one moment, even while helping my lady friend down with her outsize bag. Harry may be gallant with the ladies, but Harry don't have much trouble keeping the hair outa his eyes.

After that we got quite pally, and I was just opening a bottle of something special that the local chief of police had given me as a farewell present, when a voice like Caucasian granite demanded from the doorway whether there was a vacant seat. I said 'No', but my girl friend said 'Yes', and our friendly little circle was now one too many.

Well, as long as Olga – we were already on Christian name terms, you see – and I were alone in the compartment I didn't mind this coy habit of the Orient Express of keeping its passengers in the dark while racing through a chain of tunnels. But now that we had company, I began to feel a bit bashful about it. And with good reason – for when we got out of the next tunnel my little bag had gone.

No, I didn't raise the alarm. I didn't pull the emergency cord, either. Not yet, anyway. I just looked at my two fellow-travellers and thought things over. What worried me was not so much who'd taken the bag but how they'd gotten rid of it. The window was closed, the door was shut, the baggage rack was in plain sight, and neither the girl nor the man could have hidden it on his person. Then what? Under the seat? I dropped a coin and started looking for it. What did I find? The coin, of course. No bag.

I was still turning it over in my mind when Olga broke the silence. 'The tunnel, it has made the air rather bad, has it not? Perhaps you could open the window a bit, Monsieur?'

'Perhaps. As a rule these damn windows stick. It takes about three strong men and one derrick to raise them.'

'Perhaps the other gentleman could help.'

'I regret, but I am blind.'

That seemed to rule out the man. So while I went through the motions of trying to open the window, I watched the reflection of my girl friend in the glass. As I was saying, you have to be patient in my line of business, even if it makes you look like a fool spending half an hour trying to get a train window open – but in the end I was rewarded. Yes, it was in the big bag, of course: my little bag was in the big one . . . Very cute.

Just then we went into another tunnel. I figured that all I had to do now when we got out of it was to grab the big bag and get my money back. If the girl didn't carry a rod, that shouldn't be too tough. Anyway, that's what I thought. But when we did come out into daylight again, it turned out that Old Harry had been outsmarted for the second time. Now the big bag had disappeared. How? I'll give you one guess – through the window that I had so obligingly opened for Olga. So what now? Well, the old emergency cord, of course.

Almost before the train had stopped I was out of it and well into the tunnel. But somebody was behind me. And as I was running and stumbling through the tunnel a nasty thought occurred to me: maybe it was the blind man after all who had tossed out the bag. If so, he'd have all the advantage over me in the dark. And at that moment I stumbled over something and fell.

But what I had fallen over wasn't the bag, and what my fingers touched wasn't money, but a face – a man's face. I couldn't see who it was, but I didn't need to, for suddenly I had it all figured out. The Greek must have sent the dame with the trick bag after me to get back his dough. She had an accomplice placed in the tunnel to pick up the bag. The whole thing was timed perfectly – a bit *too* perfectly, because when Olga tossed the bag it hit her accomplice on the noddle and knocked him cold.

Just then, a voice called just behind me: 'Mr Lime! Hullo, Mr Lime!'

So help me! it was my old chum the chief of police. Pretty soon I was surrounded by policemen all patting me on the back and shouting 'Bravo'. When we got out of the tunnel the police chief made a little speech.

'Mr Lime, on behalf of the Yugoslav People's Democracy, I extend my most profound appreciation and gratitude for this astounding exhibition of quick action and bravery. Why, it must have taken enormous strength to knock out a man as powerful and dangerous as Leonov!'

'Leonov,' I said. 'You mean you know him?'

'*Know* him! Why, Mr Lime, he is our public enemy Number One. *Everybody* knows him.'

I decided to take the plunge. 'Just one thing. I wonder if any of your men have happened to stumble over a suit-case. . . ?'

'Indeed we have. A large suit-case with a fortune of money inside.'

'Thank heaven for that.'

'It was the property of his sister – a dangerous woman, sir. It is indeed fortunate that we have been able to intercept that money. It was intended, naturally, for the financing of more sabotage . . .'

'Now just a minute,' I interrupted, 'let me tell you about that money.'

'No need at all, sir. We understand everything, and the money has, of course, been confiscated by the proper authorities. And as a reward for your glorious effort, you will receive . . .'

'Yes. What will I receive?'

'The highest decoration that the People's Democracy of Yugoslavia can bestow.'

'A medal! Who wants a medal? I tell you the money is mine.'

'I beg your pardon.'

This obviously wasn't going down too good, but I tried to explain what had happened. The police chief cut me short with: 'Sir, that's a very mercenary attitude, if you'll forgive me for saying so . . .'

'I don't care,' I hollered. 'I want my money.'

'You would be very mistaken to try and set yourself against the will of the People's Government. Others have tried it, and well . . . take a piece of friendly advice, sir.'

'Well, what's the pitch?'

'Settle for the medal.'

And that is how I got me a nice big medal. Yeah, Harry Lime was a real live hero, which cost him a lot of dough.

The Smart Detective

◆

LESLIE CHARTERIS

The Saint, aka Simon Templar, 'a modern day Robin Hood', has something of the latter-day Harry Lime in his character, not being averse to breaking the law, and effecting justice in his own special way. He will, though, only steal from criminals and from time to time does help the police and other law enforcement agencies to solve their biggest cases. A handsome, physically strong man possessed of many capabilities and a striking intellect, he has been as much of a thorn in the side of authority as the criminal fraternity since his debut in Meet The Tiger in 1928. The Saint also dresses stylishly, eats and drinks well, and has a magnetic attraction for women which he exploits unashamedly. Templar has been played in the movies by three debonair leading men, George Sanders, Hugh Sinclair and Louis Hayward, while in the long-running NBC radio series, The Saint, which started in America in 1944, he was portrayed by the trio of Tom Conway, Brian Aherne and Vincent Price. It took television, though, to really do justice to Simon Templar when Roger Moore took on the role for ATV in 1963 and starred in one hundred and fourteen hour long episodes made in the following five years. Though TV has twice remade the series, first with Ian Ogilvy in The Return of The Saint (1978), and then Simon Dutton in six two-hour specials under the umbrella title, The Saint (1989), neither of these quite matched the style and panache of Moore's original.

   Leslie Charteris (1907–   ) modelled The Saint on an idealized version of himself when he was a young man and coupled this with an exhaustive study of criminology, a love of travel and the good life, to create his character, who has since become an international institution and one of the most popular characters in crime fiction. Probably The

Saint's most persistent adversary is Chief Inspector Claud Eustace Teal of Scotland Yard who is featured in the following story which appeared as an episode of the ATV series in 1965. Teal was played by the veteran actor Ivor Dean, while the 'Smart Detective' of the title, Peter Corrio, was portrayed by another versatile English performer, Brian Worth.

INSPECTOR Corrio was on the carpet. This was a unique experience for him, for he had a rather distinguished record in the Criminal Investigation Department. While he had made comparatively few sensational arrests, he had acquired an outstanding reputation in the field of tracing stolen property, and incidentally in pursuit of this speciality had earned a large number of insurance company rewards which might have encouraged the kind-hearted observer to list a very human jealousy among the chief causes of his unpopularity – he was a very smug man about his successes, and he had other vanities which were even less calculated to endear him to the other detectives whom his inspired brilliance had more than once put in the shade.

None of these things, however, were sufficient to justify his immediate superiors in administering the official flattening which they had long been yearning to bestow; and it was with some pardonable glow of satisfaction that Chief Inspector Claud Eustace Teal, who was as human as anyone else if not more so, had at last found the adequate excuse for which his soul had been pining wistfully for many moons.

For at last Inspector Corrio's smug zeal had overreached itself. He had made an entirely gratuitous, uncalled for, and unauthorized statement to a writer on the *Bulldog* which had been featured under two-column headlines and decorated with Inspector Corrio's favourite photograph of himself on the first inside sheet of that enterprising but sensation-loving weekly.

This copy of the paper lay on Mr Teal's desk while he spoke his mind to his subordinate, and he referred to it several times for the best quotations which he had marked off in blue pencil in preparation for the interview.

One of these read: 'If you ask me why this man Simon Templar was ever allowed to come back to England, I can't tell you. I don't believe in idealistic crooks any more than I believe in reformed crooks, and the Department has got enough work to do without having any more troubles of that kind on its hands. But I can tell you this. There have been a lot of changes in the system since Templar was last here, and he won't find it so easy to get away with his tricks as he did before.'

Teal read out this and other extracts in his most scorching voice, which was a very scorching voice when he put his heart into it.

'I hadn't heard the news about your being appointed Police Commissioner,' Teal said heavily. 'But I'd like to be the first to congratulate you. Of course a gentleman with your education will find it a pretty soft job.'

Inspector Corrio shrugged his shoulders sullenly. He was a dark and rather flashily good-looking man, who obviously had no illusions about the latter quality, with a wispy moustache and the slimmest figure consistent with the physical requirements of the Force.

'I was just having a chat with a friend,' he said. 'How was I to know he was going to print what I said? I didn't know anything about it until I saw it in the paper myself.'

Teal turned to page sixteen and read out from another of his blue-pencilled panels: 'Inspector Corrio is the exact reverse of the popular conception of a detective. He is a slender well-dressed man who looks rather like Clark Gable and might easily be mistaken for an idol of the silver screen.'

'You didn't know that he'd say that either, did you?' Teal inquired in tones of acid that would have seared the skin of a rhinoceros.

Inspector Corrio's face reddened. He was particularly proud of his secretaryship of the Ponder's End Amateur Players, and he had never been able to see anything humorous in his confirmed conviction that his destined home was in Hollywood and that his true vocation was that of the dashing hero of a box-office-shattering series of romantic melodramas.

Having dealt comprehensively with these lighter points, Mr Teal opened his shoulders and proceeded to the meatier business of the conference. In a series of well chosen sentences, he went on to summarize his opinion of Inspector Corrio's ancestry, past life, present value, future prospects, looks, clothes, morals, intelligence, and assorted short-comings, taking a point of view which made up in positiveness and vigour for anything which it may have lacked in absolute impartiality.

'And understand this,' he concluded. 'The Saint hasn't come home to get into any trouble. I know him and he knows me, and he knows me too well to try anything like that. And what's more, if anybody's got to take care of him I can do it. He's a grown-up proposition, and it takes a grown-up detective to look after him. And if any statements have to be made to the papers about it, I'll make them.'

Corrio waited for the storm to pass its height, which took some time longer.

'I'm sure you know best, sir – especially after the way he's often been able to help you,' he said humbly, while Teal glared at him speechlessly. 'But I have a theory about the Saint.'

'You have a what?' repeated Mr Teal, as if Corrio had uttered an indecent word.

'A theory, sir. I think the mistake that's been made all along is in trying to get something on the Saint *after* he's done a job. What we ought to do is pick out a job that he looks likely to do, watch it, and catch him red-handed. After all, his character is so well known that any real detective ought to be able to pick out the things that would interest him with his eyes shut. There's one in that paper on your desk – I noticed it this morning.'

'Are you still talking about yourself?' Teal demanded unsympathetically. 'Because if so – '

Corrio shook his head.

'I mean that man Oppenheim who owns the sweat shops. It says in the paper that he's just bought the Vanderwoude emerald collection for a quarter of a million pounds to give to his daughter for a wedding present. Knowing how Oppenheim got his money and knowing the Saint's line, it's my idea that the Saint will try to do something about those jewels – '

'And try something so feeble that even a fairy like you could catch him at it,' snarled Mr Teal discouragingly. 'Go back and do your detecting at Ponder's End, Corrio – I hear there's a bad ham out there that they've been trying to find for some time.'

If he had been less incensed with his subordinate, Mr Teal might have perceived a germ of sound logic in Corrio's theory, but he was in no mood to appreciate it. Two days later he did not even remember that the suggestion had been made; which was an oversight on his part, for it was at that time that Simon Templar did indeed develop a serious interest in the unpleasant Mr Oppenheim.

This was because Janice Dixon stumbled against him late one night as he was walking home in the general direction of Park Lane through one of the dark and practically deserted streets of Soho. He had to catch her to save her from falling.

'I'm sorry,' she muttered.

He murmured some absent-minded commonplace and straightened her up, but her weight was still heavy on his hand. When he let her go she swayed towards him and clung on to his arm.

'I'm sorry,' she repeated stupidly.

His first thought was that she was drunk, but her breath was innocent of the smell of liquor. Then he thought the accident might be only the excuse for a more mercenary kind of introduction; but he saw that her face was not made up as he would have expected it to be in that case. It was a pretty face, but so pale that it looked ghostly in the semi-darkness between the far-spaced street lamps; and he saw that she had dark circles under her eyes and that her mouth was without lipstick.

'Is anything the matter?' he asked.

'No – it's nothing. I'll be all right in a minute. I just want to rest.'

'Let's go inside somewhere and sit down.'

There was an all-night snack bar on the corner, and he took her into it. It seemed to be a great effort for her to walk, and another explanation of her unsteadiness flashed into his mind. He sat her down at the counter and ordered two cups of coffee.

'Would you like something to eat with it?'

Her eyes lighted up, and she bit her lip.

'Yes. I would. But – I haven't any money.'

'I shouldn't worry about that. We can always hold up a bank.' The Saint watched her while she devoured a sandwich, a double order of bacon and eggs, and a slice of pie. She ate intently, quickly, without speaking. Without seeming to stare at her, his keen blue eyes took in the shadows under her cheek-bones, the neat patch on one elbow of the cheap dark coat, the cracks in the leather of shoes which had long since lost their shape.

'I wish I had your appetite,' he said gently, when at last she had finished.

She smiled for the first time, rather faintly.

'I haven't had anything to eat for two days,' she said. 'And I haven't had as much to eat as this all at once for a long time.'

Simon ordered more coffee, and offered her a cigarette. He put his heels up on the top rung of his stool and leaned his elbows on his knees. She told him her name, but for the moment he didn't answer with his own.

'Out of a job?' he asked quietly.

She shook her head.

'Not yet.'

'You aren't on a diet by any chance, are you?'

'Yes. A nice rich diet of doughnuts and coffee, mostly.' She smiled rather wearily at his puzzlement. 'I work for Oppenheim.'

'Doesn't he pay you?'

'Oh, yes. But maybe you haven't heard of him. I'm a dressmaker. I work with fifty other girls in an attic in the East End, making handmade underwear. We work ten hours a day, six days a week, sewing. If you're clever and fast you can make two pieces in a day. They pay you one shilling apiece. You can buy them in Brompton Road for a pound or more, but that doesn't do us any good. I made twelve shillings last week, but I had to pay the rent for my room.'

It was Simon Templar's first introduction to the economics of the sweat shop; and hardened as he was to the ways of chisellers and profiteers the cold facts as she stated them made him feel slightly sick at his stomach. He realized that he had been too long in ignorance of the existence of such people as Mr Oppenheim.

'Do you mean to say he gets people to work for him on those terms?' he said incredulously. 'And how is it possible to live on twelve shillings a week?'

'Oh, there are always girls who'll do it if they can't get anything else. I used to get three pounds a week doing the same work in Kensington, but I was ill for a couple of weeks and they used it as an excuse to let me go. I didn't have any job at all for three months, and twelve shillings a week is better than nothing. You learn how to live on it. After a while you get used to being hungry; but when you have to buy shoes or pay a dentist's bill, and the rent piles up for a few weeks, it doesn't do you any good.'

'I seem to have heard of your Mr Oppenheim,' said the Saint thoughtfully. 'Didn't he just pay a quarter of a million pounds for a collection of emeralds?'

Her lips flickered cynically.

'That's the man. I've seen them, too – I've been working on his daughter's trousseau because I've got more experience of better class work than the other girls, and I've been going to the house to fit it. It's just one of those things that makes you feel like turning communist sometimes.'

'You've been in the house, have you?' he said, even more thoughtfully. 'And you've seen these emeralds?' He stopped himself, and drew smoke from his cigarette to trickle it thoughtfully back across the counter. When he turned to her again, his dark reckless face held only the same expression of friendly interest that it had held before. 'Where are you going to sleep to-night?'

She shrugged.

'I don't know. You see, I owe three weeks rent now, and they won't let me in until I pay it. I expect I'll take a stroll down to the Embankment.'

'It's healthy enough, but a bit draughty.' He smiled at her suddenly, with disarming frankness. 'Look here, what would you say if I suggested that we wander around to a little place close by here where I can get you a room? It's quiet and clean, and I don't live there. But I'd like to do something about you. Stay there to-night and meet me for dinner to-morrow, and let's talk it over.'

She met him the following evening; and he had to do very little more than keep his ears open to learn everything that he wanted to know.

'They're in Oppenheim's study – on the first floor. His daughter's room is next door to it, and the walls aren't very thick. He was showing them to her yesterday afternoon when I was there. He has a big safe in the study, but he doesn't keep the emeralds in it. I heard him boasting about how clever he was. He said, "Anybody who came in looking for the emeralds would naturally think they'd be in the safe, and they'd get to work on it at once. It'd take them a long time to open it, which would give us plenty of chances to catch them; but anyhow they'd be disappointed. They'd never believe that I had a quarter of a million pounds' worth of emeralds just tucked away behind a row of books on a shelf. Even the man from the detective agency doesn't know it – he thinks the safe is what he's got to look after."'

'So they have a private detective on the job, do they?' said the Saint.

'Yes. A man from Ingerbeck's goes in at seven o'clock every evening and stays till the servants are up in the morning. The butler's a pretty tough-looking customer himself, so I suppose Oppenheim thinks the house is safe enough in his hands in the day time . . . Why do you want to know all this?'

'I'm interested.'

She looked at him with an unexpected clearness of understanding.

'Is that what you meant when you said you'd like to do something about me? Did you think you could do it if you got hold of those emeralds?'

The Saint lighted a cigarette with a steady and unhurried hand, and then his blue eyes came back to her face for a moment before he answered with a very quiet and calculating directness.

'That was more or less my idea,' he said calmly.

She was neither shocked nor frightened. She studied him with a sober and matter-of-fact attention as if they were discussing where she might find another job, but a restrained intenseness with which he thought he could sympathize came into her voice. She said: 'I couldn't call anybody a criminal who did that. He really deserves to lose them. I believe I'd be capable of robbing him myself if I knew how to go about it – have you ever done anything like that before?'

'I have had a certain amount of experience,' Simon admitted mildly. 'You may have read about me. I'm called The Saint.'

'You? You're pulling my leg.' She stared at him and the amused disbelief in her face changed slowly into a weakening incredulity. 'But you might be. I saw a photograph once . . . Oh, if you only were! I'd help you to do it – I wouldn't care what it cost.'

'You can help me by telling me everything you can remember about Oppenheim's household and how it works.'

She had been there several times; and there were many useful things she remembered, which his skilful questioning helped to bring out. They went down into the back of his mind and stayed there while he talked about other things. The supremely simple, obvious, and imperfectible solution came to him a full two hours later, when they were dancing on a small packed floor off Shaftesbury Avenue.

He took her back to their table as the three-piece orchestra expired, lighted a cigarette, and announced serenely:

'It's easy. I know just how Comrade Oppenheim is going to lose his emeralds.'

'How?'

'They have a man in from Ingerbeck's at night, don't they? And he has the run of the place while everybody else is asleep. They give him breakfast in the morning when the servants get up, and then he takes a cigar and goes home. Well, the same thing can happen just once more. The guy from Ingerbeck's comes in, stays the night, and goes home. Not the usual guy, because he's sick or been run over by a truck or something. Some other guy. And when this other guy goes home, he can pull emeralds out of every pocket.'

Her mouth opened a little.

'You mean you'd do that?'

'Sure. Apart from the fact that I don't like your Mr Oppenheim, it seems to me that with a quarter of a million's worth of emeralds one could do a whole lot of amusing things which Oppenheim would never dream of. To a bloke with my imagination – '

'But when would you do it?'

He looked at his watch mechanically.

'Eventually – why not now? Or at least this evening.' He was almost mad enough to consider it; but he restrained himself. 'But I'm afraid it might be asking for trouble. It'll probably take me a day or two to find out a few more things about this dick from Ingerbeck's, and then I'll have to get organized to keep him out of the way on the night I want to go in. I should think you could call it a date for Friday.'

She nodded with a queer childish gravity.

'I believe you'd do it. You sound very sure of everything. But what would you do with the emeralds after you got them?'

'I expect we could trade them in for a couple of hot dogs – maybe more.'

'You couldn't sell them.'

'There are ways and means.'

'You couldn't sell stones like that. I'm sure you couldn't. Everything in a famous collection like that would be much too well known. If you took them into a dealer he'd recognize them at once, and then you'd be arrested.'

The Saint smiled. It has never been concealed from the lynx-eyed student of these chronicles that Simon Templar had his own very human weaknesses; and one of these was a deplorable lack of resistance to the temptation to display his unique knowledge of the devious ways of crime, like a pedlar spreading his wares in the market-place, before a suitably impressed and admiring audience.

'Not very far from here, in Bond Street,' he said, 'there's a little bar where you can find the biggest fence in England any evening between six and eight o'clock. He'll take anything you like to offer him across the table, and pay top prices for it. You could sell him the Crown Jewels if you had them. If I borrow Oppenheim's emeralds on Friday night I'll be rid of them by dinner time Saturday, and then we'll meet for a celebration and see where you'd like to go for a holiday.'

He was in high spirits when he took her home much later to the lodging house where he had found her a room the night before. There was one virtue in the indulgence of his favourite vice; talking over the details of a coup which he was freshly planning in his mind helped him to crystallize and elaborate his own ideas, gave him a charge of confidence and optimistic energy from which the final strokes of action sprung as swiftly and accurately as bullets out of a gun. When he said good night to her he felt as serene and exhilarated in spirit as if the Vanderwoude emeralds were already his own. He was in such good spirits that he had walked a block from the lodging house before he remembered that he had left her without trying to induce her to take some money for her immediate needs, and without making any arrangement to meet her again.

He turned and walked back. Coincidence, an accident of time involving only a matter of seconds, had made incredible differences to his life before: this, he realized later, was only another of those occasions when an overworked guardian angel seemed to play with the clock to save him from disaster.

The dimly lighted desert of the hall was surrounded by dense oases of potted palms, and one of these obstructions was in a direct line from the front door, so that anyone who entered quietly might easily remain unnoticed until he had circumnavigated this clump of shrubbery. The Saint, who from the ingrained habit of years of dangerous living moved silently without conscious effort, was just preparing to step around this divinely inspired decoration when he heard someone speaking in the hall and caught the sound of a name which stopped him dead in his tracks. The name was Corrio. Simon stood securely hidden behind the fronds of imported vegetation, and listened for as long as he dared to some of the most interesting lines of dialogue which he had ever overheard. When he had heard enough, he slipped out again as quietly as he had come in, and went home without disturbing Janice Dixon. He would get in touch with her the next day: for the moment he had something much more urgent to occupy his mind.

It is possible that even Inspector Corrio's smugness might have been shaken if he had known about this episode of unpremeditated eavesdropping, but this unpleasant knowledge was hidden from him. His elastic self-esteem had taken no time at all to recover from the effects of Teal's reprimand; and when Mr Teal happened to meet him on a certain Friday afternoon he looked as offensively sleek and self-satisfied as he had always been. It was beyond Teal's limits of self denial to let the occasion go by without making the use of it to which he felt he was entitled.

'I believe Oppenheim has still got his emeralds,' he remarked, with a certain feline joviality.

Inspector Corrio's glossy surface was unscratched.

'Don't be surprised if he doesn't keep them much longer,' he said. 'And don't blame me if the Saint gets away with it. I gave you the tip once, and you wouldn't listen.'

'Yes, you gave me the tip,' Teal agreed benevolently. 'When are you going out to Hollywood to play Sherlock Holmes?'

'Maybe it won't be so long now,' Corrio said darkly. 'Paragon Pictures are pretty interested in me – apparently one of their executives happened to see me playing the lead in our last show at the Ponder's End Playhouse, and they want me to take a screen test.'

Mr Teal grinned evilly.

'You're too late,' he said.

'They've already made a picture of *Little Women*.'

He had reason to regret some of his jibes the next morning, when news came in that every single one of Mr Oppenheim's emeralds had been removed from its hiding place and taken out of the house, quietly and without any fuss, in the pockets of a detective of whom the Ingerbeck agency had never heard. They had, they said, been instructed by telephone that afternoon to discontinue the service, and the required written confirmation had arrived a few hours later, written on Mr Oppenheim's own flowery letterhead and signed with what they firmly believed to be his signature; and nobody had been more surprised and indignant than they were when Mr Oppenheim, on the verge of an apoplectic fit, had rung up Mr Ingerbeck himself and demanded to know how many more crooks they had on their payroll and what the blank blank they proposed to do about it. The impostor had arrived at the house at the usual hour in the evening, explained that the regular man had been taken ill, and presented the necessary papers to accredit himself; and he had been left all night in the study, and let out at breakfast time according to the usual custom. When he went out he was worth a quarter of a million pounds as he stood up – he was according to the butler's rather hazy description, a tallish man with horn-rimmed glasses and a thick crop of red hair.

'That red hair and glasses is all nonsense,' said Corrio, who was in Chief Inspector Teal's office when the news came in. 'Just an ordinary wig and a pair of frames from any opticians. It was the Saint all right – you can see his style right through it. What did I tell you?'

'What the devil do you think you can tell *me*?' Teal roared back at him. Then he subdued himself. 'Anyway, you're crazy. The Saint's out of business.'

Corrio shrugged.

'Would you like me to take the case, sir?'

'What, you?' Mr Teal disrobed a wafer of chewing gum with the same distaste with which he might have undressed Inspector Corrio. 'I'll take the case myself.' He glowered at Corrio thoughtfully for a moment. 'Well, if you know so much about it you can come along with me. And we'll see how clever you are.'

It was a silent journey, for Teal was too full of a vague sort of wrath to speak, and Corrio seemed quite content to sit in a corner and finger his silky moustache with an infuriatingly tranquil air of being quite well satisfied with the forthcoming opportunity of demonstrating his own brilliance.

In the house they found a scene of magnificent confusion. There was the butler, who seemed to be getting blamed for having admitted the thief; there was a representative of Ingerbeck's, whose temper appeared to be fraying rapidly under the flood of wild accusations which Oppenheim was flinging at him; there was a very suave and imperturbable official of the insurance company which had covered the jewels; and there was Mr Oppenheim himself, a short, fat, yellow-faced man, dancing about like an agitated marionette, shaking his fists in an ecstasy of rage, screaming at the top of his voice and accusing everybody in sight of crimes and perversions which would have been worth at least five hundred years on Dartmoor if they could have been proved. Teal and Corrio had to listen while he unburdened his soul again from the beginning.

'And now vat you think?' he wound up, 'these dirty crooks, this insurance company vat takes all my money, they say they don't pay anything. They say they repudiate the policy. Just because I tried to keep the emeralds vere they couldn't be found, instead of leaving them in a save vat anyone can open – '

'The thing is,' explained the official of the insurance company, with his own professional brand of unruffled unctuousness, 'that Mr Oppenheim has failed to observe the conditions of the policy. It was issued on the express understanding that if the emeralds were to be kept in the house, they were to be kept in this safe and guarded by a detective from some recognized agency. Neither of these stipulations have been complied with, and in the circumstances – '

'It's a dirty swindle!' shrieked Oppenheim. 'Vat do I care about your insurance company? I vill cancel all my policies. I buy up your insurance company and throw you out in the street to starve. I offer my own reward for the emeralds. I vill pay a hundred – I mean five thousand pounds to the man who brings back my jewels!'

'Have you put that in writing yet?' asked Inspector Corrio quickly.

'No. But I do so at vonce. Bah! I vill show these dirty doublecrossing crooks – '

He whipped out his fountain pen and scurried over to the desk.

'Here, wait a minute,' said Teal, but Oppenheim paid no attention to him. Teal turned to Corrio. 'I suppose you have to be sure of the reward before you start showing us how clever you are,' he said nastily.

'No, sir. But we have to consider the theory that the robbery might have been committed with that in mind. Emeralds like those would be difficult to dispose of profitably – I can only think of one fence in London who'd handle a package of stuff like that.'

'Then why don't you pull him in?' snapped Teal unanswerably.

'Because I've never had enough evidence. But I'll take up that angle this afternoon.'

He took no further part in the routine examinations and questionings which Teal conducted with dogged efficiency, but on the way back to Scotland Yard he pressed his theory again with unusual humility.

'After all, sir, even if this isn't one of the Saint's jobs, whoever did it, they're quite likely to deal with this chap I've got in mind, and we aren't justified in overlooking it. I know you don't think much of me, sir,' said Corrio with unwonted candour, 'but you must admit that I was right a few days ago when you wouldn't listen to me, and now I think it'd be only fair for you to give me another chance.'

Almost against his will, Teal forced himself to be just.

'All right,' he said grudgingly. 'Where do we find this fence?'

'If you can be free about a quarter to five this afternoon,' said Corrio, 'I'd like you to come along.'

Simon Templar walked north along Bond Street. He felt at peace with the world. At such times as this he was capable of glowing with a vast and luxurious contentment, the same deep and satisfying tranquillity that might follow a perfect meal eaten in hunger or the drinking of a cool drink at the end of a hot day. As usually happened with him, this mood had made its mark on his clothes; and he was a very beautiful and resplendent sight as he sauntered along the sidewalk with the brim of his hat tilted piratically over his eyes, looking like some swashbuckling medieval brigand who had been miraculously transported into the twentieth century and put into modern dress without losing the swagger of a less inhibited age. In one hand he carried a brown paper parcel.

Chief Inspector Teal's pudgy hand closed on his arm near the corner of Burlington Gardens; and the Saint looked round and recognized him with a delighted and completely innocent smile.

'Why, hullo there, Claud Eustace,' he murmured. 'The very man I've been looking for.' He discovered Corrio coming up out of the background, and smiled again. 'Hi, Gladys,' he said politely.

Corrio seized his other arm and worked him swiftly and scientifically into a doorway. There was a gleam of excitement in his dark eyes. 'It looks as if my theory was right again,' he said to Teal.

Mr Teal kept his grip of the Saint's arm. His rather frog-like eyes glared at the Saint angrily, but not with the sort of anger that most people would have expected.

'You damn fool,' he said, rather damn-foolishly. 'What did you have to do it for? I told you when you came home that you couldn't get away with that stuff any more.'

'What stuff?' asked the Saint innocently.

Corrio had grabbed the parcel out of his hand, and he was tearing it open with impatient haste.

'I think this is what we're looking for,' he said.

The broken string and torn brown paper fluttered to the ground as Corrio ripped them off. When the outer wrappings were gone he was left with a cardboard box. Inside the box there was a layer of crumpled tissue paper. Corrio jerked it out and remained staring frozenly at what was finally exposed. This was a fully dressed and very lifelike doll with features that were definitely familiar. Tied around its neck on a piece of ribbon was a ticket on which was printed: 'Film Star Series, No. 12: CLARKE GABLE. 2/11.'

An expression of delirious and incredulous relief began to creep over the chubby curves of Teal's pink face – much the same expression as might have come into the face of a man who, standing close by the crater of a rumbling volcano, had seen it suddenly explode only to throw off a shower of fairy lights and coloured balloons. The corners of his mouth began to twitch, and a deep vibration like the tremor of an approaching earthquake began to quiver over his chest.

Corrio's face was black with fury. He tore out the rest of the packing paper and squeezed out every scrap of it between his fingers, snatched the doll out of the box and twisted and shook it to see if anything could have been concealed inside it. Then he flung that down also among the mounting fragments of litter on the ground. He thrust his face forward until it was within six inches of the Saint's.

'Where are they?' he snarled savagely.

'Where are who?' asked the Saint densely.

'You know damn well what I'm talking about,' Corrio said through his teeth. 'What have you done with the stuff you stole from Oppenheim's last night? Where are the Vanderwoude emeralds?'

'Oh, them,' said the Saint mildly. 'That's a funny question for *you* to ask.' He leaned lazily on the wall against which Corrio had forced him, took out his cigarette-case and looked at Teal.

'As a matter of fact,' he said calmly, 'that's what I wanted to see you about. If you're particularly interested I think I could show you where they went to.'

The laugh died away on Teal's lips, to be replaced by the startled and hurt look of a dog that has been given an unexpected bone and then kicked almost as soon as it has picked it up.

'So you do know something about that job,' he said slowly.

'I know plenty,' said the Saint. 'Let's take a cab.'

He straightened up off the wall. For a moment Corrio looked as if he would pin him back there, but Teal's intent interest countermanded the movement without speaking or even looking at him. Teal was puzzled and disturbed, but somehow the Saint's quiet voice and unsmiling eyes told him that there was something there to be taken seriously. He stepped back, and Simon walked past him unhindered and opened the door of a taxi standing by the kerb.

'Where are we going to?' asked Teal, as they turned into Piccadilly.

The Saint grinned gently, and settled back in his corner with his cigarette. He ignored the question.

'Once upon a time,' he said presently, 'there was a smart detective. He was very smart because after some years of ordinary detecting he had discovered that the main difficulty about the whole business was that you often have to find out who committed a crime, and this is liable to mean a lot of hard work and a good many disappointments.

'So this guy, being a smart fellow, thought of a much simpler method, which was more or less to persuade the criminals to tell him about it themselves. For instance, suppose a crook got away with a tidy cargo of loot and didn't want to put it away in the refrigerator for icicles to grow on: he could bring his problem to our smart detective, and our smart detective could think it over and say, "Well, Featherstonehaugh, that's pretty easy. All you do is just go and hide this loot in a dustbin on Greek Street or hang it on a tree in Hyde Park, or something like that, and I'll do a very smart piece of detecting and find it. Then I'll collect the reward and we'll go shares in it." Usually this was pretty good business for the crook, the regular fences being as miserly as they are; and the detective didn't starve on it either; but somehow it never seemed to occur to the other detectives to wonder how he did it.'

He finished speaking as the taxi drew up at a small and dingy hotel near Charing Cross.

Mr Teal was sitting forward, with his round moon-face looking like a surprised plum-pudding and his eyes fixed sleepily on the Saint's face.

'Go on,' he said gruffly.

Simon shook his head and indicated the door.

'We'll change the scene again.'

He got out and paid off the driver, and the other two followed him into the hotel. Corrio's face seemed to have gone paler under its olive tan.

Simon paused in the lobby and glanced at him.

'Will you ask for the key, or shall I? It might be better if you asked for it,' he said softly, 'because the porter will recognize you. Even if he doesn't know you by your right name.'

'I don't quite know what you're talking about,' Corrio said coldly, 'but if you think you can wriggle out of this with any of your wild stories, you're wasting your time.' He turned to Teal. 'I have got a room here, sir – I just use it sometimes when I'm kept in town late and I can't get home. It isn't in my own name, because – well, sir, you understand – I don't always want everybody to know who I am. This man has got to know about it somehow, and he's just using it to try and put up some crazy story to save his own skin.'

'All the same,' said Teal, with surprising gentleness, 'I'd like to go up. I want to hear some more of this crazy story.'

Corrio turned on his heel and went to the desk. The room was on the third floor – an ordinary cheap hotel room with the usual revolting furniture to be found in such places. Teal glanced briefly over its salient features as they entered, and looked at the Saint again.

'Go on,' he said. 'I'm listening.'

The Saint sat down on the edge of the bed and blew smoke-rings.

'It would probably have gone on a lot longer,' he said, 'if this smart detective hadn't thought one day what a supremely brilliant idea it would be to combine business with profit, and have the honour of convicting a most notorious and elusive bandit known as the Saint – not forgetting, of course, to collect the usual cash reward in the process. So he used a very good-looking young damsel – you ought to meet her sometime, Claud, she really is a peach – having some idea that the Saint would never run away very fast from a pretty face. In which he was damn right . . . She had a very well-planned hard-luck story, too, and the whole act was most professionally staged. It had all the ingredients that a good psychologist would bet on to make the Saint feel that stealing Oppenheim's emeralds was the one thing he had left glaringly undone in an otherwise complete life. Even the spade-work of the job had already been put in, so that she could practically tell the Saint how to pinch the jewels. So that our smart detective must have thought he was sitting pretty, with a sucker all primed to do the dirty work for him and take the rap if anything went wrong – besides being still there to take the rap when the smart detective made his arrest and earned the reward if everything went right.'

Simon smiled dreamily at a particularly repulsive print on the wall for a moment.

'Unfortunately I happened to drop in on this girl one time when she wasn't expecting me, and I heard her phoning a guy named Corrio to tell him I was well and truly hooked,' he said. 'On account of having read in the *Bulldog* some talk by a guy of the same name about what he was going to do to me, I was naturally interested.'

Corrio started forward.

'Look here, you – '

'Wait a minute.' Mr Teal held him back with an unexpectedly powerful arm. 'I want the rest of it. Did you do the job, Saint?'

Simon shook his head sadly. It was at that point that his narrative departed, for the very first time, from the channels of pure veracity in which it had begun its course – but Mr Teal was not to know this.

'Would I be such a sap, Claud?' he asked reproachfully. 'I knew I could probably get away with the actual robbery, because Corrio would want me to; but as soon as it was over, knowing in advance who'd done it, he'd be chasing round to catch me and recover the emeralds. So I told the girl I'd thought it all over and decided I was too busy.' The Saint sighed, as if he was still regretting a painful sacrifice. 'The rest is pure theory; but this girl gave me a cloakroom ticket from Victoria Station this morning and asked me if I'd collect a package this afternoon and take it along to an address on Bond Street. I didn't do it because I had an idea what would happen; but my guess would be that if somebody went along and claimed the parcel they'd find the emeralds in it. Not all the emeralds, probably, because that'd be too risky if I got curious and opened it; but some of them. The rest are probably here – I've been looking around since we've been here, and I think there's some new and really rather amateurish stitching in the upholstery of that chair. I could do something with that reward myself – '

Corrio barred his way as he got off the table.

'You stay where you are,' he grated. 'If you're trying to get away with some smart frame-up – '

'Just to make sure,' said the Saint, 'I fixed a dictagraph under the table yesterday. Let's see if it has anything to say.'

Teal watched him soberly as he prepared to play back the record. In Chief Inspector Teal's mind was the memory of a number of things which he had heard Corrio say, which fitted into the picture which the Saint offered him much too vividly to be easily denied.

Then the dictagraph began to play. And Teal felt a faint shiver run up his spine at the uncannily accurate reproduction of Corrio's voice.

'*Smart work, Leo . . . I bet these must be worth every penny of the price on them.*'

The other voice was unfamiliar.

'*Hell, it was easy. The layout was just like you said. But how're you goin' to fix it on the other chap?*'

'*That's simple. The girl gets him to fetch a parcel from Victoria and take it where I tell her to tell him. When he gets there, I'm waiting for him.*'

'*You're not goin' to risk givin' in all that stuff?*'

'*Oh, don't be so wet. There'll only be just enough in the parcel to frame him. Once he's caught, it'll be easy enough to plant the rest somewhere and find it.*'

Corrio's eyes were wide and staring.

'It's a plant!' he screamed hysterically. 'That's a record of the scene I played in the film test I made yesterday.'

Simon smiled politely, cutting open the upholstery of the armchair and fishing about for a leather pouch containing about two hundred thousand pounds' worth of emeralds which should certainly be there unless somebody else had found them since he chose that ideal hiding-place for his loot.

'I only hope you'll be able to prove it, Gladys,' he murmured; and watched Teal grasp Corrio's arm with purposeful efficiency.

Gideon and the Chestnut Vendor

◆

JOHN CREASEY

Commander George Gideon of Scotland Yard's CID has been described by no less an authority than Ellery Queen as 'a born detective' and a man possessing 'a built-in radar system for ratiocination – invisible antennas that pick up even the tiniest of crime waves.' He is, though, a bulky, slow-moving policeman with a sleepy-looking expression and gentle voice – but a man who should never be underestimated at any cost for once on the trail of a crime he is relentless and unforgiving. Gideon's warmth, sincerity and dedication made him a success with crime lovers immediately on his debut in 1955 *in* Gideon's Day. *The Inspector's fame was ensured when the renowned American director John Ford filmed this first novel in* 1958 *using actual London locations and the excellent Jack Hawkins in the lead role. In* 1964, *ATV transferred Gideon to the small screen as* Gideon's Way *starring John Gregson, the mild-mannered English actor familiar until then for his comedy roles. It is, though, for the twenty-six hour-long episodes as the reassuring Gideon that he is probably now best remembered by many members of the public.*

The creator of Gideon, John Creasey (1908–1973) *has been described as the most prolific writer in the crime and detective story genre, having written over six hundred books under some thirty pen names during a career which spanned forty years. He claimed to have received over seven hundred rejection slips for stories he wrote while working in clerical, factory and sales jobs before his first book was accepted in* 1932. *Apart from the the twenty-one books about Gideon, he was also the creator of a number of other series characters including Superintendent Folly, Roger West, The Toff, The Baron and Dr Palfrey. Surprisingly, Creasey wrote only a few short stories about*

*Inspector Gideon, of which the following has not been included in
book form before. It is, though, a gem with 'G.G.' in top deductive
form . . .*

OLD Ben Fairley had sold fresh roasted chestnuts for more winters
than he could remember. As a matter of fact, he remembered very
little of his seventy-odd years, for he had always lived almost entirely
in the present, whether it was good or bad. Each summer he went out
on the road, calling on those farms where he could find temporary
employment planting or hoeing or fruit picking. Each winter he came
'home,' to the rooming house near London's Covent Garden, where he
stored his barrow and brazier, bought his chestnuts at wholesale, and
roasted them.

Old Ben's pitch was near Leicester Square.

His chestnuts were always fleshy and white, brought all the way
from sun-drenched Italy, and old Ben was as fussy as a chef while
splitting them and turning them and keeping them hot.

The fire in the brazier also kept him warm.

Many people knew him, passing his barrow with a smile or a nod,
sometimes pausing to hand him a shilling or a two-shilling piece,
usually 'forgetting' to take their bag of chestnuts. Some, on the other
hand, liked chestnuts, and were not embarrassed to skin and eat them
as they pounded London's hard pavements.

Among these was George Gideon, Commander of the Criminal
Investigation Department of New Scotland Yard. From time to time,
often late at night after the theatre crowds had left and London was
quiet and empty, Gideon would stroll round the square mile which
included all Soho as well as Piccadilly Circus and Leicester Square,
almost as if he owned the ground he walked on. Certainly he loved it.
The sight of his solid massive figure, his square chin thrust forward, his
broad forehead wrinkled under iron-grey hair, was familiar to
newsdealer and pavement artist, taxi driver and night-club tout,
pedlar and policeman.

On cold nights Gideon would stop at old Ben's chestnut barrow,
pay his shillings, take a soft appetizing nut, and pop it hot and whole
into his mouth.

'Must have a palate like a piece of iron,' old Ben would say. Or:

'You're the only man I know who can open those nuts without burning his fingers. How do you do it, Mr Gideon?'

'I get a tough skin catching bad men,' Gideon would answer invariably.

They would both laugh, and Gideon would stay for a few moments, talking to old Ben, tossing the husks onto the fire and watching them blaze.

One night, only half an hour after he had left the chestnut vendor, a taxi drew up close to old Ben's barrow. Ben watched first one then two, three, four youths scramble out, and sensed some kind of trouble. Almost at once another taxi screeched to a halt at the far side of the street. This time old Ben was too busy to count how many men got out; he had grabbed the handles of his barrow and started to move off.

He did not get far.

Suddenly one of the youths pushed him aside. As old Ben staggered, another snatched at the barrow and a third began to pluck the chestnuts from their wire container. Angry now, as much as frightened, old Ben shouted a protest.

More youths rushed up, and passers-by stopped in alarm as the two groups fought. In the struggle someone pushed against the brazier and tipped it over. As old Ben ran forward to save his chestnuts, red-hot coals glowed like tracers through the air, striking against his outstretched hands.

He screamed with pain.

A police whistle shrilled out.

In five minutes old Ben Fairley, groaning and only half conscious, was being rushed to the hospital. The two opposing gangs had disappeared, and the hot coals, scattered across the pavement, were dying.

Gideon heard of this in the middle of his briefing session at New Scotland Yard at about half-past ten the next morning. It was mentioned almost in passing by a Superintendent Lloyd who was in charge of the police attempt to curtail the activities of the teen-age gangs in Soho.

'I could understand if they had a purpose,' Lloyd was saying. He was big, earnest, and Welsh. 'But they fight just for the sake of fighting. Razor blades and brass knuckles were used again last night, George.'

Gideon looked bleak. 'Did you catch any of them?'

'No. They were gone before our chaps arrived. The swine don't care what damage they do or whether they injure anybody. This time an old chestnut seller was badly burned when they knocked over his brazier.'

Gideon stiffened. 'Chestnut seller? Where was his pitch?'

'Just past the National Portrait Gallery, near Leicester Square,' the Superintendent answered.

Gideon pressed a bell on his desk and when his assistant came in he said quickly, 'A chestnut seller was burned last night near Leicester Square. Find out what his name was, where he is, and how he's doing.'

'Right,' said the assistant, a tall, lean, bony man named Lemaitre.

'Do you know the fellow?' asked the Welshman.

'If it's the man I think it is, I've known him for thirty years,' said Gideon. 'Have you put in your report yet?'

'It's being typed out now.'

'See that I get a copy,' Gideon ordered.

Very soon he learned that it was indeed Ben Fairley, that old Ben was comfortable, but that for a man of his age the shock might have grave consequences.

'His hands are burned so badly that he won't roast any more chestnuts for some time,' Lemaitre reported. 'He can see visitors, though.'

'Have we got a man with him?'

'Lloyd didn't ask for one,' Lemaitre said defensively. 'It isn't as if he were involved in any particular crime. Just these young hooligans fighting among themselves.'

Gideon grunted.

He studied the brief report, prepared as routine, as well as two statements from eyewitnesses, which also said very little. Armed with these, Gideon went to have a word with old Ben at the Charing Cross Hospital. He had never seen the man washed and shaved before. Both of Ben's hands were heavily bandaged, and he looked tired and worn; but his eyes were bright in his lined face, and his frail voice held a note of anger.

'Just rushed at me, they did, and *I'd* never done them any harm. Never even seen them before in my life!'

'We'll get them, Ben,' said Gideon; and he meant to. 'Tell me a little more, will you?'

'There's nothing more to tell,' said old Ben. 'One lot came up in one taxi and the other lot came up in another. Just rushed at me, they did.'

'How did you burn your hands?' asked Gideon.

Ben looked at him as if wondering how an intelligent man could ask such a question.

'Trying to save my chestnuts, of course. They were my capital, Mr Gideon – I needed them if I was going to stay in business.'

'I'll see that you stay in business,' promised Gideon. 'Now, Ben, what happened after that? The report says there were no chestnuts left in the basket.'

'The so-and-sos grabbed them,' said Ben, anger making his voice hoarse. 'Fancy stealing a few bobs' worth of chestnuts from an old man! How mean can you get?'

'Don't you worry about it,' said Gideon soothingly. 'Just tell me this. How many chestnuts did you have?'

'About five pounds – in weight. I mean. That would be including those the young lady gave me. But Mr Gideon – '

'Young lady?' interrupted Gideon sharply. 'What young lady? And when did she give you the chestnuts?'

'Yesterday afternoon, Mr Gideon. She came out of one of those new apartment houses at the back of Oxford Street. I've seen her several times as I've pushed my barrow past there – it's on my route to the pitch, see. "Hello, dad," she says, "I've got something for you." Then she hands me a great big bag of chestnuts. Beauties, they were – otherwise I wouldn't have sold them,' added Ben virtuously.

Gideon leaned forward. 'Now, Ben, think hard. Are you quite sure about all this?'

'''Course I'm sure!' cried Ben. 'A bit of all right, she is, with long blonde hair hanging down her back. Funny thing, life, ain't it, Mr Gideon? In the afternoon someone gives me chestnuts – in the evening someone pinches 'em, and my own with 'em.'

Gideon was looking thoughtful. 'One of the new apartment houses behind Oxford Street,' he murmured to himself. 'Blonde. Hmm.' Slowly he got to his feet. 'Yes, it's a funny life, Ben. But you take it easy. When you're well, I'll see you get all you need to start up in business again.'

Leaving the hospital Gideon hurried back to New Scotland Yard, and as soon as he reached his office he sent for Superintendent Lloyd.

'Any lead on those lads in the fight last night?' Gideon asked.

'No, Commander. Two of our chaps saw them, but they weren't the usual Soho troublemakers. That's the problem – it's contagious. What fun they got out of snatching a few chestnuts, heaven only knows.'

'Check with N.E. Division on Dicey Gamble and find out if he still lives in one of the new apartment houses behind Oxford Street,' said Gideon. 'And find out what colour his wife's hair is – she used to bleach it,' he added thoughtfully.

Lloyd looked up sharply.

'Dicey? I saw him only last week, and he's still living in that flat – must cost him a fortune. His wife's a blonde.'

'A bit of all right?' inquired Gideon. 'With long hair?'

'You've got her to a T,' said Lloyd. 'Why she ever married that thieving slob I'll never know. What's on your mind about Dicey?'

Dicey Gamble was the leader of a small group of smash-and-grab raiders who specialized in robbing jewellery shops. He had already been to prison once, and some of his 'boys' were still inside, but he could always find others to join him.

'Call it a long shot,' replied Gideon. 'Tell N.E. Division to find out if any of his gang bought any chestnuts recently. If necessary, check every grocer in the district. Get a move on, there's no time to lose.'

The Superintendent hurried out and within an hour he was on the telephone to Gideon.

'You were right, sir! One of Dicey Gamble's boys bought two pounds of chestnuts yesterday morning.'

'Good! Get all the help you need and raid Dicey's apartment straight away,' Gideon ordered. 'I'm just going home. Phone me there and let me know what happens.'

He wished, as he so often did, that he could take an active part in what was to follow; in this, at least, he envied his subordinates, who had the stimulus and excitement of physical action.

At seven o'clock that evening the police from N.E. Division and from the Yard arrived at Dicey Gamble's apartment.

Panic showed in Dicey's eyes when the Yard men appeared at his door, but the panic was quickly veiled.

'I've got nothing here, Super,' he insisted. 'You can search the place, but you won't find anything.'

Lloyd looked at him squarely. 'You won't get away with that old chestnut, Dicey.'

The colour drained from Dicey's face. Lloyd pushed past him and walked through the apartment, stopping short when he came to the kitchen. The table was covered with a sheet of newspaper, and on the newspaper was a pile of chestnuts. Dicey had obviously been in the process of cutting each nut in two — several had already been halved.

In eight of the halves, buried inside the hard nuts, were diamonds.

'There's nothing new in this game,' Gideon explained to Lloyd. 'I once knew a thief who split a hazelnut in two, put a diamond inside, and stuck the shell together. The gangs that attacked old Ben obviously weren't in it for the sheer fun — so they were in it for the chestnuts. Add to that the fact that old Ben was given chestnuts by a woman who lived in the same house as one of our cleverest jewel thieves, and it all started to make sense.'

'I'll say it made sense,' agreed Lloyd. 'Dicey and his mob had these hot diamonds and hid them in the chestnuts. One of the boys dumped them at Dicey's flat, on instructions. But Dicey was out, and as neither he nor his wife eat chestnuts, wifey gave them to old Ben.'

'Everyone says she's a bit of all right,' murmured Gideon.

Later that day, as he sat with old Ben at the Charing Cross Hospital, Gideon finished the story.

'As soon as Dicey discovered what his wife had done, he got his mob together for a raid on your barrow to get back the chestnuts – but in getting word to his boys, another gang learned what had happened and reached you first. Dicey's lot caught up with them. Simple Ben, wasn't it?'

Old Ben gave a slow, pleased smile. Perhaps when he next roasted chestnuts he would dream of a fortune in diamonds.

Light-Fingers

---◆---

FRANCIS DURBRIDGE

Paul Temple, the novelist and amateur detective, became one of the most popular characters on BBC radio during the years of the Second World War and was later successfully transferred into films and television. A clean cut, tough and sinewy man, his satisfaction comes from 'ferreting out murky truth wherever it lies at the bottom of the social burrow and giving it a figurative one-from-the-shoulder between its shifty eyes', according to his creator, Francis Durbridge. Radio Times added to this pen-picture of Temple in 1960 when introducing a new serial by claiming that, 'The "Emperor" of the private-eyes, those brave and upright incorruptibles whom the public love because they are larger than life, uncomplicated in their psyches and bound to prevail over cunning and guile, is Mr Paul Temple with his soignee little mate, Steve, working right alongside.' The radio series, in fact, flourished for thirty years from 1938 to 1968, opening with Hugh Morton and Marjorie Westbury, the latter of whom remained with the programme until its finale, despite several new Paul Temples: Carl Bernard, Barry Morse, Howard Marion Crawford, Kim Peacock and, lastly, Peter Coke. The first film, Calling Paul Temple was made in 1948, with John Bentley, the star of many low-budget post war British action movies, in the lead role. Dinah Sheridan was Steve in this picture as well as its two sequels, Paul Temple's Triumph (1950) and Paul Temple Returns (1952). She also repeated the role when she and Bentley starred in the twelve-episode BBC TV series, Paul Temple, also scripted by Durbridge, which was screened in 1968.

Francis Durbridge (1912–   ) began his career as the author of mystery novels, but his name became familiar to the public through his

*many radio, film and TV scripts, in particular the Paul Temple stories
and the adventures of his other private detective, Tim Frazer. He later
adapted a number of the Temple cases into novels and one of them,*
Paul Temple and the Front Page Men, *became a stage play. Light-
Fingers was similarly adapted from a special half-hour Christmas
broadcast in 1950 and today's readers will doubtless be amused by
the last of the three clues which Paul Temple reveals . . .*

PAUL Temple, popular novelist and famous private detective,
placed a red carnation in the buttonhole of his dinner jacket,
flicked a fleck of dust from his trousers, and carefully adjusted his
evening-dress bow. It was New Year's Eve and both the novelist and
Mrs Temple – known affectionately as Steve – had been invited to a
dinner party.

The party was to be held at Nicholas Hall, a delightful old manor
house on the Hog's Back just outside Guildford. The Hall belonged to
a friend of Paul Temple's called Sir Stephen Peters. Every year Sir
Stephen gave a New Year's Eve party and both Paul and Steve were
invited.

It was just after six o'clock when Steve climbed into the driving-seat
of her husband's new sports car and turned the bonnet of the car
southwards.

'Now drive carefully, Steve,' warned Temple. 'Remember the roads
are very treacherous at this time of the year.'

Steve smiled, for in spite of the fact that she was a careful driver, they
never started out on a journey without Temple administering a
friendly warning. As the car glided away from the kerb and made for
the open country, Steve glanced down at the illuminated clock on the
dashboard.

'How long should it take us to reach Guildford, Paul?'

There was a twinkle in Temple's eye as he said: 'We may never reach
there if you don't keep your eyes on the road!'

'If there are any more complaints about my driving, Mr Temple, I
shall insist that you get out and walk!'

Temple glanced across at his wife and chuckled softly to himself. It
was a funny thing about Steve, he reflected, although she was a very
keen driver she never seemed to be completely relaxed. Even now she

sat clutching the wheel with both hands, an expression of grim determination on her features.

When the car came to a standstill at the last set of traffic lights, just before they reached the open country, Steve did manage to relax slightly and remove her hands from the steering-wheel.

The lights changed from amber to green and the car moved forward.

Temple glanced into the driving-mirror and suddenly sat bolt upright.

'By Timothy,' he said, 'this fellow behind us seems to be in a hurry!'

Steve turned her head and noticed a black saloon car bearing down on them.

'You'll have to pull into the side, Steve!' exclaimed Temple. 'Or he'll force you into the hedge!'

As Temple spoke the overtaking car lurched forward and Steve instinctively reached for the handbrake. There was a scraping of metal and a sudden bump as the back mudguard of the saloon caught the wing of Temple's car. Steve skilfully manoeuvred the car into the side and as it came to a standstill switched on the headlights. In the distance they could see the saloon roaring its way down the country road. In a little while it was completely out of sight.

Steve sat for a moment trying to regain her breath; she was obviously a little frightened.

Temple said, very quietly: 'That was excellent driving, my dear. If you'd lost your head we should have been involved in a very nasty accident.'

'Did you notice the driver of the car?'

Temple shook his head. 'He was heavily muffled and he wore his hat right down over his eyes. I doubt very much whether I should recognize him again.' He got out of the car and surveyed the damage. The wing was scratched and there was a dent near the offside lamp.

'You've had a nasty shock, Steve. You'd better let me drive for the rest of the journey.' As he climbed into the driving-seat Temple heard the sudden whir of a motor-horn and the sound of an approaching car. Steve was already staring out of the window unable to suppress her excitement.

'Here's a police car, Paul!' she shouted. 'I believe they're chasing the man who bumped into us.'

The police car came to a sudden halt and Temple recognized his old friend Chief-Inspector Brooks.

Temple lowered the window.

'What's happened, Inspector?'

The inspector was a thickset man with a jovial face and a weather-beaten countenance. He looked more like a farmer than a police inspector and because of this his enemies frequently underrated him. Brooks was in fact a shrewd north-countryman with an intimate knowledge of the London underworld.

'There's been a robbery at Malfrey's the jewellers in New Bond Street. "Light-Fingers" Layman made a smash-and-grab. He got away with a diamond necklace worth thirty thousand pounds.'

Temple said: 'A black saloon crashed into us. It was driven by a man in a dark overcoat and a muffler over his face – was that the notorious Layman?'

The inspector nodded. 'Yes, that was "Light-Fingers" all right. Which way did he go, Temple?'

'He went straight down the road ahead,' volunteered Steve. 'The number of the car was UMX 829.'

'We know the number of the car, Mrs Temple,' said Brooks, 'but if he once makes a get-away, ten to one he'll abandon the car or change the number plates.' As the inspector spoke the police car shot forward and before Temple had even time to wave good-bye it was nearly out of sight.

'Have you heard of "Light-Fingers" Layman?' asked Steve.

Temple changed gear and the sports car once again moved forward into the centre of the road.

'I first heard of him two or three years ago when he broke into the North Midfield Bank at Exeter. "Light-Fingers" is what they call a lone operator – he works entirely on his own.'

'Would you recognize him if you saw him?'

'I very much doubt it,' said Temple. 'I've only seen photographs of him. If I remember rightly he has rather a nasty scar across the back of his left hand.'

The car gathered speed and Paul Temple found himself thinking of 'Light-Fingers' Layman; although he had never actually encountered 'Light-Fingers' the novelist knew only too well, from the confidential reports he had seen on the Exeter Case at Scotland Yard, that he was a most dangerous criminal.

After they had been driving for about a quarter of an hour Steve suddenly drew Temple's attention to the police car. It was about a hundred yards ahead of them, parked by the side of the road under a huge tree.

Temple took his foot off the accelerator.

'What's happened, Inspector?' he called.

There was a look of both annoyance and bitter disappointment on the inspector's face. He nodded towards the uniformed sergeant who was busy working the radio transmitter. 'We've got a cordon round the entire district but it looks as if "Light-Fingers" has given us the slip, Temple.'

'We'll keep our eyes open, Inspector. If we see anything suspicious I'll phone Sergeant O'Hara at Guildford.'

Ten minutes later Temple *did* see something suspicious and he was so surprised that he took his eyes off the road and grabbed Steve by the arm.

'Look where you're going, Paul!' ejaculated Steve.

Temple applied the brakes and the car came to a standstill.

He switched on the headlights.

'Do you see what I see, Steve?'

Steve turned her head and then suddenly she realized what her husband was staring at. In a little clearing, about ten or twenty yards down from the main road, stood the black saloon car. It had obviously been forced off the road, or deliberately driven off, for the front wheels rested in a narrow ditch and the radiator was embedded in the bank.

While they were watching the car a man came running up the bank and on to the road. He was a nervous, shrivelled-up little man with a clean-shaven face and long dark hair. He carried his overcoat over his left arm. The man hesitated for a moment, shielding his eyes from the glare of the headlights.

Paul Temple took careful stock of the stranger before dimming the lights. The man certainly didn't look like the notorious 'Light-Fingers' although there was a nasty cut across the lower part of his face which added a sinister touch to his appearance. The stranger hurried across to Temple and introduced himself. He explained that his name was Professor Thompson and that he was on his way to Guildford.

'I was driving along in my car when suddenly this car,' he pointed to the black saloon, 'overtook me and crashed into the ditch. I hurried down the bank to see if I could be of any assistance but to my astonishment . . .'

'The driver of the other vehicle knocked you out and stole your car,' said Temple.

The little man nodded; he looked both surprised and relieved. 'But that's exactly what happened!' he stammered. 'How on earth did you know?'

Temple told the professor about the robbery and about 'Light-Fingers' Layman, adding: 'You'd better let us drive you into Guildford, Professor.'

The professor was highly delighted at the suggestion and lost no time climbing into Temple's car. 'I should be extremely grateful if you would drive me into Guildford,' he said. 'I have a most important appointment at eight o'clock.' The little man seemed far more concerned about keeping his appointment than about the arrest of 'Light-Fingers' and the recovery of the stolen car.

'What sort of car were you driving?' asked Temple.

'It's a brand new Austin – this year's model. It's dark maroon and the registration number is EKL 974.'

'Well, that shouldn't be difficult to find,' said Temple. 'I'll contact the police as soon as we come to the next 'phone box.'

'Oh, dear!' said the professor. 'This is most disturbing. I do hope I shan't be late for my appointment!'

Paul Temple smiled, moved the gear into position and released the clutch. 'Your appointment must be a very important one, Professor.'

The professor nodded. 'I'm an antique dealer and a collector of rare coins,' he explained. 'Earlier this evening a lady telephoned me from Guildford with the exciting news that she had discovered a Queen Elizabeth Bank of England note and that she was prepared to consider a reasonable offer for it.'

'Is the note valuable?' asked Steve.

'Valuable!' The professor was obviously thunderstruck by such a question. 'It's unique!' he exclaimed. 'All my life I've been on the lookout for such a treasure.'

Temple said: 'I suppose you're anxious to contact the lady before any of the other collectors get to hear of the discovery.'

The professor looked very worried. 'That's exactly what I'm afraid of!' he said. 'I simply must get to Guildford before any of the Bond Street collectors.'

'Well, we'll do the best we can, Professor,' said Temple, 'but I'm afraid you'll have to wait while I telephone the police.'

The nearest telephone was at the crossroads a mile or so down the road. Temple stopped the car and, after pocketing the ignition key, crossed the grass plot to the telephone box.

'I want to speak to Sergeant O'Hara,' said Temple, when the telephone operator put him through to police headquarters.

Sergeant O'Hara was delighted to hear from Paul Temple for he had known Temple in the old days when the novelist had investigated the 'Front-Page-Men' affair.

'Compliments of the season!' bellowed the little Irishman, 'but what in the wide world brings you down to this part o' the country now?'

Temple spoke very quietly, and as he spoke he stared out of the telephone box at the professor and Steve who were engaged in an animated conversation.

Temple said: 'Listen, Sergeant! Steve and I are on our way to Nicholas Hall and we want you to send a police car out to meet us. We should reach the outskirts of Guildford in about a quarter of an hour.'

Although O'Hara was bewildered he sensed the tone of urgency in Temple's voice.

'Is anything the matter?' he said quietly.

Paul Temple said: 'Yes, I've got the man you're looking for – I picked him up five minutes ago.'

The sergeant gasped. He knew that Temple must be referring to 'Light-Fingers' Layman.

'By the Lord Harry!' he stammered, unable to believe his own ears. 'Not "Light-Fingers" Layman?'

' "Light-Fingers" Layman,' said Paul Temple quietly.

And ten minutes later, thanks to the astuteness of Paul Temple, the notorious 'Light-Fingers' was arrested.

*　　*　　*

Later than night, or rather in the early hours of the New Year, Paul Temple told Steve and his old friend Sir Stephen Peters why he had suspected the bogus 'professor'. 'As soon as I saw him carrying his overcoat over his left arm I was suspicious,' said Temple. 'It was a very cold night and yet obviously he was determined not to wear his coat. I realized however that the overcoat must be serving a particular purpose – it was in fact *concealing the scar on the back of his left hand.*'

'That was Clue number one,' said Steve, 'but what was the second clue, Paul?'

'The second clue,' explained Temple, 'was when the "professor" said that his car had been stolen. He described the car as a brand new model, registration number *EKL 974.* I knew that he was lying immediately he told me the registration number. *A new car would never be registered as EKL – these letters belong to the 1938 or '39 period.*'

'And the third clue?' asked Sir Stephen.

'The third clue was the most important of them all,' said Temple. 'It was when the "professor" pretended to be a collector of rare coins. He said that he was going to Guildford in order to buy a very valuable Queen Elizabeth Bank of England note.'

'Well?' said Steve, obviously puzzled.

Paul Temple smiled. '*There is no such thing as a Queen Elizabeth Bank of England note,*' he said quietly. '*Such notes did not exist in the time of Queen Elizabeth. The first Bank of England note was issued in 1694.'*

The All-Bad Hat

H. R. F. KEATING

Inspector Ganesh Ghote, the homicide expert in the Bombay CID, is a mixture of naivety and brilliance, who seems always likely to become the victim of either the tough criminals he encounters or the unfeeling superiors who order his day-to-day existence — yet somehow he still manages to succeed. As the first Indian detective in modern fiction, the debut of Inspector Ghote (it is pronounced Go-tay) in The Perfect Murder *in 1964 attracted widespread attention, and the subsequent novels with their colourful pictures of the customs and speech patterns of Indian life, not to mention the drug smugglers, kidnappers and murderers he pursues, have not disappointed the growing number of readers. The adaptation of Ghote for a BBC TV series in 1969 increased the little detective's fame still further, aided in no small degree by the excellent performance in the central role by the versatile Indian actor, Zia Mohyeddin.*

H. R. F. Keating (1926–   ) was himself an employee of the BBC engineering department before becoming a journalist and then a successful crime novelist. His reputation was made by the first of the Ghote novels, The Perfect Murder, *which won the Crime Writers' Association Best Mystery Novel Award and also a special award from the Mystery Writers of America. Several critics have referred to the Inspector as 'one of the great characters of the contemporary mystery novel' — and he is again in excellent form in this short story written in 1984.*

INSPECTOR Ghote of the Bombay CID was not a frequenter of record shops. But on this occasion he was on an important errand. It was soon to be his son Ved's birthday, and Ghote's wife, Protima, had declared that the one thing the boy really wanted as a present was a record of the title song from the new hit movie *Sant aur Badmash*, the one in which two brothers are separated soon after their birth and one becomes a holyman, a saint, a *sant*, and the other becomes a deepest-dyed villain, a *badmash*. And in the last reel they are reconciled.

But Ghote was not finding it easy to make his purchase. From loudspeakers in all four corners of the smart new shop – he had been told it was the best in Bombay – music was pounding out at maximum volume. His attempts to make anyone behind the counter hear had so far come to nothing.

At last he could stand the frustration no longer. He leant across the glossy counter, seized a young man behind it by the sides of his silk *kurta*, and drew him close.

'Please to stop all this noise,' he demanded.

'Noise?' said the young man, or rather *shouted* the young man. 'What noise is it?'

'That music. That damn music. Kindly get owner here to turn down volume.'

'I am owner,' the young man answered. 'Sole proprietor, Loafer's Delight Disc Mart.'

'Then you must turn down the volume,' Ghote shouted. 'Now.'

'Cool it, man,' the younger proprietor shouted back. 'Be cooling it. That volume's good.'

'It is bad. Bad, I tell you. I am thinking it may be offence against the law.'

'The law? You are making me laugh, man.'

Ghote felt a jet of rage fountain up inside him.

'I am an inspector of police,' he shouted.

'That is swinging, man,' the proprietor riposted. 'And I am the son of the Minister for Home.'

'Please to behave,' Ghote answered, sharply dismissing such impudence.

But whether the young man would have obeyed this injunction or not was never to be put to the test. Down near the entrance of the long, tunnel-like shop, with its smart new racks of records and tapes and its dazzling posters decorating every wall, someone else was not behaving well.

In fact, two tough-looking men, roughly dressed in contrast to the shop's smart clientele, were behaving extremely badly.

One of the record racks had already been deliberately knocked over. As the shop's young proprietor reduced the volume of his massive loudspeakers almost to nothing, more as a response to the trouble near the entrance than to Ghote's demand, Ghote was able to hear what one of the newcomers was calling out to the other.

'Hey, Chandra bhai, these stands, see how easy they tip over.'

'Yes, yes,' the other man, a turbaned Sikh, called back. 'And these posters. So nice. But, look, already they are torn.'

They were not as he spoke. But two instants later they were torn indeed, ripped right off the walls by the man himself.

'Stop,' screamed the young proprietor. 'Stop. Those are imported. Two hundred rupees each.'

Rip. Rip. Rip. Another six hundred rupees went cascading to the floor.

'All right,' Ghote said. 'I will deal with those two.'

He began making his way purposefully down the length of the narrow shop. But the place was too crowded for him to be able to get anywhere near the two troublemakers before, with cheerful shouts of 'Sorry, Mr Loafer' and 'Good-bye, Mr Loafer Delight,' they had reached the entrance and disappeared among the packed pavements of Mahatma Gandhi Road.

However, Ghote had had plenty of time to study the faces of the two goondas and had hurried back to CID Headquarters and there gone through the fat, tattered books of criminals in the Records section. It had not taken him long to find the two. The Sikh was one Iqbal Singh and the other was a certain Chandra Chagoo.

'I do not think I would have too much of difficulty to nab the pair of them, sir,' Ghote said to Assistant Commissioner of Police Samant a quarter of an hour later.

'You are not even to try, Inspector.'

Ghote blinked.

'Not to try, ACP sahib? But already I am knowing the favoured haunts of those two. I can have them behind the bars in no time at all.'

'You are not to waste your time.'

Ghote stared at the ACP across his wide, semicircular desk with its clutter of telephones, pen sets, and teacups. He really could not believe he had heard what he had.

'But, sir,' he pleaded, 'if you had seen those two goondas, the way they set about breaking up that place, sir. It was a matter of deliberate destruction at a Number One level.'

'No doubt, no doubt, Inspector. And you know why they were doing all that?'

'Protection racket, sir. The young fellow who owns the place was telling me afterwards. He had been asked to pay and said he would rely upon the police to protect him. It is a very black mark for us, sir.'

'And you know why a pair of goondas like that can get away with doing such things, Inspector?'

'No, sir,' Ghote had to answer after thinking hard.

'It is because those two goondas that you were taking such trouble to impress on your memory, Inspector, are not more than small fries only.'

'Small fries, sir?'

'Exactly, Inspector. You can nab them if you want, but when they come up before the Magistrate, what would we find?'

Ghote decided to leave the Assistant Commissioner to answer his own question.

'We would find that they are having alibis, Inspector. First-class alibis. Two, three, four seemingly respectable fellows willing to swear that at the time in question our two friends were not in Bombay even. And a damn fine advocate to back up the tale.'

'But . . . but, ACP sahib, alibis and advocates are costing very much of money. And those two did not look as if they are have more than two paisa to rub together.'

'Quite right, Inspector.'

'But then . . .'

'But the fellow they are working for has got all the paisa you could wish for.'

'And that is who, ACP?'

'It is Daddyji.'

'Daddyji, sir?'

'Yes, Inspector. Other names he has and has. But Daddyji he is known as always. If you had worked on protection racket cases before you would have known.'

'Yes, sir. He is running many many such rackets then?'

'Not so many, Inspector.'

'But, sir, if he is not running many many, then how is he so wealthy that he can afford such alibis and advocates?'

'It is because of the kind of places he is specializing in protecting, Inspector. He likes only the best. Anything that is particularly fine. Best class places only.'

'I see, sir. Yes, that is bad.'

'He *is* bad, Inspector. Daddyji *is* bad. He is nothing less than an all-bad hat.'

Until this moment, Ghote had been following the ACP's

explanation with all dutifulness. But these last words stuck in his craw. An all-bad hat? All bad? He could not find it in himself to believe it. And foolishly he ventured to express that doubt.

'But, sir, no man is altogether . . .'

'What is this, Inspector? You, a police officer. You have seen plenty of miscreants, I hope. Am I going to hear you tell me there is no such thing as an all-bad man?'

'But . . .'

Ghote thought better of it.

'No, sir.'

'Hmm. Well, I grant that most criminals are not all-bad. They are lacking in the guts to be. But that is not meaning that there are not all-bad men, and of them all, Inspector, the man by the name of Daddyji is the worst. The worst.'

'But, sir . . .'

'No. Let me tell a thing or two about Daddyji, Inspector. Have you got a father?'

'Sir, everybody is having a father. They may not still be . . .'

'Good. Well, now, perhaps you may not have had good relations with your father. But nevertheless, you were treating him always with a certain respect, isn't it?'

'Yes, sir.'

'Daddyji has a father, Inspector. He used to run the gang that Daddyji now has. A pretty tough chap, also. But then came the day when Daddyji thought it was time that he took over. Do you know where that father is now, Inspector?'

'No, sir.'

'Take a walk down to Flora Fountain, Inspector. There you would see a crippled man, propped up against the wall, selling little clay figures that he is making.'

'Yes, sir. I am knowing him. Very very popular with tourists, the figures he is making. Most lively objects.'

'And damn close to falling under Indian Penal Code, Section 292.'

'Obscene books and objects, sir. Yes, sir, I think you are right.'

'But it is not those that I am concerned with, Inspector. It is his legs.'

'His legs, sir?'

'I suppose you are too busy always looking at those figures. But that man's legs are smashed to pieces, Inspector. And it was his own son who was doing that.'

'I see, sir. Yes, a very bad hat.'

'No, Inspector. An all-bad hat. An all-bad hat. And much too clever to be nabbed by one inspector only. So, leave him . . .'

He broke off as one of the phones on his wide desk shrilled out. He picked up the receiver.

'Samant. What is it? Oh. Oh, yes, sir. Yes, Minister sahib. Yes? Yes, your son, Minister sahib. Yes, I see, sir. Yes, yes. Yes, at once. At once, Minister sahib.'

Slowly ACP Samant put down the receiver. He gave Ghote, standing neatly to attention on the far side of his desk, a slow, assessing look.

'So, Inspector, as I was telling, it is not going to be at all easy to pull in Daddyji. But we are going to do it. You are going to do it. He has a place down in Colaba. Go over there *ek dum* and get out of him something. Something to have him fairly and squarely on a first-class foolproof charge.'

So, scarcely half an hour later, Ghote was standing face to face with the man ACP Samant had pronounced to be all-bad.

Certainly, he thought – looking at the burly frame, the almost bald bullet head with the thick knife scar running above the left eyebrow, and the expression of sullen coldness in the deep-set eyes – the fellow has all the appearance of somebody who is bad. Very bad even. But all-bad?

In spite of everything the ACP had said, Ghote kept his reservations.

'Well,' he said, 'so you are the famous Daddyji I have heard and read a lot about. But you are not so big as I was expecting. You are not much taller than myself.'

'But twice as hard,' said Daddyji, his voice grinding out.

'Perhaps. But let me tell you something. However hard or not hard I am, the CID itself is harder than you, Daddyji. Than you or anyone – than any man with a man's weaknesses.'

'But I am here. And this is not Thana Gaol.'

'No, it is not. But the day for Thana Gaol is coming.'

'All kinds of days are coming. The day when elephants are flying, the day when the sea is drying up. But still I am able to do what I want.'

'But perhaps that time is going to end sooner than you think. I have a feeling that now you have gone too far.'

'I go where I like. Where do you think is too far, my little inspector?'

'I think,' Ghote said slowly, 'the Loafer's Delight Disc Mart was too far. The owner is the son of the Minister for Home.'

But his threat, if threat it was, received only a roar of uninhibited laughter from the gang boss.

'Oh,' he said, wiping his eyes, 'that I was not knowing.'

'Not when you were ordering his shop to be pulled to pieces?' Ghote slipped in.

But his ruse was by no means clever enough.

'I order, Inspector?' Daddyji answered blandly. 'But why should you be thinking that?'

'Because that is your modus operandi,' Ghote replied. 'That is the pattern you are always working to, Daddyji. We know very much about you already.'

'You know nothing.'

'Oh, perhaps not enough to get a conviction today. But no man is perfect, and one day you would make mistake.'

'Oh, yes, mistake and mistake I will make. But it will be no matter.'

'No matter?'

Daddyji shrugged.

'If I am making mistake,' he said, 'it would maybe cost me plenty plenty. But plenty plenty I have. So good-bye to catching Daddyji, Inspector.'

'Nevertheless,' Ghote said, 'I require you to answer certain questions.'

'Answers cost nothing.'

'If they are not true, they will cost you your freedom.'

But Daddyji only smiled.

'They will cost me only the price of making them true after, my little inspector,' he said. 'And lies are cheap enough.'

'We shall see. Now, where were you at three-fifteen pip emma today?'

'That is easy. I was here. I am always careful to be with friends at such times, and I was talking with a police constable I am knowing.'

'At such times?' Ghote leapt in. 'Why were you saying "at such times"?'

Daddyji smiled again.

'At such times? At afternoon times only, Inspector. It is at such times that a man feels sad, and then it is good to talk. Especially with a police constable.'

'Very well. Then tell me, when did you last see two men by the names of Iqbal Singh and Chandra Chagoo?'

'Inspector, will you say those names again?'

'You are very well knowing them.'

'Inspector, I have never heard of any such persons. Who are they, please?'

'They are the men you instructed to break up the Loafer's Delight Disc Mart.'

Daddyji looked Ghote straight in the eye.

'And you would never be able to prove that, Inspector,' he said. 'You would never be able to prove that we have ever even met.'

So Ghote hardly had anything very successful to report. And ACP Samant was not very pleased.

'And I suppose now,' he snapped, 'you are proposing to sit upon your bottom and say "no can do"'?

'No, sir,' Ghote answered firmly.

'No, sir. No, sir. Then what are you proposing to do, man?'

'Sir, from my examination of the material in Records I have come to the conclusion there is one good line still to take.'

'Records. Records. You are all alike. If it is hiding in Records with a good fan blowing down on you in the heat, you are willing to work and to work. But if it is getting out into the hot streets, you are thinking differently.'

'But, sir, I am about to go out into the hot . . . into the streets, sir. To interview the owner of the only place so far to have defied Daddyji's goondas, sir. An establishment by the name of the Galerie Sodawaterwala.'

'Galerie? Galerie? What sort of a place is that?'

'It is an art gallery, ACP sahib, and also a shop for the sale of curios and other objects.'

'Thank you for telling me, Inspector. And I suppose next you are going to inform me that Sodawaterwala is an old Parsi name. But give me credit for knowing a little bit about some things, Inspector.'

'Yes, sir. No, sir. Sorry, sir.'

'Well, what for are you standing there, man? Get out there to this Sodawaterwala Gallery and talk to the man.'

Mr Sodawaterwala seemed well named. He was a meek and mild-looking individual, evidently with all the artistic leanings of the ancient Parsi community fully developed. But he had refused to pay Daddyji's men any protection money. Even after the police guard he had been given, when he had reported the approach first, had eventually been withdrawn.

'And nothing has happened since those men were withdrawn?' Ghote asked him, with surprise.

'Ah, no, Inspector. But, you see, I took certain steps.'

'Steps?'

Mr Sodawaterwala heaved a neat little sigh.

'Inspector,' he said, 'I must confess. I hired goondas of my own.'

'Criminal types? But, Mr Sodawaterwala . . .'

'Yes, yes. But what was I to do? The very day the police guard was withdrawn, I spotted on the far pavement there the very men who had earlier demanded money. But I am glad to say, Inspector, that both the fellows I hired proved to be altogether charming chaps.'

'I am glad to hear.'

'Yes, yes. Goondas they may have been, but thoroughly willing and dependable fellows, both.'

'They may have *been*, Mr Sodawaterwala? Are they then with you no more?'

'No, no. They are here always by day. But by night, I regret to say, I have been unable to find any others as dependable.'

'But have you then left the premises unguarded at night?'

Mr Sodawaterwala suddenly smiled with tremendous impishness.

'No, no, no, indeed,' he said. 'Come this way, Inspector, and I will show you something.'

He led Ghote to an upstairs office over the big gallery showroom, throwing open its door with a flourish. And there, sitting on two stools, were what Ghote took to be at first sight a pair of the most villainous looking goondas he had ever met.

But then he stood peering in at the dimly lit room and looked again.

'They are not real?' he asked. 'They are dummies only?'

Mr Sodawaterwala giggled in glee.

'Exactly so, Inspector. Exactly so. A ruse I borrowed from my extensive reading of the crime stories of the West. The Saint, Sherlock Holmes, and so forth. These are just such models as deceived the fierce Colonel Moran when Holmes returned from the dead.'

'You were making yourself?' Ghote asked, looking more closely at the extremely lifelike heads.

'No, no, my dear sir. I have no talent in that direction. Yet I am inclined to bet that you will never guess who did indeed make these altogether excellent figures.'

'One of the artists whose work you are selling?'

'No, no. Not at all, not at all.'

'Then I am unable to guess.'

'They were made, my dear sir, by none other than my sweeper boy.'

'A sweeper. But . . .'

'Yes, yes. But how could a sweeper, a boy of the lowest class, have such a talent? You are right to ask. But, Inspector, let it be a lesson to us. Never underestimate the abilities and complexity of any human being whatsoever.'

'He made them by himself, without any assistance?' Ghote asked, looking again at the uncannily lifelike models, still only half able to believe that someone young and untutored could possess such ability.

'Something like a miracle, is it not?' the dapper little Parsi gallery owner said. 'And, more than this, the boy – he is about sixteen years of age only – came to me like a miracle.'

'How was that?' Ghote asked.

'Well, one morning a few weeks ago my old sweeper, who had been with me for years, announced suddenly that he was leaving. I offered him an increment. I offered him a better place to sleep. He had the use of this cupboard here under the stair. Look.'

Mr Sodawaterwala led Ghote to a small door under the stairs and opened it with a flourish.

'You will meet my miracle . . .' he began.

Then his voice came to an abrupt halt.

'But . . . but this is extraordinary,' he said.

'What is it?' Ghote asked, alerted by the note of bewilderment in the Parsi's tone.

'The boy, Piloo. He has gone. Look. All his few possessions, they are here no more. And his pictures. His pictures have gone.'

'What pictures are these?' Ghote asked.

'I was telling you, Inspector. Piloo came to me asking for a job just the very day that my old sweeper left so unaccountably. But quite soon I discovered that Piloo was a remarkable artist. He began to play with some scraps of modelling clay that were lying about, and he made these really excellent small pictures. Scenes of everyday life, modelled in clay. I was going to put them on display even.'

'He knew this?'

'Yes, yes. Only three days ago I told him. And now he has gone. Vanished. And I really believe he would have become the Indian Hogarth.'

Ghote stood in silent tribute for a moment to this odd event in the gallery owner's life. But he could not waste more time.

'Mr Sodawaterwala,' he said, 'when I saw those dummies of your goonda guards, an idea came into my head. Can I ask you tonight not to put them in their usual place?'

Mr Sodawaterwala visibly paled.

'But, Inspector,' he said, 'in that case I very much fear I shall be visited by those fellows who threatened me. They will break up the gallery, perhaps even attack me, myself.'

'That they should come into the gallery is my object,' Ghote answered. 'But do not take away the dummies till a late hour. Say, after midnight. Before then I will come and conceal myself on the premises.'

'And catch the fellows red-handed?' Mr Sodawaterwala brightened.

'More than that I am hoping,' Ghote said. 'I hope to catch them and to get them to admit who sent them.'

'You think you can do that, Inspector?'

'I think I must do it, Mr Sodawaterwala.'

Ghote's mind was still filled with that determination as, just after eleven that night, he cautiously approached the darkened Galerie Sodawaterwala from the rear, the key to its back door, which Mr Sodawaterwala had given him, in his hand.

But he found the little door in the narrow dark lane already unlocked. Worse, forced open.

With pounding heart, he pushed into the echoing empty premises, flashing his pocket torch here and there. All seemed to be well. Nowhere was there any sign of the damage Daddyji's men were likely to have inflicted.

But then, from somewhere up above, he thought he detected a sound. A muffled groan.

He swung the flashlight beam round, located the stairs, pounded up them. Pausing for a moment at the top, he listened. And, yes, distinctly, another groan.

He ran forward.

Mr Sodawaterwala was lying on the floor in the middle of his little upstairs office. His face was black and bloodied. One of his legs was twisted under him at an angle that it should never have been. Both his hands were a mess of open wounds.

Ghote knelt beside him.

'Mr Sodawaterwala,' he said, 'I am here. I will fetch help. Do not try to move. Where is your telephone?'

'In gallery,' the battered Parsi managed. 'Down . . .'

'Yes, yes. Downstairs. I am going. Lie back. Help will be here in a few minutes only.'

And, indeed, an ambulance arrived in answer to Ghote's urgent call in a commendably short time. But the interval had been long enough for Mr Sodawaterwala to groan out to Ghote the details of what had happened.

'Daddyji' was the first word that he managed to mutter.

'Daddyji?' Ghote asked. 'Did he come himself? Was it him who did this to you?'

'He took pleasure . . . in telling . . . telling me.'

Ghote felt a renewed sense of angry determination.

'Then we shall get him,' he said. 'I am promising you that, Mr Sodawaterwala. But how was it that he knew this was a time to come? Were those dummies still in place?'

'Yes. Yes. Still there. As instructed. But Piloo. Piloo had gone.'

'Piloo? Your sweeper boy who disappeared this afternoon? What had he to do with this?'

'Brother.'

'Brother? I do not understand.'

'Piloo Daddyji's young brother. Daddyji told me. Told me make my old sweeper leave, put the boy in instead. Spy.'

Ghote, kneeling beside the broken body of the Parsi, whom he had not liked to move, thought for a little.

'But did you not tell it was some weeks since the boy came?' he asked at last. 'He had time to make the dummies, and for you to discover he was the Indian Garth-ho.'

'Hogarth. Hogarth. Very famous British artist. Scenes of low life.'

'I am sorry. Hogarth. Yes, Hogarth. But why, if he was sent as a spy, did he not tell Daddyji long ago that you were not really guarded?'

'Because I had told him what a talent he had. He refused for a time to tell his brother.'

'Daddyji told you this?'

'Boasted. Said he was giving me extra because . . . because of that.'

'Yes, that is very like the man,' Ghote said grimly. 'But now we would nab him. With your assistance we would do it.'

'No,' groaned the battered man on the floor beside him.

'But . . . but . . . No, lie back. Mr Sodawaterwala.'

'Inspector, I will not give evidence against that man.'

'But, Mr Sodawaterwala, this is the one good chance we have. A man of your reputation, a stainless witness against that man.'

'Inspector. Not what I thought I was. Not a fighter for good through and through. Insp . . . He told me what he would do to me next time.'

So it was with feelings of deep pessimism that Ghote reported next day to ACP Samant.

'Sir, Mr Sodawaterwala is recovering well in JJ Hospital. But he is adamant, sir. He will not give evidence.'

The ACP grunted noncommittally.

'And you say this boy, this Piloo, is Daddyji's younger brother?'

'Yes, sir. But if you are thinking that here is a way into that man's heart, I do not . . .'

'Heart? Heart? I tell you, Inspector, that sort of talk does not apply in the case of Daddyji. He is an all-bad hat. Understand that.'

'Yes, sir.'

'But the boy took away from the gallery these paintings or pictures or whatever?'

'Pictures in clay, sir. Mr Sodawaterwala believes they will make him the Indian Garth . . . the Indian Hogarth, sir.'

'I dare say. I dare say. But the point is that the clay was undoubtedly the property of Mr Sodawaterwala. So the boy stole it. And we are going to put him behind the bars for that.'

Ghote felt puzzled.

'But, sir, he was not anything to do with the raid on the Minister's son's record shop, sir.'

'But is the Minister to know that, Ghote? Is he? No, no, we tell Minister sahib that the boy was one of the two brothers and that it has been convenient to bring a charge against one only, and we assure him that the culprit will catch a damn long term of Rigorous Imprisonment. That will get the Minister off our back. And that, after all, is the object of the exercise.'

'But, sir,' Ghote said, flooded with sudden dismay. 'Sir, the boy is the Indian Hogarth. If he is sent to prison, India will lose her Hogarth.'

ACP Samant brought his fist crashing down onto his desk till every brass paperweight there jumped in the air.

'Inspector,' he stormed, 'unless you get down to Colaba and arrest that boy now, India will lost her Inspector Ghote.'

Less than an hour later, Ghote was once again facing the formidable figure of Daddyji. A smiling, contemptuous Daddyji.

'I had a feeling that I would be seeing you soon, my little inspector.'

'I expect so,' Ghote returned levelly. 'But I have not come to hear where you were at eleven pip emma last night.'

That did get home to the iron-tough crook.

'Not? Not? But you must want to know. I was far away. Out at Juhu Beach. With my friends Mahesh Khandwalla, Sudhakar Dalvi, Mohamed Hai, Sudhir . . .'

'Stop. However many names you are giving, I know you were at the Galerie Sodawaterwala committing grievous bodily harm.'

Daddyji brightened at this. Here was a game where he knew the score.

'And you have witnesses?' he asked. 'As many as I have?'

'I have one witness. The best. I have the man you beat up.'

'And he will give evidence, is it?'

'Why would he not?'

Daddyji shrugged. Elaborately.

'How should I be knowing my little inspector, why this witness of yours will not tell the lies you are wanting? Perhaps it is that he is afraid.'

'Afraid of worse treatment from you,' Ghote stated blankly.

Daddyji looked back at him. He held out his wrists as if for handcuffs.

'You are going to arrest me for that then?' he asked.

'No,' Ghote said. 'Not you, Daddyji.'

Again he surprised the gang boss.

'Not me? Then who?'

'I have come to arrest your brother, Piloo.'

'Piloo? But you cannot do that. Why, my witnesses will be speaking the truth for him.'

'Not when the charge is taking away feloniously from the Galerie Sodawaterwala a quantity of art material – namely, six pictures in clay.'

Daddyji relaxed visibly.

'Oh, but take, Inspector,' he said. 'Take the boy, take.'

'Take?'

'Yes. Take, take. For some pieces of mud only, he puts himself in danger. Why should I bother with him?'

'But he is your brother.'

'Brother, smother. What is brother? He is one of my men. Or until now he was.'

Ghote looked at the broad-shouldered crook.

'Perhaps I should warn you,' he said, 'the boy is likely to get a long sentence. When someone as influential as the Minister has been insulted by him.'

'He can go to gaol for all his life. What am I caring?'

'But his pictures,' Ghote said.

'Those things. Pah!'

'But do you not know,' Ghote continued earnestly, 'that the boy has very, very great gifts. Mr Sodawaterwala says he will be the Indian Hogarth. Hogarth is a very, very famous English artist.'

'What is that to me? Here, you will be wanting your evidence, Inspector. Look under that charpoy there. That is where the boy put his bundle. You will find your pictures there.'

Ghote went and knelt beside the rope-slung bed, as much to hide his sense of disgust at Daddyji's behaviour as to get hold of the pictures. They were there, sure enough, and he dragged out the bundle and opened it up, thinking all the while, *Yes, the ACP was right. Daddyji is an all-bad man. All-bad.*

'Hey!'

Daddyji's voice came loudly from over Ghote's shoulder.

'Hey, look at that. It is me. Just as I am. It is me playing cards with

Iqbal Singh and that idiot Chandra Chagoo. See, he is losing as always. It is on his face. Wonderful, wonderful.'

Ghote looked more closely at the six hard-baked clay tablets. It was certainly true. Small though they were, it was clear beyond doubt that one of the card players was Daddyji, and that on the miniature face of the man the gang boss had pointed out there was an expression of stupid chagrin, as if indeed he was losing at the game and could not understand why.

'Inspector?' Daddyji said, with a note of sudden calculation in his voice.

'What is it?'

'Inspector, I am going to ask you to do something for me.'

'For you? You dare to ask?'

Ghote thought with rising anger of how this man was truly all-bad.

'Inspector,' Daddyji continued, oblivious of Ghote's plain opposition, 'I am asking you to take these pictures now to Mr Sodawaterwala and to tell him that, of course, Piloo did not steal them. That he brought them here to show to me only. To me, his brother who had raised him from a boy.'

'Take the pictures back? To Mr Sodawaterwala?'

Ghote felt deeply dismayed.

'Then there would be no charge against Piloo,' he said.

'That is right,' Daddyji answered cheerfully. 'And Piloo can go on and make more and more very good pictures like this. He can become the Indian Highlife.'

'Hogarth. Hogarth. But . . .'

And then an idea came to Ghote, an idea so good it was almost incredible.

'You are quite sure you are wanting me to take back these pictures?' he asked, trying to keep his voice neutral.

'But, yes, yes, yes. It is important for Piloo to have this chance. I may be a bad man, Inspector, but I am not all bad. I have some heart left for the boy.'

Quickly, Ghote gathered up the little clay tablets, wrapped them, and took them off.

He took them to Mr Sodawaterwala in his bed at the JJ Hospital.

'And, if what Daddyji told me is true,' he said after he had handed them over, 'when you get back to your gallery you would find Piloo already back there, making more pictures like these.'

Mr Sodawaterwala smiled through his bruised and battered face. A smile of great gentleness.

'But that is wonderful, Inspector,' he said. 'Wonderful. And Daddyji himself insisted that you have the pictures? It is yet more wonderful. It restores my faith in humanity.'

'Yes,' Ghote said, 'it would seem that my own belief was all the time right. There is no such thing as the all-bad man. Even Daddyji has in him some spark of goodness. You know that his father, Piloo's father, too, has a gift for modelling in clay. He is making little, somewhat obscene figures to sell to tourists at Flora Foutain. So the strain of the artist comes to the surface if only in appreciation of what is good, even in a fellow like Daddyji.'

Mr Sodawaterwala smiled again.

'But in Piloo,' he said, 'that strain has gone to the heights. Do you know what I will do for him?'

'It would be something good I am sure.'

'I hope so. I am going to hold a first-class, Number One exhibition for him. And, just as soon as I can, I will go back and put these first six pictures of his in the window of the Galerie, as a foretaste.'

'Very good, Mr Sodawaterwala. Very good. And I will see that night and day there are four-five hefty constables guarding that window.'

'Guarding?' said Mr Sodawaterwala. 'But surely, Inspector, now that Daddyji has shown he is not all-bad, there is no need for that.'

'But there is need, very much of need,' Ghote replied. 'You see, one of those pictures is very important evidence.'

'Evidence? But there is no longer a question of Piloo having stolen any clay. That is ridiculous.'

'That is ridiculous, yes. But I will tell you what is not ridiculous: a charge against Daddyji of conspiring with two individuals, namely Iqbal Singh and Chandra Chagoo, to cause damage at the Loafer's Delight Disc Mart.'

Mr Sodawaterwala looked bewildered.

'But I do not understand,' he said. 'How can one of Piloo's pictures have anything to do with such a place as the Loafer's Delight Disc Mart?'

'Because that picture shows Daddyji was a close acquaintance of those two men, something that up to now he was prepared to manufacture evidence to disprove. One of those pictures shows the three of them playing cards together, clearly as clearly.'

'Then you are going to arrest Daddyji?' Mr Sodawaterwala asked. 'But you cannot do that now.'

Ghote looked down at him on the smooth white pillow of the hospital bed.

He sighed.

'Yes, Mr Sodawaterwala,' he said, 'I can arrest him, and I will. Did you think I can let him go scot-free just because he gave Piloo his chance in life? Yes, even though it was in giving Piloo that chance that he betrayed himself, I must arrest him nevertheless. All-bad or partly good, it is my duty to put him behind the bars, and I will do it.'

Stan The Killer

———————— ◆ ————————

GEORGES SIMENON

Commissaire *Jules Maigret, the heavy-set, pipe-smoking, methodical French detective is today probably as famous as Sherlock Holmes and his exploits have been featured in almost as many radio, film and television adaptations as the Great Detective of Baker Street. The similarities do not end there, for just as Conan Doyle tried to end the life of his creation, so Georges Simenon's attempts to retire the redoubtable policeman were frustrated by the overwhelming public demand. In all, he wrote eighty-four novels and eighteen short stories about Maigret which have provided the basis for an ever-increasing number of film and TV versions. The first screen Maigret was Pierre Renoir, brother of the famous director Jean Renoir (who also produced the detective's film debut,* La Nuit du Carrefour *in 1923), and he has been followed by (in chronological order) Abel Tarride, Harry Baur, Albert Prejean, Charles Laughton, Michel Simon, Maurice Manson, Jean Gabin and Heinz Ruhmann. Then came his turn on television, and the popular conception is that Britain's Rupert Davies was the inaugurator of this new era in 1960 whereas, in fact, three other actors had preceded him on the small screen.*

The first Maigret-on-TV was surprisingly, made in America where the short story, Stan the Killer *was adapted for 'live' presentation on the hour-long weekly drama series,* The Trap, *on May 20, 1950, with the leading television actor, Herbert Berghof in the title role. It was not, by all accounts, a very auspicious debut, but two years later, on September 9, 1952 the same story was again presented on another anthology series,* Studio One, *with the later-to-be-famous 'Method' actor, Eli Wallach as Maigret. Still one more actor was to appear as the Commissioner before Rupert Davies made him a household name on*

TV. He was Basil Sydney, a veteran English theatrical actor, who played the role in the seventy-five minute pilot for the BBC series, Maigret and the Lost Life, *which was screened on December 6, 1959. Despite the press and public acclaim for Sydney's performance, he decided against continuing in the role, and so Rupert Davies was cast – and the rest is history. Since Davies' groundbreaking series of fifty-two programmes between 1960 and 1963, the role has also been played on television in a number of other countries by the following actors: Gino Cervi (in Italy), Jean Richard (France), Richard Harris (Britain), Jan Teuling (Holland), Kinya Aikawa (Japan), Boris Tenine (Russia) and the two latest additions, Michael Gambon in the Granada series and Bruno Cremer on French TV.*

Georges Simenon (1903–1989) is without doubt one of the most remarkable writers of all time – in 1972, for example, UNESCO estimated him to be the most translated author in the world and said his books had been read by upwards of five hundred million people. During his lifetime he wrote approximately two hundred and twenty titles under his own name and at least the same number of novellas under seventeen different pen names. Maigret was, initially, intended as just another character in one of his books, but instead has become one of the immortal fictional characters. Of all the Maigret short stories which might be selected for this volume, Stan the Killer *which first introduced him to a television audience seems perhaps the most appropriate . . .*

MAIGRET puffed at his pipe as he walked along slowly, hands clasped behind his back. It was not a simple matter to push his heavy body through the morning mob in the Rue Saint-Antoine, where a bright sun poured down on carts and baskets of fruits and vegetables, blocking almost the entire width of the pavement.

It was marketing time – the time for feeling artichokes and tasting cherries, the time for scallops and chops to take turns in the scales.

Salesmen in white aprons, butchers in fine checks; the smell of cheese here and a whiff of roasting coffee there; the ping of cash registers and the distrustful glances of housewives . . . and in the midst of it all the slow heavy progress of Maigret, on one of his most tormenting cases.

Across from the Rue de Birague there's a little café with three tables in front of it, called the Barrel of Burgundy. There Maigret settled himself, like any other weary passer-by. He did not even look up at the tall thin waiter who came for his order. 'Small white Mâcon,' he muttered – and who was to guess that this occasionally inept new waiter at the Barrel of Burgundy was otherwise known as Detective Janvier?

The waiter returned with the wine precariously balanced on a tray. He wiped the table with a questionable cloth, and was even so clumsy as to drop a scrap of paper on the floor. Maigret picked it up as he left, and read:

> *The woman's gone out marketing. No sign of One-Eye. The Beard left early. The three others must be still in the hotel.*

At ten in the morning the crowd was getting even worse. Next to the *Barrel*, a grocer's shop was having a sale and barkers kept entreating the passers-by to sample biscuits, cake, country cheeses.

At the corner of the Rue de Birague you could see the sign of a dingy hotel, *Rooms by the month, week or day. Payment in advance.* With doubtless intentional irony this rat-trap had chosen to call itself the Beauséjour.

Maigret sipped at his light dry white wine and stared apparently aimlessly at the teeming crowd in the spring sun. But his gaze soon settled on a window in the first floor of a house in the Rue de Birague opposite the hotel. At that window a little old man sat by a canary's cage and seemed to have no interest in life but to bask in the sun for as long as the Lord should deign to leave him alive.

And this old gentleman, who took no notice of Maigret, was Sergeant Lucas, aged some twenty years.

All this constituted a state of siege which is more commonly known to the police as a stake-out. It had lasted six days, and at least twice a day the Inspector came around for the latest news. At night his men were relieved by a patrolman, who was actually a detective from the Judiciary Police, and a wench who contrived to walk the streets without ever picking up a customer.

The crowd shoved by so close to the tiny terrace of the Barrel of Burgundy that Maigret found himself constantly obliged to pull his legs back under his chair. And now, as he did so once more, he suddenly realized that a man had sat down unnoticed at the same table. He was a little man, with red hair and sad eyes, whose mournful face had something of the clown about it.

'You again?' the Inspector grunted.

'I beg you to forgive me, Monsieur Maigrette, but I am certain that you will eventually accept the proposition which – ' He broke off to say to the waiterly Janvier, 'The same as my friend.'

He had an extremely marked Eastern European accent. He presumably suffered from throat trouble, and he constantly chewed at a cigar-shaped object impregnated with creosote.

'You're getting on my nerves!' Maigret burst out. 'Will you kindly tell me how you knew I'd come here this morning?'

'I did not know.'

'Then why are you here? Are you going to try to convince me that this is an accidental meeting?'

'No.'

The little man's yellow eyes gazed around him, staring into emptiness. He spoke in a sad voice, unvarying in pitch, as though perpetually offering condolences.

'You are not nice to me, Monseur Maigrette.'

'That isn't answering my question. How do you happen to be here this morning?'

'I followed you.'

'From Headquarters?'

'Long before that. From your home.'

'So you admit you're spying on me?'

'I am not spying on you, Monsieur Maigrette. I have far too much respect and admiration for you! I have already stated to you that I shall one day be your collaborator . . .'

And he sighed nostalgically, contemplating the artificial ash of painted wood which tipped his creosote cigar.

There'd been nothing about it in any of the papers save one; and that one, which had got the tip from the Lord knows where, uniquely complicated the Inspector's task.

> *The police have reason to believe that Stan the Killer's gang*
> *of bandits are at this moment in Paris.*

It was true enough, but silence would have been more helpful.

In four years a gang of unknown foreign nationals had attacked five farms, always in the North of France, always with the same methods.

In each case it was an isolated farm, run by elderly people. The crime invariably took place the night of a market day; and the chosen victims were always those who had sold a good number of fowls and animals and had a large sum of cash in hand.

Nothing scientific about the procedure. Brutal attack, as in the days of the highway robbers. Absolute contempt for human life. These bandits killed every human being they found on the farm, even down to the children; it was the one way of making sure they could never be identified.

Were there two of them? Or five, or eight?

In every case neighbours had noticed a small truck. One twelve-year-old claimed he had seen a one-eyed man. Some asserted that the killers wore black masks. Whatever the facts, one thing was certain: every inhabitant of each farm had had his throat sliced.

This was no business of the Paris police. This was up to the mobile units in the provinces, who worked on it for two years without remotely clarifying the mystery – a failure which did not reassure the countryside.

Then a report came in from Lille, from a colony of Polish miners. The report was vague enough; it was impossible even to establish its ultimate source.

'The Poles say that this is Stan the Killer's gang . . .'

But when the police tried to question the coal miners one by one, the men had never heard of it, or muttered, 'Well, they told me . . .'

'Who's "they"?'

'I don't know, I forget . . .'

Then came the crime near Rheims. There the gang overlooked a servant girl sleeping in the attic, who became the first survivor. She had heard the murderers talking in a language she thought was Polish. She had seen their masks through a hole in the boards; and had noticed that one of the men had only one eye and that another, a giant of a man, was extraordinarily hairy.

And so the police had come to refer to them as 'Stan the Killer,' 'The Beard,' and 'One-Eye.'

For months nothing more turned up, until a detective on the hotel squad made a discovery. His territory was the Saint-Antoine district, and in a hotel in the Rue de Birague he observed a suspicious group which included a one-eyed man and a giant whose face was literally covered with hair.

They were seemingly poor people. The bearded giant and his wife rented a room by the week; but almost every night they gave shelter to several compatriots.

Everything was strictly hush-hush – and so the next day one newspaper printed the story. The day after that Maigret found a letter in his mail – clumsily written in an almost childish hand, full of misspellings, on the cheap sort of paper sold in grocery stores:

You won't ever get Stan. Look out. Before you can take
him, he'll have time to kill off plenty more.

The letter was no hoax, Maigret was certain; it *felt* right. It had the
filthy aftertaste of the underworld.

'Be careful,' the chief advised. 'Don't rush into an arrest. The man
who's cut sixteen throats in four years won't hesitate to scatter a few
bullets around him when he sees he's done for.'

Which was why Janvier had become a waiter and Lucas a basking
old man.

The noisy life of the quarter went on with no suspicion that a
desperate man might at any moment start firing in all directions . . .
And then Michael Ozep appeared.

His first meeting with Maigret had been four days ago. He had arrived
at Headquarters and insisted on seeing the Inspector personally.
Maigret had let him wait a good two hours; but the little man was
undaunted. He entered the office, clicked his heels, bowed, and
extended his hand:

'Michael Ozep, former officer in the Polish forces, now teacher of
gymnastics in Paris – '

The Pole spoke so volubly and with so pronounced an accent that it
was sometimes impossible to follow him. He explained that he came of
very good family, that he could not go back to Poland to retrieve his
property, and that he had sunk to depths of despair because even now
he still could not accustom himself to leading a mediocre life.

'You understand, Monsieur Maigrette – ' (it was impossible to wean
him from that pronunciation) ' – I am a gentleman. Here I am forced to
give lessons to individuals of no culture and no education. I am a poor
man . . . I have decided to commit suicide.'

'A nut – ' Maigret thought to himself. An astonishing number of the
unbalanced feel the need of confiding their problems to the police; he
was used to such visits.

'I tried it three weeks ago. I threw myself into the Seine but the river
squad saw me and pulled me out.'

Maigret invented a pretext to step into the next office and phoned
the river squad. The story was true.

'Six days later I tried to gas myself, but the postman came with a
letter and opened the door. I truly *want* to kill myself, do you
understand? My existence has lost all value. A gentleman cannot
consent to live in poverty and mediocrity. Therefore I thought that you
might have need of a man like me . . .' Ozep paused.

'For what?'

'To help you to arrest Stan the Killer.'

Maigret frowned. 'You know him?'

'No. I have only heard talk about him. As a Pole, I am indignant that a man of my people should so violate the laws of hospitality. I should like to see Stan and his gang arrested. Among those who go to arrest him, some will certainly be killed. Is it not better then that it should be I, since I already desire to die?'

All Maigret found himself capable of saying was the traditional formula, 'Leave your address. I'll write you a letter.'

Michael Ozep had a furnished room in the Rue des Tournelles, not far from the Rue de Birague. The report of the investigating detective was in his favour. He had indeed been a second lieutenant in the Polish forces, but after that his trail vanished. In Paris he taught gymnastics and his suicide attempts were genuine.

Nevertheless Maigret sent him an official letter ending:

> . . . deeply regret that I cannot take advantage of your generous proposition, for which my most sincere thanks . . .

Twice since then Ozep had appeared at the Quai des Orfèvres and insisted on seeing the Inspector. The second time he had even refused to leave, claiming that he could wait as long as he was obliged to.

And now Ozep sat there, at Maigret's table, in front of the *Barrel of Burgundy*.

'I wish to prove to you, Monsieur Maigrette, that I am of some use and that you can accept my services. I have been following you for three days, and I am in a position to tell you everything that you have done during that time. I know too that the waiter who just brought my wine is one of your detectives and that there is another at the window across from us.'

Maigret clenched his pipe furiously between his teeth and kept his eyes turned away from the Pole, who went on and on in his monotonous voice. It wore Maigret out merely to listen to him, especially since the accent so distorted each syllable that he had to concentrate to follow the sense.

'You are not a Pole, Monsieur Maigrette. You do not speak the language. I earnestly desire to help you; for I cannot see the good name of my native land tarnished.'

The Inspector was beginning to choke with anger. The former second lieutenant could hardly fail to observe the fact, but he continued nevertheless:

'If you try to capture Stan, what will he do? He has two, maybe three revolvers in his pockets. He fires at everybody. Who knows how many ladies he wounds? How many little babies he kills? Then people will say that the police – '

'Will you shut up?'

'Now as for me, I am resolved to die. No one will weep for poor Ozep. You say to me, "There is Stan!" and I follow him as I have followed you. I wait for the moment when there is no one near us and I say: "You are Stan the Killer!" Then he fires at me and I shoot him in the leg. By the fact that he shoots me, you have your proof that he is Stan and you are not making a blunder. And since he is crippled by my shot – '

'Supposing I have you arrested?' Maigret broke in crudely.

'Why?'

'To get a little peace!'

'What would you say? What has poor Ozep done in violation of the laws of France which he wishes only to defend and for which he is offering up his life?'

'Stuff it!'

'I beg your pardon? Are you agreeing?'

'Not in the least.'

At that moment a woman went by, a woman with blonde hair and a clear complexion, recognizably a foreigner. She was carrying a shopping bag and was headed for a butcher's shop.

Maigret was following her with his eyes when he noticed that his companion had suddenly started to mop his brow with an enormous handkerchief.

'That is the mistress of Stan, is it not?' Ozep asked.

'Will you be quiet?'

'You have convinced yourself that this is the mistress of Stan, but you do not know which one is Stan. You think it is the one with the beard. Now the bearded one is called Boris. And the man with one eye is Sasha. He is not a Pole, he is Russian-born. If you should investigate them yourself you will learn nothing.'

No housewife shopping in the confusion of the Rue Saint-Antoine could suspect the subjects being discussed on the tiny terrace of the Barrel of Burgundy. The blonde foreigner was buying chops at a nearby butcher's stall; in her eyes there was something of that same lassitude that lay in the eyes of Ozep.

'Perhaps you fear you may be called to account if I am killed? In the first place, I have no family. In the second place, I have written a letter in which I state that I alone, and purely of my own volition, have sought this death . . .'

Poor Janvier stood on the threshold trying to think of a way of telling Maigret that there was a telephone message for him. Maigret noticed the ambiguous pantomime, but went on watching the Pole and puffing forth little clouds of pipe smoke.

'Listen, Ozep.'

'Yes, Monsieur Maigrette?'

'If you're seen again anywhere around the Rue Saint-Antoine, I'll have you arrested!'

'You are refusing this offer which I – ?'

'Get out, or I'll arrest you here and now!'

The little man rose, clicked his heels, bowed almost double, and executed a dignified retreat. Maigret had noticed one of his detectives nearby; now he signalled the man to follow the peculiar teacher of gymnastics.

At last Janvier could deliver his message. 'Lucas just phoned. He's spotted that they have guns in the room. Five Poles slept in the next room last night, leaving the door open between. Some of them had to sleep on the floor . . . Who the devil was that character you were talking to?'

'No one . . . How much?'

Janvier slipped back into character, pointing at Ozep's glass. 'You're paying monsieur's bill. . . ?'

Maigret took a taxi to Headquarters. At the door of his office he found the detective who had set out after Ozep.

'You lost him?' he roared. 'Aren't you ashamed of yourself? I give you the most childish job of shadowing and you – '

'I didn't lose him,' the detective murmured humbly.

'Where is he?'

'Here.'

'You pulled him in?'

'He pulled me.'

For Ozep had, indeed, headed directly for Headquarters, where he had placidly installed himself and his sandwich in the waiting-room, after announcing that he had an appointment with Inspector 'Maigrette.'

There's no kudos in paper work; but there may be the solution of a case.

Unwillingly, irritatedly, Maigret was adding up in one report in his own large handwriting the various information obtained in two weeks' siege of the gang.

When he set down the facts in order he could see even more easily how very little they had learned. They did not even know precisely how many individuals belonged to the gang. The earlier reports, from the people who had seen or thought they had seen the bandits near the time of the attacks, stated that there were four of them, sometimes five. It was probable that they had other accomplices, who cased the farms and markets beforehand. That brought the number to six or seven, which seemed to correspond roughly with the number who hung around the nucleus in the Rue de Birague.

There were only three regular tenants, all of whose papers seemed to be in order.

1. Boris Saft, the one the police called The Beard, who seemed to live as man and wife with the pale blonde.

2. Olga Tzerewski, twenty-eight, born in Vilno.

3. Sasha Vorontsov, known as One-Eye.

Boris the Beard and Olga occupied one room, Sasha One-Eye the next; the door between was always left open.

The young woman did the shopping every morning and cooked the meals on a gas stove.

The Beard rarely went out, but spent most of his days stretched on the iron bedstead, reading Polish language newspapers which he had one of the gang buy for him at the newspaper kiosk in the Place de la Bastille. Once the errand boy brought back an American fact-detective magazine in addition to other newspapers. They all read that.

One-Eye went out often, always followed by one of Maigret's detectives. A fact of which he was probably aware, since he never did more than take long walks through Paris, stopping in many bars but never speaking to a soul.

As for the rest, they were what Lucas called 'the floating population.' People came and went, always the same lot, four or five of them. Olga fed them, and sometimes they slept on the floor overnight. There was nothing odd about this; it happens in many hotels with poor clientèle – exiles who get together to rent a room and then put up any of their compatriots they come across.

On the floating population Maigret had a few notes:

1. The Chemist, so called because he had tried to obtain a job at a chemical plant. His clothes were badly worn, but rather well cut. For hours he would wander around the streets of Paris like a man looking for any way to earn a little money; and once, for a whole day, he was employed as a sandwich-man.

2. Spinach, named after his implausible spinach-green hat which seemed even more unlikely in view of his faded pink shirt. Spinach went out particularly in the evenings, when he picked up tips opening car doors in front of the Montmartre bars.

3. Puffy, a fat, wheezy little man, better dressed than the others.

And there were two others who visited the hotel less regularly; it was hard to say if they belonged to the gang.

Maigret stared at the notes with the exasperated feeling that the most important detail was somehow eluding him. Finally he picked up his pen again and wrote: *These people give the impression of penniless foreigners, looking for any kind of work at all. But there's always vodka in the rooms, and sometimes impressive spreads of food. Maybe the gang knows it's being watched, and is putting on an act for the police. If one of them is Stan the Killer, it is probably either The Beard or One-Eye. But this is only guesswork.*

It was without the least enthusiasm that he brought his report to the chief.

'Nothing new?'

'Nothing specific. I'd swear the rascals have spotted one of our men and are simply amusing themselves, seeing how often they can come in and go out on innocent errands. They know we can't keep a large section of the force mobilized on their account for ever. Time's on their side; they have lots of it . . .'

'You have a plan?'

'Look, chief. You'll hear people say I'm waiting for inspiration; they couldn't be more wrong. What I'm waiting for is the one significant happening that never fails to turn up. The whole thing is being there when it does turn up so that I can take advantage of it.'

'So you're waiting for a – happening?' the chief smiled. He knew his man.

'This much I'm convinced of: this *is* Stan the Killer's gang. Because of that fool reporter who keeps hanging around here they're on their guard. Now what I want to know is, why did Stan write to me? Perhaps out of sheer bravado. These killers have their pride – you might almost say, professional pride. But which of them is Stan? And why that nickname? It's more American than Polish.

'You know how I take my time before I reach any conclusions. Well, it's beginning to come . . . The last two or three days I've begun to get the feel of the psychology of these boys. Very different from French murderers.

'They need money, not to have a fling in the night spots, or to clear out of the country – but just simply to live their own lives, which to them means doing nothing, eating, drinking, sleeping, spending their days stretched out on a bed, smoking cigarettes, gossiping, and killing bottles of vodka.

'The way I see it, after their first crime they lived like this until the

money ran out; then they got ready for another job. Whenever the
funds are low, they start again, coldly, without remorse, without a
trace of pity for the old people whose throats they cut – and whose
life's savings they eat up in a few weeks or months . . . And now that
I've got the feel of it, I'm waiting. The happening may even be here
already.'

'Where?'

'In the waiting-room. The little man who calls me Maigrette and
who wants to help in the arrest, even if it costs him his skin. He claims
it's just another method of suicide.'

'A crackpot?'

'Could be. Or an accomplice of Stan's who's using this method of
keeping in touch with what we're doing.'

Maigret emptied his pipe by tapping it gently on the windowledge,
so that the ashes fell somewhere on the Quai des Orfèvres, perhaps on
the hat of a passer-by.

'He bothers me, that little man,' he added. 'I've seen his face
somewhere. It's not in our files, but I've seen it. And I've seen the girl,
too, the blonde; she's worth remembering.'

The chief leaned forward. 'We've been going on the assumption that
the blonde is Stan's mistress. You associate her and the little man. You
see the possible implication?'

'That my little man is Stan himself? Could be.'

'Are you going to accept this man's offer?'

'I think so.' The Inspector headed for the door. He felt he'd said
enough. 'You'll see, chief. I'll be amazed if we still need the stake-out
by the end of this week.'

And it was Thursday afternoon now.

'Sit down. Doesn't it get on your nerves to suck at that filthy creosote
cigar all day?'

'No, Monsieur Maigrette.'

'That "Maigrette" of yours is beginning to get me . . . However, let's
get down to business. Now, tell me, are you still set on dying?'

'Yes, Monsieur Maigrette.'

'And if I told you to go up to One-Eye and fire a bullet into his leg,
you'd do it?'

'Yes, Monsieur Maigrette. But you would first have to give me a
revolver. I am a poor man and – '

'Now suppose I tell you to go to The Beard or One-Eye and say you
have important information – that the police are coming to arrest
them?'

'Gladly, Monsieur Maigrette. I shall wait until One-Eye passes by in the street and then I shall perform my commission.'

The lowering gaze of the Inspector had no effect on the little Pole. Rarely had Maigret seen a man who combined such self-assurance with such utter serenity. Michael Ozep spoke of killing himself or of visiting the Polish gang as simply, as naturally, as he might refer to brushing his teeth.

'You've never met either of them?'

'No, Monsieur Maigrette.'

'All right. I'm going to give you the job. And if there's any trouble, it's on your head.' Maigret lowered his eyelids to conceal his too sharp interest in the other's reaction. 'In a minute we'll go together to the Rue Saint-Antoine. I'll wait for you outside. You'll go up to the room, picking a time when the woman is there alone. You'll tell her you're a fellow Pole and you happened by chance to learn that the police are raiding the hotel tonight – '

Ozep said nothing.

'You understand?'

'Yes.'

'It's all set?'

'I must confess something to you, Monsieur Maigrette . . .'

'You're turning yellow?'

'Yellow? I do not under – ah! – yes. No, I am not turning yellow. But I should prefer to arrange the matter in a different way . . . I – I am a timid man with the ladies. And the ladies are intelligent, far more intelligent than we men. Therefore, she will see that I am lying. And because I know that she will see that I am lying, I shall blush. And when I blush . . .'

Maigret sat motionless, absorbing this unlikely explanation.

'I should prefer to talk to a man. To the one with the beard, if you like, or the one you call One-Eye, or anyone at all – '

A ray of sunlight pierced slantwise through the office and lit full on Maigret's face. He seemed to be dozing, like a man whose injudiciously heavy lunch obliges him to take a siesta.

'It is exactly the same thing, Monsieur Maigrette . . .'

But Monsieur Maigret did not answer. The only sign that he was still alive was the slim blue spiral which rose from his pipe.

'I am desolated. You demand precisely the one thing which – '

'Forget it!'

'I beg your pardon?'

'I said, forget it . . . Where did you know the woman Olga Tzerewski?'

'I?'

'Answer me.'

'I do not understand what you mean . . .'

'Answer me!'

'I do not know this woman. If I knew her, I would tell you so.'

'Where did you know her?'

'I swear to you, Monsieur Maigrette, that – '

'*Where did you know her?*'

'Why have you suddenly stopped being nice to me? You talk to me so brutally! To me who came here to place myself at your disposal, to prevent Frenchmen from being murdered by a compatriot – '

'Cut the talk.'

'Monsieur, please, ask me anything else – to throw myself under a subway train – '

'I'm asking you to go and see that woman and tell her that we'll make a raid tonight.'

'And – and if I refuse?'

'Then you'd better see to it that I never lay eyes on you again.'

'Are you really going to arrest the gang tonight?'

'Probably.'

'At what time will you make the raid?'

'Let's say one in the morning.'

'I am going.'

'Where?'

'To find the woman.'

'Just a minute! We're going together.'

'It is better that I go alone. If one of them sees us, he will understand that I am assisting the police . . .'

The Pole had hardly left the office, of course, before the Inspector had set a detective at his heels. And without losing a moment Maigret hurried downstairs and leaped into a taxi.

'Corner of Rue de Birague and Rue Saint-Antoine, as fast as you can make it!'

It was a radiant afternoon. Striped awnings lent a note of colour to the shops. In their shadows dogs sprawled and napped, and all life seemed to run in slow motion. One felt that even the buses had a hard time making headway in the hot heavy air. Their wheels left tracks in the heated asphalt.

Maigret sprang out of the taxi into the house on the corner. On the second floor he opened a door without bothering to knock and found

Lucas sitting at the window, still in the rôle of a quiet and curious elderly gentleman.

The room was shabby but clean. On the table lay the remains of a cold meal that Lucas had had sent up from a delicatessen.

'Anything new, Inspector?'

'Anybody at home across the way?'

The room had been chosen for its strategic position; you could see straight into the two rooms of the Hotel Beauséjour which the Poles occupied.

In this heat all the windows of another adjoining room were unshuttered and open, revealing a young girl, scantily clad, asleep on a bed.

'Well, well, Lucas! Looks like you don't find your job too boring . . .'

A pair of field-glasses on a chair gave evidence that Lucas attended to his work conscientiously and missed no detail, however slight.

'At the moment,' said the sergeant, 'there are two of them in the rooms, but there'll be only one in a minute. The man's getting dressed. He stayed in bed all morning, as usual.'

'That's The Beard?'

'Yes. There were three of them for lunch: The Beard, the woman, and One-Eye. One-Eye left as soon as he'd eaten. Then The Beard got up and began to dress . . . Well! He's just put on a clean shirt. That doesn't happen very often.'

Maigret walked over to the window. The hairy giant was knotting his tie. You could see the man's lips move as he looked at himself in the mirror. Behind him the blonde woman was cleaning up, gathering papers and rolling them into a ball, turning off the stove, dusting the frame of a bright-coloured picture on the wall.

'If only we knew what they're saying!' Lucas sighed. 'There are times when it drives me crazy. I watch them talking and talking and they never stop.'

'The limitless resources of the police,' said Maigret dryly, 'do not include a lip-reader who knows Polish.'

'It gets on my nerves. I'm beginning to understand the torture it must be to be deaf.'

'Do you think the woman will stay there?'

'This isn't the time she usually goes out. And if she meant to, she would have put on her grey suit.'

Olga was wearing the same dark wool dress in which she had done her marketing that morning. While she cleaned up her bohemian

establishment she kept smoking a cigarette without ever taking it from
her lips, in the fashion of the habitual smoker.

'She never talks,' Maigret observed.

'This isn't the time she does that, either. It's in the evenings that she
gets to talking, when they're all gathered around her. Or a few times
when she's alone with the one I called Spinach – which doesn't happen
very often. Either I'm badly mistaken or she has a weakness for
Spinach. He's the best-looking of the lot.'

It was a strange experience to be in an unknown room like this, to
look into the lives of people and come to know their smallest gestures.

'You're getting as snoopy as a concierge, Lucas.'

'That's what I'm here for, isn't it? I can even tell you that the little
girl over there – the one who's sleeping so soundly – was making love
last night until three in the morning with a young man in a dinner
jacket who left at dawn, undoubtedly so he could get into his family's
house unnoticed . . . Hold on! Now The Beard's leaving.'

'Just look at him. He's practically elegant!'

'Not so bad. But he looks more like a foreign wrestler than a man of
the world.'

'Well, let's say a wrestler who's doing good business,' Maigret
conceded.

No goodbye kiss across the way. The man simply disappeared from
view, and a minute later he emerged on to the pavement and set off
towards the Place de la Bastille.

'Derain will pick him up,' Lucas announced, sitting there like a huge
spider at the centre of its web. 'But he knows he's being followed. He
won't do anything but walk around and maybe stop for a drink
somewhere.'

As for the woman, she had taken a road map out of a drawer and
spread it on the table.

Ozep couldn't have taken a taxi, Maigret calculated; he must have
come by Métro, in which case he should arrive at any moment. 'If he's
coming . . .' he corrected himself.

He did come. They saw him arrive, hesitate, wander up and down
the pavement, while the detective trailing him displayed great interest
in a fish stall in the Rue Saint-Antoine.

Seen from above like this, the tiny Pole seemed even thinner, even
more insignificant. Maigret experienced, for a moment, a pang of
remorse. He could hear the poor devil's voice repeating a hundred
times, in involved explanation, his famous 'Monsieur Maigrette . . .'

He was hesitating, that was obvious. He seemed even to be afraid,
staring around him with a visible anguish.

'Do you know what he's looking for?' the Inspector asked Lucas.

'The little pale fellow? No. Maybe some money to get into the hotel?'

'He's looking for me. He's saying to himself that I must be somewhere around and if by some miracle I've changed my mind . . .'

Too late now; Michael Ozep had plunged into the dark hallway of the hotel. They could follow him in their minds. He would be climbing the stairs, reaching the first floor . . .

'He's still stalling,' Maigret announced. The door should have opened before this. 'He's on the landing. He's going to knock. He's knocked – look!'

The blonde girl started, shoved the map with an instinctive movement back in the dresser, and went towards the door. For a moment they could see nothing. The two were in the invisible part of the room. Then suddenly the woman appeared. Something about her had changed. Her steps were fast, decisive. She went straight to the window, closed it, then drew the dark curtains.

Lucas turned to the Inspector with a quizzical smile. 'Well, now!' He laughed. But his smile faded as he noticed that Maigret appeared to be concerned.

'What time is it, Lucas?'

'Ten past three.'

'In your opinion, what are the chances that one of the gang will come back to the hotel in the next hour?'

'I doubt it. Unless, as I was telling you, Spinach, if he knows The Beard is out of the way. You don't look very happy.'

'I don't like the way she closed that window.'

'Are you afraid for your little Pole?'

Maigret said nothing.

'Have you thought,' Lucas went on, 'that we haven't any real proof that he is in that room? It's true we saw him go into the hotel. But he might perfectly well have gone to some other room, and somebody else came – '

Maigret shrugged his shoulders and sighed.

'What time is it, Lucas?'

'Twenty past three. Do you want to go over and see what's happening?'

'Not yet. But I'm probably going to make a fool of myself . . . Where can you telephone?'

'In the next room. He's a tailor who does piece-work for one of the big houses, so he has to have a phone.'

'Good. Try not to let him listen in. Telephone the chief, and tell him I want him to send me twenty armed men at once. They're to spread a cordon around the Hotel Beauséjour and wait for my signal.'

Maigret's expression indicated the seriousness of this order, which was so out of character, for the Inspector usually laughed at police mobilization. 'You think there'll be dirty work going on?' Lucas asked.

'If it hasn't already gone on . . .'

His eyes remained fixed on the window, on the filthy glass panes, on the crimson velvet curtains of the time of Louis Philippe.

When Lucas came back from the telephone, he found the Inspector still in the same place, still frowning thoughtfully.

'The boss says please be careful. There was a detective killed only last week, and if there should be another accident – '

'Be quiet, will you?'

'Do you think that Stan the Killer – '

'I don't think anything! I've thought so much about this case since this morning that I've got a headache. Now I'm satisfied just to have impressions; and at the moment I have the impression that some disagreeable things are happening or are about to happen.'

In the nearby room the young girl was still asleep, her mouth open, her legs bent back. Higher up, on the fourth floor, somebody was trying to play an accordian, incessantly repeating, with the same false notes, the same fox-trot refrain.

'Do you want me to go over?' Lucas suggested.

Maigret gave him a harsh look, as if his subordinate had reproached him for lack of courage.

'Do you think I'd hesitate to go myself? You're forgetting one thing: Once we're over there, it's too late. If we go and find nothing, we'll never pin anything on that gang. That's why I'm hesitating . . . If only that girl hadn't closed the window!' He suddenly lifted his eyebrows. 'Tell me: the other times, when she's been alone with a man, has she ever closed the window?'

'Never.'

'Then she hadn't any suspicion of your presence here.'

'She probably took me for just another foolish old man.'

'So it isn't the girl who had the idea of closing the window, but the character who came in.'

'Ozep?'

'Ozep or somebody else. The one who came in must have told the girl to close the window before he showed himself.'

Maigret suddenly took his hat from the chair, emptied his pipe, and scraped the bowl with his index finger.

'Where are you going, boss?'

'I'm waiting for our men to get here . . . Look! There are two of them by the bus stop. And some others in that parked taxi . . . If I stay inside five minutes without opening that window, you'll come in with our men.'

'You have your gun. . . ?'

A few moments later Lucas could see Maigret crossing the street, could see Detective Janvier notice him and break off his task of wiping the tables on the terrace.

After what seemed a miraculously short interval, the window across the way opened. Maigret signalled to his sergeant to join him.

From across the street Lucas had gathered that the room was empty save for the Inspector. He stumbled up a dark staircase through the stench of bad cooking and worse plumbing and entered the room, only to start back as he found the body of a woman stretched out at his feet.

It was as if the murderer had wished to leave his signature on his crime. The woman's throat had been cut, as with all the other victims of Stan. There was blood everywhere.

The bright picture on the wall turned out, on closer inspection, to be a portrait of Olga – even blonder, even more fresh-skinned than she had been in life. Lucas looked from the lushly alluring portrait to the unappetizing sight on the floor. He felt oddly like a drinking man who sees a bottle of fine brandy smashed.

'It was your Pole?'

Maigret shrugged his shoulders, still standing rooted in the middle of the room.

'Shall I give his description to our men so they can see that he doesn't leave the hotel? And I'd like to put a man on the roof, just in case – '

'Go ahead.'

'Shall I call the chief?'

'In a minute.'

It was no easy job to talk with Maigret when he was like this. Lucas tried to put himself in his shoes. Maigret himself had said he'd make a fool of himself. But this was worse than looking foolish. He had mobilized a large body of police when it was too late, when the crime had already been committed under Maigret's very eyes – almost with his consent, since he'd been the one who had sent Ozep into the Hotel Beauséjour.

'And if any of the gang come back, shall I arrest them?'

Maigret nodded indifferently, and at last Lucas went out.

'Where's Maigret?' the chief demanded of Lucas before he was halfway out of his car.

'In the room. Number 19 on the second floor. The people in the hotel don't know about it yet.'

A few moments later the director of the Judiciary Police found Maigret sitting in a chair in the middle of the room, two steps from the body.

'Well, my friend! It looks to me as though we are in a pretty fix!'

For answer he received a grunt.

'So the notorious killer was none other than the little man who offered you his services! You must admit, Maigret, you might have been somewhat less trustful; Ozep's attitude was suspicious to say the least . . .'

A heavy vertical furrow seamed Maigret's brow and his jaws jutted out, giving his whole face a striking quality of power.

'You think he hasn't managed to slip out of the hotel yet?'

'I'm sure of it,' said Maigret.

'You haven't searched the hotel?'

'Not yet.'

'You think he'll let himself be captured easily?'

Then Maigret's gaze moved slowly away from the window, shifted towards the director.

'If I'm wrong, the man will try to kill as many people as he can before he's arrested. If I'm not wrong, things will take care of themselves.'

'I don't understand.'

'I'll tell you again, chief: I can be wrong. Anybody can be wrong. In that case, I beg your pardon, because there's going to be trouble. There's something in this case that doesn't fit; I can feel it. If Ozep was Stan, there was no reason why . . .' His voice trailed off.

'You're staying here, Maigret?'

'Pending further instructions, yes.'

'Then I'll go and see what our men are doing outside.'

They had arrested Spinach when, as Lucas had foreseen, he had come to pay his call on the young woman. When they told him that Olga had been killed, he turned pale; but he showed no reaction when they spoke of Ozep.

A half-hour later it was One-Eye's turn to come home and be arrested on the threshold. He submitted impassively; but when they told him of the woman's death, he tried to break free from his handcuffs and leap upstairs.

'Who did it?' he shouted. 'Who killed her? One of you, wasn't it?'

'It was Ozep, alias Stan the Killer.'

The man quieted down as if by magic. He frowned as he repeated: 'Ozep?'

'You aren't going to tell us you didn't know your boss's real name?'

It was the chief in person who conducted this hasty questioning in a corridor, and he had the impression that a faint smile crossed the prisoner's lips.

Then came another of the gang, the one they called the Chemist. He simply answered all questions with an air of absolute confusion, as if he had never heard of the woman nor of Ozep nor of Stan.

Maigret was still upstairs with the dead woman, hunting for the key that would at last enable him to understand what had happened.

'All right . . .' he murmured when Lucas told him of the arrest of The Beard, who had begun by raging like a fiend and ended by bawling like a calf.

Suddenly he raised his head. 'Do you notice something, Lucas? That's four that they've arrested, and not one of them's put up any real resistance. Whereas a man like Stan – '

'But since Stan is Ozep – '

'Have you found him?'

'Not yet. We had to let all the accomplices come home before we turned the hotel upside down. Now that we have almost all of them, the big boss is laying siege. Our men are downstairs and they're going to go through everything.'

'Listen, Lucas . . .'

The sergeant had been about to leave. He paused, feeling for Maigret something akin to pity.

'One-Eye is not Stan. Spinach is not Stan. The Beard is not Stan. But I'm convinced that Stan lived in this hotel and was the focus around which the others gathered.'

Lucas said nothing. Let the Inspector have his monomania.

'If Ozep was Stan, he had no reason to come here to kill an accomplice. If he was not Stan . . .'

Suddenly Maigret rose, crossed to the wall and pulled down the brightly coloured picture of Olga. He tore away the tape that framed it, revealing lines of lettering above and below the face. He handed it to Lucas.

The sergeant knew enough English to make out both the line above:

REAL LIFE DETECTIVE CASES

and the lines below:

THE PRETTY POLE AND THE TERROR OF
TERRE HAUTE

Maigret was smiling now. 'Vanity,' he said. 'They can't ever resist it. They had to buy the magazine when they saw it on the bookstalls, and she had to frame the picture.

'I knew I'd seen her face before. I do remember the case roughly. I kept some cuttings on it. Very similar to ours. In the Middle West of America, four or five years ago. A gang attacking lonely farms, cutting throats . . . Just like ours . . . and they had a woman leader. The American press took great pleasure in describing her atrocities.'

'Then Stan. . . ?'

'. . . was Olga. Almost certainly. I'll be positive in an hour, now that I know what to look for in the office. Are you coming with me, Lucas?'

'But Ozep?' Lucas asked, as they settled back in the cab.

'It's Ozep I especially want to look up. That is, I'm hoping I'll find something about him. If he killed this woman, he must have had a motive . . . Listen, Lucas: When I wanted to send him to the others, he agreed at once. But when I gave him an errand to the woman, he refused, and I was forced to use pressure. In other words, the rest of the gang did not know him – *but the woman did*.'

It took a good half-hour to find the cuttings. Order was not Maigret's strong point.

'Read this! Always allowing for the exaggeration of the American press – they like to give the readers their money's worth – *The Female Fiend . . . The Deadly Pole . . . Girl, 23, Heads Murder Gang . . .*'

The press revelled in the exploits of the Polish girl and produced many proofs of her photogenic qualities. At eighteen Stephanie Polintskaja was already known to the Warsaw police. Around this time she met a man who married her and strove to curb her evil instincts. She had a child by him. One day the man came home from work to find that his wife had vanished, taking everything of value with her. The child's throat had been cut.

'You know who that man was?' Maigret asked.

'Ozep?'

'Here's his picture, and a good likeness. You understand now? Stephanie, nicknamed Stan, ran wild in America. How she escaped the American prisons I do not know. In any case she took refuge in France, surrounded herself with a fresh lot of brutes, and took up her old career.

'Her husband learns from the papers that she is in Paris, that the police are on her trail. Does he want to rescue her once more? I doubt it. I'm rather inclined to think that he wants to make sure that the detestable murderess of his child shall not escape punishment. That's why he offers me his services. He hasn't the guts to work alone – he needs the police to help him. And then, this afternoon, I force his hand . . .

'Face to face with his former wife, what can he do? Kill or be killed! She certainly would not hesitate to destroy the only man outside the gang who could testify against her.

'So he killed . . . And do you want to know what I think? I'm betting that they'll find him somewhere in the hotel, more or less seriously wounded. After muffing two attempts at suicide, it would amaze me if he muffed the third. Now you can go back to the hotel and – '

'No use!' It was the chief's voice. 'Ozep hanged himself in a vacant room on the fifth floor.'

'He made it,' Maigret sighed. 'Poor devil!'

'You're sorry for him?'

'Indeed I am. Especially since I'm somewhat responsible for his death . . . I don't know if it means I'm getting old, but I certainly took long enough to find the solution – '

'What solution?' the chief asked suspiciously.

'The solution to the whole problem!' Lucas intervened happily. 'The Inspector has reconstructed the case.'

'That so, Maigret?'

'It is . . . You know, I don't think I've ever been so mad at myself in my life. I felt that the solution was there, within reach, that just one little touch . . . And you all kept buzzing round me like horseflies, telling me about arrests that didn't mean a thing . . . And then I remembered the American detective magazine and the woman's face on the cover!'

Maigret took a deep breath, loaded his pipe, and asked Lucas for matches. The afternoon vigil had used up all his own.

'What do you say, chief? It's seven o'clock. Suppose we three settle down to a nice glass of beer? Provided that Lucas gets rid of his wig and makes himself respectable again.'

The Treasure Hunt

◆

EDGAR WALLACE

Mr J. G. Reeder, the investigator from the Public Prosecutor's Office, is a curious mixture of the mild and the deadly. A small, middle-aged man, with a pale, whiskered face, his unprepossessing appearance masks what he calls 'a criminal mind' and a vicious streak in his nature. Formerly at Scotland Yard, he has an almost encyclopaedic knowledge of crime and criminals which has made him one of the country's leading experts on counterfeiting, forgery and bank robberies. He is also no stranger to murder. His many brushes with the criminal underworld have resulted in a number of attempts on his life and he conceals in his nondescript suit a revolver, while inside the handle of his umbrella is a spring-loaded knife blade. The investigator made his first appearance in The Mind of Mr J. G. Reeder in 1925 and was featured in four movies in the pre-war years: George Bellamy, Gibb McLaughlin and Will Fyffe filling the rôle. In 1971, Thames Television produced a series of sixteen hour-long episodes, The Mind of J. G. Reeder, which attracted a large audience during its run and gave the unassuming-looking TV actor, Hugh Burden, the part for which he is best remembered.

Edgar Wallace (1875–1932), the hugely successful writer who had to spend his own money to publish his first novel, The Four Just Men (1905), produced over one hundred and seventy books and became known as 'The King of Thrillers'. He created many popular characters including Sanders and Bones, Surefoot Smith of the CID, Detective Oliver Rater, and the memorable pair of super-criminals, 'The Ringer' and 'The Squealer'. The J. G. Reeder story here, The Treasure Hunt, is a fine example of the extraordinary mixture of the benign and the

*vicious in his character, and formed the basis of perhaps the best of all
the episodes in the TV series . . .*

THERE is a tradition in criminal circles that even the humblest of
detective officers is a man of wealth and substance, and that his
secret hoard was secured by thieving, bribery and blackmail. It is the
gossip of the fields, the quarries, the tailor's shop, the laundry and the
bakehouse of fifty county prisons and three convict establishments,
that all highly placed detectives have by nefarious means laid up for
themselves sufficient earthly treasures to make work a hobby and their
official pittance the most inconsiderable portion of their incomes.

Since Mr J. G. Reeder had for over twenty years dealt exclusively with
bank robbers and forgers, who are the aristocrats and capitalists of the
underworld, legend credited him with country houses and immense
secret reserves. Not that he would have a great deal of money in the
bank. It was admitted that he was too clever to risk discovery by the
authorities. No, it was hidden somewhere: it was the pet dream of
hundreds of unlawful men that they would some day discover the
hoard and live happily ever after. The one satisfactory aspect of his
affluence (they all agreed) was that, being an old man – he was over
fifty – he couldn't take his money with him, for gold melts at a certain
temperature and gilt-edged stock is seldom printed on asbestos paper.

The Director of Public Prosecutions was lunching one Saturday at
his club with a judge of the King's Bench – Saturday being one of the
two days in the week when a judge gets properly fed. And the
conversation drifted to a certain Mr J. G. Reeder, the chief of the
Director's sleuths.

'He's capable,' he confessed reluctantly, 'but I hate his hat. It is the
sort that So-and-so used to wear,' he mentioned by name an eminent
politician; 'and I loathe his black frock-coat, people who see him
coming into the office think he's a coroner's officer, but he's capable.
His side-whiskers are an abomination, and I have a feeling that, if I
talked rough to him, he would burst into tears – a gentle soul. Almost
too gentle for my kind of work. He apologizes to the messenger every
time he rings for him!'

The judge, who knew something about humanity, answered with a
frosty smile.

'He sounds rather like a potential murderer to me,' he said cynically.

Here, in his extravagance, he did Mr J. G. Reeder an injustice, for Mr Reeder was incapable of breaking the law – quite. At the same time there were many people who formed an altogether wrong conception of J. G.'s harmlessness as an individual. And one of these was a certain Lew Kohl, who mixed bank-note printing with elementary burglary.

Threatened men live long, a trite saying but, like most things trite, true. In a score of cases, when Mr J. G. Reeder had descended from the witness stand, he had met the baleful eye of the man in the dock and had listened with mild interest to divers promises as to what would happen to him in the near or the remote future. For he was a great authority on forged bank-notes and he had sent many men to penal servitude.

Mr Reeder, that inoffensive man, had seen prisoners foaming at the mouth in their rage, he had seen them white and livid, he had heard their howling execrations and he had met these men after their release from prison and had found them amiable souls half ashamed and half amused at their nearly forgotten outbursts and horrific threats.

But when, in the early part of 1914, Lew Kohl was sentenced for ten years, he neither screamed his imprecations nor registered a vow to tear Mr Reeder's heart, lungs and important organs from his frail body.

Lew just smiled and his eyes caught the detective's for the space of a second – the forger's eyes were pale blue and speculative, and they held neither hate nor fury. Instead, they said in so many words:

'At the first opportunity I will kill you.'

Mr Reeder read the message and sighed heavily, for he disliked fuss of all kinds, and resented, in so far as he could resent anything, the injustice of being made personally responsible for the performance of a public duty.

Many years had passed, and considerable changes had occurred in Mr Reeder's fortune. He had transferred from the specialized occupation of detecting the makers of forged bank-notes to the more general practice of the Public Prosecutor's bureau, but he never forgot Lew's smile.

The work in Whitehall was not heavy and it was very interesting. To Mr Reeder came most of the anonymous letters which the Director received in shoals. In the main they were self-explanatory, and it required no particular intelligence to discover their motive. Jealousy, malice, plain mischief-making, and occasionally a sordid desire to benefit financially by the information which was conveyed, were behind the majority. But occasionally:

'Sir James is going to marry his cousin, and it's not three months since his poor wife fell overboard from the Channel steamer crossing to Calais. There's something very fishy about this business. Miss Margaret doesn't like him, for she knows he's after her money. Why was I sent away to London that night? He doesn't like driving in the dark, either. It's strange that he wanted to drive that night when it was raining like blazes.'

This particular letter was signed 'A Friend.' Justice has many such friends.

'Sir James' was Sir James Tithermite, who had been a director of some new public department during the war and had received a baronetcy for his services.

'Look it up,' said the Director when he saw the letter. 'I seem to remember that Lady Tithermite was drowned at sea.'

'On the nineteenth of December last year,' said Mr Reeder solemnly. 'She and Sir James were going to Monte Carlo, breaking their journey in Paris. Sir James, who has a house near Maidstone, drove to Dover, garaging the car at the Lord Wilson Hotel. The night was stormy and the ship had a rough crossing – they were half-way across when Sir James came to the purser and said that he had missed his wife. Her baggage was in the cabin, her passport, rail ticket and hat, but the lady was not found, indeed was never seen again.'

The Director nodded.

'I see, you've read up the case.'

'I remember it,' said Mr Reeder. 'The case is a favourite speculation of mine. Unfortunately I see evil in everything and I have often thought how easy – but I fear that I take a warped view of life. It is a horrible handicap to possess a criminal mind.'

The Director looked at him suspiciously. He was never quite sure whether Mr Reeder was serious. At that moment, his sobriety was beyond challenge.

'A discharged chauffeur wrote that letter, of course,' he began.

'Thomas Dayford, of 179, Barrack Street, Maidstone,' concluded Mr Reeder. 'He is at present in the employ of the Kent Motor-Bus Company, and has three children, two of whom are twins and bonny little rascals.'

The Chief laughed helplessly.

'I'll take it that you *know!*' he said. 'See what there is behind the letter. Sir James is a big fellow in Kent, a Justice of the Peace, and he has powerful political influences. There is nothing in this letter, of course. Go warily, Reeder – if any kick comes back to this office, it goes on to you – intensified!'

Mr Reeder's idea of walking warily was peculiarly his own. He travelled down to Maidstone the next morning, and, finding a bus that passed the lodge gates of Elfreda Manor, he journeyed comfortably and economically, his umbrella between his knees. He passed through the lodge gates, up a long and winding avenue of poplars, and presently came within sight of the grey manor house.

In a deep chair on the lawn he saw a girl sitting, a book on her knees, and evidently she saw him, for she rose as he crossed the lawn and came towards him eagerly.

'I'm Miss Margaret Letherby – are you from – ?' She mentioned the name of a well-known firm of lawyers, and her face fell when Mr Reeder regretfully disclaimed connection with those legal lights.

She was as pretty as a perfect complexion and a round, not too intellectual, face could, in combination, make her.

'I thought – do you wish to see Sir James? He is in the library. If you ring, one of the maids will take you to him.'

Had Mr Reeder been the sort of man who could be puzzled by anything, he would have been puzzled by the suggestion that any girl with money of her own should marry a man much older than herself against her own wishes. There was little mystery in the matter now. Miss Margaret would have married any strong-willed man who insisted.

'Even me,' said Mr Reeder to himself, with a certain melancholy pleasure.

There was no need to ring the bell. A tall, broad man in a golfing suit stood in the doorway. His fair hair was long and hung over his forehead in a thick flat strand; a heavy tawny moustache hid his mouth and swept down over a chin that was long and powerful.

'Well?' he asked aggressively.

'I'm from the Public Prosecutor's office,' murmured Mr Reeder. 'I have had an anonymous letter.'

His pale eyes did not leave the face of the other man.

'Come in,' said Sir James gruffly.

As he closed the door he glanced quickly first to the girl and then to the poplar avenue.

'I'm expecting a fool of a lawyer,' he said, as he flung open the door of what was evidently the library.

His voice was steady; not by a flicker of eyelash had he betrayed the slightest degree of anxiety when Reeder had told his mission.

'Well – what about this anonymous letter? You don't take much notice of that kind of trash, do you?'

Mr Reeder deposited his umbrella and flat-crowned hat on a chair

before he took a document from his pocket and handed it to the
baronet, who frowned as he read. Was it Mr Reeder's vivid
imagination, or did the hard light in the eyes of Sir James soften as he
read?

'This is a cock and bull story of somebody having seen my wife's
jewellery on sale in Paris,' he said. 'There is nothing in it. I can account
for every one of my poor wife's trinkets. I brought back the jewel case
after that awful night. I don't recognize the handwriting: who is the
lying scoundrel who wrote this?'

Mr Reeder had never before been called a lying scoundrel, but he
accepted the experience with admirable meekness.

'I thought it untrue,' he said, shaking his head. 'I followed the details
of the case very thoroughly. You left here in the afternoon – '

'At night,' said the other brusquely. He was not inclined to discuss
the matter, but Mr Reeder's appealing look was irresistible. 'It is only
eighty minutes' run to Dover. We got to the pier at eleven o'clock,
about the same time as the boat train, and we went on board at once. I
got my cabin key from the purser and put her ladyship and her baggage
inside.'

'Her ladyship was a good sailor?'

'Yes, a very good sailor; she was remarkably well that night. I left
her in the cabin dozing, and went for a stroll on the deck – '

'Raining very heavily and a strong sea running,' nodded Reeder, as
though in agreement with something the other man had said.

'Yes – I'm a pretty good sailor – anyway, that story about my poor
wife's jewels is utter nonsense. You can tell the Director that, with my
compliments.'

He opened the door for his visitor, and Mr Reeder was some time
replacing the letter and gathering his belongings.

'You have a beautiful place here, Sir James – a lovely place. An
extensive estate?'

'Three thousand acres.' This time he did not attempt to disguise his
impatience. 'Good afternoon.'

Mr Reeder went slowly down the drive, his remarkable memory at
work.

He missed the bus which he could easily have caught, and pursued
an apparently aimless way along the winding road which marched
with the boundaries of the baronet's property. A walk of a quarter of a
mile brought him to a lane shooting off at right angles from the main
road, and marking, he guessed, the southern boundary. At the corner
stood an old stone lodge, on the inside of a forbidding iron gate. The
lodge was in a pitiable state of neglect and disrepair. Tiles had been

dislodged from the roof, the windows were grimy or broken, and the little garden was overrun with docks and thistles. Beyond the gate was a narrow, weed-covered drive that trailed out of sight into a distant plantation.

Hearing the clang of a letter-box closing, he turned to see a postman mounting his bicycle.

'What place is this?' asked Mr Reeder, arresting the postman's departure.

'South Lodge – Sir James Tithermite's property. It's never used now. Hasn't been used for years – I don't know why; it's a short cut if they happen to be coming this way.'

Mr Reeder walked with him towards the village, and he was a skilful pumper of wells, however dry; and the postman was not dry by any means.

'Yes, poor lady! She was very frail – one of those sort of invalids that last out many a healthy man.'

Mr Reeder put a question at random and scored most unexpectedly.

'Yes, her ladyship was a bad sailor. I know because every time she went abroad she used to get a bottle of that stuff people take for sea-sickness. I've delivered many a bottle till Raikes the chemist stocked it – "Pickers' Travellers' Friend," that's what it was called. Mr Raikes was only saying to me the other day that he'd got half a dozen bottles on hand, and he didn't know what to do with them. Nobody in Climbury ever goes to sea.'

Mr Reeder went on to the village and idled his precious time in most unlikely places. At the chemist's, at the blacksmith's shop, at the modest building yard. He caught the last bus back to Maidstone, and by great good luck the last train to London.

And, in his vague way, he answered the Director's query the next day with:

'Yes, I saw Sir James: a very interesting man.'

This was on the Friday. All day Saturday he was busy. The Sabbath brought him a new interest.

On this bright Sunday morning, Mr Reeder, attired in a flowered dressing-gown, his feet encased in black velvet slippers, stood at the window of his house in Brockley Road and surveyed the deserted thoroughfare. The bell of a local church, which was accounted high, had rung for early Mass, and there was nothing living in sight except a black cat that lay asleep in a patch of sunlight on the top of the house opposite. The hour was seven-thirty, and Mr Reeder had been at his desk since six, working by artificial light, the month being October towards the close.

From the half-moon of the window bay he regarded a section of the Lewisham High Road and as much of Tanners Hill as can be seen before it dips past the railway bridge into sheer Deptford.

Returning to his table, he opened a carton of the cheapest cigarettes and, lighting one, puffed in an amateurish fashion. He smoked cigarettes rather like a woman who detests them but feels that it is the correct thing to do.

'Dear me,' said Mr Reeder feebly.

He was back at the window, and he had seen a man turn out of Lewisham High Road. He had crossed the road and was coming straight to Daffodil House – which frolicsome name appeared on the door-posts of Mr Reeder's residence. A tall, straight man, with a sombre brown face, he came to the front gate, passed through and beyond the watcher's range of vision.

'Dear me!' said Mr Reeder, as he heard the tinkle of a bell.

A few minutes later his housekeeper tapped on the door.

'Will you see Mr Kohl, sir?' she asked.

Mr J. G. Reeder nodded.

Lew Kohl walked into the room to find a middle-aged man in a flamboyant dressing-gown sitting at his desk, a pair of pince-nez set crookedly on his nose.

'Good morning, Kohl.'

Lew Kohl looked at the man who had sent him to seven and a half years of hell, and the corner of his thin lips curled.

''Morning, Mr Reeder.' His eyes flashed across the almost bare surface of the writing-desk on which Reeder's hands were lightly clasped. 'You didn't expect to see me, I guess?'

'Not so early,' said Reeder in his hushed voice, 'but I should have remembered that early rising is one of the good habits which are inculcated by penal servitude.'

He said this in the manner of one bestowing praise for good conduct.

'I suppose you've got a pretty good idea of why I have come, eh? I'm a bad forgetter, Reeder, and a man in Dartmoor has time to think.'

The older man lifted his sandy eyebrows, the steel-rimmed glasses on his nose slipped further askew.

'That phrase seems familiar,' he said, and the eyebrows lowered in a frown. 'Now let me think – it was in a melodrama, of course, but was it "Souls in Harness" or "The Marriage Vow"?'

He appeared genuinely anxious for assistance in solving this problem.

'This is going to be a different kind of play,' said the long-faced Lew through his teeth. 'I'm going to get you, Reeder – you can go along and tell your boss, the Public Prosecutor. But I'll get you sweet! There will be no evidence to swing me. And I'll get that nice little stocking of yours, Reeder!'

The legend of Reeder's fortune was accepted even by so intelligent a man as Kohl.

'You'll get my stocking! Dear me, I shall have to go barefooted,' said Mr Reeder, with a faint show of humour.

'You know what I mean – think that over. Some hour and day you'll go out, and all Scotland Yard won't catch me for the killing! I've thought it out – '

'One has time to think in Dartmoor,' murmured Mr J. G. Reeder encouragingly. 'You're becoming one of the world's thinkers, Kohl. Do you know Rodin's masterpiece – a beautiful statue throbbing with life – '

'That's all.' Lew Kohl rose, the smile still trembling at the corner of his mouth. 'Maybe you'll turn this over in your mind, and in a day or two you won't be feeling so gay.'

Reeder's face was pathetic in its sadness. His untidy sandy-grey hair seemed to be standing on end; the large ears, that stood out at right angles to his face, gave the illusion of quivering movement.

Lew Kohl's hand was on the door-knob.

'*Womp!*'

It was the sound of a dull weight striking a board; something winged past his cheek, before his eyes a deep hole showed in the wall, and his face was stung by flying grains of plaster. He spun round with a whine of rage.

Mr Reeder had a long-barrelled Browning in his hand, with a barrel-shaped silencer over the muzzle, and he was staring at the weapon open-mouthed.

'Now how on earth did that happen?' he asked in wonder.

Lew Kohl stood trembling with rage and fear, his face yellow-white.

'You – you swine!' he breathed. 'You tried to shoot me!'

Mr Reeder stared at him over his glasses.

'Good gracious – you think that? Still thinking of killing me, Kohl?'

Kohl tried to speak but found no words, and, flinging open the door, he strode down the stairs and through the front entrance. His foot was on the first step when something came hurtling past him and crashed to fragments at his feet. It was a large stone vase that had decorated the window-sill of Mr Reeder's bedroom. Leaping over the debris of stone and flower mould, he glared up into the surprised face of Mr J. G. Reeder.

'I'll get you!' he spluttered.

'I hope you're not hurt?' asked the man at the window in a tone of concern. 'These things happen. Some day and some hour – '

As Lew Kohl strode down the street, the detective was still talking.

Mr Stan Bride was at his morning ablutions when his friend and sometime prison associate came into the little room that overlooked Fitzroy Square.

Stan Bride, who bore no resemblance to anything virginal, being a stout and stumpy man with a huge red face and many chins, stopped in the act of drying himself and gazed over the edge of the towel.

'What's the matter with you?' he asked sharply. 'You look as if you'd been chased by a busy. What did you go out so early for?'

Lew told him, and the jovial countenance of his room-mate grew longer and longer.

'You poor fish!' he hissed. 'To go after Reeder with that stuff! Don't you think he was waiting for you? Do you suppose he didn't know the very moment you left the Moor?'

'I've scared him, anyway,' said the other, and Mr Bride laughed.

'Good scout!' he sneered. 'Scare that old person!' (He did not say 'person.') 'If he's as white as you, he *is* scared! But he's not. Of course he shot past you – if he'd wanted to shoot you, you'd have been stiff by now. But he didn't. Thinker, eh – he's given you somep'n' to think about.'

'Where that gun came from I don't – '

There was a knock at the door and the two men exchanged glances.

'Who's there?' asked Bride, and a familiar voice answered.

'It's that busy from the Yard,' whispered Bride, and opened the door.

The 'busy' was Sergeant Allford, CID, an affable and portly man and a detective of some promise.

''Morning, boys – not been to church, Stan?'

Stan grinned politely.

'How's trade, Lew?'

'Not so bad.' The forger was alert, suspicious.

'Come to see you about a gun – got an idea you're carrying one, Lew – Colt automatic R.7/94318. That's not right, Lew – guns don't belong to this country.'

'I've got no gun,' said Lew sullenly.

Bride had suddenly become an old man, for he also was a convict on licence, and the discovery might send him back to serve his unfinished sentence.

'Will you come a little walk to the station, or will you let me go over you?'

'Go over me,' said Lew, and put out his arms stiffly whilst the detective rubbed him down.

'I'll have a look round,' said the detective, and his 'look round' was very thorough.

'Must have been mistaken,' said Sergeant Allford. And then, suddenly: 'Was that what you chucked into the river as you were walking along the Embankment?'

Lew started. It was the first intimation he had received that he had been 'tailed' that morning.

Bride waited till the detective was visible from the window crossing Fitzroy Square; then he turned in a fury on his companion.

'Clever, ain't you! That old hound knew you had a gun – knew the number. And if Allford had found it you'd have been "dragged" and me too!'

'I threw it in the river,' said Lew sulkily.

'Brains – not many but some!' said Bride, breathing heavily. 'You cut out Reeder – he's hell and poison, and if you don't know it you're deaf! Scared him? You big stiff! He'd cut your throat and write a hymn about it.'

'I didn't know they were tailing me,' growled Kohl; 'but I'll get him! And his money too.'

'Get him from another lodging,' said Bride curtly. 'A crook I don't mind, being one; a murderer I don't mind, but a talking jackass makes me sick. Get his stuff if you can – I'll bet it's all invested in real estate, and you can't lift houses – but don't talk about it. I like you, Lew, up to a point; you're miles before the point and out of sight. I don't like Reeder – I don't like snakes, but I keep away from the Zoo.'

So Lew Kohl went into new diggings on the top floor of an Italian's house in Dean Street, and here he had leisure and inclination to brood upon his grievances and to plan afresh the destruction of his enemy. And new plans were needed, for the schemes which had seemed so watertight in the quietude of a Devonshire cell showed daylight through many crevices.

Lew's homicidal urge had undergone considerable modification. He had been experimented upon by a very clever psychologist – though he never regarded Mr Reeder in this light, and, indeed, had the vaguest idea as to what the word meant. But there were other ways of hurting Reeder, and his mind fell constantly back to the dream of discovering this peccant detective's hidden treasure.

It was nearly a week later that Mr Reeder invited himself into the Director's private sanctum, and that great official listened spellbound while his subordinate offered his outrageous theory about Sir James

Tithermite and his dead wife. When Mr Reeder had finished, the Director pushed back his chair from the table.

'My dear man,' he said, a little irritably, 'I can't possibly give a warrant on the strength of your surmises – not even a search warrant. The story is so fantastic, so incredible, that it would be more at home in the pages of a sensational story than in a Public Prosecutor's report.'

'It was a wild night, and yet Lady Tithermite was not ill,' suggested the detective gently. 'That is a fact to remember, sir.'

The Director shook his head.

'I can't do it – not on the evidence,' he said. 'I should raise a storm that'd swing me into Whitehall. Can't you do anything – unofficially?'

Mr Reeder shook his head.

'My presence in the neighbourhood has been remarked,' he said primly. 'I think it would be impossible to – er – cover up my traces. And yet I have located the place, and could tell you within a few inches –'

Again the Director shook his head.

'No, Reeder,' he said quietly, 'the whole thing is sheer deduction on your part. Oh, yes, I know you have a criminal mind – I think you have told me that before. And that is a good reason why I should not issue a warrant. You're simply crediting this unfortunate man with your ingenuity. Nothing doing!'

Mr Reeder sighed and went back to his bureau, not entirely despondent, for there had intruded a new element into his investigations.

Mr Reeder had been to Maidstone several times during the week, and he had not gone alone; though seemingly unconscious of the fact that he had developed a shadow, for he had seen Lew Kohl on several occasions, and had spent an uncomfortable few minutes wondering whether his experiment had failed.

On the second occasion an idea had developed in the detective's mind, and if he were a laughing man he would have chuckled aloud when he slipped out of Maidstone station one evening and, in the act of hiring a cab, had seen Lew Kohl negotiating for another.

Mr Bride was engaged in the tedious but necessary practice of so cutting a pack of cards that the ace of diamonds remained at the bottom, when his former co-lodger burst in upon him, and there was a light of triumph in Lew's cold eye which brought Mr Bride's heart to his boots.

'I've got him!' said Lew.

Bride put aside the cards and stood up.

'Got who?' he asked coldly. 'And if it's killing, you needn't answer, but get out!'

'There's no killing.'

Lew sat down squarely at the table, his hands in his pockets, a real smile on his face.

'I've been trailing Reeder for a week, and that fellow wants some trailing!'

'Well?' asked the other, when he paused dramatically.

'I've found his stocking!'

Bride scratched his chin, and was half convinced.

'You never have?'

Lew nodded.

'He's been going to Maidstone a lot lately, and driving to a little village about five miles out. There I always lost him. But the other night, when he came back to the station to catch the last train, he slipped into the waiting-room and I found a place where I could watch him. What do you think he did?'

Mr Bride hazarded no suggestion.

'He opened his bag,' said Lew impressively, 'and took out a wad of notes as thick as that! He'd been drawing on his bank! I trailed him up to London. There's a restaurant on the station and he went in to get a cup of coffee, with me keeping well out of his sight. As he came out of the restaurant he took out his handkerchief and wiped his mouth. He didn't see the little book that dropped, but I did. I was scared sick that somebody else would see it, or that he'd wait long enough to find it himself. But he went out of the station and I got that book before you could say "knife." Look!'

It was a well-worn little notebook, covered with faded red morocco. Bride put out his hand to take it.

'Wait a bit,' said Lew. 'Are you in this with me fifty-fifty, because I want some help?'

Bride hesitated.

'If it's just plain thieving, I'm with you,' he said.

'Plain thieving — and sweet,' said Lew exultantly, and pushed the book across the table.

For the greater part of the night they sat together talking in low tones, discussing impartially the methodical book-keeping of Mr J. G. Reeder and his exceeding dishonesty.

The Monday night was wet. A storm blew up from the south-west, and the air was filled with falling leaves as Lew and his companion footed the five miles which separated them from the village. Neither carried any impedimenta that was visible, yet under Lew's waterproof coat was a kit of tools of singular ingenuity, and Mr Bride's coat pockets were weighted down with the sections of a powerful jemmy.

They met nobody in their walk, and the church bell was striking eleven when Lew gripped the bars of the South Lodge gates, pulled himself up to the top and dropped lightly on the other side. He was followed by Mr Bride, who, in spite of his bulk, was a singularly agile man. The ruined lodge showed in the darkness, and they passed through the creaking gates to the door and Lew flashed his lantern upon the keyhole before he began manipulation with the implements which he had taken from his kit.

The door was opened in ten minutes and a few seconds later they stood in a low-roofed little room, the principal feature of which was a deep, grateless fire-place. Lew took off his mackintosh and stretched it over the window before he spread the light in his lamp, and, kneeling down, brushed the debris from the hearth, examining the joints of the big stone carefully.

'This work's been botched,' he said. 'Anybody could see that.'

He put the claw of the jemmy into a crack and levered up the stone, and it moved slightly. Stopping only to dig a deeper crevice with a chisel and hammer he thrust the claw of the jemmy farther down. The stone came up above the edge of the floor and Bride slipped the chisel underneath.

'Now together,' grunted Lew.

They got their fingers beneath the hearthstone and with one heave hinged it up. Lew picked up the lamp and, kneeling down, flashed a light into the dark cavity. And then:

'Oh, my God!' he shrieked.

A second later two terrified men rushed from the house into the drive. And a miracle had happened, for the gates were open and a dark figure stood squarely before them.

'Put up your hands, Kohl' said a voice, and hateful as it was to Lew Kohl, he could have fallen on the neck of Mr Reeder.

At twelve o'clock that night Sir James Tithermite was discussing matters with his bride-to-be: the stupidity of her lawyer, who wished to safeguard her fortune, and his own cleverness and foresight in securing complete freedom of action for the girl who was to be his wife.

'These blackguards think of nothing but their fees,' he began, when his footman came in unannounced, and behind him the Chief Constable of the county and a man he remembered seeing before.

'Sir James Tithermite?' said the Chief Constable unnecessarily, for he knew Sir James very well.

'Yes, Colonel, what is it?' asked the baronet, his face twitching.

'I am taking you into custody on a charge of wilfully murdering your wife, Eleanor Mary Tithermite.'

* * *

'The whole thing turned upon the question as to whether Lady Tithermite was a good or a bad sailor,' explained J. G. Reeder to his chief. 'If she were a bad sailor, it was unlikely that she would be on the ship, even for five minutes, without calling for the stewardess. The stewardess did not see her ladyship, nor did anybody on board, for the simple reason that she was not on board! She was murdered within the grounds of the Manor; her body was buried beneath the hearthstone of the old lodge, and Sir James continued his journey by car to Dover, handing over his packages to a porter and telling him to take them to his cabin before he returned to put the car into the hotel garage. He had timed his arrival so that he passed on board with a crowd of passengers from the boat train, and nobody knew whether he was alone or whether he was accompanied, and, for the matter of that, nobody cared. The purser gave him his key, and he put the baggage, including his wife's hat, into the cabin, paid the porter and dismissed him. Officially, Lady Tithermite was on board, for he surrendered her ticket to the collector and received her landing voucher. And then he discovered she had disappeared. The ship was searched, but of course the unfortunate lady was not found. As I remarked before – '

'You have a criminal mind,' said the Director good-humouredly. 'Go on, Reeder.'

'Having this queer and objectionable trait, I saw how very simple a matter it was to give the illusion that the lady was on board, and I decided that, if the murder was committed, it must have been within a few miles of the house. And then the local builder told me that he had given Sir James a little lesson in the art of mixing mortar. And the local blacksmith told me that the gate had been damaged, presumably by Sir James's car – I had seen the broken rods and all I wanted to know was when the repairs were effected. That she was beneath the hearth in the lodge I was certain. Without a search warrant it was impossible to prove or disprove my theory, and I myself could not conduct a private investigation without risking the reputation of our department – if I may say "our",' he said apologetically.

The Director was thoughtful.

'Of course, you induced this man Kohl to dig up the hearth by pretending you had money buried there. I presume you revealed that fact in your notebook? But why on earth did he imagine that you had a hidden treasure?'

Mr Reeder smiled sadly.

'The criminal mind is a peculiar thing,' he said, with a sigh. 'It harbours illusions and fairy stories. Fortunately, I understand that mind. As I have often said – '

Van Der Valk and the False Caesar

◆ ————————◆———————— ◆

NICOLAS FREELING

Chief Inspector Van der Valk of the Amsterdam Police is a humanistic detective who always tries to look at both sides in any crime. He is a concerned criminologist, but nevertheless willing to try unorthodox methods of detection which quite often brings him into confrontation with the officialdom that he so heartily dislikes. Van der Valk has been getting results – and admirers – since his debut in Love in Amsterdam *was published in 1962. He has become equally successful on television, inspiring two different series with fine leading men. The better known of the two,* Van der Valk, *was launched by Thames Television with thirteen hour-long episodes in 1972 filmed on location and starring the likeable blond actor, Barry Foster, who has continued the role in subsequent series. A similar series was also made by West German TV in 1983 with another excellent British actor, the former star of* Bouquet of Barbed Wire (1973), *Frank Finlay, playing the Dutch policeman.*

Nicolas Freeling (1927–) lived in Holland for a number of years which explains the authenticity of the background to his stories, and was inspired to write his first Van der Valk novel out of a sense of outrage at being unjustly arrested and charged with theft. Freeling is a great admirer of Maigret and has admitted the influence of Georges Simenon's work on his own character. He also worked in the hotel business for a number of years before achieving success as a writer and apart from making Van der Valk something of a gourmet has provided him with a wife who is highly intelligent and an excellent cook and – as in the case of Van der Valk and the False Caesar – *is quite often able to help him in the solving of a case . . .*

'NOW look,' said Van der Valk quietly across his desk, ' a simple unsupported charge of hanky-panky is not enough – if the police listened every time they got that there'd be no end to it. I'm not saying for an instant you might be acting from malice or spite, but you do see my point, huh? An official inquiry, casting doubt on a death, is already very serious. Then publicity, gossip, conjecture – not to mention a charge of false prosecution.'

'I know', said the young man helplessly. 'But it's too much for me. My father gathered and ate mushrooms for thirty years – and then suddenly he dies from eating mushrooms. It's just too big for me to swallow. I cannot – I will not – believe in a mistake.'

Van der Valk stared at him for a long minute, then slowly took a piece of paper, slowly unclipped his pen, and stabbed the air with it. 'Make a statement – only the things of which you are reasonably certain. Sign it. If it should later show untruth or distortion you could be in big trouble – you accept that?'

'Yes,' the young man said resignedly.

'And if anything does show up, and if I decided to act on it, you realize the very heavy responsibility you would be taking on? You've really weighed all the possible consequences? . . . Very well, I'll take your statement and it will be carefully studied, but that's all I can promise you. Now, you say your father ate these mushroom dishes often. Did anybody ever share them?'

'I did, usually. Only that night I wasn't there. Nobody else ever did – they had a terror of them.'

'He cooked the mushrooms himself?'

'As a rule, yes. Sometimes she did, if he were tired or busy. This time she did.'

'And which mushrooms were they, exactly?'

'One only. A Caesar. A big Caesar – best there is. He was very proud of having found it.'

'He told you that?'

'He was in coma when I arrived. She told me – but I recognized it. Huge orange thing.'

'But an amanita?'

'A perfectly safe amanita. I've had them before, though not often.'

'He had nausea, you say, and drunkenness. Then he fell asleep?'

'Yes. He behaved as though he were drunk. But I called the doctor –
he'd had no more than usual, a small bottle of burgundy. The doctor
said yes, it might be muscarine poisoning, and he injected atropine. He
said there was a serum but that it was difficult to get – antiphalline. He
came back about four hours later – he'd been everywhere for it. But by
the time the doctor returned it was too late. I don't blame him; he did
his best.'

'So your father died, in a drunken heavy sleep passing into coma,
about ten to twelve hours after eating. Very well. Now tell me –'

Ordinarily Van der Valk never mentioned his work at home. But
Arlette was something of a mushroom expert herself – Frenchwoman,
countrywoman. She would be interested.

'Sounds very queer. An expert wouldn't make a mistake like that.
There is a false orange, a false Caesar – two in fact, the flykiller and the
panther. But anybody with experience can tell the difference.'

'What about the phalloids?'

'Entirely different – they're pale, brownish or greenish. There's a
safe pale one, but it's difficult to tell – and a good red one too which is
very like the panther. But not a Caesar – you'd need to be really stupid
to mistake a wicked amanita for a Caesar.'

'Is the poisoning always the same?'

'No, not a bit. The phalloids are the horrible ones – destroy your
liver. Doesn't show for about twelve hours and then it's too late. You
die about three days later. There is a serum.'

'Yes, the doctor tried to get the serum. But he couldn't.'

'He doesn't know mushrooms. The panther isn't phalline at all, so
the serum's irrelevant, no use at all. And you die much quicker – in a
few hours and in a coma. Muscarine, I think, and it's easier to treat. If
you get the doctor in time you don't die at all.'

'Know what the treatment is?

'Atropine, I believe.'

'Yes, that checks. That's what the doctor gave him.'

'Wait a moment,' said Arlette slowly. 'I'm trying to remember
something. I think I've heard that if you're poisoned with a panther or
a flykiller, then atropine is all wrong – makes it even worse. You better
look it up.'

'A Dutch doctor might not know that.'

'A French one might not know it either – unless he were a
countryman.'

Van der Valk got all the tomes out and spent an hour studying. 'True
enough. Here in the natural history book. There's a muscarine

syndrome, and for that the treatment is atropine. But there's also a panther syndrome, and for that atropine is bad. But it's confusing, because the panther also contains muscarine. The phalloids are quite different, of course.'

'Nobody would mistake a phalloid for a Caesar,' insisted Arlette. 'I don't even see how anyone could mistake a panther for a Caesar.'

'Would getting the wrong treatment kill him?'

'Of course not – but it wouldn't stop him from dying either.'

'What about *after* the mushroom was cooked? You couldn't tell then, could you?'

'I don't know,' said Arlette simply. 'I've never cooked one.'

'I asked about it – thought you'd be interested. Done in oil – with tomatoes, garlic, parsley.'

'Then it would be impossible to tell,' she said with certainty. 'It would go yellowish orange – yes, it would look like a Caesar.'

It *might* have been an accident of treatment – and one couldn't accuse a doctor of not recognizing the false Caesar. It *might* have been a mistake – when old, Arlette had said, or after rain, the colours were much the same, but an experienced picker would never have taken the risk. And it was possible – possible – that a panther had been substituted for the Caesar.

Only an exhumation order would decide – and Van der Valk could see the magistrate's face if he came up with that rigmarole! And there would always remain the doubt – the victim *might* have picked the panther himself.

It was better, was it not, that a murderer go free than that innocent people, and a doctor who had done his best, should all have their lives ruined? Wasn't it?

Certainly it was. Once Van der Valk started it would be impossible to stop. Exactly like a bobsled run. Which killed people too, sometimes.

'Oddly enough I've mushrooms for supper,' said Arlette.

'Not tonight. I know I'm being childish – but not tonight.'

And she mourned all evening, because of the waste.

The Footsteps That Ran

◆————————◆

DOROTHY L. SAYERS

Lord Peter Death Bredon Wimsey, the Eton educated younger son of the Duke of Denver, has been called the most dashing and sophisticated detective in crime fiction. The Radio Times *has gone further, describing him in 1987 as, 'this monocled milord who combines Sherlock Holmes's brainpower with the Scarlet Pimpernel's pluck, in the silly-ass guise of a Bertie Wooster.' And just as Holmes needs Watson and Wooster could not survive without Jeeves, so Lord Peter is inseparable from his 'confidential man', the ex-Army sergeant, Bunter. Wimsey became an amateur detective almost by chance after distinguished military service, when his knowledge of criminology made him a man to seek out by the innocent when they were in an incriminating situation. Following his first appearance in* Whose Body? *(1923), the eccentric and witty aristocrat was soon the best known amateur detective in London (based in a sumptuous flat at 110, Piccadilly) as well as becoming an increasingly popular character with readers. The first Lord Peter film,* The Silent Passenger, *was made in 1935 with Peter Haddon in the lead role and Aubrey Mather as Bunter. Robert Montgomery appeared as a more staid mi'lord in* Busman's Honeymoon *(1940), but it was the grandiloquent actor Seymour Hicks as Bunter who stole the picture. It was not until 1973 that Wimsey made his debut on television, and the BBC adaptations of four of the novels featuring the sleuth (*Clouds of Witness, The Unpleasantness at the Bellona Club, The Nine Tailors *and* Murder Must Advertise*) were all excellently set in the Twenties, memorably served by the former comedy actor, Ian Carmichael, and proved essential watching for millions of viewers. In 1987, the BBC made a second series from the novel,* Strong Poison, *with Edward Petherbridge as Wimsey and Richard Morant playing Bunter.*

Dorothy Sayers (1893–1957) is today numbered among the 'Queens of Crime Fiction', although she was far more dedicated to her other literary writing – mainly to do with religious subjects – and once claimed that she 'only dabbled in crime novels to make money'. A formidable scholar at Oxford University, she initially worked in a London advertising agency (where she was responsible for coining the famous phrase 'Guinness is good for you'), but it was the success of Lord Peter Wimsey whom she conceived in 1920 which gave her the independence to write. Of her short tales about the amateur detective and his servant, The Footsteps That Ran *probably shows Bunter, a trained mechanic, photographer and cook, at his most resourceful in helping his Lordship solve a murder in what Ellery Queen has described as 'one of the best short stories about Lord Peter Wimsey.'*

M R Bunter withdrew his head from beneath the focusing cloth. 'I fancy that will be quite adequate, sir,' he said deferentially, 'unless there are any further patients, if I may call them so, which you would wish put on record.'

'Not to-day,' replied the doctor. He took the last stricken rat gently from the table, and replaced it in its cage with an air of satisfaction. 'Perhaps on Wednesday, if Lord Peter can kindly spare your services once again – '

'What's that?' murmured his lordship, withdrawing his long nose from the investigation of a number of unattractive-looking glass jars. 'Nice old dog,' he added vaguely. 'Wags his tail when you mention his name, what? Are these monkey-glands, Hartman, or a south-west elevation of Cleopatra's duodenum?'

'You don't know anything, do you?' said the young physician, laughing. 'No use playing your bally-fool-with-an-eyeglass tricks on me, Wimsey. I'm up to them. I was saying to Bunter that I'd be no end grateful if you'd let him turn up again three days hence to register the progress of the specimens – always supposing they do progress, that is.'

'Why ask, dear old thing?' said his lordship. 'Always a pleasure to assist a fellow-sleuth, don't you know. Trackin' down murderers – all in the same way of business and all that. All finished? Good egg! By the way, if you don't have that cage mended you'll lose one of your patients – Number five. The last wire but one is workin' loose – assisted by the intelligent occupant. Jolly little beasts, ain't they? No need of dentists – wish I was a rat – wire much better for the nerves than that fizzlin' drill.'

Dr Hartman uttered a little exclamation.

'How in the world did you notice that, Wimsey? I didn't think you'd even looked at the cage.'

'Built noticin' – improved by practice,' said Lord Peter quietly. 'Anythin' wrong leaves a kind of impression on the eye; brain trots along afterwards with the warnin'. I saw that when we came in. Only just grasped it. Can't say my mind was glued on the matter. Shows the victim's improvin', anyhow. All serene, Bunter?'

'Everything perfectly satisfactory, I trust, my lord,' replied the manservant. He had packed up his camera and plates, and was quietly restoring order in the little laboratory, whose fittings – compact as those of an ocean liner – had been disarranged for the experiment.

'Well,' said the doctor, 'I am enormously obliged to you, Lord Peter, and to Bunter too. I am hoping for a great result from these experiments, and you cannot imagine how valuable an assistance it will be to me to have a really good series of photographs. I can't afford this sort of thing – yet,' he added, his rather haggard young face wistful as he looked at the great camera, 'and I can't do the work at the hospital. There's no time; I've got to be here. A struggling GP can't afford to let his practice go, even in Bloomsbury. There are times when even a half-crown visit makes all the difference between making both ends meet and having an ugly hiatus.'

'As Mr Micawber said,' replied Wimsey, ' "Income twenty pounds, expenditure nineteen, nineteen, six – result: happiness; expenditure twenty pounds, ought, six – result: misery." Don't prostrate yourself in gratitude, old bean; nothin' Bunter loves like messin' round with pyro and hyposulphite. Keeps his hand in. All kinds of practice welcome. Finger-prints and process plates spell seventh what-you-may-call-it of bliss, but focal-plane work on scurvy-ridden rodents (good phrase!) acceptable if no crime forthcoming. Crimes have been rather short lately. Been eatin' our heads off, haven't we, Bunter? Don't know what's come over London. I've taken to prying into my neighbour's affairs to keep from goin' stale. Frightened the postman into a fit the other day by askin' him how his young lady at Croydon was. He's a married man, livin' in Great Ormond Street.'

'How did you know?'

'Well, I didn't really. But he lives just opposite to a friend of mine – Inspector Parker; and his wife – not Parker's; he's unmarried; the postman's, I mean – asked Parker the other day whether the flyin' shows at Croydon went on all night. Parker, bein' flummoxed, said "No," without thinkin'. Bit of a give-away, what? Thought I'd give the poor devil a word in season, don't you know. Uncommonly thoughtless of Parker.'

The doctor laughed. 'You'll stay to lunch, won't you?' he said. 'Only cold meat and salad, I'm afraid. My woman won't come Sundays. Have to answer my own door. Deuced unprofessional, I'm afraid, but it can't be helped.'

'Pleasure,' said Wimsey, as they emerged from the laboratory and entered the dark little flat by the back door. 'Did you build this place on?'

'No,' said Hartman; 'the last tenant did that. He was an artist. That's why I took the place. It comes in very useful, ramshackle as it is, though this glass roof is a bit sweltering on a hot day like this. Still, I had to have something on the ground floor, cheap, and it'll do till times get better.'

'Till your vitamin-experiments make you famous, eh?' said Peter cheerfully. 'You're goin' to be the comin' man, you know. Feel it in my bones. Uncommonly neat little kitchen you've got, anyhow.'

'It does,' said the doctor. 'The lab makes it a bit gloomy, but the woman's only here in the daytime.'

He led the way into a narrow little dining-room, where the table was laid for a cold lunch. The one window at the end farthest from the kitchen looked out into Great James Street. The room was little more than a passage, and full of doors – the kitchen door, a door in the adjacent wall leading into the entrance-hall, and a third on the opposite side, through which his visitor caught a glimpse of a moderate-sized consulting-room.

Lord Peter Wimsey and his host sat down to table, and the doctor expressed a hope that Mr Bunter would sit down with them. That correct person, however, deprecated any such suggestion.

'If I might venture to indicate my own preference, sir,' he said, 'it would be to wait upon you and his lordship in the usual manner.'

'It's no use,' said Wimsey. 'Bunter likes me to know my place. Terrorizin' sort of man, Bunter. Can't call my soul my own. Carry on, Bunter; we wouldn't presume for the world.'

Mr Bunter handed the salad, and poured out the water with a grave decency appropriate to a crusted old tawny port.

It was a Sunday afternoon in that halcyon summer of 1921. The sordid little street was almost empty. The ice-cream man alone seemed thriving and active. He leaned luxuriously on the green post at the corner, in the intervals of driving a busy trade. Bloomsbury's swarm of able-bodied and able-voiced infants was still; presumably within-doors, eating steamy Sunday dinners inappropriate to the tropical weather. The only disturbing sounds came from the flat above, where heavy footsteps passed rapidly to and fro.

'Who's the merry-and-bright bloke above?' enquired Lord Peter presently. 'Not an early riser, I take it. Not that anybody is on a Sunday mornin'. Why an inscrutable Providence ever inflicted such a ghastly day on people livin' in town I can't imagine. I ought to be in the country, but I've got to meet a friend at Victoria this afternoon. Such a day to choose. ... Who's the lady? Wife or accomplished friend? Gather she takes a properly submissive view of woman's duties in the home, either way. That's the bedroom overhead, I take it.'

Hartman looked at Lord Peter in some surprise.

''Scuse my beatly inquisitiveness, old thing,' said Wimsey. 'Bad habit. Not my business.'

'How did you – ?'

'Guesswork,' said Lord Peter, with disarming frankness. 'I heard the squawk of an iron bedstead on the ceiling and a heavy fellow get out with a bump, but it may quite well be a couch or something. Anyway, he's been potterin' about in his stocking feet over these few feet of floor for the last half-hour, while the woman has been clatterin' to and fro, in and out of the kitchen and away into the sittin'-room, with her high heels on, ever since we've been here. Hence deduction as to domestic habits of the first-floor tenants.'

'I thought,' said the doctor, with an aggrieved expression, 'you'd been listening to my valuable exposition of the beneficial effects of Vitamin B, and Lind's treatment of scurvy with fresh lemons in 1755.'

'I was listenin',' agreed Lord Peter hastily, 'but I heard the footsteps as well. Fellow's toddled into the kitchen – only wanted the matches, though; he's gone off into the sittin'-room and left her to carry on the good work. What was I sayin'? Oh, yes! You see, as I was sayin' before, one hears a thing or sees it without knowin' or thinkin' about it. Then afterwards one starts meditatin', and it all comes back, and one sorts out one's impressions. Like those plates of Bunter's. Picture's all there, l – la – what's the word I want, Bunter?'

'Latent, my lord.'

'That's it. My right-hand man, Bunter; couldn't do a thing without him. The picture's latent till you put the developer on. Same with the brain. No mystery. Little grey books all my respected grandmother!

Little grey matter's all you want to remember things with. As a matter of curiosity, was I right about those people above?'

'Perfectly. The man's a gas-company's inspector. A bit surly, but devoted (after his own fashion) to his wife. I mean, he doesn't mind hulking in bed on a Sunday morning and letting her do the chores, but he spends all the money he can spare on giving her pretty hats and fur coats and what not. They've only been married about six months. I was called in to her when she had a touch of 'flu in the spring, and he was almost off his head with anxiety. She's a lovely little woman, I must say – Italian. He picked her up in some eating-place in Soho, I believe. Glorious dark hair and eyes: Venus sort of figure; proper contours in all the right places; good skin – all that sort of thing. She was a bit of a draw to that restaurant while she was there, I fancy. Lively. She had an old admirer round here one day – awkward little Italian fellow, with a knife – active as a monkey. Might have been unpleasant, but I happened to be on the spot, and her husband came along. People are always laying one another out in these streets. Good for business, of course, but one gets tired of tying up broken heads and slits in the jugular. Still, I suppose the girl can't help bring attractive, though I don't say she's what you might call stand-offish in her manner. She's sincerely fond of Brotherton, I think, though – that's his name.'

Wimsey nodded inattentively. 'I suppose life is a bit monotonous here,' he said.

'Professionally, yes. Births and drunks and wife-beatings are pretty common. And all the usual ailments, of course. Just at present I'm living on infant diarrhoea chiefly – bound to, this hot weather, you know. With the autumn, 'flu and bronchitis set in. I may get an occasional pneumonia. Legs, of course, and varicose veins – God!' cried the doctor explosively, 'if only I could get away, and do my experiments!'

'Ah!' said Peter, 'where's that eccentric old millionaire with a mysterious disease, who always figures in the novels? A lightning diagnosis – a miraculous cure – "God bless you, doctor; here are five thousand pounds" – Harley Street – '

'That sort doesn't live in Bloomsbury,' said the doctor.

'It must be fascinatin', diagnosin' things,' said Peter thoughtfully. 'How d'you do it? I mean, is there a regular set of symptoms for each disease, like callin' a club to show you want your partner to go no trumps? You don't just say: "This fellow's got a pimple on his nose, therefore he has fatty degeneration of the heart – "''

'I hope not,' said the doctor drily.

'Or is it more like gettin' a clue to a crime?' went on Peter. 'You see somethin' – a room, or a body, say, all knocked about anyhow, and there's a damn sight of symptoms of somethin' wrong, and you've got just to pick out the ones which tell the story?'

'That's more like it,' said Dr Hartman. 'Some symptoms are significant in themselves – like the condition of the gums in scurvy, let us say – others in conjunction with – '

He broke off, and both sprang to their feet as a shrill scream sounded suddenly from the flat above, followed by a heavy thud. A man's voice cried out lamentably; feet ran violently to and fro; then, as the doctor and his guests stood frozen in consternation, came the man himself – falling down the stairs in his haste, hammering at Hartman's door.

'Help! Help! Let me in! My wife! He's murdered her!'

*   *   *

They ran hastily to the door and let him in. He was a big, fair man, in his shirt-sleeves and stockings. His hair stood up, and his face was set in bewildered misery.

'She is dead – dead. He was her lover,' he groaned. 'Come and look – take her away – Doctor! I have lost my wife! My Maddalena – ' He paused, looked wildly for a moment, and then said hoarsely, 'Someone's been in – somehow – stabbed her – murdered her. I'll have the law on him, doctor. Come quickly – she was cooking the chicken for my dinner – Ah-h-h!'

He gave a long, hysterical shriek, which ended in a hiccupping laugh. The doctor took him roughly by the arm and shook him. 'Pull yourself together, Mr Brotherton,' he said sharply. 'Perhaps she is only hurt. Stand out of the way!'

'Only hurt?' said the man, sitting heavily down on the nearest chair. 'No – no – she is dead – little Maddalena – Oh, my God!'

Dr Hartman had snatched a roll of bandages and a few surgical appliances from the consulting-room, and he ran upstairs, followed closely by Lord Peter. Bunter remained for a few moments to combat hysterics with cold water. Then he stepped across to the dining-room window and shouted.

'Well, wot is it?' cried a voice from the street.

'Would you be so kind as to step in here a minute, officer?' said Mr Bunter. 'There's been murder done.'

*   *   *

When Brotherton and Bunter arrived upstairs with the constable, they found Dr Hartman and Lord Peter in the little kitchen. The doctor was kneeling beside the woman's body. At their entrance he looked up, and shook his head.

'Death instantaneous,' he said. 'Clean through the heart. Poor child. She cannot have suffered at all. Oh, constable, it is very fortunate you are here. Murder appears to have been done – though I'm afraid the man has escaped. Probably Mr Brotherton can give us some help. He was in the flat at the time.'

The man has sunk down on a chair, and was gazing at the body with a face from which all meaning seemed to have been struck out. The policeman produced a notebook.

'Now, sir,' he said, 'don't let's waste any time. Sooner we can get to work the more likely we are to catch our man. Now, you was 'ere at the time, was you?'

Brotherton stared a moment, then, making a violent effort, he answered steadily:

'I was in the sitting-room, smoking and reading the paper. My – *she* – was getting the dinner ready in here. I heard her give a scream, and I rushed in and found her lying on the floor. She didn't have time to say anything. When I found she was dead, I rushed to the window, and saw the fellow scrambling away over the glass roof there. I yelled at him, but he disappeared. Then I ran down – '

''Arf a mo',' said the policeman. 'Now, see 'ere, sir, didn't you think to go after 'im at once?'

'My first thought was for her,' said the man. 'I thought maybe she wasn't dead. I tried to bring her round – ' His speech ended in a groan.

'You say he came in through the window,' said the policeman.

'I beg your pardon, officer,' interrupted Lord Peter, who had been apparently making a mental inventory of the contents of the kitchen. 'Mr Brotherton suggested that the man went *out* through the window. It's better to be accurate.'

'It's the same thing,' said the doctor. 'It's the only way he could have come in. These flats are all alike. The staircase door leads into the sitting-room, and Mr Brotherton was there, so the man couldn't have come that way.'

'And,' said Peter, 'he didn't get in through the bedroom window, or we should have seen him. We were in the room below. Unless, indeed, he let himself down from the roof. Was the door between the bedroom and the sitting-room open?' he asked suddenly, turning to Brotherton.

The man hesitated a moment. 'Yes,' he said finally. 'Yes, I'm sure it was.'

'Could you have seen the man if he had come through the bedroom window?'

'I couldn't have helped seeing him.'

'Come, come, sir,' said the policeman, with some irritation, 'better let *me* ask the questions. Stands to reason the fellow wouldn't get in through the bedroom window in full view of the street.'

'How clever of you to think of that,' said Wimsey. 'Of course not. Never occurred to me. Then it must have been this window, as you say.'

'And, what's more, here's his marks on the window-sill,' said the constable triumphantly, pointing to some blurred traces among the London soot. 'That's right. Down he goes by that drain-pipe, over the glass roof down there – what's that the roof of?'

'My laboratory,' said the doctor. 'Heavens! to think that while we were there at dinner this murdering villain – '

'Quite so, sir,' agreed the constable. 'Well, he'd get away over the wall into the court be'ind. 'E'll 'ave been seen there, no fear; you needn't anticipate much trouble in layin' 'ands on 'im, sir. I'll go round there in 'arf a tick. Now then, sir' – turning to Brotherton – ''ave you any idea wot this party might have looked like?'

Brotherton lifted a wild face, and the doctor interposed.

'I think you ought to know, constable,' he said, 'that there was – well, not a murderous attack, but what might have been one, made on this woman before – about eight weeks ago – by a man named Marincetti – an Italian waiter – with a knife.'

'Ah!' The policeman licked his pencil eagerly. 'Do you know this party as 'as been mentioned?' he enquired of Brotherton.

'That's the man,' said Brotherton, with concentrated fury. 'Coming here after my wife – God curse him! I wish to God I had him dead here beside her!'

'Quite so,' said the policeman. 'Now, sir' – to the doctor – ''ave you got the weapon wot the crime was committed with?'

'No,' said Hartman, 'there was no weapon in the body when I arrived.'

'Did *you* take it out?' pursued the constable, to Brotherton.

'No,' said Brotherton, 'he took it with him.'

'Took it with 'im,' the constable entered the fact in his notes. 'Phew! Wonderful 'ot it is in 'ere, ain't it, sir?' he added, mopping his brow.

'It's the gas-oven, I think,' said Peter mildly. 'Uncommon hot thing, a gas-oven, in the middle of July. D'you mind if I turn it out? There's the chicken inside, but I don't suppose you want – '

Brotherton groaned, and the constable said: 'Quite right, sir. A man wouldn't 'ardly fancy 'is dinner after a thing like this. Thank you, sir. Well now, doctor, wot kind of weapon do you take this to 'ave been?'

'It was a long, narrow weapon – something like an Italian stiletto, I imagine,' said the doctor, 'about six inches long. It was thrust in with great force under the fifth rib, and I should say it had pierced the heart centrally. As you see, there has been practically no bleeding. Such a wound would cause instant death. Was she lying just as she is now when you first saw her, Mr Brotherton?'

'On her back, just as she is,' replied the husband.

'Well, that seems clear enough,' said the policeman. 'This 'ere Marinetti, or wotever 'is name is, 'as a grudge against the poor young lady – '

'I believe he was an admirer,' put in the doctor.

'Quite so,' agreed the constable. 'Of course, these foreigners are like that – even the decentest of 'em. Stabbin' and such-like seems to come nateral to them, as you might say. Well, this 'ere Marinetti climbs in 'ere, see the poor young lady standin' 'ere by the table all alone, gettin' the dinner ready; 'e comes in be'ind, catches 'er round the waist, stabs 'er – easy job, you see; no corsets nor nothink – she shrieks out, 'e pulls 'is stiletty out of 'er an' makes tracks. Well, now we've got to find 'im, and by your leave, sir, I'll be gettin' along. We'll 'ave 'im by the 'eels before long, sir, don't you worry. I'll 'ave to put a man in charge 'ere, sir, to keep folks out, but that needn't worry you. Good mornin', gentlemen.'

'May we move the poor girl now?' asked the doctor.

'Certainly. Like me to 'elp you, sir?'

'No. Don't lose any time. We can manage.' Dr Hartman turned to Peter as the constable clattered downstairs. 'Will you help me, Lord Peter?'

'Bunter's better at that sort of thing,' said Wimsey, with a hard mouth.

The doctor looked at him in some surprise, but said nothing, and he and Bunter carried the still form away. Brotherton did not follow them. He sat in a grief-stricken heap, with his head buried in his hands. Lord Peter walked about the little kitchen, turning over the various knives and kitchen utensils, peering into the sink bucket, and apparently taking an inventory of the bread, butter, condiments, vegetables, and so forth which lay about in preparation for the Sunday meal. There were potatoes in the sink, half peeled, a pathetic witness to the quiet domestic life which had been so horribly interrupted. The colander was filled with green peas. Lord Peter turned these things over with an inquisitive finger, gazed into the smooth surface of a bowl of dripping as though it were a divining-crystal, ran his hands several times right through a bowl of flour – then drew his pipe from his pocket and filled it slowly.

The doctor returned, and put his hand on Brotherton's shoulder.

'Come,' he said gently, 'we have laid her in the other bedroom. She looks very peaceful. You must remember that, except for that moment of terror when she saw the knife, she suffered nothing. It is terrible for you, but you must try not to give way. The police – '

'The police can't bring her back to life,' said the man savagely. 'She's dead. Leave me alone, curse you! Leave me alone, I say!'

He stood up, with a violent gesture.

'You must not sit here,' said Hartman firmly. 'I will give you something to take, and you must try to keep calm. Then we will leave you, but if you don't control yourself – '

After some further persuasion, Brotherton allowed himself to be led away.

'Bunter,' said Lord Peter, as the kitchen door closed behind them, 'do you know why I am doubtful about the success of those rat experiments?'

'Meaning Dr Hartman's, my lord?'

'Yes. Dr Hartman has a theory. In any investigation, my Bunter, it is most damnably dangerous to have a theory.'

'I have heard you say so, my lord.'

'Confound you – you know it as well as I do! What is wrong with the doctor's theories, Bunter?'

'You wish me to reply, my lord, that he only sees the facts which fit in with theory.'

'Thought-reader!' exclaimed Lord Peter bitterly.

'And that he supplies them to the police, my lord.'

'Hush!' said Peter, as the doctor returned.

*   *   *

'I have got him to lie down,' said Dr Hartman, 'and I think the best thing we can do is to leave him to himself.'

'D'you know,' said Wimsey, 'I don't cotton to that idea, somehow.'

'Why? Do you think he's likely to destroy himself?'

'That's as good a reason to give as any other, I suppose,' said Wimsey, 'when you haven't got any reason which can be put into words. But my advice is, don't leave him for a moment.'

'But why? Frequently, with a deep grief like this, the presence of other people is merely an irritant. He begged me to leave him.'

'Then for God's sake go back to him,' said Peter.

'Really, Lord Peter,' said the doctor, 'I think I ought to know what is best for my patient.'

'Doctor,' said Wimsey, 'this is not a question of your patient. A crime has been committed.'

'But there is no mystery.'

'There are twenty mysteries. For one thing, when was the window-cleaner here last?'

'The window-cleaner?'

'Who shall fathom the ebony-black enigma of the window-cleaner?' pursued Peter lightly, putting a match to his pipe. 'You are quietly in your bath, in a state of more or less innocent nature, when an intrusive head appears at the window, like the ghost of Hamilton Tighe, and a gruff voice, suspended between earth and heaven, says "Good morning, sir." Where do window-cleaners go between visits? Do they hibernate, like busy bees? Do they – ?'

'Really, Lord Peter,' said the doctor, 'don't you think you're going a bit beyond the limit?'

'Sorry you feel like that,' said Peter, 'but I really want to know about the window-cleaner. Look how clear these panes are.'

'He came yesterday, if you want to know,' said Dr Hartman, rather stiffly.

'You are sure?'

'He did mine at the same time.'

'I thought as much,' said Lord Peter. 'In the words of the song:

> 'I thought as much,
> It was a little – window-cleaner.

In that case,' he added, 'it is absolutely imperative that Brotherton should not be left alone for a moment. Bunter! Confound it all, where's that fellow got to?'

The door into the bedroom opened.

'My lord?' Mr Bunter unobtrusively appeared, as he had unobtrusively stolen out to keep an unobtrusive eye upon the patient.

'Good,' said Wimsey. 'Stay where you are.' His lackadaisical manner had gone, and he looked at the doctor as four years previously he might have looked at a refractory subaltern.

'Dr Hartman,' he said, 'something is wrong. Cast your mind back. We were talking about symptoms. Then came the scream. Then came the sound of feet running. *Which direction did they run in?*'

'I'm sure I don't know.'

'Don't you? Symptomatic, though, doctor. They have been

troubling me all the time, subconsciously. Now I know why. They ran *from the kitchen.*'

'Well?'

'Well! And now the window-cleaner – '

'What about him?'

'Could you swear that it wasn't the window-cleaner who made those marks on the sill?'

'And the man Brotherton saw – ?'

'Have we examined your laboratory roof for his footsteps?'

'But the weapon? Wimsey, this is madness! Someone took the weapon.'

'I know. But did you think the edge of the wound was clean enough to have been made by a smooth stiletto? It looked ragged to me.'

'Wimsey, what are you driving at?'

'There's a clue here in the flat – and I'm damned if I can remember it. I've seen it – I know I've seen it. It'll come to me presently. Meanwhile, don't let Brotherton – '

'What?'

'Do whatever it is he's going to do.'

'But what is it?'

'If I could tell you that I could show you the clue. Why couldn't he make up his mind whether the bedroom door was open or shut? Very good story, but not quite thought out. Anyhow – I say, doctor, make some excuse, and strip him, and bring me his clothes. And send Bunter to me.'

The doctor stared at him, puzzled. Then he made a gesture of acquiescence and passed into the bedroom. Lord Peter followed him, casting a ruminating glance at Brotherton as he went. Once in the sitting-room, Lord Peter sat down on a red velvet arm-chair, fixed his eyes on a gilt-framed oleograph, and became wrapped in contemplation.

Presently Bunter came in, with his arms full of clothing. Wimsey took it, and begn to search it, methodically enough, but listlessly. Suddenly he dropped the garments, and turned to the manservant.

'No,' he said, 'this is a precaution, Bunter mine, but I'm on the wrong tack. It wasn't here I saw – whatever I did see. It was in the kitchen. Now, what was it?'

'I could not say, my lord, but I entertain a conviction that I was also, in a manner of speaking, conscious – not consciously, my lord, if you understand me, but still conscious of an incongruity.'

'Hurray!' said Wimsey suddenly. 'Cheer-oh! for the sub-conscious what's-his-name! Now let's remember the kitchen. I cleared out of it because I was gettin' obfuscated. Now then. Begin at the door. Fryin'-pans and sauce-pans on the wall. Gas-stove – oven goin' – chicken inside. Rack of wooden spoons on the wall, gas-lighter, pan-lifter. Stop me when I'm gettin' hot. Mantelpiece. Spice-boxes and stuff. Anything wrong with them? No. Dresser. Plates. Knives and forks – all clean; flour dredger – milk-jug – sieve on the wall – nutmeg-grater. Three-tier steamer. Looked inside – no grisly secrets in the steamer.'

'Did you look in all the dresser drawers, my lord?'

'No. That could be done. But the point is, I *did* notice somethin'. What did I notice? That's the point. Never mind. On with the dance – let joy be unconfined! Knife-board. Knife-powder. Kitchen table. Did you speak?'

'No,' said Bunter, who had moved from his attitude of wooden deference.'

'Table stirs a chord. Very good. On table. Choppin'-board. Remains of ham and herb stuffin'. Packet of suet, Another sieve. Several plates. Butter in a glass dish. Bowl of drippin' – '

'Ah!'

'Drippin' – ! Yes, there was – '

'Something unsatisfactory, my lord – '

'About the drippin'! Oh, my head! What's that they say in *Dear Brutus*, Bunter? "Hold on to the workbox." That's right. Hold on to the drippin'. Beastly slimy stuff to hold on to – Wait!'

There was a pause.

'When I was a kid,' said Wimsey, 'I used to love to go down into the kitchen and talk to old cookie. Good old soul she was, too. I can see her now, gettin' chicken ready, with me danglin' my legs on the table. *She* used to pluck an' draw 'em herself. I revelled in it. Little beasts boys are, ain't they, Bunter? Pluck it, draw it, wash it, stuff it, tuck its little tail through its little what-you-may-call-it, truss it, grease the dish – Bunter?'

'My lord!'

'Hold on to the dripping!'

'The bowl, my lord – '

'The bowl – visualize it – what was wrong?'

'It was full, my lord!'

'Got it – got it – *got* it! The bowl was full – smooth surface. Golly! I knew there was something queer about it. Now why shouldn't it be full? Hold on to the – '

'The bird was in the oven.'

'Without dripping!'

'Very careless cookery, my lord.'

'The bird – in the oven – no dripping. Bunter! Suppose it was never put in till after she was dead? Thrust in hurriedly by someone who had something to hide – horrible!'

'But with what object, my lord?'

'Yes, why? That's the point. One more mental association with the bird. It's just coming. Wait a moment. Pluck, draw, wash, stuff, tuck up, truss – By God!'

'My lord?'

'Come on, Bunter. Thank Heaven we turned off the gas!'

He dashed through the bedroom, disregarding the doctor and the patient, who sat up with a smothered shriek. He flung open the oven door and snatched out the baking-tin. The skin of the bird had just begun to discolour. With a little gasp of triumph, Wimsey caught the iron ring that protruded from the wing, and jerked out – the six-inch spiral skewer.

The doctor was struggling with the excited Brotherton in the doorway. Wimsey caught the man as he broke away, and shook him into the corner with a jiu-jitsu twist.

'Here is the weapon,' he said.

'Prove it, blast you!' said Brotherton savagely.

'I will,' said Wimsey. 'Bunter, call in the policeman whom you will find at the door. Doctor, we shall need your microscope.'

*   *   *

In the laboratory the doctor bent over the microscope. A thin layer of blood from the skewer had been spread upon the slide.

'Well?' said Wimsey impatiently.

'It's all right,' said Hartman. 'The roasting didn't get anywhere near the middle. My God, Wimsey, yes, you're right – round corpuscles, diameter $\frac{1}{3621}$ – mammalian blood – probably human – '

'Her blood,' said Wimsey.

*   *   *

'It was very clever, Bunter,' said Lord Peter, as the taxi trundled along on the way to his flat in Piccadilly. 'If that fowl had gone on roasting a bit longer the blood-corpuscles might easily have been destroyed beyond all hope of recognition. It all goes to show that the unpremeditated crime is usually the safest.'

'And what does your lordship take the man's motive to have been?'

'In my youth,' said Wimsey meditatively, 'they used to make me read the Bible. Trouble was, the only books I ever took to naturally were the ones they weren't over and above keen on. But I got to know the Song of Songs pretty well by heart. Look it up, Bunter; at your age it won't hurt you; it talks sense about jealousy.'

'I have perused the work in question, your lordship,' replied Mr Bunter, with a sallow blush. 'It says, if I remember rightly: "*Jealousy is cruel as the grave.*"'

The Eye of Apollo

◆

G. K. CHESTERTON

There is, at first glance, no more unlikely detective than the Roman Catholic priest, Father Brown. His bland face and empty eyes, his almost dull-witted manner and gentle speech, seem to make him a person who could be easily outwitted or fooled. But inside his simple clerical garb beats a brave heart and a quick brain. His method of approach to detection is to try to get inside the mind of the criminal and he sees his mission as trying to make wrongdoers repent rather than having them arrested. His greatest triumph came early in his career when he outsmarted the French criminal mastermind, Flambeau, 'the most famous thief in Europe', who then reformed and became Father Brown's devoted assistant on many subsequent cases. After his initial appearance in 1911 in The Innocence of Father Brown, *the little priest soon won admirers all over the world, including Ellery Queen who declared him to be one of 'the three greatest detectives in fiction' – the other two being Edgar Allan Poe's pioneer sleuth Auguste Dupin and Sherlock Holmes. The priest has subsequently been played in films three times: by Walter Connolly in* Father Brown, Detective *(1934); by Alec Guinness in the best screen adaptation,* Father Brown *(1954); and in two German adaptations made in the Sixties starring Heinz Ruhmann. He has twice been featured on television, most successfully in Britain when ATV produced twenty-six hour-long episodes of* Father Brown *in 1974 with the versatile Kenneth More giving a faithful interpretation of the thoughtful cleric. An attempt by NBC to relocate him in New York in a ninety-six-minute special,* Father Brown, Detective *(1980) with Bernard Hughes in the lead was rated 'watchable but overlong' by the critics and did not generate enough interest to launch the projected series.*

The prolific G. K. Chesterton (1874–1936), who was an artist, journalist, critic, poet, novelist and short story writer, combined his interest in criminology with his devout Catholic faith in creating Father Brown. A gregarious and popular man, Chesterton also gave mystery fiction the stories of 'The Club of Queer Trades' and a more orthodox crime fighter in the 'gentleman detective', Horne Fisher. The Father Brown story here, The Eye of Apollo, *in which he and Flambeau confront a bogus religious leader, is of especial interest because it comes near to answering one of the biggest mysteries about the priest – his first name – and also brings him very close to being outwitted by the villain . . .*

THAT singular smoky sparkle, at once a confusion and a transparency, which is the strange secret of the Thames, was changing more and more from its grey to its glittering extreme as the sun climbed to the zenith over Westminster, and the two men crossed Westminster Bridge. One man was very tall and the other very short; they might even have been fantastically compared to the arrogant clock-tower of Parliament and the humbler humped shoulders of the Abbey, for the short man was in clerical dress. The official description of the tall man was M. Hercule Flambeau, private detective, and he was going to his new offices in a new pile of flats facing the Abbey entrance. The official description of the short man was the Rev. J. Brown, attached to St Francis Xavier's Church, Camberwell, and he was coming from a Camberwell death-bed to see the new offices of his friend.

The building was American in its sky-scraping altitude, and American also in the oiled elaboration of its machinery of telephones and lifts. But it was barely finished and still understaffed: only three tenants had moved in; the office just above Flambeau was occupied, as also was the office just below him; the two floors above that and the three floors below were entirely bare. But the first glance at the new tower of flats caught something much more arresting. Save for a few relics of scaffolding, the one glaring object was erected outside the office just above Flambeau's. It was an enormous gilt effigy of the human eye, surrounded with rays of gold, and taking up as much room as two or three office windows.

'What on earth is that?' asked Father Brown, and stood still.

'Oh, a new religion,' said Flambeau, laughing; 'one of those new religions that forgive your sins by saying you never had any. Rather like Christian Science, I should think. The fact is that a fellow calling himself Kalon (I don't know what his name is, except that it can't be that) has taken the flat just above me. I have two lady typewriters underneath me, and this enthusiastic old humbug on top. He calls himself the New Priest of Apollo, and he worships the sun.'

'Let him look out,' said Father Brown. 'The sun was the cruellest of all the gods. But what does that monstrous eye mean?'

'As I understand it, it is a theory of theirs,' answered Flambeau, 'that a man can endure anything if his mind is quite steady. Their two great symbols are the sun and the open eye; for they say that if a man were really healthy he could stare at the sun.'

'If a man were really healthy,' said Father Brown, 'he would not bother to stare at it.'

'Well, that's all I can tell you about the new religion,' went on Flambeau carelessly. 'It claims, of course, that it can cure all physical diseases.'

'Can it cure the one spiritual disease?' asked Father Brown, with a serious curiosity.

'And what is the one spiritual disease?' asked Flambeau, smiling.

'Oh, thinking one is quite well,' said his friend.

Flambeau was more interested in the quiet little office below him than in the flamboyant temple above. He was a lucid Southerner, incapable of conceiving himself as anything but a Catholic or an atheist; and new religions of a bright and pallid sort were not much in his line. But humanity was always in his line, especially when it was good-looking; moreover, the ladies downstairs were characters in their way. The office was kept by two sisters, both slight and dark, one of them tall and striking. She had a dark, eager and aquiline profile, and was one of those women whom one always thinks of in profile, as of the clean-cut edge of some weapon. She seemed to cleave her way through life. She had eyes of startling brilliancy, but it was the brilliancy of steel rather than of diamonds; and her straight, slim figure was a shade too stiff for its grace. Her younger sister was like her shortened shadow, a little greyer, paler, and more insignificant. They both wore a business-like black, with little masculine cuffs and collars. There are thousands of such curt, strenuous ladies in the offices of London, but the interest of these lay rather in their real than their apparent position.

For Pauline Stacey, the elder, was actually the heiress of a crest and half a county, as well as great wealth; she had been brought up in castles and gardens, before a frigid fierceness (peculiar to the modern woman) had driven her to what she considered a harsher and a higher existence. She had not, indeed, surrendered her money; in that there would have been a romantic or monkish abandon quite alien to her masterful utilitarianism. She held her wealth, she would say, for use upon practical social objects. Part of it she had put into her business, the nucleus of a model typewriting emporium; part of it was distributed in various leagues and causes for the advancement of such work among women. How far Joan, her sister and partner, shared this slightly prosaic idealism no one could be very sure. But she followed her leader with a dog-like affection which was somehow more attractive – with its touch of tragedy – than the hard, high spirits of the elder. For Pauline Stacey had nothing to say to tragedy; she was understood to deny its existence.

Her rigid rapidity and cold impatience had amused Flambeau very much on the first occasion of his entering the flats. He had lingered outside the lift in the entrance-hall waiting for the lift-boy, who generally conducts strangers to the various floors. But this bright-eyed falcon of a girl had openly refused to endure such official delay. She said sharply that she knew all about the lift, and was not dependent on boys – or on men either. Though her flat was only three floors above, she managed in the few seconds of ascent to give Flambeau a great many of her fundamental views in an off-hand manner; they were to the general effect that she was a modern working woman and loved modern working machinery. Her bright black eyes blazed with abstract anger against those who rebuke mechanic science and ask for the return of romance. Everyone, she said, ought to be able to manage machines, just as she could manage the lift. She seemed almost to resent the fact of Flambeau opening the lift-door for her; and that gentleman went up to his own apartments smiling with somewhat mingled feeling at the memory of such spit-fire self-dependence.

She certainly had a temper, of a snappy, practical sort; the gestures of her thin, elegant hands were abrupt or even destructive. Once Flambeau entered her office on some typewriting business, and found she had just flung a pair of spectacles belonging to her sister into the middle of the floor and stamped on them. She was already in the rapids of an ethical tirade about the 'sickly medical notions' and the morbid admission of weakness implied in such an apparatus. She dared her sister to bring such artificial, unhealthy rubbish into the place again. She asked if she was expected to wear wooden legs or false hair or glass eyes; and as she spoke her eyes sparkled like the terrible crystal.

Flambeau, quite bewildered with this fanaticism, could not refrain from asking Miss Pauline (with direct French logic) why a pair of spectacles was a more morbid sign of weakness than a lift, and why if science might help us in the one effort, it might not help us in the other.

'That is *so* different,' said Pauline Stacey loftily. 'Batteries and motors and all those things are marks of the force of man – yes, Mr Flambeau, and the force of women, too! We shall take our turn at these great engines that devour distance and defy time. That is high and splendid – that is really science. But these nasty props and plasters the doctors sell – why, they are just badges of poltroonery. Doctors stick on legs and arms as if we were born cripples and sick slaves. But I was free-born, Mr Flambeau! People only think they need these things because they have been trained in fear instead of being trained in power and courage, just as the silly nurses tell children not to stare at the sun, and so they can't do it without blinking. But why among the stars should there be one star I may not see? The sun is not my master, and I will open my eyes and stare at him whenever I choose.'

'Your eyes,' said Flambeau, with a foreign bow, 'will dazzle the sun.' He took pleasure in complimenting this strange stiff beauty, partly because it threw her a little off her balance. But as he went upstairs to his floor he drew a deep breath and whistled, saying to himself: 'So she has got into the hands of that conjurer upstairs with his golden eye.' For, little as he knew or cared about the new religion of Kalon, he had heard of his special notion about sun-gazing.

He soon discovered that the spiritual bond between the floors above and below him was close and increasing. The man who called himself Kalon was a magnificent creature, worthy, in a physical sense, to be the pontiff of Apollo. He was nearly as tall even as Flambeau, and very much better looking, with a golden beard, strong blue eyes, and a mane flung back like a lion's. In structure he was the blond beast of Nietzsche, but all this animal beauty was heightened, brightened and softened by genuine intellect and spirituality. If he looked like one of the great Saxon kings, he looked like one of the kings that were also saints. And this despite the cockney incongruity of his surroundings; the fact that he had an office half-way up a building in Victoria Street; that the clerk (a commonplace youth in cuffs and collars) sat in the outer room, between him and the corridor; that his name was on a brass plate, and the gilt emblem of his creed hung above his street, like the advertisement of an oculist. All this vulgarity could not take away from the man called Kalon the vivid oppression and inspiration that came from his soul and body. When all was said, a man in the presence of this quack did feel in the presence of a great man. Even in the loose jacket-suit of linen that he wore as a workshop dress in his office he was a fascinating and formidable figure; and when robed in the white vestments and crowned with the golden circlet, in which he daily saluted the sun, he really looked so splendid that the laughter of the street people sometimes died suddenly on their lips. For three times in the day the new sun-worshipper went out on his little balcony, in the face of all Westminster, to say some litany to his shining lord: once at daybreak, once at sunset, and once at the shock of noon. And it was while the shock of noon still shook faintly from the towers of Parliament and parish church that Father Brown, the friend of Flambeau, first looked up and saw the white priest of Apollo.

Flambeau had seen quite enough of these daily salutations of Phœbus, and plunged into the porch of the tall building without even looking for his clerical friend to follow. But Father Brown, whether from a professional interest in ritual or a strong individual interest in tomfoolery, stopped and stared up at the balcony of the sun-worshipper, just as he might have stopped and stared up at a Punch and Judy. Kalon the Prophet was already erect, with argent garments and uplifted hands, and the sound of his strangely penetrating voice could be heard all the way down the busy street uttering his solar litany. He was already in the middle of it; his eyes were fixed upon the flaming disk. It is doubtful if he saw anything or anyone on this earth; it is substantially certain that he did not see a stunted, round-faced priest who, in the crowd below, looked up at him with blinking eyes. This was perhaps the most startling difference between even these two far divided men. Father Brown could not look at anything without blinking; but the priest of Apollo could look on the blaze at noon without a quiver of the eyelid.

'O sun,' cried the prophet, 'O star that art too great to be allowed among the stars! O fountain that flowest quietly in that secret spot that is called space. White father of all white unwearied things, white flames and white flowers and white peaks. Father, who art more innocent than all thy most innocent and quiet children; primal purity, into the peace of which – '

A rush and crash like the reversed rush of a rocket was cloven with a strident and incessant yelling. Five people rushed into the gate of the mansions as three people rushed out, and for an instant they all deafened each other. The sense of some utterly abrupt horror seemed for a moment to fill half the street with bad news – bad news that was all the worse because no one knew what it was. Two figures remained still after the crash of commotion: the fair priest of Apollo on the balcony above, and the ugly priest of Christ below him.

At last the tall figure and titanic energy of Flambeau appeared in the doorway of the mansions and dominated the little mob. Talking at the top of his voice like a fog-horn, he told somebody or anybody to go for a surgeon; and as he turned back into the dark and thronged entrance his friend Father Brown slipped in insignificantly after him. Even as he ducked and dived through the crowd he could still hear the magnificent melody and monotony of the solar priest still calling on the happy god who is the friend of fountains and flowers.

Father Brown found Flambeau and some six other people standing round the enclosed space into which the lift commonly descended. But the lift had not descended. Something else had descended; something that ought to have come by a lift.

For the last four minutes Flambeau had looked down on it; had seen the brained and bleeding figure of that beautiful woman who denied the existence of tragedy. He had never had the slightest doubt that it was Pauline Stacey; and, though he had sent for a doctor, he had not the slightest doubt that she was dead.

He could not remember for certain whether he had liked her or disliked her; there was so much both to like and dislike. But she had been a person to him, and the unbearable pathos of details and habit stabbed him with all the small daggers of bereavement. He remembered her pretty face and priggish speeches with a sudden secret vividness which is all the bitterness of death. In an instant, like a bolt from the blue, like a thunderbolt from nowhere, that beautiful and defiant body had been dashed down the open well of the lift to death at the bottom. Was it suicide? With so insolent an optimist it seemed impossible. Was it murder? But who was there in those hardly inhabited flats to murder anybody? In a rush of raucous words, which he meant to be strong and suddenly found weak, he asked where was that fellow Kalon. A voice, habitually heavy, quiet and full, assured him that Kalon for the last fifteen minutes had been away up on his balcony worshipping his god. When Flambeau heard the voice, and felt the hand of Father Brown, he turned his swarthy face and said abruptly:

'Then, if he has been up there all the time, who can have done it?'

'Perhaps,' said the other, 'we might go upstairs and find out. We have half an hour before the police will move.'

Leaving the body of the slain heiress in charge of the surgeons, Flambeau dashed up the stairs to the typewriting office, found it utterly empty, and dashed up to his own. Having entered that, he returned with a new and white face to his friend.

'Her sister,' he said with an unpleasant seriousness, 'her sister seems to have gone out for a walk.'

Father Brown nodded. 'Or, she may have gone up to the office of that sun man,' he said. 'If I were you I should just verify that, and then let us talk it over in your office. No,' he added suddenly, as if remembering something; 'shall I ever get over that stupidity of mine? Of course, in their office downstairs.'

Flambeau stared; but he followed the little father downstairs to the empty flat of the Staceys, where that impenetrable pastor took a large red-leather chair in the very entrance, from which he could see the stairs and landings, and waited. He did not wait very long. In about four minutes three figures descended the stairs, alike only in their solemnity: The first was Joan Stacey, the sister of the dead woman – evidently she *had* been upstairs in the temporary temple of Apollo; the second was the priest of Apollo himself, his litany finished, sweeping down the empty stairs in utter magnificence – something in his white robes, beard and parted hair had the look of Doré's Christ leaving the Pretorium; the third was Flambeau, black browed and somewhat bewildered.

Miss Joan Stacey, dark, with a drawn face and hair prematurely touched with grey, walked straight to her own desk and set out her papers with a practical flap. The mere action rallied everyone else to sanity. If Miss Joan Stacey was a criminal, she was a cool one. Father Brown regarded her for some time with an odd little smile, and then, without taking his eyes off her, addressed himself to somebody else.

'Prophet,' he said, presumably addressing Kalon, 'I wish you would tell me a lot about your religion.'

'I shall be proud to do it,' said Kalon, inclining his still crowned head, 'but I am not sure that I understand.'

'Why, it's like this,' said Father Brown, in his frankly doubtful way. 'We are taught that if a man has really bad first principles, that must be partly his fault. But, for all that, we can make some difference between a man who insults his quite clear conscience more or less crowded with sophistries. Now, do you really think that murder is wrong at all?'

'Is this an accusation?' asked Kalon very quietly.

'No,' answered Brown, equally gently, 'it is the speech for the defence.'

In the long and startled stillness of the room the prophet of Apollo slowly rose, and really it was like the rising of the sun. He filled that room with his light and life in such a manner that a man felt he could as easily have filled Salisbury Plain. His robed form seemed to hang the whole room with classic draperies; his epic gesture seemed to extend it into grander perspectives, till the little black figure of the modern cleric seemed to be a fault and an intrusion, a round, black blot upon some splendour of Hellas.

'We meet at last, Caiaphas,' said the prophet. 'Your church and mine are the only realities on this earth. I adore the sun, and you the darkening of the sun; you are the priest of the dying, and I of the living God. Your present work of suspicion and slander is worthy of your coat and creed. All your church is but a black police; you are only spies and detectives seeking to tear from men confessions of guilt, whether by treachery or torture. You would convict men of crime, I would convict them of innocence. You would convince them of sin, I would convince them of virtue.

'Reader of the books of evil, one more word before I blow away your baseless nightmares for ever. Not even faintly could you understand how little I care whether you can convict me or no. The things you call disgrace and horrible hanging are to me no more than an ogre in a child's toybook to a man once grown up. You said you were offering the speech for the defence. I care so little for the cloudland of this life that I will offer you the speech for the prosecution. There is but one thing that can be said against me in this matter, and I will say it myself. The woman that is dead was my love and my bride; not after such manner as your tin chapels call lawful, but by a law purer and sterner than you will ever understand. She and I walked another world from yours, and trod places of crystal while you were plodding through tunnels and corridors of brick. Well, I know that policemen, theological and otherwise, always fancy that where there has been love there must soon be hatred; so there you have the first point made for the prosecution. But the second point is stronger; I do not grudge it you. Not only is it true that Pauline loved me, but it is also true that this very morning, before she died, she wrote at that table a will leaving me and my new church half a million. Come, where are the handcuffs? Do you suppose I care what foolish things you do with me? Penal servitude will only be like waiting for her at a wayside station. The gallows will only be going to her in a headlong car.'

He spoke with the brain-shaking authority of an orator, and Flambeau and Joan Stacey stared at him in an amazed admiration. Father Brown's face seemed to express nothing but extreme distress; he looked at the ground with one wrinkle of pain across his forehead. The prophet of the sun leaned easily against the mantelpiece and resumed:

'In a few words I have put before you the whole case against me – the only possible case against me. In fewer words still I will blow it to pieces, so that not a trace of it remains. As to whether I have committed this crime, the truth is in one sentence: I could not have committed this crime. Pauline Stacey fell from this floor to the ground at five minutes past twelve. A hundred people will go into the witness-box and say that I was standing out upon the balcony of my own rooms above from just before the stroke of noon to a quarter-past –the usual period of my public prayers. My clerk (a respectable youth from Clapham, with no sort of connexion with me) will swear that he sat in my outer office all the morning, and that no communication passed through. He will swear that I arrived a full ten minutes before the hour, fifteen minutes before any whisper of the accident, and that I did not leave the office or the balcony all that time. No one ever had so complete an alibi: I could subpœna half Westminster. I think you had better put the handcuffs away again. The case is at an end.

'But last of all, that no breath of this idiotic suspicion remain in the air, I will tell you all you want to know. I believe I do know how my unhappy friend came by her death. You can, if you choose, blame me for it, or my faith and philosophy at least; but you certainly cannot lock me up. It is well known to all students of the higher truths that certain adepts and *illuminati* have in history attained the power of levitation – that is, of being self-sustained upon the empty air. It is but a part of that general conquest of matter which is the main element in our occult wisdom. Poor Pauline was of an impulsive and ambitious temper. I think, to tell the truth, she thought herself somewhat deeper in the mysteries than she was; and she has often said to me, as we went down in the lift together, that if one's will were strong enough, one could float down as harmlessly as a feather. I solemnly believe that in some ecstasy of noble thoughts she attempted the miracle. Her will, or faith, must have failed her at the crucial instant, and the lower law of matter had its horrible revenge. There is the whole story, gentlemen, very sad and, as you think, very presumptuous and wicked, but certainly not criminal or in any way connected with me. In the shorthand of the police-courts, you had better call it suicide. I shall always call it heroic failure for the advance of science and the slow scaling of heaven.'

It was the first time Flambeau had ever seen Father Brown vanquished. He still sat looking at the ground, with a painful and corrugated brow, as if in shame. It is impossible to avoid the feeling which the prophet's winged words had fanned, that here was a sullen, professional suspector of men overwhelmed by a prouder and purer spirit of natural liberty and health. At last he said, blinking as if in bodily distress: 'Well, if that is so, sir, you need do no more than take the testamentary paper you spoke of and go. I wonder where the poor lady left it.'

'It will be over there on her desk by the door, I think,' said Kalon, with that massive innocence of manner that seemed to acquit him wholly. 'She told me specially she would write it this morning, and I actually saw her writing as I went up in the lift to my own room.'

'Was her door open then?' asked the priest, with an eye on a corner of the matting.

'Yes,' said Kalon calmly.

'Ah! it has been open ever since,' said the other, and resumed his silent study of the mat.

'There is a paper over here,' said the grim Miss Joan, in a somewhat singular voice. She had passed over to her sister's desk by the doorway, and was holding a sheet of blue foolscap in her hand. There was a sour smile on her face that seemed unfit for such a scene or occasion, and Flambeau looked at her with a darkening brow.

Kalon the prophet stood away from the paper with that royal unconsciousness that had carried him through. But Flambeau took it out of the lady's hand and read it with the utmost amazement. It did, indeed, begin in the formal manner of a will, but after the words 'I give and bequeath all of which I die possessed' the writing abruptly stopped with a set of scratches, and there was no trace of the name of any legatee. Flambeau, in wonder, handed this to his friend, who glanced at it and silently gave it to the priest of the sun.

An instant afterwards that pontiff, in his splendid sweeping draperies, had crossed the room in two great strides, and was towering over Joan Stacey, his blue eyes standing from his head.

'What monkey tricks have you been playing here?' he cried. 'That's not all Pauline wrote.'

They were startled to hear him speak in quite a new voice, with a Yankee shrillness in it; all his grandeur and good English had fallen from him like a cloak.

'That is the only thing on her desk,' said Joan, and confronted him steadily with the same smile of evil favour.

Of a sudden the man broke out into blasphemies and cataracts of incredulous words. There was something shocking about the dropping of his mask; it was like a man's real face falling off.

'See here!' he cried in broad American, when he was breathless with cursing; 'I may be an adventurer, but I guess you're a murderess. Yes, gentlemen, here's your death explained, and without any levitation. The poor girl is writing a will in my favour; her cursed sister comes in, struggles for the pen, drags her to the well, and throws her down before she can finish it. Sakes! I reckon we want the handcuffs after all.'

'As you have truly remarked,' replied Joan, with ugly calm, 'your clerk is a very respectable young man, who knows the nature of an oath; and he will swear in any court that I was up in your office arranging some typewriting work for five minutes before and five minutes after my sister fell. Mr Flambeau will say he found me there.'

There was a silence.

'Why, then,' cried Flambeau, 'Pauline was alone when she fell, and it was suicide!'

'She was alone when she fell,' said Father Brown, 'but it was not suicide.'

'Then how did she die?' asked Flambeau impatiently.

'She was murdered.'

'But she was all alone,' objected the detective.

'She was murdered when she was all alone,' answered the priest.

All the rest stared at him, but he remained sitting in the same old dejected attitude, with a wrinkle in his round forehead and an appearance of impersonal shame and sorrow; his voice was colourless and sad.

'What I want to know,' cried Kalon, with an oath, 'is when the police are coming for this bloody and wicked sister. She's killed her flesh and blood; she's robbed me of half a million that was just as sacredly mine as – '

'Come, come, prophet,' interrupted Flambeau, with a kind of sneer; 'remember that all this world is a cloudbank.'

The hierophant of the sun-god made an effort to climb back on to his pedestal. 'It is not the mere money,' he cried, 'though that would equip the cause throughout the world. It is also my beloved one's wishes. To Pauline all this was holy. In Pauline's eyes – '

Father Brown suddenly sprang erect, so that his chair fell over flat behind him. He was deathly pale, yet he seemed fired with a hope; his eyes shone.

'That's it!' he cried in a clear voice. 'That's the way to begin. In Pauline's eyes – '

The tall prophet retreated before the tiny priest in an almost mad disorder. 'What do you mean? How dare you?' he cried repeatedly.

'In Pauline's eyes,' repeated the priest, his own shining more and more. 'Go on – in God's name, go on. The foulest crime the fiends ever prompted feels lighter after confession; and I implore you to confess. Go on, go on – in Pauline's eyes – '

'Let me go, you devil!' thundered Kalon, struggling like a giant in bonds. 'Who are you, you cursed spy, to weave your spiders' webs round me, and peep and peer? Let me go.'

'Shall I stop him?' asked Flambeau, bounding towards the exit, for Kalon had already thrown the door wide open.

'No; let him pass,' said Father Brown, with a strange deep sigh that seemed to come from the depths of the universe. 'Let Cain pass by, for he belongs to God.'

There was a long-drawn silence in the room when he had left it, which was to Flambeau's fierce wits one long agony of interrogation. Miss Joan Stacey very coolly tidied the papers on her desk.

'Father,' said Flambeau at last, 'it is my duty, not my curiosity only – it is my duty to find out if I can, who committed the crime.'

'Which crime?' asked Father Brown.

'The one we are dealing with, of course,' replied his impatient friend.

'We are dealing with two crimes,' said Brown; 'crimes of a very different weight – and by very different criminals.'

Miss Joan Stacey, having collected and put away her papers, proceeded to lock up her drawer. Father Brown went on, noticing her as little as she noticed him.

'The two crimes,' he observed, 'were committed against the same weakness of the same person, in a struggle for her money. The author of the larger crime found himself thwarted by the small crime; the author of the smaller crime got the money.'

'Oh, don't go on like a lecturer,' groaned Flambeau, 'put it in a few words.'

'I can put it in one word,' answered his friend.

'Miss Joan Stacey skewered her business-like black hat on to her head with a business-like black frown before a little mirror, and, as the conversation proceeded, took her handbag and umbrella in an unhurried style, and left the room.

'The truth is in one word, and a short one,' said Father Brown. 'Pauline Stacey was blind.'

'Blind!' repeated Flambeau, and rose slowly to his whole huge stature.

'She was subject to it by blood,' Brown proceeded. 'Her sister would have started eyeglasses if Pauline would have let her; but it was her special philosophy or fad that one must not encourage such diseases by yielding to them. She would not admit the cloud; or she tried to dispel it by will. So her eyes got worse and worse with straining; but the worst strain was to come. It came with this precious prophet, or whatever he calls himself, who taught her to stare at the hot sun with the naked eye. It was called accepting Apollo. Oh, if these new pagans would only be old pagans, they would be a little wiser! The old pagans knew that mere naked Nature-worship has a cruel side. They knew that the eye of Apollo can blast and blind.'

There was a pause, and the priest went on in a gentle and even broken voice: 'Whether or no that devil deliberately made her blind, there is no doubt that he deliberately killed her through her blindness. The very simplicity of the crime is sickening. You know he and she went up and down in those lifts without official help; you know also how smoothly and silently the lifts slide. Kalon brought the lift to the girl's landing, and saw her, through the open door, writing in her slow, sightless way the will she had promised him. He called out to her cheerily that he had the lift ready for her, and she was to come out when she was ready. Then he pressed a button and shot soundlessly up to his own floor, walked through his own office, out on to his own balcony, and was safely praying before the crowded street when the poor girl, having finished her work, ran gaily out to where her lover and lift were to receive her, and stepped – '

'Don't!' cried Flambeau.

'He ought to have got half a million by pressing that button,' continued the little father in the colourless voice in which he talked of such horrors; 'but that went smash. It went smash because there happened to be another person who also wanted the money, and who also knew the secret about poor Pauline's sight. There was one thing about that will that I think nobody noticed: although it was unfinished and without a signature, the other Miss Stacey and some servant of hers had already signed it as witnesses. Joan had signed first, saying Pauline could finish it later, with a typical feminine contempt for legal forms. Therefore, Joan wanted her sister to sign the will without real witnesses. Why? I thought of the blindness, and felt sure she had wanted Pauline to sign in solitude because she had wanted her not to sign at all.

'People like the Staceys always use fountain pens; but this was specially natural to Pauline. By habit and her strong will and her memory she could still write almost as well as if she saw; but she could not tell when her pen needed dipping. Therefore, her fountain pens were carefully filled by her sister – all except this fountain pen. This was carefully *not* filled by her sister; the remains of the ink held out for a few lines and then failed altogether. And the prophet lost five hundred thousand pounds and committed one of the most brutal and brilliant murders in human history for nothing.'

Flambeau went to the open door and heard the official police ascending the stairs. He turned and said: 'You must have followed everything devilish close to have traced the crime to Kalon in ten minutes.'

Father Brown gave a sort of start.

'Oh! to him,' he said. 'No; I had to follow rather close to find out about Miss Joan and the fountain pen. But I knew Kalon was the criminal before I came into the front door.'

'You must be joking!' cried Flambeau.

'I'm quite serious,' answered the priest. 'I tell you I knew he had done it, even before I knew what he had done.'

'But why?'

'These pagan stoics,' said Brown reflectively, 'always fail by their strength. There came a crash and a scream down the street, and the priest of Apollo did not start or look round. I did not know what it was; but I knew that he was expecting it.'

Guilt-Edged Blonde

◆

ROSS MACDONALD

Lew Archer could be called the first environmentally-friendly private detective, for in numerous cases he has used his knowledge of natural history – in particular his love for wild life such as birds, animals, trees and flowers – to bring to justice those who endanger the environment. With the public's growing awareness of 'green issues' in the Sixties and Seventies, Archer became arguably the most famous private eye of the time, and certainly by eschewing undue violence and sexual promiscuity endeared himself to a large audience of readers. The first of his cases, The Moving Target *(1949) filled in the details of his earlier life as a policeman in Long Beach, California, a job he lost when he could no longer put up with the corrupt administration. As a private investigator he succeeds by painstaking enquiry and questioning, always being ready to sympathize with those unwittingly drawn into crime. The first screen portrayal of Lew Archer was provided by Paul Newman in* Harper *(1966) in which his name was inexplicably changed in an otherwise excellent version of* The Moving Target. *Newman reprised the role in* The Drowning Pool *in 1975. A year earlier, the private investigator was brought to television by NBC as* The Underground Man *with Peter Graves in the lead role. Despite the hefty audience figures for this TV special and the fact that it gave rise to a series,* Archer, *Graves was mysteriously replaced by Brian Keith and his tough portrayal of the detective brought it to an end after just six episodes. This rather unhappy TV exposure has done nothing to harm Lew Archer's popularity with the reading public, however, and NBC, ever optimistic, have recently been discussing the possibility of another shot at a series.*

Ross Macdonald (1915–) has admitted that his detective

embodies many of his own concerns about ecology and he, too, has fought authority over industrial encroachment in Santa Barbara, California where he lives. Ross, whose real name is Kenneth Miller, was an avid reader of mysteries as a child – Sherlock Holmes being his favourite – and apart from a string of crime stories he has also published a number of mainstream novels under his real name which have become bestsellers and led to him being cited as a major American novelist by several of the most prestigious journals such as The New York Times *and* Newsweek. *As Ross Macdonald, too, he has lifted the detective short story to new dimensions as is evident in the following intriguing Lew Archer case . . .*

A MAN was waiting for me at the gate at the edge of the runway. He didn't look like the man I expected to meet. He wore a stained tan windbreaker, baggy slacks, a hat as squashed and dubious as his face. He must have been forty years old, to judge by the grey in his hair and the lines around his eyes. His eyes were dark and evasive, moving here and there as if to avoid getting hurt. He had been hurt often and badly, I guessed.

'You Archer?'

I said I was. I offered him my hand. He didn't know what to do with it. He regarded it suspiciously, as if I was planning to try a Judo hold on him. He kept his hands in the pockets of his windbreaker.

'I'm Harry Nemo.' His voice was a grudging whine. It cost him an effort to give his name away. 'My brother told me to come and pick you up. You ready to go?'

'As soon as I get my luggage.'

I collected my overnight bag at the counter in the empty waiting room. The bag was very heavy for its size. It contained, besides a toothbrush and spare linen, two guns and the ammunition for them. A .38 special for sudden work, and a .32 automatic as a spare.

Harry Nemo took me outside to his car. It was a new seven-passenger custom job, as long and black as death. The windshield and side windows were very thick, and they had the yellowish tinge of bullet-proof glass.

'Are you expecting to be shot at?'

'Not me.' His smile was dismal. 'This is Nick's car.'

'Why didn't Nick come himself?'

He looked around the deserted field. The plane I had arrived on was a flashing speck in the sky above the red sun. The only human being in sight was the operator in the control tower. But Nemo leaned toward me in the seat, and spoke in a whisper:

'Nick's a scared pigeon. He's scared to leave the house. Ever since this morning.'

'What happened this morning?'

'Didn't he tell you? You talked to him on the phone.'

'He didn't say very much. He told me he wanted to hire a bodyguard for six days, until his boat sails. He didn't tell me why.'

'They're gunning for him, that's why. He went to the beach this morning. He has a private beach along the back of his ranch, and he went down there by himself for his morning dip. Somebody took a shot at him from the top of the bluff. Five or six shots. He was in the water, see, with no gun handy. He told me the slugs were splashing around him like hailstones. He ducked and swam under water out to sea. Lucky for him he's a good swimmer, or he wouldn't of got away. It's no wonder he's scared. It means they caught up with him, see?'

'Who are "they," or is that a family secret?'

Nemo turned from the wheel to peer into my face. His breath was sour, his look incredulous. 'Hell, don't you know who Nick is? Didn't he tell you?'

'He's a lemon-grower, isn't he?'

'He is now.'

'What did he used to be?'

The bitter beaten face closed on itself. 'I oughtn't to be flapping at the mouth. He can tell you himself if he wants to.'

Two hundred horses yanked us away from the kerb. I rode with my heavy leather bag on my knees. Nemo drove as if driving was the one thing in life he enjoyed, rapt in silent communion with the engine. It whisked us along the highway, then down a gradual incline between geometrically painted lemon groves. The sunset sea glimmered red at the foot of the slope.

Before we reached it, we turned off the blacktop into a private lane which ran like a straight hair-parting between the dark green trees. Straight for half a mile or more to a low house in a clearing.

The house was flat-roofed, made of concrete and fieldstone, with an attached garage. All its windows were blinded with heavy draperies. It was surrounded with well-kept shrubbery and lawn, the lawn with a ten-foot wire fence surmounted by barbed wire.

Nemo stopped in front of the closed and padlocked gate, and

honked the horn. There was no response. He honked the horn again.

About halfway between the house and the gate a crawling thing came out of the shrubbery. It was a man, moving very slowly on hands and knees. His head hung down almost to the ground. One side of his head was bright red, as if he had fallen in paint. He left a jagged red trail in the gravel of the driveway.

Harry Nemo said, 'Nick!' He scrambled out of the car. 'What happened, Nick?'

The crawling man lifted his heavy head and looked at us. Cumbrously, he rose to his feet. He came forward with his legs spraddled and loose, like a huge infant learning to walk. He breathed loudly and horribly, looking at us with a dreadful hopefulness. Then he died on his feet, still walking. I saw the change in his face before it struck the gravel.

Harry Nemo went over the fence like a weary monkey, snagging his slacks on the barbed wire. He knelt beside his brother and turned him over and palmed his chest. He stood up shaking his head.

I had my bag unzipped and my hand on the revolver. I went to the gate, 'Open up, Harry.'

Harry was saying, 'They got him,' over and over. He crossed himself several times. 'The dirty bastards.'

'Open up,' I said.

He found a key ring in the dead man's pocket and opened the padlocked gate. Our dragging footsteps crunched the gravel. I looked down at the specks of gravel in Nicky Nemo's eyes, the bullet hole in his temple.

'Who got him, Harry?'

'I dunno. Fats Jordan, or Artie Castola, or Faronese. It must have been one of them.'

'The Purple Gang.'

'You called it. Nicky was their treasurer back in the thirties. He was the one that didn't get into the papers. He handled the payoff, see. When the heat went on and the gang got busted up, he had some money in a safe-deposit box. He was the only one that got away.'

'How much money?'

'Nicky never told me. All I know, he come out here before the war and bought a thousand acres of lemon land. It took them fifteen years to catch up with him. He always knew they were gonna, though. He knew it.'

'Artie Castola got off the Rock last spring.'

'You're telling me. That's when Nicky bought himself the bullet-proof car and put up the fence.'

'Are they gunning for you?'

He looked around at the darkening groves and the sky. The sky was streaked with running red, as if the sun had died a violent death.

'I dunno,' he answered nervously. 'They got no reason to. I'm as clean as soap. I never been in the rackets. Not since I was young, anyway. The wife made me go straight, see?'

'I said, 'We better get into the house and call the police.'

The front door was standing a few inches ajar. I could see at the edge that it was sheathed with quarter-inch steel plate. Harry put my thoughts into words.

'Why in hell would he go outside? He was safe as houses as long as he stayed inside.'

'Did he live alone?'

'More or less alone.'

'What does that mean?'

He pretended not to hear me, but I got some kind of answer. Looking through the doorless arch into the living room, I saw a leopardskin coat folded across the back of the chesterfield. There were red-tipped cigarette butts mingled with cigar butts in the ashtrays.

'Nicky was married?'

'Not exactly.'

'You know the woman?'

'Naw.' But he was lying.

Somewhere behind the thick walls of the house there was a creak of springs, a crashing bump, the broken roar of a cold engine, grinding of tyres in gravel. I got to the door in time to see a cerise convertible hurtling down the driveway. The top was down, and a yellow-haired girl was small and intent at the wheel. She swerved around Nick's body and got through the gate somehow, with her tyres screaming.

I aimed at the right rear tyre, and missed. Harry came up behind me. He pushed my gun arm down before I could fire again. The convertible disappeared in the direction of the highway.

'Let her go,' he said.

'Who is she?'

He thought about it, his slow brain clicking almost audibly. 'I dunno. Some pig that Nicky picked up someplace. Her name is Flossie or Florrie or something. She didn't shoot him, if that's what you're worried about.'

'You know her pretty well, do you?'

'The hell I do. I don't mess with Nicky's dames.' He tried to work up a rage to go with the strong words, but he didn't have the makings. The

best he could produce was petulance. 'Listen, mister, why should you
hang around? The guy that hired you is dead.'

'I haven't been paid, for one thing.'

'I'll fix that.'

He trotted across the lawn to the body and came back with an
alligator billfold. It was thick with money.

'How much?'

'A hundred will do it.'

He handed me a hundred-dollar bill. 'Now how about you scram,
bud, before the law gets here?'

'I need transportation.'

'Take Nicky's car. He won't be using it. You can park it at the
airport and leave the key with the agent.'

'I can, eh?'

'Sure. I'm telling you you can.'

'Aren't you getting a little free with your brother's property?'

'It's my property now, bud.' A bright thought struck him, dis-
organizing his face. 'Incidentally, how would you like to get off of my
land?'

'I'm staying, Harry. I like this place. I always say it's people that
make a place.'

The gun was still in my hand. He looked down at it.

'Get on the telephone, Harry. Call the police.'

'Who do you think you are, ordering me around? I took my last
order from anybody, see?' He glanced over his shoulder at the dark
and shapeless object on the gravel, and spat venomously.

'I'm a citizen, working for Nicky. Not for you.'

He changed his tune very suddenly. 'How much to go to work for
me?'

'Depends on the line of work.'

He manipulated the alligator wallet. 'Here's another hundred. If
you got to hang around, keep the lip buttoned down about the dame,
eh? Is it a deal?'

I didn't answer, but I took the money. I put it in a separate pocket by
itself. Harry telephoned the county sheriff.

He emptied the ashtrays before the sheriff's men arrived, and stuffed
the leopardskin coat into the woodbox. I sat and watched him.

We spent the next two hours with loud-mouthed deputies. They
were angry with the dead man for having the kind of past that
attracted bullets. They were angry with Harry for being his brother.
They were secretly angry with themselves for being inexperienced and
incompetent. They didn't even uncover the leopardskin coat.

Harry Nemo left the courthouse first. I waited for him to leave, and tailed him home, on foot.

Where a leaning palm tree reared its ragged head above the pavements there was a court lined with jerry-built frame cottages. Harry turned up the walk between them and entered the first cottage. Light flashed on his face from inside. I heard a woman's voice say something to him. Then light and sound were cut off by the closing door.

An old gabled house with boarded-up windows stood opposite the court. I crossed the street and settled down in the shadows of its veranda to watch Harry Nemo's cottage. Three cigarettes later a tall woman in a dark hat and a light coat came out of the cottage and walked briskly to the corner and out of sight. Two cigarettes after that she reappeared at the corner on my side of the street, still walking briskly. I noticed that she had a large straw handbag under her arm. Her face was long and stony under the streetlight.

Leaving the street, she marched up the broken sidewalk to the veranda where I was leaning against the shadowed wall. The stairs groaned under her decisive footsteps. I put my hand on the gun in my pocket, and waited. With the rigid assurance of a WAC corporal marching at the head of her platoon, she crossed the veranda to me, a thin high-shouldered silhouette against the light from the corner. Her hand was in her straw bag, and the end of the bag was pointed at my stomach. Her shadowed face was a gleam of eyes, a glint of teeth.

'I wouldn't try it if I were you,' she said. 'I have a gun here, and the safety is off, and I know how to shoot it, mister.'

'Congratulations.'

'I'm not joking.' Her deep contralto rose a notch. 'Rapid fire used to be my speciality. So you better take your hands out of your pockets.'

I showed her my hands, empty. Moving very quickly, she relieved my pocket of the weight of my gun, and frisked me for other weapons.

'Who are you, mister?' she said as she stepped back. 'You can't be Arturo Castola, you're not old enough.'

'Are you a policewoman?'

'I'll ask the questions. What are you doing here?'

'Waiting for a friend.'

'You're a liar. You've been watching my house for an hour and a half. I tabbed you through the window.'

'So you went and bought yourself a gun?'

'I did. You followed Harry home. I'm Mrs Nemo, and I want to know why.'

'Harry's the friend I'm waiting for.'

'You're a double liar. Harry's afraid of you. You're no friend of his.'

'That depends on Harry. I'm a detective.'

She snorted. 'Very likely. Where's your buzzer?'

'I'm a private detective,' I said. 'I have identification in my wallet.'

'Show me. And don't try any tricks.'

I produced my photostat. She held it up to the light from the street, and handed it back to me. 'So you're a detective. You better do something about your tailing technique. It's obvious.'

'I didn't know I was dealing with a cop.'

'I was a cop,' she said. 'Not any more.'

'Then give me back my .38. It cost me seventy dollars.'

'First tell me, what's your interest in my husband? Who hired you?'

'Nick, your brother-in-law. He called me in Los Angeles today, said he needed a bodyguard for a week. Didn't Harry tell you?'

She didn't answer.

'By the time I got to Nick, he didn't need a bodyguard, or anything. But I thought I'd stick around and see what I could find out about his death. He was a client, after all.'

'You should pick your clients more carefully.'

'What about picking brothers-in-law?'

She shook her head stiffly. The hair that escaped from under her hat was almost white. 'I'm not responsible for Nick or anything about him. Harry is my responsibility. I met him in line of duty and I straightened him out, understand? I tore him loose from Detroit and the rackets, and I brought him out here. I couldn't cut him off from his brother entirely. But he hasn't been in trouble since I married him. Not once.'

'Until now.'

'Harry isn't in trouble now.'

'Not yet. Not officially.'

'What do you mean?'

'Give me my gun, and put yours down. I can't talk into iron.'

She hesitated, a grim and anxious woman under pressure. I wondered what quirk of fate or psychology had married her to a hood, and decided it must have been love. Only love would send a woman across a dark street to face down an unknown gunman. Mrs Nemo was horsefaced and ageing and not pretty, but she had courage.

She handed me my gun. Its butt was soothing to the palm of my hand. I dropped it into my pocket. A gang of boys at loose ends went by in the street, hooting and whistling purposelessly.

She leaned toward me, almost as tall as I was. Her voice was a low sibilance forced between her teeth:

'Harry had nothing to do with his brother's death. You're crazy if you think so.'

'What makes you so sure, Mrs Nemo?'

'Harry couldn't, that's all. I know Harry, I can read him like a book. Even if he had the guts, which he hasn't, he wouldn't dare to think of killing Nick. Nick was his older brother, understand, the successful one in the family.' Her voice rasped contemptuously. 'In spite of everything I could do so or say, Harry worshipped Nick right up to the end.'

'Those brotherly feelings sometimes cut two ways. And Harry had a lot to gain.'

'Not a cent. Nothing.'

'He's Nick's heir, isn't he?'

'Not as long as he stays married to me. I wouldn't let him touch a cent of Nick Nemo's filthy money. Is that clear?'

'It's clear to me. But is it clear to Harry?'

'I made it clear to him, many times. Anyway, this is ridiculous. Harry wouldn't lay a finger on that precious brother of his.'

'Maybe he didn't do it himself. He could have had it done for him. I know he's covering for somebody.'

'Who?'

'A blonde girl left the house after we arrived. She got away in a cherry-coloured convertible. Harry recognized her.'

'A cherry-coloured convertible?'

'Yes. Does that mean something to you?'

'No. Nothing in particular. She must have been one of Nick's girls. He always had girls.'

'Why would Harry cover for her?'

'What do you mean, cover for her?'

'She left a leopardskin coat behind. Harry hid it, and paid me not to tell the police.'

'Harry did that?'

'Unless I'm having delusions.'

'Maybe you are at that. If you think Harry paid that girl to shoot Nick, or had anything – '

'I know. Don't say it. I'm crazy.'

Mrs Nemo laid a thin hand on my arm. 'Anyway, lay off Harry. Please. I have a hard enough time handling him as it is. He's worse than my first husband. The first one was a drunk, believe it or not.' She glanced at the lighted cottage across the street, and I saw one-half of her bitter smile. 'I wonder what makes a woman go for the lame ducks the way I did.'

'I wouldn't know, Mrs Nemo. Okay, I lay off Harry.'

But I had no intention of laying off Harry. When she went back to her cottage, I walked around three-quarters of the block and took up a new position in the doorway of a dry-cleaning establishment. This time I didn't smoke. I didn't even move, except to look at my watch from time to time.

Around eleven o'clock the lights went out behind the blinds in the Nemo cottage. Shortly before midnight the front door opened and Harry slipped out. He looked up and down the street and began to walk. He passed within six feet of my dark doorway, hustling along in a kind of furtive shuffle.

Working very cautiously, at a distance, I tailed him downtown. He disappeared into the lighted cavern of an all-night garage. He came out of the garage a few minutes later, driving an old Chevrolet.

My money also talked to the attendant. I drew an old Buick which would still do seventy-five. I proved that it would as soon as I hit the highway. I reached the entrance to Nick Nemo's private lane in time to see Harry's lights approaching the dark ranchhouse.

I cut my lights and parked at the roadside a hundred yards below the entrance to the lane, and facing it. The Chevrolet reappeared in a few minutes. Harry was still alone in the front seat. I followed it blind as far as the highway before I risked my lights. Then down the highway to the edge of town.

In the middle of the motel and drive-in district he turned off onto a side road and in under a neon sign which spelled out *TRAILER COURT* across the darkness. The trailers stood along the bank of a dry creek. The Chevrolet stopped in front of one of them, which had a light in the window. Harry got out with a spotted bundle under his arm. He knocked on the door of the trailer.

I U-turned at the next corner and put in more waiting time. The Chevrolet rolled out under the neon sign and turned toward the highway. I let it go.

Leaving my car, I walked along the creek bank to the lighted trailer. The windows were curtained. The cerise convertible was parked on its far side. I tapped on the aluminium door.

'Harry?' a girl's voice said. 'Is that you, Harry?'

I muttered something indistinguishable. The door opened, and the yellow-haired girl looked out. She was very young, but her round blue eyes were heavy and sick with hangover, or remorse. She had on a nylon slip, nothing else.

'What is this?'

She tried to shut the door. I held it open.

'Get away from here. Leave me alone. I'll scream.'

'All right. Scream.'

She opened her mouth. No sound came out. She closed her mouth again. It was small and fleshy and defiant. 'Who are you? Law?'

'Close enough. I'm coming in.'

'Come in then, damn you. I got nothing to hide.'

'I can see that.'

I brushed in past her. There were dead Martinis on her breath. The little room was a jumble of feminine clothes, silk and cashmere and tweed and gossamer nylon, some of them flung on the floor, others hung up to dry. The leopardskin coat lay on the bunk bed, staring with innumerable bold eyes. She picked it up and covered her shoulders with it. Unconsciously, her nervous hands began to pick the wood chips out of the fur.

'Harry did you a favour, didn't he?' I said.

'Maybe he did.'

'Have you been doing any favours for Harry?'

'Such as?'

'Such as knocking off his brother?'

'You're way off the beam, mister. I was very fond of Uncle Nick.'

'Why run out on the killing then?'

'I panicked,' she said. 'It would happen to any girl. I was asleep when he got it, see, passed out if you want the truth. I heard the gun go off. It woke me up, but it took me quite a while to bring myself to and sober up enough to put my clothes on. By the time I made it to the bedroom window, Harry was back, with some guy.' She peered into my face. 'Were you the guy?'

I nodded.

'I thought so. I thought you were law at the time. I saw Nick lying there in the driveway, all bloody, and I put two and two together and got trouble. Bad trouble for me, unless I got out. So I got out. It wasn't nice to do, after what Nick meant to me, but it was the only sensible thing. I got my career to think of.'

'What career is that?'

'Modelling. Acting. Uncle Nick was gonna send me to school.'

'Unless you talk, you'll finish your education at Corona. Who shot Nick?'

A thin edge of terror entered her voice. 'I don't know, I tell you. I was passed out in the bedroom. I didn't see nothing.'

'Why did Harry bring you your coat?'

'He didn't want me to get involved. He's my father, after all.'

'Harry Nemo is your father?'

'Yes.'

'You'll have to do better than that. What's your name?'

'Jeannine, Jeannine Larue.'

'Why isn't your name Nemo if Harry is your father? Why do you call him Harry?'

'He's my stepfather, I mean.'

'Sure,' I said. 'And Nick was really your uncle, and you were having a family reunion with him.'

'He wasn't any blood relation to me. I always called him uncle, though.'

'If Harry's your father, why don't you live with him?'

'I used to. Honest. This is the truth I'm telling you. I had to get out on account of the old lady. The old lady hates my guts. She's a real creep, a square. She can't stand for a girl to have any fun. Just because my old man was a rummy – '

'What's your idea of fun, Jeannine?'

She shook her feathercut hair at me. It exhaled a heavy perfume which was worth its weight in blood. She bared one pearly shoulder and smiled an artificial hustler's smile. 'What's yours? Maybe we can get together.'

'You mean the way you got together with Nick?'

'You're prettier than him.'

'I'm also smarter, I hope. Is Harry really your stepfather?'

'Ask him if you don't believe me. Ask him. He lives in a place on Tule Street – I don't remember the number.'

'I know where he lives.'

But Harry wasn't at home. I knocked on the door of the frame cottage and got no answer. I turned the knob, and found that the door was unlocked. There was a light behind it. The other cottages in the court were dark. It was long past midnight, and the street was deserted. I went into the cottage, preceded by my gun.

A ceiling bulb glared down on sparse and threadbare furniture, a time-eaten rug. Besides the living room, the house contained a cubbyhole of a bedroom and a closet kitchenette. Everything in the poverty-stricken place was pathetically clean. There were moral mottoes on the walls, and one picture. It was a photograph of a towheaded girl in a teen-age party dress. Jeannine, before she learned that a pretty face and a sleek body could buy her the things she wanted. The things she thought she wanted.

For some reason I felt sick. I went outside. Somewhere out of sight an old car engine muttered. Its muttering grew on the night. Harry Nemo's rented Chevrolet turned the corner under the streetlight. Its front wheels were weaving. One of the wheels climbed the kerb in front of the cottage. The Chevrolet came to a halt at a drunken angle.

I crossed the sidewalk and opened the car door. Harry was at the wheel, clinging to it desperately as if he needed it to hold him up. His chest was bloody. His mouth was bright with blood. He spoke through it thickly:

'She got me.'

'Who got you, Harry? Jeannine?'

'No. Not her. She was the reason for it, though. We had it coming.'

Those were his final words. I caught his body as it fell sideways out of the seat. Laid it out on the sidewalk and left it for the cop on the beat to find.

I drove across town to the trailer court. Jeannine's trailer still had light in it, filtered through the curtains over the windows. I pushed the door open.

The girl was packing a suitcase on the bunk bed. She looked at me over her shoulder, and froze. Her blonde head was cocked like a frightened bird's, hypnotized by my gun.

'Where are you off to, kid?'

'Out of this town. I'm getting out.'

'You have some talking to do first.'

She straightened up. 'I told you all I know. You didn't believe me. What's the matter, didn't you get to see Harry?'

'I saw him. Harry's dead. Your whole family is dying like flies.'

She half turned and sat down limply on the disordered bed. 'Dead? You think I did it?'

'I think you know who did. Harry said before he died that you were the reason for it all.'

'Me the reason for it?' Her eyes widened in false naïveté, but there was thought behind them, quick and desperate thought. 'You mean Harry got killed on account of me?'

'Harry and Nick both. It was a woman who shot them.'

'God,' she said. The desperate thought behind her eyes crystallized into knowledge. Which I shared.

The aching silence was broken by a big diesel rolling by on the highway. She said above its roar:

'That crazy old bat. So *she* killed Nick.'

'You're talking about your mother. Mrs Nemo.'

'Yeah.'

'Did you see her shoot him?'

'No. I was blotto like I told you. But I saw her out there this week, keeping an eye on the house. She's always watched me like a hawk.'

'Is that why you were getting out of town? Because you knew she killed Nick?'

'Maybe it was. I don't know. I wouldn't let myself think about it.'

Her blue gaze shifted from my face to something behind me. I turned. Mrs Nemo was in the doorway. She was hugging the straw bag to her thin chest.

Her right hand dived into the bag. I shot her in the right arm. She leaned against the door frame and held her dangling arm with her left hand. Her face was granite in whose crevices her eyes were like live things caught.

The gun she dropped was a cheap .32 revolver, its nickel plating worn and corroded. I spun the cylinder. One shot had been fired from it.

'This accounts for Harry,' I said. 'You didn't shoot Nick with this gun, not at that distance.'

'No.' She was looking down at her dripping hand. 'I used my old police gun on Nick Nemo. After I killed him, I threw the gun into the sea. I didn't know I'd have further use for a gun. I bought that little suicide gun tonight.'

'To use on Harry?'

'To use on you. I thought you were on to me. I didn't know until you told me that Harry knew about Nick and Jeannine.'

'Jeannine is your daughter by your first husband?'

'My only daughter.' She said to the girl, 'I did it for you, Jeannine. I've seen too much – the awful things that can happen.'

The girl didn't answer.

'I can understand why you shot Nick,' I said, 'but why did Harry have to die?'

'Nick paid him,' she said. 'Nick paid him for Jeannine. I found Harry in a bar an hour ago, and he admitted it. I hope I killed him.'

'You killed him, Mrs Nemo. What brought you here? Was Jeannine the third on your list?'

'No. No. She's my own girl. I came to tell her what I did for her. I wanted her to know.'

She looked at the girl on the bed. Her eyes were terrible with pain and love.

The girl said in a stunned voice, 'Mother. You're hurt. I'm sorry.'

'Let's go, Mrs Nemo,' I said.

The World Series Murder

◆

REX STOUT

The gargantuan detective Nero Wolfe – he is described as being just under six foot tall and weighing one seventh of a ton – is a man devoted to the very best food and solving the very hardest cases. A person of fastidious tastes, he lives in some luxury in a house on West 35th Street in New York, where his put-upon assistant, Archie Goodwin – who also chronicles his exploits – does much of the leg work (chasing suspects as well as girls) to bring Wolfe the clues that will enable him to solve his cases. Wolfe is said to hate work and unnecessary exercise, but is passionately dedicated to growing orchids. His mastery of languages, his ability to fathom the most obscure clues and his love-hate relationship with both the police and the criminal fraternity, make him a wholly unique figure who was immediately enjoyed by readers when he made his debut in Fer-de-lance *in 1934.* Meet Nero Wolfe *(1936) was the first movie about the detective featuring a somewhat slimmer Edward Arnold in the title role; while the rather more corpulent Walter Connolly starred in the second,* The League of Frightened Men, *which was made a year later. Lionel Stander played Archie Goodwin in both pictures. In 1943, American radio embraced the fat man in* The Adventures of Nero Wolfe, *a weekly, half-hour programme which starred Santos Ortega during its first season and Sydney Greenstreet thereafter. Again there was a single Archie Goodwin, Everett Sloane. ABC TV introduced the detective to the small screen in 1977 in* Nero Wolfe, *an adaptation of the novel,* The Doorbell Rang, *with Thayer David and Tom Mason. Three years later, NBC screened a thirteen-episode series of hour-long dramas with William Conrad and Lee Horsley which was faithful to the original stories but did not continue beyond its first season.*

Rex Stout (1886–1975), despite his surname, was as thin as Nero Wolfe was fat, and unlike his character loved hard work. Both, though, shared a passion for good food and gardening. Stout had a variety of menial jobs until, finding himself almost penniless during the Depression, he started selling articles and stories to magazines, and finally made his name when Fer-de-lance *was serialized in the* Saturday Evening Post. *At the time of his death, his books were said to have sold more than forty-five million copies. The World Series Murder is one of the best of the Nero Wolfe stories and was adapted for both the original radio programme and the William Conrad TV series.*

AT the end of the sixth innings the score was Boston eleven, New York one. I would not have believed that the day would ever come when, seated in a lower box between home and first, at the seventh and deciding game of a World Series between New York and Boston, I would find myself glomming a girl. I am by no means above glomming a girl if she is worthy, but not at a ball game, where my mind is otherwise occupied. That awful day, though, I did.

The situation was complex and will have to be explained. It was a mess even before the game started. Pierre Mondor, owner of a famous restaurant in Paris, was visiting New York and was our house guest at Nero Wolfe's old brownstone on West 35th Street. He got the notion, somehow, that Wolfe had to take him to a baseball game, and Wolfe as his host couldn't refuse. Tickets were no problem, since Emil Chisholm, oil millionaire and part owner of the New York team, considered himself deeply in Wolfe's debt on account of a case we had handled for him a few years back.

So that October afternoon, a Wednesday, I got the pair of them – the noted private detective and the noted chef – up to the ball park. It was twenty past one, only ten minutes to game time, and the stands were jammed. I motioned to Mondor, and he slid in and sat. Wolfe stood and glared down at the wooden slats and metal arms. Then he glared at me.

'Are you out of your senses?' he demanded.

'I warned you,' I said coldly. 'It was designed for men, not mammoths.'

He tightened his lips, moved his bulk, lowered it, and tried to squeeze between the arms. No. He grasped the rail in front with both hands, wriggled loose, and perched on the edge of the seat.

Mondor called to me across the great expanse of Wolfe's back: 'I depend with confidence on you, Arshee! You must make clear as it develops! What are the little white things?'

I love baseball, I love the New York team, I had fifty bucks up on that game, but I would have got up and gone but for one thing: It was working hours and Wolfe pays my salary, and there were too many people, some of them alive and loose, who felt strongly that he had already lived too long. He is seldom out in the open, easy to get at, and when he is I like to be nearby. So I gritted my teeth and stuck.

The ground crew finished smoothing off and hauled their drags away; the umpires did a huddle, the home team trotted out on the field to their stations; the throng gave with a lusty, excited roar; we all stood up for *The Star-Spangled Banner*, and then sat down again. After southpaw Ed Romeike, 22–4 for the season, had burned a few over for the range, Lew Baker, the catcher, fired it to Tiny Garth at second. The Boston lead-off man came to the white line, the plate umpire said go, and Romeike looked around at the field, toed the rubber, went into his tricky wind-up, and shot a fast one over the outside corner for strike one. The crowd let out a short, sharp yell.

My personal nightmare was bad enough. Mondor was our guest, and trying to tell a foreigner what a base on balls is during a World Series game, with two men on, two down, and Oaky Asmussen at bat, is hard on the nerves. As for Wolfe, it wasn't so much the sight of him there in his concentrated misery; it was the certainty that by tomorrow he would have figured out a way to blame it on me, and that would start a feud.

Bad enough, but more was to come, and not for me alone. One fly had plopped into the soup even before the game started, when the line-up was announced and Tiny Garth was named for second base, with no explanation. A buzz of amazement had filled the stands. Why not Nick Ferrone? Ferrone, a lanky, big-eared kid just up from the bush five months back, had fielded and batted himself so far to the front that it was taken for granted he would be voted rookie of the year. He had been spectacular in the first six games of the Series, batting 427. Where was he today? Why Garth?

Then the game. That was no personal nightmare of mine; it was all too public. In the first inning Con Prentiss, New York's shortstop, bobbled an easy grounder, and two minutes later Lew Baker, the catcher, trying to nab a runner at second, threw the ball six feet over

Garth's head into the outfield. With luck the visitors scored only one run. In the second inning Nat Neill, centre fielder, misjudged a fly he could have walked under, tried to run in three directions at once, and had to chase it to the fence; and soon after that, Prentiss grabbed a hard-hit ball on the hop and hurled it into the dirt three paces to the left of third base. By the time they got three out, Boston had two more runs.

As the New York team came in for their turn at bat in the second, bitter sarcasms from the stands greeted them. Then our section was distracted by an incident. A man in a hurry came plunging down the aisle, bumping my elbow as he passed, and pulled up alongside a front box occupied by six men, among them the Mayor of New York and oilman Emil Chisholm, who had provided our tickets. The man spoke into the ear of Chisholm, who looked anything but happy. Chisholm said something to his boxmates, arose, and beat it up the aisle double-quick, followed by cutting remarks from nearby fans who had recognized him. As my eyes went back to the arena, Con Prentiss, New York shortstop, swung at a floater and missed by a mile.

There is no point in my retailing the agony. As I said, at the end of the sixth the score was eleven to one. Romeike was hurling all right, but his support would have been pitiful on a sand lot. Joe Eston, the third baseman, and Nat Neill had each made two errors, and Con Prentiss and Lew Baker three apiece. As they came to the dugout in the sixth one wit yelled, 'Say it ain't true, Joe!' at Eston, and the crowd recognizing that classic moan to Shoeless Joe Jackson, let out a howl. They were getting really rough. As for me, I had had plenty of the tragedy out on the diamond and was looking around for something less painful, when I caught sight of the girl, in a box off to my right.

I glommed her, not offensively. There were two of them. One was a redhead who would start to get plump in a couple of years; almost worthy, but not quite. The other one, the glommee, had light-brown hair and dark-brown eyes, and was fully qualified. I had the feeling that she was not a complete stranger, that I had seen her somewhere before, but couldn't place her.

The pleasure it gave me to look at her was not pure, because it was adulterated with resentment. She looked happy. Her eyes sparkled. Apparently she liked the way things were going. There is no law barring enemy fans from a ball park, but I resented it. Nevertheless, I continued the glommation. She was the only object I had seen there that day, on or off the field, that didn't make me want to shut my eyes.

Something came between her and me. A man stopped at my elbow, and asked my ear: 'Are you Archie Goodwin?'

I told him yes.

'Is that Nero Wolfe?'

I nodded.

'Mr Chisholm wants him in the clubhouse, quick.'

I reflected for two seconds, decided that this was straight from heaven, and slid forward to tell Wolfe: 'Mr Chisholm invites us to the clubhouse. We'll avoid the crush. There's a chair there. He wants to see you.'

He didn't growl, 'What about?' He didn't even growl. He muttered something to Mondor, pulled himself erect, and side-stepped past me to the aisle. Mondor came after him. The courier led the way and I brought up the rear. As we went up the concrete steps single file a shout came from somewhere on the left:

'Go get 'em, Nero! Sic 'em!'

Such is fame . . .

'This is urgent!' Emil Chisholm squeaked. 'It's urgent.'

There was no chair in the club-room of the size Wolfe likes and needs, but there was a big leather couch, and he was on it, breathing hard and scowling. Mondor was seated over against the wall, out of it. Chisholm, a hefty, broad-shouldered guy, with a wide, thick mouth and a long, straight nose, was too upset to stand or sit, so he was boiling around. I was standing near an open window. Through it came a sudden swelling roar from the crowd out in the stands.

'Shut that window!' Chisholm barked.

I did so.

'I'm going home,' Wolfe stated in his most conclusive tone. 'But not until they have left. Perhaps, if you will tell me briefly – '

'We've lost the Series!' Chisholm shouted.

Wolfe closed his eyes, and opened them again. 'If you'll keep your voice down,' he suggested. 'I've had enough noise today. If losing the Series is your problem, I'm afraid I can't help.'

'No. Nobody can.' Chisholm stood facing him. 'I blew up. I'm sorry. I've got to get hold of myself. This is what happened: Out there before the game Art got a suspicion – '

'Art?'

'Art Kinney, our manager. Naturally, he was watching the boys like a hawk, and he got a suspicion something was wrong. That first – '

'Why was he watching them like a hawk?'

'That's his job! He's manager!' Chisholm realized he was shouting again, stopped, clamped his jaw, and clenched his fists. After a second he went on: 'Also, Nick Ferrone has disappeared. He was here with them in the clubhouse, he had got into uniform; then, after they went

out to the dugout, he just wasn't there. Art sent Doc Soffer back here to
get him, but he couldn't find him. He was simply gone. Art had to put
Garth as second base. Naturally, he was on edge, and he noticed things
– the way some of the boys looked and acted – that made him
suspicious. Then – '

A door opened and a guy came running in, yelling, 'Fitch hit one and
Neill let it get by, and Asmussen scored! Fitch went on to third!'

I recognized him, chiefly by his crooked nose, which had got in the
way of a line drive back in the twenties, when he was a star in-fielder. It
was Beaky Durkin, now a New York scout with a new lease on life
because he had dug up Nick Ferrone out in Arkansas.

Chisholm yelled at him, 'Get out!' He took a threatening step. 'Get
out! . . . Hey, Doc! Come in here!'

Durkin, backing out, collided with a man in the doorway. This was
Doc Soffer, New York's veteran medico, bald, wearing black-rimmed
glasses; he had a long torso and short legs. Entering, he looked as if his
ten best-paying patients had just died on him.

'I can't sweat it, Doc,' Chisholm told him. 'I'm going nuts! This is
Nero Wolfe. You tell him.'

'Who are you?' Wolfe demanded.

Soffer stopped before him. 'I'm Dr Horton Soffer,' he said, clipping
it. 'Four of my men have been drugged. They're out there now, trying
to play ball, and they can't.' He stopped, looking as if he were about to
break down and cry, gulped, and went on:

'They didn't seem right, there in the dugout. I noticed it and so did
Kinney. That first inning there was no doubt about it, something was
wrong. The second inning it was even worse – and the same four men,
Baker, Prentiss, Neill, and Eston. I got an idea, and came here to
investigate. You see that cooler?'

He pointed to a big, white-enamelled refrigerator standing against a
wall.

Wolfe nodded. 'Well?'

'It contains mostly an assortment of drinks in bottles. I know my
men's habits, every little habit they've got and every big one, too. I
know that after they get into uniform before a game those four men –
the four I named – have the habit of getting a bottle of Beebright out of
the cooler.'

'What is Beebright?'

'It's a carbonated drink that's supposed to have honey in it instead
of sugar. Each of those four men drinks a bottle of it, or part of one,
before he goes out to the field, practically without exception. And it
was those four that were off – terrible! I never saw anything like

it. That's how I got my idea. I told Kinney, and he said to come and see.

'Usually the clubhouse boy cleans up here after the men leave for the field, but this being the deciding game of the World Series, today he didn't. Stuff was scattered around – as you see, it still is – and there was a Beebright bottle there on that table with a little left in it. It didn't smell wrong, and I didn't want to waste any tasting. I had sent for Mr Chisholm, and when he came we decided what to do. He sent for Beaky Durkin, who had a seat in the grandstand, because he knew Ferrone better than anyone else. We thought he might have some idea that would help explain what had happened to Ferrone and those four other boys. I took the Beebright down the street to a drugstore, and made two tests. The first one, Ranwez's, didn't prove anything, but that was probably because it is limited – '

'Negatives may be skipped,' Wolfe muttered.

'I'm telling you what I did,' Soffer snapped. 'Ranwez's test took over half an hour. The second, Ekkert's, took less. I did it twice, to check. It was conclusive. The Beebright contained sodium phenobarbital. I couldn't get the quantity, in a hurry like that, but on a guess it was two grains, possibly a little more, in the full bottle. Anyone can get hold of it. Certainly that would be no problem for a bigtime gambler who wanted to clean up on a World Series game.'

Chisholm swore, audibly.

Doc Soffer nodded. 'And somebody put it in the bottles, knowing those four men would drink it just before the game. All he had to do was remove the caps, drop the tablets in, replace the caps, and shake the bottles a little – not much, because it's very soluble. They must have been placed in the refrigerator not much before noon; otherwise someone else might have drunk them. Besides, if they were fixed very far in advance, the drinks would have gone stale and the men would have noticed it. So it must have been someone – '

Chisholm had marched to the window. He whirled and yelled, 'Ferrone did it! He did it and lammed!'

Doc Soffer said, 'I don't know about that, but I've got to tell Art – ' He almost ran from the room.

Beaky Durkin appeared again. He came through the door and halted, facing Chisholm. He was trembling and his face was white, all but the crooked nose.

'Not Nick,' he said hoarsely. 'Not that boy. Nick didn't do it!'

'Oh, no?' Chisholm was bitter. 'Did I ask you? A fine rookie of the year you brought in from Arkansas! Where is he? Bring him here and let me get my hands on him! Go find him!'

Beaky looked bewildered. 'Go where?'

'How do I know? He's your pet, not mine,' Chisholm said savagely. 'Get him and bring him in and I'll offer him a new contract – that will *be* a contract. Now beat it!'

Durkin lifted helpless hands, but turned and left the room.

Wolfe grunted. 'Sit down, please,' he told Chisholm. 'When I address you I want to look at you, and my neck is not elastic . . . Thank you, sir. You want to hire me for a job?'

'Yes. I want – '

'Please. Is this correct? Four of your best players, drugged as described by Dr Soffer, could not perform properly, and as a result a game is lost and a World Series?'

'We're losing it.' Chisholm's head swung toward the window and back again. 'Art's pulling out the drugged men, but of course it's lost.'

'And you assume a gambler or a group of gamblers is responsible. How much could he or they win on a game?'

'On today's game, any amount. Fifty thousand, or double that, easy.'

'I see. Then you need the police. At once.'

Chisholm shook his head. 'I don't want to. Baseball is a wonderful game, the best and cleanest game on earth. This is the dirtiest thing that's happened in baseball in thirty years, and it's got to be handled right and handled fast. You're the best detective in the business, and you're right here. With a swarm of cops trooping in, who knows what'll happen! If we have to have them later, all right, but now you're here. Go to it!'

Wolfe was frowning. 'You think this Nick Ferrone did it.'

'I don't know!' Chisholm was yelling again. 'How do I know what I think? He's a harebrained kid just out of the sticks, and he's disappeared. What does that look like?'

Wolfe nodded. 'Very well.' He drew a deep sigh. 'I can at least make some gestures, and see.' He aimed a finger at the door Beaky Durkin and Doc Soffer had used. 'Is that an office?'

'It leads to Kinney's office – the manager's.'

'Then it has a phone. You will call police headquarters and report the disappearance of Nick Ferrone, and ask them to find him. Such a job, when urgent, is beyond my resources. Tell them nothing more for the present if you want it that way. Where do the players change clothing?'

'Through there.' Chisholm indicated another door. 'That's the locker room. The shower room is beyond.'

Wolfe's eyes came to me: 'Archie. You will look around all premises adjoining this room. This room you can leave to me.'

'Anything in particular?' I asked.

'No. You have good eyes and a head of sorts. Use them.'

'I could wait to phone the police,' Chisholm suggested, 'until you –'

'No,' Wolfe snapped. 'In ten minutes you can have every cop in New York looking for Mr Ferrone, and it will cost you ten cents. Spend it. I charge more for less.'

Chisholm went out, through the door at the left. I thought I might as well start in that direction, and followed him across a hall and into another room. It was good-sized, furnished with desk, chairs, and accessories. Beaky Durkin sat in a corner with his ear to a radio tuned low, and Doc Soffer was there with him. Chisholm barked, 'Shut that thing off!' and crossed to a desk with a phone.

Under other circumstances I would have enjoyed having a look at the office of Art Kinney, the New York manager, but I was on a mission and there was too big an audience. I about-faced and backtracked to the clubroom. As I crossed to the door in the far wall, Wolfe was standing by the open door of the refrigerator with a bottle of Beebright in his hand, holding it at arm's length, sneering at it, and Mondor was beside him.

I passed through the door and was in a room both long and wide, with two rows of lockers, benches and stools, and a couple of chairs. The locker doors were marked with numbers and names. I tried three; they were locked. Through a doorway at the left was the shower room. I went to the far end, glancing in at each of the shower stalls, was disappointed to see no pillbox that might have contained sodium phenobarbital, and returned to the locker room.

In the middle of the row on the right was the locker marked 'Ferrone'. Its door was locked. With my portable key collection I could have operated, but I don't take it along to ball games, and nothing on my personal ring was usable. It seemed to me that the inside of that locker was the first place that needed attention, so I returned to the clubroom, made a face at Wolfe as I went by, and entered Kinney's office. Chisholm had finished phoning and was seated at a desk, staring at the floor. Beaky Durkin and Doc Soffer had their ears glued to the radio.

I asked Chisholm, 'Have you got a key to Ferrone's locker?'

His head jerked up. 'No. I think Kinney has a master key. I don't know where he keeps it.'

'Fifteen to two,' Durkin informed us, or maybe he was just talking to himself. 'New York batting in the ninth, two down. Garth got a home run, bases empty. It's all –'

'Shut up!' Chisholm yelled at him.

Since Kinney would soon be with us, and since Ferrone's locker had first call, I thought I might as well wait there for him. However, with our client sitting there glaring at me it would be well to display some interest and energy, so I moved. I went to the filing cabinets and looked them over. I opened a door, saw a hall leading to stairs going down, and shut the door. I crossed to another door in the opposite wall, and opened that.

Since I hadn't the faintest expectation of finding anything pertinent beyond that door, let alone a corpse, I must have made some sign of surprise, but if so it wasn't noticed. I stood for three seconds, then slipped inside and squatted long enough to get an answer to the main question. I arose, backed out, and addressed Soffer: 'Take a look here, Doc. I think he's dead.'

He made a noise, stared, and moved. I marched into the clubroom and crossed to the couch where Wolfe was sitting.

'Found something,' I told him. 'Nick Ferrone, in uniform, on the floor of a closet, with a baseball bat alongside him and his head smashed in. He's dead, according to me, but Doc Soffer is checking, if you want an expert opinion.'

Wolfe grunted. 'Call the police.'

'Yes, sir. A question: Any minute the ballplayers will be coming in here. The cops won't like it if they mess around. Do we care? It won't be Cramer. This is the Bronx, not Manhattan. Do we – ?'

A bellow, Chisholm's, came through: 'Wolfe! Come in here!'

Wolfe got up, growling. 'We owe the police nothing, but we have a client – I think we have. I'll see. Meanwhile, you stay here. Everyone entering this room remains, under surveillance.' He headed for Kinney's office.

Another door opened, the one in the west wall, and Nat Neill, New York's centre fielder, entered the clubroom, his jaw set and his eyes blazing. Following him came Lew Baker, the catcher. Behind them on the stairs, was a clatter of footsteps.

The game was over. New York had lost . . .

Another thing I don't take along to ball games is a gun, but that day there was a moment when I wished I had. After an ordinary game, even a lost one, I suppose the team might have been merely irritated if, on getting to the clubhouse, they found a stranger backed up against the door to the locker room telling them they could not pass. But that day they were ready to plug one another, so why not a stranger?

The first dozen were ganging me, about to start using hands, when Art Kinney, the manager, appeared. He strode, tight-lipped, through to his office and the gang let up to consider; all but Bill Moyse, the second-string catcher, six-feet-two and over two hundred pounds. He had come late, after Kinney. He strode up to me, making fists, and announced that his wife was waiting for him, he was going in to change, and either I would move or he would move me.

One of his teammates called: 'Show him her picture, Bill! That'll move him!'

Moyse whirled and leaped. Hands grabbed for him but he kept going. Whether he reached his target or not I can't say, because, first, I was staying put and it was quite a mix-up, and, second, I was seeing something that wasn't present. The mention of Moyse's wife and her picture had done it. What I was seeing was a picture of a girl that had appeared in the *Gazette* a couple of months back, with a caption tagging her as the showgirl bride of William Moyse, the ballplayer; and it was the girl I had been glomming in a nearby box when the summons had come from Chisholm. No question about it. That was interesting.

Meanwhile, Moyse was doing me a service by making a diversion. Three or four men had hold of him, and others were gathered around his target, Con Prentiss, the shortstop. They were all jabbering. Prentiss, who was wiry and tough, was showing his teeth in a grin, not an attractive one. Moyse suddenly whirled again and was heading back for me. It was useless to start slugging that mountain of muscle, and I was set to try blocking him, when a loud voice came from the doorway to the manager's office: 'Here! Attention, all of you!'

It was Art Kinney. His face was absolutely white and his neck cords were twitching, as they all turned toward him.

'I'm full up,' he said, half hysterical. 'This is Nero Wolfe, the detective. He'll tell you something.'

Muttering began as Kinney stepped aside and Wolfe took his place in the doorway. The great man's eyes swept over them, and then he spoke:

'You deserve an explanation, gentlemen, but the police are coming and there's not much time. You have just lost a ball game by knavery. Four of you were drugged, in a drink called Beebright, and could not perform properly. You will learn – '

They drowned him out. It was an explosion of astonished rage.

'Gentlemen!' Wolfe thundered. 'Will you listen?' He glowered. 'You will learn more of that later, but there is something more urgent. The dead body of one of your colleagues, Mr Nick Ferrone, has been discovered on these premises. He was murdered. It is supposed, naturally, that the two events, the drugging and the murder, are connected. In any case, if you do not know what a murder investigation means to everyone within reach, innocent or not, you are about to learn. For the moment you will not leave this room. When the police arrive they will tell you – '

Heavy feet were clomping in the hall. The door swung open and a uniformed cop stepped in, followed by three others. The one in front, a sergeant, halted and demanded indignantly: 'What's all this? Where is it?'

The team looked at the cops, and hadn't a word to say . . .

Inspector Hennessy of Bronx Homicide was tall and straight, silver-haired, with a bony face and quick-moving grey eyes. Two years before he had told Nero Wolfe that if he ever again tried poking into a murder in the Bronx he would be escorted to the Harlem River and dunked. But when, at nine o'clock that evening, Hennessy breezed through the clubroom, passing in front of the leather couch where Wolfe was seated, with a ham sandwich in one hand and a bottle of beer in the other, he didn't even toss him a glance. He was much too busy.

The Police Commissioner was in Manager Kinney's office with Chisholm and others. The Bronx District Attorney and an assistant were in the locker room, along with an assortment of Homicide men, giving various athletes their third or fourth quiz. There were still a couple of dozen city employees in the clubhouse, though the scientists – the photographers and fingerprint hounds – had all finished and gone.

I had standing as the finder of the corpse, but also I was a part of Wolfe. Technically, Wolfe was not poking into a murder; he had been hired by Chisholm, before the corpse had been found, to find out who had doped the ballplayers. However, in gathering facts for relay to Wolfe I had not discriminated. I saw Nick Ferrone's locker opened and the contents examined, with no startling disclosures.

While I was in Kinney's office watching a basket squad load the corpse and carry it out, I heard a lieutenant on the phone giving instructions for a roundup of gamblers throughout the metropolitan area. A little later I picked up a bunch of signal statements from a table, and sat down and read them through, without anyone noticing. By that time the commissioner and the district attorney had arrived, and they had eight or nine quiz posts going in the various rooms, and Hennessy was doing his best to keep it organized.

I collected all I could for Wolfe. The bat that had been used to crack Ferrone's skull was no stock item, but a valued trophy. With it, years back, there had been belted a grand slam home run that had won a pennant, and it had been displayed on a wall rack in the manager's office. The murderer could have simply grabbed it from the rack. It had no usable fingerprints. Of eight bottles of Beebright left in the cooler, the two in front had been doped and the other six had not. No other drinks had been tampered with. Everyone had known of the liking of those four – Baker, Prentiss, Neill, and Eston – for Beebright, and their habit of drinking a bottle of it before a game. No good prints. No sign anywhere of a container of sodium phenobarbital tablets.

There were a thousand other negatives; for instance, the clubhouse boy, Jimmie Burr. The custom was that when he wasn't around, the players would put chits in a little box for what they took; and he hadn't been around. For that game someone had got him a box seat, and he had beat it to the grandstand while most of the players were in the locker room, changing. A sergeant jumped on it: Who had got him out of the way by providing a ticket for a box seat? But it had been Art Kinney himself.

Around eight o'clock they turned a big batch loose. Twenty men, including coaches and the bat boy, were allowed to go to the locker room to change, under surveillance, and then let out, with instructions to keep available. They were not in the picture as it then looked.

It was established that Ferrone had arrived at the clubhouse shortly after one o'clock and had got into uniform; a dozen of the men had been in the locker room with him. He had been present during a pre-game session with Kinney in the clubroom, and no one remembered seeing him leave afterwards. When they trooped out and down the stairs and emerged onto the field, Ferrone's absence was not noticed until they had been in the dugout for some minutes.

As the cops figured it, he couldn't have been slammed with a baseball bat in Kinney's office only a few yards away, while the team was in the clubroom, and therefore all who had unquestionably left for the field with the gang, and had stayed there, were in the clear until further notice. With them went Pierre Mondor, who had wanted to see a ball game and had picked a beaut.

As I said, when Inspector Hennessy breezed through the clubroom at nine o'clock, coming from the locker room and headed for Kinney's office, he didn't even toss a glance at the leather couch where Wolfe and I were seated. He disappeared. But soon he was back again, speaking from the doorway: 'Come in here, will you, Wolfe?'

'No,' Wolfe said. 'I'm eating.'

'The commissioner wants you.'

'Is he eating?' Waiting for no reply, Wolfe turned his head and bellowed, 'Mr Skinner! I'm dining!'

It wasn't very polite, I thought, to be sarcastic about the sandwiches and beer Chisholm had provided. Hennessy started a remark which indicated that he agreed with me, but it was interrupted by the appearance of Commissioner Skinner at his elbow. Hennessy stepped in and aside, and Skinner approached the couch, followed by Chisholm.

Skinner kept it friendly: 'I've just learned that four men who were told they could go are still here: Baker, Prentiss, Neill, and Eston. When Inspector Hennessy asked them why, they told him that Mr Chisholm had asked them to stay. Mr Chisholm says that he did so at your suggestion. He understood that you wanted to speak with them after our men have all left. Is that correct?'

Wolfe nodded. 'I made it quite plain, I thought.'

'M-m.' The commissioner regarded him. 'You see, I know you fairly well. You wouldn't dream of hanging on here half the night to speak with those men merely as a routine step in an investigation. And, besides, at Mr Chisholm's request you have already been permitted to speak with them, and with several others. You're cooking something. Those are the four men who were drugged, but they left the clubhouse for the field with the rest of the team, so the way we figure it, none of them killed Ferrone. How do you figure it?'

Wolfe swallowed the last of a well-chewed bite. 'I don't.'

Hennessy growled and set his jaw.

Skinner said, 'I don't believe it,' with his tone friendlier than his words. 'You're cooking something,' he insisted. 'What's the play with those four men?'

Wolfe shook his head. 'No, sir.'

Hennessy took a step forward. 'Look,' he said; 'this is the Bronx. You don't turn *this* murder into a parlour game.'

Wolfe raised brows at him. 'Murder? I am not concerned with murder. Mr Chisholm hired me to investigate the drugging of his employees. The two events may, of course, be connected, but the murder is your job. And they were not necessarily connected. I understand that a man named Moyse is in there now with the district attorney' – Wolfe aimed a thumb at the door to the locker room – 'because it has been learned that he has twice within a month assaulted Mr Ferrone physically through resentment at Ferrone's interest in his wife, injudiciously displayed. And that Moyse did not leave the clubhouse with the others, but arrived at the dugout three or four minutes later, just before Ferrone's absence was noticed. For your murder, Mr Hennessy, that should be a help; but it doesn't get me on with my job – disclosure of the culprit who drugged the drinks. Have you charged Mr Moyse?'

'No.' Hennessy was curt. 'So you're not interested in the murder?'

'Not as a job, since it's not mine. But if you want a comment from a specialist, you're closing your lines too soon.'

'We haven't closed any lines.'

'You let twenty men walk out of here. You are keeping Moyse for the reasons given. You are keeping Dr Soffer, I suppose, because when Ferrone was missed in the dugout Soffer came here to look for him, and he could have found him here alive and killed him. You are keeping Mr Durkin, I suppose again, because he, too, could have been here alone with Ferrone. He says he left the clubhouse shortly before the team did and went to his seat in the grandstand, and stayed there. Has he been either contradicted or corroborated?'

'No.'

'Then you regard him as vulnerable on opportunity?'

'Yes.'

'Are you holding Mr Chisholm for the same reason?'

Chisholm made a noise. Skinner and Hennessy stared. Skinner said, 'We're not holding Mr Chisholm.'

'You should be, for consistency,' Wolfe declared. 'This afternoon, when I reached my seat in the stands, at twenty minutes past one, the mayor and others were there in a nearby box, but Mr Chisholm was not. He arrived a few minutes later. He has told me that when he arrived with his party, about one o'clock, he had the others escorted to the stands, that he started for the clubhouse for a word with his employees, that he was delayed by the crowd and decided it was too late, and then proceeded to the box. If the others are vulnerable on opportunity, so is he.'

They made remarks, all three of them, not appreciative.

Wolfe put the beer bottle to his lips, tilted it, and swallowed. He put the bottle down empty.

'I was merely,' he said mildly, 'commenting on the murder as a specialist. As for my job, learning who drugged the drinks, I haven't even made a start. How could I in this confounded hubbub? Trampled by an army. I have been permitted to sit here and talk to people, yes, with a succession of your subordinates standing behind me breathing down my neck. Pfui!'

'Very rude, I'm sure,' Hennessy said dryly. 'The commissioner has asked you, what's the play with those four men?'

Wolfe shook his head. 'Not only those four. I included others in my request to Mr Chisholm: Dr Soffer, Mr Kinney, Mr Durkin, and of course Mr Chisholm himself. I am not arranging a parlour game. I make a living as a professional detective, and I need their help on this job I've undertaken. I think I know why – engrossed as you are with the most sensational case you've had in years – you're spending all this time chatting with me: You suspect I'm contriving a finesse. Well, I am.'

'You are?'

'Yes.' Wolfe suddenly was peevish. 'Haven't I sat here for five hours submerged in your pandemonium? Haven't you all the facts that I have, and many more besides? Haven't you thousands of men to command – and I but one? One little fact strikes me, as apparently it has not struck you, and in my forlorn desperation I decide to test my interpretation of it. For that test I need help, and I ask Mr Chisholm to provide it.'

'We'll be glad to help,' Skinner offered. 'Which fact, and how do you interpret it?'

'No, sir.' Wolfe was positive. 'It is my one slender chance to earn a fee. I intend – '

'But we may not know this fact.'

'Certainly you do. I have stated it explicitly during this conversation, but I won't point at it for you. If I did you'd spoil it for me, and, slender as it is, I intend to test it. I am not beset with the urgency of murder, as you are, but I'm in a fix. I don't need a motive strong enough to incite a man to murder, merely one to persuade him to drug some bottled drinks – mildly, far from lethally. A thousand dollars? Twenty thousand? That would be only a fraction of the possible winnings on a World Series game. As for opportunity, anyone at all could have slipped in here late this morning, before others had arrived, with drugged bottles of that drink and put them in the cooler – and earned a fortune. Those twenty men you let go, Mr Hennessy – how many of them can you say positively did not drug the drinks?'

The inspector was scowling at him. 'I can say that I don't think any of them killed Ferrone.'

'Ah, but I'm not after the murderer; that's your job.' Wolfe upturned a palm. 'You see why I am driven to a forlorn finesse?'

We all turned, as a man came in from the locker room. District Attorney Megalech of the Bronx was as masterful as they come and bald as a doorknob. He strode across and told Skinner and Hennessy he wanted to speak with them, took an elbow of each, and steered them through the door to Kinney's office. Chisholm, uninvited, wheeled and followed them.

Wolfe reached for a sandwich and I arose and stood looking down at him. I asked, 'How good is this fact you're saving up?'

'Not very.' He chewed and swallowed. 'Good enough to try if we get nothing better. Evidently they have nothing at all. You heard them.'

'Yeah. You told them they have all the facts you have, but they haven't. The one I gave you about Mrs Moyse? That's not the one you're interpreting privately?'

'No.'

'She might still be around, waiting. I might possibly get something better than the one you're saving. Shall I go try?'

He grunted. I took it for a yes, and moved. Outside the hall door stood a cop. I addressed him: 'I'm going down to buy Mr Wolfe a pickle. Do I need to be passed out or in?'

'You?' He used only the right half of his mouth for talking. 'Shoot your way through. Huh?'

'Right. Many thanks.' I went . . .

It was dumb to be so surprised, but I was. I might have known that the news that New York had been doped out of the game and the Series, and that Nick Ferrone, the rookie of the year, had been murdered, would draw a record mob. Downstairs inside the entrance there were sentries, and outside a regiment was stretched into a cordon. I was explaining to a sergeant who I was and telling him I would be returning, when three desperate men, one of whom I recognized, came springing at me. All they wanted was the truth, the whole truth, and nothing but the truth. I had to get really rude. I have been clawed at by newspapermen more than once, but I had never seen them quite as hungry as they were that October night. As they wouldn't shake loose, I dived through the cordon and into the mob.

It looked hopeless. The only parked cars in sight on that side of the street were police cars. I pushed through to the fringe of the throng and made my way two blocks south. Having made inquiries of two members of the team hours before, I knew what I was looking for: a light-blue sedan.

I crossed the street and headed for the parking plaza. Two cops in the cordon gave me a look, but it wasn't the plaza they were guarding and I marched on through. In the dim light I could see three cars over at the north end. Closer up, one was a light-blue sedan. I went up to it. Two females on the front seat were gazing at me through the window, and one of them was my glommee. The radio was on. I opened the door and said hello.

'Who are you?' she demanded.

'My name's Archie Goodwin. I'll show credentials if you are Mrs William Moyse.'

'What if I am?'

She was rapidly erasing the pleasant memory I had of her. Not that she had turned homely in a few hours, but her expression was not only unfriendly but sour, and her voice was not agreeable. I got out my wallet and extracted my licence card. 'If you are who I think you are,' I said, 'this will identify me.'

'Okay, your name's Goodman.' She ignored the card. 'So what?'

'Not Goodman.' I pronounced it for her: 'Archie Goodwin. I work for Nero Wolfe, who is up in the clubhouse. I just came from there. Why not turn off the radio?'

'I'd rather turn you off,' she said bitterly.

Her companion, the redhead who had been with her in the box, reached for the knob, and the radio died. 'Look, Lila,' she said earnestly; 'you're acting like a sap. Invite him in. He may be human. Maybe Bill sent him.'

'What did Walt tell us?' Lila snapped at her. 'Nero Wolfe is there working with the cops.' She came back to me: 'Did my husband send you? Prove it.'

I put a foot on the edge of the frame, not aggressively. 'That's one reason,' I said, 'why Mr Wolfe can't stand women. The way they flop around, intellectually. I didn't say your husband sent me. He didn't. He couldn't even if he wanted to, because for the past hour he has been kept in the locker room conversing with a gathering of homicide hounds, and still is. Mr Wolfe sent me. But in a way it's a personal problem I've got, and no one but you can help me.'

'*You*'ve got a personal problem! *You* have! Take it away.'

'I will if you say so, but wait till I tell you. Up to now they have only one reason for picking on your husband. The players left the clubhouse for the field in a bunch – all but one of them, who left later and got to the dugout a few minutes after the others. It was Bill Moyse. They all agreed on that, and Bill admits it. The cops figure that he had seen or heard something that made him suspect Nick Ferrone of doping the drinks – you know about that? That the Beebright was doped?'

'Yes. Walt Goidell told me.' She gestured toward the redhead. 'Helen's husband. He's on the team.'

'And that he stayed behind with Ferrone to put it to him, and Nick got tough, and he got tougher, with a baseball bat. That's how the cops figure it, and that's why they're after Bill. But I have a private reason, confided only to Nero Wolfe, to think that the cops have got it twisted. Mr Wolfe is inclined to agree with me, but he hasn't told the cops, because he has been hired by Chisholm and wants to earn a fat fee. My private slant is that if Bill did kill Ferrone – please note the 'if' – it wasn't because he caught Ferrone doping the drinks, but the other way around. Ferrone caught Bill doping the drinks, and was going to spill it, and Bill killed him.'

She was goggling at me. 'You have the nerve – !'

'Hold it. I'm telling you. This afternoon at the game I was in a box. By the sixth inning I had had plenty of the game and looked around for something to take my mind off it, and I saw an extremely attractive girl. I looked at her some more. I had a feeling that I had seen her before, but couldn't place her. The score was eleven to one, the home team were flat on their faces, and that lovely specimen was exactly what my eyes needed – except for one flaw. She was having a swell time. Her whole face and manner showed it. She liked what was happening out on the field.'

She was trying to say something, but I raised my voice a little: 'Wait till I tell you. Later, after the game, in the clubhouse, Bill Moyse said his wife was waiting for him, and someone made a crack about showing me her picture. Then it clicked. I remembered seeing a picture of his bride in the *Gazette*, and it was the girl I had seen in the stands. Then, later, I had a chance to ask some of the players some questions, and I learned that she usually drove to games in Bill's light-blue sedan and waited for him after the game. It puzzled me that it made the wife of a New York player happy to see his team getting walloped in the deciding game of a World Series, and Mr Wolfe agreed. Why were you tickled stiff to see them losing?'

'I wasn't.'

'It's perfectly ridiculous,' the redhead snorted.

I shook my head. 'That won't do. Mr Wolfe accepts my judgment on girls, and I have told him you were happy. If I go back and report that you flatly deny it, I don't see how he can do anything but tell the cops, and that will be bad. They'll figure that you wanted New York to lose because you knew Bill did, and why. Then, of course, they'll refigure the murder and get a new answer – that Ferrone found out that Bill had doped the drinks, and Bill killed him. They'll start on Bill all over again and – '

'Stop it!'

'I was only saying, if they – '

The redhead horned in, then. 'How dumb can you get?' she demanded. 'You say you know girls! Do you know baseball girls? I'm one! I'm Helen Goidell, Walt's wife. I would have liked to slap Lila this afternoon, sitting there gloating, much as I love her. But I'm not a sap like you! She's not married to the team, she's married to Bill! Lew Baker had batted 132 in the first six games of the Series, and he had made four errors and had nine bases stolen on him, and still they wouldn't give Bill a chance. Lila had sat through those six games praying to see Bill walk out – and not once! What did she care about the Series? She wanted to see Bill in it. And look at Baker this afternoon! If he had been doped, all right, but Lila didn't know it then. All she knew was that Bill was probably going to get his chance. What you know about girls, you nitwit!'

She was blazing.

'I'm still willing to learn,' I said agreeably. 'Is she right, Mrs Moyse?'

'Yes.'

'Then I am, too, on the main point? You were pleased to see New York losing?'

'I said she was right.'

'Yeah. Then I've still got a problem. If I accept your version, and report to Wolfe accordingly, he'll accept it, too. Whether you think I know girls or not, he does. So that's some responsibility for me. What if you're a lot smoother and trickier than I think you are? Your husband is suspected of murder, and they're still working on him. What if he's guilty and they manage to squeeze out of you what they need to hook him? How will I look if they do? Any suggestions?'

Lila had none. She sat with her head lowered, silent.

'You sound almost human,' Helen Goidell said.

'That's deceptive,' I told her. 'I turn it on and off. If I thought she had something Mr Wolfe could use I'd stop at nothing, even hair-pulling. But at the moment I really don't think she has. I think she's pure and innocent and wholesome. Her husband is another matter. For her sake, I hope he wriggles out of it somehow, but I'm not taking any bets. The cops seem to like him, and I know cops as well as I do girls.' I removed my foot from the car frame. 'So long and so forth.' I turned to go.

'Wait a minute.' It was Lila.

I turned back. Her head was up.

'Is this straight?' she asked.

'Is what straight?'

'You're going to tell Mr Wolfe you're satisfied about me?'

'Well. Satisfied is quite a word. I'm going to tell him I have bought your explanation of your happiness at the game – or, rather, Mrs Goidell's.'

'You could be a liar.'

'Not only could be, I often am, but not at the moment.'

She regarded me. 'Maybe you can tell me about Bill,' she said. 'They don't really think he killed Nick Ferrone, do they?'

'They think maybe he did.'

'I know he didn't.'

'Good for you. But you weren't there, so you don't have a vote.'

She nodded. She was being hard and practical. 'Are they going to arrest him? Will they really charge him with murder?'

'I can't say. But Bill is the leading candidate.'

'Then I've got to do something. I wish I knew what he's telling them. Do you know?'

'Only that he's denying he knows anything about it. He says he left the clubhouse after the others had gone, because he went back to the locker room to change to other shoes.'

She shook her head. 'I don't mean that. I mean, whether he told them –' She stopped. 'No. I know he didn't. He wouldn't. He knows something and I know it, too, about a man trying to fix that game. Only, he wouldn't tell, on account of me. I have to go and see someone downtown. Will you come along?'

'To see who?'

'I'll tell you on the way.'

Helen Goidell blurted, 'For heaven's sake, Lila, do you know what you're saying?'

If Lila replied I missed it, for I was on my way around the car. It was a little headstrong to dash off with a damsel, leaving Wolfe up there with mass-production sandwiches, warm beer, and his one measly little fact he was saving up, but this might be really hot.

By the time I got around to the other door Helen had it open and was getting out. Her feet on the ground, she turned to speak: 'I don't want any part of this, Lila. I do not! I wish I'd gone with Walt instead of staying with you!'

She turned and trotted off, towards the street. I climbed in and pulled the door shut.

'She'll tell Walt,' Lila said.

I nodded. 'Yeah. But does she know where we're going?'

'No.'

'Then let's go.'

She started the engine, levered to reverse, and backed the car.

Under ordinary circumstances she was probably a pretty good driver, but that night wasn't ordinary for her. Swinging right, there was a little click on my side as we grazed the fender of a stopped car. Rolling up the grade, we slipped between two taxis, clearing by an inch, and both hackmen yelled at her. Stopping for a light at the crest, she turned her head and spoke:

'It's my Uncle Dan. His name is Gale. He came last night and asked me –'

She fed gas and we shot forward, but a car heading uptown and squeezing the light was suddenly there smack in our path. With a lightning reflex her foot hit the brake, the other car zipped by with at least a foot to spare, she fed gas again, and the sedan jerked forward.

I asked her, 'Taking the Highway?'

'Yes, it's quicker.'

'It will be if you make it. Just concentrate on that and let the details wait.'

She got to the downtown side of the highway without any actual contact with other vehicles, turned into the left lane and stepped on it. The speedometer said fifty-five when she spoke again.

'If I go ahead and tell you, I can't change my mind. He wanted me to persuade Bill to fix the game. He said he'd give us ten thousand dollars. I didn't even want to tell Bill, but he insisted, so I did. I knew what Bill would say – '

She broke off to do some expert weaving, swerving to the middle lane, then a sprint, then swinging back to the left again in front of a couple of cars that had slowed her down to under fifty.

'Look,' I told her; 'you could gain up to two minutes this way with luck, but getting stopped and getting a ticket would take at least ten. You're driving, okay, but don't try to talk, too.'

She didn't argue, but she held the pace. I twisted around to keep an eye on the rear through the window, and stayed that way clear to 57th Street. We rolled down the ramp and a block south, turned left on 56th Street, had a green light at Eleventh Avenue, and went through. A little short of Tenth Avenue we turned into the kerb and stopped. Lila reached for the hand brake and gave it a yank.

'Let's hear it,' I said. 'Enough to go on. Is Uncle Dan a gambler?'

'No.' Her face turned to me. 'I'm afraid of him.'

'Then what is he?'

'He runs a drugstore. He owns it. That's where we're going to see him. My father and mother died when I was just a kid, and Uncle Dan has been good to me – as good as he could. If it hadn't been for him I'd have been brought up in an orphans' home. Of course, Bill wanted to tell Art Kinney last night, but he didn't on account of me, and that's why he's not telling the cops.'

'Maybe he is telling them, or soon will.'

She shook her head. 'I know Bill. We decided we wouldn't tell, and that settled it. Uncle Dan made me promise we wouldn't tell before he said what he wanted.'

I grunted. 'Even so, he was crowding his luck, telling you two about the programme before signing you up. If he explained the idea of doping the Beebright – '

'But he didn't! He didn't say how it was to be done. He didn't get that far, because Bill said nothing doing, as I knew he would.'

I eyed her. 'This was last night?'

'Yes.'

'What time?'

'Around eight o'clock. We had dinner early with Helen and Walt Goidell, and when we got home Uncle Dan was there waiting for us.'

'Where's home?'

'Our apartment on Seventy-ninth Street. He spoke to me alone first, and then insisted I had to ask Bill.'

'And Bill turned him down flat?'

'Of course he did!'

'Bill didn't see him alone later?'

'Of course not!'

'All right, don't bite. I need to know. Now what?'

'We're going to see him. We're going to tell him that we have to tell the cops, and we're going to try to get him to come along. That's why I wanted you with me, because I'm afraid of him – I mean, I'm afraid he'll talk me out of it. But they've got to know that Bill was asked to fix the game and he wouldn't. If it's hard on Uncle Dan that's too bad, but I can't help it. I'm for Bill, all the way.'

I was making myself look at her, for discipline. I was having the normal male impulses at the sight and sound of a good-looking girl in trouble, and they were worse than normal because I was partly responsible. I had given her the impression that the cops were about set to take her Bill on the big one, which was an exaggeration. I hadn't mentioned that one reason they were keeping him was his reaction to the interest Nick Ferrone had shown in her, which of course had no bearing on anyone's attempt to fix a ball game. True, she had been in a mess before I had got to her, but I had shoved her in deeper. What she needed now was understanding and sympathy, and I was all she had. Which was I, a man or a detective?

'Okay,' I said, 'let's go see Uncle Dan.'

The engine was running. She released the hand brake, fed gas, and we rolled. Three minutes got us to Eighth Avenue, where we turned downtown. The car slowed and she pulled in at the kerb.

'There it is.' She pointed. 'Gale's Pharmacy.'

It was ten paces down. There were lights in the window, but otherwise it looked drab. I got out and held the door, and she joined me on the sidewalk. She put a hand on my arm.

'You're staying right with me,' she stated.

'Absolutely,' I assured her. 'I'm good with uncles.'

As we crossed to the entrance and went inside I was feeling not fully dressed. I have a routine habit of wearing a gun when I'm on a case involving people who may go to extremes, but, as I said, I do not go armed to ball games. However, at first sight of Daniel Gale I did not put him in that category. His drugstore was so narrow that a fat man would have had to squeeze between the soda-fountain stools and the central showcase, and that made it look long, but it wasn't. Five or six customers were on the stools, and the soda jerk was busy.

At the cosmetics counter on the left, a woman was being waited on by a little guy with a pale, tight-skinned face, wearing glasses.

'That's him,' Lila whispered to me.

We waited near the door. Uncle Dan, concentrating on the customer, hadn't seen us. Finally the customer made her choice and, as he tore off paper to wrap the purchase, his eyes lifted and he saw Lila. Also, he saw me, beside her. He froze. He held it, rigid, for seconds, then came to, went on with the wrapping job, and was handed a bill by the customer. While he was at the cash register Lila and I crossed to the counter. As he handed the woman her change, Lila spoke:

'Uncle Dan, I've got to tell you – '

She stopped because he was gone. Without speaking, he turned and made for the rear, disappeared behind a partition, and a door closed. I didn't like it, but didn't want to start a commotion by hurdling the counter, so I stepped to the end and circled, went to the door that had closed, and turned the knob. It was locked. There I was, out at first, unless I was prepared to smash the door in.

The soda jerk called, 'Hey, Mac, come out of that!'

'It's all right,' Lila told him. 'I'm his niece – Mr Gale is my Uncle Dan.'

'I never saw you before, lady . . . You, Mac, come out here where you belong! Whose uncle are you?'

A couple of the fountain customers gave him his laugh. Then the door I was standing by popped open and Uncle Dan was there, beside me.

'Henry!' he called.

'Right here!' the soda jerk called back.

'Take over for a while – I'll be busy. Come here, Lila, will you?'

Lila circled the end of the counter and approached us. There wasn't room enough to be gallant and let her pass, so I followed Gale through the door into the back room ahead of her. It was small, and the stacks of shipping cartons and other objects took most of what space there was. The rows of shelves were crammed with packaged merchandise, except those along the right wall, which held labelled bottles. Gale stopped near the door, and Lila and I went on by.

'We don't want to be disturbed,' Gale said, and bolted the door.

'Why not?' I inquired.

He faced me, and from a distance of five arms' lengths, with Lila between us, I had my first good view of the eyes behind the specs. They were cold and deadly.

'Because,' he was telling me, 'this is a private matter. You see, I recognized you, Mr Goodwin. Your face is not as well known as your employer's, but it has been in the papers on several occasions, and you were in my mind on account of the news. The radio bulletins have included the detail that Nero Wolfe and his assistant were present and engaged by Mr Chisholm. So when I saw you with my niece I realized we should talk privately. But you're an impulsive young man, and for fear you may not like what I say, I make conditions. I shall stay here near the door. You will move to that packing case back of you and sit on it, with your hands in sight and making no unnecessary movements. My niece will put the chair here in front of me and sit on it, facing you, between you and me. That way I will feel free to talk.'

I thought he was batty. As a setup against one of my impulses, including a gun if I had had one, it made no sense at all. I backed up to the packing case and lowered myself, resting my hands on my knees to humour him. When Lila saw me complying she moved the chair, the only one there, as directed, and sat with her back to her uncle. He, himself, went to a narrow counter, picked up a bottle of colourless liquid, removed the glass stopper, held it to his nose, and sniffed.

'I do not have fainting spells,' he said apologetically, 'but at the moment I am a little unstrung. Seeing my niece here with you was a real shock for me. I came back here to consider what it might mean, but reached no conclusion. Perhaps you'll explain?'

'Your niece will. Tell him, Lila.'

She started to twist around in the chair, but he commanded her: 'No, my dear, stay as you were. Face Mr Goodwin.' He took another sniff at the bottle.

She obeyed. 'It's Bill,' she said. 'They're going to arrest him for murder, and they mustn't. They won't, if we tell them how you offered to pay him for fixing the game and he wouldn't do it. He won't tell them, on account of me, so we have to. I know I promised you I wouldn't, but now I've got to. You see how it is, Uncle Dan; I've got to.'

'You haven't told the police?'

'No. I thought the best way was to come and get you to go with me. I was afraid to come alone, because I know how bad it will be for you, but it will be worse for Bill if we don't. Don't you see, Uncle – ?'

'Keep your back turned, Lila. I insist on it. That's right; stay that way.' He had been talking in an even low tone, but now his voice became thin and strained: 'I'll tell you why I want your back to me – so I can't see your face . . . Remember, Goodwin, don't move! . . . This is a bottle of pure sulphuric acid. I was smelling it just to explain why I had it; of course, it has no smell. I suppose you know what it will do. This bottle is nearly full, and I'm holding it carefully, because one drop on your skin will scar you for life. That's why I want your back to me. Lila. I'm very fond of you, and I don't want to see your face if I have to use this acid. If you move, Lila dear, I'll use it. Or you, Goodwin; especially you. I hope you both understand?'

His hand holding the bottle hovered inches above her head. She looked as if she might keel over, and I urged her, 'Sit tight, Lila, and don't scream.'

'Yes,' Uncle Dan said approvingly. 'I should have mentioned that. Screaming would be as bad as moving. I had to tell you about the acid before I discussed matters. I'm not surprised at your fantastic suggestion, Lila, because I know how foolish you can be, but I'm surprised at you, Goodwin. How could you expect me to consent to my complete ruin? Did Lila persuade you that I am an utter fool?'

'I guess she must have,' I admitted. 'What kind of man are you?'

He proceeded to tell me, and I pretended to listen. I also tried to keep my eyes on his pale, tight-skinned face, but that wasn't easy, because they were fascinated by the bottle he was holding. Meanwhile, my brain was buzzing. Unless he was plain loony the only practical purpose of the bottle must be to gain time – and for what?

'. . . and I will,' he was saying. 'This won't kill you, Lila dear, but it will be horrible, and I don't want to do it unless I have to. Only, you mustn't think I won't. You don't really know me very well, because to you I'm just Uncle Dan. You didn't know that I once had a million dollars and I was an important and dangerous man. There were people who knew me and feared me, but I was unlucky. I have gambled and made fortunes, and lost them. That affects a man's nerves. It changes a man's outlook on life. I borrowed enough money to buy this place, and for years I worked hard and did well – well enough to pay it all back. But that was my ruin. I owed nothing and had a little cash and decided to celebrate by losing one hundred dollars to some old friends – just one hundred dollars, but I didn't lose. I won several thousand. After that I went on, and lost what I had won, and I lost this place.

'So I don't own this place; my friends do. They are very old friends, and they gave me a chance to get this place back. I'm telling you about this, Lila dear, because I want you to understand. I came to you and

Bill with that offer because I had to, and you promised me, you swore you would tell no one. I have been an unlucky man, and sometimes a weak one, but I am never going to be weak again – Don't move!'

Lila, who had lifted her head a little, stiffened. I sat gazing at Gale. Obviously, he was stalling for time, but what could he expect to happen? It could be only one thing: he expected somebody to come. He expected help.

As soon as he had seen us he had scooted back here to phone somebody. Help was on the way, the kind of help that would deal with Lila and me efficiently and finally; and big-time gamblers who could provide ten grand to fix a game are just the babies to be ready with that kind of help.

Either he was loony or that was it. But then what? They might come any second; they might be entering the drugstore right now. Any second a knock on the door might come . . .

Gale was talking: 'I didn't think you'd tell, Lila, after all I've done for you. You promised me you wouldn't. Now, of course, you've told Goodwin and it can't be helped. If I just tip this bottle – '

'Nuts,' I said emphatically, but not raising my voice. 'You haven't got it staged right.' I had my eyes straight on his specs. 'Maybe you don't want to see her face, but the way you've got her, with her back to you, it's no good. What if she suddenly ducked, and dived forward? You might get some on her clothes or her feet, but the chair would be in your way. Have you considered that? . . . Better still, what if she suddenly darted sideways in between those cartons? The instant she moved I'd be moving, too, and that would take her out of my path. She'd be taking a chance, but that would be better than sitting there waiting for the next act. Unquestionably, it would be better for her to go sideways – with her head down and her arms out. You see how bum your arrangement is? But if you make her turn and face you – '

She moved. She went sideways, to her left, her head down and her arms out, diving for the cartons.

I lost a tenth of a second because I hadn't dared to pull my feet back ready for the spring, but that was all I lost. I didn't leap, I just went, with all the force my leg muscles could give it. My target was the bottom of the left front leg of the chair, and I went in flat, face down, and had the leg before he could get under way. The impact of the chair knocked him back against the door, and I kept going and grabbed his ankle and jerked.

Of course, the bottle could have landed right on me, but I had to get him off his feet. As I yanked his ankle I kept my face down, and he tumbled. The next thing I knew I was on top of him, pinning him, with

a grip on his throat, looking around for the bottle. It had never reached
the floor. It had landed on a carton six feet to my right and lay there on
its side, the stuff gurgling out. The floor slanted toward the wall, so no
flood threatened me.

'Okay, Lila,' I said. 'I need help.'

She was scrambling to her feet. 'Did he – did it – ' She giggled.

'No. If you have hysterics I'll tell Bill. Slap yourself; I can't.'

But he – '

'Shut up. Company's coming and we've got to get out of here. I want
some adhesive tape quick.' She started looking on shelves and in
drawers. 'Watch your step,' I told her. 'That stuff's spreading to the
floor . . . When I said I was good with uncles I didn't mean uncles like
him. He's a lulu. He – '

'Here it is.'

'Good girl. Tear off a piece six inches long . . . that's it. Now across
his mouth good and tight, diagonally. Now one the other way. . . .
That ought to do it, thank you, nurse. Now find some nice sterile
bandage.'

She found that, too, and held his arms while I sat on his knees and
tied his ankles. Then I fastened his wrists behind him and anchored the
strip of bandage to the handle of a locked drawer. I squatted for a look
at the tape on his mouth, gave it a rub, stood up, went to the door, and
pushed the bolt.

'Come on,' I told her.

I opened the door and she passed through. I followed and pulled the
door to. There were customers on the fountain stools, and Henry was
selling a man a pack of cigarettes. I paused on my way to the street
door to tell him that Mr Gale would be out soon, then opened the door
to Lila. On the sidewalk I told her to wait in the car while I made a
phone call.

Up twenty paces was a bar and grill. I went in, found a phone booth,
dialled Manhattan Homicide, asked for Sergeant Purley Stebbins, and
got him. He wanted to know if I was still up at the ball park.

I told him no. 'Where I am,' I said, 'is top secret. I'm giving you a hot
one.' I gave him the address of Gale's Pharmacy. 'Get a prowl car there
fast, and plenty of reinforcements. Gale, the owner, on information
received, was the go-between for the gamblers who fixed the ball
game. He's in the back room of his store, gagged and tied.'

'Is *this* a gag?'

'No. The reason for the hurry is that I think Gale sent for a rescue
squad to deal with certain parties who are no longer there, and it
would be nice to get there in time to welcome them. So PD cars should

not park in front. Be sure to tell them not to step in the stuff on the floor that looks like water, because it's sulphuric acid. That's all. Got the address?'

'Yes. Where are you? And – '

'Sorry, I've got a date. This could make you a lieutenant. Step on it.'

I went out and back to the car. Lila was on the driver's side, gripping the steering wheel with both hands.

'Move over,' I said. 'I'll do the driving this time.'

She slid across, and I got in and pulled the door to. I sat. Half a minute went by.

'Where are we going?' she asked. Her voice was so weak I barely got it.

'Uptown. Where Bill is.' Maybe he was.

'Why don't we start?'

'I phoned for cops. If others come before the cops do I want to get a look at them. In case I forget it later, I want to mention that that was a beautiful dive you made, and the timing couldn't have been better. I'm for you, only spiritually of course, since you're happily married.'

'I want to get away from here. I want to see Bill.'

'You will. Relax.'

We sat, but not for long. It couldn't have been more than four minutes before a pair of cops swung around the corner, headed for the entrance to Gale's Pharmacy, and then entered. I pushed the starter button . . .

It was only half an hour short of midnight when I stopped the car at the kerb across the street from the main entrance to the ball park. The mob had dwindled to a few small knots, and of the long line of police cars only three were left. Two cops were having a tête-à-tête in front of the entrance.

Lila was a quick mover. She had got out and circled the car to my side by the time I hit the pavement. I gave her the ignition key and we were crossing the street when suddenly she let out a squawk and started to run. I took another step, and stopped. Bill Moyse was there, emerging from the entrance, with a dick on either side of him and one behind. Lila ended her run in a flying leap and was on him. The startled dicks grabbed for her, and the two uniformed cops started toward them.

I would have liked to deliver Lila to Wolfe, or at least to Hennessy, but there was a fat chance of tearing her loose from her second-string catcher. Also, I did not care to get hung up explaining to a bunch of underlings how I happened to be chauffeuring for Mrs Moyse, so I detoured around the cluster, made it inside the entrance, and headed for the clubhouse stairs. Hearing heavy footsteps above, starting down, and voices, one of them Hennessy's, I slipped quietly behind a pillar.

Surely Stebbins had informed the Bronx of my phone call about the situation at Gale's Pharmacy, and so surely Hennessy would be inquisitive enough to want to take me along wherever he was going. I didn't risk peeking around the pillar, but, judging from the footsteps, there were four or five men. As soon as they had faded out I went on up the stairs. I was not chipper. I did not have Lila. I had been gone more than two hours. Wolfe might have gone home. They might all be gone.

But they weren't. Wolfe was in the clubroom, on the leather couch, and Chisholm was standing. As I entered, their heads turned to me.

'The police are looking for you,' Wolfe said coldly.

'Uh-huh.' I played it indifferent. 'I just dodged a squad.'

'Why did you go to that drugstore?'

I raised the brows. 'Oh, you've heard about it?'

'Yes. Mr Hennessy did, and he was kind enough to tell me.' He was dripping sarcasm. 'It is a novel experience, learning of your movements through the courtesy of a policeman.'

'I was too busy to phone.' I glanced at Chisholm. 'Maybe I should report privately.'

'This is getting to be a farce,' Chisholm growled. His tie was crooked, his eyes were bloodshot, and he had a smear of mustard at the side of his mouth.

'No,' Wolfe said, to me, not to Chisholm. 'Go ahead. But be brief.'

I obeyed. With the training and experience I have had I can report a day of dialogue practically verbatim, but he had said to be brief, so I condensed it, including all essentials.

'Then you don't know whether Gale was actually involved or not. When he failed with Mr and Mrs Moyse he may have quit trying.'

'I doubt it.'

'You could have resolved the doubt. You were sitting on him. Or you could have brought him here.'

I might have made three or four cutting remarks if an outsider hadn't been present. I stayed calm. 'Maybe I didn't make it clear,' I conceded generously. 'It was ten to one he had phoned for help, the kind of help that would leave no doubts to resolve, and it might have come any second. Not that I was scared – I was too busy – but I wanted to see you once more so I could resign. I resign.'

'Bosh.' Wolfe put his hands on the leather seat for leverage and raised himself to his feet. 'Very well. I'll have to try it.'

Chisholm put in, 'Inspector Hennessy said to notify him immediately if Goodwin showed up.'

Wolfe wheeled on him, snarling. 'Am I working for you? Yes! Notify Mr Hennessy? Bah!' He turned and strode through the door that led to Art Kinney's office.

Chisholm and I fell in behind.

They were all in there. The four who were famous athletes didn't look very athletic just at present. Their sap had started draining with the first inning of that awful ball game, and it hadn't stopped for more than ten hours. Lew Baker, catcher, and Con Prentiss, short-stop, were perched on a desk. Joe Eston, third baseman, and Nat Neill, centre-fielder, were on chairs.

Art Kinney, the manager, was standing over by a window. Doc Soffer was seated at Kinney's desk, bent over, with his elbows on his knees and his face covered by his hands. Beaky Durkin was propped against a table, saggy and bleary-eyed.

'It had better be good,' someone said. I didn't know who, because I was placing a chair for Wolfe where he could see them all without straining his neck. When he was in it, with nothing to spare between the arms, I crossed to a vacant seat over by the radio. Chisholm was there, at my right.

Wolfe's head moved from side to side and back again. 'I hope,' he said grumpily, 'you're not expecting too much.'

'I'm through expecting,' Kinney muttered.

Wolfe nodded. 'I know how you feel, Mr Kinney. All of you. You are weary and low in spirit. You have been personally and professionally humiliated. You have all been talked at too much. I'm sorry I have to prolong it, but I had to wait until the police were gone. Also, since I have no evidence, I had to let them complete their elaborate and skilled routine in search of some. They got none. Actually, they have nothing but a druggist that Mr Goodwin got for them.'

'They've got Bill Moyse,' Con Prentiss rumbled.

'Yes, but on suspicion, not on evidence. Of course I admit, because I must, that I am in the same fix. I, too, have a suspicion but no evidence, only mine is better-grounded. I suspect one of you eight men of drugging the drinks and killing Ferrone. What I – '

They made enough noise to stop him. He held up a palm.

'If you please, gentlemen. I have a question to put. I suspect one of you, but I have no evidence and no way of getting any speedily. That is why I asked Mr Chisholm to keep you here for consultation with me after the departure of the police. I wanted to ask you: Do you want to help? I would like to tell you the reason for my suspicion and ask you to help me get evidence to support it. I think you can if you will. Well?'

'One of *us*?' Joe Eston demanded.

It was interesting to see them. Naturally, they all had an impulse, all but one, anyway, to look around at faces, but no two of them handled it exactly alike. Chisholm looked straight and full at each in turn. Beaky Durkin sent quick little glances here and there. Doc Soffer, frowning and pursing his lips, turned his head slowly left to right.

'Go ahead!' Kinney blurted. 'Have you got something or not?'

'Yes, I have something,' Wolfe assured him, 'But I don't know how good it is. Without your help it is no good at all.'

'We'll help if we can. Let's hear it.'

'Well. First the background. Were the two events – the drugging of the drinks and the murder – connected? The reasonable supposition is yes, until and unless it is contradicted. If they were connected, how? Did Ferrone drug the drinks, and did one of his team-mates discover it and, enraged, go for him with the bat? It seems unlikely.'

Wolfe focused on Beaky Durkin: 'Mr Durkin, you knew Ferrone better than anyone else. You discovered him and got him here. You were his roommate and counsellor. You told me that because of his brilliant performance this season his salary for next year would be doubled; that his heart was set on winning today's game and the Series; that winning or losing meant a difference of some two thousand dollars to him personally; that his Series money would pay his debts, with some to spare; and that, knowing him intimately, you are positive that he could not have been bribed to drug the drinks. Is that correct?'

'It sure is.' Durkin was hoarse and cleared his throat. 'Nick was a swell kid.' He looked around as if ready for an argument, but nobody started one.

'Do any of you dispute it?' Wolfe asked.

They didn't.

'Then without evidence it is idiotic to assume that he drugged the drinks. The alternative, suppose that the two events were connected, is the reverse: that someone drugged the drinks and Ferrone knew or suspected it and was going to expose him, and was killed. That is how I see it. Call him X. X could have – '

'Don't beat around the bush,' Kinney blurted. 'Name him!'

'Presently. X could have put the drugged drinks in the cooler any time during the late morning, as opportunity offered. What led Ferrone to suspect him of skulduggery may not be known, but conjecture offers a wide choice. Ferrone's suspicion may have been only superficial, but to X any suspicion whatever was a mortal menace, knowing, as he did, what was going to happen on the ball field. When Ferrone questioned him he had to act. The two were, of course, in this room together, at the time the rest of you were leaving the clubroom for the field or shortly after. X was, as so many have been, the victim of progressive emergency. At first he needed only money, and to get it he stooped to scoundrelism; but it betrayed him into needing the life of a fellow man.'

'Cut the rhetoric,' Chisholm snapped. 'Name him.'

Wolfe nodded. 'Naming him is easy. But it is pointless to name him, and expose myself to an action for slander, unless I can enlist your help. As I said, I have no evidence. All I have is a fact about one of you, a fact known to all of you and to the police, which seems to me to point to guilt. But I admit that other interpretations are conceivable. You are better judges of that than I am, and I'm going to present it for your consideration.'

He aimed his gaze at Baker and Prentiss, perched on a desk, raised a hand, slowly, and scratched the tip of his nose. His eyes moved to pin Doc Soffer. His head jerked to the left, to focus on Chisholm, and the right, to Beaky Durkin. He spoke:

'I'll illustrate my meaning. Take you, Mr Durkin. You have accounted for yourself, but you have been neither contradicted nor corroborated. You say you left the clubhouse shortly before the team did and went to your seat in the grandstand.'

'That's right.' Durkin was still hoarse. 'And I didn't kill Nick.'

'I didn't say you did. I am merely expounding. You say you remained in your seat, watching the game, until the third inning, when you went sent for by Mr Chisholm to come to the clubhouse. That, too, is neither contradicted nor corroborated. Certainly you were there when you were sent for, but there is no proof that you had been there continuously since the game started and even before.'

'I don't know about proof, but I was. I can probably find the guy that was sitting next to me.'

'You didn't leave your seat once during that time?'

'I did not.'

Wolfe looked around. 'Well, gentlemen. That's the fact I can't explain. Can you?'

They were gawking at him. 'Do we have to?' Baker demanded.

'Someone does.' Wolfe's voice sharpened: 'Consider the situation. Consider the relationship of those two men. The discovery of Ferrone is Durkin's proudest achievement as a baseball scout. He fosters him and treasures him. Today, now yesterday, at the game that was to be the climax of Ferrone's triumphant season, Durkin is in the clubroom and sees Ferrone there in uniform, with the others, young, sound, mighty, valiant. He leaves the clubhouse and goes to a seat in the grandstand. Before long the loudspeaker announces that Garth, not Ferrone, will play second base. Durkin keeps his seat. The players take the field, and the game starts, with no Ferrone. Durkin keeps his seat. They play the first inning badly. Durkin keeps his seat. They play the second inning badly. Durkin keeps – '

'Good lord!' Art Kinney yelled.

'Exactly.' Wolfe lifted a hand. 'Please, gentlemen, keep your seats. It is clearly fantastic. The announcement that Garth would play second base could have been taken by Durkin merely as a blunder, but when they took the field without Ferrone his consternation would have been insupportable. The one thing he couldn't possibly have done was to stay in his seat. Why did you, Mr Durkin?'

'I couldn't think – ' He tried to clear his throat and almost choked. 'What could I do?'

'I don't know. I said I can't explain what you did do, but I can try. Suppose the nonappearance of Ferrone was no surprise to you, because you knew where he was and what had happened to him. Suppose, further, you were in a state of severe systemic shock because you had murdered him. I submit that explanation of your keeping your seat is plausible. Can you offer any other?'

Durkin took two steps. 'Look here,' he said; 'you can't sit there and accuse me of a thing like that. I don't have to stay and take it, and I'm not going to.'

He started for the door, but Lew Baker was suddenly there in his path. 'Back up, Beaky. I said back up!'

Beaky did so, literally. He backed until his rump hit the edge of the table. He groped for support and braced himself.

Wolfe was grim. 'I was supposing, Mr Durkin, not accusing. But I am now ready to accuse, and I do. I explained, when I was calling you X, how and why you acted.' His eyes moved. 'Gentlemen, I ask you to look at him. Look at his face, his eyes. Look at his hands, clutching the table in dismay and despair. Yes, I accuse him. I say that that man drugged your drinks, caused you to lose your game, and, threatened with exposure, murdered your teammate.'

They were all on their feet, including Art Kinney. They were making threatening sounds.

'Wait!' Wolfe said sharply, and they turned to him. 'I must warn you, you approach him at your peril, for I have no proof. It will be gratifying to press a confession out of him, but a confession is not evidence, and we need some. I suggest that you try for it. He did it for money, and surely he was paid something in advance, unless he is a fool. Where is it? Certainly not on his person, since you have all been searched, but it is somewhere, and it would do admirably. Where is it?'

Lew Baker got to Durkin ahead of the others. He told him in a thin, tight voice, so tight it twanged, 'I wouldn't want to touch you, Beaky, you dirty rat. Where is it? Where's the jack?'

'Lew, I swear to – '

'Skip it! You fixed us, did you? And Nick – you fixed him. I'd hate to touch you, but if I do – '

The others were there, Kinney and Doc Soffer with them, crowding in on Durkin, who had pulled back onto the table, still gripping the edge. I went to the end of the table and stood. They were all strong and hard, and their nervous systems had had a tough day. Aside from the killing of Nick Ferrone, this was the bird who had made them play ball like half-witted apes in the most important game of their lives, to an audience of fifty million.

'Give me room, fellows,' Nat Neill said. 'I'm going to plug him.'

Durkin didn't flinch. His jaw was quivering and his eyes looked sick, but he didn't flinch.

'This is wrong,' Con Prentiss said. 'He wants us to hurt him. He'd like to be knocked cold. He's not a coward; he's just a snake.'

'It's a moral question,' Joe Eston said. 'That's the way to handle it.'

Art Kinney shouldered between two of them to get his face within ten inches of Durkin's. 'Look, Beaky. You've been in baseball thirty years. You know everybody in the majors and we know you. What do you think's going to happen? Where could you light? We've got you here now and we're going to keep you. I'll send for the whole team. How will you like that?'

'I want a lawyer,' Durkin said.

Neill roared. 'He wants a lawyer! I'm going to clip him!'

'No, Beaky, no lawyers,' Kinney said. 'I'll send for the boys and we'll lock the doors. Where's the money? Where is it?'

Durkin's head went forward, down. Kinney put a fist under his chin and yanked it up and held it. 'No, you don't. Look at me. We've got you, but even if we didn't where could you go? Where are you going to sleep and eat?'

'Let me hold his chin,' Neill requested. 'I'll fix it for him.'

'Shut up,' Eston told him. 'It's a moral question.'

Kinney's fist was still propping Durkin's chin. 'I think,' he said, 'the boys ought to have a look at you. They won't be sleeping anyhow, not tonight. Con, get on the phone and find them. You, too, Lew, the one in the clubroom. Get 'em here – get all of 'em you can. And tell them not to spill it. We don't want any cops yet.'

'No!' Durkin squawked.

'No what, Beaky?' Kinney removed his fist.

'I didn't mean to kill Nick.' He was slobbering. 'I swear I didn't, Art. He suspected. He found out I bet a grand against us and he threw it at me. I brought him here to explain. But he wouldn't believe me and was going to tell you, and he got sore and came at me, and I grabbed the bat just to stop him, and when I saw he was dead – You've got to believe me, Art. I didn't want to kill Nick!'

'You got more than a grand for doping the drinks.'

'I'm coming clean, Art. You can check me and I'm coming clean. I got five grand and I've got five more coming. I had to have it, Art, because the bookies had me down and I was sunk. I was listed good if I didn't come through. I had it on me, but with the cops coming I knew we'd be frisked, so I ditched it. You see I'm coming clean, Art. I ditched it there in the radio. I stuffed it in through a slot.'

There was a scramble and a race. Prentiss tangled with a chair and went down with it, sprawling. Nat Neill won. He jerked the radio around and started clawing at the back, but the panel was screwed on.

'Here,' I said, 'I've got a – '

He hauled off and swung with his bare fists; he yanked, and half the panel came off. He looked inside and started to stick his hand in, but I shouldered him, good and hard, and sent him sideways. The others were there, three of them, surrounding me.

'Well?' Wolfe called.

'A good, fat roll,' I told him and the world. 'The one on the outside is a C.'

Beaky Durkin, left to himself on the table, suddenly moved fast. He was on his feet and streaking for the door. Joe Eston, who had claimed it was a moral issue, leaped for him as if he had been a blazing line drive trying to get by, got to him, and landed with his right.

'That will do,' Wolfe said, as one who had earned the right to command. 'Thank you gentlemen. Archie, get Mr Hennessy.'

I went to Kinney's desk and reached for the phone. At the instant my fingers touched it, it rang. So instead of dialling I lifted it and feeling cocky, told it, 'Nero Wolfe's Bronx office, Goodwin speaking.'

'This is Inspector Hennessy. Is Durkin there?'

I said yes.

'Fine. Hold him, and hold him good. We cracked Gale and he spilled everything. Durkin is it. Gale got to him and bought him. You'll get credit for getting Gale – that'll be all right – but I'll appreciate it if you'll hold off and let it be announced officially. We'll be there for Durkin in five minutes.'

'He's stretched out here on the floor. Mr Wolfe hung it on him. Also, we have found a roll of lettuce he cached in the radio.'

I hung up and turned to Wolfe: 'That was Hennessy. They broke Gale and he unloaded. He gave them Durkin and they're coming for him.

'The trouble is this: Which of us crossed the plate first, you with your one little fact, or me with my druggist? You can't deny that Hennessy's call came before I started to dial him. How can we settle it?'

We can't. That was months ago, and it's not settled yet.

The Man Who Was Hammered

◆

JACK TREVOR STORY

Sexton Blake, once referred to as 'the world's longest serving detective', has changed his dress style somewhat since his first appearance in 1893 in The Missing Millionaire *where he set off in search of clues as a sturdy figure with a high-crowned bowler, elastic-sided boots and a heavy walking stick. His hawk-like features, high forehead and penetrating blue-grey eyes have not changed over the years, but his clothing has kept pace with fashion. Blake has also always had a youthful assistant, Tinker, and a long-suffering landlady, Mrs Bardell, both little changed by the passing years. In all, he is said to have been involved in more cases than any other sleuth – almost four thousand, consisting of two hundred and fifty million words written by several hundred writers including Harry Blyth (who created Blake as an imitation of Sherlock Holmes and even gave him a Baker Street residence), Edgar Wallace, Peter Cheyney, Leslie Charteris, John Creasey, Delano Ames and Jack Trevor Story. When the last of the twice monthly novelettes about him was published in 1963 it was claimed that more than five hundred million issues had been sold in the seventy years since his debut. Among the detective's many admirers was Dorothy L. Sayers who described the Blake saga as, 'the nearest approach to a national folklore, conceived as the centre for a cycle of loosely-connected romances in the Arthurian manner.' Praise indeed for a character who had started his career in the pages of a weekly paper called* The Halfpenny Marvel *where he was billed as 'the office-boys' Sherlock Holmes'!*

Over the years at least two dozen films have been made about the sleuth, beginning with a silent picture, Sexton Blake, Detective *in 1909 starring C. Douglas Carlisle, whose role was repeated in later years by such diverse actors as Douglas Payne, Langhorne Burton, George Curzon and David Farrar. In 1939, Curzon also played Blake in the radio serial,* Enter Sexton Blake (1939), *though he was replaced by Arthur Young the following year in* A Case For Sexton Blake. *It was not until 1968 that Blake reached television audiences when Rediffusion launched a twenty-six-part series of twenty-five minute stories entitled* Sexton Blake, *starring Laurence Payne with Roger Foss as Tinker. The following year, Thames screened a six-part series,* Sexton Blake and the Puff Adder *again starring Payne and Foss and some exotic location shooting in Tangier. The BBC also utilized the universal appeal of the detective a decade later by producing* Sexton Blake and the Demon God *in six parts with Jeremy Clyde ('He makes a very good Sexton Blake with his 1930's face and high cheekbones which go well with middle parted hair and starched collar,'* The Times *of September 15, 1978 reported) and Philip Davis as Tinker. The flamboyant writer and journalist Jack Trevor Story (1917–1991), well-known for his novels* The Trouble With Harry (1949) *and* Live Now, Pay Later (1960), *also contributed some of the most entertaining of the Sexton Blake novelettes including* The Big Steal, The Blonde and The Boodle *and* Violence in Quiet Places. *His* The Man Who Was Hammered *is one of the best of the short stories to feature Blake.*

'EXCUSE me, Officer – '
The cultured voice, the pleasantness of its tone, brought Constable Charles Penn round in considerable surprise. One did not expect to hear speech of that quality in the district of Hoxton he was patrolling then.

'Sir?' he asked automatically.

The stranger was as tall as himself, and pretty well as broad, although much older. Obviously a gentleman, Penn thought.

'I'm looking for a place called Mabon's Court, Officer. Do you happen to know it?'

'Mabon's Court?' Penn stared at the stranger through the murk of mist and rain. He gave a short laugh. 'Yes, I know Mabon's Court, sir, but – are you sure you've got the right name?' he asked. 'I mean – it's pretty bad down there.'

'Yes, so I understand; but that's the place I'm after. Would you mind directing me there?'

'Certainly, sir!' Penn turned and pointed down the dark road ahead. 'If you continue straight down there, sir, to the fourth turning on the right, you'll find Lister Street. Turn down there, sir, cross the road, and you'll find that Mabon's Court is either the six or seventh building on the left-hand side.'

'Thank you very much, Officer. It's a foul night, isn't it?'

'You're right, it is, sir!' Penn agreed fervently. 'And you're going to a pretty foul spot!' he added mentally as he watched the well-clad stranger stride away quickly into the darkness. 'A doctor, maybe,' he thought as he continued his patrol. He had that look about him, and something of a doctor's quiet authority. Certainly no one of his quality, apart from a doctor, would be likely to have business with anyone living in Mabon's Court. The lousiest tenement in all Hoxton it was. Why, even the police never went there except in pairs!

The constable hitched his cape higher about his frozen ears and plodded steadily on. He hated night work, anyway – particularly in the winter – and it was worse still in this district. He glanced at his watch – ten minutes past eleven. It must have been a pretty urgent call that had got that doctor out to Mabon's Court at this time of night.

Always supposing he was a doctor.

A couple of hours later, returning to make a point on the corner of Biggin Street and Water Lane, the constable came through Lister Street and thought again of the man who had asked him the way to Mabon's Court. As he passed the building he looked up at its dingy, dilapidated façade, and automatically shone his torch through the open door on to the worn stone stairs which led to the flats above. A shocking place it was. Absolutely unfit for human habitation, with the paper and plaster hanging off the walls and pools of water lying stagnant in what was euphemistically called the 'hall'. With a shudder of disgust – tempered by a feeling of pity for the poor dregs of humanity who were compelled to live in such surroundings – he switched off his torch and crossed to the other side of the road. But he had barely found the kerb and mounted the pavement when he stopped – warned by some sixth sense that he was no longer alone.

He flashed his torch ahead of him, and behind. Then he swung it sideways along the wall, and suddenly the breath caught cold in his throat.

A man was lying face downwards in the doorway of an empty shop. There was a thin trickle of red oozing ominously from underneath him. Penn stepped nearer, his eyes taking in the great red stain that was spreading slowly over the back of the man's overcoat. Then he turned him over.

A moment later he reached for his whistle.

It was the 'doctor' who had spoken to him earlier on. He was dead. Stabbed in the back.

Murdered!

Mrs Bardell eyed the caller with considerable misgiving. Taxi-drivers, bookies' touts, even sandwich-men, she was pretty well accustomed to – for no house in London could claim a greater variety of visitors than the famous house in Baker Street that was the residence of Sexton Blake and his almost equally well-known assistant, Tinker. But broken-down tramps and vagabonds – ?

'I must see him!' the man on the doorstep insisted, his voice at strange variance with his dilapidated appearance. 'The name is Fletcher, and my business is in connection with the Hoxton murder.'

At the word 'murder' Blake's landlady brightened considerably. As she frequently said, she lived on murders!

'Wait a minute, then,' she said in her most imposing voice. 'I will acquaint Mr Blake of your request.' She left him on the doorstep and sailed in to inform her illustrious employer that a Mr Fletcher was without. 'I think 'e must be in disguise,' she added, 'becos although 'e looks like a na'porth o' dirt, 'e speaks like a gent.'

'Fletcher – ?' the private investigator repeated. 'The Hoxton murder – ?'

'That there what's in the paper this mornin', sir. Poor gent by the name o' Williams – stabbed in the back 'e were, poor dear.'

The detective thought for a moment. He was, of course, perfectly familiar with the Hoxton affair, so far as the papers had reported it. But why this man should come to him about it, seeing that he was not engaged upon the case . . .

'All right,' he decided suddenly. 'Show him into the consulting-room, Mrs Bardell. I may as well see him.'

Mrs Bardell accordingly returned to the front door, and when a minute or two later Blake went through into the consulting-room the man was already there.

'Mr Fletcher?' Blake asked, completely ignoring his visitor's disreputable appearance.

'Maurice Fletcher, Mr Blake.'

The detective motioned him to a seat. The fellow had spoken his name with an emphasis which suggested that Blake ought to be familiar with it, yet, look at the man as he might, neither face nor name conveyed anything to the detective's mind.

'I'm afraid you don't remember me,' he said then. And when Blake shook his head: 'I'm not surprised,' he added drily. 'For one thing it is fifteen years since I last sat in this chair. And for another – well, circumstances are not what they were with me, as you can see for yourself. Actually, Mr Blake, I am the Fletcher end of the once well-known firm of stockbrokers, Williams & Fletcher, of 39 Old Moorgate Street, EC4. And it is just about fifteen years ago that I came to see you to ask your help in – '

'Tracing your partner,' Blake cut in quickly. 'Now I remember you, Mr Fletcher. I'm sorry. Of course I remember you. Your partner disappeared, didn't he? And it is a matter for regret that I was never able to find him for you. I remember coming to the conclusion that he was dead.'

'Yes, that is so. He absconded with the entire cash resources of the firm, and he's never been heard of from that day to this – or, rather, from that day until last night.'

'You mean that he has returned?' Blake asked in quick surprise. 'You have heard from him?'

'He came back last night, Mr Blake,' the other said slowly. 'He's dead now.'

'Dead?' Blake echoed, aware of a tiny alarm bell ringing deep down in his awareness.

'He was murdered – last night – within fifty yards of where I am living. Haven't you seen this morning's papers? The Hoxton murder? Williams?'

Blake rose slowly to his feet. Now he understood, and his eyes narrowed. Williams, of course! Williams – once of Williams & Fletcher – so that was the man who had been killed. He remembered the firm's luxurious offices in Old Moorgate Street. Remembered, too, the smart, up-to-the-minute business man this present scarecrow had been at that time. Williams & Fletcher – that had been the firm. And now Williams was lying murdered, while Fletcher. . . ?

'I believe that at any moment I shall be arrested and charged with Williams' murder,' Fletcher said for himself, as though reading the unspoken question in the detective's eyes. 'I am under the gravest suspicion. I had the opportunity and the motive. I cannot deny that Leslie Williams ruined me. I cannot deny that I hated him. I cannot deny that at the time it happened, when my hate was at white heat, if only I could have found him I would have killed him with less compunction than I would kill a dog . . . but not now. Now I am completely indifferent to everybody and everything. If Leslie Williams were to walk into this room now I verily believe that I should scarcely bother to look at him. And yet – and this is the part I have to make you believe – when I heard his voice on the stairs last night, and saw his face, I ran away and went out by the back stairs rather than stop to speak to him. That is the truth, Mr Blake. But I'm afraid the police do not believe me.'

In the silence which followed that extraordinary confession the door opened and Tinker came in. At sight of Blake's curious visitor he would instantly have withdrawn, save that the detective checked him. He had been on a job out Brixton way, and was still wearing his hat and overcoat.

'Did you want me?' Blake asked him.

Tinker hunched his shoulders.

'Well, no,' he said, glancing again at the tatterdemalion in the chair. 'Except that we seem to be under observation, guv'nor. There's a squad car about one hundred yards down the street, and a couple of plain-clothes men watching the front door. I wondered what was up.'

'Does that mean that they're – waiting for me?' Maurice Fletcher asked under his breath.

Blake went out and had a look. When he came back again his face was grave.

'You told me, I think,' he said quietly to the anxious man, 'that you know nothing whatever about your late partner's death. Is that statement completely true, Mr Fletcher?'

'I swear it, Mr Blake! I know no more about it than you know yourself. I saw him, it's true. I also heard him. But as to killing him – no! I know nothing whatever about it.'

'I see.' Blake sat down again, his manner suddenly brisk. 'Very well,' he invited. 'In that case, you'd better tell me exactly what happened.'

'Right from the beginning, you mean?'

'No, that won't be necessary. I think I remember the beginning of the affair. You were an old-established and prosperous firm of stockbrokers until your partner suddenly cleared off and left you flat. He went off with everything you possessed. Within six months you were hammered, and – forgive me – you never got back. In the beginning you did try, but the task was impossible. You've slipped further and further down the ladder until . . .'

'Until I can slip no further,' Fletcher nodded when the detective paused. 'Yes, that's a pretty fair summary of my life since Williams walked out on me. In the last fifteen years I've tried my hand at most things, and failed at each one of them. Finally, two years ago, I took a

room in Hoxton – in a tenement block known as Mabon's Court – and
I've been there ever since, living on a small allowance made me by a
relative whose fortune I made for him twenty and more years ago.
Bread on the water – so to speak.'

He paused and wiped his thin lips. He couldn't be a day more than
fifty-five, Blake reckoned, yet he looked seventy. He was bowed and
broken, white-haired and watery-eyed. Yet there was something
attractive about him in spite of his looks and his careless, unshaven,
dilapidated appearance. Perhaps it was his voice, which was still soft
and pleasant to the ear. Or it may have been the facility with which he
expressed himself.

'How do you know that Williams was coming to see you last night?'
Blake asked him. 'Or – what is infinitely more important – how do the
police know?'

'He told them – or practically told them,' the other replied. He
related how, late last night, a well-dressed stranger had asked a
constable the way to Mabon's Court, and the constable had told him.
A couple of hours later the same constable had discovered the same
well-dressed stranger lying murdered in a doorway not fifty yards
from the entrance to Mabon's Court. In his pocket was an identity
card in the name of Leslie Williams, with a Mayfair address, and a
cheque book on a Mayfair branch of the Bank of Canada.

'But that doesn't necessarily mean that he was coming to Mabon's
Court to see you,' Blake pointed out quickly.

'Of itself – no, Mr Blake. But, unfortunately, he asked for me. He
knocked up the people on the ground floor, immediately inside the
entrance, and asked if they knew which room Maurice Fletcher
occupied. They told him Number 17, on the second floor, and he
started up the stairs to find me.'

'Did you say that you heard him asking that question?'

'Heard him and saw him! I must have entered the place only a
minute or so before he arrived there, because I was still mounting the
stairs round the "well" when I heard someone knocking on the door of
Number 1. I leaned over the railings and looked down, and when
Number 1 opened his door I saw him.'

'And recognized him?' Blake asked incredulously. 'After fifteen
years? And when you could only see the top of his hat?'

Fletcher shook his head.

'No,' he said. 'But I recognized him when he asked for me. I knew his
voice in a moment. And when Number 1 pointed up the stairs, and
Williams looked up to see where he was pointing, the light from the
open door fell full on his upturned face, and I knew that it was he.'

'And then. . . ?'

'How shall I say? I think I must have lived a lifetime in the next few seconds. I can't even begin to describe my feelings – though mainly, I guess, I was stunned by the suddenness of it all, because for years and years I had come to think of him as being dead. I knew amazement, bewilderment, consternation – but over and above all else I knew an ungovernable urge to get out of it before he found me and I had to speak to him. I don't know what I was afraid of, but I knew that I couldn't bear him to find me there. So I ran up the remaining stairs, dived through my room, and went out through the back door on to the fire-escape.'

'What did you do then?'

'I don't know – that's the trouble. I think I went out into the High Street, but after that – no, I can't remember. I just walked on and on: I don't know where I went.'

'What time did you get back?'

'I don't know. I have no clock, in any event – I go by a clock in the High Street which I can see from my window. All I can tell you is that it was still dark outside; that my door was on the latch – just as I'd left it – and the oil-lamp was smoking on the table. I use an oil-lamp, by the way, because it gives heat as well as light. It saves coal.'

'Was the lamp burning when you ran into the room after seeing Williams?'

'Yes. You see, when I went out originally I was only going for a minute or two just to warm up before turning in. Matter of fact, there's a night-watchman in the next street, and I intended to chat to him for a minute or two beside his fire. I did chat to him.'

'Can he vouch for that?'

'Oh yes. But I left there at about a quarter past eleven, so that there's no point in it, don't you see?'

Blake nodded, and was silent for a time, thinking. He glanced at Tinker, who was staring at Fletcher thoughtfully. No getting away from it, the fellow had all the motive on earth – but had he done it? That was the question. Time, place, opportunity – all three were perfect. On the other hand, he did not strike the experienced detective as being the kind of man who would do murder save under the strongest provocation. Question was: had Williams given him the provocation?

He was still pondering the matter when there was a ring at the front door. Tinker went out to answer it, and came back with the information that Inspector Paine of the Hoxton Division would like a word with Sexton Blake.

'Show him in,' said the detective, with a warning glance at Maurice
Fletcher.

Fletcher half rose in his chair, but with a shrug sat down again. His
manner said as plainly as any words could have done: 'What is to be
will be.'

'Ah!' said Inspector Paine a moment later when he perceived him
sitting there. He was a big, burly man, a typical Detective-Inspector,
inclined to be just the least shade truculent. 'Maurice Fletcher,' he was
beginning officially, 'I hold a warrant for your arrest upon a charge of
murd – ' but then Blake stopped him.

'Just a moment, Inspector,' he begged. 'I am the last man on earth to
interfere with you in the execution of your duty – as of course you
know. On the other hand, before you execute that warrant you hold,
would you mind telling me upon what grounds you are basing your
charge? Is the motive revenge? Revenge for something that happened
fifteen years ago?'

The inspector frowned and shook his head. However, the reputation of Sexton Blake was so high in official quarters that at last he
shrugged his broad shoulders and decided to acquiesce to the
detective's request.

'No, sir,' he said bluntly. 'It's robbery.'

'Robbery – ?' Blake and Fletcher echoed in unison, and the inspector
nodded.

'It has come to our knowledge,' he said, 'that late yesterday
afternoon the murdered man drew from his bank no less a sum than
ten thousand pounds – all in one-hundred-pound notes. We have
traced his movements very carefully indeed, and we are confident that
when he entered Mabon's Court the dead man had at any rate the bulk
of that money on his person. Our charge against Maurice Fletcher is
that he spoke with Leslie Williams, discovered that he had the money
on him, murdered him in the street outside, and then robbed him of the
notes.'

'It is quite useless, I take it, to assure you that this is the first I have
heard of such notes?' Fletcher asked quietly. 'Or to say again that I had
no word with Leslie Williams either in the building or out of it last
night?'

'Quite useless, I'm afraid,' the inspector assured him. 'We have
proof to the contrary.'

'What proof?' It was Blake who asked the question.

'We've found two of the notes in his room. One under the
floorboards, and a second behind a patch of broken plaster in the wall
above his bed. The numbers have been checked, and both appear on

the list of those issued by the bank to Leslie Williams late yesterday afternoon.'

Tinker's lips formed into a soundless whistle, but Blake said nothing. He was watching Fletcher as he sat gaping in his chair.

'In my – room?' the wretched man jerked out at last. He was white as a sheet. He appeared to be on the verge of collapse. 'But this is – ridiculous!' he whispered. 'It's a lie! By heavens, it's a trick just to bolster up your case! I tell you again that I never spoke to Williams! While as for robbing him – '

'Ten thousand, did you say, Inspector?' Blake cut him short.

'Ten thousand, Mr Blake.'

The private detective nodded. He glanced at Fletcher, who was watching him with bated breath.

'That's odd,' he mused. 'Very odd, Inspector – because if my memory serves me correctly that is exactly the sum that Leslie Williams stole from Fletcher's safe fifteen years ago. Isn't that so, Fletcher?'

'Why – why, yes, it is,' the other answered, his eyes wide. 'By heavens, it was ten thousand – and I can prove it!' he added more forcibly.

'So that if Williams was making a secret journey to Mabon's Court with ten thousand pounds in his pocket, there's just the chance that he was intending to make the *amende honorable*, Inspector. In which case, why should Fletcher either rob him or murder him?'

For a full minute the inspector remained silent, but then he brushed the suggestion aside. He dealt in facts rather than theories, and the discovery of those two notes in Fletcher's room was a fact there was no getting round.

'All that's for the jury to decide,' he said brusquely. 'Meanwhile, I hold a warrant – '

'Quite so,' Blake cut in on the instant. 'But I've a suggestion to make to you, inspector, which, if it does no good, will at least do no harm. You have some men outside, I think? You have? I thought so. Well, now, what about allowing two of them to sit here with Maurice Fletcher while you and I take another look round that room of his in Mabon's Court? I tell you frankly, I believe there is something missing in this story. Or,' he added when the inspector said nothing, 'what about taking him with us?'

'Yes, I don't mind taking him with us; although I'm sure you're making a mistake, Mr Blake.'

'I'll risk that,' was all the private detective said. 'Let's go, shall we?'

Mabon's Court – in spite of what the ex-stockbroker had told him about it – came as a distinct shock to Sexton Blake. Poverty he had been prepared for, dirt even. But not for the appalling squalor and filth that he actually found there. It seemed almost impossible to believe that a man of Maurice Fletcher's birth and upbringing could ever have lived in such a place for two long years. It was more like a native barracks than a block of English flats.

'It was about here that I looked over and saw him,' Fletcher said as they mounted the cracked and worn stone steps to the second floor.

Blake paused for a moment to look over the iron railing into the well below. Just as Fletcher had described, the door of Number 1 was plainly visible from where he was standing. And he could easily imagine that the face of anyone looking up the stairs from that position would be discernible in the same way – and doubly so at night when the light from the hall would be full upon him.

Then they went up to Fletcher's room.

For a minute or so Blake stood on the threshold looking about him – and if he had been surprised before he was horrified now at the revelation of the conditions under which the man was living. The room was no more than twelve feet square, and beyond a rough deal table, a deal chair, and a tumbled bed it was entirely innocent of furniture. There was not even a carpet on the floor. The table was littered with the remains of a meal – bread-crumbs were everywhere, save in one small spot where they appeared to have been swept off on to the bare boards as though to make room for somebody sitting down. The oil-lamp, smelling vilely, stood dirty and sooted at one end of the table. The place stank.

'Not the Ritz, perhaps,' Maurice Fletcher observed crookedly. 'But all I can afford, Mr Blake. As for the dirt,' he added, observing the detective's nose wrinkle, 'it's amazing what the human body can become accustomed to without even noticing it.'

'Shut up, you!' snapped the inspector, taking Blake by the arm and showing him where the two notes had been found. The first had been discovered beneath a loose floorboard in one corner of the room. The second, it seemed, behind the plaster where a chunk of perhaps a foot square had broken away at some earlier period. 'One in each of those,' the inspector said. 'And the rest we reckon he took away with him and hid outside. Sooner or later we shall find them – but those two'll do to be going on with.'

The private detective nodded, but said nothing. That broken plaster was quite the most noticeable feature of the bare walls, and not even a child could miss the loose floorboard. Of course, criminals do make childish mistakes or they would never be caught – but even so, he could not see Maurice Fletcher being quite so obvious as that!

'What do you imagine he did with the remainder of the notes?' he asked at last. 'And why keep those two in particular?'

Inspector Paine hunched his shoulders. His smile suggested that the private detective had still a great deal to learn that was an open book to the professional police.

'He's fenced them,' he said. 'He's no fool, you know – and he'd realize in a moment that notes of that size would be traceable. As for the two he kept – that's an old failing with men of his type, Mr Blake. He kept those two so that he could take them out in secret and assure himself again and again that at last he'd really got his hands on money. I've seen it a dozen times, and it always gets 'em in the end.'

'But why hide them in such an obvious place, Inspector?'

'I don't suppose he ever thought we'd search here.'

'I can't agree.' The private detective's tone was crisp and decisive. They were alone together now, save for Tinker, since by a wave of his hand the inspector had instructed his men to take Fletcher outside to wait for them on the landing. 'You are forgetting, Inspector, that Fletcher knew – knew for certain sure – that his old partner was coming up to this room to see him. He heard him ask for him. He actually saw him, down there in the entrance, and knew that whoever lives in Number 1 would be able to give evidence that the stranger had asked for Maurice Fletcher and had actually started up the stairs towards his room. Isn't it plain, therefore, that – if, as you say, he killed the man – he would know from the very outset that he would be the first man to fall under suspicion?'

'I dunno,' the inspector hedged after a brief silence. 'It mightn't have occurred to him.'

'Yet you said yourself that he was no fool!'

'Yes, I know. But – '

'It won't do, Paine!' Blake snapped off the conversation and commenced a careful survey of the room. At the table he paused for a time gravely considering that little patch that had been swept free of bread and crumbs. Then suddenly he dropped to his hands and knees and made a minute inspection of the bare floorboards immediately beneath that bit of the table, gradually working outwards until he came to an abrupt halt.

'Could I have a word with Fletcher?' he asked the inspector a minute or two later.

The inspector's gesture inferred that it didn't matter whether he did or not, the result would still be the same. Nevertheless, he called to his men to bring the prisoner in.

'Oh, Fletcher,' Blake said casually, 'I want to write a note. Would you mind lending me a pen and ink?'

The ex-stockbroker stared.

'Pen and ink?' he echoed. He looked round his room and smiled. 'Sorry,' he said, 'I haven't either, Mr Blake.'

'No pen or ink, man?'

'I never use them – I'm sorry. I don't suppose I've written a letter in the last ten years.'

'As I thought!' Blake swung round on the watching inspector. 'Now then, sir,' he said, and from the altered tone of his voice Tinker knew that he had discovered something important. 'Among the effects found on the murdered man's body was a fountain-pen, I think? Am I correct?'

'He certainly had a fountain-pen – yes,' the other agreed slowly.

'Filled, I think, with blue ink?' Blake smiled. 'Rather bluer than usual, maybe? And it was either beginning to run dry or was not in perfect working order?'

Inspector Paine frowned. It was clear that he did not relish this curious cross-examination, yet even so he had to agree that the pen was certainly running dry and that the little ink they had found in it was definitely bluer than usual.

'He also had, I think, a letter without an envelope, or maybe a pocket-book from which a leaf is missing?'

'He had a letter without an envelope,' the inspector snapped back. 'But how do you know – ?'

'Because he used the envelope here, Inspector, for the purpose of writing a letter to Maurice Fletcher,' the private detective explained easily. 'He had nothing else to write on, so he used that. He arrived here from downstairs to find the door shut but a light showing from underneath it, yet when he knocked there was no answer – because the occupant of the room, as he has told you, was already making his way down the fire-escape. Anyway, having come so far and so secretly to make this *amende honorable* for his past sins, Williams was not to be put off so easily. He knocked again – I think he knocked very loudly. Then, in desperation, he tried the door, found it was not locked, and calmly walked inside to wait for Fletcher's return.'

'This, of course, is all theory,' cut in Inspector Paine with a thin smile of indulgence, but Blake shook his head.

'On the contrary, I think you will find it all fact, Inspector,' he said. 'Anyway, to continue. Having walked inside and found the room empty, he decided to wait – and I think he waited for a very long time. But at last, seeing that Fletcher still remained absent, he decided to leave him a note – and, I think, a couple of one-hundred-pound notes as proof of his good intentions.'

'Oh yeah?' grinned Paine, suddenly catching the other's drift.

'That, at least, is my belief, Inspector – but when he came to look round he could find nothing to write with or anything to write on. So he took out his own fountain-pen, opened out one of his letters, sat down in this chair here, swept this bit of the table clear of breadcrumbs and so forth, and started to write his message on the inside of the slit envelope . . . but then the pen wouldn't work!'

'Too bad!' jibed the inspector. 'What did he do then?'

'He did what you or I or anyone else would have done in similar circumstances, Inspector,' Blake smiled. 'He shook it towards the floor. He shook the ink down the barrel, and in doing that – as nearly aways happens – he shook some on to the floor.'

'Where?' snapped the other, his voice suddenly taut.

'Precisely where one would expect to find it – beside the chair, Inspector. There, you see! One large spot and two smaller ones, all three of very blue ink and all three quite fresh. I am confident that chemical analysis of those three ink-stains will prove the ink to have come from Williams' pen. Furthermore, the very fact that Williams sat here writing proves conclusively that Fletcher was not in the room with him; or why would he have to write at all?'

'Well, as to that, Fletcher might have been threatening him,' Paine retorted truculently. 'Compelling him to write a confession or something.'

'Had Fletcher gone to Williams' flat – yes, that possibility might have held good. But not when Williams took the trouble to come to Fletcher's flat, Inspector, after fifteen long years of it! I say again that Williams sought out Fletcher last night with the one object of making an *amende honorable*. That's why he came here, and that's why he brought with him the exact amount of hard cash that he stole from Fletcher's safe fifteen years ago.'

'Yes, but wait a minute!' the professional cracked in triumphantly. 'Agreeing all that, Mr Blake – and even agreeing that Fletcher wasn't in the room when Williams wrote to him – if he did indeed write to him, where's the letter he wrote? Why hasn't he produced it? What's he done with it?'

'There was never any letter here, I'm afraid,' Fletcher spoke up slowly for himself. 'At least, none that I've seen.'

'And you told me back in Mr Blake's own house that you'd never even seen the two notes we found in this room, didn't you?' crowed the inspector. 'So that puts that off the map as well! You found neither the letter nor the notes, because obviously if you had done you'd have said so when I first questioned you.'

'I agree entirely with what you say, Inspector,' Blake put in unexpectedly. 'In fact, that is the whole of my ease. Fletcher did not find the letter, nor the two notes – for the simple reason that when Fletcher got back from his walk last night both letter and notes were gone!'

'Gone?' echoed the other. 'You mean that Williams – changed his mind?'

'No. I mean that they were stolen.'

Inspector Paine stared blankly. 'Stolen?' he said, then he pulled himself together, and gave a short laugh. 'Heavens,' he protested, 'I don't think you can expect to put that one over on me, Mr Blake. To begin with, nobody knew he was even up here!'

'Then what about the people who sent him up – the people in Number 1?' Tinker interposed quickly. 'They knew he was here. They'd seen him start up the stairs.'

'And not only them,' Blake added. 'You may be sure that Williams knocked pretty vigorously on that door before it occurred to him to try the knob. And from what I know of places like this, such knockings would be bound to attract attention from near neighbours.'

'Oh, but hang it all, Mr Blake – '

'Wait a minute, Inspector! Maurice Fletcher has assured me that he did not kill his one-time partner, nor did he even know that he had come here bringing money – and I'm bound to say that I believe him. But if Fletcher didn't murder him, who did? Manifestly, robbery was the motive of the crime; but who could have known that Williams had all that money on him? Or even any money at all? And why was he killed going away from this place instead of when he was coming to it?'

'Well,' shrugged the inspector after a brief silence, 'why was he?'

Sexton Blake smiled.

'Because the man who murdered him did not know that he had the money until he had seen him waving it about in this room.'

'I don't get that, Blake.'

'Yet it's simple enough, Inspector – and that's why I say that in all human probability Williams left those two hundred-pound notes in the letter he wrote. He must have left them, or why should he take the wad of notes from his pocket at all? He took the wad of notes from his pocket in order to leave two in that envelope for Fletcher, as an earnest of his good intentions – and somebody saw him doing it – '

'How?'

'Through the keyhole.'

'But my dear Blake – ?'

'Just a minute, Inspector – let me finish. If you try that keyhole for yourself you will find that the whole of this table is in view, together with the chair. Therefore anyone keeping watch from outside would have seen Williams writing his note, seen him take out that vast wad of money, seen him peel off two notes, and return the rest to his pocket. He couldn't help but see him – because it was night, remember, and Williams was working in the full light of that lamp.'

'And who do you suggest would be watching him, Mr Blake?'

The private investigator caught the jibe in the inspector's voice and his own manner sharpened perceptibly.

'Inspector Paine,' he said, 'your acquaintance with this class of tenement is greater perhaps than my own. And I'm sure you'll agree that no well-dressed stranger could come here at half past eleven at night and start banging on a tenant's door without his nearest neighbours sitting up and taking notice? Well, that is what happened here. Someone heard Williams knocking on that door, and later he saw him enter and close the door behind him. His curiosity was aroused: likewise his business instinct. So when all was quiet again that man crept out and applied his eye to the keyhole to see what was going on.'

'And he saw Williams flashing ten thousand quid around, eh?'

'Exactly. He saw this well-dressed stranger leaving two Bank of England notes in a torn envelope, and he saw him replace the rest in his pocket. And straightway he made his plans. No doubt he saw even then that the blame would fall on Fletcher. No doubt he thought the stranger and Fletcher were working some deep-laid racket together –what else could he think, knowing nothing of the partnership that had once existed between the two? It would look an absolute cert to him. So he waited until Williams left the room, dived in and collared both letter and notes, and then quickly followed down the stairs into the street.'

'And stabbed him for the remainder of the money, you mean?'

'Stabbed him for the remainder of the money,' Blake agreed. 'He caught him up on the far side of the road – not caring how near the block he killed him, since the blame would fall plumb on Fletcher – robbed him, and then hurried back to his own room. There, I think, his first task would be to read the letter Williams had written; and it was then that he would learn for the first time of the connection between the two men and understand how a second motive would become applicable to Fletcher – that of revenge on the man who had wronged him so bitterly.

'And that, I think, explains why he brought those two banknotes back again and hid them where he was certain the police would find them,' Blake went on judiciously. 'To ensure his own safety he deliberately sacrificed two hundred pounds of his loot in order to put Fletcher's neck still further into the noose. Those two banknotes would damn Fletcher utterly, he reckoned – and they almost did,' he added with a sidelong glance at Inspector Paine.

The inspector sniffed, but did not deny it. Presently he walked over and stood staring at the three ink-stains, vaguely irritated that he himself had not appreciated their significance. On the other hand, how was he to know that Fletcher had never written a letter in ten years!

Suddenly he wheeled round.

'I'm bound to admit that you've put up a most plausible theory, Mr Blake,' he said somewhat peevishly. 'On the other hand, it is only theory – and will remain theory until you can prove it by arresting whoever did kill Williams.'

'I agree,' Blake answered. 'And that must be our next task, Inspector. Fortunately,' he added, 'I do not think it will be a very protracted task, because if I'm right, the murderer almost certainly lives in this building. In fact, I'll go further than that – and say that he almost certainly lives on this landing. Have you interviewed the people living on either side of this room, and the ones living opposite?'

'We've interviewed nobody so far – there appeared to be no need.'

Blake smiled.

'Then I think we'd better make a start,' he suggested gently. 'Don't you?'

They ran him to earth that same night, in a common lodging-house out Walham Green way – a thin, ferrety-faced man, tight-lipped and shifty-eyed, an old offender, long known to the police as the Southall Slasher. It appeared that for some weeks past he had been living in the room almost directly opposite the one occupied by Maurice Fletcher –'hiding out' there, in fact, since the room was not really his at all, he had merely taken it over for the time being from a man he knew who was doing six months' 'hard' on a burglary charge.

A wiser man would have stayed there, but the Southall Slasher had never been renowned for wisdom. He had remained there just long enough to know that a warrant had been issued for Fletcher's arrest, and then – very foolishly as it transpired – had tied up his few belongings in a handkerchief and quietly faded from the scene. No doubt he had thought himself safe. Or it may have been that he was getting nervous about the Bank of England notes he had stitched into his ancient overcoat. In any event, whatever the reason, he had decided to get out then and there – and that is what put Blake and the rest on his track.

With untiring patience they trailed him from haunt to haunt across London. They inquired for him at every address where he was known, and at several where he was not – until, towards midnight, they ran him to earth in the Walham Green lodging-house, where he had just gone to bed. And even then it was touch and go.

'Stick 'em up!' Inspector Paine roared as he saw the Slasher's hand dive beneath his pillow. There was a crash and a roar and a yard of blue flame, but the bullet spanged into the wall a good inch over the inspector's head – and in a moment they were all over him. Snarling and cursing, they pinned him down while Sexton Blake tore the old overcoat from beneath his pillow and quickly extracted banknote after banknote from where they had been stitched into the lining.

And finally he came upon something else, at sight of which he whistled – it was nothing less than the opened-out envelope upon which Leslie Williams had written what was destined to be his last letter. In it he told Fletcher that he had brought him back the ten thousand he had stolen from the firm's safe fifteen years ago, but that not finding him in, he was enclosing two hundred pounds with the letter and would come back with the remainder at eleven o'clock the following night. He had prospered, he wrote, but had never been able to forget the injury he had done his one-time partner all those years ago.

It was that letter that hanged the Southall Slasher, though, oddly enough – it came out at the trial – he had kept it because, having no name on it, he had thought that it would account for his possession of the money should he ever be challenged with having stolen it! It had never occurred to him that he might be arrested for the actual murder.

Nor was that the only odd feature of the crime, for as Blake said some time later, when he was discussing the affair with a new and rehabilitated Maurice Fletcher:

'The thing that strikes me as being so amazing is that, having prospered mightily for fifteen years on the proceeds of his crime, Williams should be murdered on the very night when he had determined to make full restitution!'

The Garage Racketeers

◆

GEOFFREY WEBB & EDWARD J. MASON

The intrepid private detective and occasional special agent, Dick Barton (formerly Captain Richard Barton of the Commandos) was the hero of the BBC's first daily radio serial and in seven hundred and eleven episodes between 1946 to 1951 became a legend: loved by listeners of all ages and frequently deplored by educationalists and clergymen. Aided by two assistants, Jock Anderson and Snowy White, the series was unforgettable for both the tight spots that the three men managed to get themselves into – and out of – but also the signature tune, The Devil's Gallop *by Charles Williams which opened and closed each cliff-hanging episode with the refrain of, 'Dum-de-dum Dah! Dum-de-dum . . .' Noel Johnson was the first broadcaster to play Barton, with Alex McCrindle and John Mann as Jock and Snowy, and he was followed by two others, Duncan Carse and Gordon Davis, before the series ended. Such was the popularity of Barton in the late Forties that three feature films were also made of his exploits,* Dick Barton, Special Agent *(1948),* Dick Barton Strikes Back *(1949) and* Dick Barton at Bay *(1950), all starring Don Stannard. It was not until a quarter of a century later, though, in 1978 that Dick Barton became a television star with former Shakespearean actor Tony Vogel in the lead role playing him as a square-jawed, no-nonsense investigator in trench coast and fedora. Vogel, who had experience in previous TV crime series including* Paul Temple, The New Avengers *and* The Return of The Saint, *had James Cosmo and Anthony Heaton as co-stars. The series was set firmly in the post-war era in which it had first emerged and generated a whole new group of fans who also created a huge demand for tapes of the original radio episodes, thus ensuring the legend lived on . . .*

Although Geoffrey Webb and Edward J. Mason wrote the scripts for Dick Barton, *he had actually been created by Norman Collins (1907–   ), the Controller of the BBC Light Programme and famous for his novel,* London Belongs To Me *(1945), who wanted to feature a 'cloak and dagger soap opera' every evening. Gradually the idea of a two-fisted private investigator took shape, although he went through several name changes from Rex Drake to Peter Fenton and Roger Barton before Collins himself suggested the evocative Dick Barton. Norman Collins later went into television, but always retained his affection for Barton, as did the scriptwriters, Webb and Mason, who turned one of the most exciting radio stories into the following dramatic tale . . .*

A T the wheel of Barton's sleek, powerful car, Jock Anderson suddenly assumed an intent, watchful expression. Then he reduced the car's speed and shrugged ruefully. As the machine slid to a stop:

'What's up, 'Aggis?' queried Snowy.

'Listen,' said Jock. He switched off the engine and in the sudden silence a faint hissing noise could be heard.

'Puncture, eh?' said Barton from the back seat. 'What made you notice it, Jock?'

'She was bumping a bit on the front offside,' replied the Scot, opening the driving door and easing himself out of the seat. 'Only had 'em blown up this morning, too!'

A moment later the three of them were gazing disgustedly at a large rusty nail which was embedded in the tyre of the front offside wheel. Fortunately the spare wheel was in good order and, working quickly and efficiently, the car was roadworthy again within five minutes.

Jock looked enquiringly at Barton.

'What say, Mr Barton?' he asked. 'Think we'd better get the tyre repaired right away? We'd be in a mess if we had another burst now.'

Dick Barton nodded.

'You're right, Jock. Better to be safe than sorry. We'll pop round to Nicky's garage. It's no distance from here and old Nicky will be glad to see us again.'

Nicky Grant had good reason to remember Barton and Co. At a

time when the garage-proprietor had been right down on his luck –
shortly after his demobilization from the same unit in which Dick and
Snowy had served – he had asked Barton for help in clearing his
outstanding debts and starting afresh. Feeling sorry for his ex-
comrade-in-arms, Dick had come to the rescue, with the result that
Nicky had very quickly been able to repay the loan and build up a
sound and lucrative little business.

As the car approached the garage, Snowy suddenly sat up with a
jerk.

'Do you see what I see, 'Aggis?' he asked.

Jock whistled softly, then murmured: 'Gosh, Mr Barton – looks like
we've dropped in on Nicky Grant at an awkward moment.'

He drew the car into the kerbside and the three companions
regarded Nicky Grant and his garage with sympathetic eyes.

It seemed that a huge, American Diesel-engined lorry had decided to
go backward instead of forward after filling up. As a result the window
of Nicky's establishment was completely shattered and one of the
petrol pumps was leaning over at a drunken angle. Nicky himself
appeared to be arguing his case with a massive and obviously
unsympathetic lorry-driver as Dick, Snowy and Jock approached
them unobserved.

'Just too bad, son,' the lorry-driver was saying. 'Just one of those
things. Sorry and all that.'

What Nicky lacked in inches he made up for in guts, as Dick and
Snowy well knew. He was very angry right now and the lorry-driver's
size in no way deterred him!

'I know these waggons,' he said, indicating the big lorry, 'and the
reverse gear is nowhere near the forward gears. You deliberately
backed into my place and I know why.'

The driver picked up his cap from the front wheel of his lorry, dusted it
carefully and placed it at a jaunty angle on his bullet head. Then he
looked down at Nicky Grant and grinned. It wasn't a pleasant grin.

'You know the answer son,' he said. 'You should insure yourself
with Benny – then this sort of thing wouldn't happen.'

'Why you dirty gangster . . .' Nicky began.

The big man brought the back of his hand sharply across the lips of
the little garage-owner.

'Don't say things like that or I might get rough,' he said. 'I don't
like . . .'

What he liked and disliked, Nicky was never to know – for just at
that precise moment the lorry driver received an open-handed cuff on
the ear which made his head sing.

'You mustn't act like that, chum,' said Barton, mildly. 'T'isn't fair to hit people smaller than yourself.'

With an oath the big man turned on Barton – then stopped as he saw Snowy and Jock standing by.

'Three to one, eh?' he said.

Snowy and Jock stepped politely aside and left the field clear for Dick and the lorry driver.

'We're strangers around here,' said Jock apologetically to the infuriated bully. 'This isn't our quarrel, honest.'

He pointed to Barton.

'This is the bloke you want to argue with,' he continued. '*He* hit you – not us.'

Snowy nodded innocently and agreed.

'S'right, mate,' he confirmed. 'He's the geezer what just poked you in the ear. Nothing to do with us.'

The lorry driver took fresh heart at this. Barton, although a hefty enough individual, was no match in size or weight for the transport man. His unpleasant grin returned. Then – obviously considering that surprise in attack is worth a multitude of arguments – he hurled himself at Dick Barton without warning.

It was a big mistake. A very big mistake indeed.

Without seeming to move from the spot on which he was standing, Barton reached out with both hands and used the big man's own impetus to increase the effectiveness of his throw.

The lorry driver sailed through the air for several feet before landing head-first on the concrete pavement.

Barton looked down at the recumbent figure and shook his head sadly. Then he turned to Nicky Grant, whose expression of angry despair had changed to one of joyous welcome.

'Don't think much of your friends, Nicky,' said Barton, disapprovingly. 'How'd you come to mix up with characters like him?'

Nicky's expression changed again.

'It's Chicago gangster stuff all over again, sir,' he said, heavily. Then – nodding towards the unconscious lorry driver – 'He's one of Benny's boys.'

Dick, Snowy and Jock looked at each other and then back at Nicky. They shook their heads.

'Sorry, Nicky,' Barton said. 'But we've never heard of Benny – so "Benny's boys" don't ring a bell with us. Who might Benny be?'

For a moment the little man seemed undecided whether to speak. Then, with a helpless shrug, he turned to Barton.

'You might as well know the lot, sir,' he said. 'Got nothing to lose now, anyway.' He paused for a moment, then continued. 'Benny is doing his best to become the King of the Rackets so far as garages are concerned. He goes around to small one-man concerns like mine and offers to "look after us" providing we pay him – say – two hundred pounds. If we agree – all well and good – we have no trouble until the next request for two hundred pounds. If we refuse, as I did – then . . .' Nicky nodded towards the smashed window and the damaged petrol pump. '. . . then Benny sees that we suffer for it.'

Dick Barton thought quietly for a moment, weighing up the facts Nicky Grant had presented. Then: 'And I s'pose this is only the beginning?' he asked. 'If you still refuse to pay "protection money", then our friend Benny will go on and on until you haven't any business left?'

Nicky shrugged again.

'That's about it, sir,' he agreed.

'Why not contact the police?' Jock asked.

'Just what I intended doing,' said Nicky – 'but once Benny gets the impression that you're not going to "play ball" with him – he doesn't give you much time to do anything. Only ten minutes ago I refused to pay over any money to Benny. Three minutes after I'd refused – *this* happened. Benny's boys must have been waiting down the street with this lorry all ready. That's how they work. Don't give you time to make a real decision. They just hit you – good and hard. Then you don't feel like going to the police in case you might get something worse next time. See?'

Dick, Snowy and Jock were just about to probe further into the matter when the giant lorry roared into life behind them. For a brief moment while Nicky Grant had been explaining matters to them, their attention had been diverted from the bullying lorry driver. The effect of this gentleman's encounter with the concrete pavement had plainly been over-estimated by Barton and Co. – for, seizing his opportunity, the man had crept into his driving seat, started up the motor and now seemed intent on using the vehicle as an instrument of destruction. With murderous intent he directed it at the three friends and the little proprietor.

'Jump!' yelled Barton, and seeing that Nicky stood wavering uncertainly in the path of the oncoming vehicle, he picked up the little man bodily and leapt aside. Snowy also jumped clear, but Jock – better placed than the others for offensive action – hopped onto the running board and reached for the steering-wheel. The driver was ready for such action, though, and lashed out with one fist just as Jock landed. Taken off balance the Scotsman tried desperately to regain a foothold on the careering vehicle but without success. He fell to the ground and the rear wheels of the heavy lorry missed his head by inches. Then the lorry was away, hurtling down the street with a clash of hurriedly changed gears.

Barton dashed towards his own car, calling to Jock and Snowy to follow suit – then he stopped and pointed with some annoyance to the offside front tyre – the tyre they had replaced only a few minutes earlier.

It was quite flat.

Jock, dusting himself down ruefully, looked across at his Chief.

'One thing – we've got the number,' he pointed out. 'He won't get far once we put the Flying Squad on to him.'

Dick nodded, then turned to Nicky who was still gazing in the direction the lorry had gone and muttering half-audible imprecations.

'Suppose you tell us the whole story from the beginning, while you fix these two punctures, Nicky?' he suggested.

Nicky Grant sighed.

'Sure, sir,' he said dejectedly. 'But I don't think you'll be able to do a lot of good. What's more – I've got a feeling this is only the beginning so far as I'm concerned. Big Benny won't sit down under this. I shall get it right in the neck now.'

'In that case, chum,' said Snowy cheerfully. 'The thing to do is to make sure Big Benny gets it in the neck first!'

From the empty windows of a blitz-damaged house nearby, Big Benny put down his binoculars and spat disgustedly. He had been watching the whole drama that had just been enacted at Nicky's garage. At his side a flashily-dressed blonde girl was busily adding a further quota of lipstick to an already over-burdened pair of lips.

'Of all the luck!' he complained. 'Whaddya think, Sheila – just as we're giving that sucker a quiet little lesson, three mugs have to turn up and spoil everything!'

'I got eyes of my own,' said the girl, shortly. 'And I'll tell you something, Benny. Those three mugs, as you call 'em, ain't such mugs as all that.'

'You mean you know 'em?' questioned the racketeer.

'Who doesn't?' countered his lady friend. 'Those three gentlemen happen to be Dick Barton, Snowy and Jock.'

Benny whistled incredulously.

'What's more,' went on Sheila, 'If you take my tip you'll take a couple of months rest and lie low from now on. If Barton starts chasing you, you've had it.'

Benny smiled a superior smile and proceeded to pick his teeth with a match-stick.

'You don't know little Benny, sweetheart,' he told her. 'If anybody's "had it" – it's not Benny. It's Barton!'

Sheila resumed her redecorating operations with the aid of a small mirror.

'There are cemeteries full of people who went around talking like that, Benny,' she murmured. 'Take my tip – lie low.'

Benny reddened slightly. He was getting peeved. He didn't like the idea of his own girlfriend comparing his ability unfavourably with that of someone else. If anybody was going to be the Big Shot – then it was Benny and no one else. He squared his padded shoulders and adjusted the glaring necktie so that more of its horrific pattern became visible.

'I think we'll put Mr Nosey-Parker Barton out of the way right now in fact,' he said. 'Come on, Sheila.'

'What are you going to do, Benny?' she asked dubiously. 'I'm not sticking my neck out for you or anybody.'

Benny dived his hand into one of the deep pockets of his 'spivvy' overcoat, then drew it out holding a small firework.

'They call it a "Victory Flare", ducks,' he said. 'And that's just what it's going to be. Dick Barton's going to be sorry he ever tried to butt in on Benny's racket.'

Sheila shook her head disbelievingly as Benny turned and began to pick his way over the rubble towards where his car stood. Then she put away her lipstick and mirror and followed him.

But she didn't seem at all happy. To Sheila's simple mind it was going to take more than a penny firework to put the fear of death into Dick Barton. Still, Big Benny's ideas did sometimes work out all right. Sometimes.

After Nicky Grant had finished telling the story of how Big Benny and his gang had victimized small garage owners, Barton and Co. were quiet for a few moments. Then: 'And everybody's scared to go to the police, eh?' said Barton. 'Nobody has the nerve to make an official complaint?'

Nicky shook his head gloomily.

'They're all small garage owners like myself,' he explained. 'Even if the police had caught up with Benny – the damage to the property would already have been done.'

'Well – the police are on to the job *now*, anyway,' said Jock. 'Inspector Burke's got all his boys on the lookout for that lorry, and he'll be along here himself very shortly.'

The 'tooting' of a motor horn disturbed the conversation and Nicky went to serve petrol from one of his serviceable pumps. Meanwhile, Dick, Snowy and Jock continued their task of repair on the two punctured tyres.

No one noticed the low black saloon car which drove slowly past the garage entrance.

It passed the petrol pump from which Nicky was serving at the very moment that the garage proprietor began to spurt petrol into the customer's tank.

Then things happened very quickly.

Big Benny – his wide-brimmed trilby hat pulled low over his face – lit the Victory Flare and, as it burst into flame, threw it with careful accuracy at the petrol pipe Nicky Grant was using.

Instantly the jet of petrol became a jet of searing flame, which in its turn transformed the customer's petrol tank into a blazing fire. Nicky himself – badly burned about the hands and face – dropped the nozzle of the petrol pipe and staggered about blindly as Dick and Jock rushed to his rescue.

Snowy, appreciating the situation at once and realizing that the black saloon car held the instigators of the trouble, picked up the first missile he could lay hands on and hurled it after the retreating car. The missile happened to be a jar full of white paint with which Nicky had been preparing a signboard. Snowy's aim was true and the jar smashed itself on the back of the black car, splashing the spare wheel cover and the mudguards and making the car itself a conspicuous object. Then Snowy turned to help his fire-fighting pals.

The fire was quickly extinguished, but poor Nicky was in considerable pain.

'This is what comes of upsetting Big Benny,' he gasped, as Barton treated his burns. 'The trouble is that as soon as all the other garage owners hear about this, they'll do what Benny tells 'em to do. They won't risk a "doing" like this.'

'Can't hardly blame 'em, can you?' said Snowy reasonably.

'Police boys arriving,' said Jock – pointing to a police car which was heading towards them. 'Where do we go from here, Mr Barton?'

Dick looked grim.

'We go wherever Big Benny goes, Jock,' he said. 'And we keep on going – until brother Benny is in jail.'

Then he turned to salute Inspector Burke, who was approaching the scene.

'Hello, Burke, old son,' he greeted. 'We want an ambulance right away and a warning to all your cars to watch out for a black Triumph saloon which looks as though somebody's poured a bucket of white paint over the back of it.'

The Inspector nodded quickly and turned back towards the police car.

'I'll get 'em cracking on that first, then, Dick,' he said, 'You can give me all the griff afterwards.'

Snowy grinned approvingly at the retreating figure of the Detective Inspector.

'One thing about ole Burkey,' he said. ''E don't waste time askin' questions and fillin' up forms, does 'e? Believes in gettin' on with the job!'

Nicky Grant lifted himself painfully so that he was leaning on one elbow.

'Tell you what, sir,' he said to Barton. 'I think you'll find my cousin is the next on Benny's list. Name of Carter. Keeps a garage along Campden End Road.'

'Got his phone number?' queried Barton. 'And the full address?'

Nicky nodded.

'Got a card in my jacket pocket,' he said. 'Only it ain't a "him" – it's a "her". Rita, her name is – Rita Carter. She spoke to me on the phone this morning and from the way she talked I reckon Benny's got her marked down as one of his next jobs.'

Jock shook his head sadly.

'If only they'd realize that they play the gangster's own game by not going to the police,' he complained. 'They help to keep the racketeers in business that way.'

Barton looked down at the bandages which swathed the hands and face of Nicky Grant.

'There are times when one can see their point of view, though, Jock,' he murmured. 'But there's one thing very certain. Very certain indeed. The activities of Mr Benny must come to a full stop. The sooner the better.'

And looking at the expression on Dick Barton's face just at that moment, Nicky Grant felt glad he wasn't in Big Benny's shoes.

At first, when Rita Carter met Barton and Co. and Inspector Burke, she was not anxious to have their assistance. As Nicky Grant had foreseen, the news of what had happened at Nicky's garage was already public property, and Rita Carter – as she frankly confessed – preferred to pay 'protection' money to Big Benny rather than lose her entire business.

Eventually, however, she was persuaded to co-operate with the forces of law and order and Barton and Co. learned that some of Benny's boys would be along at approximately ten p.m. to collect one hundred pounds in one pound notes from her.

'That is,' she concluded. 'Unless they've spotted you here now and reported it to Big Benny. In that case I might as well go along and buy myself a nice wreath!'

Burke smiled.

'We don't want you to do anything except what Benny's told you to do, Miss Carter,' he said. 'You're a willing victim. You are going to pay up and like it. What *we* do is nothing whatever to do with you and you shan't be made to suffer for it.'

Rita Carter tried to smile as though she had no qualms, but it was a poor effort. She'd heard a lot about Big Benny – and not very much about Dick Barton. So far as she was concerned she wished Nicky Grant had kept his mouth shut. She watched as the four men climbed into their car and drove off. Maybe everything would be all right, she thought hopefully. Maybe.

She walked back into the main garage and suddenly her heart missed a beat. Something moved near the big breakdown lorry.

'Who . . . who's there?' she called.

There was a chuckle.

Then into the dimly lighted office a figure strolled casually.

Rita watched without moving as the man approached. He was wearing a long black overcoat, padded at the shoulders, and a gay silk muffler. A thin, pencil-line moustache adorned his upper lip and the inevitable black trilby pulled down over the baggy eyes.

'Not thinkin' of double-crossin' anybody, was you, ducks?' enquired this individual.

Rita Carter shook her head dumbly.

'Didn't think you would,' sneered the man. 'Benny wouldn't like it if you done that.'

'Wha . . . what d'you want?' asked the girl.

The man held out his hand.

'Two hundred nicker. *Now*,' he said. 'We was goin' to let you off with *one* hundred – but you been talkin' to coppers an' we don't like that.'

'*I* didn't say anything . . . *they* talked to *me*,' stammered the frightened girl. 'I didn't tell them anything.'

'Two hundred nicker. Now,' said the man coldly, and once again held out his hand.

With a stifled sob, Rita Carter went into the office and began to count out the notes. What else could she do?

As though sensing her desperation, the man approached her and there was a click as he flashed out a cut-throat razor.

'I got a message for you, ducks,' he said. 'Now listen careful. You're bein' watched from now on, see? And if you make one false move between now and ten pip emma – well . . .' he clicked the razor significantly. 'See what I mean?' he concluded.

She handed him the money and backed away. Those notes represented weeks of hard work and she hated the idea of handing them over so tamely. On the other hand the prospect of making a closer acquaintance with the open razor discouraged more adventurous action.

The spiv grinned.

'Now you're learning, ducks,' he said, stuffing the money into his overcoat pocket. 'I'll take this along to Benny and maybe he won't be quite so mad at you. You been a very sensible girl – handin' over the dough without any trouble. I'll put a good word in for you with Benny. P'r'aps he won't ask for any more money from you . . . not for weeks and weeks.'

'But I can't pay any more money,' said the girl desperately. 'I shall be bankrupt. I can't spare any more.'

The crook turned away.

'I daresay you'd find a few pennies if you was – er – persuaded properly,' he said. 'G'night ducks. Sweet dreams.'

He strode jauntily out of the main garage, feeling pleased with himself. The big advantage about threatening defenceless girls was that they so rarely showed fight.

It was at this point in his reverie that things began to go wrong. Someone very rudely knocked his hat off. Just like that, without warning.

'So sorry,' murmured Barton, quietly. 'I thought there was a man underneath it.' He handed back the black trilby to the astonished gangster. 'I see now I was wrong.'

The crook reached for his cut-throat razor, but Barton acted first. Exactly what happened the spiv wasn't sure; he only knew that at one moment he was holding his razor – and the next he was nursing a sprained wrist.

'You mustn't use these things,' said Barton shocked. 'You might cut yourself.'

He waved the open razor dangerously near to the crook's long pointed nose, and the man whimpered in alarm.

As Snowy, Jock and Inspector Burke approached, Barton spoke again in a quiet, menacing tone.

'We figured that Benny would have someone parked around this place to report developments, sonny,' he said. 'And it looks as though we were dead right.'

'What are you going to do?' quavered the spiv, all his bravado gone.

Burke interrupted: ''Tisn't what we're going to do, brother,' he said. 'It's what we're expecting *you* to do.'

He stuck his face close to the gangster's.

'If you've got any sense,' he continued. 'You'll take us to Big Benny. What's more, you'll take us there right away.'

Snowy, meanwhile, was emptying the man's pockets.

'The judges don't like robbery with violence,' he pointed out. 'Use your loaf, Sweeney Todd, and turn King's Evidence.'

The crook nodded eagerly.

'Yes . . . all right,' he agreed. 'I'll talk, but you got to give me protection from Big Benny.'

Somewhere near at hand a car backfired.

A quaint look of surprise spread over the face of the crook. His eyes widened. He seemed about to say something, but didn't.

'Well . . . go on . . .' urged Burke.

But instead of going on, the spiv seemed to give way gradually at the knees.

He sagged down on to the pavement, and as he lay on his back, the light from the garage enabled them to see the bullet hole in his overcoat. It was over the crook's heart.

Jock was first to notice the car which was parked some distance away. It was a low black saloon car, and on one of the rear mudwings was a smudgy white patch, which might have been caused by the over-hasty removal of wet white paint.

'There they go,' yelled Jock, and with a brief word to Burke regarding a later meeting at the flat, Dick and Snowy pelted after the Scot as he piled in and started the engine.

Burke looked after them regretfully as the car roared in pursuit of the black saloon, then he turned his attention once again to the mortally wounded crook.

Although the car from which the shot had been fired now had a substantial lead – the driver of it made the mistake of taking a route along a straight major road. As a result Jock, at the wheel of Barton's car, was able to spot the black limousine fairly quickly. It was now purely a question of which car had most power under the bonnet, unless a police car complicated matters by butting in.

As they neared the outskirts of the city, the traffic thinned, and Jock's foot pressed harder and harder on the accelerator. Very gradually they began to overhaul the black saloon.

Barton uttered a brief word of warning.

'Better keep as low as possible in your seats,' he muttered. 'Once they realize that we're overtaking 'em, they might begin shooting.'

As he finished speaking, there was a spurt of flame from the car in front, and a metallic clang from their own front mudguard.

'Only wants one of those bullets to hit a front tyre at this speed,' murmured Snowy, 'and I reckon we should go for a Burton in a big way.'

Another spurt of flame and a faint whine as the bullet sped past them seemed to prove that the crooks were thinking along the same lines.

Jock rocked the steering wheel gently from side to side and the car pursued a zig-zag course, making it a difficult target. Then the road began to wind upwards and the man in front decided not to waste any ammunition.

Both cars were now travelling at high speed, but it was plain that Barton's car was the more powerful of the two, and with Jock's expert handling the distance between them gradually lessened.

'We're reaching the top of the hill any minute now, Jock,' said Barton. 'Can't keep up this speed. You know what this gradient's like.'

'Yes,' grunted Jock. 'Wonder if the bloke in front knows it? If not he's going to get a nasty shock.'

The hill which lay directly ahead was a nasty brute. Dick, Snowy and Jock knew it of old. Not only was it very steep – but halfway down there was a sharp turn to the right. If taken at too high a speed there was a real danger of hitting the brick wall which bordered the lefthand side of the road. The fact that this wall was constantly being repaired bore evidence to the fact that too many drivers were in the habit of disregarding the warning signs at the top of the hill.

Jock reduced the car's speed and peered ahead.

'He's not slowing down, y'know,' he said.

Snowy and Dick Barton leaned forward to get a better view of the car ahead. Their own car was now just beginning the steep descent. The black saloon in front seemed to be increasing rather than reducing its speed.

'They're stark staring mad!' said Barton. 'They can't make the bend at that speed.'

Suddenly the headlights of the leading car blazed with increased intensity.

'Must have had 'em dipped until now,' said Snowy.

In the powerful rays the road ahead was brilliantly illuminated and it seemed to the watchers in the car behind that for the first time the crooks really appreciated the danger that lay in front of them.

'Too late . . . too *late!*' Jock muttered.

The black saloon was now almost at the sharp right-angled bend, and its speed was much too great.

The driver pulled desperately at the wheel and stamped on his brakes.

Then, as Dick, Snowy and Jock watched with fascinated horror, the black car skidded over on two wheels.

For a moment it looked as though they might make it. Then the speed at which they had been travelling exerted its full effect. The car went right over on to its left side, hit the brick wall and went straight through.

By the time the three companions reached the hole in the wall it was too late to do anything but watch.

Some twenty feet below them, the wreck of the car had become a blazing inferno. In some way the petrol tank had spread its contents over the vehicle and one of the men may have been smoking. At all events – even if the crooks had survived the terrific impact of the crash – the fire must have finished them.

'Well,' murmured Snowy, philosophically, 'if Big Benny is down there in that lot, we can pack up and go home. The "protection racket" is finished!'

But unfortunately Big Benny wasn't.

Sheila watched her companion anxiously as he paced angrily up and down.

'I told you to lie low when Barton came into it,' she reminded him.

Benny waved her aside impatiently.

'We got to put him out of the way,' he said. 'We got to.'

Sheila yawned.

'You said all that before,' she pointed out. 'And where has it got us? I'll tell you. It's got us into a spot where we've lost a perfectly good car and three of our best men. If you ask me – Barton is winning on points, Benny.'

'On points, yes,' agreed Big Benny. 'But in this sort of fight it's the knockout that wins.'

'Well – don't ask me to come in on any of your crazy stunts,' said Sheila.

Benny looked at her.

'Matter of fact that's just what I *am* going to do,' he said slowly. 'And what's more – if you know what's good for you, you'll do just as you're told. *Just* as you're told,' he repeated.

Sheila looked up at him, startled.

'What d'you mean?' she enquired.

'This is what I mean,' said Benny. 'Now listen. This is what you gotta do. And I want it done properly – with no slip-ups. Or else . . .'

He eyed her threateningly.

'You goin' to do what I say?' he questioned. 'Are you?'

For a moment she seemed inclined to argue. Then – seeing his face grow more and more menacing – she nodded at him.

'I'll help you, Benny,' she said. 'You know that!'

Benny smiled his unpleasant smile.

'That's a good girl,' he said approvingly.

Dick, Snowy and Jock had just finished tea when the front door bell rang. A moment later Snowy ushered in a pretty but rather flashily-dressed girl who looked thoroughly frightened.

'Mr Barton. . . ?' she queried, looking from one to the other.

Barton nodded. 'What is it?' he asked.

Sheila clutched his arm.

'Mr Barton, I can put you on to Big Benny,' she said urgently. 'I know where he is – and I know where he's going to be tonight.'

The three friends waited politely, saying nothing.

'I can take you to him,' she said. 'Honest I can.'

Barton watched her closely.

'And who might you be?' he asked.

'I'm Sheila – Benny's girlfriend that was,' she replied. 'But I'm not now – I don't hold with murder. I want him put behind bars. He's mad, that Benny . . . mad.'

Barton turned to the phone.

'I'll get the police . . .' he began – but she interrupted him.

'No!' she said fiercely. 'Call the police and you get no help from me. I'm not helping coppers, not little Sheila. I'll help *you* – but if you rope in the police I'm saying nothing.'

She said it as though she meant it.

'Where will Benny be tonight?' asked Barton.

'Come with me and I'll take you to the place,' the girl told him.

Snowy laughed.

'And walk straight into an ambush, eh?' he said.

Sheila moved towards the door.

'If that's how you feel,' she said, 'All right – forget it. Sorry I spoke. But I'll tell you this. Benny is going to a garage tonight to offer some "protection" to the garage owner. He's going by himself because the boys are on another job. Still – if you don't want to know – well – think no more about it.'

Barton stepped between her and the door.

'All right,' he said. 'You win. Take us to Benny.'

Sheila made them stop at a crossroads.

'The garage is about a quarter of a mile down that road on the left-hand side – the Wayside Garage,' she said.

Barton looked at his watch.

'It's half past six,' he said. 'You say Benny will be there any time now?'

'That's right,' said Sheila. She seemed nervous and ill at ease.

Nearby a newsboy was selling evening papers.

'Get me a paper, Jock,' said Barton casually. 'See what's won the three-thirty.'

'What horse did you back?' asked Jock, equally casual.

'Burke's the Boy,' said Barton.

'Doesn't stand an earthly,' grinned the Scot as he left the car. A few moments later he was back again with a paper.

'Told you so,' he said. 'Burke's the Boy is an also-ran.'

Barton shrugged ruefully.

'Ah, well,' he murmured. 'Maybe there'll be a reward for catching Big Benny. I think we'll go along now and lie in wait for him, eh, miss?'

Sheila nodded eagerly.

Barton pondered for a second.

'No,' he went on. 'On second thoughts we'll wait here a little longer – another quarter of an hour. If he hasn't come along by then we'll push ahead. Better to catch him in the act,' he added vaguely.

Fifteen minutes later, to the girl's unmistakable relief, Barton decided to move in to the garage. He gave the word to Jock and they drove slowly down the road. At length – following Sheila's guidance – Jock drove into a large, well-equipped garage. The place was a big, three storey building, the whole of the ground floor being taken up with a repair shop.

Two men came forward and looked at Barton.

'Evenin', Mr Barton,' said one of them.

Barton grinned.

''Fraid I don't know you,' he said. 'But you seem to know me all right.'

From the front of the garage there came a dull clang as the iron doors were closed.

'Yes – we know you, Mr Interfering Barton!' said Big Benny, stepping out from behind a wooden partition.

Jock prepared to go into action, but Barton's hand restrained him.

'Looks as though we walked into an ambush,' he remarked cheerfully to Sheila.

The girl shrugged and lit a cigarette.

'Put that out!' snarled Benny. 'You'll see why in a minute.'

From various hiding places a number of tough-looking customers began to emerge. None of them looked particularly friendly so far as Dick, Snowy and Jock were concerned.

'Get out of that car and stand in front of us, the three of you,' ordered Benny.

At a nod from Barton, Snowy and Jock did as they were told.

Benny lurched forward and sneered at Barton.

'This time you've had it, sonny-boy,' he said.

'Take your ugly face out of my way, Benny,' said Barton quietly. 'It offends me.'

Benny scowled and thrust his face even nearer to Barton's.

'Listen, mug . . .' he began.

Barton didn't want to listen. Instead he planted his fist with considerable force right in the middle of Big Benny's face. Benny fell over backwards and then sat up on the garage floor nursing a bleeding nose. He looked murderous.

Meanwhile, Snowy and Jock, following Barton's lead – began mixing it with the other crooks. It was a hopeless battle from the outset – Barton and Co. were outnumbered by three to one. Even so, they gave a very good account of themselves, before the three of them were overpowered and safely tied up. Four of the crooks were taking no further interest in the proceedings.

Big Benny stood over them – a scarlet handkerchief still pressed to his nose. He aimed a savage kick at Barton, then said: 'Bring me the petrol pipe, Lefty.'

Sheila started.

'Why, Benny?' she asked.

'We're going to have a fire,' said Benny. 'This place is well insured, don't worry.'

He took the nozzle of the pipe from the petrol pump.

'Nobody smoking, is there?' he asked, looking round.

Nobody was.

Then calmly – as though he were watering the garden, Benny began to spray Dick, Snowy and Jock with petrol. The acrid fumes of the spirit filled the building. Soon Barton's clothes – and those of Snowy and Jock were saturated.

'OK', said Benny. 'You'll burn all right now.'

Barton looked up at him.

'You'll swing for this, Benny,' he said.

Benny sprayed the petrol liberally around the garage.

'Got to catch me first,' he said.

'We'll do that all right,' said a quiet voice, suddenly.

Benny and his gang swung round towards the iron doors. Unobserved by the crooks, Inspector Burke and a force of police had managed to creep in through the office entrance.

'Good ole Burke,' yelled Snowy delightedly. 'We knew you'd do it!'

One of Benny's men reached for his gun.

'Don't fire,' shouted Benny, panic-stricken. 'The whole place will go up if you do. Follow me . . .' and with surprising speed he dashed towards a flight of stairs in the corner of the repair shop. Several of his men followed.

Burke busied himself cutting the cords which held Barton and Co.

'Don't worry,' he said in response to Barton's look of surprise. 'This place is surrounded. They can't get away.'

'Sooner we're out of here the better, though,' said Snowy. 'One spark and we go up in flames.'

'Outside, everybody,' ordered Burke. 'This place isn't safe until the petrol fumes have cleared. There's no hurry so far as Benny and his boys are concerned. They've got to come down eventually.'

Between them they pushed Barton's car out of the garage. The three of them reeked of petrol.

Meanwhile – from a window of the top storey, Benny challenged the police.

'Come and get us if you want us!' he shouted, and waved a revolver. 'Come on, copper!' he added. 'Let's see how brave you are!'

Sheila, meanwhile, was standing near the Inspector. She seemed dazed by the sudden turn events had taken. Then suddenly she snatched herself away from the two policemen who were guarding her and raced across the garage towards the stairs Benny had used. She had almost reached them when her foot slipped on a patch of oil. Falling, she clutched desperately at some steel rods, bringing them down with her, just as the two policemen reached her and jerked her to her feet again.

'Quickly!' yelled Barton suddenly.

He had noticed that one of the steel rods, in falling, had dislodged a piece of metal near a bench upon which a number of car batteries were standing. The metal fell flat on top of the batteries.

As it caused a short circuit between the positive and negative terminals of one of the batteries, a shower of blue sparks went up. Then there was a dull roar and the entire ground floor of the building seemed to be one solid wall of flame.

Instinctively Dick Barton hurled himself forward to the rescue of the two policemen and the girl.

'You chump!' shouted Snowy, hanging on to his chief. 'You can't go near that lot with your clothes soaked in petrol. Use your loaf, sir!'

Reluctantly Barton allowed himself to be held back, then he sighed with relief as the two policemen came staggering through the flames carrying the unconscious Sheila.

Inspector Burke took charge.

'Look, you three,' he urged. 'Get into the car before a stray spark turns you all into blazing torches!' And he shepherded Dick, Snowy and Jock into their car.

A shrill scream from the top of the burning building made them look up.

Kneeling on a window sill, Big Benny, mad with terror, was alternately praying, pleading and cursing. He seemed to have taken the window as his own property, regardless of the other members of his gang who were up there with him. As Barton and Co. watched the cowardly gangster screaming and shouting with fright, someone inside the room seemed to be trying to force their way past him and out of the window. Frenziedly Benny tried to push the man back again, but plainly the room was filling with smoke and the crook concerned was desperate for fresh air. For a few moments Benny struggled to regain possession of the window sill. Then it happened.

Someone inside the room lashed out with his fist at the gangster as he knelt on the window sill. With a wild cry Big Benny tried to clutch the window – the drainpipe – anything, but without success. His huge, ungainly body came hurtling to the ground and thudded onto the concrete pavement, where it lay very still.

'And that,' remarked Barton to Inspector Burke, 'would appear to be that! So perish all racketeers. What say, Inspector?'

And Inspector Burke fully agreed.

Sheila opened her eyes painfully and regarded Snowy and Jock as they tried to make her comfortable. Then she gazed past them at Barton.

'Tell me . . .' she whispered. 'How did the police know where to come?'

Jock grinned, and pointed to Burke.

'Meet Inspector Burke,' he said. 'Remember: Burke's the Boy!'

Sheila smiled faintly.

'You told the newsboy to phone the police?' she asked.

'S'right,' said Snowy. 'Then we waited for fifteen minutes till we saw 'em drive up behind us. Get it?'

Sheila smiled again.

'I told Benny he was wasting his time trying to beat Barton,' she murmured. 'But he wouldn't listen. I'll bet he wishes he'd listened to me now.'

Jock looked out of the car window at the gangster's body spreadeagled on the ground.

'I'll bet he does,' said Jock.

Hazell and the Patriot

◆————◆————◆

P. B. YUILL

The appearance in 1978 of Hazell, a former cop turned private detective, opened up a new era of crime dramas on British television. A tough and abrasive character with an irrepressible Cockney exuberance who operates in the sleezier areas of London, Hazell is frequently involved in violence and is not above taking the law into his own hands to solve a case. His relationship with the police – particularly his former colleagues – is an uneasy and often hostile one. The TV series from Thames Television in which he appeared, attempted to transpose a character who was not unlike Phillip Marlowe into the kind of London streets that most nearly matched those of Chandler's downtown Los Angeles. The ten hour-long stories achieved high audience figures, and while many viewers considered them good entertainment, there were others, including several newspaper reviewers, who attacked the series for its violence. The craggy television actor Nicholas Ball played Hazell with considerable verve and was well supported by the versatile Roddy McMillan.

The books by 'P. B. Yuill' on which the series was based concealed the identities of former London newspaper journalist, Gordon Williams, author of several filmed novels including The Straw Dogs (1971); and Terry Venables, the former professional footballer, club manager and now boss of Tottenham Hotspur FC. Williams' knowledge of police procedures and Venables' East London background, plus their natural wit, were ideally suited in the creation of Hazell's cases, and it has been a source of regret to many readers and viewers that the subsequent different demands on the time of the two men has curtailed more stories. This typical short story of a bit of

Hazell 'business' was written at the time of the launching of the TV series.

ON the Tube to Dot Wilmington's office that August morning I'd read over somebody's shoulder in the *Mirror* where another of our pop geniuses was moving out to dodge tax.

Reluctantly, of course.

'No, I'm not desperate for work,' I said to the short, dumpy woman with the dyed blonde hair. 'I got at least eighty quid in the iron tank and the garage only wants ninety for clutch work. Plus I got about a hundred and fifty owing to me on a job I did . . .'

'All right, you're desperate,' Dot said.

We stared at each other across her desk. The window behind her was open to let in a cool breeze but any air moving outside was hotter than three in a bed.

'Business is terrible all round,' she said. 'That was your mistake, not becoming a brewer or a bureaucrat.'

'Or a rocker.'

'There's an electrical wholesaler in Acton — somebody's weeding out the stock. How's your double-entry bookkeeping?'

'Nine times nine is . . . ninety-nine?'

'Didn't you make two grand out of the crook you saved from the heavies?'

'Paid off the motor, didn't I? A week in Jersey . . . soon goes. Anyway, it was you phoned me, remember.'

Outside on the ledge two pigeons muttered among themselves about the drought. It did just cross my mind that Dot was enjoying all this. I'd once been on the staff of her security consultancy, seventy-five quid a week on the muck and bullet line.

Then she brought up a file from the carpet.

'Bad debts,' she said, shoving it across the desk. 'I usually bung 'em to a smart cookie called Vinnie Rae on a split-commission basis. Penny ante stuff most of it, not even worth the small-claims court. As a favour to me she might let you take a couple — twenty per cent of anything you recover. I'll ring and tell her you're coming over . . .'

'Her?'

'Yeah – and a word of warning, lover boy. Karate was her best subject at Roedean.'

'All go with you women nowadays, innit?'

Sicilian Avenue is an arched passage off Southampton Row in the no-man's land west of Tottenham Court Road. Little businesses, a stamp-collectors' shop, a restaurant with outside tables, a touch of the Continongs if you didn't look too hard. Naturally the developers had wanted to destroy it a couple of years back.

One good thing about the country being bust – you can count on seeing the same building two weeks in a row.

Vinnie Rae had told Dot she'd be having coffee outside.

I spotted her partner first.

Jason. Black mostly, with a bit of brown, very sleek and shiny. Bit of a gay dog judging by the way his big eyes said hello.

She was cream mostly, what you might call a biggish girl, very healthy, in a pale blue denim suit and white shoes.

'Vinnie Rae?' I said standing well away from the hound. 'James Hazell . . .'

'Ah yes.' She squinted up at me. The dog checked my credit-rating and decided I wasn't worth burying for later. 'Do have a seat . . . it's all right, Jason only goes for the throat if I raise a finger.'

'What does he go for if you raise two fingers?'

'A lady never raises two fingers.'

I sat down and put the folder on the table.

'Had any experience of debt-collecting?'

'Collecting new ones every day.'

She smiled.

Up to the table came this second hound, mostly black, very sleek, very shiny. Only this one had a dry nose. And big shades.

'All hail,' he said dramatically, clicking his heels and sliding into a seat. He was wearing a black shirt open to the navel, with a gold ornament on a chain dangling down his hairy chest. From his flared jeans he brought out a bundle of readies, which he slapped down beside her coffee-cup.

'Four hundred and twenty-five, full settlement!'

'Well *done*, Roger,' she said. 'Never thought you'd crack it.'

'I knew it would take something special,' he said modestly, with a little wave of his hand. 'I steam into his reception . . .' He held both hands behind his back . . . 'I steam past his plush secretary and there he is behind his desk. "You again?" he says sarcastically. "Yes, me again, Mr Slippery" . . . then I go *whoosh*!' He brought his right hand down smack on the table. 'First axe – smack into polished cedar! "Better give me the doings or this one" ' – he brought his left hand up – ' "is for your *skull*!" Paid up like a lamb!'

'Poetry in motion,' Vinnie murmured, starting to thumb notes off the bundle. She slung him around seventy or eighty fives and oncers. The way they disappeared into his skyrocket his jeans might have had jaws.

'And I had to buy two axes,' he said, quite reasonably I thought. Vinnie wasn't impressed.

'Deduct them.'

'*Tax*?' He stood up and gave her a clenched fist salute. 'Those about to die of Socialism salute you!'

His slimline buttocks jigged away through the tables. 'Roger's an out-of-work actor – he can make a bad debt seem like a death warrant.'

Then she came back to me. 'Oh yes.' She opened the file. 'All right – here's an old friend you can have a beginner's bash at.' She handed me the sheet of paper. 'A mere two hundred and thirty pounds but you only have to go as far as Oxford Street . . .'

'What's the . . . er . . . form?'

'Question of psychology really. No violence.'

'Yeah? What do you call smashing axes into desks?'

She smiled and touched the hound's chin. 'We call that applied psychology, don't we, Jason?'

I got away without being retrieved . . .

You'll find a lot of buildings like it in the West End, tucked away in odd corners. The notice-board listed everything from escort agencies to cut-rate carpets, cheap fares to Australia, palms read (crystal ball by special arrangement), a yoga health clinic, several secretarial agencies . . . and Mr Dornford's little conglomerate.

I went up to the fourth floor. On the way I passed three or four silent Indians. The businessman sort. Most of the doors looked a bit damaged – it's a safe bet any building like that in the pulsating West End echoes at night to the traditional sounds of splintering panels and jemmied hinges.

Mr Dornford was in 39. Judging by the number of companies with notices on his door his office had to be slightly bigger than the Vickers building. Travel and insurance mostly.

I knocked.

He was about sixty-five, dark suit, white hair combed back with a strict parting, a moustache the colour of old piano keys, a regimental tie with the kind of knot that makes fingernails yell for help.

A gentleman of the old school, no doubt about it.

'Mr Dornford?'

'He's gone. What's it about?'

Two silent Indians came along the corridor. He gave them a bit of a glare. They slid past me.

'Gone?'

'Knew what he was doing,' he said, quite viciously, staring at the disappearing Indians. 'I bought his businesses – '

'Gresham's office equipment reckon he owes them – '

'Sorry, can't help you.'

He was going to shut the door. For twenty per cent of two hundred and thirty quid I was willing to risk causing offence. I put my hand on the door.

'Where is he then?'

'He drops in occasionally to collect his mail – write to him. Now, unfashionable as it may seem, I have work to do.'

'They've tried writing – he never replies.'

'Can't blame him, postage rates these days. Now . . .'

'If you bought the business you'd be legally responsible . . .'

'I bought only the goodwill – the ill-will as it turned out.'

Behind him in the office a phone rang. He turned to look at it. On the wall I caught a glimpse of a framed photograph of a young geezer in uniform.

'If he comes in I'll ask him for his address – best I can do,' he said . . .

Half an hour later I was going into Vinnie Rae's office on the third floor above Sicilian Avenue. She was on the phone. The Dobermann was on the floor. The bundle of notes was on her desk.

I was on edge.

But the hound gave me the benefit of the doubt.

'Funny how people never complain about our forty per cent until the money's been recovered,' she was saying. She gave me a little wave, pointing me in the direction of a small purple sofa with wooden arms.

They say animals can smell fear.

Maybe Jason had a cold in the nose.

'Well I have two hundred and fifty-five pounds here for you,' she said, thumbing the notes. I reached the sofa without provoking Jason. Vinnie laughed. 'Oh no no no no,' she said, giving me a wink, 'we deduct at source. Cash business, no cheques – and *no* bad debts . . . very good.'

She rang off.

'Well?'

'Bit hot.'

She stretched her arms. Her denim suit seemed a bit tight.

I dunno why, I looked quickly at Jason.

Oh yeah he knew what I was thinking. He sort of sneered. There was only one dirty dog in the room and it wasn't him.

'Dornford's sold out to an old geezer called Telford,' I said. 'Telford's getting me an address for Dornford.'

She managed a frown and smile at the same time.

'And what're you going to do while you're waiting for the address?'

'I dunno . . . maybe try another one . . .'

She sighed. 'Dot did say you needed a bit of help.'

'I'll register as a charity I expect.'

'I *hate* to tamper with masculine pride and all that but . . . Telford – one of the old brigade? Seedy but a certain air of previous distinction? Pushing seventy perhaps? Moustache, white hair?'

It was paper-hat time. The kind with a big D.

She smiled ever so sweetly.

'We don't have time for looking and learning in this racket,' she said.

So back I went to Oxford Street.

This time it was Plan B . . . steam in like a fist with a smile on its face.

Knock knock.

'Who is it?'

'Hazell.'

'You're beginning to be a nuisance.'

I got down in a crouch and looked through his letter-box. He was on the other side of the room, looking at me over a desk.

'You going to let me in, Mr Dornford?'

'I told you – my name's Telford.'

'And mine's Lawrence of Bethnal Green.'

'Oh . . . oh very well.'

As he opened the door a teenage person came along the corridor. Hard to say what sex, pale face, green hair.

'Did you see that?' Dornford let his head fall. I closed the door. 'What *is* the country coming to?'

'To a halt. Anyway, this debt of yours . . .'

He snorted as if I'd made a bad joke. He went to the window. 'When I think of all the wonderful men I saw dying around me in the desert – the lifeblood of a proud nation seeping into the sand . . . *now*? Has it ever occurred to you – who would fly the Spitfires today?'

'Look . . .'

'Long-haired layabouts. Poofs. Hermaprodites with green hair. Thieves – in this rat-hole they'd steal the paint off the woodwork. The only ones that will work are these dusky devils – place is full of 'em. Is this the Britain we fought and died for?'

'You owe Gresham's two hundred and thirty quid.'

He waved a gentlemanly hand. 'Is that the only motivation we have left – money, money, money?'

'Let me put it this way. You pay your debt and I'll buy British.'

'Haven't got it, old boy. Business is abominable.'

'You had an electric typewriter out of them . . .'

'Stolen. Burglars. Kicked the door down.'

'The insurance . . .'

'I insured with my own company.' He heaved with silent laughter. 'My insurance company's gone bust!'

I decided to cut out the social niceties.

'I think you're an old bleeding fraudsman,' I said heavily. 'Don't give me all that dying in the desert crap . . .'

He nodded and walked to his desk. He sat down, folded his arms and closed his eyes.

'Well, get on with it,' he said.

'Get on with what?'

'The rough stuff. That's what they pay you for, isn't it? Go on – you represent the new morality. Kick an old man whose only crime was to fall behind with his payments.'

'Fall behind? You never got under starters' orders!'

'They should never have encouraged a man of my age to incur such a debt. That's how they make their money, you know – tempting people into commitments with seductive blandishments and then . . .' He opened his eyes. 'Does your work make you feel *proud*?'

I walked across to his desk and thumped my fist down. It was supposed to make him . . . well, not exactly putting the frighteners in but letting him know.

I hurt my knuckles as it happened.

'Can't you pay *anything*?' I said.

He brought a wallet out from his hip-pocket and opened it wide. 'My daily entitlement,' he said, sliding out a solitary pound note. 'My own fault – I should've packed in years ago, but when you have a sick wife . . .'

I had the pound out of his hand.

'Let's talk about the balance.'

'I *could* break into a small building society account that my wife and I hoped would see us through . . . very bleak at our age . . . you young chaps never think it will happen to you . . .'

'Look, mate,' I said, wagging my finger at him, 'I want the money.'

He had a bright idea.

'Man in your line – how are you off for insurance?'

Honest to God. He was trying to sell me insurance.

'I'll act as broker – you pay me the initial premium and I'll give you back my commission – it won't cover the whole debt but it's a start, isn't it?'

The phone rang. He picked it up, still looking at me with his small blue eyes. His hand had blue veins and looked slightly warped. It shook a bit. His eyes were watery.

'Oh hello,' he said into the phone, 'how is my wife?' He listened. 'Oh . . . confirmed, is it? . . . Well yes, one has had to prepare oneself for the worst . . . yes, thank you very much for phoning.'

He put down the phone. Somebody knocked at the door. He motioned at me to keep quiet.

'Mr Dornford? It's Captain McInnes.'

'The block manager,' Dornford said, going to the door.

They'd have made a fine pair of book-ends, only the Captain was fatter.

'Just thought I'd tell you, old chap – two offices done over last night. I'm chucking out this damned security mob – oh, busy are you?'

'It's all right . . .'

The Captain gave me a look. 'No, won't disturb you, Dornford. You seem to be the only other white man in this teeming bazaar. May drop by later.'

Dornford shut the door. He shook his head. 'In a way I'm glad my time's about over,' he said cheerfully, 'this isn't what I was used to. Oh well . . .'

He went to the window.

He looked much older, standing there against the sunshine. Call me a naïve sentimental fool but there was something stopping me from putting the boot in.

I did have a spin through his wallet. Didn't even have a credit card, just junk.

'No, I don't envy you your youth,' he said. 'I had my best days in a much better world. Different class.'

'Oh ballocks.'

I got up and went to the door. I wasn't put in this world to terrorize old geezers with shaky hands, was I?

'Going?'

'Yeah.'

We looked at each other. I don't know why, I found myself laughing.

I went back to his desk and put the pound note down.

He nodded wisely.

'Thank you.'

I left with that good deed feeling. Sort of clean, you know what I mean?

'You got *what*?' Vinnie demanded.

She was back outside having coffee and a pastry.

'One sov.'

'One pound?'

'Yup.'

'Very good . . . you've earned twenty pee.'

'No I haven't. I gave it back.'

'What?'

'I don't think I got the stomach for this debt-gathering caper. Better send him the old axe trick.'

'Dot said you were a bit of a romantic but . . . a debt-collector giving the money *back*? You might get in the *Guinness Book of Records*.'

I raised my hand. The waiter came over. I ordered a cup of tea. Jason was on the deck, tongue hanging out. A girl passed in a white summer dress. One thing about all this heat, legs were coming out of hiding.

'I like to think of myself as a professional,' I said. 'Enquiry agent I suppose you'd call it. You know – missing poodles, missing husbands, who stole the priceless eggcups? Some old guy living in a dream world. . . ? I mean, he actually expected me to whack him about.'

'Drink your tea,' she said, 'we're going for a little walk. You can tell me about these lofty ideals of yours.'

Oxford Street on a hot August afternoon. All your foreigners and that, come to sunny Britain for a bargain. She had Jason on a chain. People do tend to dodge a Dobermann. Vinnie seemed amused by something.

I was sweating a bit by the time we turned into Dornford's building. On the stairs we met these two way-out characters, Indians – but something else. White surgeons' masks, white robes, little white mops over their shoulders.

'Jains,' Vinnie said.

'Who's Jane?'

'No it's a religious sect. They believe in the sanctity of life. The masks are to stop flies getting into their mouths. The mops are to wipe the ground in front of each step in case they tramp on an ant.'

'You'd learn that kind of stuff at Roedean I expect.'

'My father was Indian Army.'

'He could come here for a reunion.'

'He's having it in Heaven.'

'Sorry about that.'

'I'm not.'

When Dornford saw the hound he tried to close the door. Jason didn't exactly knock him down and trot all over him but he wasn't standing any nonsense.

'What's all this?' Dornford demanded, getting the desk between himself and our four-legged friend.

'I believe you've been giving our Mr Hazell a hard time,' Vinnie said.

'I explained to Mr Hazell . . .'

'I'm afraid Mr Hazell is learning our business. You can take this as a compliment.'

'Compliment?'

'I am the final sanction. Vinnie and the Dobermann.' She cocked a finger at Jason. 'Good dog.'

Jason did his imitation of the MGM lion. Dornford looked ready to get up on the desk.

'I appeal to you – as a man of reason,' he stammered.

'You don't appeal to me,' Vinnie said. 'Now – can we settle this matter once and for all?'

'I told Mr Hazell – I'm in no position to . . .'

'What a lovely view of dirty walls,' she said, looking out at the well behind the building. 'Are we going to be here long enough to get to like it?'

'I daresay I could make some kind of proposal . . .'

Vinnie took a deep breath, shaking her head.

'It's too late for proposals, Mr Dornford. I'm instructed to collect the whole amount. It's not the principle, it's the money. Do you like Dobermann pinschers? They have a bad reputation but by and large they're quite sensible. Jason can count up to ten. Talk, Jason, talk.'

The hound barked.

'This is outright intimidation,' Dornford said. There was a note of complaint in his voice. I began to think this Vinnie was a bit strong.

It took them long enough but once women find the way in . . . look out.

'No, it has to be a lot worse than this before it's intimidation, Mr Dornford,' Vinnie said.

'Bringing a brute like that in here? That's bad enough in my book. Are you willing to get yourself involved in this sort of thing, Mr Hazell?'

I shrugged. 'Better give the dog a bone, Mr Dornford.'

'Let me make two things quite clear, young woman. I am not paying you a penny and I'm also going to make sure Gresham's pay heavily for this gross intrusion . . . demanding money with menaces is the legal description.'

'False pretences is the legal description for assuming a false name,' Vinnie said.

The old geezer was beat.

Vinnie didn't wait till he was down.

'There's also an electric typewriter bought on hire-purchase . . .'

'The burglar took it.'

'Why didn't you tell Gresham's?'

'I don't know, I don't know.' He was really suffering.

'Look, Vinnie,' I began, 'he doesn't . . .'

Hope came into his face.

'Perhaps you're too easily gulled for our business, Mr Hazell,' she said. She turned on Dornford. 'Two hundred and thirty pounds.'

I cannot tell a lie, I was pretty sure I'd have to stop her putting the hound on him. Obviously he didn't have the money –

If my face had fallen any further I would have been tramping on my nose.

The old rascal sat down, pulled out a wallet, opened up a cheque book, and started to write.

A different wallet!

'To cash,' she said pleasantly.

He muttered something, then tore off the cheque.

Hardly looking at it she handed it back. 'You forgot the date.'

'Oh, did I? Terrible thing, old age,' he said. Somebody had just topped him up with oil. He gave her an old-fashioned smile this time.

She examined the cheque, then handed it to me.

'Jason and I will wait till Mr Hazell brings back the cash,' she said. 'You can ring the bank.'

It was twenty past three.

As I went out the door he started telling her about some package holiday deal he was promoting for the Greek Islands . . .

She drove me back that evening, after a couple of drinks. Aston Martin – of course. As a woman driver she was about as indecisive as Dirty Harry.

'Aren't you asking me in for a drink?' she said when we reached my gaff. I was kipping down in Paddington that month, short-term rental furnished till I copped enough for a proper flat.

'Will Jason be all right?'

'Give him a pint of milk, he'll be happy.'

'Couldn't we leave him out here? Give him a pedestrian to chew on . . .'

'I think you're scared of Jason.'

'I'm not too sure about you either.'

She patted me on the back.

'It has to be a lot worse before it's intimidation.'

As I say, now women have twigged to what it's all about they're *worse* than men. Not only did she say I couldn't expect more than five per cent, considering it was her who screwed the readies out of Dornford, she didn't muck about when it came to the old sack race.

'Don't you like aggressive women?' she asked sweetly. Her fingernails were making grooves on my back.

'This shirt only came back from the laundry yesterday. Do you mind?'

'Sorry.'

'That's better,' I said, taking it off. 'Can we blindfold Jason or something?'

'Once you've worked together a few times you'll get to love him.'

'I'll be a bit busy for a while,' I said.

'Yes, where is the bedroom?'

'My life – are you hinting at something?'

Jason watched us going into the bedroom.

I waited till afterwards to tell her.

'You did me a good turn as it happens,' I said, 'they've been having a lot of break-ins at Dornford's building. The manager reckons it's always the same bloke. Thirty quid a night we agreed on. Not bad, eh?'

'To catch a burglar? Stuck in that dump night after night? I can do better for you than that – '

'Anything I can do you can do debtor? By the way, maybe none of my business . . . but why *did* Dot send me round to you?'

'She'd told me a few things about you.'

'Such as?'

'None of your business. Why go touting for other work? I've a backlog of people like Dornford.'

'Women bosses? Dogs for partners? Terrorizing old men? Enough shit in this life without making a career out of it . . . I always say.'

'If that's how you feel . . .'

She made a move to get out of bed. She was a big strong girl but . . .

Somebody's got to fly the Spitfires, haven't they?

Rumpole and the Hanging Judge

◆

JOHN MORTIMER

Horace Rumpole has been called the antithesis of Perry Mason, a barrister who is disreputable in appearance and practice, yet notwithstanding that a formidable wit, sage and raconteur. Known, simply, as 'Rumpole of the Bailey' he is admired for his defence of hopeless causes (he will only accept defence briefs) and his table-talk in Pommeroy's wine bar where he drowns his frustrations in Chateau Fleet Street. Since his early triumph as a youthful barrister in the case of The Penge Bungalow Murder, *Rumpole has skirmished with all manner of legal adversaries, hard-hearted judges and dodgy clients –though his most fearsome opponent still remains his wife, Hilda: 'She Who Must Be Obeyed'. His battle cries have become famous, too, the resounding 'Never plead Guilty!' or punning, 'An Englishman's gin-bottle is his castle!'. As a result of his fame on TV, Rumpole has now become a cult hero – albeit an unlikely one – and even has a 'Rumpole Society of America', whose members (over five hundred at last count) have crossed the Atlantic to visit the places featured in the stories such as the Old Bailey and El Vino's, the Fleet Street wine bar which is the original of Pommeroy's. To these fans, Rumpole is the quintessential Englishman, a true eccentric, not to mention a champion of the underdog.*

The actual creation of Rumpole by John Mortimer (1923–), himself a barrister as well as a novelist and dramatist, is like all good mystery stories something of a puzzle. It is said he evolved from a single BBC Play for Today in 1976, although there were elements of him to be found in a radio and TV play, The Dock Brief, *shown in 1957. Be this as it may, it was Thames Television who launched a series of hour-long plays,* Rumpole of the Bailey, *in 1978, with the inspired casting of Leo McKern in the title role. Since then the triumphs and failures of the irascible barrister – including his ongoing feud with Mr Justice Bullingham – have proved essential viewing. Several attempts by John Mortimer to terminate the character have been overwhelmed by public demand, perhaps most notably in 1981 when Thames produced a one hundred and twenty minute special, Rumpole's Return in which the old war-horse came back from supposed retirement in Florida to score a notable triumph over Bullingham. In the following story, Rumpole tangles with another redoubtable judge in the shape of Mr Justice Truscott . . .*

IT was said of Mr Justice Truscott that he always ordered muffins for tea at his club after passing a death sentence.

Sir Fennimore Truscott has now, happily, dropped off the twig but I don't believe death to be a particularly good excuse and I am prepared to speak as much ill of the old sweetheart now as I was when he sat upon the bench taking snuff, sneezing into a silk bandana, grunting at junior counsel and handing out intolerable sentences. When I read his obituary in *The Times* I couldn't restrain a moderate feeling of contentment at the death of one who, as I told my wife Hilda (She Who Must Be Obeyed), was widely regarded in the legal profession as Judge Jeffreys without the jokes.

Not that 'Frightful Fen' was without jokes entirely. He just didn't make much use of them in Court. As an after-dinner speaker at Sheriffs' gatherings his anecdotes would send the ladies scurrying from the room in hot flushes as he embarked, yet again, on the story of the bestiality case he tried in Truro, or the hilarious rape he heard in Devizes. To those of a forgiving nature Fennimore Truscott might then have been described as of a jovial, even Rabelaisian disposition, but the atmosphere in his Court was about as cheerful as a baby's funeral.

All the same his outrageous rudeness did occasionally achieve a sort of sharpness which might have been called wit by sympathetic observers. I was not, as you may have gathered, to be numbered among these tolerant persons, and that was not only because of the outrageous treatment I received at his hands (I have had more stand up rows, misdirections, interruptions and deterrent sentences from old 'Fen' than I have had bottles of Pommeroy's Plonk) but because he was, as you will no doubt recall, the man who hanged Martin Muschamp.

I suppose to anyone under forty the name of Marty Muschamp won't mean anything in particular; but in the remote days when we still believed in death as a short, sharp measure of Penal Reform, young Muschamp was, for a brief moment in our legal history, a sort of star with his photograph on the front page of the *News of the World*. His slow but inevitable progress towards the scaffold was watched by the populace over their Sunday breakfasts with the sort of tremulous, second-hand excitement which was the next best thing to a first-floor window in Newgate Street during the working life of Jack Ketch.

Marty, although he had, as I say, attained executable years, was said to have the mental age of a child of ten. He had a girl friend, a mistress indeed, called Louise Natley who, from the photographs provided, was not only somewhat under par in the glamour department, but had that curious expression, that mixture of resentment, docility and ill-tempered resignation which seems, in a curious way to be the hall mark of the murderee.

Earlier on the night in question Marty and Louise had been heard quarrelling in a coffee bar near the street in Putney where they both lived. Later they admittedly went for a walk together on Wimbledon Common. Marty's evidence was that they had had another quarrel and Louise ran off and left him. He said he sat on a seat for a long while smoking and thinking things over and then got up and started vaguely looking for her.

He found her legs, without any particular difficulty, sticking out of a clump of laurels. When he uncovered the rest of Louise it was clear that she had been sexually assaulted and strangled. He knelt beside her to see if she were still breathing and that is how, he told the police after a good many lies and denials that he had ever been near the body, Louise's blood came to be on his shirt cuffs and trousers.

It was the sort of case, after all, which might have been lost by the most fearless advocate before the fairest tribunal. Martin was not defended, unfortunately, by Horace Rumpole, then enjoying a certain well deserved notoriety as the victor in the Penge Bungalow Murders. His counsel, a youngish QC used to appearing for such respected bodies as building societies and banks, was unnerved at the frosty reception given to those whose client for the day is an alleged teenage murderer and rapist.

Marty Muschamp was found guilty. His father organized a petition with three thousand signatures but the Home Secretary of the day, a worried ex-headmaster of the Labour persuasion, saw no reason why the law should not take its course. Martin Muschamp vanished from this earth and from the front pages for a while.

Five years later a man named Heathers, picked up for a number of similar crimes, confessed to having found Louise wandering alone on Wimbledon Common and raped and killed her. The description he gave of his victim was convincing; influential persons wrote letters to *The Times*, a television film was made on the subject and there was an inquiry, after which Marty Muschamp, buried within the prison walls, failed to hear the good news that his innocence had been established. The inquiry was at pains to point out that Mr Justice Truscott had conducted the trial with perfect impartiality on the evidence as it was known to him at the time, and that no blame attached to him whatever.

The abolition of the death penalty, and the fact that murder trials are now conducted in what old Truscott once described in one of his inimitable after-dinner speeches as 'a sort of holiday atmosphere', has taken most of the pep out of detective stories ('The shadow of ten years in the nick began to fall across the swarthy face of Quentin Lazarotti' is not the sort of line that appeals greatly to your average lady writer of whodunnits; such authoresses prefer the drama of the noose). It has also meant a huge drop in box office takings and a falling away of audiences which I have noticed at my more recent murder trials.

In fact the case I did at Grimble Assizes, one of the last murders the old Hanging Darling ever tried in this world (God help us if he is now performing some judicial function on the Other Side) took place in an almost empty courtroom. There was only one man in the public gallery, but he was a most conscientious attender. He was in his place dead on ten o'clock each morning and stayed until Truscott rose at four thirty, when he would stand, bow smartly to the Judge and walk away alone.

He was a gaunt, thin-faced man with red hair going grey and he wore, in spite of the courtroom's oppressive central heating, a frayed overcoat and a checked woollen muffler at all times. He had pale blue eyes and they were fixed throughout the proceedings on the ageing and frequently scowling face of Mr Justice Truscott.

We were not able, I'm afraid, to put on a particularly fascinating show for our dedicated fan. The murder was the result of a fight outside a pub at closing time, it involved the use of some rather choice language and a broken Guinness bottle, and like the vast majority of killings was remote from any plot used by a lady writer of whodunnits, being more accurately described as a rather dreary case of common assault with disastrous consequences.

Even the prisoner seemed unable to show a great deal of interest in the events as they unfolded, the jury sat in soporific silence, the bespectacled young prosecutor presented the case with all the riveting oratory of a lecturer taking an evening class on double-entry book-keeping. It didn't seem the sort of show that could keep even our solitary spectator glued to his seat.

Such entertainment value as existed was provided by his lordship. He went through the whole repertoire of judicial tricks and gave us all the golden oldies of judicial behaviour. He fawned on the jury ('Members of the jury, you and I may have to spend a few days together. Now if any of you require a short break for any reason you won't hesitate to tell me, will you?').

He treated prosecuting and defence counsel with impartial con-tempt. When the prosecutor went carefully through a witness's statement he said, 'With a small amount of reasonable preparation, Mr Arkell, we could have got through that witness in half the time.' When I was doing moderately well with my cross-examination he'd say, 'It's hardly in your client's best interests to labour every detail, is it, Mr Rumpole?'

If the prosecution made a good point he'd find it was an excellent moment to adjourn so that the jury could brood on it during lunch. If yours truly scored a minor hit he would do his best to minimize its effect with a series of laborious and carefully worded questions, ending with a triumphant glare at the jury and a long time spent recording it in his notebook.

Around the third day of the trial I was cross-examining a copper in a reasonably uncontroversial, desultory fashion and venturing to suggest that some of my client's less well-chosen phrases ('So I made up my mind to bash the Mick on the head and looked around for a bottle' was one of them) had in fact been composed at the station by officers with some talent for stage dialogue and a burning zeal to secure a conviction.

'Mr Rumpole!' There was a noise from the bench like the rumbling eruption of some almost extinct volcano. 'Are you seriously suggesting that this *young* officer is seeking to mislead this jury?'

At this point something snapped inside Rumpole. I had had enough of the old darling's interruptions, and if I were going down I might as well sink with all guns blazing.

'I really can't see what his being *young* has got to do with it, my Lord.' I bowed with exaggerated politeness. 'I never heard there was an age limit for inventing a prisoner's verbals. It may well be something that comes fairly early on in the course of police training in the fair city of Grimble.'

There wasn't even a titter from the twelve honest citizens in the jury box, indeed they looked at me rather as a bench of canons might look at a member of the congregation who has just blown an almighty raspberry at the bishop during the course of his Lenten address.

I was surprised, however, to receive no further rebuke from the bench. Indeed, I thought I saw, about the long thin line of the judicial mouth, something which might even be interpreted as a smile. I continued to go through the formalities of challenging the police note book and as I did so the usher handed me a note from the judge. I glanced at it, not sure if it was to announce my immediate committal for contempt or to tell me that my flies were undone. 'Dear Rumpole,' I read in his lordship's meticulous handwriting, 'if you're free during the adjournment perhaps you'd care to lunch at the Lodgings?'

'He was sat beside me in the cinema, sir', said this girl complainant, in the Indecent Assault, 'and he put his hand up my skirt'. 'Very well', said the old Recorder with his eye on the clock. 'I suggest we leave it there until five past two'.

I gave a token smile. Truscott's story was not a new one. I had been looking forward to a restful lunch in the Grimble Arms, a pub opposite the back entrance of the Law Courts and to a solitary pint of draught Guinness and a portion of steak and kidney pie. Instead I had been whisked with his scarlet lordship and police outriders to a Victorian manor house in the suburbs, that gloomy lodging where Truscott J. served his own particular sentence of imprisonment. He made a stab at a chop, dropped gravy on his chin and then looked at me and said, after a long silence, 'I like the way you're doing this case, Rumpole. You understand what it's all about. Courage'.

I felt for the claret. It was a tribute I'd never sought or expected.

'You need courage to do both our jobs. Courage to take a view of a case and stick to it . . .'

'Even though it may be mistaken?'

'Mistakes can usually be put right'. Truscott speared a potato.

'Nowadays, perhaps. It wasn't possible though . . . in some of your old cases', I said with as much malignity as I could manage.

'You're thinking of Muschamp'. He was ahead of me. He seemed smaller without his wig on, and much older. His head was bald and wrinkled but his eye was bright and quick like a bird's.

'I'd feel exactly the same about the Muschamp case today. The idea of the girl wandering off and getting killed by someone else! It was an impossible coincidence.'

'Apparently not impossible.' I felt that the Judge was asking me for something, possibly approval. 'Of course, the death penalty made that sort of mistake a little hard to put right.'

'The death penalty. . . . People talk a lot about the death penalty. They don't remember that hard cases make bad laws. Nothing wrong with the death penalty. It needed facing up to, of course, but for us it was simply part of the job, wasn't it?'

'Part of *your* job.' I was an advocate and able to avoid final responsibility.

'Not a part that gave me any particular satisfaction, of course. You may have heard a ridiculous story about muffins. Quite without foundation. You haven't been able to get muffins at the Army and Navy Club since before the war! You a gardener, Rumpole?'

'I'm afraid not.' Indeed, our alleged mansion flat in the Gloucester Road provided little scope for the herbaceous border. I was still a little surprised at the development of his lordship's argument.

'I'm a rose man myself,' he told me. 'Of course it's been a little difficult to get round all the pruning, since my wife died. Anyway,' he returned to the subject like a man with a pimple he can't resist touching, 'it was never my decision. The jury'd found Muschamp guilty . . .'

'But of course you directed the jury.'

'Oh yes,' he admitted.

'You told them he'd frequently broken the law by having an affair with a girl under sixteen . . .'

'I thought that showed . . . a certain ruthlessness.'

'But didn't it make it somewhat unlikely that he'd go to the trouble of raping her?'

I asked the question, but I still wasn't entirely sure what was happening. Had the old darling sought me out because he wanted to be questioned by someone who has, I must in all modesty admit, something of a talent for cross-examination?

'She wouldn't agree to his rogering her that night, you see,' the judge explained. 'So they'd had a quarrel.'

'You make it all sound extremely simple.'

'I like to keep things simple in the law.' He smiled. 'Then I find juries understand them better.'

'And so why did he kill her?'

'So that she wouldn't give evidence against him.'

'Of course.' A perfectly simple explanation. The only trouble with it was that it turned out to be wrong.

'Anyway.' None too soon his lordship lifted his table napkin and wiped the spot of gravy off his chin. 'It was the jury's decision, as I said.'

I remembered the newspaper reports and the helpless anger I'd felt when reading them. Truscott had told the jury at least three times in his summing-up that they might find it hard to believe the defendant's evidence. Now he had raised the subject and I had no objection to reminding him of what he'd said.

'Muschamp lied outrageously to the police,' he defended himself. 'At first he told them he'd never been on the common with the girl at all. I was perfectly entitled to point that out, surely?'

Alone at the lunch table in the dark, chilly dining room, with the port between us and the clock ticking on the mantelpiece, we seemed to be undergoing an extraordinary change of roles. I had been appointed the judge by whom Fennimore Truscott was apparently anxious, after all these years, to be acquitted. I said nothing, but I pulled the watch out of my pocket; judgment was no part of my profession.

'Yes, we must get back,' he agreed. 'I thought, Rumpole, you might care to see this.'

He went over to a sideboard then and found the silver framed photograph he must always have taken on circuit with him. He showed me a rose garden by a Surrey house and two schoolgirls, rather plain children in cotton frocks and cardigans, frowning at the camera.

'The Mrs Sam Macready's flowering well, don't you think? Oh, and that's two of the grandchildren.'

What I was being shown was the evidence in mitigation. The facts that he grew roses and could breed a third generation of female Truscotts with cold eyes and thin, lipless mouths that might, any day, snap in some irreversible judgment were apparently to be put to his credit. I took careful note of all he said, but the least sentence I thought I could pass on him was silence.

So I said nothing, or not, at any rate, until we were settled, in embarrassing proximity, in the back of the creaking Daimler.

'There's a man in court who comes to listen to every moment of our trial. He pays the most extraordinary attention to you, Judge. Have you any idea who he is?'

'No. Really?' Truscott looked out of the window, uninterested. 'I hadn't noticed.'

I asked that, like all good questions, because I already knew the answer. I had discovered who our dedicated visitor was because I had heard an usher whisper a name, and I could just remember the distraught and pathetic face of a man hopelessly holding up a petition with three thousand signatures on the front page of the *News of the World*.

Our devoted spectator was there when we got back to court and he was listened intently while Truscott J., reverting to form, showed no sign whatever of having shared a chop and a glass of claret with me, or of having urged his cause before me as an unlikely tribunal.

I was not greatly disturbed by 'Frightful Fen' that afternoon. He had, to be sure, his own appalling fate, and apparently went on circuit forever accompanied by an accusing figure, a man haunting him and reminding him, in every subsequent case, of an old, irreversible mistake. The justice of it, I had to admit, pleased me and in this implacable pursuit I did feel that a judicial crime was in some way absolved. Mr Justice Truscott was like a hunted man, a criminal on the run, and his elderly, wrinkled head shrank into his stiff collar and ermine trimmed gown like the retracting head of a tortoise. For a moment I felt almost ready to forgive him.

There was, of course, a great deal to forgive. The old darling not only interrupted my speech to the jury three times; he dozed ostentatiously during the moving bits of my peroration and when it came to the summing up he was ever ready with the boot. A great deal of his elegant footwork was done by gesture and tone of voice. 'Of course the defendant *says*, members of the jury, that he was quite unaware of the fact that he had picked up any sort of weapon, and you *may even* believe him' (hopeless rolling of the eyes towards heaven and the strong implication that if you believe that you must be off your chump).

Much of the defence case was put with a weary sigh of, 'Perhaps *you* can accept that, members of the jury. It's entirely a matter for *you*.' After they had heard the evidence of 'that very decent young police officer. You may remember the one with the small moustache,' the outcome was no longer in doubt, nor was it delayed for very long.

After I had said goodbye to my client I went to drown the memories of a case which could never be rated among the Rumpole triumphs at the dark and stuffy little bar, with its hissing coal fires and comforting sawdust-covered floor where I had been denied my usual luncheon. I ordered a large rum and lit up a small cigar, and I was sitting with the golden spirit flooding into my veins and the familiar ash falling gently on to the waistcoat, when our constant audience came into the bar, stood near me and ordered a half of mild ale. I saw how large his hands were and that his exposed wrists were red and bony.

'You're right, Mr Muschamp,' I said, my tongue a little loosened by a second double. 'He's an unmitigated bastard!'

'Why, sir. Who would you be talking about?' The man's voice was so gentle I thought he was making an Irishman's joke.

'Why, Mr Justice "Frightful Fen" Truscott, of course. Don't you always watch him in court?'

'Sure, I always watch him. He's a fine man! A just man! I like to see him when he's working in London and as I have a married sister up in Grimble I take the opportunity to follow him on the Assize. I find it a legal education. There's not a judge sitting with a finer sense of fair play. Now admit it, your man was as guilty as hell, now wasn't he, Mr Rumpole?'

'Maybe *he* was. But your son . . .'

'I don't blame him for that. Not for one minute.' Mr Muschamp had not hesitated and his voice remained gentle as ever.

'You don't?' I choked incredulously on a recently reordered rum.

'No, he explained that to me.'

'He explained. . . ?'

'Oh yes. I behaved foolishly once. I got up in his court and I shouted at him. About Marty. He had me into his room and he explained. That they had all done their best for my boy on the facts as they knew them. It wasn't the law was at fault, he said, and he only had his job to do. Well, you can't blame the doctor if the patient has an accident at work, can you, Mr Rumpole?'

'Perhaps not but . . .'

'Hard cases make bad laws. He explained that to me, Mr Rumpole.' And then Mr Muschamp spoke with a tolerant smile. 'I'm in favour of hanging myself. It's what they need. Some of these young thugs . . .'

'Do you mean to tell me,' I emptied my glass before trying to catch the drift of the evidence, 'that you haunt old Truscott's court because you have such an enormous *admiration* for him?'

'Oh yes. It's a pleasure to me to see such a fair man in action. You admire him too, don't you, Mr Rumpole, if you're honest about it?'

'Admire him? No. If I'm honest about it, no.'

'Oh come,' Mr Muschamp took a delicate sip from the edge of his beer mug, 'I'm sure you do, otherwise you wouldn't have quarrelled with him so nicely.'

I went back to the Station Hotel (all the discomforts of all-night musical plumbing, deaf waiters and firewood in the mattresses) and soaked myself for a long time in a hot bath before catching a train back to London and She Who Must Be Obeyed. I wanted to be made clean of the memories of that extraordinary encounter; but what was it exactly that I was anxious to forget? Was it the humility that could pardon greater wrongs than I had ever suffered, or was it man's endless capacity to respect cruelty and injustice? Was it, perhaps, a revulsion at that forgiveness which is almost an insult to compassion? I turned the hot water tap with my great toe and did my best to wash away the grime of Grimble.

Great Aunt Allie's Flypapers

◆

P. D. JAMES

Commander Adam Dalgliesh is a shrewd, cultured, late middle-aged police detective whose mixture of physical presence and intuitive skills have helped him solve some of the most malicious, intriguing and hate-filled cases of murder in recent crime fiction. The accounts of his cases reveal Dalgliesh as a punctiliously bleak policeman who looks with a cool eye on death, and as a man who learned early in his career that it was those who people love most who cause them the most suffering. He invariably seems to expose pain during his enquiries and often encounters several people who could have committed the crime, each harbouring murderous desires and devices within them. The policeman's debut on television in 1983 in the seven-part mini-series based on Death of an Expert Witness *(which was set in the unlikely seeming locale of a forensic science laboratory) proved a triumph for both Anglia TV as well as the actor who played him, Roy Marsden, the former star of the series* Airline. *Although the novels featuring the dour detective already had a very considerable readership, the success of the series enormously enhanced his popularity and led to several further TV adaptations including* Shroud for a Nightingale *(1983),* Cover Her Face *(1985) and* The Black Tower *(1985).*

Baroness Phyllis Dorothy James (1920–), who was made a Life Peer in 1990, has been referred to as 'one of the Queens of Crime' and the natural successor to Agatha Christie. She has admitted to enjoying detective stories when she was a girl, and says that Dorothy L. Sayers was one of her influences. Although she won a prize for story writing when she was sixteen, the illness of her husband as a result of injuries he sustained during the Second World War precluded any ideas of a literary career and instead she worked in the civil service for forty

years, first in hospital administration and then at the Home Office, in
the police and forensic science departments. It was probably inevitable
that crime fiction should be P. D. James' chosen subject when she at
last had the time to write, introducing Adam Dalgliesh in 1962 in
Cover Her Face. *Her success since that time – and the fame of her*
detective – has been remarkable. Great Aunt Allie's Flypapers *is a*
rare short story featuring Dalgliesh which was first published in a
women's magazine in 1969, and its reappearance here will surely
delight all admirers of P. D. James' exceptional talent.

'YOU see, my dear Adam,' explained the Canon gently, as he
walked with Chief Superintendent Dalgliesh under the Vicarage
elms: 'Useful as the legacy would be to us, I wouldn't feel happy in
accepting it if Great Aunt Allie came by her money in the first place by
wrongful means.'

What the Canon meant was that he and his wife wouldn't be happy
to inherit Great Aunt Allie's fifty thousand pounds if, sixty-seven years
earlier, she had poisoned her elderly husband with arsenic in order to
get it. As Great Aunt Allie had been accused and acquitted of just that
charge in a 1902 trial which, for her Hampshire neighbours, had
rivalled the Coronation as a public spectacle, the Canon's scruples
were not altogether irrelevant. Admittedly, thought Dalgliesh, most
people faced with the prospect of fifty thousand pounds would be
happy to subscribe to the commonly held convention that, once an
English Court has pronounced its verdict, the final truth of the matter
had been established once and for all. There may possibly be a higher
judicature in the next world but hardly in this. And so Hubert Boxdale
would normally be happy to believe. But, faced with the prospect of an
unexpected fortune, his scrupulous conscience was troubled. The
gentle but obstinate voice went on:

'Apart from the moral principle of accepting tainted money, it
wouldn't bring us happiness. I often think of that poor woman, driven
restlessly round Europe in her search for peace, of that lonely life and
unhappy death.'

Dalgliesh recalled that Great Aunt Allie had moved in a predictable
pattern with her retinue of servants, current lover and general
hangers-on from one luxury Riviera hotel to the next, with stays in

Paris or Rome as the mood suited her. He was not sure that this orderly programme of comfort and entertainment could be described as being restlessly driven round Europe or that the old lady had been primarily in search of peace. She had died, he recalled, by falling overboard from a millionaire's yacht during a rather wild party given by him to celebrate her eighty-eighth birthday. It was perhaps not an edifying death by the Canon's standards, but Dalgliesh doubted whether she had, in fact, been unhappy at the time. Great Aunt Allie (it was impossible to think of her by any other name), if she had been capable of coherent thought, would probably have pronounced it a very good way to go.

But this was hardly a point of view he could put forward comfortably to his present companion.

Canon Hubert Boxdale was Superintendent Adam Dalgliesh's godfather. Dalgliesh's father had been his Oxford contemporary and life-long friend. He had been an admirable godfather: affectionate, uncensorious, genuinely concerned. In Dalgliesh's childhood, he had always been mindful of birthdays and imaginative about a small boy's pre-occupations and desires.

Dalgliesh was very fond of him and privately thought him one of the few really good men he had known. It was only surprising that the Canon had managed to live to seventy-one in a carnivorous world in which gentleness, humility and unworldliness are hardly conducive to survival, let alone success. But his goodness had in some sense protected him. Faced with such manifest innocence, even those who exploited him, and they were not a few, extended some of the protection and compassion they might show to the slightly subnormal.

'Poor old darling,' his daily woman would say, pocketing pay for six hours when she had worked five and helping herself to a couple of eggs from his refrigerator. 'He's really not fit to be let out alone.' It had surprised the then young and slightly priggish Detective Constable Dalgliesh to realize that the Canon knew perfectly well about the hours and the eggs, but thought that Mrs Copthorne, with five children and an indolent husband, needed both more than he did. He also knew that if he started paying for five hours she would promptly work only four and extract another two eggs, and that this small and only dishonesty was somehow necessary to her self-esteem. He was good. But he was not a fool.

He and his wife were, of course, poor. But they were not unhappy, indeed it was a word impossible to associate with the Canon. The death of his two sons in the 1939 war had saddened but not destroyed him. But he had anxieties. His wife was suffering from disseminated sclerosis and was finding it increasingly hard to manage. There were comforts and appliances which she would need. He was now, belatedly, about to retire and his pension would be small. A legacy of fifty thousand pounds would enable them both to live in comfort for the rest of their lives and would also, Dalgliesh had no doubt, give them the pleasure of doing more for their various lame dogs. Really, he thought, the Canon was an almost embarrassingly deserving candidate for a modest fortune. Why couldn't the dear, silly old noodle take the cash and stop worrying? He said cunningly: 'Great Aunt Allie was found not guilty, you know, by an English jury. And it all happened nearly seventy years ago. Couldn't you bring yourself to accept their verdict?'

But the Canon's scrupulous mind was totally impervious to such sly innuendos. Dalgliesh told himself that he should have remembered what, as a small boy, he had discovered about Uncle Hubert's conscience – that it operated as a warning bell and that, unlike most people, Uncle Hubert never pretended that it hadn't sounded or that he hadn't heard it or that, having heard it, something must be wrong with the mechanism.

'Oh, I did, while she was alive. We never met, you know. I didn't wish to force myself on her. After all, she was a wealthy woman. My grandfather made a new will on his marriage and left her all he possessed. Our ways of life were very different. But I usually wrote briefly at Christmas and she sent a card in reply. I wanted to keep some contact in case, one day, she might want someone to turn to, and would remember that I am a priest.'

And why should she want that, thought Dalgliesh. To clear her conscience? Was that what the dear old boy had in mind? So he must have had some doubts from the beginning. But of course he had; Dalgliesh knew something of the story, and the general feeling of the family and friends was that Great Aunt Allie had been extremely lucky to escape the gallows.

His own father's view, expressed with reticence, reluctance and compassion, had not in essentials differed from that given by a local reporter at the time.

'How on earth did she expect to get away with it? Damned lucky to escape topping if you ask me.'

'The news of the legacy came as a complete surprise?' asked Dalgliesh.

'Indeed, yes. I only saw her once at that first and only Christmas, six weeks after her marriage when my grandfather died. We always talk of her as Great Aunt Allie but in fact, as you know, she married my grandfather. But it seemed impossible to think of her as a step-grandmother.

'There was the usual family gathering at Colebrook Croft at the time I was there with my parents and my twin sisters. I was barely four and the twins were just eight months old. I can remember nothing of my grandfather or of his wife. After the murder – if one has to use that dreadful word – my mother returned home with us children, leaving my father to cope with the police, the solicitors and the newsmen. It was a terrible time for him. I don't think I was even told that my grandfather was dead until about a year later. My old nurse, Nellie, who had been given Christmas as a holiday to visit her own family, told me that, soon after my return home. I asked her if grandfather was now young and beautiful for always. She, poor woman, took it as a sign of infant prognostication and piety. Poor Nellie was sadly superstitious and sentimental, I'm afraid. But I knew nothing of Grandfather's death at the time and certainly can recall nothing of that Christmas visit or of my new step-grandmother. Mercifully, I was little more than a baby when the murder was done.'

'She was a music-hall artist, wasn't she?' asked Dalgliesh.

'Yes, and a very talented one. My grandfather met her when she was working with a partner in a hall in Cannes. He had gone to the South of France, with his manservant, for his health. I understood that she extracted a gold watch from his chain and, when he claimed it, told him that he was English, had recently suffered from a stomach ailment, had two sons and a daughter, and was about to have a wonderful surprise. It was all correct except that his only daughter had died in childbirth leaving him a granddaughter, Marguerite Goddard.'

'That was all easily guessable from Boxdale's voice and appearance,' said Dalgliesh. 'I can only suppose the surprise was the marriage?'

'It was certainly a surprise, and a most unpleasant one for the family. It is easy to deplore the snobbishness and the conventions of another age and, indeed, there was much in Edwardian England to deplore, but it was not a propitious marriage. I think of the difference in background, education and way of life, the lack of common interests. And there was the disparity of age. Grandfather had married a girl just three months younger than his own granddaughter. I cannot wonder that the family were concerned, that they felt that the union could not, in the end, contribute to the contentment or happiness of either party.'

And that was putting it charitably, thought Dalgliesh. The marriage certainly hadn't contributed to their happiness. From the point of view of the family, it had been a disaster. He recalled hearing of an incident when the local vicar and his wife, a couple who had actually dined at Colebrook Croft on the night of the murder, first called on the bride. Apparently old Augustus Boxdale had introduced her, saying: 'Meet the prettiest little variety artiste in the business. Took a gold watch and notecase off me without any trouble. Would have had the elastic out of my pants if I hadn't watched out. Anyway, she stole my heart, didn't you, sweetheart?'

All this was accompanied by a hearty slap on the rump and a squeal of delight from the lady who had promptly demonstrated her skill by extracting the Reverend Arthur Venables' bunch of keys from his left ear.

Dalgliesh thought it tactful not to remind the Canon of this story. 'What do you wish me to do, sir?' he enquired.

'It's asking a great deal I know when you're so busy. But if I had your assurance that you believed in Aunt Allie's innocence, I should feel happy about accepting the bequest. I wondered if it would be possible for you to see the records of the trial. Perhaps it would give you a clue. You're so clever at this sort of thing.'

He spoke without flattery but with an innocent wonder at the strange vocations of men. Dalgliesh was, indeed, very clever at this sort of thing. A dozen or so men at present occupying security wings in HM prisons could testify to Chief Superintendent Dalgliesh's cleverness as, indeed, could a handful of others walking free whose defending counsel had been in their own way as clever as Chief Superintendent Dalgliesh. But to re-examine a case over sixty years old seemed to require clairvoyance rather than cleverness. The trial judge and both learned counsels had been dead for over fifty years. Two world wars had taken their toll. Four reigns had passed. It was highly probable that, of those who had slept under the roof of Colebrook Croft on that fateful Boxing Day night of 1901, only the Canon still survived. But the old man was troubled and had sought his help, and Dalgliesh, with a day or two's leave due to him, had the time to give it.

'I'll do what I can,' he promised.

The transcript of a trial which had taken place sixty-seven years ago took time and trouble to obtain even for a Chief Superintendent of the Metropolitan Police. It provided little comfort for the Canon. Mr Justice Bellows had summed up with that avuncular simplicity with which he was wont to address juries, regarding them as a panel of well-intentioned but cretinous children. And the facts could have been

comprehended by any child. Part of the summing up set them out with
lucidity:

'And so, gentlemen of the jury, we come to the night of December
26th. Mr Augustus Boxdale, who had perhaps indulged a little
unwisely on Christmas Day, had retired to bed in his dressing room
after luncheon, suffering from a recurrence of the slight indigestive
trouble which had afflicted him for most of his life. You will have
heard that he had taken luncheon with the members of his family and
ate nothing which they, too, did not eat. You may feel you can acquit
luncheon of anything worse than over-richness.

'Dinner was served at eight pm promptly, as was the custom at
Colebrook Croft. There were present at that meal Mrs Augustus
Boxdale, the deceased's bride; his elder son Captain Maurice Boxdale
wit his wife; his younger son the Reverend Henry Boxdale, with his
wife; his granddaughter Miss Marguerite Goddard; and two neighbours, the Reverend and Mrs Arthur Venables.

'You have heard how the accused took only the first course at
dinner, which was ragout of beef, and then, at about eight-twenty, left
the dining room to sit with her husband. Shortly after nine o'clock she
rang for the parlour maid, Mary Huddy, and ordered a basin of gruel
to be brought up to Mr Boxdale. You have heard that the deceased was
fond of gruel, and indeed as prepared by Mrs Muncie, the cook, it
sounds a most nourishing dish for an elderly gentleman of weak
digestion.

'You have heard Mrs Muncie describe how she prepared the gruel
according to Mrs Beeton's admirable recipe and in the presence of
Mary Huddy in case, as she said, "The master should take a fancy to it
when I'm not at hand and you had to make it". After the gruel had
been prepared, Mrs Muncie tasted it with a spoon and Mary Huddy
carried it upstairs to the main bedroom together with a jug of water to
thin the gruel if it were too strong. As she reached the door, Mrs
Boxdale came out, her hands full of stockings and underclothes. She
has told you that she was on her way to the bathroom to wash them
through. She asked the girl to put the basin of gruel on the washstand
by the window and Mary Huddy did so in her presence. Miss Huddy
has told us that, at the time she noticed the bowl of fly papers soaking
in water and she knew that this solution was one used by Mrs Boxdale
as a cosmetic wash. Indeed, all the women who spent that evening in
the house, with the exception of Mrs Venables, have told you that they
knew that it was Mrs Boxdale's practice to prepare this solution of fly
papers.

'Mary Huddy and the accused left the bedroom together and you have heard the evidence of Mrs Muncie that Miss Huddy returned to the kitchen after an absence of only a few minutes. Shortly after nine o'clock, the ladies left the dining room and entered the drawing room to take coffee. At nine-fifteen pm, Miss Goddard excused herself to the company and said that she would go to see if her grandfather needed anything. The time is established precisely because the clock struck the quarter hour as she left and Mrs Venables commented on the sweetness of its chime. You have also heard Mrs Venables' evidence and the evidence of Mrs Maurice Boxdale and Mrs Henry Boxdale that none of the ladies left the drawing room during the evening, and Mr Venables has testified that the three gentlemen remained together until Miss Goddard appeared about three-quarters of an hour after to inform them that her grandfather had become very ill and to request that the doctor be sent for immediately.

'Miss Goddard has told you that, when she entered her grandfather's room, he was just finishing his gruel and was grumbling about its taste. She got the impression that this was merely a protest at being deprived of his dinner rather than that he genuinely considered that there was something wrong with the gruel. At any rate, he finished most of it and appeared to enjoy it despite his grumbles.

'You have heard Miss Goddard describe how, after her grandfather had had as much as he wanted of the gruel, she took the bowl next door and left it on the washstand. She then returned to her grandfather's bedroom and Mr Boxdale, his wife and his granddaughter played three-handed whist for about three-quarters of an hour.

'At ten o'clock Mr Augustus Boxdale complained of feeling very ill. He suffered from griping pains in the stomach, from sickness and from looseness of the bowels. As soon as the symptoms began Miss Goddard went downstairs to let her uncles know that her grandfather was worse and to ask that Doctor Eversley should be sent for urgently. Doctor Eversley has given you his evidence. He arrived at Colebrook Croft at ten-thirty pm when he found his patient very distressed and weak. He treated the symptoms and gave what relief he could but Mr Augustus Boxdale died shortly before midnight.

'Gentlemen of the jury, you have heard Marguerite Goddard describe how, as her grandfather's paroxysms increased in intensity, she remembered the gruel and wondered whether it could have disagreed with him in some way. She mentioned this possibility to her elder uncle, Captain Maurice Boxdale. Captain Boxdale has told you how he handed the bowl with its residue of gruel to Doctor Eversley with the request that the doctor should lock it in a cupboard in the library, seal the lock and keep the key. You have heard how the contents of the bowl were later analysed and with what results.'

An extraordinary precaution for the gallant captain to have taken, thought Dalgliesh, and a most perspicacious young woman. Was it by chance or by design that the bowl hadn't been taken down to be washed up as soon as the old man had finished with it? Why was it, he wondered, that Marguerite Goddard hadn't rung for the parlour maid and requested her to remove it? Miss Goddard appeared the only other suspect. He wished he knew more about her.

But, except for those main protagonists, the characters in the drama did not emerge very clearly from the trial report. Why, indeed, should they? The British accusatorial system of trial is designed to answer one question: is the accused guilty beyond reasonable doubt of the crime charged? Exploration of the nuances of personality, speculation and gossip have no place in the witness box. The two Boxdale brothers came out as very dull fellows indeed. They and their estimable, respectable sloping-bosomed wives had sat at dinner in full view of each other from eight until after nine o'clock (a substantial meal, that dinner) and had said so in the witness box, more or less in identical words. The ladies' bosoms might have been heaving with far from estimable emotions of dislike, envy, embarrassment or resentment of the interloper. If so, they didn't tell the court.

But the two brothers and their wives were clearly innocent, even if a detective of that time could have conceived of the guilt of a gentlefolk so well respected, so eminently respectable. Even their impeccable alibis had a nice touch of social and sexual distinction. The Rev. Arthur Venables had vouched for the gentlemen, his good wife for the ladies. Besides, what motive had they? They could no longer gain financially by the old man's death. If anything, it was in their interests to keep him alive in the hope that disillusion with his marriage or a return to sanity might occur to cause him to change his will. So far Dalgliesh had learned nothing that could cause him to give the Canon the assurance for which he hoped.

It was then that he remembered Aubrey Glatt. Glatt was a wealthy amateur criminologist who had made a study of all the notable Victorian and Edwardian poison cases. He was not interested in anything earlier or later, being as obsessively wedded to his period as any serious historian, which indeed he had some claim to call himself. He lived in a Georgian house in Winchester – his affection for the Victorian and Edwardian age did not extend to its architecture – and was only three miles from Colebrook Croft. A visit to the London

Library disclosed that he hadn't written a book on the case but it was improbable that he had totally neglected a crime close at hand and so in period. Dalgliesh had occasionally helped him with the technical details of police procedure. Glatt, in response to a telephone call, was happy to return the favour with the offer of afternoon tea and information.

Tea was served in his elegant drawing room by a parlour maid wearing a frilly cap with streamers. Dalgliesh wondered what wage Glatt paid her to persuade her to wear it. She looked as if she could have played a role in any of his favourite Victorian dreams and Dalgliesh had an uncomfortable thought that arsenic might be dispensed with the cucumber sandwiches. Glatt nibbled away and was expansive.

'It's interesting that you should have taken this sudden and, if I may say so, somewhat inexplicable interest in the Boxdale murder. I got out my notebook on the case only yesterday. Colebrook Croft is being demolished to make way for a new housing estate and I thought I would visit it for the last time. The family, of course, haven't lived there since the 1914–18 war. Architecturally, it's completely un-distinguished but one grieves to see it go. We might drive over after tea if you are agreeable.

'I never wrote my book on the case, you know. I planned a work entitled *The Colebrook Croft Mystery* or *Who Killed Augustus Boxdale?* But the answer was all too obvious.'

'No real mystery?' suggested Dalgliesh.

'Who else could it have been but Allegra Boxdale? She was born Allegra Porter, you know. Do you think her mother could have been thinking of Byron? I imagine not. There's a picture of her on page two of the notebook by the way, taken by a photographer in Cannes on her wedding day. I call it beauty and the beast.'

The old photograph had scarcely faded and Great Aunt Allie half-smiled at Dalgliesh across nearly seventy years. Her broad face with its wide mouth and rather snub nose was framed by two wings of dark hair swept high and topped, in the fashion of the day, by an immense flowered hat. The features were too coarse for real beauty but the eyes were magnificent, deep set and well spaced, and the chin round and determined. Beside this vital young Amazon poor Augustus Boxdale, clutching his bride as if for support, was but a very frail and under-sized beast. Their pose was unfortunate. She almost looked as if she were about to fling him over her shoulder.

Glatt shrugged. 'The face of a murderess? I've known less likely ones. Her Counsel suggested, of course, that the old man had poisoned his own gruel during the short time she left it on the washstand to cool while she visited the bathroom. But why should he? All the evidence suggests that he was in a state of post-nuptial euphoria, poor senile old booby. Our Augustus was in no hurry to leave this world, particularly by such an agonizing means. Besides, I doubt whether he even knew the gruel was there. He was in bed next door in his dressing room, remember.'

Dalgliesh asked: 'What about Marguerite Goddard? There's no evidence about the exact time when she entered the bedroom.'

'I thought you'd get on to that. She could have arrived while her step-grandmother was in the bathroom, poisoned the gruel, hidden herself either in the main bedroom or elsewhere until it had been taken in to Augustus, then joined her grandfather and his bride as if she had just come upstairs. It's possible, I admit. But it is unlikely. She was less inconvenienced than any of the family by her grandfather's second marriage. Her mother was Augustus Boxdale's eldest child who married, very young, a wealthy patent medicine manufacturer. She died in childbirth and the husband only survived her by a year. Marguerite Goddard was an heiress. She was also most advantageously engaged to Captain the Honourable John Brize-Lacey. Marguerite Goddard, young, beautiful, in possession of the Goddard fortune, not to mention the Goddard emeralds and the eldest son of a Lord, was hardly a serious suspect. In my view Defence Counsel, that was Roland Gort Lloyd, remember, was wise to leave her strictly alone.'

'A memorable defence, I believe.'

'Magnificent. There's no doubt Allegra Boxdale owed her life to Gort Lloyd. I know that concluding speech by heart:

' "Gentlemen of the Jury, I beseech you in the sacred name of Justice to consider what you are at. It is your responsibility, and yours alone, to decide the fate of this young woman. She stands before you now, young, vibrant, glowing with health, the years stretching before her with their promise and their hopes. It is in your power to cut off all this as you might top a nettle with one swish of your cane. To condemn her to the slow torture of those last waiting weeks; to that last dreadful walk; to heap calumny on her name; to desecrate those few happy weeks of marriage with the man who loved her so greatly; and to cast her into the final darkness of an ignominious grave.'

'Pause for dramatic effect. Then the crescendo in that magnificent voice. "And on what evidence gentlemen? I ask you." Another pause. Then the thunder. "On what evidence?" '

'A powerful defence,' said Dalgliesh. 'But I wonder how it would go down with a modern judge and jury.'

'Well, it went down very effectively with that 1902 jury. Of course, the abolition of capital punishment has rather cramped the more histrionic style. I'm not sure that the reference to topping nettles was in the best of taste. But the jury got the message. They decided that, on the whole, they preferred not to have the responsibility of sending the accused to the gallows. They were out six hours reaching their verdict and it was greeted with some applause. If any of those worthy citizens had been asked to wager five pounds of their own good money on her innocence, I suspect it would have been a different matter. Allegra Boxdale had helped him, of course. The Criminal Evidence Act, passed three years earlier, enabled him to put her in the witness box. She wasn't an actress of a kind for nothing. Somehow, she managed to persuade the jury that she had genuinely loved the old man.'

'Perhaps she had,' suggested Dalgliesh. 'I don't suppose there had been much kindness in her life. And he was kind.'

'No doubt, no doubt. But love!' Glatt was impatient. 'My dear Dalgliesh! He was a singularly ugly old man of sixty-nine. She was an attractive girl of twenty-one!'

Dalgliesh doubted whether love, that iconoclastic passion, was susceptible to this kind of simple arithmetic but he didn't argue. Glatt went on: 'The prosecution couldn't suggest any other romantic attachment. The police got in touch with her previous partner, of course. He was discovered to be a bald, undersized little man, sharp as a weasel, with a buxom wife and five children. He had moved down the coast after the partnership broke up and was now working with a new girl. He said regretfully that she was coming along nicely, thank you gentlemen, but would never be a patch on Allie and that, if Allie got her neck out of the noose and ever wanted a job, she knew where to come. It was obvious, even to the most suspicious policeman, that his interest was professional. As he said: "What was a grain or two of arsenic between friends?"

'The Boxdales had no luck after the trial. Captain Maurice Boxdale was killed in 1916 leaving no children, and the Reverend Edward lost his wife and their twin daughters in the 1918 influenza epidemic. He survived until 1932. The boy Hubert may still be alive, but I doubt it. That family always were a sickly lot.

'My greatest achievement, incidentally, was in tracing Marguerite Goddard. I hadn't realized that she was still alive. She never married Brize-Lacey or, indeed, anyone else. He distinguished himself in the 1914–18 war, came successfully through and eventually married an eminently suitable young woman, the sister of a brother officer. He inherited the title in 1925 and died in 1953. But Marguerite Goddard may be alive now for all I know. She may even be living in the same modest Bournemouth hotel where I found her. Not that my efforts in tracing her were rewarded. She absolutely refused to see me. That's the note that she sent out to me, by the way. Just there.'

It was meticulously pasted into the notebook in its chronological order and carefully annotated. Aubrey Glatt was a natural researcher; Dalgliesh couldn't help wondering whether this passion for accuracy might not have been more rewarding spent other than in the careful documentation of murder.

The note was handwritten in an elegant upright hand, the strokes black and very thin but clear and unwavering.

Miss Goddard presents her compliments to Mr Aubrey Glatt. She did not murder her grandfather and has neither the time nor the inclination to gratify his curiosity by discussing the person who did.

Aubrey Glatt said: 'After that extremely disobliging note, I felt there was really no point in going on with the book.'

Glatt's passion for Edwardian England obviously extended to a wider field than its murders and they drove to Colebrook Croft high above the green Hampshire lanes in an elegant 1910 Daimler. Aubrey wore a thin tweed coat and deerstalker hat and looked, Dalgliesh thought, rather like a Sherlock Holmes, with himself as attendant Watson.

'We are only just in time, my dear Dalgliesh,' he said when they arrived. 'The engines of destruction are assembled. That ball on the chain looks like the eyeball of God, ready to strike. Let us make our number with the attendant artisans. You will have no wish to trespass, will you?'

The work of demolition had not yet begun but the inside of the house had been stripped and plundered, the great rooms echoed to their footsteps like gaunt and deserted barracks after the final retreat. They moved from room to room, Glatt mourning the forgotten glories of an age he had been born too late to enjoy; Dalgliesh with his mind on the somewhat more immediate and practical concerns.

The design of the house was simple and formalized. The first floor, on which were most of the main bedrooms, had a long corridor running the whole length of the facade. The master bedroom was at the southern end with two large windows giving a distant view of Winchester Cathedral tower. A communicating door led to a small dressing room.

The main corridor had a row of four identical large windows. The brass curtain rods and wooden rings had been removed (they were collectors' items now) but the ornate carved pelmets were still in place. Here must have hung pairs of heavy curtains giving cover to anyone who wished to slip out of view. And Dalgliesh noted with interest that one of the windows was exactly opposite the door of the main bedroom. By the time they had left Colebrook Croft and Glatt had dropped him at Winchester Station, Dalgliesh was beginning to formulate a theory.

His next move was to trace Marguerite Goddard if she were still alive. It took him nearly a week of weary searching, a frustrating trail along the South Coast from hotel to hotel. Almost everywhere his enquiries were met with defensive hostility. It was the usual story of a very old lady who had become more demanding, arrogant and eccentric as her health and fortune waned; an unwelcome embarrassment to manager and fellow guests alike. The hotels were all modest, a few almost sordid. What, he wondered, had become of the legendary Goddard fortune?

From the last landlady he learned that Miss Goddard had become ill, really very sick indeed, and had been removed six months previously to the local district general hospital. And it was there that he found her.

The ward sister was surprisingly young, a petite, dark-haired girl with a tired face and challenging eyes.

'Miss Goddard is very ill. We've put her in one of the side wards. Are you a relative? If so, you're the first one who has bothered to call and you're lucky to be in time. When she is delirious she seems to expect a Captain Brize-Lacey to call. You're not he, are you?'

'Captain Brize-Lacey will not be calling. No, I'm not a relative. She doesn't even know me. But I would like to visit her if she's well enough and is willing to see me. Could you please give her this note.'

He couldn't force himself on a defenceless and dying woman. She still had the right to say no. He was afraid she would refuse him. And if she did, he might never learn the truth. He wrote four words on the back page of his diary, signed them, tore out the page, folded it and handed it to the Sister.

She was back very shortly.

'She'll see you. She's weak, of course, and very old, but she's perfectly lucid now. Only please don't tire her.'

'I'll try not to stay too long.'

The girl laughed: 'Don't worry. She'll throw you out soon enough if she gets bored. The chaplain and the Red Cross librarian have a terrible time with her. Third room on the left. There's a stool to sit on under the bed. We will ring the bell at the end of visiting time.'

She bustled off, leaving him to find his own way. The corridor was very quiet. At the far end he could glimpse through the open door of the main ward the regimented rows of beds, each with its pale blue coverlet, the bright glow of flowers on some of the tables, and the laden visitors making their way in pairs to each bedside. There was a faint buzz of welcome, a hum of conversation. But no one was visiting the side wards. Here, in the silence of the aseptic corridor, Dalgliesh could smell death.

The woman propped high against the pillows in the third room on the left no longer looked human. She lay rigidly, her long arms disposed like sticks on the coverlet. This was a skeleton clothed with a thin membrane of flesh beneath whose yellow transparency the tendons and veins were as plainly visible as an anatomist's model. She was nearly bald and the high-domed skull under its spare down of hair was as brittle and vulnerable as a child's. Only the eyes still held life, burning in their deep sockets with an animal vitality. But when she spoke her voice was distinctive and unwavering, evoking as her appearance never could the memory of imperious youth.

She took up his note and read aloud four words: 'It was the child. You are right, of course. The four-year-old Hubert Boxdale killed his grandfather. You signed this note Adam Dalgliesh. There was no Dalgliesh connected with the case.'

'I am a detective of the Metropolitan Police. But I'm not here in any official capacity. I have known about this case for a number of years from a dear friend. I have a natural curiosity to learn the truth. And I have formed a theory.'

'And now, like that poseur Aubrey Glatt, you want to write a book?'

'No. I shall tell no one. You have my promise.'

Her voice was ironic.

'Thank you. I am a dying woman, Mr Dalgliesh. I tell you that, not to invite your sympathy which it would be an impertinence for you to offer and which I neither want nor require, but to explain why it no longer matters to me what you say or do. But I, too, have a natural curiosity. Your note, cleverly, was intended to provoke it. I should like to know how you discovered the truth.'

Dalgliesh drew the visitors' stool from under the bed and sat down beside her. She did not look at him. The skeleton hands still holding his note did not move.

'Everyone in Colebrook Croft who could have killed Augustus Boxdale was accounted for, except the one person whom nobody considered, the small boy. He was an intelligent, articulate child. He was almost certainly left to his own devices. His nurse did not accompany the family to Colebrook Croft and the servants who were there over Christmas had extra work and also the care of the delicate twin girls. The boy probably spent much time with his grandfather and the new bride. She, too, was lonely and disregarded. He could have trotted around with her as she went about her various activities. He could have watched her making her arsenical face wash and, when he asked, as a child will, what it was for, could have been told "to make me young and beautiful". He loved his grandfather but he must have known that the old man was neither young nor beautiful. Suppose he woke up on that Boxing Day night overfed and excited after the Christmas activities? Suppose he went to Allegra Boxdale's room in search of comfort and companionship and saw there the basin of gruel and the arsenical mixture together on the washstand? Suppose he decided that here was something he could do for his grandfather?'

The voice from the bed said quietly:

'And suppose someone stood unnoticed in the doorway and watched him.'

'So you were behind the window curtains on the landing looking through the open door?'

'Of course. He knelt on the chair, two chubby hands clasping the bowl of poison, pouring it with infinite care into his grandfather's gruel. I watched while he replaced the linen cloth over the basin, got down from the chair, replaced it with careful art against the wall and trotted out into the corridor and back to the nursery. About three seconds later, Allegra came out of the bathroom and I watched while she carried the gruel in to my grandfather. A second later I went into the main bedroom. The bowl of poison had been a little heavy for Hubert's small hands to manage and I saw that a small pool had been spilt on the polished top of the washstand. I mopped it up with my handkerchief. Then I poured some of the water from the jug into the poison bowl to bring up the level. It only took a couple of seconds and I was ready to join Allegra and my grandfather in the bedroom and sit with him while he ate his gruel.

'I watched him die without pity and without remorse. I think I hated them both equally. The grandfather who had adored, petted and indulged me all through my childhood and deteriorated into this disgusting old lecher, unable to keep his hands off this woman even when I was in the room. He had rejected me and his family, jeopardized my engagement, made our name a laughing stock in the County, and all for a woman that my grandmother wouldn't have employed as a kitchen maid. I wanted them both dead. And they were both going to die. But it would be by other hands than mine. I could deceive myself that it wasn't my doing.'

Dalgliesh asked: 'When did she find out?'

'She knew that evening. When my grandfather's agony began she went outside for the jug of water. She wanted a cool cloth for his head. It was then that she noticed that the level of water in the jug had fallen and that a small pool of liquid on the washstand had been mopped up. I should have realized that she would have seen that pool. She had been trained to register every detail. She thought at the time that Mary Huddy had spilt some of the water when she set down the tray and the gruel. But who but I could have mopped it up? And why?'

'And when did she face you with the truth?'

'Not until after the trial. Allegra had magnificent courage. She knew what was at stake. But she also knew what she stood to gain. She gambled with her life for a fortune.'

And then Dalgliesh understood what had happened to the Goddard inheritance.

'So she made you pay?'

'Of course. Every penny. The Goddard fortune, the Goddard emeralds. She lived in luxury for sixty-seven years on my money. She ate and dressed on my money. When she moved with her lovers from hotel to hotel it was on my money. She paid them with my money. And if she has left anything, which I doubt, it is my money. My grandfather left very little. He had been senile and had let money run through his fingers like sand.'

'And your engagement?'

'It was broken, you could say by mutual consent. A marriage, Mr Dalgliesh, is like any other legal contract. It is most successful when both parties are convinced they have a bargain. Captain Brize-Lacey was sufficiently discouraged by the scandal of a murder in the family. He was a proud and highly conventional man. But that alone might have been accepted with the Goddard fortune and the Goddard emeralds to deodorize the bad smell. But the marriage couldn't have succeeded if he had discovered that he had married socially beneath him, into a family with a major scandal and no compensating fortune.'

Dalgliesh said: 'Once you had begun to pay you had no choice but to go on. I see that. But why did you pay? She could hardly have told her story. It would have meant involving the child.'

'Oh no! That wasn't her plan at all. She never meant to involve the child. She was a sentimental woman and she was fond of Hubert. No, she intended to accuse me of murder outright. Then, if I decided to tell the truth, how would it help me? After all, I wiped up the spilled liquid, I topped up the bowl. She had nothing to lose remember, neither life nor reputation. They couldn't try her twice. That's why she waited until after the trial. It made her secure for ever.

'But what of me? In the circles in which I moved at that time reputation was everything. She needed only to breathe the story in the ears of a few servants and I was finished. The truth can be remarkably tenacious. But it wasn't only reputation. I paid in the shadow of the gallows.'

Dalgliesh asked, 'But could she ever prove it?'

Suddenly she looked at him and gave an eerie screech of laughter. It tore at her throat until he thought the taut tendons would snap violently.

'Of course she could! You fool! Don't you understand? She took my handkerchief, the one I used to mop up the arsenic mixture. That was her profession, remember. Some time during that evening, perhaps when we were all crowding around the bed, two soft plump fingers insinuated themselves between the satin of my evening dress and my flesh and extracted that stained and damning piece of linen.'

She stretched out feebly towards the bedside locker. Dalgliesh saw what she wanted and pulled open the drawer. There on the top was a small square of very fine linen with a border of hand-stitched lace. He took it up. In the corner was her monogram delicately embroidered. And half of the handkerchief was still stiff and stained with brown.

She said: 'She left instructions with her solicitors that this was to be returned to me after her death. She always knew where I was. But now she's dead. And I shall soon follow. You may have the handkerchief, Mr Dalgliesh. It can be of no further use to either of us now.'

Dalgliesh put it in his pocket without speaking. As soon as possible he would see that it was burnt. But there was something else he had to say. 'Is there anything you would wish me to do? Is there anyone you want told, or to tell? Would you care to see a priest?'

Again there was that uncanny screech of laughter but softer now:

'There's nothing I can say to a priest. I only regret what I did because it wasn't successful. That is hardly the proper frame of mind for a good confession. But I bear her no ill will. One should be a good loser. But I've paid, Mr Dalgliesh. For sixty-seven years I've paid. And in this world, young man, the rich only pay once.'

She lay back as if suddenly exhausted. There was a silence for a moment. Then she said with sudden vigour: 'I believe your visit has done me good. I would be obliged if you'd return each afternoon for the next three days. I shan't trouble you after that.'

Dalgliesh extended his leave with some difficulty and stayed at a local inn. He saw her each afternoon. They never spoke again of the murder. And when he came punctually at two pm on the fourth day it was to be told that Miss Goddard had died peacefully in the night with apparently no trouble to anyone. She was, as she had said, a good loser.

A week later, Dalgliesh reported to the Canon.

'I was able to see a man who has made a detailed study of the case. I have read the transcript of the trial and visited Colebrook Croft. And I have seen one other person, closely connected with the case but who is now dead. I know you will want me to respect confidence and to say no more than I need.'

The Canon murmured his quiet assurance. Dalgliesh went on quickly.

'As a result I can give you my word that the verdict was a just verdict and that not one penny of your grandfather's fortune is coming to you through anyone's wrong doing.'

He turned his face away and gazed out of the window. There was a long silence. The old man was probably giving thanks in his own way. Then Dalgliesh was aware of his godfather speaking. Something was being said about gratitude, about the time he had given up to the investigation.

'Please don't misunderstand me, Adam. But when the formalities have been completed I should like to donate something to a charity named by you, one close to your heart.'

Dalgliesh smiled. His contributions to charity were impersonal; a quarterly obligation discharged by banker's order. The Canon obviously regarded charities as so many old clothes; all were friends but some fitted better and were consequently more affectionately regarded than others.

But inspiration came:

'It's good of you to think of it, Sir. I rather liked what I learned about Great Aunt Allie. It would be pleasant to give something in her name. Isn't there a society for the assistance of retired and indigent variety artists, conjurers and so on?'

The Canon, predictably, knew that there was and could name it.

Dalgliesh said: 'Then I think, Canon, that Great Aunt Allie would have agreed that a donation in her name would be entirely appropriate.'

Jemima Shaw at the Sunny Grave

❖

ANTONIA FRASER

Jemima Shore is a beautiful investigative reporter for Megalith Television whose enquiries have a habit of landing her in the midst of a crime. First brought into contact with the seamy side of life as a teenager when she exposed a drug running racket in a Catholic convent school, Jemima was never in any doubt that her future lay in television though the trail of criminals, blackmailers and murderers who have crossed her path over the years since then are not quite what she had expected. Jemima has a beguiling charm and a determined streak in her nature that can unravel clues in the most unlikely places and lull the guilty into a false sense of security. Her work is likely to take her into a dusty museum or to some exotic location abroad – but still crime seems to dog her footsteps. In Mrs Bancroft, her beloved but highly possessive cleaning lady, Jemima has a sensible, down-to-earth influence, and in Detective Chief Inspector J. H. Portsmouth – 'Pompey of the Yard' – a frequently invaluable friend in a tight corner. Thames Television launched their twelve, hour-long series, Jemima Shore Investigates, adapted from the novels by Antonia Fraser in 1983, and ensured the success of the productions by casting the strikingly attractive red-headed English actress Patricia Hodge in the title role.

Lady Antonia Fraser (1932–) was, of course, best known for her excellent children's books and historical biographies – including Mary Queen of Scots *(1969) which won the James Tait Black Memorial Prize for Biography – before she utilized her interest in the arts, crime fiction and television in the continuing series of tales about Jemima Shore. The story which follows also mixes these elements in a particularly puzzling case for the glamorous investigator . . .*

'THIS is your graveyard in the sun – ' The tall young man standing
in her path was singing the words lightly but clearly. It took
Jemima Shore a moment to realize exactly what message he was
intoning to the tune of the famous calypso. Then she stepped back. It
was a sinister and not particularly welcoming little parody.

>'This is my island in the sun
>Where my people have toiled since time begun – '

Ever since she had arrived in the Caribbean, she seemed to have had
the tune echoing in her ears. How old was it? How many years was it
since the inimitable Harry Belafonte had first implanted it in
everybody's consciousness? No matter. Whatever its age, the calypso
was still being sung today with charm, vigour, and a certain
relentnessness on Bow Island, and on the other West Indian islands she
had visited in the course of her journey.

It was not the only tune to be heard, of course. The loud noise of
music, she had discovered, was an inseparable part of Caribbean life,
starting with the airport. The heavy, irresistible beat of the steel band,
the honeyed wail of the singers; all this was happening somewhere if
not everywhere all over the islands late into the night: the joyous
sound of freedom, of dancing, of drinking (rum punch), and, for the
tourists at any rate, the sound of holiday.

It wasn't the sound of holiday for Jemima Shore, Investigator. Or
not officially so. That was all to the good, Jemima being one of those
people temperamentally whose best holidays combined some work
with a good deal of pleasure. She could hardly believe it when
Megalith Television, her employers, had agreed to a programme
which took her away from freezing Britain to the sunny Caribbean in
late January. This was a reversal of normal practice, by which Cy
Fredericks, Jemima's boss – and the effective boss of Megalith – was
generally to be found relaxing in the Caribbean in February while
Jemima herself, if she got there at all, was liable to be despatched there
in the inconvenient humidity of August. And it was a fascinating
project to boot. This was definitely her lucky year.

'This is my island in the sun – ' But what the young man facing her
had actually sung was 'your *graveyard* in the sun.' Hers? Or whose?

Since the man was standing between Jemima and the historic grave she had come to visit, it was possible that he was being proprietorial as well as aggressive. On second thoughts, surely not. It was a joke, a cheerful joke on a cheerful, very sunny day. But the young man's expression was, it seemed to her, more threatening than that.

Jemima gazed back with that special sweet smile so familiar to viewers of British television. (These same viewers were also aware from past experience that Jemima, sweet as her smile might be, stood no nonsense from anyone, at least not on her programme.) On closer inspection, the man was not really as young as all that. She saw someone of perhaps roughly her own age – early thirties. He was white, although so deeply tanned that she guessed he wasn't a tourist but one of the small loyal European population of Bow Island, a place fiercely proud of its recent independence from a much larger neighbour.

The stranger's height, unlike his youth, was not an illusion. He towered over Jemima and she herself was not short. He was also handsome, or would have been except for an oddly formed, rather large nose with a high bridge to it and a pronounced aquiline curve. But if the nose marred the regularity of his features, the impression left was not unattractive. He was wearing whitish cotton shorts, like more or less every male on Bow Island, black or white. His orange T-shirt bore the familiar island logo or crest: the outline of a bow in black and a black hand drawing it back. Beneath the logo was printed one of the enormous variety of local slogans – cheerful again – designed to make a play upon the island's name. This one read: THIS IS THE END OF THE SUN-BOW!

No, in that friendly T-shirt, he was surely not intending to be aggressive.

In that case, the odd thing about the whole encounter was that the stranger still stood absolutely still in Jemima's path. She could glimpse the large stone Archer Tomb just behind him, which she recognized from the postcards. For a smallish place, Bow Island was remarkably rich in historic relics. Nelson in his time had visited it with his fleet, for like its neighbours Bow Island had found itself engulfed in the Napoleonic Wars. Two hundred or so years before that, first British, then French, then British again had invaded and settled the island which had once belonged to Caribs, and before that Arawaks. Finally, into this melting pot, Africans had been brought forcibly to work the sugar plantations on which its wealth depended. All these elements in various degrees had gone to make up the people now known casually among themselves as the Bo'landers.

The Archer Tomb, the existence of which had in a sense brought Jemima across the Atlantic, belonged to the period of the second – and final – British settlement. Here was buried the most celebrated Governor in Bow Island's history, Sir Valentine Archer. Even its name commemorated his long reign. Bow Island had originally been called by the name of a saint, and while it was true the island was vaguely formed in the shape of a bow it was Governor Archer who had made the change: to signify ritually that this particular archer was in command of this particular bow.

Jemima knew that the monument, splendidly carved, would show Sir Valentine Archer with Isabella, his wife, beside him. This double stone bier was capped with a white wood structure reminiscent of a small church, done either to give the whole monument additional importance – although it must always have dominated the small churchyard by its sheer size – or to protect it from the weather. Jemima had read that there were no Archer children inscribed on the tomb, contrary to the usual Seventeenth Century practice. This was because, as a local historian delicately put it, Governor Archer had been as a parent to the entire island. Or in the words of another purely local calypso:

> 'Across the sea came old Sir Valentine –
> He came to be your daddy, and he came to be mine.'

In short, no one monument could comprise the progeny of a man popularly supposed to have sired over a hundred children, legitimate and illegitimate. The legitimate line was, however, now on the point of dying out. It was to see Miss Isabella Archer, officially at least the last of her race, that Jemima had come to the Caribbean. She hoped to make a programme about the old lady and her home, Archer Plantation House, alleged to be untouched in its decoration these fifty years. She wanted also to interview her generally about the changes Miss Archer had seen in her lifetime in this part of the world.

'Greg Harrison,' said the man standing in Jemima's path suddenly. 'And this is my sister, Coralie.' A girl who had been standing unnoticed by Jemima in the shade of the arched church porch stepped rather shyly forward. She, too, was extremely brown and her blonde hair, whitened almost to flax by the sun, was pulled back into a ponytail. His sister. Was there a resemblance? Coralie Harrison was wearing a similar orange T-shirt, but otherwise she was not much like her brother. She was quite short, for one thing, and her features were appealing rather than beautiful – and, perhaps fortunately, she lacked her brother's commanding nose.

'Welcome to Bow Island, Miss Shore,' she began. But her brother interrupted her. He put out a hand, large, muscular, and burnt to nut colour by the sun.

'I know why you're here and I don't like it,' said Greg Harrison. 'Stirring up forgotten things. Why don't you leave Miss Izzy to die in peace?' The contrast between his apparently friendly handshake and the hostile, if calmly spoken words was disconcerting.

'I'm Jemima Shore,' she said, though he obviously knew that. 'Am I going to be allowed to inspect the Archer Tomb? Or is it to be across your dead body?' Jemima smiled again with sweetness.

'*My* dead body!' Greg Harrison smiled back in his turn. The effect, however, was not particularly warming. 'Have you come armed to the teeth, then?' Before she could answer, he began to hum the famous calypso again. Jemima imagined the words: 'This is your graveyard in the sun.' Then he added: 'Might not be such a bad idea, that, when you start to dig up things that should be buried.'

Jemima decided it was time for action. Neatly sidestepping Greg Harrison, she marched firmly toward the Archer Tomb. There lay the carved couple. She read: 'Sacred to the memory of Sir Valentine Archer, first Governor of this island, and his only wife, Isabella, daughter of Randal Oxford, gentleman.' She was reminded briefly of her favourite Philip Larkin poem about the Arundel Monument, beginning, 'The Earl and Countess lie in stone – ' and ending, 'All that remains of us is love.'

But that couple lay a thousand miles away in the cloistered cool of Chichester Cathedral. Here the hot tropical sun burnt down on her naked head. She found she had taken off her large straw hat as a token of respect and quickly clapped it back on again. Here, too, in contrast to the very English-looking stone church with pointed Gothic windows beyond, there were palm trees among the graves instead of yews, their slender trunks bending like giraffes' necks in the breeze. She had once romantically laid white roses on the Arundel Monument. It was as the memory of the gesture returned to her that she spied the heap of bright pink and orange hibiscus blossoms lying on the stone before her. A shadow fell across it.

'Tina puts them there.' Greg Harrison had followed her. 'Every day she can manage it. Most days. Then she tells Miss Izzy what she's done. Touching, isn't it?' But he did not make it sound as if he found it especially touching. In fact, there was so much bitterness, even malevolence, in his voice that for a moment, standing as she was in the sunny graveyard, Jemima felt quite chilled. 'Or is it revolting?' he added, the malevolence now quite naked.

'Greg,' murmured Coralie Harrison faintly, as if in protest.

'Tina?' Jemima said. 'That's Miss Archer's – Miss Izzy's – companion. We've corresponded. For the moment I can't remember her other name.'

'She's known as Tina Archer these days, I think you'll find. When she wrote to you, she probably signed the letter Tina Harrison.' Harrison looked at Jemima sardonically but she had genuinely forgotten the surname of the companion – it was, after all, not a particularly uncommon one.

They were interrupted by a loud hail from the road. Jemima saw a young black man at the wheel of one of the convenient roofless minis everyone seemed to drive around Bow Island. He stood up and started to shout something.

'Greg! Cora! You coming on to –' She missed the rest of it – something about a boat and a fish. Coralie Harrison looked suddenly radiant, and for a moment even Greg Harrison actually looked properly pleased.

He waved back. 'Hey, Joseph. Come and say hello to Miss Jemima Shore of BBC Television!'

'Megalith Television,' Jemima interrupted, but in vain. Harrison continued: 'You heard, Joseph. She's making a programme about Miss Izzy.'

The man leapt gracefully out of the car and approached up the palm-lined path. Jemima saw that he, too, was extremely tall. And like the vast majority of the Bo'landers she had so far met, he had the air of being a natural athlete. Whatever the genetic mix in the past of Carib and African and other people that had produced them, the Bo'landers were certainly wonderful-looking. He kissed Coralie on both cheeks and patted her brother on the back.

'Miss Shore, meet Joseph –' but even before Greg Harrison had pronounced the surname, his mischievous expression had warned Jemima what it was likely to be '– Joseph Archer. Undoubtedly one of the ten thousand descendants of the philoprogenitive old gentleman at whose tomb you are so raptly gazing.' All that remains of us is love indeed, thought Jemima irreverently as she shook Joseph Archer's hand – with all due respect to Philip Larkin, it seemed that a good deal more remained of Sir Valentine than that.

'Oh, you'll find we're all called Archer round here,' murmured Joseph pleasantly. Unlike Greg Harrison, he appeared to be genuinely welcoming. 'As for Sir Val-en-tine –' he pronounced it syllable by syllable like the calypso '– don't pay too much attention to the stories.' Otherwise, how come we're not all living in that fine old Archer Plantation House?'

'Instead of merely my ex-wife. No, Coralie, don't protest. I could kill her for what she's doing.' Again Jemima felt a chill at the extent of the violence in Greg Harrison's voice. 'Come, Joseph, we'll see about that fish of yours. Come on, Coralie.' He strode off, unsmiling, accompanied by Joseph, who did smile. Coralie, however, stopped to ask Jemima if there was anything she could do for her. Her manner was still shy but in her brother's absence a great deal more friendly. Jemima also had the strong impression that Coralie Harrison wanted to communicate something to her, something she did not necessarily want her brother to hear.

'I could perhaps interpret, explain – ' Coralie stopped. Jemima said nothing. 'Certain things,' went on Coralie. 'There are so many layers in a place like this. Just because it's small, an outsider doesn't always understand – '

'And I'm the outsider? Of course I am.' Jemima had started to sketch the tomb for future reference, something for which she had a minor but useful talent. She forbore to observe truthfully, if platitudinously, that an outsider could also sometimes see local matters rather more clearly than those involved – she wanted to know what else Coralie had to say. Would she explain, for example, Greg's quite blatant dislike of his former wife?

But an impatient cry from her brother now in the car beside Joseph meant that Coralie for the time being had nothing more to add. She fled down the path and Jemima was left to ponder with renewed interest on her forthcoming visit to Isabella Archer of Archer Plantation House. It was a visit which would include, she took it, a meeting with Miss Archer's companion, who, like her employer, was currently dwelling in comfort there.

Comfort! Even from a distance, later that day, the square, low-built mansion had a comfortable air. More than that, it conveyed an impression of gracious and old-fashioned tranquillity. As Jemima drove her own rented mini up the long avenue of palm trees – much taller than those in the churchyard – she could fancy she was driving back in time to the days of Governor Archer, his copious banquets, parties, and balls, all served by black slaves.

At that moment, a young woman with coffee-coloured skin and short black curly hair appeared on the steps. Unlike the maids in Jemima's hotel who wore a pastiche of bygone servants' costume at dinner – brightly coloured dresses to the ankle, white-muslin aprons, and turbans – this girl was wearing an up-to-the-minute scarlet halter-top and cutaway shorts revealing most of her smooth brown legs. Tina Archer: for so she introduced herself.

It did not surprise Jemima Shore one bit to discover that Tina Archer – formerly Harrison – was easy to get on with. Anyone who left the hostile and graceless Greg Harrison was already ahead in Jemima's book. But with Tina Archer chatting away at her side, so chic and even trendy in her appearance, the revelation of the interior of the house was far more of a shock to her than it would otherwise have been. There was nothing, nothing at all, of the slightest modernity about it. Dust and cobwebs were not literally there perhaps, but they were suggested in its gloom, its heavy wooden furniture – where were the light cane chairs so suitable to the climate? – and above all in its desolation. Archer Plantation House reminded her of poor Miss Havisham's time-warp home in *Great Expectations*. And still worse, there was an atmosphere of sadness hanging over the whole interior. Or perhaps it was mere loneliness, a kind of sombre, sterile grandeur you felt must stretch back centuries.

All this was in violent contrast to the sunshine still brilliant in the late afternoon, the rioting bushes of brightly coloured tropical flowers outside. None of it had Jemima expected. Information garnered in London had led her to form quite a different picture of Archer Plantation House, something far more like her original impression, as she drove down the avenue of palm trees, of antique mellow grace.

Just as Jemima was adapting to this surprise, she discovered the figure of Miss Archer herself to be equally astonishing. That is to say, having adjusted rapidly from free and easy Tina to the mouldering, sombre house, she now had to adjust with equal rapidity all over again. For the very first inspection of the old lady, known by Jemima to be at least eighty, quickly banished all thoughts of Miss Havisham. Here was no aged, abandoned bride, forlorn in the decaying wedding-dress of fifty years before. Miss Izzy Archer was wearing a coolie straw hat, apparently tied under her chin with a duster, a loose white man's shirt, and faded blue jeans cut off at the knee. On her feet were a pair of what looked like child's brown sandals. From the look of her, she had either just taken a shower wearing all this or been swimming. She was dripping wet, making large pools on the rich carpet and dark, polished boards of the formal drawing room, all dark-red brocade and swagged, fringed curtains, where she had received Jemima. It was possible to see this even in the filtered light seeping through the heavy brown shutters which shut out the view of the sea.

'Oh, don't fuss so, Tina dear,' exclaimed Miss Izzy impatiently – although Tina had, in fact, said nothing. 'What do a few drops of water matter? Stains? What stains?' (Tina still had not spoken.) 'Let the government put it right when the time comes.'

Although Tina Archer continued to be silent, gazing amiably, even cheerfully, at her employer, nevertheless in some way she stiffened, froze in her polite listening attitude. Instinctively Jemima knew that she was in some way upset.

'Now don't be silly, Tina, don't take on, dear.' The old lady was now shaking herself free of water like a small but stout dog. 'You know what I mean. If you don't, who does – since half the time I don't know what I mean, let alone what I say. You can put it all right one day, is that better? After all, you'll have plenty of money to do it. You can afford a few new covers and carpets.' So saying, Miss Izzy, taking Jemima by the hand and attended by the still-silent Tina, led the way to the farthest dark-red sofa. Looking remarkably wet from top to toe, she sat down firmly in the middle of it.

It was in this way that Jemima first realized that Archer Plantation House would not necessarily pass to the newly independent government of Bow Island on its owner's death. Miss Izzy, if she had her way, was intending to leave it all, house and fortune, to Tina. Among other things, this meant that Jemima was no longer making a programme about a house destined shortly to be a national museum – which was very much part of the arrangement that had brought her to the island and had, incidentally, secured the friendly cooperation of that same new government. Was all this new? How new? Did the new government know? If the will had been signed, they must know.

'I've signed the will this morning, dear,' Miss Archer pronounced triumphantly, with an uncanny ability to answer unspoken questions. 'I went swimming to celebrate. I always celebrate things with a good swim – so much more healthy than rum or champagne. Although there's still plenty of *that* in the cellar.'

She paused. 'So there you are, aren't you, dear? Or there you will be. Here you will be. Thompson says there'll be trouble, of course. What can you expect these days? Everything is trouble since independence. Not that I'm against independence, far from it. But everything new brings new trouble here in addition to all the old troubles, so that the troubles get more and more. On Bow Island, no troubles ever go away. Why is that?'

But Miss Izzy did not stop for an answer. 'No, I'm all for independence and I shall tell you all about that, my dear' – she turned to Jemima and put one damp hand on her sleeve – 'on your programme. I'm being a Bo'lander born and bred, you know.' It was true that Miss Izzy, unlike Tina for example, spoke with the peculiar, slightly sing-song intonation of the islanders – not unattractive to Jemima's ears.

'I was born in this very house eighty-two years ago in April,' went on Miss Izzy. 'You shall come to my birthday party. I was born during a hurricane. A good start! But my mother died in childbirth, they should never have got in that new-fangled doctor, just because he came from England. A total fool he was, I remember him well. They should have had a good Bo'lander midwife, then my mother wouldn't have died and my father would have had sons – '

Miss Izzy was drifting away into a host of reminiscences – and while these were supposed to be what Jemima had come to hear, her thoughts were actually racing off in quite a different direction. Trouble? What trouble? Where did Greg Harrison, for example, stand in all this – Greg Harrison who wanted Miss Izzy to be left to 'die in peace?' Greg Harrison who had been married to Tina and was no longer? Tina Archer, now heiress to a fortune.

Above all, why was this forthright old lady intending to leave everything to her companion? For one thing, Jemima did not know how seriously to treat the matter of Tina's surname. Joseph Archer had laughed off the whole subject of Sir Valentine's innumerable descendants. But perhaps the beautiful Tina was in some special way connected to Miss Izzy. She might be the product of some rather more recent union between a rakish Archer and a Bo'lander maiden. More recent than the Seventeenth Century, that is.

Her attention was wrenched back to Miss Izzy's reminiscing monologue by the mention of the Archer Tomb.

'You've seen the grave? Tina has discovered it's all a fraud. A great big lie, lying under the sun – yes, Tina dear, you once said that. Sir Valentine Archer, my great great great – ' An infinite number of greats followed before Miss Izzy finally pronounced the word 'grandfather', but Jemima had to admit that she did seem to be counting. 'He had a great big lie perpetuated on his tombstone.'

'What Miss Izzy means – ' This was the first time Tina had spoken since they entered the darkened drawing room. She was still standing, while Jemima and Miss Izzy sat.

'Don't tell me what I mean, child,' rapped out the old lady; her tone was imperious rather than indulgent. Tina might for a moment have been a plantation worker two hundred years earlier rather than an independent-minded girl in the late Twentieth Century. 'It's the inscription which is a lie. She wasn't his only wife. The very inscription should have warned us. Tina wants to see justice done to poor little Lucie Anne and so do I. Independence indeed! I've been independent all my life and I'm certainly not stopping now. Tell me, Miss Shore, you're a clever young woman from television. Why do you bother to contradict something unless it's true all along? That's the way you work all the time in television, don't you?'

Jemima was wondering just how to answer this question diplomatically and without traducing her profession when Tina firmly, and this time successfully, took over from her employer.

'I read history at university in the UK, Jemima. Genealogical research is my speciality. I was helping Miss Izzy put her papers in order for the museum – or what was to be the museum. Then the request came for your programme and I began to dig a little deeper. That's how I found the marriage certificate. Old Sir Valentine *did* marry his young Carib mistress, known as Lucie Anne. Late in life – long after his first wife died. That's Lucie Anne who was the mother of his youngest two children. He was getting old, and for some reason he decided to marry her. The church, maybe. In its way, this has always been a God-fearing island. Perhaps Lucie Anne, who was very young and very beautiful, put pressure on the old man, using the church. At any rate, these last two children of all the hundreds he sired would have been legitimate!'

'And so?' questioned Jemima in her most encouraging manner.

'I'm descended from Lucie Anne – and Sir Valentine, of course.' Tina returned sweet smile for sweet smile. 'I've traced that, too, from the church records – not too difficult, given the strength of the church here. Not too difficult for an expert, at all events. Oh, I've got all sorts of blood, like most of us round here, including a Spanish grandmother and maybe some French blood, too. But the Archer descent is perfectly straightforward and clear.'

Tina seemed aware that Jemima was gazing at her with respect. Did she, however, understand the actual tenor of Jemima's thoughts? This is a formidable person, Jemima was reflecting. Charming, yes, but formidable. And ruthless, maybe, on occasion. Jemima was also, to be frank, wondering just how she was going to present this sudden change of angle in her programme on Megalith Television. On the one hand, it might now be seen as a romantic rags-to-riches story, the discovery of the lost heiress. On the other hand, just supposing Tina Archer was not so much an heiress as an adventuress? In that case, what would Megalith – what did Jemima Shore – make of a bright young woman putting across a load of false history on an innocent old lady? In those circumstances, Jemima could understand how the man by the sunny grave might display his contempt for Tina Archer.

'I met Greg Harrison by the Archer Tomb this morning,' Jemima commented deliberately. 'Your ex-husband, I take it.'

'Of course he's her ex-husband.' It was Miss Izzy who chose to answer. 'That no-good. Gregory Harrison has been a no-good since the day he was born. And that sister of his. Drifters. Not a job between them. Sailing. Fishing. As if the world owes them a living.'

'Half sister. Coralie is his half sister. And she works in a hotel boutique.' Tina spoke perfectly equably, but once again Jemima guessed that she was in some way put out. 'Greg is the no-good in that family.' For all her calm, there was a hint of suppressed anger in her reference to her former husband. With what bitterness that marriage must have ended!

'No-good, the pair of them. You're well out of that marriage, Tina dear,' exclaimed Miss Izzy. 'And do sit down, child – you're standing there like some kind of housekeeper. And where is Hazel, anyway? It's nearly half past five. It'll begin to get dark soon. We might go down to the terrace to watch the sun sink. Where is Henry? He ought to be bringing us some punch. The Archer Plantation punch, Miss Shore – wait till you taste it. One secret ingredient, my father always said – '

Miss Izzy was happily returning to the past.

'I'll get the punch,' said Tina, still on her feet. 'Didn't you say Hazel could have the day off? Her sister is getting married over at Tamarind Creek. Henry has taken her.'

'Then where's the boy? Where's what's-his-name? Little Joseph.' The old lady was beginning to sound petulant.

'There isn't a boy any longer,' explained Tina patiently. 'Just Hazel and Henry. As for Joseph – well, little Joseph Archer is quite grown up now, isn't he?'

'Of course he is! I didn't mean that Joseph – he came to see me the other day. Wasn't there another boy called Joseph? Perhaps that was before the war. My father had a stable boy – '

'I'll get the rum punch.' Tina vanished swiftly and gracefully.

'Pretty creature,' murmured Miss Izzy after her. 'Archer blood. It always shows. They do say the best-looking Bo'landers are still called Archer.'

But when Tina returned, the old lady's mood had changed again.

'I'm cold and damp,' she declared. 'I might get a chill sitting here. And soon I'm going to be all alone in the house. I hate being left alone. Ever since I was a little girl I've hated being alone. Everyone knows that. Tina, you have to stay to dinner. Miss Shore, you must stay, too. It's so lonely here by the sea. What happens if someone breaks in? – Don't frown, there are plenty of bad people about. That's one thing that hasn't gotten better since independence.'

'Of course I'm staying,' replied Tina easily. 'I've arranged it with

Hazel.' Jemima was wondering guiltily if she, too, ought to stay. But it was the night of her hotel's weekly party on the beach – barbecue followed by dancing to a steel band. Jemima, who loved to dance in the Northern Hemisphere, was longing to try it here. Dancing under the stars by the sea sounded idyllic. Did Miss Izzy really need extra company? Her eyes met those of Tina Archer across the old lady's strawhatted head. Tina shook her head slightly.

After a sip of the famous rum punch – whatever the secret ingredient, it was the strongest she had yet tasted on the island – Jemima was able to make her escape. In any case, the punch was having a manifestly relaxing effect on Miss Izzy herself. She became rapidly quite tipsy and Jemima wondered how long she would actually stay awake. The next time they met must be in the freshness of a morning.

Jemima drove away just as the enormous red sun was rushing down below the horizon. The beat of the waves from the shore pursued her. Archer Plantation House was set in a lonely position on its own spit of land at the end of its own long avenue. She could hardly blame Miss Izzy for not wanting to be abandoned there. Jemima listened to the sound of the waves until the very different noise of the steel band in the next village along the shore took over. That transferred her thoughts temporarily from recent events at Archer Plantation House to the prospect of her evening ahead. One way or another, for a brief space of time, she would stop thinking altogether about Miss Isabella Archer.

That was because the beach party was at first exactly what Jemima had expected – relaxed, good-natured, and noisy. She found her cares gradually floating away as she danced and danced again with a series of partners, English, American, and Bo'lander, to the beat of the steel band. That rum punch of Miss Izzy's, with its secret ingredient, must have been lethal because its effects seemed to stay with her for hours. She decided she didn't even need the generous profferings of the hotel mixture – a good deal weaker than Miss Izzy's beneath its lavish surface scattering of nutmeg. Others, however, decided that the hotel punch was exactly what they did need. All in all, it was already a very good party long before the sliver of the new moon became visible over the now-black waters of the Caribbean. Jemima, temporarily alone, tilted back her head as she stood by the lapping waves at the edge of the beach and fixed the moon in her sights.

'You going to wish on that new little moon?' She turned. A tall man – at least a head taller than she was – was standing beside her on the sand. She had not heard him, the gentle noise of the waves masking his approach. For a moment she didn't recognize Joseph Archer in his loose flowered shirt and long white trousers, so different did he look from the fisherman encountered that noon at the graveside.

In this way it came about that the second part of the beach party was quite unexpected, at least from Jemima's point of view.

'I ought to wish. I ought to wish to make a good programme, I suppose. That would be a good, professional thing to do.'

'Miss Izzy Archer and all that?'

'Miss Izzy, Archer Plantation House, Bow Island – to say nothing of the Archer Tomb, old Sir Valentine, and all that,' She decided not to mention Tina Archer and all that for the time being.

'All that!' He sighed. 'Listen, Jemima – it's good, this band. We're saying it's about the best on the island these days. Let's be dancing, shall we? Then you and me can talk about all that in the morning. In my office, you know.'

It was the distinct authority with which Joseph Archer spoke quite as much as the mention of his office which intrigued Jemima. Before she lost herself still further in the rhythm of the dance – which she had a feeling that with Joseph Archer to help her she was about to do – she must find out just what he meant. And, for that matter, just who he was.

The second question was easily answered. It also provided the answer to the first. Joseph Archer might or might not go fishing from time to time when he was off-duty, but he was also a member of the newly formed Bo'lander government. Quite an important one, in fact. Important in the eyes of the world in general, and particularly important in the eyes of Jemima Shore, Investigator. For Joseph Archer was the minister dealing with tourism, his brief extending to such matters as conservation, the Bo'lander historic heritage, and – as he described it to her – 'the future National Archer Plantation House Museum.'

Once again it didn't seem the appropriate moment to mention Tina Archer and her possible future ownership of the plantation house. As Joseph himself had said, the morning would do for all that. In his office in Bowtown.

They danced on for a while, and it was as Jemima had suspected it would be: something to lose herself in, perhaps dangerously so. The tune to 'This is my island in the sun' was played and Jemima never once heard the graveyard words in her imagination. Then Joseph Archer, most politely and apparently regretfully, said he had to leave. He had an extremely early appointment – and not with a fish, either, he added with a smile. Jemima felt a pang which she hoped didn't show. But there was plenty of time, wasn't there? There would be other nights and other parties, other nights on the beach as the moon waxed to full in the two weeks she had before she must return to England.

Jemima's personal party stopped, but the rest of the celebration went on late into the night, spilling onto the sands, even into the sea, long after the sliver of the moon had vanished. Jemima, sleeping fitfully and visited by dreams in which Joseph Archer, Tina, and Miss Izzy executed some kind of elaborate dance, not at all like the kind of island jump-up she had recently been enjoying, heard the noise in the distance.

Far away on Archer Plantation's lonely peninsula, the peace was broken not by a steel band but by the rough sound of the waves bashing against the rocks at its farthest point. A stranger might have been surprised to see that the lights were still on in the great drawing room, the shutters having been drawn back once the sun was gone, but nobody born on Bow Island – a fisherman out to sea, for example – would have found it at all odd. Everyone knew that Miss Izzy Archer was frightened of the dark and liked to go to bed with all her lights blazing. Especially when Hazel had gone to her sister's wedding and Henry had taken her there – another fact of island life which most Bo'landers would have known.

In her room overlooking the sea, tossing in the big four-poster bed in which she had been born over eighty years ago, Miss Izzy, like Jemima Shore, slept fitfully. After a while, she got out of bed and went to one of the long windows. Jemima would have found her nightclothes, like her swimming costume, bizarre, for Miss Izzy wasn't wearing the kind of formal Victorian nightdress which might have gone with the house. Rather, she was 'using up,' as she quaintly put it, her father's ancient burgundy-silk pyjamas, purchased many æons ago in Jermyn Street. And as the last Sir John Archer, Baronet, had been several feet taller than his plump little daughter, the long trouser legs trailed on the floor behind her.

Miss Issy continued to stare out of the window. Her gaze followed the direction of the terrace, which led in a series of parterres, once grandly planted, now overgrown, down to the rocks and the sea. Although the waters themselves were mostly blackness, the Caribbean night was not entirely dark. Besides, the light from the drawing-room windows streamed out onto the nearest terrace. Miss Izzy rubbed her eyes, then she turned back into the bedroom, where the celebrated oil painting of Sir Valentine hung over the mantelpiece dominated the room. Rather confusedly – she must have drunk far too much of that punch – she decided that her ancestor was trying to encourage her to be valiant in the face of danger for the first time in her life. She, little Isabella Archer, spoilt and petted Izzy, his last legitimate descendant – no, not his last legitimate descendant, but the habits of a lifetime were difficult to break – was being spurred on to something courageous by the hawklike gaze of the fierce old autocrat.

But I'm so old, thought Miss Izzy. Then: But not *too* old. Once you let people know you're not, after all, a coward –

She looked out of the window once more. The effects of the punch were wearing off. Now she was quite certain of what she was seeing. Something dark, darkly clad, dark-skinned – What did it matter, someone dark had come out of the sea and was now proceeding silently in the direction of the house.

I must be brave, thought Miss Izzy. She said aloud: 'Then he'll be proud of me. His brave girl.' Whose brave girl? No, not Sir Valentine's – Daddy's brave girl. Her thoughts began to float away again into the past. I wonder if Daddy will take me on a swim with him to celebrate?

Miss Izzy started to go downstairs. She had just reached the door of the drawing room and was standing looking into the decaying red-velvet interior, still brightly illuminated, at the moment when the black-clad intruder stepped into the room through the open window.

Even before the intruder began to move softly toward her, dark-gloved hands outstretched, Miss Izzy Archer knew without doubt in her rapidly beating old heart that Archer Plantation, the house in which she had been born, was also the house in which she was about to die.

'Miss Izzy Archer is dead. Some person went and killed her last night. A robber, maybe.' It was Joseph Archer who broke the news to Jemima the next morning.

He spoke across the broad desk of his formal office in Bowtown. His voice was hollow and distant, only the Bo'lander sing-song to connect him with Jemima's handsome dancing partner of the night before. In his short-sleeved but official-looking white shirt and dark trousers, he looked once again completely different from the cheerful ragged fisherman Jemima had first encountered. This was indeed the rising young Bo'lander politician she was seeing: a member of the newly formed government of Bow Island. Even the tragic fact of the death – the murder, as it seemed – of an old lady seemed to strike no chord of emotion in him.

Then Jemima looked again and saw what looked suspiciously like tears in Joseph Archer's eyes.

'I just heard myself, you know. The Chief of Police, Sandy Marlow, is my cousin.' He didn't attempt to brush away the tears. If that was what they were. But the words were presumably meant as an explanation. Of what? Of shock? Grief? Shock he must surely have experienced, but grief? Jemima decided at this point that she could at least inquire delicately about his precise relationship to Miss Izzy.

It came back to her that he had visited the old lady the week previously, if Miss Izzy's rather vague words concerning 'Little Joseph' were to be trusted. She was thinking not so much of a possible blood relationship as some other kind of connection. After all, Joseph Archer himself had dismissed the former idea in the graveyard. His words about Sir Valentine and his numerous progeny came back to her: 'Don't pay too much attention to the stories. Otherwise, how come we're not all living in that fine old Archer Plantation House?' At which Greg Harrison had commented with such fury: 'Instead of merely my ex-wife.' The exchange made more sense to her now, of course, that she knew of the position of Tina Harrison, now Tina Archer, in Miss Izzy's will.

The will! Tina would now inherit! And she would inherit in the light of a will signed the very morning of the day of Miss Izzy's death. Clearly, Joseph had been correct when he dismissed the claim of the many Bo'landers called Archer to be descended in any any meaningful fashion from Sir Valentine. There was already a considerable difference between Tina, the allegedly sole legitimate descendant other than Miss Izzy, and the rest of the Bo'lander Archers. In the future, with Tina come into her inheritance, the gap would widen even more.

It was extremely hot in Joseph's office. It was not so much that Bow Island was an unsophisticated place as that the persistent breeze made air-conditioning generally unnecessary. The North American tourists who were beginning to request air-conditioning in the hotels, reflected Jemima, would only succeed in ruining the most perfect kind of natural ventilation. But a government office in Bowtown was rather different. A huge fan in the ceiling made the papers on Joseph's desk stir uneasily. Jemima felt a ribbon of sweat trickle down beneath her long loose white T-shirt, which she had belted as a dress to provide some kind of formal attire to call on a Bo'lander minister in working hours.

By this time, Jemima's disbelieving numbness on the subject of Miss Izzy's murder was wearing off. She was struck by the frightful poignancy of that last encounter in the decaying grandeur of Archer

Plantation House. Worse still, the old lady's pathetic fear of loneliness
was beginning to haunt her. Miss Izzy had been so passionate in her
determination not to be abandoned. 'Ever since I was a little girl I've
hated being alone. Everyone knows that. It's so lonely here by the sea.
What happens if someone breaks in?'

Well, someone had broken in. Or so it was presumed. Joseph
Archer's words: 'A robber, maybe.' And this robber – maybe – had
killed the old lady in the process.

Jemima began hesitantly: 'I'm so sorry, Joseph. What a ghastly
tragedy! You knew her? Well, I suppose everyone round here must
have known her – '

'All the days of my life, since I was a little boy. My mama was one of
her maids. Just a little thing herself, and then she died. She's in that
churchyard, you know, in a corner. Miss Izzy was very good to me
when my mama died, oh, yes. She was kind. Now you'd think that
independence, *our* independence, would be hard for an old lady like
her, but Miss Izzy she just liked it very much. "England's no good to
me any more, Joseph," she said, "I'm a Bo'lander just like the rest of
you." '

'You saw her last week, I believe. Miss Izzy told me that herself.'

Joseph gazed at Jemima steadily – the emotion had vanished. 'I went
to talk with her, yes. She had some foolish idea of changing her mind
about things. Just a fancy, you know. But that's over. May she rest in
peace, little old Miss Izzy. We'll have our National Museum now,
that's for sure, and we'll remember her with it. It'll make a good
museum for our history. Didn't they tell you in London, Jemima?'
There was pride in his voice as he concluded: 'Miss Izzy left everything
in her will to the people of Bow Island.'

Jemima swallowed hard. Was it true? Or rather, was it still true?
Had Miss Izzy really signed a new will yesterday? She had been quite
circumstantial on the subject, mentioning someone called Thompson
– her lawyer, no doubt – who thought there would be 'trouble' as a
result. 'Joseph,' she said, 'Tina Archer was up at Archer Plantation
House yesterday afternoon, too.'

'Oh, that girl, the trouble she made, tried to make. Tina and her
stories and her fine education and her history. And she so pretty!'
Joseph's tone was momentarily violent but he finished more calmly.
'The police are waiting at the hospital. She's not speaking yet, she's not
even conscious.' Then even more calmly: 'She's not so pretty now, I
hear. That robber beat her, you see.'

It was hotter than ever in the Bowtown office and even the papers on
the desk were hardly stirring in the waft of the fan. Jemima saw

Joseph's face swimming before her. She absolutely must not faint – she never fainted. She concentrated desperately on what Joseph Archer was telling her, the picture he was recreating of the night of the murder. The shock of learning that Tina Archer had also been present in the house when Miss Izzy was killed was irrational, she realized that. Hadn't Tina promised the old lady she would stay with her?

Joseph was telling her that Miss Izzy's body had been found in the drawing room by the cook, Hazel, returning from her sister's wedding at first light. It was a grisly touch that because Miss Izzy was wearing red-silk pyjamas – her daddy's – and all the furnishings of the drawing room were dark-red as well, poor Hazel had not at first realized the extent of her mistress's injuries. Not only was there blood everywhere, there was water, too – pools of it. Whatever – whoever – had killed Miss Izzy had come out of the sea. Wearing rubber shoes – or flippers – and probably gloves as well.

A moment later, Hazel was in no doubt about what had hit Miss Izzy. The club, still stained with blood, had been left lying on the floor of the front hall. (She herself, deposited by Henry, had originally entered by the kitchen door.) The club, although not of Bo'lander manufacture, belonged to the house. It was a relic, African probably, of Sir John Archer's travels in other parts of the former British Empire, and hung heavy and short-handled on the drawing-room wall. Possibly Sir John had in mind to wield it against unlawful intruders but to Miss Izzy it had been simply one more family memento. She never touched it. Now it had killed her.

'No prints anywhere,' Joseph said. 'So far.'

'And Tina?' asked Jemima with dry lips. The idea of the pools of water stagnant on the floor of the drawing room mingled with Miss Izzy's blood reminded her only too vividly of the old lady when last seen – soaking wet in her bizarre swimming costume, defiantly sitting down on her own sofa.

'The robber ransacked the house. Even the cellar. The champagne cases Miss Izzy boasted about must have been too heavy, though. He drank some rum. The police don't know yet what he took – silver snuff-boxes maybe, there were plenty of those about.' Joseph sighed. 'Then he went upstairs.'

'And found Tina?'

'In one of the bedrooms. He didn't hit her with the same weapon – lucky for her, as he'd have killed her just like he killed Miss Izzy. He left that downstairs and picked up something a good deal lighter. Probably didn't reckon on seeing her or anyone there at all. 'Cept for Miss Izzy, that is. Tina must have surprised him. Maybe she woke up.

Robbers – well, all I can say is that robbers here don't generally go and kill people unless they're frightened.'

Without warning, Joseph slumped down in front of her and put his head in his hands. He murmured something like: 'When we find who did it to Miss Izzy – '

It wasn't until the next day that Tina Archer was able to speak even haltingly to the police. Like most of the rest of the Bow Island population, Jemima Shore was informed of the fact almost immediately. Claudette, manageress of her hotel, a sympathetic if loquacious character, just happened to have a niece who was a nurse. But that was the way information always spread about the island – no need for newspapers or radio, this private telegraph was far more efficient.

Jemima had spent the intervening twenty-four hours swimming rather aimlessly, sunbathing, and making little tours of the island in her mini. She was wondering at what point she should inform Megalith Television of the brutal way in which her projected programme had been terminated and make arrangements to return to London. After a bit, the investigative instinct, that inveterate curiosity which would not be stilled, came to the fore. She found she was speculating all the time about Miss Izzy's death. A robber? A robber who had also tried to kill Tina Archer? Or a robber who had merely been surprised by her presence in the house? What connection, if any, had all this with Miss Izzy's will?

The will again. But that was one thing Jemima didn't have to speculate about for very long. For Claudette, the manageress, also just happened to be married to the brother of Hazel, Miss Izzy's cook. In this way, Jemima was apprised – along with the rest of Bow Island, no doubt – that Miss Izzy had indeed signed a new will down in Bowtown on the morning of her death, that Eddie Thompson, the solicitor, had begged her not to do it, that Miss Izzy *had* done it, that Miss Izzy had still looked after Hazel all right, as she had promised (and Henry who had worked for her even longer), and that some jewellery would go to a cousin in England, 'seeing as Miss Izzy's mother's jewels were in an English bank anyway since long back.' But for the rest, well, there would be no National Bo'lander Museum now, that was for sure. Everything else – that fine old Archer Plantation House, Miss Izzy's fortune, reputedly enormous but who knew for sure? – would go to Tina Archer.

If she recovered, of course. But the latest cautious bulletin from Claudette via the niece-who-was-a-nurse, confirmed by a few other loquacious people on the island, was that Tina Archer *was* recovering. The police had already been able to interview her. In a few days she would be able to leave the hospital. And she was determined to attend Miss Izzy's funeral, which would be held, naturally enough, in that little English-looking church with its incongruous tropical vegetation overlooking the sunny grave. For Miss Izzy had long ago made clear her own determination to be buried in the Archer Tomb, along with Governor Sir Valentine and 'his only wife, Isabella.'

'As the last of the Archers. But she still had to get permission since it's a national monument. And of course the government couldn't do enough for her. So they gave it. Then. Ironic, isn't it?' The speaker making absolutely no attempt to conceal her disgust was Coralie Harrison. 'And now we learn that she wasn't the last of the Archers, not officially, and we shall have the so-called Miss Tina Archer as chief mourner. And while the Bo'lander government desperately looks for ways to get round the will and grab the house for their precious museum, nobody quite has the bad taste to go ahead and say no – no burial in the Archer Tomb for naughty old Miss Izzy. Since she hasn't, after all, left the people of Bow Island a penny.'

'It should be an interesting occasion,' Jemima murmured. She was sitting with Coralie Harrison under the conical thatched roof of the hotel's beach bar. This was where she first danced, then sat out with Joseph Archer on the night of the new moon – the night Miss Izzy had been killed. Now the sea sparkled under the sun as though there were crystals scattered on its surface. Today there were no waves at all and the happy water-skiers crossed and re-crossed the wide bay with its palm-fringed shore. Enormous brown pelicans perched on some stakes which indicated where rocks lay. Every now and then, one would take off like an unwieldy aeroplane and fly slowly and inquisitively over the heads of the swimmers. It was a tranquil, even an idyllic scene, but somewhere in the distant peninsula lay Archer Plantation House, not only shuttered but now, she imagined, also sealed by the police.

Coralie had sauntered up to the bar from the beach. She traversed the few yards with seeming casualness – all Bo'landers frequently exercised their right to promenade along the sands unchecked (as in most Caribbean islands, no one owned any portion of the beach in Bow Island, even outside the most stately mansion like Archer Plantation House, except the people). Jemima, however, was in no doubt that this was a planned visit. She had not forgotten that first meeting, and Coralie's tentative approach to her, interrupted by Greg's peremptory cry.

It was the day after the inquest on Miss Izzy's death. Her body had been released by the police and the funeral would soon follow. Jemima admitted to herself that she was interested enough in the whole Archer family, and its various branches, to want to attend it, quite apart from the tenderness she felt for the old lady herself, based on that brief meeting. To Megalith Television, in a telex from Bowtown, she had spoken merely of tying up a few loose ends resulting from the cancellation of her programme.

There had been an open verdict at the inquest. Tina Archer's evidence in a sworn statement had not really contributed much that wasn't known or suspected already. She had been asleep upstairs in one of the many fairly derelict bedrooms kept ostensibly ready for guests. The bedroom chosen for her by Miss Izzy had not faced onto the sea. The chintz curtains in this back room, bearing some dated rosy pattern from a remote era, weren't quite so bleached and tattered since they had been protected from the sun and salt.

Miss Izzy had gone to bed in good spirits, reassured by the fact that Tina Archer was going to spend the night. She had drunk several more rum punches and had offered to have Henry fetch some of her father's celebrated champagne from the cellar. As a matter of fact, Miss Izzy often made this offer after a few draughts of punch, but Tina reminded her that Henry was away and the subject was dropped.

In her statement, Tina said she had no clue as to what might have awakened the old lady and induced her to descend the stairs – it was right out of character in her own opinion. Isabella Archer was a lady of independent mind but notoriously frightened of the dark, hence Tina's presence at the house in the first place. As to her own recollection of the attack, Tina had so far managed to dredge very few of the details from her memory – the blow to the back of the head had temporarily or permanently expunged all the immediate circumstances from her consciousness. She had a vague idea that there had been a bright light, but even that was rather confused and might be part of the blow she had suffered. Basically, she could remember nothing between going to bed in the tattered, rose-patterned four-poster and waking up in hospital.

Coralie's lip trembled. She bowed her head and sipped at her long drink through a straw – she and Jemima were drinking some exotic mixture of fruit juice, alcohol free, invented by Matthew, the barman. There was a wonderful soft breeze coming in from the sea and Coralie was dressed in a loose flowered cotton dress, but she looked hot and angry. 'Tina schemed for everything all her life and now she's got it. That's what I wanted to warn you about that morning in the churchyard – don't trust Tina Archer, I wanted to say. Now it's too late, she's got it all. When she was married to Greg, I tried to like her, Jemima, honestly I did. Little Tina, so cute and so clever, but always trouble – '

'Joseph Archer feels rather the same way about her, I gather,' Jemima said. Was it her imagination or did Coralie's face soften slightly at the sound of Joseph's name?

'Does he? I'm glad. He fancied her, too, once upon a time. She is quite pretty.' Their eyes met. 'Well, not all that pretty, but if you like the type – ' Jemima and Coralie both laughed. The fact was that Coralie Harrison was quite appealing, if you liked *her* type, but Tina Archer was ravishing by any standards.

'Greg absolutely loathes her now, of course,' Coralie continued firmly, 'especially since he heard the news about the will. When we met you that morning up at the church he'd just been told. Hence, well, I'm sorry, but he was very rude, wasn't he?'

'More hostile than rude.' But Jemima had begun to work out the timing. 'You mean your brother knew about the will *before* Miss Izzy was killed?' she exclaimed.

'Oh, yes. Someone from Eddie Thompson's office told Greg – Daisy Marlow, maybe, he takes her out. Of course, we all knew it was on the cards, except we hoped Joseph had argued Miss Izzy out of it. And he *would* have argued her out of it given time. That museum is everything to Joseph.'

'Your brother and Miss Izzy – that wasn't an easy relationship, I gather.'

Jemima thought she was using her gentlest and most persuasive interviewer's voice, but Carolie countered with something like defiance: 'You sound like the police!'

'Why, have they – ?'

'Well, of course they have!' Coralie answered the question before Jemima had completed it. 'Everyone knows that Greg absolutely hated Miss Izzy – blamed her for breaking up his marriage, for taking little Tina and giving her ideas!'

'Wasn't it rather the other way around – Tina delving into the family records for the museum and then my programme? You *said* she was a schemer.'

'Oh, I *know* she was a schemer! But did Greg? He did not. Not then. He was besotted with her at the time, so he had to blame the old lady. They had a frightful row – very publicly. He went round to the house one night, went in by the sea, shouted at her. Hazel and Henry heard, so then everyone knew. That was when Tina told him she was going to get a divorce and throw in her lot with Miss Izzy for the future. I'm afraid my brother is rather an extreme person – his temper is certainly extreme. He made threats – '

'But the police don't think – ' Jemima stopped. It was clear what she meant.

Coralie swung her legs off the bar stool. Jemima handed her the huge straw bag with the archer logo on it and she slung it over her shoulder in proper Bo'lander fashion.

'How pretty,' Jemima commented politely.

'I sell them at the hotel on the North Point. For a living.' The remark sounded pointed. 'No,' Coralie went on rapidly before Jemima could say anything more on that subject, 'of course the police don't *think*, as you put it. Greg might have assaulted Tina – but Greg kill Miss Izzy when he knew perfectly well that by so doing he was handing his ex-wife a fortune? No way. Not even the Bo'lander police would believe that.'

That night Jemima Shore found Joseph Archer again on the beach under the stars. But the moon had waxed since their first encounter. Now it was beginning to cast a silver pathway on the waters of the night. Nor was this meeting unplanned as that first one had been. Joseph had sent her a message that he would be free and they had agreed to meet down by the bar.

'What do you say I'll take you on a night drive round our island, Jemima?'

'No. Let's be proper Bo'landers and walk along the sands.' Jemima wanted to be alone with him, not driving past the rows of lighted tourist hotels, listening to the eternal beat of the steel bands. She felt reckless enough not to care how Joseph himself would interpret this change of plan.

They walked for some time along the edge of the sea, in silence except for the gentle lap of the waves. After a while, Jemima took off her sandals and splashed through the warm receding waters, and a little while after that Joseph took her hand and led her back onto the sand. The waves grew conspicuously rougher as they rounded the point of the first wide bay. They stood for a moment together, Joseph and Jemima, he with his arm companionably around her waist.

'Jemima, even without that new moon, I'm going to wish – ' Then Joseph stiffened. He dropped the encircling arm, grabbed her shoulder, and swung her around. 'Jesus, oh sweet Jesus, do you see that?'

The force of his gesture made Jemima wince. For a moment she was distracted by the flickering moonlit swathe on the dark surface of the water. There were multitudinous white – silver – horses out beyond the land where high waves were breaking over an outcrop of rocks. She thought Joseph was pointing out to sea. Then she saw the lights.

'The Archer house!' she cried. 'I thought it was shut up!' It seemed that all the lights of the house were streaming out across the promontory on which it lay. Such was the illumination that you might have supposed some great ball was in progress, a thousand candles lit as in the days of Governor Archer. More sombrely, Jemima realized that was how the plantation house must have looked on the night of Miss Izzy's death. Tina Archer and others had borne witness to the old lady's insistence on never leaving her house in darkness. The night her murderer had come in from the sea, this is how the house must have looked to him.

'Come on!' said Joseph. The moment of lightness – or loving, perhaps? – had utterly vanished. He sounded both grim and determined.

'To the police?'

'No, to the house. I need to know what's happening there.'

As they half ran along the sands, Joseph said, 'This house should have been *ours*.'

Ours: the people of Bow Island.

His restlessness on the subject of the museum struck Jemima anew since her conversation with Coralie Harrison. What would a man – or a woman, for that matter – do for an inheritance? And there was more than one kind of inheritance. Wasn't a national heritage as important to some people as a personal inheritance to others? Joseph Archer was above all a patriotic Bo'lander. And he had not known of the change of will on the morning after Miss Izzy's death. She herself had evidence of that. Might a man like Joseph Archer, a man who had already risen in his own world by sheer determination, decide to take the law into his own hands in order to secure the museum for his people while there was still time?

But to kill the old lady who had befriended him as a boy? Batter her to death? As he strode along, so tall in the moonlight, Joseph was suddenly a complete and thus menacing enigma to Jemima.

They had reached the promontory, had scrambled up the rocks, and had got as far as the first terrace when all the lights in the house went out. It was as though a switch had been thrown. Only the cold eerie glow of the moon over the sea behind them remained to illuminate the bushes, now wildly overgrown, and the sagging balustrades.

But Joseph strode on, helping Jemima up the flights of stone steps, some of them deeply cracked and uneven. In the darkness, Jemima could just see that the windows of the drawing room were still open. There had to be someone in there behind the ragged red-brocade curtains which had been stained by Miss Izzy's blood.

Joseph, holding Jemima's hand, pulled her through the centre window.

There was a short cry like a suppressed scream and then a low sound, as if someone was laughing at them there in the dark. An instant later, all the lights were snapped on at once.

Tina was standing at the door, her hand at the switch. She wore a white bandage on her head like a turban – and she wasn't laughing, she was sobbing.

'Oh, it's you, Jo-seph and Je-mi-ma Shore.' For the first time, Jemima was aware of the sing-song Bo'lander note in Tina's voice. 'I was so fright-ened.'

'Are you all right, Tina?' asked Jemima hastily, to cover the fact that she had been quite severely frightened herself. The atmosphere of angry tension between the two other people in the room, so different in looks yet both of them, as it happened, called Archer, was almost palpable. She felt she was in honour bound to try to relieve it. 'Are you all alone?'

'The police said I could come.' Tina ignored the question. 'They have finished with everything here. And besides – ' her terrified sobs had vanished, there was something deliberately provocative about her as she moved toward them ' – why ever not?' To neither of them did she need to elaborate. The words 'since it's all mine' hung in the air.

Joseph spoke for the first time since they had entered the room. 'I want to look at the house,' he said harshly.

'Jo-seph Archer, you get out of here. Back where you came from, back to your off-ice and that's not a great fine house.' Then she addressed Jemima placatingly, in something more like her usual sweet manner. 'I'm sorry, but, you see, we've not been friends since way back. And, besides, you gave me such a shock.'

Joseph swung on his heel. 'I'll see you at the funeral, Miss Archer.' He managed to make the words sound extraordinarily threatening.

That night it seemed to Jemima Shore that she hardly slept, although the threads of broken, half remembered dreams disturbed her and indicated that she must actually have fallen into some kind of doze in the hour before dawn. The light was still grey when she looked out of her shutters. The tops of the tall palms were bending – there was quite a wind.

Back on her bed, Jemima tried to recall just what she had been dreaming. There had been some pattern to it: she knew there had. She wished rather angrily that light would suddenly break through into her sleepy mind as the sun was shortly due to break through the eastern fringe of palms on the hotel estate. No gentle, slow-developing, rosy-fingered dawn for the Caribbean: one brilliant low ray was a herald of what was to come, and then, almost immediately, hot relentless sunshine for the rest of the day. She needed that kind of instant clarity herself.

Hostility. That was part of it all – the nature of hostility. The hostility, for example, between Joseph and Tina Archer the night before, so virulent and public – with herself as the public – that it might almost have been managed for effect.

Then the management of things: Tina Archer, always managing, always a schemer (as Coralie Harrison had said – and Joseph Archer, too). That brought her to the other couple in this odd, four-pointed drama: the Harrisons, brother and sister, or rather *half* brother and sister (a point made by Tina to correct Miss Izzy).

More hostility: Greg, who had once loved Tina and now loathed her. Joseph, who had once also perhaps loved Tina. Coralie, who had once perhaps – very much perhaps, this one – loved Joseph and certainly loathed Tina. Cute and clever little Tina, the Archer Tomb, the carved figures of Sir Valentine and his wife, the inscription. Jemima was beginning to float back into sleep, as the four figures, all Bo'landers, all sharing some kind of common past, began to dance to a calypso whose wording, too, was confused:

> 'This is your graveyard in the sun
> Where my people have toiled since time begun – '

An extraordinarily loud noise on the corrugated metal roof above her head recalled her, trembling, to her senses. The racket had been quite immense, almost as if there had been an explosion or at least a missile fired at the chalet. The thought of a missile made her realize that it had in fact been a missile: it must have been a coconut which had fallen in such a startling fashion on the corrugated roof. Guests were officially warned by the hotel against sitting too close under the palm trees, whose innocuous-looking fronds could suddenly dispense their heavily lethal nuts. COCONUTS CAN CAUSE INJURY ran the printed notice.

That kind of blow on my head would certainly have caused injury thought Jemima, if not death.

Injury, if not death. And the Archer Tomb: my only wife.

At that moment, straight on cue, the sun struck low through the bending fronds to the east and onto her shutters. And Jemima realized not only why it had been done but how it had been done. Who of them all had been responsible for consigning Miss Izzy Archer to the graveyard in the sun.

The scene by the Archer Tomb a few hours later had that same strange mixture of English tradition and Bo'lander exoticism which had intrigued Jemima on her first visit. Only this time she had a deeper, sadder purpose than sheer tourism. Traditional English hymns were sung at the service, but outside a steel band was playing at Miss Izzy's request. As one who had been born on the island, she had asked for a proper Bo'lander funeral.

The Bo'landers, attending in large numbers, were by and large dressed with that extreme formality – dark suits, white shirts, ties, dark dresses, dark straw hats, even white gloves – which Jemima had observed in churchgoers of a Sunday and in the Bo'lander children, all of them neatly uniformed on their way to school. No Bow Island T-shirts were to be seen, although many of the highly coloured intricate and lavish wreaths were in the bow shape of the island's logo. The size of the crowd was undoubtedly a genuine mark of respect. Whatever the disappointments of the will to their government, to the Bo'landers Miss Izzy Archer had been part of their heritage.

Tina Archer wore a black scarf wound round her head which almost totally concealed her bandage. Joseph Archer, standing far apart from her and not looking in her direction, looked both elegant and formal in his office clothes, a respectable member of the government. The Harrisons stood together, Coralie with her head bowed. Greg's defiant aspect, head lifted proudly, was clearly intended to give the lie to any suggestions that he had not been on the best of terms with the woman whose body was now being lowered into the family tomb.

As the coffin – so small and thus so touching – vanished from view, there was a sigh from the mourners. They began to sing again: a hymn, but with the steel band gently echoing the tune in the background.

Jemima moved discreetly in the crowd and stood by the side of the tall man.

'You'll never be able to trust her,' she said in a low voice. 'She's managed you before, she'll manage you again. It'll be someone else who will be doing the dirty work next time. On you. You'll never be able to trust her, will you? Once a murderess, always a murderess. You may wish one day you'd finished her off.'

The tall man looked down at her. Then he looked across at Tina Archer with one quick savagely doubting look. Tina Archer Harrison, his only wife.

'Why you – ' For a moment, Jemima thought Greg Harrison would actually strike her down there at the graveside, as he had struck down old Miss Izzy and – if only on pretence – struck down Tina herself.

'Greg darling.' It was Coralie Harrison's pathetic, protesting murmur. 'What are you saying to him?' she demanded of Jemima in a voice as low as Jemima's own. But the explanations – for Coralie and the rest of Bow Island – of the conspiracy of Tina Archer and Greg Harrison were only just beginning.

The rest was up to the police, who with their patient work of investigation would first amplify, then press, finally concluding the case. And in the course of the investigations, the conspirators would fall apart, this time for real. To the police fell the unpleasant duty of disentangling the new lies of Tina Archer, who now swore that her memory had just returned, that it had been Greg who had half killed her that night, that she had had absolutely nothing to do with it. And Greg Harrison denounced Tina in return, this time with genuine ferocity. 'It was her plan, her plan all along. She managed everything. I should never have listened to her!'

Before she left Bow Island, Jemima went to say goodbye to Joseph Archer in his Bowtown office. There were many casualties of the Archer tragedy beyond Miss Izzy herself. Poor Coralie was one: she had been convinced that her brother, for all his notorious temper, would never batter down Miss Izzy to benefit his ex-wife. Like the rest of Bow Island, she was unaware of the deep plot by which Greg and Tina would publicly display their hostility, advertise their divorce, and all along plan to kill Miss Izzy once the new will was signed. Greg, ostentatiously hating his ex-wife, would not be suspected, and Tina, suffering such obvious injuries, could only arouse sympathy.

Another small casualty, much less important, was the romance which just might have developed between Joseph Archer and Jemima Shore. Now, in his steamingly hot office with its perpetually moving fan, they talked of quite other things than the new moon and new wishes.

'You must be happy you'll get your museum,' said Jemima.

'But that's not at all the way I wanted it to happen,' he replied. Then

Joseph added: 'But you know, Jemima, there has been justice done. And in her heart of hearts Miss Izzy did really want us to have this National Museum. I'd have talked her round to good sense again if she had lived.'

'That's why they acted when they did. They didn't dare wait, given Miss Izzy's respect for you,' suggested Jemima. She stopped, but her curiosity got the better of her. There was one thing she had to know before she left. 'The Archer Tomb and all that. Tina being descended from Sir Valentine's lawful second marriage. Is that true?'

'Yes, it's true. Maybe. But it's not important to most of us here. You know something, Jemima? I, too, am descended from that well known second marriage. Maybe. And a few others maybe. Lucie Anne had two children, don't forget, and Bo'landers have large families. It was important to Tina Archer, not to me. That's not what I want. That's all past. Miss Izzy was the last of the Archers, so far as I'm concerned. Let her lie in her tomb.'

'What *do* you want for yourself? Or for Bow Island, if you prefer.'

Joseph smiled and there was a glimmer there of the handsome fisherman who had welcomed her to Bow Island, the cheerful dancing partner. 'Come back to Bow Island one day, Jemima. Make another programme about us, our history and all that, and I'll tell you then.'

'I might just do that,' said Jemima Shore.

The Case of the Perfect Maid

◆

AGATHA CHRISTIE

Miss Marple, the archetypal English gentlewoman, is also probably the most famous female detective in literature, a gentle, almost frail-looking spinster lady with a deceiving fluster who flourishes on gossip and is no stranger to every kind of human evil. St Mary Mead where she lives is, on the surface, a typical English village – but beneath that surface fester all sorts of wrongdoing which from time to time demand Miss Marples' extraordinary intellect and years of study of human nature to resolve. Miss Marple has by now been adapted from the printed page into all the mediums of entertainment: starting with the radio in 1942 when she was featured in Armchair Detective, *and seven years later on the stage when Barbara Mullen (who would become famous as the housekeeper Janet McPherson in the TV series,* Dr Finlay's Casebook) *played her in* The Murder at the Vicarage. *On the screen, the redoubtable Margaret Rutherford created an enduring image of her as an eccentric lady of bustling energy and wobbling chins in a series of four pictures made between 1962 and 1964. Curiously, Miss Marple had already made her TV debut then – in America in 1956 when the weekly anthology show,* Goodyear Playhouse, *adapted* A Murder Is Announced, *with the astonishing piece of casting of Lancashire-born singer, Gracie Fields, in the lead role! Another member of the cast was a young man later to become famous playing The Saint and James Bond, Roger Moore. Two American actresses have subsequently appeared as the spinster sleuth on TV, Angela Lansbury and Helen Hayes, before Britain's veteran actress Joan Hickson began what is now regarded as the definitive portrayal in 1984 with the mini-series of* The Body in the Library. *Other adaptations have followed reaffirming the magic of both the original stories and Miss Hickson's performance.*

Agatha Christie (1890–1976), whose centenary was celebrated recently with a host of special events, once admitted that Miss Marple was based on her own grandmother, a very Victorian lady who possessed a knowledge of criminality that was the amazement of her granddaughter. In the sixteen novels and collections of short stories about Miss Marple, Agatha Christie created a character who lives and breathes on the printed page as much as she now does on the screen. In the following story, Miss Marple tackles a case in company with Detective Inspector Slack, a character who has proved extremely popular in the Joan Hickson series played by David Horovitch.

'OH, if you please, Madam, could I speak to you a moment?'
It might be thought that this request was in the nature of an absurdity, since Edna, Miss Marple's little maid, was actually speaking to her mistress at the moment.

Recognizing the idiom, however, Miss Marple said promptly, 'Certainly, Edna, come in and shut the door. What is it?'

Obediently shutting the door, Edna advanced into the room, pleated the corner of her apron between her fingers, and swallowed once or twice.

'Yes, Edna?' said Miss Marple encouragingly.

'Oh, please, Ma'am, It's my cousin, Gladdie.'

'Dear me,' said Miss Marple, her mind leaping to the worst – and, alas, the most usual conclusion. 'Not – not in trouble?'

Edna hastened to reassure her. 'Oh, no ma'am, nothing of that kind. Gladdie's not that kind of girl. It's just that she's upset. You see, she's lost her place.'

'Dear me, I am sorry to hear that. She was at Old Hall, wasn't she, with the Miss – Misses – Skinner?'

'Yes, ma'am, that's right, ma'am. And Gladdie's very upset about it – very upset indeed.'

'Gladys has changed places rather often before, though, hasn't she?'

'Oh, yes, ma'am. She's always one for a change, Gladdie is. She never seems to get really settled, if you know what I mean. But she's always been the one to give the notice, you see!'

'And this time it's the other way round?' asked Miss Marple dryly.

'Yes, ma'am, and it's upset Gladdie something awful.'

Miss Marple looked slightly surprised. Her recollection of Gladys, who had occasionally come to drink tea in the kitchen on her 'days out', was a stout, giggling girl of unshakably equable temperament.

Edna went on. 'You see, ma'am, it's the way it happened – the way Miss Skinner looked.'

'How,' inquired Miss Marple patiently, 'did Miss Skinner look?'

This time Edna got well away with her news bulletin.

'Oh, ma'am, it was ever such a shock to Gladdie. You see, one of Miss Emily's brooches was missing, and such a hue and cry for it as never was, and of course nobody likes a thing like that to happen; it's upsetting, ma'am, if you know what I mean. And Gladdie's helped search everywhere, and there was Miss Lavinia saying she was going to the police about it, and then it turned up again, pushed right to the back of a drawer in the dressing-table, and very thankful Gladdie was.

'And the very next day as ever was a plate got broken, and Miss Lavinia she bounced out right away and told Gladdie to take a month's notice. And what Gladdie feels is it couldn't have been the plate and that Miss Lavinia was just making an excuse of that, and that it must be because of the brooch and they think as she took it and put it back when the police was mentioned, and Gladdie wouldn't do such a thing, not never she wouldn't, and what she feels is as it will get round and tell against her and it's a very serious thing for a girl, as you know, ma'am.'

Miss Marple nodded. Though having no particular liking for the bouncing, self-opinioned Gladys, she was quite sure of the girl's intrinsic honesty and could well imagine that the affair must have upset her.

Edna said wistfully, 'I suppose, ma'am, there isn't anything you could do about it? Gladdie's in ever such a taking.'

'Tell her not to be silly,' said Miss Marple crisply. 'If she didn't take the brooch – which I'm sure she didn't – then she has no cause to be upset.'

'It'll get about,' said Edna dismally.

Miss Marple said, 'I – er – am going up that way this afternoon. I'll have word with the Misses Skinner.'

'Oh, thank you, madam,' said Edna.

Old Hall was a big Victorian house surrounded by woods and park land. Since it had been proved unlettable and unsalable as it was, an enterprising speculator had divided it into four flats with a central hot water system, and the use of 'the grounds' to be held in common by the tenants. The experiment had been satisfactory. A rich and eccentric old lady and her maid occupied one flat. The old lady had a passion for birds and entertained a feathered gathering to meals every day. A retired Indian judge and his wife rented a second. A very young couple, recently married, occupied the third, and the fourth had been taken only two months ago by two maiden ladies of the name of Skinner. The four sets of tenants were only on the most distant terms with each other, since none of them had anything in common. The landlord had been heard to say that this was an excellent thing. What he dreaded were friendships followed by estrangements and subsequent complaints to him.

Miss Marple was acquainted with all the tenants, though she knew none of them well. The elder Miss Skinner, Miss Lavinia, was what might be termed the working member of the firm. Miss Emily, the younger, spent most of her time in bed suffering from various complaints which, in the opinion of St Mary Mead, were largely imaginary. Only Miss Lavinia believed devoutly in her sister's martyrdom and patience under affliction, and willingly ran errands and trotted up and down to the village for things that 'my sister had suddenly fancied.'

It was the view of St Mary Mead that if Miss Emily suffered half as much as she said she did, she would have sent for Doctor Haydock long ago. But Miss Emily, when this was hinted to her, shut her eyes in a superior way and murmured that her case was not a simple one – the best specialists in London had been baffled by it – and that a wonderful new man had put her on a most revolutionary course of treatment and that she really hoped her health would improve under it. No humdrum GP could possibly understand her case.

'And it's my opinion,' said the outspoken Miss Hartnell, 'that she's very wise not to send for him. Dear Doctor Haydock, in that breezy manner of his, would tell her that there was nothing the matter with her and to get up and not make a fuss! Do her a lot of good!'

Failing such arbitrary treatment, however, Miss Emily continued to lie on sofas, to surround herself with strange little pill boxes, and to reject nearly everything that had been cooked for her and ask for something else – usually something difficult and inconvenient to get.

The door was opened to Miss Marple by 'Gladdie', looking more depressed than Miss Marple had ever thought possible. In the sitting-room (a quarter of the late drawing-room, which had been partitioned into a dining-room, drawing-room, bathroom, and housemaid's cupboard), Miss Lavinia rose to greet Miss Marple.

Lavinia Skinner was a tall, gaunt, bony female of fifty. She had a gruff voice and an abrupt manner.

'Nice to see you,' she said. 'Emily's lying down – feeling low today, poor dear. Hope she'll see you, it would cheer her up, but there are times when she doesn't feel up to seeing anybody. Poor dear, she's wonderfully patient.'

Miss Marple responded politely. Servants were the main topic of conversation in St Mary Mead, so it was not difficult to lead the conversation in that direction. Miss Marple said she had heard that that nice girl, Gladys Holmes, was leaving.

Miss Lavinia nodded. 'Wednesday week. Broke things, you know. Can't have that.'

Miss Marple sighed and said we all had to put up with things nowadays. It was so difficult to get girls to come to the country. Did Miss Skinner really think it was wise to part with Gladys?

'Know it's difficult to get servants,' admitted Miss Lavinia. 'The Devereuxs haven't got anybody – but then, I don't wonder – always quarrelling, jazz on all night – meals any time – that girl knows nothing of housekeeping. I pity her husband! Then the Larkins have just lost their maid. Of course, what with the judge's Indian temper and his wanting chota hazri, as he calls it, at six in the morning and Mrs Larkin always fussing, I don't wonder at that, either. Mrs Carmichael's Janet is a fixture, of course – though in my opinion she's the most disagreeable woman, and absolutely bullies the old lady.'

'Then don't you think you might reconsider your decision about Gladys? She really is a nice girl. I know all her family; very honest and superior.'

Miss Lavinia shook her head.

'I've got my reasons,' she said importantly.

Miss Marple murmured, 'You missed a brooch, I understand – '

'Now, who has been talking? I suppose the girl has. Quite frankly, I'm almost certain she took it. And then got frightened and put it back – but, of course, one can't say anything unless one is sure.' She changed the subject. 'Do come and see Miss Emily, Miss Marple. I'm sure it would do her good.'

Miss Marple followed meekly to where Miss Lavinia knocked on a door, was bidden enter, and ushered her guest into the best room in the flat, most of the light of which was excluded by half-drawn blinds. Miss Emily was lying in bed, apparently enjoying the half-gloom and her own indefinite sufferings.

The dim light showed her to be a thin, indecisive-looking creature, with a good deal of greyish-yellow hair untidily wound around her head and erupting into curls, the whole thing looking like a bird's nest of which no self-respecting bird could be proud. There was a smell in the room of Eau de Cologne, stale biscuits, and camphor.

With half-closed eyes and in a thin, weak voice, Emily Skinner explained that this was 'one of her bad days.'

'The worst of ill health is,' said Miss Emily in a melancholy tone, 'that one knows what a burden one is to everyone around one.

'Lavinia is very good to me. Lavvie dear, I do so hate giving trouble but if my hot-water bottle could only be filled in the way I like it – too full it weighs on me so – on the other hand, if it is not sufficiently filled, it gets cold immediately!'

'I'm sorry, dear. Give it to me. I will empty a little out.'

'Perhaps, if you're doing that, it might be refilled. There are no rusks in the house, I suppose – no, no, it doesn't matter. I can do without. Some weak tea and a slice of lemon – no lemons? No, really, I couldn't drink tea without lemon. I think the milk was slightly turned this morning. It has put me right against milk in my tea. It doesn't matter. I can do without my tea. Only I do feel so weak. Oysters, they say, are nourishing. I wonder if I could fancy a few? No, no, too much bother to get hold of them so late in the day. I can fast until tomorrow.'

Lavinia left the room murmuring something incoherent about bicycling down to the village.

Miss Emily smiled feebly at her guest and remarked that she did hate giving anyone any trouble.

Miss Marple told Edna that evening that she was afraid her embassy had met with no success.

She was rather troubled to find that rumours as to Gladys's dishonesty were already going around the village.

In the post office, Miss Wetherby tackled her, 'My dear Jane, they gave her a written reference saying she was willing and sober and respectable, but saying nothing about honesty. That seems to me most significant! I hear there was some trouble about a brooch. I think there must be something in it, you know, because one doesn't let a servant go nowadays unless it's something rather grave. They'll find it most difficult to get anyone else. Girls simply will not go to Old Hall. They're nervous coming home on their days out. You'll see, the Skinners won't find anyone else, and then, perhaps that dreadful hypochrondriac sister will have to get up and do something!'

Great was the chagrin of the village when it was made known that the Misses Skinner had engaged, from an agency, a new maid who, by all accounts, was a perfect paragon.

'A three years' reference recommending her most warmly, she

prefers the country, and actually asks less wages than Gladys. I really feel we have been most fortunate.'

'Well, really,' said Miss Marple, to whom these details were imparted by Miss Lavinia in the fishmonger's shop. 'It does seem too good to be true.'

It then became the opinion of St Mary Mead that the paragon would cry off at the last minute and fail to arrive.

None of these prognostications came true, however, and the village was able to observe the domestic treasure, by name, Mary Higgins, driving through the village in Reed's taxi to Old Hall. It had to be admitted that her appearance was good. A most respectable-looking woman, very neatly dressed.

When Miss Marple next visited Old Hall, on the occasion of recruiting stall-holders for the vicarage fete, Mary Higgins opened the door. She was certainly a most superior-looking maid, at a guess forty years of age, with neat black hair, rosy cheeks, a plump figure discreetly arrayed in black with a white apron and cap – 'quite the good, old-fashioned type of servant,' as Miss Marple explained afterward, and with the proper, inaudible, respectful voice, so different from the loud but adenoidal accents of Gladys.

Miss Lavinia was looking far less harassed than usual and, although she regretted that she could not take a stall owing to her preoccupation with her sister, she nevertheless tendered a handsome monetary contribution, and promised to produce a consignment of penwipers and babies' socks.

Miss Marple commented on her air of well-being.

'I really feel I owe a great deal to Mary. I am so thankful I had the resolution to get rid of that other girl. Mary is really invaluable. Cooks nicely and waits beautifully and keeps our little flat scrupulously clean – mattresses turned over every other day. And she is really wonderful with Emily!'

Miss Marple hastily inquired after Emily.

'Oh, poor dear, she has been very much under the weather lately. She can't help it, of course, but it really makes things a little difficult sometimes. Wanting certain things cooked and then, when they come, saying she can't eat now – and then wanting them again half an hour later and everything spoiled and having to be done again. It makes, of course, a lot of work – but fortunately Mary does not seem to mind at all. She's used to waiting on invalids, she says, and understands them. It is such a comfort.'

'Dear me,' said Miss Marple. 'You are fortunate.'

'Yes, indeed. I really feel Mary has been sent to us as an answer to prayer.'

'She sounds to me,' said Miss Marple, 'almost too good to be true. I should – well, I should be a little careful if I were you.'

Lavinia Skinner failed to perceive the point of this remark. She said, 'Oh! I assure you I do all I can to make her comfortable. I don't know what I should do if she left.'

'I don't expect she'll leave until she's ready to leave,' said Miss Marple and stared very hard at her hostess.

Miss Lavinia said, 'If one has no domestic worries, it takes such a load off one's mind, doesn't it? How is your little Edna shaping?'

'She's doing quite nicely. Not much ahead, of course. Not like your Mary. Still I do know all about Edna because she's a village girl.'

As she went out into the hall she heard the invalid's voice fretfully raised. 'This compress has been allowed to get quite dry – Doctor Allerton particularly said moisture continually renewed. There, there, leave it. I want a cup of tea and a boiled egg – boiled only three minutes and a half, remember, and send Miss Lavinia to me.'

The efficient Mary emerged from the bedroom and, saying to Lavinia, 'Miss Emily is asking for you, madam,' proceeded to open the door for Miss Marple, helping her into her coat and handing her her umbrella in the most irreproachable fashion.

Miss Marple took the umbrella, dropped it, tried to pick it up, and dropped her bag, which flew open. Mary politely retrieved various odds and ends – a handkerchief, an engagement book, an old-fashioned leather purse, two shillings, three pennies, and a striped piece of peppermint rock.

Miss Marple received the last with some signs of confusion.

'Oh, dear, that must have been Mrs Clement's little boy. He was sucking it, I remember, and he took my bag to play with. He must have put it inside. It's terribly sticky, isn't it?'

'Shall I take it, madam?'

'Oh, would you? Thank you so much.'

Mary stooped to retrieve the last item, a small mirror upon recovering which Miss Marple exclaimed fervently, 'How lucky, now, that that isn't broken.'

She thereupon departed, Mary standing politely by the door holding a piece of striped rock with a completely expressionless face.

For ten days longer St Mary Mead had to endure hearing of the excellencies of Miss Lavinia's and Miss Emily's treasure.

On the eleventh day, the village awoke to its big thrill.

Mary, the paragon, was missing! Her bed had not been slept in, and the front door was found ajar. She had slipped out quietly during the night.

And not Mary alone was missing! Two brooches and five rings of Miss Lavinia's; three rings, a pendant, a bracelet and four brooches of Miss Emily's were missing, also!

It was the beginning of a chapter of catastrophe.

Young Mrs Devereux had lost her diamonds which she kept in an unlocked drawer and also some valuable furs given to her as a wedding present. The judge and his wife also had had jewellery taken and a certain amount of money. Mrs Carmichael was the greatest sufferer. Not only had she some very valuable jewels but she also kept in the flat a large sum of money which had gone. It had been Janet's evening out, and her mistress was in the habit of walking round the gardens at dusk calling to the birds and scattering crumbs. It seemed clear that Mary, the perfect maid, had had keys to fit all the flats!

There was, it must be confessed, a certain amount of ill-natured pleasure in St Mary Mead. Miss Lavinia had boasted so much of her marvellous Mary.

'And all the time, my dear, just a common thief!'

Interesting revelations followed. Not only had Mary disappeared into the blue, but the agency who had provided her and vouched for her credentials was alarmed to find that the Mary Higgins who had applied to them and whose references they had taken up had, to all intents and purposes, never existed. It was the name of a bona fide servant who had lived with a bona fide sister of a dean, but the real Mary Higgins was existing peacefully in a place in Cornwall.

'Damned clever, the whole thing,' Inspector Slack was forced to admit. 'And, if you ask me, that woman works in with a gang. There was a case of much the same kind in Northumberland a year ago. Stuff was never traced, and they never caught her. However, we'll do better than that in Much Benham!'

Inspector Slack was always a confident man.

Nevertheless, weeks passed, and Mary Higgins remained triumphantly at large. In vain Inspector Slack redoubled that energy that so belied his name.

Miss Lavinia remained tearful. Miss Emily was so upset, and felt so alarmed by her condition that she actually sent for Doctor Haydock.

The whole of the village was terribly anxious to know what he thought of Miss Emily's claims to ill health, but naturally could not ask him. Satisfactory data came to hand on the subject, however, through Mr Meek, the chemist's assistant, who was walking out with

Clara, Mrs Price-Ridley's maid. It was then known that Doctor Haydock had prescribed a mixture of asafoetida and valerian which, according to Mr Meek, was the stock remedy for malingerers in the army!

Soon afterwards it was learned that Miss Emily, not relishing the medical attention she had had, was declaring that in the state of her health she felt it her duty to be near the specialist in London who understood her case. It was, she said, only fair to Lavinia.

The flat was put up for subletting.

It was a few days after that that Miss Marple, rather pink and flustered, called at the police station in Much Benham and asked for Inspector Slack.

Inspector Slack did not like Miss Marple. But he was aware that the chief constable, Colonel Melchett, did not share that opinion. Rather grudgingly, therefore, he received her.

'Good afternoon, Miss Marple, what can I do for you?'

'Oh, dear,' said Miss Marple, 'I'm afraid you're in a hurry.'

'Lots of work on,' said Inspector Slack, 'but I can spare a few moments.'

'Oh, dear,' said Miss Marple. 'I hope I shall be able to put what I say properly. So difficult, you know, to explain oneself, don't you think? No, perhaps you don't. But you see, not having been educated in the modern style – just a governess, you know, who taught one the dates of the kings of England and general knowledge – Doctor Brewer – three kinds of diseases of wheat – blight, mildew – now what was the third – was it smut?'

'Do you want to talk about smut?' asked Inspector Slack and then blushed.

'Oh, no, no.' Miss Marple hastily disclaimed any wish to talk about smut. 'Just an illustration, you know. And how needles are made, and all that. Discursive, you know, but not teaching one to keep to the point. Which is what I want to do. It's about Miss Skinner's maid, Gladys, you know.'

'Mary Higgins,' said Inspector Slack.

'Oh, yes, the second maid. But it's Gladys Holmes I mean – rather an impertinent girl and far too pleased with herself but really strictly honest, and it's so important that that should be recognized.'

'No charge against her so far as I know,' said the Inspector.

'No, I know there isn't a charge – but that makes it worse. Because, you see, people go on thinking things. Oh, dear – I knew I should explain badly. What I really mean is that the important thing is to find Mary Higgins.'

'Certainly,' said Inspector Slack. 'Have you any ideas on the subject?'

'Well, as a matter of fact, I have,' said Miss Marple. 'May I ask you a question? Are fingerprints of no use to you?'

'Ah,' said Inspector Slack, 'that's where she was a bit too artful for us. Did most of her work in rubber gloves or housemaid's gloves, it seems. And she'd been careful – wiped off everything in her bedroom and on the sink. Couldn't find a single fingerprint in the place!'

'If you did have her fingerprints, would it help?'

'It might, madam. They may be known at the Yard. This isn't her first job, I'd say!'

Miss Marple nodded brightly. She opened her bag and extracted a small cardboard box. Inside it, wedged in cotton wool, was a small mirror.

'From my handbag,' said Miss Marple. 'The maid's prints are on it. I think they should be satisfactory – she touched an extremely sticky substance a moment previously.'

Inspector Slack stared. 'Did you get her fingerprints on purpose?'

'Of course.'

'You suspected her then?'

'Well, you know it did strike me that she was a little too good to be true. I practically told Miss Lavinia so. But she simply wouldn't take the hint! I'm afraid, you know, Inspector, that I don't believe in paragons. Most of us have our faults – and domestic service shows them up very quickly!'

'Well,' said Inspector Slack, recovering his balance, 'I'm obliged to you, I'm sure. We'll send these up to the Yard and see what they have to say.'

He stopped. Miss Marple had put her head a little on one side and was regarding him with a good deal of meaning.

'You wouldn't consider, I suppose, Inspector, looking a little nearer home?'

'What do you mean, Miss Marple?'

'It's very difficult to explain, but when you come across a peculiar thing you notice it. Although, often, peculiar things may be the merest trifles. I've felt that all along, you know; I mean about Gladys and the brooch. She's an honest girl; she didn't take that brooch. Then why did Miss Skinner think she did? Miss Skinner's not a fool; far from it! Why was she so anxious to let a girl go who was a good servant when servants are hard to get? It was peculiar, you know. So I wondered. I wondered a good deal. And I noticed another peculiar thing! Miss Emily's a hypochondriac, but she's the first hypochondriac who hasn't sent for some doctor or other at once. Hypochrondriacs love doctors. Miss Emily didn't!'

'What are you suggesting, Miss Marple?'

'Well, I'm suggesting, you know, that Miss Lavinia and Miss Emily are peculiar people. Miss Emily spends nearly all her time in a dark room. And if that hair of hers isn't a wig, I – I'll eat my own back switch! And what I say is this – it's perfectly possible for a thin, pale, grey-haired, whining woman to be the same as a black-haired, rosy-cheeked, plump woman. And nobody that I can find ever saw Miss Emily and Mary Higgins at one and the same time.

'Plenty of time to get impressions of all the keys, plenty of time to find out all about the other tenants, and then – get rid of the local girl. Miss Emily takes a brisk walk across country one night and arrives at the station as Mary Higgins next day. And then, at the right moment, Mary Higgins disappears, and off goes the hue and cry after her. I'll tell you where you'll find her, Inspector. On Miss Emily Skinner's sofa! Get her fingerprints if you don't believe me, but you'll find I'm right! A couple of clever thieves, that's what the Skinners are – and no doubt in league with a clever post and rails or fence or whatever you call it. But they won't get away with it this time! I'm not going to have one of our village girl's character for honesty taken away like that! Gladys Holmes is as honest as the day, and everybody's going to know it! Good afternoon!'

Miss Marple had stalked out before Inspector Slack had recovered.

'Whew!' he muttered. 'I wonder if she's right?'

He soon found out that Miss Marple was right again.

Colonel Melchett congratulated Slack on his efficiency, and Miss Marple had Gladys come to tea with Edna and spoke to her seriously on settling down in a good situation when she got one.

The Snapdragon and the C.I.D.

◆

MARGERY ALLINGHAM

Albert Campion is another of the pre-War detectives initially seen as a 'silly ass' whose pleasant smile and owl-like glasses mask an intrepid nature and investigative mind. The son of an aristocratic family, Campion began his early years as an amateur detective posing as a conman under the unlikely aliases of Tootles Ash or Mornington Dodd apparently to confuse the criminal fraternity – but soon abandoned this modus operandi to adopt the personality of a self-assured investigator ever ready to help those who found themselves in trouble and sought him out at his flat near Piccadilly Circus. He is often aided in his enquiries by his Cockney valet, Magersfontein Lugg, a reformed criminal, and Inspector Stanislaus Oates of Scotland Yard, whose successful association with Campion assists his own rise in the ranks of the police force. Like Miss Marple, Albert Campion made his radio debut in Armchair Detective *in the mid-Forties, but although a film was made in 1956 of one of the books in which he appears,* Tiger in the Smoke, *starring Donald Sinden, his character was completely omitted! The sleuth had, in fact, to wait until 1988 to be featured on television in the BBC series,* Campion, *with the former* All Creatures Great And Small *and* Dr Who *star, Peter Davison, in the lead role. Andrew Burt made a similarly excellent Inspector Oates and Brian Glover co-starred as Lugg.*

Margery Allingham (1904–1966) is often listed with Dorothy L. Sayers and Agatha Christie as one of the 'Queens of Crime', though her early career was devoted to journalism and historical novels in the footsteps of her father, the successful editor of The New London Journal, *who encouraged her undoubted talent. Her first crime stories were contributions to the long-running Sexton Blake saga, and it was in 1929 that she introduced Campion in* The Crime at Black Dudley, *which was followed by a further twenty-seven novels and collections of stories. A number of tales featuring the versatile Campion were, though, left uncollected at the time of Miss Allingham's death, of which the following, with Inspector Oates playing an important role, is one of the best.*

'MURDER under the mistletoe – and the man who must have done it couldn't have done it. That's my Christmas and I don't feel merry, thank you very much all the same.' Superintendent Stanislaus Oates favoured his old friend Mr Albert Campion with a pained smile and sat down in the chair indicated.

It was the afternoon of Christmas Day and Mr Campion, only a trifle more owlish than usual behind his horn-rims, had been fetched down from the children's party which he was attending at his brother-in-law's house in Knightsbridge to meet the Superintendent who had moved heaven and earth to find him.

'What do you want?' Mr Campion inquired facetiously. 'A little pocket conjuring?'

'I don't care if you do it swinging from a trapeze. I just want a reasonable explanation.' Oates was rattled. His dyspeptic face with the perpetually sad expression was slightly flushed and not with festivity. He plunged into his story.

'About eleven last night a crook called Sampson was found shot dead in the back of a car in a garage under a small drinking club in Alcatraz Mews, named the Humdinger. A large bunch of mistletoe which had been lying on the front seat ready to be driven home, had been placed on top of the body partially hiding it – which was why it hadn't been found before. The gun, fitted with a silencer, but wiped of prints, was found under the front seat. The dead man was recognized at once by the owner of the car who is also the owner of the club. He was her current boy friend. She is quite a well-known West End character called "Girlski". What did you say?'

'I said "Oe-er",' murmured Mr Campion. 'One of the Eumenides, no doubt?'

'No.' Oates spoke innocently. 'She's not a Greek. Don't worry about her. Just keep your mind on the facts. She knows, as we do, that the only person who wanted to kill Sampson is a nasty little snake called Krait. He has been out of circulation for the best of reasons. Sampson turned Queen's evidence against him in a matter concerning a conspiracy to rob Her Majesty's mails and when he was released last Tuesday he came out breathing retribution.'

'Not the Christmas spirit,' said Mr Campion inanely.

'That is exactly what *we* thought,' Oates agreed. 'So about five o'clock yesterday afternoon two of our chaps, hearing that he was at the Humdinger where he might have been expected to make trouble, dropped along there and brought him in "to help our inquiries" and he's been in ever since. Well, now. We have at least a dozen reasonably sober witnesses to prove that Krait did not meet Sampson at the club. Sampson had been there earlier in the afternoon but he left about a quarter to four saying he'd got to do some shopping but promising to return. Fifteen minutes or so later Krait came in and stayed there in full view of Girlski and the customers until our ministering angels turned up and collected him. Now what do you say?'

'Too easy.' Mr Campion was suspicious. 'Krait killed Sampson just before he came in himself. The two met in the dusk outside the club. Krait forced Sampson into the garage and possibly into the car and shot him out of hand. With the way the traffic has been lately he'd hardly have attracted attention had he used a mortar let alone a gun with a silencer. He wiped the weapon, chucked it in the car, threw the mistletoe over the corpse and went up to Girlski and the rest to renew old acquaintance and establish an alibi. Your chaps, arriving when they did, must have appeared welcome.'

Oates nodded. 'We thought that. That *is* what happened. That is why this morning's development has set me gibbering. We have now two unimpeachable witnesses who swear that the dead man was in Chipperwood West at six last evening delivering some Christmas purchases he had made on behalf of a neighbour. That is a whole hour after Krait was put under arrest. The assumption is that Sampson returned to Alcatraz Mews some time later in the evening and was killed by someone else – which I do not believe. Unfortunately the Chipperwood West witnesses are not the kind of people we are going to shake. One of them is a friend of yours. She asked our Inspector if he knew you because you were "so good at crime and all that nonsense".'

'Good Heavens!' Mr Campion spoke piously as the explanation of the Superintendent's unlikely visitation was made plain to him. 'I don't think I know Chipperwood West.'

'It's a suburb which is becoming fashionable. Have you ever heard of Lady Larradine?'

'Old Lady 'ell?' Mr Campion let the joke of his salad days escape without being noticed by either of them. 'I don't believe it. She must be dead by this time!'

'There's a type of woman who never dies before you do,' said Oates with apparent sincerity. 'She's quite a dragon I understand from our Inspector. However, she isn't the actual witness. There are two of them. Brigadier Brose is one. Ever heard of him?'

'I don't think I have.'

'My information is that you'd remember him if you'd met him. We'll find out. I'm taking you with me, Campion. I hope you don't mind?'

'My sister will hate it. I'm due to be Father Christmas in about an hour.'

'I can't help that.' Oates was adamant. 'If a bunch of silly crooks want to get spiteful at the festive season someone must do the homework. Come and play Father Christmas with me. It's your last chance. I'm retiring in the summer.'

He continued in the same vein as they sat in the back of a police car threading their way through the deserted Christmas streets where the lamps were growing bright in the dusk.

'I've had bad luck lately,' he said seriously. 'Too much. It won't help my memoirs if I go out in a blaze of no-enthusiasm.'

'You're thinking of the Phaeton robbery,' Mr Campion suggested. 'What are you calling the memoirs? *Man-eaters of the Yard*?'

Oates's mild old eyes brightened but not greatly. 'Something of the kind,' he admitted. 'But no one could be blamed for not solving that blessed Phaeton business. Everyone concerned was bonkers. A silly old musical star, for thirty years the widow of an eccentric Duke, steps out into her London garden one autumn morning leaving the street door wide open and all her most valuable jewellery, collected from strongrooms all over the country, lying in a brown paper parcel on her bureau in the first room off the hall. Her excuse was that she was just going to take it to the Bond Street auctioneers and was carrying it herself for safety! The thief was equally mental to lift it.'

'It wasn't saleable?'

'Saleable! It couldn't even be broken up. The stuff is just about as well-known as the Crown Jewels. Great big enamels which the old Duke had collected at great expense. No fence would stay in the same room with them, yet, of course, they are worth the earth as every newspaper has told us at length ever since they were pinched!'

'He didn't get anything else either, did he?'

'He was a madman.' Oates dismissed him with contempt. 'All he gained was the old lady's housekeeping money for a couple of months which was in her handbag – about a hundred and fifty quid – and the other two items which were on the same shelf, a soapstone monkey and a plated paper-knife. He simply wandered in, took the first things he happened to see and wandered out again. Any sneak thief, tramp or casual snapper-upper could have done it and who gets blamed? Me!'

He looked so woebegone that Mr Campion changed the subject hastily. 'Where are we going?' he inquired. 'To call on her ladyship? Do I understand that at the age of one hundred and forty-six or whatever it is she is cohabiting with a Brig? Which war?'

'I can't tell you,' Oates was literal as usual. 'It could be the South African. They're all in a nice residential hotel. It's the sort of place that is very popular with the older members of the landed gentry just now.'

'When you say "landed" you mean as in Fish?'

'Roughly, yes. Elderly people, living on capital. About forty of them. This place used to be called "The Haven" and has now been taken over by two ex-society widows and renamed "The Ccraven" with two Cs. It's a select hotel-cum-Old-Ducks' Home for "Mother's Friends". You know the sort of place?'

'I can envisage it. Don't say your murdered chum from the Humdinger lived there too?'

'No, he lived in a more modest outfit whose garden backs on the Ccraven's grounds. The Brigadier and one of the other residents, a Mr Charlie Taunton who has become a bosom friend of his, were in the habit of talking to Sampson over the wall. Taunton is a lazy man who seldom goes out and has little money but he very much wanted to get some gifts for his fellow guests – something in the nature of little jokes from the chain stores, I understand – but he dreaded the exertion of shopping for them and Sampson appears to have offered to get him some little items wholesale and to deliver them by six o'clock on Christmas Eve in time for him to package them up and hand them to Lady Larradine who was dressing the tree at seven.'

'And you say that Sampson actually did this?' Mr Campion sounded bewildered.

'Both old gentlemen swear to it. They insist they went down to the wall at six and Sampson handed the parcel over as arranged. My Inspector is an experienced man and he doesn't think we shall shake either of them.'

'That leaves Krait with a complete alibi. How did these Chipperwood witnesses hear of Sampson's death?'

'Routine. The local police called at Sampson's home address this morning to report the death only to discover the place closed. The landlady and her family are away for the holiday and Sampson himself was due to spend it with Girlski. The police stamped about a bit no doubt, making sure of all this and in the course of their investigations they were seen and hailed by the two old boys in the other garden. The two were shocked to hear that their kind acquaintance was dead and volunteered the information that he was with them at six.'

Mr Campion looked blank. 'Perhaps they don't keep the same hours as anybody else,' he suggested. 'Old people can be highly eccentric.'

Oates shook his head. 'We thought of that. My Inspector, who came down the moment the local police reported, insists that they are perfectly normal and quite positive. Moreover, they had the purchases. He saw the packages already on the tree. Lady Larradine pointed them out to him when she asked after you. She'll be delighted to see you, Campion.'

'I can hardly wait!'

'You don't have to,' said Oates grimly as they pulled up before a huge Edwardian villa. 'It's all yours.'

'My dear boy! You haven't aged any more than I have!' Lady Larradine's tremendous voice, one of her chief terrors as he recollected, echoed over the crowded first-floor room where she received them. There she stood in an outmoded but glittering evening gown looking as always, exactly like a spray-flecked seal. 'I knew you'd come,' she bellowed. 'As soon as you got my oblique little SOS. How do you like our little hideout? Isn't it *fun*! Moira Spryg-Fysher and Janice Poole-Poole wanted something to do so we all put our pennies in it and here we are!'

'Almost too marvellous,' murmured Mr Campion in all sincerity. 'We really want a word with Brigadier Brose and Mr Taunton.'

'Of course you do and so you shall! We're all waiting for the Christmas tree. Everybody will be there for that in about ten minutes in the drawing-room. My dear, when we came they were calling it the Residents' Lounge!'

Superintendent Oates remained grave. He was startled to discover that the Dragon was not only fierce but also wily. The news that her apparently casual mention of Mr Campion to the Inspector had been a ruse to get hold of him shocked the innocent policeman. He retaliated by insisting that he must see the witnesses at once. Lady Larradine silenced him with a friendly roar. 'My dear man, you can't. They've gone for a walk. I always turn men out of the house after Christmas luncheon. They'll soon be back. The Brigadier won't miss his Tree!

Ah. Here's Fiona. This is Janice Poole-Poole's daughter, Albert. Isn't she a pretty girl?'

Mr Campion saw Miss Poole-Poole with relief knowing of old that Oates was susceptible to the type. The newcomer was young and lovely and even her back-combed hair-do and the fact that she appeared to have painted herself two black eyes failed to spoil the exquisite smile she bestowed on the helpless officer.

'Fabulous to have you really here,' she said and sounded as if she really meant it. While he was still recovering Lady Larradine led him to the window.

'You can't see it because it's pitch dark,' she said, 'but out there, down the garden, there's a wall and it was over it that the Brigadier and Mr Taunton spoke to Mr Sampson at six o'clock last night. No one liked the man Sampson. I think poor Mr Taunton was almost afraid of him. Certainly he seems to have died very untidily!'

'But he did buy Mr Taunton's Christmas gifts for him?'

The dragon lifted a webby eyelid. 'You have already been told that. At six last night Mr Taunton and the Brigadier went to meet him to get the box. I got them into their mufflers so I know! I had the packing paper ready too, for Mr Taunton to take up to his room . . . Rather a small one on the third floor.' She lowered her voice to reduce it to the volume of distant traffic. 'Not many pennies but a dear little man!'

'Did you see these presents, Ma'am?'

'Not before they were wrapped! That would have spoiled the surprise!'

'I shall have to see them.' There was a mulish note in the Superintendent's voice which the lady was too experienced to ignore. 'I've thought how to do that without upsetting anybody,' she said brightly. 'The Brigadier and I will cut the presents from the Tree and Fiona will be handing them round. All Mr Taunton's little gifts are in the very distinctive black and gold paper I bought from Millie's Boutique and so, Fiona, you must give every package in gold and black paper not to the person to whom it is addressed but to the Superintendent. Can you do that, dear?'

Miss Poole-Poole seemed to feel the task difficult but not impossible and the trusting smile she gave Oates cut short his objections like the sun melting frost.

'Splendid!' The Dragon's roar was hearty. 'Give me your arm, Superintendent. You shall take me down.'

As the procession reached the hall it ran into the Brigadier himself. He was a large, pink man, affable enough, but of a martial type and he bristled at the Superintendent. 'Extraordinary time to do your business – middle of Christmas Day!' he said after acknowledging the introductions.

Oates inquired if he had enjoyed his walk.

'Talk?' said the Brigadier. 'I've not been talking. I've been asleep in the card-room. Where's old Taunton?'

'He went for a walk, Athole dear,' bellowed the Dragon gaily.

'So he did. You sent him! Poor feller.'

As the old soldier led the way to the open door of the drawing-room it occurred to both the visitors that the secret of Lady Larradine's undoubted attraction for him lay in the fact that he could hear *her* if no one else. The discovery cast a new light altogether on the story of the encounter with Sampson in the garden.

Meanwhile they had entered the drawing-room and the party had begun. As Mr Campion glanced at the company, ranged in a full circle round a magnificent tree loaded with gifts and sparkling like a waterfall, he saw face after familiar face. They were old acquaintances of the dizzy nineteen-thirties whom he had mourned as gone for ever when he thought of them at all. Yet here they all were, not only alive but released by great age from many of the restraints of convention. He noticed that every type of head-gear from night-cap to tiara was being sported with fine individualistic enthusiasm. But Lady Larradine gave him no time to look about. She proceeded with her task immediately.

Each guest had been provided with a small invalid table beside his armchair and Oates, reluctant but wax in Fiona's hands, was no exception. He found himself seated between a mountain in flannel and a wraith in mauve mink, waiting his turn with the same beady-eyed avidity.

Christmas tree procedure at the Ccraven proved to be well organized. The Dragon did little work herself. Armed with a swagger stick she merely prodded parcel after parcel hanging amid the boughs while the task of detaching them was performed by the Brigadier who handed them to Fiona. Either to add to the excitement or perhaps to muffle any unfortunate comment on gifts received by the uninhibited company, jolly Christmas music was played throughout and under cover of the noise Mr Campion was able to tackle his hostess.

'Where is Taunton?' he whispered.

'Such a nice little man. Most presentable but just a little teeny-weeny bit dishonest.' Lady Larradine ignored his question but continued to put him in the picture at speed, whilst supervising the Tree at the same time. 'Fifty-seven convictions, I believe, but only small ones. I only got it all out of him last week. Shattering! He'd been so *useful* amusing the

Brigadier. When he came he looked like a lost soul with no luggage but after no time at all he settled in perfectly.' She paused and stabbed at a ball of coloured cellophane with her stick before returning to her startled guest.

'Albert. I am terribly afraid poor Mr Taunton took that dreadful jewellery of Maisie Phaeton's. It appears to have been entirely her fault. He was merely wandering past her house, feeling in need of care and attention. The door was wide open and he found himself inside, picking up a few odds and ends. When he discovered from all that fuss in the newspapers what it was he had got hold of – how well known it was, I mean – he was quite horrified and had to hide. And where better than here with us where he never had to go out?'

'Where indeed!' Mr Campion dared not glance across the room to where the Superintendent was unwrapping his black and gold parcels. 'Where is he now?'

'Of course, I hadn't the faintest idea what was worrying the man until he confessed,' the Dragon went on stonily. 'Then I realized that something would have to be done at once to protect everybody. The wretch had hidden all that frightful stuff in our tool-shed for three months, not daring to keep it in the house and to make matters worse, the impossible person at the end of the garden, Mr Sampson, had recognized him and *would* keep speaking. Apparently people in the – er – underworld all know each other just as those of us in – er – other closed circles do.'

Mr Campion, whose hair was standing on end, had a moment of inspiration. 'This absurd rigmarole about Taunton getting Sampson to buy him some Christmas gifts wholesale was your idea!' he said accusingly.

The Dragon stared. 'It seemed the best way of getting Maisie's jewellery back to her without any one person being solely involved,' she said frankly. 'I knew we should all recognize the things the moment we saw them and I was certain that after a lot of arguments we should decide to pack them up and send them round to her. But, if there *was* any repercussion, we should *all* be in it (quite a formidable array, dear) and the blame could be traced to Mr Sampson if absolutely necessary. You see the Brigadier is convinced that Sampson *was* there last night. Mr Taunton very cleverly left him on the lawn and went behind the tool-shed and came back with the box.'

'How completely immoral!'

The Dragon had the grace to look embarrassed. 'I don't think the Sampson angle would ever have arisen,' she said. 'But if it had, Sampson was quite a terrible person. Almost a blackmailer. Utterly dishonest and inconsiderate. Think how he has spoiled everything and endangered us all by getting himself killed on the one afternoon when we said he was here, so that the police were brought in. Just the one thing I was trying to avoid. When the Inspector appeared this morning I was so upset I thought of you!'

In his not unnatural alarm Mr Campion so far forgot himself as to touch her sleeve. 'Where is Taunton now?'

The Dragon threshed her train. 'Really, boy! What a fidget you are! If you must know, I gave him his Christmas present – every penny I had in cash for he was broke again, he told me – and sent him for a nice long walk after lunch. Having seen the Inspector here this morning he was glad to go.' She paused and a gentle gleam came into her hooded eyes. 'If that Superintendent has the stupidity to try to find him when once Maisie has her monstrosities back none of us will be able to identify him I'm afraid. And there's another thing. If the Brigadier should be forced to give evidence I am sure he will stick to his guns about Mr Sampson being down the garden here at six o'clock last night. He believes he was. That would mean that someone very wicked would have to go unpunished, wouldn't it? Sampson was a terrible person but no one should have killed him.'

Mr Campion was silenced. He glanced fearfully across the room.

The Superintendent was seated at his table wearing the strained yet slap-happy expression of a man with concussion. On his left was a pile of black and gilt wrappings, on his right a rajah's ransom in somewhat specialized form. From where he stood Mr Campion could see two examples amid the rest; a breastplate in gold, pearl and enamel in the shape of a unicorn in a garden and an item which looked like a plover's egg in tourmaline encased in a ducal coronet. There was also a soapstone monkey and a silver paper-knife.

Much later that evening Mr Campion and the Superintendent drove quietly back to headquarters. Oates had a large cardboard box on his knee. He clasped it tenderly.

He had been silent for a long time when a thought occurred to him.

'Why did they take him into the house in the first place?' he said. 'An elderly crook looking lost! No luggage!'

Mr Campion's pale eyes flickered behind his spectacles.

'Don't forget the Duchess's housekeeping money,' he murmured. 'I should think he offered one of the widows who really run that place the first three months' payment in cash, wouldn't you? That must be an impressive phenomenon in that sort of business, I fancy.'

Oates caught his breath and fell silent once more until presently he burst out again.

'Those people! That woman!' he exploded. 'When they were younger they led me a pretty dance – losing things or getting themselves swindled. But now they're old they take the blessed biscuit! Do you see how she's tied my hands, Campion?'

Mr Campion tried not to grin.

'Snapdragons are just permissible at Christmas,' he said. 'Handled with extreme caution they burn very few fingers it seems to me.' He tapped the cardboard box. 'And some of them provide a few plums for retiring coppers, don't they, Superintendent?'

The Adventure of the Clapham Cook

◆

AGATHA CHRISTIE

Hercule Poirot, the egocentric and immaculately dressed Belgian detective with his egg-shaped head and old world courtesy, is another of the great characters of crime fiction. This small man – just a few inches over five feet tall – with his twirled moustache, his inimitable use (or abuse!) of the English language, and the amazing reasoning power of his 'little grey calls' has been a favourite in print and on the screen for over seventy years. Based in London and assisted by his old friend, Captain Hastings, who also recounts his cases, Poirot gets great satisfaction from his uneasy relationship with Inspector Japp of Scotland Yard whom he frequently outwits. His own self-belief is unshakeable, though on the rare occasions when he does make a mistake, he is inconsolable. Poirot has had a long history in the world of entertainment: making his London stage debut in 1928 in Alibi (an adaptation of The Murder of Roger Ackroyd) with the portly Charles Laughton in the starring role; and then in 1940 on radio played by Lionel Gamlin. On the screen a tall, handsome Irish actor named Austin Trevor was totally miscast as the first film Poirot in three movies made between 1931 and 1934, but he was subsequently played much near to character by Tony Randall, Albert Finney, Ian Holm and Peter Ustinov. Once again, it was to be an American series which introduced Poirot to television in an adaptation of the case of The Disappearance of Mr Davenheim. In this pioneer General Electric Theatre production in April 1962, character actor Martin Gabel was cast as the little detective with Nina Foch as the apparently distraught Mrs Davenheim who calls on Poirot's help to find her missing husband. It was not to be until January 1989, however, that the definitive impersonation was seen on the small screen with David

Suchet's debut in The Adventure of the Clapham Cook. *The success of this LWT TV series has grown with each succeeding episode, all of them enhanced by Suchet's brilliant and painstaking impersonation, plus Hugh Fraser's excellent performances as Captain Hastings.*

Agatha Christie also had a real-life model for Hercule Poirot – a man among the Belgian refugees she saw near her home in Devon during the First World War – and like a number of other crime writers plotted the death of her famous detective long before her own end: in Final Curtain *which she wrote in 1940 but which was not published until 1975. Of all Poirot's cases in the forty-two volumes of novels and short stories about him which might be included in this Omnibus,* The Adventure of the Clapham Cook *which introduced David Suchet's definitive performance seems, perhaps, the most appropriate . . .*

AT the time that I was sharing rooms with my friend Hercule Poirot, it was my custom to read aloud to him the headlines in the morning newspaper, the *Daily Blare*

The *Daily Blare* was a paper that made the most of any opportunity for sensationalism. Robberies and murders did not lurk obscurely in its back pages. Instead they hit you in the eye in large type on the front page.

ABSCONDING BANK CLERK DISAPPEARS WITH FIFTY THOUSAND POUNDS' WORTH OF NEGOTIABLE SECURITIES, I read.

HUSBAND PUTS HIS HEAD IN GAS-OVEN. UNHAPPY HOME LIFE. MISSING TYPIST. PRETTY GIRL OF TWENTY-ONE. WHERE IS EDNA FIELD?

'There you are, Poirot, plenty to choose from. An absconding bank clerk, a mysterious sucide, a missing typist – which will you have?'

My friend was in a placid mood. He quietly shook his head.

'I am not greatly attracted to any of them, *mon ami*. Today I feel inclined for the life of ease. It would have to be a very interesting problem to tempt me from my chair. See you, I have affairs of importance of my own to attend to.'

'Such as?'

'My wardrobe, Hastings. If I mistake not, there is on my new grey suit the spot of grease – only the unique spot, but it is sufficient to trouble me. Then there is my winter overcoat – I must lay him aside in the powder of Keatings. And I think – yes, I think – the moment is ripe for the trimmings of my moustaches – and afterwards I must apply the pomade.'

'Well,' I said, strolling to the window, 'I doubt if you'll be able to carry out this delirious programme. That was a ring at the bell. You have a client.'

'Unless the affair is one of national importance, I touch it not,' declared Poirot with dignity.

A moment later our privacy was invaded by a stout red-faced lady who panted audibly as a result of her rapid ascent of the stairs.

'You're M. Poirot?' she demanded, as she sank into a chair.

'I am Hercule Poirot, yes, madame.'

'You're not a bit like what I thought you'd be,' said the lady, eyeing him with some disfavour. 'Did you pay for the bit in the paper saying what a clever detective you were, or did they put it in themselves?'

'Madame!' said Poirot, drawing himself up.

'I'm sorry, I'm sure, but you know what these papers are nowadays. You begin reading a nice article "What a bride said to her plain unmarried friend", and it's all about a simple thing you buy at the chemist's and shampoo your hair with. Nothing but puff. But no offence taken, I hope? I'll tell you what I want you to do for me. I want you to find my cook.'

Poirot stared at her; for once his ready tongue failed him. I turned aside to hide the broadening smile I could not control.

'It's all this wicked dole,' continued the lady. 'Putting ideas into servants' heads, wanting to be typists and what nots. Stop the dole, that's what I say. I'd like to know what *my* servants have to complain of – afternoon and evening off a week, alternate Sundays, washing put out, same food as we have – and never a bit of margarine in the house, nothing but the very best butter.'

She paused for want of breath and Poirot seized his opportunity. He spoke in his haughtiest manner rising to his feet as he did so.

'I fear you are making a mistake, madame. I am not holding an inquiry into the conditions of domestic service. I am a private detective.'

'I know that,' said our visitor. 'Didn't I tell you I wanted you to find my cook for me? Walked out of the house on Wednesday, without so much as a word to me, and never came back.'

'I am sorry, madame, but I do not touch this particular kind of business. I wish you good morning.'

Our visitor snorted with indignation.

'That's it, is it, my fine fellow? Too proud, eh? Only deal with Government secrets and countesses' jewels? Let me tell you a servant's every bit as important as a tiara to a woman in my position. We can't all be fine ladies going out in our motors with our diamonds and our pearls. A good cook's a good cook – and when you lose her, it's as much to you as her pearls are to some fine lady.'

For a moment or two it appeared to be a toss up between Poirot's dignity and his sense of humour. Finally he laughed and sat down again.

'Madame, you are in the right, and I am in the wrong. Your remarks are just and intelligent. This case will be a novelty. Never yet have I hunted a missing domestic. Truly here is the problem of national importance that I was demanding of fate just before your arrival. *En avant*! You say this jewel of a cook went out on Wednesday and did not return. That is the day before yesterday.'

'Yes, it was her day out.'

'But probably, madame, she has met with some accident. Have you inquired at any of the hospitals?'

'That's exactly what I thought yesterday, but this morning, if you please, she sent for her box. And not so much as a line to me! If I'd been at home, I'd not have let it go – treating me like that! But I'd just stepped out to the butcher.'

'Will you describe her to me?'

'She was middle-aged, stout, black hair turning grey – most respectable. She'd been ten years in her last place. Eliza Dunn, her name was.'

'And you had had – no disagreement with her on the Wednesday?'

'None whatever. That's what makes it all so queer.'

'How many servants do you keep, madame?'

'Two. The house-parlourmaid, Annie, is a very nice girl. A bit forgetful and her head full of young men, but a good servant if you keep her up to her work.'

'Did she and the cook get on well together?'

'They had their ups and downs, of course – but on the whole, very well.'

'And the girl can throw no light on the mystery?'

'She says not – but you know what servants are – they all hang together.'

'Well, well, we must look into this. Where did you say you resided, madame?'

'At Clapham; 88 Prince Albert Road.'

'*Bien*, madame, I will wish you good morning, and you may count upon seeing me at your residence during the course of the day.'

Mrs Todd, for such was our new friend's name, then took her departure. Poirot looked at me somewhat ruefully.

'Well, well, Hastings, this is a novel affair that we have here. The Disappearance of the Clapham Cook! Never, *never*, must our friend Inspector Japp get to hear of this!'

He then proceeded to heat an iron and carefully removed the grease spot from his grey suit by means of a piece of blotting-paper. His moustaches he regretfully postponed to another day, and we set out for Clapham.

Prince Albert Road proved to be a street of small prim houses, all exactly alike, with neat lace curtains veiling the windows, and well polished brass knockers on the doors.

We rang the bell at Number 88, and the door was opened by a neat maid with a pretty face. Mrs Todd came out in the hall to greet us.

'Don't go, Annie,' she cried. 'This gentleman's a detective and he'll want to ask you some questions.'

Annie's face displayed a struggle between alarm and a pleasurable excitement.

'I thank you, madame,' said Poirot bowing. 'I would like to question your maid now – and to see her alone, if I may.'

We were shown into a small drawing-room, and when Mrs Todd, with obvious reluctance, had left the room, Poirot commenced his cross-examination.

'*Voyons, Mademoiselle Annie*, all that you shall tell us will be of the greatest importance. You alone can shed any light on the case. Without your assistance I can do nothing.'

The alarm vanished from the girl's face and the pleasurable excitement became more strongly marked.

'I'm sure, sir,' she said, 'I'll tell you anything I can.'

'That is good.' Poirot beamed approval on her. 'Now, first of all what is your own idea? You are a girl of remarkable intelligence. That can be seen at once! What is your own explanation of Eliza's disappearance?'

Thus encouraged, Annie fairly flowed into excited speech.

'White slavers, sir, I've said so all along! Cook was always warning me against them. "Don't you sniff no scent, or eat any sweets – no matter how gentlemanly the fellow!" Those were her words to me. And now they've got her! I'm sure of it. As likely as not, she's been shipped to Turkey or one of them Eastern places where I've heard they like them fat!'

Poirot preserved an admirable gravity.

'But in that case – and it is indeed an idea! – would she have sent for her trunk?'

'Well, I don't know, sir. She'd want her things – even in those foreign places.'

'Who came for the trunk – a man?'

'It was Carter Paterson, sir.'

'Did you pack it?'

'No, sir, it was already packed and corded.'

'Ah! That's interesting. That shows that when she left the house on Wednesday, she had already determined not to return. You see that, do you not?'

'Yes, sir.' Annie looked slightly taken aback. 'I hadn't thought of that. But it might still have been white slavers, mightn't it, sir?' she added wistfully.

'Undoubtedly!' said Poirot gravely. He went on: 'Did you both occupy the same bedroom?'

'No, sir, we had separate rooms.'

'And had Eliza expressed any dissatisfaction with her present post to you at all? Were you both happy here?'

'She'd never mentioned leaving. The place is all right – ' The girl hesitated.

'Speak freely,' said Poirot kindly. 'I shall not tell your mistress.'

'Well, of course, sir, she's a caution, Missus is. But the food's good. Plenty of it, and no stinting. Something hot for supper, good outings, and as much frying-fat as you like. And anyway, if Eliza did want to make a change, she'd never have gone off this way, I'm sure. She'd have stayed her month. Why, Missus could have a month's wages out of her for doing this!'

'And the work, it is not too hard?'

'Well, she's particular – always poking round in corners and looking for dust. And then there's the lodger, or paying guest as he's always called. But that's only breakfast and dinner, same as Master. They're out all day in the City.'

'You like your master?'

'He's all right – very quiet and a bit on the stingy side.'

'You can't remember, I suppose, the last thing Eliza said before she went out?'

'Yes, I can. "If there's any stewed peaches over from the dining-room," she says, "we'll have them for supper, and a bit of bacon and some fried potatoes." Mad over stewed peaches, she was. I shouldn't wonder if they didn't get her that way.'

'Was Wednesday her regular day out?'

'Yes, she had Wednesdays and I had Thursdays.'

Poirot asked a few more questions, then declared himself satisfied. Annie departed, and Mrs Todd hurried in, her face alight with curiosity. She had, I felt certain, bitterly resented her exclusion from the room during our conversation with Annie. Poirot, however, was careful to soothe her feelings tactfully.

'It is difficult,' he explained, 'for a woman of exceptional intelligence such as yourself, madame, to bear patiently the roundabout methods we poor detectives are forced to use. To have patience with stupidity is difficult for the quick-witted.'

Having thus charmed away any little resentment on Mrs Todd's part, he brought the conversation round to her husband and elicited the information that he worked with a firm in the City and would not be home until after six.

'Doubtless he is very disturbed and worried by this unaccountable business, eh? Is it not so?'

'He's never worried,' declared Mrs Todd. ' "Well, well, get another, my dear." That's all *he* said! He's so calm that it drives me to distraction sometimes. "An ungrateful woman," he said. "We were well rid of her." '

'What about the other inmates of the house, madame?'

'You mean Mr Simpson, our paying guest? Well, as long as he gets his breakfast and his evening meal all right, *he* doesn't worry.'

'What is his profession, madame?'

'He works in a bank.' She mentioned its name, and I started slightly, remembering my perusal of the *Daily Blare*.

'A young man?'

'Twenty-eight, I believe. Nice quiet young fellow.'

'I should like to have a few words with him, and also with your husband, if I may. I will return for that purpose this evening. I venture to suggest that you should repose yourself a little, madame, you look fatigued.'

'I should just think I am! First the worry about Eliza, and then I was at the sales practically all yesterday, and you know what *that* is, M. Poirot, and what with one thing and another and a lot to do in the house, because of course Annie can't do it all – and very likely she'll give notice anyway, being unsettled in this way – well, what with it all, I'm tired out!'

Poirot murmured sympathetically, and we took our leave.

'It's a curious coincidence,' I said, 'but that absconding clerk, Davis, was from the same bank as Simpson. Can there be any connection, do you think?'

Poirot smiled.

'At the one end, a defaulting clerk, at the other a vanishing cook. It is hard to see any relation between the two, unless possibly Davis visited Simpson, fell in love with the cook, and persuaded her to accompany him on his flight!'

I laughed. But Poirot remained grave.

'He might have done worse,' he said reprovingly. 'Remember, Hastings, if you are going into exile, a good cook may be of more comfort than a pretty face!' He paused for a moment and then went on. 'It is a curious case, full of contradictory features. I am interested – yes, I am distinctly interested.'

That evening we returned to 88 Prince Albert Road and interviewed both Todd and Simpson. The former was a melancholy lantern-jawed man of forty-odd.

'Oh! Yes, yes,' he said vaguely. 'Eliza. Yes. A good cook, I believe. And economical. I make a strong point of economy.'

'Can you imagine any reason for her leaving you so suddenly?'

'Oh, well,' said Mr Todd vaguely. 'Servants, you know. My wife worries too much. Worn out from always worrying. The whole problem's quite simple really. "Get another, my dear," I say. "Get another." That's all there is to it. No good crying over spilt milk.'

Mr Simpson was equally unhelpful. He was a quiet inconspicuous young man with spectacles.

'I must have seen her, I suppose,' he said. 'Elderly woman, wasn't she? Of course, it's the other one I see always, Annie. Nice girl. Very obliging.'

'Were those two on good terms with each other?'

Mr Simpson said he couldn't say, he was sure. He supposed so.

'Well, we get nothing of interest there, *mon ami*,' said Poirot as we left the house. Our departure had been delayed by a burst of vociferous repetition from Mrs Todd who repeated everything she had said that morning at rather greater length.

'Are you disappointed?' I asked. 'Did you expect to hear something?'

Poirot shook his head.

'There was a possibility, of course,' he said. 'But I hardly thought it likely.'

The next development was a letter which Poirot received on the following morning. He read it, turned purple with indignation, and handed it to me.

> *Mrs Todd regrets that after all she will not avail herself of Mr Poirot's services. After talking the matter over with her husband she sees that it is foolish to call in a detective about a purely domestic affair. Mrs Todd encloses a guinea for consultation fee.*

'Aha!' cried Poirot angrily. 'And they think to get rid of Hercule Poirot like that! As a favour – a great favour – I consent to investigate their miserable little twopenny-halfpenny affair – and they dismiss me *comme ça*! Here, I mistake not, is the hand of Mr Todd. But I say no! – thirty-six times no! I will spend my own guineas, thirty-six hundred of them if need be, but I will get to the bottom of this matter!'

'Yes,' I said. 'But how?'

Poirot calmed down a little.

'*D'abord*,' he said, 'we will advertise in the papers. Let me see – yes – something like this: "If Eliza Dunn will communicate with this address, she will hear of something to her advantage." Put it in all the papers you can think of, Hastings. Then I will make some little inquiries of my own. Go, go – all must be done as quickly as possible!'

I did not see him again until the evening, when he condescended to tell me what he had been doing.

'I have made inquiries at the firm of Mr Todd. He was not absent on Wednesday, and he bears a good character – so much for him. Then Simpson, on Thursday he was ill and did not come to the bank, but he was there on Wednesday. He was moderately friendly with Davis. Nothing out of the common. There does not seem to be anything there. No. We must place our reliance on the advertisement.'

The advertisement duly appeared in all the principal daily papers. By Poirot's orders it was to be continued every day for a week. His eagerness over this uninteresting matter of a defaulting cook was extraordinary, but I realized that he considered it a point of honour to persevere until he finally succeeded. Several extremely interesting cases were brought to him about this time, but he declined them all. Every morning he would rush at his letters, scrutinize them earnestly and then lay them down with a sigh.

But our patience was rewarded at last. On the Wednesday following Mrs Todd's visit, our landlady informed us that a person of the name of Eliza Dunn had called.

'*Enfin*!' cried Poirot. 'But make her mount then! At once. Immediately.'

Thus admonished, our landlady hurried out and returned a moment or two later, ushering in Miss Dunn. Our quarry was much as described: tall, stout, and eminently respectable.

'I came in answer to the advertisement,' she explained. 'I thought there must be some muddle or other, and that perhaps you didn't know I'd already got my legacy.'

Poirot was studying her attentively. He drew forward a chair with a flourish.

'The truth of the matter is,' he explained, 'that your late mistress, Mrs Todd, was much concerned about you. She feared some accident might have befallen you.'

Eliza Dunn seemed very much surprised.

'Didn't she get my letter then?'

'She got no word of any kind.' He paused, and then said persuasively: 'Recount to me the whole story, will you not?'

Eliza Dunn needed no encouragement. She plunged at once into a lengthy narrative.

'I was just coming home on Wednesday night and had nearly got to the house, when a gentleman stopped me. A tall gentleman he was, with a beard and a big hat. "Miss Eliza Dunn?" he said. "Yes," I said. "I've been inquiring for you at Number 88," he said. "They told me I might meet you coming along here. Miss Dunn, I have come from Australia specially to find you. Do you happen to know the maiden name of your maternal grandmother?" "Jane Emmott," I said. "Exactly," he said. "Now, Miss Dunn, although you may never have heard of the fact, your grandmother had a great friend, Eliza Leech. This friend went to Australia where she married a very wealthy settler. Her two children died in infancy, and she inherited all her husband's property. She died a few months ago, and by her will you inherit a house in this country and a considerable sum of money."

'You could have knocked me down with a feather,' continued Miss Dunn. 'For a minute, I was suspicious, and he must have seen it, for he smiled. "Quite right to be on your guard, Miss Dunn," he said. "Here are my credentials." He handed me a letter from some lawyers in Melbourne, Hurst and Crotchet, and a card. He was Mr Crotchet. "There are one or two conditions," he said. "Our client was a little eccentric, you know. The bequest is conditional on your taking possession of the house (it is in Cumberland) before twelve o'clock tomorrow. The other condition is of no importance – it is merely a stipulation that you should not be in domestic service." My face fell. "Oh, Mr Crotchet," I said. "I'm a cook. Didn't they tell you at the house?" "Dear, dear," he said. "I had no idea of such a thing. I thought you might possibly be a companion or governess there. This is very unfortunate – very unfortunate indeed."

' "Shall I have to lose all the money?" I said, anxious like. He thought for a minute or two. "There are always ways of getting round the law, Miss Dunn," he said at last. "We lawyers know that. The way out here is for you to have left your employment this afternoon." "But my month?" I said. "My dear Miss Dunn," he said with a smile. "You can leave an employer any minute by forfeiting a month's wages. Your mistress will understand in view of the circumstances. The difficulty is *time*! It is imperative that you should catch the eleven-five from King's Cross to the North. I can advance you ten pounds or so for the fare, and you can write a note at the station to your employer. I will take it to her myself and explain the whole circumstances." I agreed, of course, and an hour later I was in the train, so flustered that I didn't know whether I was on my head or my heels. Indeed by the time I got to Carlisle, I was half inclined to think the whole thing was one of those confidence tricks you read about. But I went to the address he had given me – solicitors they were, and it was all right. A nice little house, and an income of three hundred a year. These lawyers knew very little, they'd just got a letter from a gentleman in London instructing them to hand over the house to me and one-hundred-and-fifty pounds for the first six months. Mr Crotchet sent up my things to me, but there was no word from Missus. I supposed she was angry and grudged me my bit of luck. She kept back my box too, and sent my clothes in paper parcels. But there, of course if she never had my letter, she might think it a bit cool of me.'

Poirot had listened attentively to this long history. Now he nodded his head as though completely satisfied.

'Thank you, mademoiselle. There had been, as you say, a little muddle. Permit me to recompense you for your trouble.' He handed her an envelope. 'You return to Cumberland immediately? A little word in your ear. *Do not forget how to cook.* It is always useful to have something to fall back upon in case things go wrong.'

'Credulous,' he murmured, as our visitor departed, 'but perhaps not more than most of her class.' His face grew grave. 'Come, Hastings, there is no time to be lost. Get a taxi while I write a note to Japp.'

Poirot was waiting on the doorstep when I returned with the taxi.

'Where are we going?' I asked anxiously.

'First, to despatch this note by special messenger.'

This was done, and re-entering the taxi Poirot gave the address to the driver.

'Eight-eight Prince Albert Road, Clapham.'

'So we are going there?'

'*Mais oui*. Though frankly I fear we shall be too late. Our bird will have flown, Hastings.'

'Who is our bird?'

Poirot smiled.

'The inconspicuous Mr Simpson.'

'What?' I exclaimed.

'Oh, come now, Hastings, do not tell me that all is not clear to you now!'

'The cook was got out of the way, I realize that,' I said, slightly piqued. 'But why? *Why* should Simpson wish to get her out of the house? Did she know something about him?'

'Nothing whatever.'

'Well, then – '

'But he wanted something that she had.'

'Money? The Australian legacy?'

'No, my friend – something quite different.' He paused a moment and then said gravely: '*A battered tin trunk* . . .'

I looked sideways at him. His statement seemed so fantastic that I suspected him of pulling my leg, but he was perfectly grave and serious.

'Surely he could buy a trunk if he wanted one,' I cried.

'He did not want a new trunk. He wanted a trunk of pedigree. A trunk of assured respectability.'

'Look here, Poirot,' I cried, 'this really is a bit thick. You're pulling my leg.'

He looked at me.

'You lack the brains and the imagination of Mr Simpson, Hastings. See here: On Wednesday evening, Simpson decoys away the cook. A printed card and a printed sheet of notepaper are simple matters to obtain, and he is willing to pay one-hundred-and-fifty pounds and a year's house rent to assure the success of his plan. Miss Dunn does not recognize him – the beard and the hat and the slight colonial accent completely deceive her. That is the end of Wednesday – except for the trifling fact that Simpson has helped himself to fifty thousand pounds' worth of negotiable securities.'

'*Simpson* – but it was *Davis* – '

'If you will kindly permit me to continue, Hastings! Simpson knows that the theft will be discovered on Thursday afternoon. He does not go to the bank on Thursday, but he lies in wait for Davis when he comes out to lunch. Perhaps he admits the theft and tells Davis he will return the securities to him – anyhow he succeeds in getting Davis to come to Clapham with him. It is the maid's day out, and Mrs Todd was at the sales, so there is no one in the house. When the theft is discovered and Davis is missing, the implication will be overwhelming. Davis is the thief! Mr Simpson will be perfectly safe, and can return to work on the morrow like the honest clerk they think him.'

'And Davis?'

Poirot made an expressive gesture, and slowly shook his head.

'It seems too cold-blooded to be believed, and yet what other explanation can there be, *mon ami*. The one difficulty for a murderer is the disposal of the body – and Simpson had planned that out beforehand. I was struck at once by the fact that although Eliza Dunn obviously meant to return that night when she went out (witness her remark about the stewed peaches) *yet her trunk was all ready packed when they came for it*. It was Simpson who sent word to Carter Paterson to call on Friday and it was Simpson who corded up the box on Thursday afternoon. What suspicion could possibly arise? A maid leaves and sends for her box, it is labelled and addressed ready in her name, probably to a railway station within easy reach of London. On Saturday afternoon, Simpson, in his Australian disguise, claims it, he affixes a new label and address and redespatches it somewhere else, again "to be left till called for". When the authorities get suspicious, for excellent reasons, and open it, all that can be elicited will be that a bearded colonial despatched it from some junction near London. There will be nothing to connect it with 88 Prince Albert Road. Ah! Here we are.'

Poirot's prognostications had been correct. Simpson had left two days previously. But he was not to escape the consequences of his crime. By the aid of wireless, he was discovered on the *Olympia*, en route to America.

A tin trunk, addressed to Mr Henry Wintergreen, attracted the attention of railway officials at Glasgow. It was opened and found to contain the body of the unfortunate Davis.

Mrs Todd's cheque for a guinea was never cashed. Instead Poirot had it framed and hung on the wall of our sitting-room.

'It is to me a little reminder, Hastings. Never to despise the trivial – the undignified. A disappearing domestic at one end – a cold-blooded murder at the other. To me, one of the most interesting of my cases.'

When The Wedding Was Over

◆

RUTH RENDELL

Detective Chief Inspector Wexford is a tall, rather ungainly man getting on for sixty whose body has a tendency to fat and whose face has been described quite unequivocally as 'rather ugly'. His base is the police station at Kingsmarkham in the county of Sussex, and he is a painstakingly thorough investigator with an eye for the unlikely clue. Most of Wexford's cases have confined him to his own patch, but he does occasionally run into crime on holiday or when abroad. His assistant on all the local cases is Detective Inspector Mike Burden, a thin, handsome, if rather ascetic-looking man, some twenty years younger. The pair, who like nothing better than mulling over clues and motives while downing a pint in their local, the 'Olive and Dove', always look strikingly different: Wexford untidy in a suit that seems in need of ironing, and Burden forever sartorially immaculate. 'A tramp and a Beau Brummell' is one description that has been given of this unlikely but undeniably effective partnership. Introduced first in the novel, From Doon with Death *(1964), Wexford and Burden were brought to television in 1990 by TVS in the series entitled* The Ruth Rendell Mysteries. *Cast as the most English of Chief Inspectors was George Baker – who was actually born in Varna, Bulgaria, and came to television via a stage debut at the tender age of fifteen and some leading roles in popular British films of the Fifties including* The Dambusters, A Hill in Korea *and* No Time for Tears. *Mike Burden, the other half of the duo, was played by the versatile film and TV actor, Christopher Ravenscroft.*

Ruth Rendell (1930–   ) has admitted that Wexford has strong similarities to her own father, a highly moral, intellectual man, with a fondness for quoting from books with the erudition of a Cambridge

professor. Despite her acknowledged position as one of the 'Queens of
Crime Fiction' – she has received eight major awards for her work –
Ruth Rendell does not enjoy comparisons with Agatha Christie, but
has a great admiration for Georges Simenon, having taught herself
French by reading the Maigret novels in the original! Indeed, it has
been said that Wexford, like Maigret, tries to build up a psychological
portrait of the criminal he is pursuing by observing all his or her little
foibles. The various skills of both Wexford and Burden are to be seen
in When the Wedding Was Over *in which the Chief Inspector also puts*
his knowledge of literature to good effect . . .

'MATRIMONY,' said Chief Inspector Wexford, 'begins with
dearly beloved and ends with amazement.'

His wife, sitting beside him on the bridegroom's side of the church,
whispered, 'What did you say?'

He repeated it. She steadied the large floral hat which her husband
had called becoming but not exactly conducive to *sotto voce*
intimacies. 'What on earth makes you say that?'

'Thomas Hardy. He said it first. But look in your Prayer Book.'

The bridegroom waited, hang-dog, with his best man. Michael
Burden was very much in love, was entering this second marriage with
someone admirably suited to him, had agreed with his fiancée that
nothing but a religious ceremony would do for them, yet at forty-four
was a little superannuated for what Wexford called 'all this white
wedding gubbins'. There were two hundred people in the church.
Burden, his best man and his ushers were in morning dress. Madonna
lilies and stephanotis and syringa decorated the pews, the pulpit and
the chancel steps. It was the kind of thing that is properly designed for
someone twenty years younger. Burden had been through it before
when he *was* twenty years younger. Wexford chuckled silently,
looking at the anxious face above the high white collar. And then as
Dora, leafing through the marriage service, said, 'Oh, I *see*,' the
organist went from voluntaries into the opening bars of the Lohengrin
march and Jenny Ireland appeared at the church door on her father's
arm.

A beautiful bride, of course. Seven years younger than Burden,
blonde, gentle, low-voiced, and given to radiant smiles. Jenny's father

gave her hand into Burden's and the Rector of St Peter's began: 'Dearly beloved, we are gathered together . . .'

While bride and groom were being informed that marriage was not for the satisfaction of the carnal lusts, and that they must bring up their children in a Christian manner, Wexford studied the congregation. In front of himself and Dora sat Burden's sister-in-law, Grace, whom everyone had thought he would marry after the death of his first wife. But Burden had found consolation with a red-headed woman, wild and sweet and strange, gone now God knew where, and Grace had married someone else. Two little boys now sat between Grace and that someone else, giving their parents a full-time job keeping them quiet.

Burden's mother and father were both dead. Wexford thought he recognized, from one meeting a dozen years before, an aged aunt. Beside her sat Dr Crocker and his wife, beyond them and behind were a crowd whose individual members he knew either only by sight or not at all. Sylvia, his elder daughter, was sitting on his other side, his grandsons between her and their father, and at the central aisle end of the pew, Sheila Wexford of the Royal Shakespeare Company. Wexford's actress daughter, who on her entry had commanded nudges, whispers, every gaze, sat looking with unaccustomed wistfulness at Jenny Ireland in her clouds of white and wreath of pearls.

'I, Michael George, take thee, Janina, to my wedded wife, to have and to hold from this day forward . . .'

Janina. *Janina?* Wexford had supposed her name was Jennifer. What sort of parents called a daughter Janina? Turks? Fans of Dumas? He leaned forward to get a good look at these philonomatous progenitors. They looked ordinary enough, Mr Ireland apparently exhausted by the effort of giving the bride away, Jenny's mother making use of the lace handkerchief provided for the specific purpose of crying into it those tears of joy and loss. What romantic streak had led them to dismiss Elizabeth and Susan and Anne in favour of – Janina?

'Those whom God hath joined together, let no man put asunder. Forasmuch as Michael George and Janina have consented together in holy wedlock . . .'

Had they been as adventurous in the naming of their son? All Wexford could see of him was a broad back, a bit of profile, and now a hand. The hand was passing a large white handkerchief to his mother. Wexford found himself being suddenly yanked to his feet to sing a hymn.

'O, Perfect Love, all human thought transcending,
Lowly we kneel in prayer before Thy throne . . .'

These words had the effect of evoking from Mrs Ireland audible sobs. Her son – hadn't Burden said he was in publishing? – looked embarrassed, turning his head. A young woman, strangely dressed in black with an orange hat, edged past the publisher to put a consoling arm round his mother.

'O Lord, save Thy servant and Thy handmaid.'

'Who put their trust in Thee,' said Dora and most of the rest of the congregation.

'O Lord, send them help from Thy holy place.'

Wexford, to show team spirit, said, 'Amen,' and when everyone else said, 'And evermore defend them,' decided to keep quiet in future.

Mrs Ireland had stopped crying. Wexford's gaze drifted to his own daughters, Sheila singing lustily, Sylvia, the Women's Liberationist, with less assurance as if she doubted the ethics of lending her support to so archaic and sexist a ceremony. His grandsons were beginning to fidget.

'Almighty God, who at the beginning did create our first parents, Adam and Eve . . .'

Dear Mike, thought Wexford with a flash of sentimentality that came to him perhaps once every ten years, you'll be OK now. No more carnal lusts conflicting with a puritan conscience, no more loneliness, no more worrying about those selfish kids of yours, no more temptation-of-St-Anthony stuff. For is it not ordained as a remedy against sin, and to avoid fornication, that such persons as have not the gift of continency may marry and keep themselves undefiled?

'For after this manner in the old time the holy women who trusted in God . . .'

He was quite surprised that they were using the ancient form. Still, the bride had promised to obey. He couldn't resist glancing at Sylvia.

'. . . being in subjection to their own husbands . . .'

Her face was a study in incredulous dismay as she mouthed at her sister 'unbelievable' and 'antique'.

'. . . Even as Sarah obeyed Abraham, calling him Lord, whose daughters ye are as long as ye do well, and are not afraid with any amazement.'

At the Olive and Dove hotel there was a reception line to greet guests. Mrs Ireland smiling, re-rouged and restored, Burden looking like someone who has had an operation and been told the prognosis is excellent, Jenny serene as a bride should be.

Dry sherry and white wine on trays. No champagne. Wexford remembered that there was a younger Ireland daughter, absent with her husband in some dreadful place – Botswana? Lesotho? No doubt all the champagne funds had been expended on her. It was a buffet lunch, but a good one. Smoked salmon and duck and strawberries. Nobody, he said to himself, has ever really thought of anything better to eat than smoked salmon and duck and strawberries unless it might be caviare and grouse and syllabub. He was weighing the two menus against one another, must without knowing it have been thinking aloud, for a voice said:

'Asparagus, trout, apple pie.'

'Well, maybe,' said Wexford, 'but I do like meat. Trout's a bit insipid. You're Jenny's brother, I'm sorry I don't remember your name. How d'you do?'

'How d'you do? I know who you are. Mike told me. I'm Amyas Ireland.'

So that funny old pair hadn't had a one-off indulgence when they had named Janina. Again Wexford's thoughts seemed revealed to this intuitive person.

'Oh, I know,' said Ireland, 'but how about my other sister? She's called Cunegonde. Her husband calls her Queenie. Look, I'd like to talk to you. Could we get together a minute away from all this crush? Mike was going to help me out, but I can't ask him now, not when he's off on his honeymoon. It's about a book we're publishing.'

The girl in black and orange, Burden's nephews, Sheila Wexford, Burden's best man and a gaggle of children, all carrying plates, passed between them at this point. It was at least a minute before Wexford could ask, 'Who's we?' and another half-minute before Amyas Ireland understood what he meant.

'Carlyon Brent,' he said, his mouth full of duck. 'I'm with Carlyon Brent.'

One of the largest and most distinguished of publishing houses. Wexford was impressed. 'You published the Vandrian, didn't you, and the de Coverley books?'

Ireland nodded. 'Mike said you were a great reader. That's good. Can I get you some more duck? No? I'm going to. I won't be a minute.' Enviously Wexford watched him shovel fat-rimmed slices of duck breast on to his plate, take a brioche, have second thoughts and take another. The man was as thin as a rail too, positively emaciated.

'I look after the crime list,' he said as he sat down again. 'As I said, Mike half-promised . . . This isn't fiction, it's fact. The Winchurch case?'

'Ah.'

'I know it's a bit of a nerve asking, but would you read a manuscript for me?'

Wexford took a cup of coffee from a passing tray. 'What for?'

'Well, in the interests of truth. Mike was going to tell me what he thought.' Wexford looked at him dubiously. He had the highest respect and the deepest affection for Inspector Burden but he was one of the last people he would have considered as a literary critic. 'To tell me what he thought,' the publisher said once again. 'You see, it's worrying me. The author has discovered some new facts and they more or less prove Mrs Winchurch's innocence.' He hesitated. 'Have you ever heard of a writer called Kenneth Gandolph?'

Wexford was saved from answering by the pounding of a gavel on the top table and the beginning of the speeches. A great many toasts had been drunk, several dozen telegrams read out, and the bride and groom departed to change their clothes before he had an opportunity to reply to Ireland's question. And he was glad of the respite, for what he knew of Gandolph, though based on hearsay, was not prepossessing.

'Doesn't he write crime novels?' he said when the enquiry was repeated. 'And the occasional examination of a real-life crime?'

Nodding, Ireland said, 'It's good, this script of his. We want to do it for next spring's list. It's an eighty-year-old murder, sure, but people are still fascinated by it. I think this new version could cause quite a sensation.'

'Florence Winchurch was hanged,' said Wexford, 'yet there was always some margin of doubt about her guilt. Where does Gandolph get his fresh facts from?'

'May I send you a copy of the script? You'll find all that in the introduction.'

Wexford shrugged, then smiled. 'I suppose so. You do realize I can't do more than maybe spot mistakes in forensics? I did say maybe, mind.' But his interest had already been caught. It made him say, 'Florence was married at St Peter's, you know, and she also had her wedding reception here.'

'And spent part of her honeymoon in Greece.'

'No doubt the parallel ends there,' said Wexford as Burden and Jenny came back into the room.

Burden was in a grey lounge suit, she in pale blue sprigged muslin. Wexford felt an absurd impulse of tenderness towards him. It was partly caused by Jenny's hat which she would never wear again, would never have occasion to wear, would remove the minute they got into the car. But Burden was the sort of man who could never be happy with a woman who didn't have a hat as part of her 'going-away' costume. His own clothes were eminently unsuitable for flying to Crete in June. They both looked very happy and embarrassed.

Mrs Ireland seized her daughter in a crushing embrace.

'It's not for ever, Mother,' said Jenny. 'It's only for two weeks.'

'Well, in a way,' said Burden. He shook hands gravely with his own son, down from university for the weekend, and planted a kiss on his daughter's forehead. Must have been reading novels, Wexford thought, grinning to himself.

'Good luck, Mike,' he said.

The bride took his hand, put a soft cool kiss on to the corner of his mouth. Say I'm growing old but add, Jenny kissed me. He didn't say that aloud. He nodded and smiled and took his wife's arm and frowned at Sylvia's naughty boys like the patriarch he was. Burden and Jenny went out to the car which had Just Married written in lipstick on the rear window and a shoe tied on the back bumper.

There was a clicking of handbag clasps, a flurry of hands, and then a tempest of confetti broke over them.

It was an isolated house, standing some twenty yards back from the Myringham road. Plumb in the centre of the façade was a plaque bearing the date 1896. Wexford had often thought that there seemed to have been positive intent on the part of late-Victorian builders to design and erect houses that were not only ugly, complex and inconvenient, but also distinctly sinister in appearance. The Limes, though well-maintained and set in a garden as multi-coloured, cushiony and floral as a quilt, nevertheless kept this sinister quality. Khaki-coloured brick and grey slate had been the principal materials used in its construction. Without being able to define exactly how, Wexford could see that, in relation to the walls, the proportions of the sash windows were wrong. A turret grew out of each of the front corners and each of these turrets was topped by a conical roof, giving the place the look of a cross between Balmoral castle and a hotel in Kitzbuehl. The lime trees which gave it its name had been lopped so many times since their planting at the turn of the century that now they were squat and misshapen.

In the days of the Winchurches it had been called Paraleash House. But this name, of historical significance on account of its connection with the ancient manor of Paraleash, had been changed specifically as a result of the murder of Edward Winchurch. Even so, it had stood empty for ten years. Then it had found a buyer a year or so before the First World War, a man who was killed in that war. Its present owner had occupied it for half a dozen years, and in the time intervening between his purchase of it and 1918 it had been variously a nursing home, the annexe of an agricultural college and a private school. The owner was a retired brigadier. As he emerged from the front door with two Sealyhams on a lead, Wexford retreated to his car and drove home.

It was Monday evening and Burden's marriage was two days old. Monday was the evening of Dora's pottery class, the fruits of which, bruised-looking and not invariably symmetrical, were scattered haphazardly about the room like windfalls. Hunting along the shelves for G. Hallam Saul's *When the Summer is Shed* and *The Trial of Florence Winchurch* from the Notable British Trials series, he nearly knocked over one of those rotund yet lop-sided objects. With a sigh of relief that it was unharmed, he set about refreshing his memory of the Winchurch case with the help of Miss Saul's classic.

Florence May Anstruther had been nineteen at the time of her marriage to Edward Winchurch and he forty-seven. She was a good-looking fair-haired girl, rather tall and Junoesque, the daughter of a Kingsmarkham chemist – that is, a pharmacist, for her father had kept a shop in the High Street. In 1895 this damned her as of no account in the social hierarchy, and few people would have bet much on her chances of marrying well. But she did. Winchurch was a barrister who, at this stage of his life, practised law from inclination rather than from need. His father, a Sussex landowner, had died some three years before and had left him what for the last decade of the nineteenth century was an enormous fortune, two hundred thousand pounds. Presumably, he had been attracted to Florence by her youth, her looks and her ladylike ways. She had been given the best education, including six months at a finishing school, that the chemist could afford. Winchurch's attraction for Florence was generally supposed to have been solely his money.

They were married in June 1895 at the parish church of St Peter's, Kingsmarkham, and went on a six-months honeymoon, touring Italy, Greece and the Swiss Alps. When they returned home Winchurch took a lease of Sewingbury Priory while building began on Paraleash House, and it may have been that the conical roofs on those turrets were inspired directly by what Florence had seen on her alpine travels. They moved into the lavishly furnished new house in May 1896 and Florence settled down to the life of a Victorian lady with a wealthy husband and a staff of indoor and outdoor servants. A vapid life at best, even if alleviated by a brood of children. But Florence had no children and was to have none.

Once or twice a week Edward Winchurch went up to London by the train from Kingsmarkham, as commuters had done before and have been doing ever since. Florence gave orders to her cook, arranged the flowers, paid and received calls, read novels and devoted a good many hours a day to her face, her hair and her dress. Local opinion of the couple at that time seemed to have been that they were as happy as most people, that Florence had done very well for herself and knew it, and Edward not so badly as had been predicted.

In the autumn of 1896 a young doctor of medicine bought a practice in Kingsmarkham and came to live there with his unmarried sister. Their name was Fenton. Frank Fenton was an extremely handsome man, twenty-six years old, six feet tall, with jet black hair, a Byronic eye and an arrogant lift to his chin. The sister was called Ada, and she was neither good-looking nor arrogant, being partly crippled by poliomyelitis which had left her with one leg badly twisted and paralysed.

It was ostensibly to befriend Ada Fenton that Florence first began calling at the Fentons' house in Queen Street. Florence professed great affection for Ada, took her about in her carriage and offered her the use of it whenever she had to go any distance. From this it was an obvious step to persuade Edward that Frank Fenton should become the Winchurches' doctor. Within another few months young Mrs Winchurch had become the doctor's mistress.

It was probable that Ada knew nothing, or next to nothing, about it. In the eighteen-nineties a young girl could be, and usually was, very innocent. At the trial it was stated by Florence's coachman that he would be sent to the Fentons' house several times a week to take Miss Fenton driving, while Ada's housemaid said that Mrs Winchurch would arrive on foot soon after Miss Fenton had gone out and be admitted rapidly through a french window by the doctor himself. During the winter of 1898 it seemed likely that Frank Fenton had performed an abortion on Mrs Winchurch, and for some months afterwards they met only at social gatherings and occasionally when Florence was visiting Ada. But their feelings for each other were too strong for them to bear separation and by the following summer they were again meeting at Fenton's house while Ada was out, and now also at Paraleash House on the days when Edward had departed for the law courts.

Divorce was difficult but by no means impossible or unheard-of in 1899. At the trial Frank Fenton said he had wanted Mrs Winchurch to ask her husband for a divorce. He would have married her in spite of the disastrous effect on his career. It was she, he said, who refused to consider it on the grounds that she did not think she could bear the disgrace.

In January 1900 Florence went to London for the day and, among other purchases, bought at a grocer's two cans of herring fillets marinaded in a white wine sauce. It was rare for canned food to appear in the Winchurch household, and when Florence suggested that these herring fillets should be used in the preparation of a dish called *Filets de hareng marinés à Rosette*, the recipe for which she had been given by Ada Fenton, the cook, Mrs Eliza Holmes, protested that she could prepare it from fresh fish. Florence, however, insisted, one of the cans was used, and the dish was made and served to Florence and Edward at dinner. It was brought in by the parlourmaid, Alice Evans, as a savoury or final course to a four-course meal. Although Florence had shown so much enthusiasm about the dish, she took none of it. Edward ate a moderate amount and the rest was removed to the kitchen where it was shared between Mrs Holmes, Alice Evans and the housemaid, Violet Stedman. No one suffered any ill-effects. The date was 30 January 1900.

Five weeks later on 5 March Florence asked Mrs Holmes to make the dish again, using the remaining can, as her husband had liked it so much. This time Florence too partook of the marinaded herrings, but when the remains of it were about to be removed by Alice to the kitchen, she advised her to tell the others not to eat it as she 'thought it had a strange taste and was perhaps not quite fresh'. However, although Mrs Holmes and Alice abstained, Violet Stedman ate a larger quantity of the dish than had either Florence or Edward.

Florence, as was her habit, left Edward to drink his port alone. Within a few minutes a strangled shout was heard from the dining room and a sound as of furniture breaking. Florence and Alice Evans and Mrs Holmes went into the room and found Edward Winchurch lying on the floor, a chair with one leg wrenched from its socket tipped over beside him and an overturned glass of port on the table. Florence approached him and he went into a violent convulsion, arching his back and baring his teeth, his hands grasping the chair in apparent agony.

John Barstow, the coachman, was sent to fetch Dr Fenton. By this time Florence was complaining of stomach pains and seemed unable to stand. Fenton arrived, had Edward and Florence removed upstairs and asked Mrs Holmes what they had eaten. She showed him the empty herring fillet can, and he recognized the brand as that by which a patient of a colleague of his had recently been infected with botulism, a virulent and usually fatal form of food poisoning. Fenton immediately assumed that it was *bacillus botulinus* which had attacked the Winchurches, and such is the power of suggestion that Violet Stedman now said she felt sick and faint.

Botulism causes paralysis, difficulty in breathing and a disturbance of the vision. Florence appeared to be partly paralysed and said she had double vision. Edward's symptoms were different. He continued to have spasms, was totally relaxed between spasms, and although he had difficulty in breathing and other symptoms of botulism, the onset had been exceptionally rapid for any form of food poisoning. Fenton, however, had never seen a case of botulism, which is extremely rare, and he supposed that the symptoms would vary greatly from person to person. He gave jalap and cream of tartar as a purgative and, in the absence of any known relatives of Edward Winchurch, he sent for Florence's father, Thomas Anstruther.

If Fenton was less innocent than was supposed, he had made a mistake in sending for Anstruther, for Florence's father insisted on a second opinion, and at ten o'clock went himself to the home of that very colleague of Fenton's who had recently witnessed a known case of botulism. This was Dr Maurice Waterfield, twice Fenton's age, a popular man with a large practice in Stowerton. He looked at Edward Winchurch, at the agonized grin which overspread his features, and as Edward went into his last convulsive seizure, pronounced that he had been poisoned not by *bacillus botulinus* but by strychnine.

Edward died a few minutes afterwards. Dr Waterfield told Fenton that there was nothing physically wrong with either Florence or Violet Stedman. The former was suffering from shock or 'neurasthenia', the latter from indigestion brought on by over-eating. The police were informed, an inquest took place, and after it Florence was immediately arrested and charged with murdering her husband by administering to him a noxious substance, to wit *strychnos nux vomica*, in a decanter of port wine.

Her trial took place in London at the Central Criminal Court. She was twenty-four years old, a beautiful woman, and was by then known to have been having a love affair with the young and handsome Dr Fenton. As such, she and her case attracted national attention. Fenton had by then lost his practice, lost all hope of succeeding with another in the British Isles, and even before the trial his name had become a by-word, scurrilous doggerel being sung about him and Florence in the music halls. But far from increasing his loyalty to Florence, this seemed to make him the more determined to dissociate himself from her. He appeared as the prosecution's principal witness, and it was his evidence which sent Florence to the gallows.

Fenton admitted his relationship with Florence but said that he had told her it must end. The only possible alternative was divorce and ultimately marriage to himself. In early January 1900 Florence had been calling on his sister Ada, and he had come in to find them looking through a book of recipes. One of the recipes called for the use of herring fillets marinaded in white wine sauce, the mention of which had caused him to tell them about a case of botulism which a patient of Dr Waterfield was believed to have contracted from eating the contents of a can of just such fillets. He had named the brand and advised his sister not to buy any of that kind. When, some seven weeks later, he was called to the dying Edward Winchurch, the cook had shown him an empty can of that very brand. In his opinion, Mrs Winchurch herself was not ill at all, was not even ill from 'nerves' but was shamming. The judge said that he was not there to give his opinion, but the warning came too late. To the jury the point had already been made.

Asked if he was aware that strychnine had therapeutic uses in small quantities, Fenton said he was but that he kept none in his dispensary. In any case, his dispensary was kept locked and the cupboards inside it locked, so it would have been impossible for Florence to have entered it or to have appropriated anything while on a visit to Ada. Ada Fenton was not called as a witness. She was ill, suffering from what her doctor, Dr Waterfield, called 'brain fever'.

The prosecution's case was that, in order to inherit his fortune and marry Dr Fenton, Florence Winchurch had attempted to poison her husband with infected fish, or fish she had good reason to suppose might be infected. When this failed she saw to it that the dish was provided again, and herself added strychnine to the port decanter. It was postulated that she obtained the strychnine from her father's shop, without his knowledge, where it was kept in stock for the destruction of rats and moles. After her husband was taken ill, she herself simulated symptoms of botulism in the hope that the convulsions of strychnine poisoning would be confused with the paralysis and impeded breathing caused by the bacillus.

The defence tried to shift the blame to Frank Fenton, at least to suggest a conspiracy with Florence, but it was no use. The jury were out for only forty minutes. They pronounced her guilty, the judge sentenced her to death, and she was hanged just twenty-three days later, this being some twenty years before the institution of a Court of Appeal.

After the execution Frank and Ada Fenton emigrated to the United States and settled in New England. Fenton's reputation had gone before him. He was never again able to practise as a doctor but worked as the travelling representative of a firm of pharmaceutical manufacturers until his death in 1932. He never married. Ada, on the other hand, surprisingly enough, did. Ephraim Hurst fell in love with her in spite of her sickly constitution and withered leg. They were married in the summer of 1902 and by the spring of 1903 Ada Hurst was dead in childbirth.

By then Paraleash House had been re-named The Limes and lime trees planted to conceal its forbidding yet fascinating façade from the curious passer-by.

The parcel from Carlyon Brent arrived in the morning with a very polite covering letter from Amyas Ireland, grateful in anticipation. Wexford had never before seen a book in this embryo stage. The script, a hundred thousand words long, was bound in red, and through a window in its cover appeared the provisional title and the author's name: *Poison at Paraleash, A Reappraisal of the Winchurch Case* by Kenneth Gandolph.

'Remember all that fuss about Gandolph?' Wexford said to Dora across the coffee pot. 'About four years ago?'

'Somebody confessed a murder to him, didn't they?'

'Well, maybe. While a prison visitor, he spent some time talking to Paxton, the bank robber, in Wormwood Scrubs. Paxton died of cancer a few months later, and Gandolph then published an article in a newspaper in which he said that during the course of their conversations, Paxton had confessed to him that he was the perpetrator of the Conyngford murder in 1962. Paxton's widow protested, there was a heated correspondence, MPs wanting the libel laws extended to libelling the dead, Gandolph shouting about the power of truth. Finally, the by then retired Detective Superintendent Warren of Scotland Yard put an end to all further controversy by issuing a statement to the press. He said Paxton couldn't have killed James Conyngford because on the day of Conyngford's death in Brighton Warren's sergeant and a constable had had Paxton under constant surveillance in London. In other words, he was never out of their sight.'

'Why would Gandolph invent such a thing, Reg?' said Dora.

'Perhaps he didn't. Paxton may have spun him all sorts of tales as a way of passing a boring afternoon. Who knows? On the other hand, Gandolph does rather set himself up as the elucidator of unsolved crimes. Years ago, I believe, he did find a satisfactory and quite reasonable solution to some murder in Scotland, and maybe it went to his head. Marshall, Groves, Folliott used to be his publishers. I wonder if they've refused this one because of the Paxton business, if it was offered to them and they turned it down?'

'But Mr Ireland's people have taken it,' Dora pointed out.

'Mm-hm. But they're not falling over themselves with enthusiasm, are they? They're scared. Ireland hasn't sent me this so that I can check up on the police procedural part. What do I know about police procedure in 1900? He's sent it to me in the hope that if Gandolph's been up to his old tricks I'll spot what they are.'

The working day presented no opportunity for a look at *Poison at Paraleash*, but at eight o'clock that night Wexford opened it and read Gandolph's long introduction.

Gandolph began by saying that as a criminologist he had always been aware of the Winchurch case and of the doubt which many felt about Florence Winchurch's guilt. Therefore, when he was staying with friends in Boston, Massachusetts, some two years before and they spoke to him of an acquaintance of theirs who was the niece of one of the principals in the case, he had asked to be introduced to her. The niece was Ada Hurst's daughter, Lina, still Miss Hurst, seventy-four years old and suffering from a terminal illness.

Miss Hurst showed no particular interest in the events of March 1900. She had been brought up by her father and his second wife and had hardly known her uncle. All her mother's property had come into her possession, including the diary which Ada Fenton Hurst had kept for three years prior to Edward Winchurch's death. Lina Hurst told Gandolph she had kept the diary for sentimental reasons but that he might borrow it and after her death she would see that it passed to him.

Within weeks Lina Hurst did die and her stepbrother, who was her executor, had the diary sent to Gandolph. Gandolph had read it and had been enormously excited by certain entries because in his view they incriminated Frank Fenton and exonerated Florence Winchurch. Here Wexford turned back a few pages and noted the author's dedication: *In memory of Miss Lina Hurst, of Cambridge, Massachusetts, without whose help this reappraisal would have been impossible.*

More than this Wexford had no time to read that evening, but he returned to it on the following day. The diary, it appeared, was a five-year one. At the top of each page was the date, as it might be 1 April, and beneath that five spaces each headed 18 . . . There was room for the diarist to write perhaps forty or fifty words in each space, no more. On the 1 January page in the third heading down, the number of the year, the eight had been crossed out and a nine substituted, and so it went on for every subsequent entry until March 6, after which no more entries were made until the diarist resumed in December 1900, by which time she and her brother were in Boston.

Wexford proceeded to Gandolph's first chapters. The story he had to tell was substantially the same as Hallam Saul's, and it was not until he came to chapter five and the weeks preceding the crime that he began to concentrate on the character of Frank Fenton. Fenton, he suggested, wanted Mrs Winchurch for the money and property she would inherit on her husband's death. Far from encouraging Florence to seek a divorce, he urged her never to let her husband suspect her preference for another man. Divorce would have left Florence penniless and homeless and have ruined his career. Fenton had known that it was only by making away with Winchurch and so arranging things that the death appeared natural, that he could have money, his profession and Florence.

There was only his word for it, said Gandolph, that he had spoken to Florence of botulism and had warned her against these particular canned herrings. Of course he had never seriously expected those cans to infect Winchurch, but that the fish should be eaten by him was necessary for his strategy. On the night before Winchurch's death, after dining with his sister at Paraleash House, he had introduced strychnine into the port decanter. He had also, Gandolph suggested, contrived to bring the conversation round to a discussion of food and to fish dishes. From that it would have been a short step to get Winchurch to admit how much he had enjoyed *Filets de hareng marinés à la Rosette* and to ask Florence to have them served again on the following day. Edward, apparently would have been highly likely to take his doctor's advice, even when in health, even on such a matter as what he should eat for the fourth course of his dinner, while Edward's wife did everything her lover, if not her husband, told her to do.

It was no surprise to Frank Fenton to be called out on the following evening to a man whose spasms only he would recognize as symptomatic of having swallowed strychnine. The arrival of Dr Waterfield was an unlooked-for circumstance. Once Winchurch's symptoms had been defined as arising from strychnine poisoning there was nothing left for Fenton to do but shift the blame on to his mistress. Gandolph suggested that Fenton attributed the source of the strychnine to Anstruther's chemist's shop out of revenge on Anstruther for calling in Waterfield and thus frustrating his hopes.

And what grounds had Gandolph for believing all this? Certain entries in Ada Hurst's diary. Wexford read them slowly and carefully.

For 27 February 1900, she had written, filling the entire small space: *Very cold. Leg painful again today. FW sent round the carriage and had John drive me to Pomfret. Compton says rats in the cellars and the old stables. Dined at home with F who says rats carry leptospiral jaundice, must be got rid of.* 28 February: *Drove in FW's carriage to call on old Mrs Paget. FW still here, having tea with F when I returned. I hope there is no harm in it. Dare I warn F?* 29 February: *F destroyed twenty rats with strychnine from his dispensary. What a relief!* 1 March: *Poor old Mrs Paget passed away in the night. A merciful release. Compton complained about the rats again. Warmer this evening and raining.* There was no entry for 2 March. 3 March: *Annie gave notice, she is getting married. Shall be sorry to lose her. Would not go out in carriage for fear of leaving FW too much alone with F. To bed early as leg most painful.* 4 March: *My birthday. 26 today and an old maid now, I think. FW drove over, brought me beautiful Indian shawl. She is always kind. Invited F and me to dinner tomorrow.* There was no entry for 5 March, and the last entry for nine months was the one for 6 March: *Dined last night at Paraleash House, six guests besides ourselves and the Ws. F left cigar case in the dining room, went back after seeing me home. I hope and pray there is no harm.*

Gandolph was evidently basing his case on the entries for 29 February and 6 March. In telling the court he had no strychnine in his dispensary, Fenton had lied. He had had an obvious opportunity for the introduction of strychnine into the decanter when he returned to Paraleash House in pursuit of his mislaid cigar case, and when he no doubt took care that he entered the dining room alone.

The next day Wexford re-read the chapters in which the new information was contained and he studied with concentration the section concerning the diary. But unless Gandolph were simply lying about the existence of the diary or of those two entries – things which he would hardly dare to do – there seemed no reason to differ from his inference. Florence was innocent, Frank Fenton the murderer of Edward Winchurch. But still Wexford wished Burden were there so that they might have one of their often acrimonious but always fruitful discussions. Somehow, with old Mike to argue against him and put up opposition, he felt things might have been better clarified.

And the morning brought news of Burden, if not the inspector himself, in the form of a postcard from Agios Nikolaios. The blue Aegean, a rocky escarpment, green pines. Who but Burden, as Wexford remarked to Dora, would send postcards while on his honeymoon? The post also brought a parcel from Carlyon Brent. It contained books, a selection from the publishing house's current list as a present for Wexford, and on the compliments slip accompanying them, a note from Amyas Ireland. *I shall be in Kingsmarkham with my people at the weekend. Can we meet? AI.* The books were the latest novel about Regency London by Camilla Barnet; *Put Money in Thy Purse*, the biography of Vassili Vandrian, the financier; the memoirs of Sofya Bolkinska, Bolshoi ballerina; an omnibus version of three novels of farming life by Giles de Coverley; the *Cosmos Book of Stars and Calendars*, and Vernon Trevor's short stories, *Raise me up Samuel*. Wexford wondered if he would ever have time to read them, but he enjoyed looking at them, their handsome glossy jackets, and smelling the civilized, aromatic, slightly acrid print smell of them. At ten he phoned Amyas Ireland, thanked him for the present and said he had read *Poison at Paraleash*.

'We can talk about it?'

'Sure. I'll be at home all Saturday and Sunday.'

'Let me take you and Mrs Wexford out to dinner on Saturday night,' said Ireland.

But Dora refused. She would be an embarrassment to both of them, she said, they would have their talk much better without her, and she would spend the evening at home having a shot at making a coil pot on her own. So Wexford went alone to meet Ireland in the bar of the Olive and Dove.

'I suppose,' he said, accepting a glass of Moselle, 'that we can dispense with the fiction that you wanted me to read this book to check on police methods and court procedure? Not to put too fine a point on it, you were apprehensive Gandolph might have been up to his old tricks again?'

'Oh, well now, come,' said Ireland. He seemed thinner than ever. He looked about him, he looked at Wexford, made a face, wrinkling up nose and mouth. 'Well, if you must put it like that – yes.'

'There may not have been any tricks, though, may there? Paxton couldn't have murdered James Conyngford, but that doesn't mean he didn't tell Gandolph he did murder him. Certainly the people who give Gandolph information seem to die very conveniently soon afterwards. He picks on the dying, first Paxton, then Lina Hurst. I suppose you've seen this diary?'

'Oh, yes. We shall be using prints of the two relevant pages among the illustrations.'

'No possibility of forgery?'

Ireland looked unhappy. 'Ada Hurst wrote a very stylized hand, what's called a *ronde* hand, which she had obviously taught herself. It would be easy to forge. I can't submit it to handwriting experts, can I? I'm not a policeman. I'm just a poor publisher who very much wants to publish this reappraisal of the Winchurch case if it's genuine – and shun it like the plague if it's not.'

'I think it's genuine.' Wexford smiled at the slight lightening in Ireland's face. 'I take it that it was usual for Ada Hurst to leave blanks as she did for March 2nd and March 5th?'

Ireland nodded. 'Quite usual. Every month there'd have been half a dozen days on which she made no entries.' A waiter came up to them with two large menus. 'I'll have the *bouillabaisse* and the lamb *en croûte* and the *médaillon* potatoes and french beans.'

'Consommé and then the parma ham,' said Wexford austerely. When the waiter had gone he grinned at Ireland. 'Pity they don't do *Filets de hareng marinés à la Rosette.* It might have provided us with the authentic atmosphere.' He was silent for a moment, savouring the delicate tangy wine. 'I'm assuming you've checked that 1900 genuinely was a Leap Year?'

'All first years of a century are.'

Wexford thought about it. 'Yes, of course, all years divisible by four are Leap Years.'

'I must say it's a great relief to me you're so happy about it.'

'I wouldn't quite say that,' said Wexford.

They went into the dining room and were shown, at Ireland's request, to a sheltered corner table. A waiter brought a bottle of Château de Portets 1973. Wexford looked at the basket of rolls, croissants, little plump brioches, miniature wholemeal loaves, Italian sticks, swallowed his desire and refused with an abrupt shake of the head. Ireland took two croissants.

'What exactly do you mean?' he said.

'It strikes me as being odd,' said the chief inspector, 'that in the entry for February 29th Ada Hurst says that her brother destroyed twenty rats with strychnine, yet in the entry for March 1st that Compton, whom I take to be the gardener, is still complaining about the rats. Why wasn't he told how effective the strychnine had been? Hadn't he been taken into Fenton's confidence about the poisoning? Or was twenty only a very small percentage of the hordes of rats which infested the place?'

'Right. It is odd. What else?'

'I don't know why, on March 6th, she mentions Fenton's returning for the cigar case. It wasn't interesting and she was limited for space. She doesn't record the name of a single guest at the dinner party, doesn't say what any of the women wore, but she carefully notes that her brother had left his cigar case in the Paraleash House dining room and had to go back for it. Why does she?'

'Oh, surely because by now she's nervous whenever Frank is alone with Florence.'

'But he wouldn't have been alone with Florence, Winchurch would have been there.'

They discussed the script throughout the meal, and later pored over it, Ireland with his brandy, Wexford with coffee. Dora had been wise not to come. But the outcome was that the new facts were really new and sound and that Carylon Brent could safely publish the book in the spring. Wexford got home to find Dora sitting with a wobbly looking half-finished coil pot beside her and deep in the *Cosmos Book of Stars and Calendars*.

'Reg, did you know that for the Greeks the year began on Midsummer Day? And that the Chinese and Jewish calendars have twelve months in some years and thirteen in others?'

'I can't say I did.'

'We avoid that, you see, by using the Gregorian Calendar and correct the error by making every fourth year a Leap Year. You really must read this book, it's fascinating.'

But Wexford's preference was for the Vassili Vandrian and the farming trilogy, though with little time to read he hadn't completed a single one of these works by the time Burden returned on the following Monday week. Burden had a fine even tan but for his nose which had peeled.

'Have a good time?' asked Wexford with automatic politeness.

'What a question,' said the inspector, 'to ask a man who has just come back from his honeymoon. Of course I had a good time.' He cautiously scratched his nose. 'What have you been up to?'

'Seeing something of your brother-in-law. He got me to read a manuscript.'

'Ha!' said Burden. 'I know what that was. He said something about it but he knew Gandolph'd get short shrift from me. A devious liar if ever there was one. It beats me what sort of satisfaction a man can get out of the kind of fame that comes from foisting on the public stories he *knows* aren't true. All that about Paxton was a pack of lies, and I've no doubt he bases this new version of the Winchurch case on another pack of lies. He's not interested in the truth. He's only interested in being known as the great criminologist and the man who shows the police up for fools.'

'Come on, Mike, that's a bit sweeping. I told Ireland I thought it would be OK to go ahead and publish.'

Burden's face wore an expression that was almost a caricature of sophisticated scathing knowingness. 'Well, of course, I haven't seen it,

I can't say. I'm basing my objection to Gandolph on the Paxton affair. Paxton never confessed to any murder and Gandolph knows it.'

'You can't say that for sure.'

Burden sat down. He tapped his fist lightly on the corner of the desk. 'I *can* say. I knew Paxton, I knew him well.'

'I didn't know that.'

'No, it was years back, before I came here. In Eastbourne, it was, when Paxton was with the Garfield gang. In the force down there we knew it was useless ever trying to get Paxton to talk. He *never* talked. I don't mean he just didn't give away any info, I mean he didn't answer when you spoke to him. Various times we tried to interrogate him he just maintained this total silence. A mate of his told me he'd made it a rule not to talk to policemen or social workers or lawyers or any what you might call establishment people, and he never had. He talked to his wife and his kids and his mates all right. But I remember once he was in the dock at Lewes Assizes and the judge addressed him. He just didn't answer – he wouldn't – and the judge, it was old Clydesdale, sent him down for contempt. So don't tell me Paxton made any sort of confession to Kenneth Gandolph, not *Paxton*.'

The effect of this was to reawaken all Wexford's former doubts. He trusted Burden, he had a high opinion of his opinion. He began to wish he had advised Ireland to have tests made to determine the age of the ink used in the 29 February and 6 March entries, or to have the writing examined by a handwriting expert. Yet if Ada Hurst had had a stylized hand self-taught in adulthood ... What good were handwriting experts anyway? Not much, in his experience. And of course Ireland couldn't suggest to Gandolph that the ink should be tested without offending the man to such an extent that he would refuse publication of *Poison at Paraleash* to Carlyon Brent. But Wexford was suddenly certain that those entries were false and that Gandolph had forged them. Very subtly and cunningly he had forged them, having judged that the addition to the diary of just thirty-four words would alter the whole balance of the Winchurch case and shift the culpability from Florence to her lover.

Thirty-four words. Wexford had made a copy of the diary entries and now he looked at them again. 29 February: *F destroyed twenty rats with strychnine from his dispensary. What a relief!* 6 March: *F left cigar case in the dining room, went back after seeing me home. I hope and pray there is no harm.* There were no anachronisms – men certainly used cigar cases in 1900 – no divergence from Ada's usual style. The word 'twenty' was written in letters instead of two figures. The writer, on 6 March, had written not about that day but about the day before. Did that amount to anything? Wexford thought not, though he pondered on it for most of the day.

That evening he was well into the last chapter of *Put Money in Thy Purse* when the phone rang. It was Jenny Burden. Would he and Dora come to dinner on Saturday? Her parents would be there and her brother.

Wexford said Dora was out at her pottery class, but yes, they would love to, and had she had a nice time in Crete?

'How sweet of you to ask,' said the bride. 'No one else has. Thank you, we had a lovely time.'

He had meant it when he said they would love to, but still he didn't feel very happy about meeting Amyas Ireland again. He had a notion that once the book was published some as yet unimagined Warren or Burden would turn up and denounce it, deride it, laugh at the glaring giveaway he and Ireland couldn't see. When he saw Ireland again he ought to say, don't do it, don't take the risk, publish and be damned can have another meaning than the popular one. But how to give such a warning with no sound reason for giving it, with nothing but one of those vague feelings, this time of foreboding, which had so assisted him yet run him into so much trouble in the past? No, there was nothing he could do. He sighed, finished his chapter and moved on to the farmer's fictionalized memoirs.

Afterwards Wexford was in the habit of saying that he got more reading done during that week than he had in years. Perhaps it had been a way of escape from fretful thought. But certainly he had passed a freakishly slack week, getting home most nights by six. He even read Miss Camilla Barnet's *The Golden Reticule*, and by Friday night there was nothing left but the *Cosmos Book of Stars and Calenders*.

It was a large party, Mr and Mrs Ireland and their son, Burden's daughter Pat, Grace and her husband and, of course, the Burdens themselves. Jenny's face glowed with happiness and Aegean sunshine. She welcomed the Wexfords with kisses and brought them drinks served in their own wedding present to her.

The meeting with Amyas Ireland wasn't the embarrassment Wexford had feared it would be – had feared, that is, up till a few minutes before he and Dora had left home. And now he knew that he couldn't contain himself till after dinner, till the morning, or perhaps worse than that – a phone call on Monday morning. He asked his hostess if she would think him very rude if he spoke to her brother alone for five minutes.

She laughed. 'Not rude at all. I think you must have got the world's most wonderful idea for a crime novel and Ammy's going to publish it. But I don't know where to put you unless it's the kitchen. And you,' she said to her brother, 'are not to eat anything, mind.'

'I couldn't wait,' Wexford said as they found themselves stowed away into the kitchen where every surface was necessarily loaded with the constituents of dinner for ten people. 'I only found out this evening at the last minute before we were due to come out.'

'It's something about the Winchurch book?'

Wexford said eagerly, 'It's not too late, is it? I was worried I might be too late.'

'Good God, no. We hadn't planned to start printing before the autumn.' Ireland, who had seemed about to disobey his sister and help himself to a macaroon from a silver dish, suddenly lost his appetite. 'This is serious?'

'Wait till you hear. I was waiting for my wife to finish dressing.' He grinned. 'You should make it a rule to read your own books, you know. That's what I was doing, reading one of those books you sent me and that's where I found it. You won't be able to publish *Poison at Paraleash*.' The smile went and he looked almost fierce. 'I've no hesitation in saying Kenneth Gandolph is a forger and a cheat and you'd be advised to have nothing to do with him in future.'

Ireland's eyes narrowed. 'Better know it now than later. What did he do and how do you know?'

From his jacket pocket Wexford took the copy he had made of the diary entries. 'I can't prove that the last entry, the one for March 6th that says, *F left cigar case in the dining room, went back after seeing me home*, I can't prove that's forged, I only think it is. What I know for certain is a forgery is the entry for February 29th.'

'Isn't that the one about strychnine?'

'*F destroyed twenty rats with strychnine from his dispensary. What a relief!*'

'How do you know it's forged?'

'Because the day itself didn't occur,' said Wexford. 'In 1900 there was no February 29th, it wasn't a Leap Year.'

'Oh, yes, it was. We've been through all that before.' Ireland sounded both relieved and impatient. 'All years divisible by four are Leap Years. All century years are divisible by four and 1900 was a century year. 1897 was the year she began the diary, following 1896 which was a Leap Year. Needless to say, there was no February 29th in 1897, 1898 or 1899 so there must have been one in 1900.'

'It wasn't a Leap Year,' said Wexford. 'Didn't I tell you I found this out through that book of yours, the *Cosmos Book of Stars and*

Calendars? There's a lot of useful information in there, and one of the bits of information is about how Pope Gregory composed a new civil calendar to correct the errors of the Julian Calendar. One of his rulings was that every fourth year should be a Leap Year except in certain cases . . .'

Ireland interrupted him. 'I don't believe it!' he said in the voice of someone who knows he believes every word.

Wexford shrugged. He went on, 'Century years were not to be Leap Years unless they were divisible not by four but by four hundred. Therefore, 1600 would have been a Leap Year if the Gregorian Calendar had by then been adopted, and 2000 will be a Leap Year, but 1800 was not and 1900 was not. So in 1900 there was no February 29th and Ada Hurst left the space on that page blank for the very good reason that the day following February 28th was March 1st. Unluckily for him, Gandolph, like you and me and most people, knew nothing of this as otherwise he would surely have inserted his strychnine entry into the blank space of March 2nd and his forgery might never have been discovered.'

Ireland slowly shook his head at man's ingenuity and perhaps his chicanery. 'I'm very grateful to you. We should have looked fools, shouldn't we?'

'I'm glad Florence wasn't hanged in error,' Wexford said as they went back to join the others. 'Her marriage didn't begin with dearly beloved, but if she was afraid at the end it can't have been with any amazement.'

Morse's Greatest Mystery

◆————————◆

COLIN DEXTER

The introverted and intelligent Inspector Morse is a phenomenon in both detective story and television terms. The TV programme in which he features is the only detective series which has been a success in a two-hour format, while the character's brooding intensity makes him probably the only manic depressive crime fighter. Not without good reason has he been called 'the Bow Street Hamlet'! The Inspector is also a man tormented by a youthful romance in his early days as a student in Oxford which is said to be part of the reason for his solitary nature, losing himself whenever he can in his music (Wagner), books and taste for fine wine. Morse is also a vulnerable man beneath his stern exterior, though he is dedicated to his profession and intensely loyal to his subordinates — although his long-suffering assistant, Sergeant Lewis, frequently finds this difficult to believe. The irascible Inspector first caught the general public's attention when the densely plotted and complex novel Service for All the Dead *won the Crime Writers' Association Silver Dagger award for 1979. Then, in 1987, Inspector Morse reached the TV screen thanks to ITV and the excellent casting of John Thaw, and has since earned some of the largest audience ratings for any drama programme. Thaw had earlier become well-known for his tough, unsmiling roles in two successful TV crime series:* Thick as Thieves *(1974) in which he co-starred for a season with Bob Hoskins, and fifty-two episodes of* The Sweeney, *co-starring Dennis Waterman — though in neither of these did he win the acclaim he has received for playing Inspector Morse. John was also fortunate in finding a perfect foil in Kevin Whately as Sergeant Lewis.*

Colin Dexter (1930–) the creator of Morse, was for some years a University administrator at Cambridge, yet chose to set his detective stories in the 'rival' university town of Oxford. As a life-long crossword puzzle devotee and deviser (as well as being three times national champion in the Ximenes clue-writing competition) Dexter also furnishes his crime novels with similar word games and, indeed, believes there is a strong correlation between crosswords and who-dunits. It has been said of Inspector Morse that his inquiries have 'a therapeutic thrust, as if his quest was really for the meaning of life.' The perceptiveness of this remark is excellently brought home in this final story featuring the man who is undeniably the detective with the largest viewing figures on television at the time of writing.

HE had knocked diffidently at Morse's north Oxford flat. Few had been invited into those book-lined, Wagner-haunted rooms, and even he – Sergeant Lewis – had never felt himself an over-welcome guest. Even at Christmas time. Not that it sounded much like the season of goodwill as Morse waved Lewis inside and concluded his ill-tempered conversation with the unfortunate bank manager.

'Look! If I keep a couple of hundred in my current acount, that's *my* look-out. I'm not even asking for any interest on it. All I *am* asking is that you don't stick these bloody bank charges on when I go – what, once, twice a year? – into the red. It's not that I'm mean with money –' Lewis's eyebrows ascended a centimetre – 'but if you charge me again I want you to ring and tell me *why*!'

Morse banged down the receiver and sat silent.

'You don't sound as if you've caught much of the Christmas spirit,' ventured Lewis.

'I don't like Christmas – never have.'

'You staying in Oxford, sir?'

'I'm going to decorate.'

'What – decorate the Christmas cake?' enquired Lewis.

'Decorate the kitchen. I don't like Christmas cake – never did.'

'You sound more like Scrooge every minute, sir.'

'*And* I shall read a Dickens' novel – I always do over Christmas. Re-read, rather.'

'If I were just starting on Dickens, which one. . . ?'

'I'd put *Bleak House* first, *Little Dorrit* second . . .'

The phone rang and Morse's secretary at HQ informed him that he'd won a fifty-pound gift token in the police charity raffle, and this time Morse cradled the receiver with considerably better grace.

' "Scrooge", did you say, Lewis? I'll have you know I bought five tickets – a quid apiece! – in that charity raffle.'

'I bought five tickets myself, sir.'

Morse smiled complacently: 'Let's be more charitable, Lewis! It's supporting these causes that's important – not *winning*.'

'I'll be in the car, sir,' said Lewis quietly. In truth, he was beginning to feel irritated. Morse's irascibility he could stomach; but he couldn't stick hearing much more about Morse's selfless generosity!

Morse's old car was in dock again ('Too mean to buy a new one!' his colleagues claimed) and it was Lewis's job that day to ferry the chief inspector around; doubtless, too, if things went to form, to treat him to the odd pint or two. Which indeed appeared a fair probability, since Morse had so managed things that Tuesday morning that their arrival at The George would coincide with opening time. As they drove out past the railway station, Lewis told Morse what he'd managed to discover about the previous day's events . . .

The patrons of The George had amassed four hundred pounds in aid of the Littlemore Charity for Mentally Handicapped Children, and this splendid total was to be presented to the charity's secretary at the end of the week, with a photographer promised from the *Oxford Times* to record the grand occasion. Mrs Michaels, the landlady, had been dropped by her husband at the bank in Carfax at about ten-thirty am, and had there exchanged a motley assemblage of coins and notes for forty brand-new tenners.

After this, she had bought several items, including grapes for a daughter just admitted to hospital, before catching a minibus back home, where she had arrived just after midday. The money, in a long white envelope, was in her shopping bag together with her morning's purchases. Her husband had not yet returned from the local cash-and-carry store, and on re-entering The George, via the saloon bar, Mrs Michaels had heard the telephone ringing. Thinking that it was probably the hospital, she had dumped her bag on the bar counter and rushed to answer it. On her return, the envelope was gone.

At the time of the theft, there had been about thirty people in the saloon bar, including the regular OAPs, the usual cohort of pool-playing unemployables and a pre-Christmas party from a local firm. And – yes! – from the very beginning Lewis had known that the chances of recovering the money were virtually nil. Even so, the three perfunctory interviews which Morse conducted appeared to Lewis to be sadly unsatisfactory.

After listening a while to the landlord's unilluminating testimony, Morse asked him why it had taken him so long to conduct his business at the cash-and-carry; and although the explanation given seemed perfectly adequate, Morse's dismissal of this first witness had seemed almost offensively abrupt.

And no man could have been more quickly or more effectively antagonized than the temporary barman – on duty the previous morning – who refused to answer Morse's brusque enquiry about the present state of his overdraft.

What, then, of the attractive auburn-haired Mrs Michaels? After a rather lopsided smile had introduced Morse to her regular if slightly nicotine-stained teeth, that distressed lady had been unable to fight back her tears as she sought to explain to Morse why she'd insisted on some genuine notes for the publicity photographer instead of a magnified phoney cheque.

But *wait*! Something dramatic had just happened to Morse – Lewis could see that: as if the light had suddenly shined upon a man who hitherto had sat in darkness. Morse now asked – amazingly – whether by any chance the good lady possessed a pair of bright green, high-heeled, leather shoes; and when she replied that, yes, she did, Morse smiled serenely, as though he had solved the secret of the universe, and promptly summoned into the lounge bar not only the three he'd just interviewed but all those now in The George who had been drinking there the previous morning.

As they waited, Morse asked for the serial numbers of the stolen notes, and Lewis passed over a scrap of paper on which some figures had been hastily scribbled in blotchy Biro. 'For Christ's sake, man!' hissed Morse, 'didn't they teach you to write at school?'

Lewis breathed heavily, counted to five, and then painstakingly rewrote the numbers on a piece of virgin paper: 773741–773780. At which numbers Morse glanced cursorily before sticking the paper in his pocket and proceeding to address The George's regulars.

He was virtually certain, he said, of who had stolen the money. What he was *absolutely* sure about was exactly where the money was *at that very moment*. He had the serial numbers of the notes – but that was of no importance whatsoever now. The thief might well have been tempted to spend the money earlier – but not any more! And why not? Because at this Christmas time that person *no longer had the power to resist his better self*!

In that bar, stilled now and silent as the grave itself, the faces of Morse's audience seemed mesmerized – and remained so as Morse gave his precise instructions that the stolen notes should be replaced in their original envelope and returned, he cared not by what means, to Sergeant Lewis's office at Thames Valley Police headquarters *within the next twenty-four hours*..

As they drove back, Lewis could restrain his curiosity no longer: 'You really *are* confident that. . . ?'

'Of course!'

'I never seem to be able to put the clues together myself, sir.'

'Clues? What clues, Lewis? I didn't know we had any.'

'Well, shoes, for example – how do they fit in?'

'Who said they fitted in anywhere? It's just that I used to know an auburn-haired beauty who had six – six, Lewis! – pairs of bright green shoes. They suited her, she said.'

'So . . . they've got nothing to do with the case at all?'

'Not so far as I know,' muttered Morse.

The next morning a white envelope was delivered to Lewis's office, though no one at reception could recall when or whence it had arrived. Lewis immediately rang Morse to congratulate him on the happy outcome of the case.

'There's just one thing, sir. I'd kept that scrappy bit of paper with the serial numbers on it, and these are brand-new notes all right – but not the same ones!'

'Really?' Morse sounded supremely unconcerned.

'You're not worried about it?'

'Good Lord, no! You just get that money back to ginger-knob at The George, and tell her to settle for a jumbo cheque next time! Oh – and one other thing, Lewis. I'm on *leave*. So no interruptions from anybody – understand?'

'Yes, sir. And er . . . Happy Christmas, sir!'

'And to you, old friend!' replied Morse quietly.

The bank manager rang just before lunch that same day. 'It's about the four hundred pounds you withdrew yesterday, Inspector. I did promise to ring about any further bank charges . . .'

'I explained to the girl,' protested Morse. 'I needed the money quickly.'

'Oh, it's perfectly all right. But you did say you'd call in this morning to transfer . . .'

'Tomorrow! I'm up a ladder with a paint brush at the moment.'

Morse put down the receiver and sank bank in the armchair with the crossword again. But his mind was far away, and some of the words he himself had spoken kept echoing around his brain: something about one's better self . . . And he smiled, for he knew that this would be a Christmas he might enjoy almost as much as the children up at

Littlemore, perhaps. He had solved so many mysteries in his life. Was he now, he wondered, beginning to glimpse the solution to the greatest mystery of them all?

ACKNOWLEDGEMENTS

◆

The Editor and publishers are grateful to the following authors and agents for permission to include copyright stories in this collection: William Morrow & Co Inc for "The Footprint in the Sky" by John Dickson Carr; Victor Gollancz Ltd for "The Adventure of the Emperor's Dice" by Ellery Queen, "The Footsteps That Ran" by Dorothy L. Sayers, and "The World Series Murder" by Rex Stout; Leland Hayward Inc for "Too Many Have Lived" by Dashiell Hammett; Davis Publications Inc for "The Case of the Irate Witness" by Erle Stanley Gardner, "The All-Bad Hat" by H.R.F. Keating, and "The Guilt-Edged Blonde" by Ross Macdonald; American Leisure Concepts Inc for "Walk Softly, Strangler" by Robert Hart Davis; Viking Penguin for "Marlowe Takes on the Syndicate" by Raymond Chandler and "Rumpole and the Hanging Judge" by John Mortimer; United Newspapers Magazine Corp for "Not – Tonight – Danger" by Brett Halliday; Sigmund Miller for "It's in the Bag" by Orson Welles; Leslie Charteris for "The Smart Detective"; Hodder & Stoughton Ltd for "Gideon and the Chestnut Vendor" by John Creasey; Associated Newspapers Ltd for "Light-Fingers" by Francis Durbridge; Hamish Hamilton for "Stan the Killer" by Georges Simenon; Curtis Brown for "Van der Valk and the False Caeser" by Nicholas Freeling; Fleetway Publications for "The Man Who Was Hammered" by Jack Trevor Story; BBC Enterprises for "The Garage Racketeers" by Geoffrey Webb & Edward J. Mason; Macmillan London Ltd for "Hazell and the Patriot" by P. B. Yuill; Elaine Green Ltd for "Great Aunt Allie's Flypapers" by P. D. James; Weidenfeld & Nicolson for "Jemima Shore and the Sunny Grave" by Antonia Fraser; Aitken & Stone Ltd for "The Case of the Perfect Maid" and "The Adventure of the Clapham Cook" by Agatha Christie; Peters, Fraser & Dunlop for "When The Wedding Was Over" by Ruth Rendell; TV Times for "Morse's Greatest Mystery" by Colin Dexter. While every care has been taken in establishing copyright holders, in the case of any accident infringement interested parties should contact the Editor in care of the publishers.